Balance Book 1: Cracked Roots

Jordan Franklin

Contents

Part 2

Tender Shoots

I have been dreaming in green,

Far across the forest,

In and out of the sea.

Prologue

D AUN'ATHYN VON ANDRON WATCHED the fleet of ships growing smaller and smaller as they sped westward into the setting sun. Although it hurt his eyes to look at the golden shimmer on the water, he couldn't turn away, not until both the sun and the ships had vanished together beyond the horizon. The darkness that spread across the sea seemed to spread from inside himself. And even though Daun knew that Rhae'vyn would mock him for crying, he didn't care. He couldn't help it.

His sister found him there, atop the tallest tower of the palace, staring at the dark void spread out in front of him, a hollow look in his eyes. She had a glowbe in her hand, orange like hot coals, and Daun could see worry on her face in the amber light. But she smiled at him.

"I knew I'd find you here," she said.

Daun gave her a confused look.

"You came here the last two summers when the Raccorin entourage departed. I'm sorry, Dauny. I know you and Rhae'vyn are—friends."

Daun looked at his sister, his little sibling that had just flowered a year earlier, and he found it was still hard to think of her as an adult. How much did she know about his relationship with the Raccorin princess?

"Mads, I—" he said, but she put up her hand.

"Don't worry, Dauny. You know I won't tell Father. But be careful. I saw the way Cru'chuck watched you and Rhae'vyn this summer. He knows something's going on."

"You know I don't care about the Pradishar and their purity laws."

Mads looked incredulous. "You think I do? But Father and Mother certainly do. Most of Andramere does, too. As crown prince, you have to play along. Or Balance Authority will find someone else who will."

Daun sighed. "I hate when you're right. Thanks, Mads." He forced a smile, but he couldn't keep it up. "I just—I feel like I don't even have the energy to stand, to move about, to think or feel. I'm nothing without her."

"Rhae'vyn will be back next summer. King Rhakksees never misses his month on Andramere."

"But I can't wait that long. I can't wait a month, much less a year."

"You've done it before," Mads said, matter of factly.

"It's different now. It's been different for awhile. We aren't scamps playing at flirtation. This is real love."

"Love?" Mads chuckled. "Are you sure it's not obsession? Love is patient, Dauny. Love doesn't make you miserable, it saves you from misery."

"You need to stop reading books and experience the world for yourself," Daun snapped.

Mads opened her mouth slightly in surprise, and Daun, seeing the pain in her eyes, realized what he'd done.

"Oh Mads, you know I didn't mean that. I'm just a cranky old idiot who doesn't deserve an amazing sib like you. Will you forgive me?"

Mads gave him a small smile. "Since you're having a bad night, I'll let it go. But only if you'll come downstairs and put on a good face for Father. He asked to see you."

"Then I suppose I must," he said. "Thanks for shaking me out of my funk. I owe you one."

Mads took her brother's arm.

"Come on," she said. "You have a big year ahead. Time should fly."

Daun smiled. "You know, you're probably right."

"I'm always right," Mads said.

He was grateful to his sister for cheering him up, and he followed her down the winding stairs to the upper hall, then took a lift alone to the main wing of the palace and walked the remainder of the way to their parent's private quarters. When Daun entered and saw the look on his father's face, the cheer was suddenly gone, replaced not with that black hole of despair that had swallowed him earlier, but with a feeling that he ought to feel like he'd done something wrong. When he saw the priestin Cru'chuck was there too, he clenched his teeth and tried to control his breathing.

Quellan von Andron, high doge of Andramere, dismissed the priestin.

Once they were alone, he fixed his gaze on his son but said nothing.

Daun squirmed but didn't look away.

Finally his father spoke.

"Cru'chuck tells me you and the Raccorin princess have become close."

Daun didn't have to answer, his mind gave him away. He could feel his father's awareness on his crystamin—feel him touching his thoughts and sampling his emotions. He hardened his mind and pushed back against his father.

"Submit," Quellan said. The tone carried a threat of violence. Daun stopped resisting. Quellan probed into his mind, angrily sifting through his memories, snatching them from him. He could sense his father experiencing his memories as if he'd lived them himself, peering out his eyes and ears and nose and skin, as he and Rhae'vyn kissed, and held each other, trembling.

Quellan broke the connection and turned away.

Daun tried to catch his breath. His father had done this before, of course, but this was the first time he'd seen something intimate, something special, something that wasn't for him to experience. And he couldn't figure out why he didn't feel angry, only dirty. And heartbroken.

All those thoughts left Daun's mind when he realized his father was laughing—was looking at him, smiling.

"That old fool priestin," Quellan said. "He had me convinced you were plotting to elope. But now I see it's nothing but a bit of harmless fun."

"I love her," Daun said.

His father kept laughing, but he narrowed his eyes, just a little. "If it makes you happy to think so, but I felt how you felt, and I know youthful lust when I see it, sharp but shallow, intense but fleeting. Call it what you will, I see no problem with some harmless fun while you're both unmarried. But try to be a little less conspicuous. Purity laws might not outright prohibit interracial lovemaking, but you know it's frowned upon by your future subjects and by Balance's citizens. We have enough trouble controlling rumors as it is."

Daun shook his head. "But I love her."

Quellan stopped smiling. "Let it go, son. I'll make this clear once and then never again: I will not permit any member of my family to jeopardize our mandate with Balance Authority. We rule this island because the Pradishar say we can rule this island. The von Androns have ruled Andramere for millennia and my reign will not be the last. Are we clear?"

Daun nodded, furious that he was crying.

"Dismissed," his father said, turning away.

Cru'chuck was standing outside when Daun emerged, his eyes gently twitching, but the old priestin ignored him and Daun was grateful for it. Wiping away his tears, he ran through the halls and down the stairs, out of the palace and into the old grove that spread up the hillside between the palace and the sea. He followed the trail through the darkness, struggling to see, til he found the little cabin nestled among the trees, where he slumped against the wall and wept. When he was finally tired of crying—finally tired of everything—he let sleep take him, his last thought on Rhae'vyn, her hand behind his head, pulling him in for a kiss.

When he woke the next morning, Daun knew something wonderful had happened. Just when he'd thought it was over—had to be over—he suddenly had a piece of Rhae'vyn, a piece of himself, growing out of him. He fingered the fruit where it hung below a newly bloomed flower, wide open across his abdomen, and his mind was full of the possibilities that such an object promised.

I can't, he thought. *It would be a Bhizini. A halfbreed. An outcast! Still, I don't have to decide anything until the taprin is ready to cut. There's no harm in planting it, watching the little spratlyn grow. Just for fun.*

So Daun'athyn spent the next few days fashioning a sprouting patch in the old grove, making sure the conditions were just right, putting a small fence around the soil, before finally plucking the fruit from his belly and placing it in the hole he'd dug with his own hands. He pushed the soil over the fruit, sprinkled on some water, and said a prayer to Trevian.

Even if it never sprouts, he thought, on the third day in a row he'd come back to check the patch, *at least I didn't toss it away to the birds. At least I tried.*

On the seventh day, a tender green shoot had peeked up out of the soil, and Daun cried when he saw it.

⁕⁕⁕⁕⁕

Daun'athyn never knew time could go so slowly. His father had insisted he start his annual and become a monkin—the doge was always trying to please the Pradishar, and it made Daun sick—but he'd agreed if only to have something to do. But he found the rituals boring, the lessons distracting. He wanted to be thinking about Rhae'vyn, not prayers and methods.

Every weekend, Daun headed up into the old grove, to the little cabin at the heart of the thicket, intending to pull up the growing spratlyn he'd planted there. But every time he saw the little green shrub, each week looking more and more like a Verdillion, he just couldn't do it.

Next week, he told himself.

He knew the spratlyn needed looking after while he was busy with his annual. Daun needed someone he could trust, someone without a crystamin, someone he knew would never betray him. Mads was the obvious choice—she'd never bonded with a crystal, not even the one held exclusively by the von Andron family—but he didn't dare get his sister in trouble. So he chose his old nanny instead. She had raised him, loved him as a parent, and doted on him still. She would help. He knew she would.

"My prince is quiet this morning," Motty said, as they headed up the pathway through the old grove the next day. "Don't want to tell me what this is about?"

"I already told you, it's a surprise," he said.

"Another Bhizini you're helping escape the clutches of Balance Authority?"

"Not exactly," Daun said, looking away from her.

She sighed but said nothing.

When they reached the cabin, Daun led Motty down to the sprouting patch he'd prepared, to the small but fast-growing spratlyn he'd planted.

Motty inhaled sharply but said nothing, only stared for a long time, a troubled look on her face. Finally she composed herself and spoke.

"My prince, what is this?"

"My scamp," he said.

She nodded slowly. "You know the laws against self-reproduction."

"It's not a duplicant," he said.

Motty looked at him then, unable to hide her surprise.

"Why hide it here then?"

"Because it's Rhae'vyn's," he said.

Motty's dull green face grew paler.

"Dauny—my prince—why?"

"Because it's Rhae'vyn's," he said again.

"And the princess knows of this?"

Daun shook his head and Motty closed her eyes for a long time.

"Why did you bring me here today?"

"Isn't it obvious? I need someone to look after it."

"You intend to keep growing it? To cut the taprin?"

"Yes. And no. I mean, I don't know. I just want to see what it looks like. To see—what our scamp would look like. But when the time comes, I won't cut the taprin. I'll let it wither away, I promise. It's just a bit of harmless fun."

Motty gave him a look that said everything she was unable to voice.

"I'm going to regret this," she said, finally.

"I knew I could count on you," he said.

"I will make sure the spratlyn is tended," she said. "But I beg my prince to change his mind, to pull it up now, to forget all about this, this—" But she trailed off when she saw his face.

"I knew I could count on you," he said again.

❧✦❧

The weeks turned into months, and the months into seasons, and as spring grew old and Zenithra approached with the new year, Daun'athyn could hardly contain his excitement. His annual had concluded and he was officially a monkin of the Pradishar, with a brand new purple and gray crystamin in his forehead to prove it. His father was pleased, the dogedom of Andramere was pleased, but Daun'athyn's mind had only been on one thing, and that was Rhae'vyn.

By now the spratlyn he'd planted looked like a scamp, a tiny version of a Verdillion. The branches looked like little arms and legs, and the small face looked like him—like Rhae'vyn. He came up to the grove whenever he could get away, sometimes every day, just to stare at the little thing, the life that he and Rhae'vyn had created with their love. And even though the skin was unmistakably Bhizini—a splotchy pattern of dull greens from Daun's own Andrasian heritage mixed with the bright green of the Raccorin—he didn't care. It was his own flesh, his own family. And the thought of that being that he'd created never coming into the world, never drinking up the sunshine, never laughing, never loving—no.

And so Daun took the ceremonial dagger his family had used to cut the taprin of every von Andron for thousands of years, hid the knife in his robes, and brought it with him to the grove.

"You have to live," he whispered, as he held the dagger against the flesh of the taprin, which had turned soft and pink, ready to be sliced. "I don't even know you yet. I only know I love you more than life itself."

He twisted the taprin around the blade, took a deep breath, and with a quick flick of his wrist, he cut through the pink flesh.

The scamp opened its eyes, looked up at the sky, and fill Daun's ears with its cries.

Daun picked up his scamp and held it against him, his eyes burning with tears, his heart singing as it had never sang before.

A week later, the Raccorin fleet sailed into the Bay of Bliss, ferrying King Rhakksees and his royal family into Andramere. Daun'athyn was almost sick with anticipation. With the palace abuzz with preparations for their arrival, he'd managed to spend the better part of the week with his scamp, who was growing fast and had already learned to walk, perch, click, grunt, and hiss. It would be another year before it could speak.

Motty had more or less moved into the cabin to take care of the scamp, and as the arrival of the Raccorin royal family approached, she surprised Daun by grabbing him by both arms, her face contorted with tears.

"I'm begging you, Dauny—my prince—you mustn't tell the princess of the little one."

Daun couldn't help but chuckle. "Why are you so upset?" he said, taking her hands in his own. "There's nothing to worry about. Rhae'vyn and I are in love."

Motty pulled her hands away and began to wring them together.

"Raccorin tempers can be difficult," she said, "and those of the royal family are legendary. She didn't consent to this scamp. Trust me Dauny—trust me as you did when you were just a little scamp, running into my arms whenever you were scared or lonely. Trust me and don't tell her."

But Daun'athyn would not be convinced, no matter how hard Motty tried. Finally she hardened her face, dried her tears, and began to clean up the cabin, ignoring Daun's continued attempts to convince her otherwise.

Poor old thing, Daun thought. *She's never been in love. She doesn't understand. Besides, Rhae'vyn will feel as I felt when I saw our scamp for the first time. How could someone not love their own offspring?*

And so he headed back toward the palace, his long year of waiting finally over, his heart overflowing with happiness, a song on his lips as he thought of seeing Rhae'vyn, holding her again, and telling her the good news.

She was every bit as beautiful as he remembered, and for a moment, he felt a pang of guilt that he'd not been as excited about her arrival as he normally would have been, distracted as he'd been with the duties of parenting.

The Raccorin royal family always traveled with what seemed like half the royal court, which was why his father the doge tried to avoid these official greeting ceremonies. They took hours, and nobody enjoyed them. Nobody.

Daun'athyn could hardly sit still. Whenever Rhae'vyn looked his way, he blushed, and she even gave him a smile a time or two.

He finally had a chance to speak with her among the crowd.

"I have a surprise for you," he said.

Her eyes lit up. "You always know just what I need! It's been a long trip. We traveled nonstop from P'anorum this time." She lowered her voice. "I could sure use some loving. But later—we have duties to perform." She winked at him.

"Sneak away with me now?"

She laughed. "Someone's got bugs in their petals! But you're crazy. There're eyes everywhere, and too many of them with crystals attached. We don't know who's watching."

"Then tonight. When the party's grown wild and darkness can be your cover. The old grove. Follow the pathway up the hill. I'll be waiting."

"No promises," she said.

Late that evening, well into the festivities, Daun'athyn told his mother he wasn't feeling well, and his father gave him permission to retire. Once out of the great hall, he headed for the woods. When he reached the cabin, he found Motty on the porch, the scamp in her lap, the two gently rocking back and forth.

Motty took the scamp inside and he sat in the chair and stared into the empty darkness, listening to the buzzing of the insects and the hooting of the owls, and wondering if

Rhae'vyn would show. As the hour grew late, he found himself sleepy in spite of his nerves, and he was about to call it a night and return to the palace when she came up the pathway, a small glowbe in her hand, the warm orange light like a candle, flickering in the darkness.

"What is this place?" she said. "Are you living out here in the woods?" She gave him a strange look.

"It's a retreat," he said. "A place to be alone. Without having to go halfway across the city to see you in private."

"But we're still on the palace grounds."

"Nobody comes here, I promise. We're safe."

"Well, alright then," she said, grinning. She practically leapt into his arms. "So good to see you again, sweet Daun'athyn. Kind Daun'athyn. Beautiful Daun'athyn." Her eyes were glowing.

"Have you been eating bhiza?" he said, struggling to keep his voice flat.

Rhae'vyn giggled. "Just a little. Now then, what's your surprise? Is it under here?" She grabbed at his robe.

Daun slapped her hand away. "Stop. No. This isn't how I wanted this to happen."

"What to happen? Why are you acting so strangely?"

"Maybe we should wait," he said.

She sighed and rolled her eyes. "Why do you always try to make this complicated?"

"I don't," he said. "I just—"

Rhae'vyn put up her hand and looked at the hut.

"Is someone here?" she said.

"Just Motty, my old nanny," he said.

There was a cry from inside, and Daun'athyn saw a panicked look in her eyes.

"Come out," Daun said, and his old nanny stepped through the door onto the porch, the scamp in her arms, fussing softly.

He looked at Rhae'vyn, waiting to see her expression, her smile. But her mouth was wide open and her bright green face had drained of color, so that she looked vaguely Andrasian in the warm light of the glowbe.

"Daun'athyn," she said, barely a whisper. "Is that what I think it is."

"Our scamp, yes," he said.

"Your scamp," she said quickly. "Yours, not mine. I have no scamp. I have no scamp!"

"Easy, Rhae. I know—"

"You know *nothing*," she screamed. "I told you I didn't want a commitment the last time I was here. You think that meant I wanted a scamp with you?"

"I know," he said. "But when I fruited, I—please, don't be mad—I couldn't resist. It was—a piece of you. And look—" He took the scamp from Motty. "Look at that sweet face. It looks just like you, don't you think?"

Rhae'vyn drew back her lips and hissed. "That halfbreed freak is no scamp of mine. And I'll spill your sap myself if you tell anyone it is."

Daun'athyn felt this throat pinching shut, his heart racing so fast he didn't think he could breath. "No," he said. "No. Look. Look how beautiful—"

But Rhae'vyn's face had twisted into a sneer, and her eyes were hard and full of malice. And rage.

"If you've ever loved me—if you've ever been my friend—ever cared even the slightest bit for me—"

"I love you, you know that," he said. "Rhae, please—"

"If that's true—if that's really true—then you'll tie a weight around that foul thing and toss it into the sea!"

Daun'athyn started to cry, a choking sob, his eyes burning with tears. "How could you say that? How, Rhae'vyn, how? Your own sap? Your own flesh!"

"I'll do it myself," she screamed, lunging at Daun'athyn and slashing at the scamp with her nails. She was larger than him, and taller. Stronger too. But he was quicker, and she was woozy from the bhiza. He spun backward, out of her reach, and shifting the scamp into his left arm, he spun his weight around and swung with his right hand, hitting Rhae'vyn in the chest. She fell back into one of the columns on the porch and slumped to the ground.

He handed the scamp to Motty, then tore a strip of fabric from his robe and tied Rhae'vyn's hands together around the column. Then he stood and paced, looking at Rhae'vyn, at Motty, at Rhae'vyn again. Motty refused to look at him, and she took the scamp back inside, then returned alone, a worried look on her wrinkled old face.

There was no way this could end well. He needed help.

"Watch her," he said. "I'll be back as soon as I can."

When he reached the palace, a few stragglers were still in the great hall, but the hosts had retired for the night, and the music had stopped. He went to the servant's quarters and ordered them to fetch his mother. The servant returned and told Daun'athyn his parents would see him.

When he entered their chambers, he could tell they'd already been asleep.

"This better be important," his father said.

"What's going on, Dauny, love? You're shaking." His mother was frowning, but there was fear in her eyes.

"I've—done something stupid."

"Something stupid?" Quellan von Andron said. "And it can't wait til the morning?"

"It can't. I've—had a scamp," he said.

His mother's eyes widened.

"With a Raccorin," he added, and his mother gasped.

"With princess Rhae'vyn," he said.

His mother put her hand over her mouth.

"Does anyone know?" Quellan said.

"Just Motty."

"I warned you not to defy me," his father said, but then he sighed. "You know son, this sort of thing happens more often than you'd realize. You need to be more careful when you dispose of your fruit. But it's no big fuss. Just take a weight, fasten it to the little brute's leg, and toss it off the southern cliff. Send the evidence to the bottom of the sea, and the problem is solved."

When the doge saw Daun's face, he frowned. "No need to be so upset, son," he said. "It's just a Bhizini. Surely—surely you don't want to keep the wretched thing?"

Daun said nothing.

"Princess Rhae'vyn then?" Quellan looked incredulous. "You might be a fool, but surely she knows better."

"She told me the same thing you did, when she found out."

His father's face hardened. "Are you telling me that you grew the fruit *on purpose*? I know you said you were in love, but Sweet Trevian! You planted it? Without her knowledge? Have you lost your mind?"

"I wanted a scamp," Daun said. "Her scamp."

His father narrowed his eyes to slits and pressed his lips together. "Where's the princess?" he hissed.

Daun looked at the ground.

"Where?" The edge in his father's voice took his breath away.

He swallowed hard. "Tied up in the west wood."

Quellan grabbed his son by the throat. "You foolish bastard! I'll kill the scamp myself!"

Daun's mother dropped to her knees, crying for mercy, for peace, for sanity. The guards, hearing the commotion, came into the chamber with the old priestin Cru'chuck.

"Are you alright, my lord?" the priestin asked. His eyes were twitching as he spoke.

Aga'thyn stood and touched her husband's face, then shot a sideways glance at the priestin.

"Leave us," Quellan said.

Cru'chuck scowled, his eyes still twitching, but he turned to obey.

When the door closed, Quellan turned back to Daun'athyn.

"Let me be perfectly clear with you, son. You have two choices, and only two choices. One, you take that creature and you toss it in the sea, you release the princess immediately, and you go and beg forgiveness from King Rhakksees. Heir or not, you've violated the sanctity of guest privilege, the norms of Andramere and the Andrasian Republic, even the laws of Balance Authority. You'll take responsibility for this, even if it means King Rhakksees wants your head on his wall."

"And the second choice?"

Quellan's eyes were murderous. "You'd even ask?" he hissed. "Leave this palace. This city. This island. And never return. You're no longer my son. No longer a von Andron. You're dead to us all."

Aga'thyn wept when she saw Daun's face. "Oh Dauny love, it's only a Bhizini. It'll only grow up to be an outcast, a pirate, a savage, abused and hated and feared by the whole world. Do it a favor now, before it's too late, and cast it into the sea. Save the honor of our family, and face the consequences for your actions. Oh please son, I know you'll do the right thing. Tell me you'll do the right thing!"

"High doge," Daun said. "Mother. It was an honor being a von Andron."

Quellan reached for Daun but he ducked away and out the back through his parent's bedchamber.

"Guards!" Quellan screamed. "Guards! Traitor! Treason! Seal off the grounds! Bring me—"

But Daun'athyn was sprinting—sprinting for the old grove, sprinting for his scamp, for his life, for his future. And there was sadness and grief and rage and murder in his heart.

When he emerged from the palace, the sky was lit with orange and red, and an angry plume of smoke billowed upward over the forest. Loud cracks seemed to split the night in two.

The woods are on fire. The woods are on fire!

He ran across the palace gardens, up the pathway, past the first trees of the old grove, the flames in front of him racing down the hillside, the trees popping into ash as it spread.

Daun'athyn said a prayer to Trevian, and leapt into the inferno.

Part 1
Withered Seeds

Chapter 1

From Deep Beneath and Far Beyond

Fin'roq woke to the sound of waves on the cliffs, the clattering of palm leaves at the harbor below, and the whispers and sighs of the east wind as it passed across the old lava flow and through the ruins of the palace behind him. His branches swayed along with the breeze, the leaftips squiggling back and forth like a school of fish with each gust and swirl. He lingered there a moment longer, his eyes closed, letting his mottled green skin feast on the afternoon light, before he withdrew his branches under his arms and pulled his rootpads up into his feet. He took a few careful steps to loosen up his legs, then walked to the edge of the promenade for a better look at the village.

His home sat within the shell of an old crater, the lowest of the three volcanic peaks which made up the island. The harbor, which came in through the broken south wall of the crater, was empty as always, the surface of the water feathered in the wind, a pattern of white foamy arches. On the northern shore was a small strip of sand, a narrow golden crescent wedged between the deep blue of the harbor and the medley of green jungle that covered every last visible inch of the surrounding land. Fin'roq could see the row of huts at the back of the beach, their yellow palm-thatched awnings like dead trees among the foliage.

Behind the village stood the other two peaks, their tops shrouded in cloud. The Crag, an emerald cone clothed in the thick briars and ancient groves of the Swarthen Forest, rose just behind the rim of the crater in which the village sat. And to the north and east, rising nearly twice the height of the Crag, stood P'anorum Peak, its sheer sides encrusted with crystalized lava, orange with streaks of red and black. The jagged edges were so bright in the sunshine that the mountain still seemed to burn over thirty years after the last eruption.

Fin'roq squinted and followed the lava flow along the eastern edge of the Crag, down along the rim of the crater, across the royal estate, and into the sea. Of the entire island, only the very back of the palace, the Crag, and the harbor were uncovered. The ruins of the palace stuck out of the lava like a rusty thumb, the portico over the porch like a cracked nail, the moss growing in the pits of the frieze a fungus that time and neglect had allowed to root.

He turned back to the harbor and gazed down at the beach, where he could see the villagers sunning themselves on the sand. Jock'imo had the grill at his tavern roaring—a small gray smear emanated from the chimney and disappeared in the breeze. Even with all the sunshine Fin had just eaten, he felt hungry for roasted rhingamis. Why couldn't he go to their stupid festival anyway? It's not like Balance Authority would know they had allowed someone like him to attend. He felt the anger surge up in his chest.

What's a rhingami or two, anyway, he thought. *I could snag a few without anyone noticing.*

"Don't prove 'em right, Fin," a voice growled beside him.

Fin'roq looked at the old Raccorin with surprise, not so much at what he'd said but that he'd voluntarily spoken to him at all. Grizmond was standing next to him on the promenade, tall and wide and wrinkled, his bright green face furrowed, as it always was, with a look of displeasure. His wrinkled brow made the two deep pits in his forehead look puckered and misshapen, and Fin'roq wondered yet again what they had looked like, the crystals that had once been there. Nobody else on the island had one.

"How'd you know what I was planning?" Fin said.

"I didn't," he said. "But I could tell by your looks you was angry—and determined. Bad combination, that."

"They won't miss a rhingami or two. I'll bring you one."

Grizmond grunted. "And when you're taking your lashes for crashing their festival?"

"They won't catch me."

"Maybe not this time. You're sneaky, I'll give you that. But eventually they will. You've flowered now, Fin'roq. You aren't a little scamp under foot anymore. Scamps they'll tolerate. But a flowered Bhizini? Don't give 'em a reason, least not over a bite of food."

Fin could feel his face burning and he looked away. Grizmond grunted again and walked back to his perch on the end of the promenade, where he could see the open ocean to the east, south, and west. Fin wondered why he'd spoken to him today. The old Raccorin always came up to watch the seas, and Fin'roq usually came with him, if only because Grizmond would reliably ignore him. They'd spend the days around the porch of the old palace, staring at the water, listening to the breakers on the cliff and the rumbles of thunder from the afternoon rains in the Swarthen Forest. Fin'roq would doze in the warm sunshine, but Grizmond always stayed intent on the horizon, watching. He'd answer no questions, would say little in response to anything Fin'roq said to him, but Fin didn't mind. It was better than the open hostility shown by almost everyone else.

He looked down at the harbor again and clenched his teeth. The celebration would be over at the end of the day and he'd be allowed to return to his hut, return to village life, little that there was to speak of. So he clutched the stones underfoot with his rootpads and was prepared to unfurl his branches for one more late afternoon snack when Grizmond called to him.

The old Raccorin was waving at him, urging him over to the lookout point where he was perched. "Tell me what your young eyes see," he said.

Fin'roq knew what to expect—a cloud on the water, a school of fish, a pod of water-stallions jumping and playing—anything other than a ship. No ship had been spotted in the three decades since P'anorum erupted. There'd been no sign that Balance Authority knew about the handful of survivors left on the island, and no indication whatsoever that the Raccorin Empire cared the slightest about reoccupying what was now little more than a lava-encrusted mountain in the middle of a distant sea. Not even the dreaded Bhizini pirates had been sighted, which made Fin'roq wonder why they were so feared by the villagers, and why he was so hated for looking like them.

Grizmond pointed out to the southwest. The wind was still brisk, the water choppy and strewn across with white caps, but the skies over the sea were clear with no clouds around to cast shadows. Fin'roq immediately saw what Grizmond was pointing at, along the thin, hazy strip of the horizon, between the deep blue of the ocean below and the turquoise of the sky above.

"It looks like a pale gray triangle," Fin'roq said. "If it were stormy, I'd swear it was just a cloud." He looked at the old Raccorin.

"A Pradishar cata'rin," Grizmond said, his bright green face drawing tight, which smoothed out his wrinkles and made him look younger than he was. "Though it's hard to be sure. Could be the Dyna'arin, I guess. Definitely not Bhizini."

Fin'roq watched the shape changing, growing larger. "Whatever it is, it's heading our way," he said.

Grizmond hissed and scowled. "The village must be warned."

Fin'roq's heart was racing and he struggled to catch his breath. "But the festival. I can't. They won't believe me."

"They'll be grateful you warned them."

He wanted to believe that was true.

"And you're faster than me," Grizmond said. "You know your way through the tunnels, don't you? Take 'em, if it's quicker."

Fin'roq looked embarrassed. He thought he'd kept that a secret. He opened his mouth to protest but Grizmond clutched him around the wrist, and Fin could tell from his grip that the old Raccorin was serious. "Go!" he growled, and Fin'roq turned and ran, down the promenade, across the porch, and into the ruins of the palace. The noise of the sea fell away and the sound of the wind turned into a low, mournful moaning—a sound which Fin knew came from the east wind as it passed over the lava flow, but which had convinced the villagers many decades ago that the palace had filled up with Mund'umbrian shades eager to devour them, and nobody but he and Grizmond would go near it.

The hall was lit in the back by sunbeams that passed through the crystalline lava and through the old windows of the palace, and Fin'roq sprinted into the crimson light, over a heap of rubble and down into the hollowed out passageways and empty lava tubes that crisscrossed the island. The tunnels were dark, too dark to see, but Fin had spent years in them, learning to navigate them, the precise angles to turn when the pathway forked or twisted around, where the steps were and how long they went on, so that he remembered each important route as a series of numbers. Armed with that knowledge, blindness meant nothing to him, and he walked into the dark depths of the island with confidence.

Only this time he had to slow himself on the descent lest his large paces throw off his numbers. And so, as he counted his way down the stairs, down through the old royal passageway to the harbor, it finally hit him, the news he was meant to deliver—a ship was coming to P'anorum!

And his mind went blank.

He froze in mid-step.

Fin'roq had never thought it possible that a ship would come, at least not since he was very young. As a scamp, he'd fantasized almost daily about it—his parents, come to rescue him. He and all the villagers would sail away together, saved. They'd go to distant Balan Su, the capital of the world, and there Fin'roq would join the Pradishar and study the faiths as a monkin. He'd dreamed it so many times, he'd been so sure it would happen, but he'd long since given up on it.

Could he believe it was possible again?

That would have to wait. The villagers. They needed to be warned.

He lowered his foot, realizing he'd lost count and feeling like a fool. He hissed, knowing if Grizmond beat him down the trail to deliver the news, he'd lose his chance to gain favor with the others. So he gripped the stone tightly with the rootpads on his left foot while lowering his right foot until it touched the ground. Then he quickly dropped his rootpads into the stone while pulling them out of the left foot, so that he was able to stride forth into the unknown with at least an anchor of sorts. But he wasn't prepared for the fork in the pathway, and he hit the cleft between the two routes hard with his face. His cheek tore on the sharp edge, and sap started to flow down his neck. The shock of the impact startled him, and he pulled out his rootpads, wrenching sideways into the left pathway and taking a tumble down several steps. He landed facedown, and when he looked up, he could see light in the distance.

Fin got to his feet, touched his cheek, and realized that only his pride had been seriously injured. At least nobody had been around to see him stumble. He promised he'd be more careful next time as he hurried toward the light. The tunnel's exit had partially collapsed long ago and the foliage had grown so thick overhead and along the sides that he could emerge into the jungle alongside the landing of the stair without being spotted. He looked up toward the palace and saw Grizmond coming down the trail.

Fin'roq took the final few steps that curved around and back onto the sand and sprinted toward the huts at the middle of the beach. He could see the older Verdillions congregated around Jock'imo's tavern while his peers were out on the sand tossing rings. Whisk was banging his drums and Whenton blowing his flute, and Milder was dancing in slow circles in front of them. She stopped when she saw Fin'roq and the music faded out. Her eyes were wide, and when he looked at the other villagers, he could see Roe and Kryll looking murderous, Milli surprised, and Gabs outraged.

He reached Jock'imo's tavern, panting for air. Durq came from inside the hut, glaring, and he didn't see Roe approaching from the beach until he felt the impact, a hard kick to his left knee. He cried out and dropped onto the sand, and Roe fell over on top of him, driving his knee into his flower. Fin opened his mouth to scream but Roe wrapped his fingers around his throat and began to squeeze.

"You fucking halfbreed, how dare you interrupt Nadira?" Roe said, his dull green face turning muddy with rage.

Kryll loomed overhead, his eyes narrowed, and he kicked Fin'roq in the side.

Gabs laughed.

Fin'roq extended a single branch from the underside of his arm, brought it up along Roe's side, and began to slip it around his waist, to grab him and pull him off of him, but Roe leaned close to Fin's ear.

"Please, please try it," he whispered. "I'm begging you."

Fin pulled his branch back under his arm and let the tears fall freely. Durq's face appeared above him, a look of disgust pinching his dull green cheeks. "You'd better have a good reason for this interference," he said. "Roe."

Roe abruptly let go of him and rose to his feet, and Fin turned on his side, coughing and gasping and trying not to vomit. His crushed flower felt like a knife was stuck in his belly, twisting every time he tried to breath. "Ship," he managed to sputter. "Ship coming."

Prissica, who had come to stand behind Durq, let out a wail that made Fin flinch. Her pale green face was puckered in anguish and she pointed a finger at Fin'roq, her hand trembling. "You vile beast," she screamed. "How dare you tease. How dare you!"

Fin'roq went to speak but Roe tackled him again, pushing his head down in the sand and pulling his arms behind his back and up into the air, til he was sure Roe would snap his fibers. He screamed but it only blew sand back into his mouth, choking him.

Prissica was weeping and the others were furious. Fin held his breath, tried not to panic, and cursed Grizmond for not believing him. He knew they'd overreact. He knew they wouldn't trust him.

A lone voice spoke in his defense. "Stop. Wait. Let him go," Milli Mor'n said. "Look, it's Grizmond! The old Raccorin is running. I think Fin's telling the truth."

Fin'roq heard a few of the others gasping, and Roe let him go. He got to his knees, spat out the sand, and looked down the beach to see Grizmond moving along the shore of the harbor, taking great strides. Prissica's mouth was opening and closing like a fish out of water as she looked from Fin'roq to Grizmond to Fin'roq again.

"Ship!" Grizmond called as he approached, breathing heavily, and Prissica began to wail again.

"What have you seen?" Durq said. "Speak!"

"A shape, on the southwestern horizon, moving this way. Definitely of Guild design. It'll be here by sundown."

Aar'ryn Ruu'n pushed his way through the others and stood by Durq. "Don't you see, my friends, our prayers to Trevian have been answered. He has sent his church to deliver us from exile." His eyes were shining and his wide, bright Raccorin cheeks were flushed.

"I said Guild design, I didn't say it was Pradishar," Grizmond said. "We can't know their intentions until they're here."

"Dyna'arin, Corkin, Pradishar. It's all Balance. It's all Trevian's hands," Aar'ryn Ruu'n said. "At long last, deliverance has come. And I can finally be a priestin in name, if not already in practice."

"Careful, Ruu'n," Durq said. "Only bishrops name priestins. I don't want our rescuers thinking us heretics."

"We should consider they might be hostile," Grizmond said.

Aar'ryn Ruu'n laughed and rolled his eyes.

"Hostile for you, maybe," Durq said. "But for citizens of Balance Authority?"

Prissica had gathered her wits and she took Durq by the arm. "What about *that one*," she said, pointing at Fin'roq and crinkling her nose. "We can't have a Bhizini in our midst. If the Pradishar see it, they might consider us enemies, and sail away—or attack us—before we have a chance to explain."

"There's nothing to explain," Durq said. "The Bhizini has no business being here."

"Send him to Bhea Bell," Grizmond said.

"She has no business being here, either," Durq said.

"Let's offer their heads to our rescuers," Roe said, staring at Fin'roq with a hungry look.

Fin looked at the others, at Whisk and Whenton, at Milder and Prissica, at Jock'imo and Aar'ryn and Milli and Gabs, at Kryll and Roe and Durq. Only Milli Mor'n seemed horrified at the suggestion.

Sweet Trevian, were his peers, his townsfolk, his—he didn't know what to call them but he thought of them all as friends, as the only family he had—would they so easily kill him?

He knew he should be scared, but he couldn't help but cry.

"Tell your son to back off," Grizmond said to Durq. "Nobody's getting their heads chopped today."

"Roe is a flowered Verdillion, not some scamp underfoot," Durq said. "So he'll take no orders from me. Besides, he has a good idea, why should I dissuade him?"

Grizmond pulled his sword from its scabbard just as Roe grabbed Fin'roq and held a dagger at his throat.

"Hurt my father, and I kill the Bhizini," Roe said.

"Young fool," Grizmond growled, "you hurt the Bhizini, I kill you and your father. Who's the one with more to lose?"

"You filthy slave, how dare you threaten a citizen?" Durq said, and he unsheathed his own blade.

They stood staring at each other while Fin'roq held his breath. Nobody spoke, and the only sound was the gentle slapping of the water at the edge of the sand and the rustling of the palm leaves in the breeze. Fin closed his eyes and for a moment, it was any other day on P'anorum, any other day of his uneventful life, those long days that, he now realized, had gone unappreciated.

The tension broke when a long stream of blue and orange flame shot over their heads, along with a heat blast, brief but so intense that Fin felt his entire body wilting. He thought the ship must have arrived and begun firing, but the whorl had come from the tavern and not from the harbor.

"Glad I got your attention," Bhea Bell said.

Fin couldn't believe it. In his entire life, Bhea had never set foot in the village. And yet here she was, tall and sinewy, her long gray and white hair fibers flowing around her mottled face like sea foam in the breeze. Her skin was a speckled medley of bright and dull and dark greens, and though ancient, she had a youthful glow about her. In each hand she held a small enflamer, one trained on Durq, the other on Roe.

Fin'roq had never been so glad to see her.

"Now all three of ya idiots put them weapons away before you hurt yourselves," Bhea said. "Acting like damn fools when you got a ship on the way."

"Stay out of this, Bhizini," Durq said. "None of us here need a beetle extracted or a tincture brewed. Just head back to your forest and let us take care of our own affairs." But he sheathed his weapon, and Roe let go of Fin'roq's neck.

Bhea chuckled. "I already heard Roe threaten to kill me and Fin'roq both. You wasn't exactly talking him out of it. I think that makes it my affair now too, don't it?"

Durq avoided looking at Bhea and eyed the enflamers in her hands instead. "I'd like to know how an old Bhizini witch got her claws on two of the Guild's finest weapons." Durq whistled. "What other secrets have you been keeping from us?"

"Fin'roq and I—we're going now," Bhea said.

Roe hissed but when Bhea looked at him, he dropped his eyes to the sand.

"Fin, are you hurt, my sprout?" Bhea asked.

Fin shook his head no.

"Well, come on then."

"You can't take him," Durq said. It came out as a whisper.

Bhea laughed again, then narrowed her eyes and hardened her face. "You gonna stop me, big sprout?"

Durq looked away, his pale green cheeks blushing brown.

"Anyone?" Bhea said, looking around, but they all turned away from her gaze. "Shame. After all these years, I was hoping to test these little ones out on a live specimen." She looked at the enflamers and smirked, then glanced at Grizmond for a moment. "Come on, Fin," she said, and he hurried to her side, looking down, trying to keep the tears inside. But they came out anyway, and fell heavily into the sand.

❧ ☙

Bhea said nothing on the long climb out of the crater, nearly five hundred steps cut into the stone, in zigzags back and forth, steeper and steeper. The foliage pressed in on the stair from both sides, so that Fin'roq's wide shoulders brushed the leaves and he occasionally had to crouch to avoid the hanging tangle of branches that arched overhead. He'd made this climb so many times he could have done it with his eyes closed, and yet today he struggled to keep pace with Bhea. When they reached the top, another stair descended the back of the rim into a narrow valley between the crater and the Crag. The great lava flow was off to the east, a shiny wall glowing ruby in the late afternoon light.

"You alright, my sprout?" Bhea said. She stopped and turned to look at him. "Lemme see ya." She pulled a cloth from her robe and dabbed at the cut on his cheek.

"I fell, in the tunnels," he said. "That's how I cut my face."

"They just scared is all," Bhea said. "Most of 'em, at least."

Fin started to cry again, and Bhea wrapped him in a tight hug, gently stroking his long hair fibers. She smelled like cloves and cinnamon and smoke and coconuts and the sea, and Fin nuzzled his head in her neck and felt like a scamp again, warm and safe with his Bhea.

"Turn around now, let me see them hair fibers of yours," Bhea said. "Got 'em all tangled up, ya did. We get to my place, I'll brush 'em out for ya, do 'em up however you want me to."

"They wanted to kill me," he said.

Bhea didn't say anything for a moment. "All of 'em?"

"Well, no. Grizmond, he was about to fight Durq to save me. I—couldn't believe it."

"Anyone else?"

"Milli Mor'n. She told them to stop attacking me." Fin'roq thought of Milli and sighed. He always did that when he thought of her. She was the only one of his four peers growing up who wasn't openly hostile to him. She even smiled at him sometimes, and would talk to him if the others weren't around.

"So you see, it ain't all bad," Bhea said.

"Except Balance Authority has come to rescue them," Fin said. "Do you think—I mean, it's been over thirty years—maybe Balance Authority has changed the laws? Maybe Bhizini are welcome now?"

Bhea made a sound of disapproval. "Fin'roq, my little sprout, Balance been around a long, long, *long* old time. 9,999 years. Can you imagine it? 9,999 years of peace between the Raccorin Empire and the Andrasian Republic. And 9,999 years of excluding Bhizini from their territories, killing us just for sailing in open seas should we cross one of their damn shipping lanes. No my sprout, Balance ain't changin', least not to befriend the Bhizini."

Fin'roq said nothing, his face burning.

"Let's get going," Bhea said. "We'll talk more when we get to my place."

Fin nodded. "What have you been doing, Bhea? You haven't sent for me in months and Grizmond wouldn't tell me why. I thought maybe you'd died or something."

"Just been so busy, my sprout, and I sure am sorry about it. You can come stay with me as long as you want now, you heard me?"

Fin managed a small smile.

"There we go," Bhea said. "Glad to see you grinnin' again. And listen here, this'll keep the grin on your face. Baboo's waiting for us, up ahead at my garden."

Fin'roq grabbed Bhea's arm and started skipping down the path, and she laughed. They headed for the northwest, down the back of the rim and into the Swarthen Forest. The trail narrowed as it leveled out and passed through thickets dark and cool and wet, and now the path was lined with ferns and strung about with dangling vines, and toadstools popped out of the wet soil under the trees. Later the trail opened again along stretches where he could see out and up, to the Crag overhead wrapped tight in dark clouds and to the sea down below, still spangled with white caps. He could hear the gentle purr of the waves hitting the cliffs, just barely audible over the buzzing of bugs, the gurpling of ghu frogs, the hoots of monkeys, and all the other songs of the canopy.

Soon Fin could hear the gushing of water too, and the path reached an arched stone bridge across a deep gorge, the rocks covered in moss and worn down with footsteps. Below, the Ka'Hala sang as it rushed through the narrow canyon it had carved out over the millennia, on its short journey down through the heart of the Swarthen and off the edge of the cliff to the ocean below.

On the far side of the bridge, an old stone arch was flanked with two small towers, as old as the bridge itself, which served as a doorway of sorts into Bhea's estate. Not far from the canyon's edge, the forest gave way to a plot of cleared land, a well-tended garden on the slopes leading downward, all the way to the edge of the cliff overlooking the sea. The plot was terraced on the upper half where the terrain was steeper, and on the lower part, the land flattened out and there were beds of herbs and spices and rock patches with mosses and ferns. A small channel from the Ka'Hala flowed into the garden and into a long, winding pond, where fountains sprinkled and misted the surrounding areas, and where large stone slabs with rhupan grew, all interspersed with bright flowers of pink and orange and purple and white. On the far side of the garden, the terrain dropped away sharply off an escarpment and into dense forest beyond. Near the cliffside at the bottom of the garden was a flagstone patio with a large table, a dipping pool, and a long view out to the ocean and the reef. On clear days you could see all the way to the tree-clad atolls on the edge of the Swirling Sea.

When Fin'roq crossed the bridge, passed through the arches, and headed out into the garden, he could see his friend standing on the patio's edge, arms up and branches unfurled, staring out to sea. Baboo looked like a miniature tandavin, with a saffron robe similar in color to the bark that covered the rooted ones on the gruynfeld. Bhea said he was probably as old as one too, and the youngest tandavin was at least 180 years old, so Baboo was old. And yet he looked like a scamp still far from flowering. Fin'roq remembered when he'd caught up and passed him in height, while his strange friend never grew, never changed at all.

"Baboo!" Fin shouted, skipping along the flagstone path to the patio.

Baboo lowered his branches as he turned, but kept his arms out wide, and Fin ran into them for a big hug. He picked Baboo up and twirled him around in the air, and Baboo grabbed Fin's shoulders and did a flip over his head, landing on his feet with a goofy grin on his face.

"How many times do I gotta tell ya, no acrobatics by the edge!" Bhea shouted, but she was smiling.

"Oh Baboo, thank Trevian you're here," Fin said.

"I'm always here," he said, then he did a cartwheel and stuck his tongue out at Bhea.

She wagged her finger at him, still grinning.

"There's a ship, an actual ship, coming to P'anorum. It's probably already in the harbor by now," Fin said.

"I know," Baboo said. He pointed toward the southwest. "I watched it coming." He took Fin's hand and smiled at him. "No need to worry, Fin friend. You're safe."

"That's right," Bhea said. "Ain't nothin' to worry about. You listen to your Baboo if you won't listen to your Bhea."

"That's easy for you both to say," Fin said. "You almost never leave this garden." He looked at Baboo. "And you randomly vanish away into the Swarthen Forest for months at a time. Neither of you are part of the community, so you don't have anything to lose. But me—am I supposed to spend the rest of my life here, with only the two of you? No offense, you know I love you both, more than anyone! But I want more. I want—love. I want to have a family. I want to be a monkin and serve Trevian. I want to see Balan Su, to see Andramere, to see all the places from the books and the scrolls. How am I supposed to do any of that, if they all leave me behind?"

Bhea had a stricken look on her face, and Fin blushed. "I'm sorry for yelling," he said.

"That's okay, my little sprout,," she said. "Just breathe. Take a moment and breathe it out."

Baboo started making a big show of taking deep breaths and exhaling them loudly, and Fin chuckled.

"You always manage to cheer me up," he said. "I guess I should be grateful. I couldn't ask for better companions to be stranded here with, even if it means giving up on all my dreams. I guess I should have given up on those long ago."

Baboo shrugged and stood on his head, but Bhea turned away and said nothing.

❧ ☙

Days went by without any word from the village. Fin'roq thought he'd lose his mind with anticipation. His appetite was gone. He could hardly sleep at night. The ship was all he thought about—well, mostly. Bhea Bell was keeping him so busy he didn't have time for much else. He was equal parts grateful and furious with her for it. But as a full week had come and gone and still no word from the village, his consternation was quickly turning to despair.

He got up every day as soon as the sky was light, he and Baboo both, and with the long brooms in hand, set to sweeping off the patio and the flagstone pathways that crisscrossed the garden. They had a lot of ground to cover, and by the time they finished, Bhea always had a delicious breakfast laid out on the table, first with hot steaming jha'ala, then rhupan porridge, and finally cool fizzy spring water with a squeeze of citrus to wash down the meal. Before they'd finished their fizzies, Bhea would clear the table and replace the dishes with books and scrolls, quills and ink pots. She'd lecture for awhile, then leave them to read and write on their own while she prepared lunch.

Afternoons were spent among the terraces, collecting ingredients for food and tinctures, or down in the grotto, storing and preparing and brewing. After dinner, they'd help Bhea light the glowbes around the garden, then she'd bring out her basket with games and they'd play together on the table under the stars, Baboo getting up to dance after every game, win or lose. Bhea would serve bhiza cookies after a few games, Fin's favorite treat, and he'd taken to having a few more than he should, but Bhea never said anything about it like she did when he was still a scamp.

Even with the extra bhiza cookies, and even being exhausted from all the work he'd been doing, he still found himself wide awake whenever he went to his sleeping hut. He'd raise his arms and unfurl his branches, let his rootpads slip down into the soil, then close his eyes and panic.

They were going to leave him. They were all going to leave him. They were going to be gone, forever. He'd never know the love of another. He'd never see the world, never join the Pradishar. Never study in the capital.

The hours would pass as he perched there, struggling to get enough air, feeling the sap pulsing in his neck, trying to figure out what to do, what to do, Sweet Trevian, what to do. But answers never came before sleep somehow overtook him.

And then Baboo was gone again, back to wherever he went when he wasn't at Bhea's, gone for who knew how long. Fin'roq knew there was nothing strange about him leaving. In fact a whole week with him had been something of a rare treat. But why had he left now? Couldn't Baboo see how much he needed a friend? That he was hardly holding it together?

But no. Baboo was never upset, never worried, never convinced anything was serious. He would have stayed if Fin had asked, but otherwise it wouldn't have occurred to him to do so.

"He'll be back 'fore you know it," Bhea said, setting out the breakfast on the table.

"I'm about to lose my mind," Fin said. "I can't take it anymore. I have to go back. I have to see if anyone's left. Can you understand that I'm dying here?"

Bhea gave him a tired look, and she opened her mouth to say something when a loud knocking came from the gate by the bridge. Fin'roq jumped to his feet but Bhea hissed at him. "I'll be answerin' that, thank ya much," she said. "You sit on down and eat your breakfast, you heard me?"

Fin lowered his eyes but didn't hide his scowl. Bhea hurried for the gate, and he watched as she opened a small peephole to look out. She shut the hole and opened the main gate, and Fin'roq almost squealed when he saw Grizmond enter the garden. He blinked quickly to stop the tears from stinging his eyes.

"You're still here," he said when the old Raccorin sat down at the table.

Grizmond grunted in affirmation.

"The ship?" Fin asked.

"Gone," Grizmond said.

Fin swallowed in a thick throat and took a sip of his fizzy before speaking, but Bhea beat him to it.

"And the others?" she said.

Grizmond sighed. "Everyone's still on P'anorum."

"Tell me everything," Bhea said.

"It was the Pradishar, all right. They came right on into the harbor and then just floated there, for more'n a day, without hailing us, nothing. Aar'ryn Ruu'n got so agitated he got one of the cano'rins and he and Roe paddled out to the ship. They took 'em aboard, and it was another five days before they were heard from again. We all thought Prissica was gonna have a breakdown. But then Aar'ryn and Roe came back to shore in their cano'rin, beaming like they'd just been kissed by Astra'bel. And damnit all if they hadn't been Joined! Both of 'em, with Pradishar crystamins in their foreheads. They hadn't hardly stepped ashore when the cata'rin opened wide it's gurgitator and sailed on out of the harbor. Nobody could believe it, except Aar'ryn and Roe, who stood there grinning like idiots.

"Well, next thing you know, Aar'ryn's up there preaching like a priestin, claiming Trevian had chosen him for a special mission, chosen us all for a mission. And that once the mission was over, everyone would be rescued, taken back to Balance Territories. Saved."

Bhea hissed. "You better start makin' sense," she said.

"I'm afraid it don't make much," Grizmond said. "Seems—well, it seems the Pradishar aren't willing to just up and rescue everyone. Seems they want something first. Aar'ryn and Roe won't say much, but they're looking for something. And," he looked at Fin'roq, "they need Fin's help to find it."

Fin'roq chuckled. "Is this a joke? You think I'd help them leave the island? Help them abandon me here?"

Grizmond looked at Bhea and half-sighed, half-growled before turning back to Fin. "That part makes even less sense," he said. "Seems—well, it seems they're willing to take you to Balan Su, even let you enroll as a monkin at the Pruu'patch. Providing you get 'em what they want."

Fin's heart seemed to stop beating, his lungs to drain of air, even the sound of the Ka'Hala crashing into the surf against the cliffside below seemed to fade to a whisper.

"I don't understand. What are they looking for?" he said.

"For you," Bhea said. Her mottled face had drained of color, the anger melting away into an expression Fin'roq couldn't quite place.

Grizmond gaped at Bhea, then quickly scowled again. "I don't know what they're looking for, only that it's beneath the island, down in the tunnels, and you're the only one who's been brave enough to go down there."

Fin'roq blushed at the praise, something Grizmond had never offered him before, and he could feel his ears burning. He sat in silence, wondering if he was still in the sleeping patch, yet to wake for another day of desperation.

Bhea pushed the food around on her plate, a distant look in her eyes. Fin'roq went over and sat next to her and put his head on her shoulder. "I can't believe it," he said. "It sounds—too perfect, doesn't it."

"Then there's still hope," Bhea said.

"What should I do?"

"I can't tell you that, my sprout. You've flowered now. You aren't a little scamp running about my ankles. I can't protect you no more. It's you gotta make your own decisions now. But here's what I can offer, love. You go on back to the village, talk to the others, see how you feel about things. And remember what I'm always tellin' ya—don't listen to what they sayin', look at what they doin', you wanna get to know a plant."

"Why would they be looking for me, Bhea?" he asked, and she looked up, wincing.

"Oh my sprout, the Pradishar are always huntin' Bhizini," she said. "I was just scared is all. Guess I'll always be thinking of you as a scamp. Like you was my own."

Fin hugged her and Bhea hugged him back, squeezing him so tightly he had to pat her on the shoulder to get her to ease up.

⌇⌇⌇⌇⌇ ⌇⌇⌇⌇⌇

Bhea insisted that Fin'roq stay for his studies, so Grizmond returned in the late afternoon to accompany him back to the village. The old Raccorin said nothing on the walk, occasionally grunting in response to Fin'roq's chatter.

When they climbed the short stair to the rim of the crater and started down the zigzagging pathway toward the village, Fin could see smoke rising from Jock'imo's tavern and hear the music from Whisk's drums and Whenton's flute. The western rim cast a shadow on the harbor, cutting across the beach and right over the village, slowly spreading eastward.

Fin'roq stopped, a tight feeling in his stomach. "They're having a festival," he said. "I shouldn't go down. They'll be angry."

Grizmond put his hand on his shoulder. "Not today they won't," he said.

Fin nodded and started back down the stairs, zigging and zagging through the foliage, counting as he went. When he reached the sand and started up the beach for the tavern, he could see the other villagers turn, stop, and stare, and Whisk and Whenton stopped playing. The tight feeling in Fin's stomach was back, and he looked to Grizmond, wondering if he'd been mistaken.

When he turned back toward the tavern, Aar'ryn Ruu'n was hurrying across the sand, arms wide, an enormous grin on his bright Raccorin face. On his forehead was a small round crystal, about the size of Fin's fingertip. The inside was a deep violet while the edges faded to gray, like a purple orb amidst a raincloud on his bright green skin.

"Welcome Fin'roq, welcome," Aar'ryn cried. "You'll have to forgive the others for not greeting you as I do. They didn't think you'd really come is all."

"I'm sorry to interrupt your festival," he said. "Are you sure it's okay I'm here?"

Aar'ryn laughed loudly. "Fin'roq, Fin'roq," he said, "this festival is for you."

Fin looked around at the other villagers, who had come closer but were still holding back, not sure what to do. Only Milli Mor'n was smiling at him, and he blushed, his heart thudding in his ears.

"Hi everyone," he said, staring at Milli and waving awkwardly, his arm feeling like it didn't belong to him—his voice like it came from somewhere else—his face like it was on fire.

Durq walked over to him, his narrow Andrasian cheeks pulled into a smirk which quickly broke into a toothy smile. "Welcome, Fin'roq," he said, and that was all it took for the others to come round. They all greeted him in turn, even putting their hands on his chest in the formal way as none of them ever had before. Even Prissica touched him, and instead of crinkling her nose in his presence, she looked almost radiant, her eyes warm and twinkling. Fin'roq felt the skin on his back and neck tingling.

"There's our savior," she said, winking. "The only one of us brave enough." She scowled at Durq.

He put his hands up. "I don't know the way is all. And my ankle gives me trouble sometimes, you know that. I'd probably twist it and end up petrifying under there."

"Whisk, Whenton, strike up the music," Aar'ryn said. "Jock'imo, get those rhingamis on the grill. The rest of you, give Fin'roq some space. You've got all evening to catch up."

"I don't mind," Fin said, but Aar'ryn had already put his arm around his shoulders and was leading him up the beach, away from the others.

"Of course you don't, Fin," he said. "Can I call you Fin? Wonderful. Not to worry, we'll return to the festival soon, I just need a moment of your time first. Let's go down to the old sharlum where we can speak privately. What do you say?"

Fin looked back to see what Grizmond was doing but he was busy talking to Jock'imo. So he shrugged and followed Aar'ryn up to the western end of the beach, where a small stair led to a flat rocky outcropping on the water's edge. Bougainvillea grew thick in the foliage around the edges, all purple flowers in honor of the Pradishar. The space had been used as a sharlum for as long as Fin'roq could remember, with Aar'ryn Ruu'n as the pretend priest. The villagers would gather here at high noon, every third day, to hear passages from the Pruu'log and to sing the old songs. Fin'roq was never invited, but always sat nearby, listening to the words through the thorny vines of the bougainvillea.

And yet now he was invited inside. Now the fake priestin had a Pradishar crystal. No more pretending. What could Aar'ryn Ruu'n see with that crystal? What was it like to have one? Fin'roq longed to know.

"What are the Pradishar looking for?" Fin asked once they were inside the sharlum.

Aar'ryn chuckled. "Old Grizmond's been running his mouth, eh? The fool never speaks when I need him to, then he goes and says too much when I need him not to."

"You didn't want me to know?"

Aar'ryn giggled. "Of course I wanted you to know. But in the proper time. The last thing I wanted you to think was that our intentions were impure. The others are convinced their fate is in your hands, but I know that our fate is in Trevian's hands, and his hands alone. I've served the master blindly, for decades, on faith alone. But now I have a piece of him inside of me." He touched the crystal on his forehead. "Now I see as I've never seen before." His eyes were twitching.

"Then what do you need me for?"

Aar'ryn seemed to return from far away and his eyes fell still. He looked at Fin'roq without saying anything.

Roe came up the steps into the sharlum, and when Fin saw him, his stomach clenched up and he held his breath, waiting. An encounter with Roe almost always meant an assault of some kind or other. But he had a calm look on his face and the corners of his eyes were crinkled into a smile. He had a violet and gray crystal nearly identical to Ruu'n's, but the gray edges faded seamlessly into his ashen-green Andrasian skin.

"We need you to take Aar'ryn Ruu'n and me down into the tunnels," Roe said, walking over to Fin'roq and placing his hands on Fin's chest in greeting.

Fin placed his own hands on Roe's chest and was surprised at how warm he felt, how soft his skin was, and he couldn't help blushing.

"But that's only a little thing," Roe said. "Believe it or not, the captain of the ship and the one who Joined us to the crystal was a Bhizini, Fin'roq. A Bhizini, but also a Pradishar priestin. Times are changing in Balance Territories. Now that I'm a monkin of the Pradishar—now that I can see as I never could before—I see that I've been wrong in how I've treated you, Fin'roq. Do you think you can forgive me?"

Roe hadn't moved his hands from Fin's chest, and Fin had hardly taken a breath while Roe spoke. Was he telling the truth? He looked at Roe, at his smile, his eyes, his annoyingly handsome face, and he nodded. "Forgiven," he said. Then he turned to Aar'ryn. "Is it true? There's a Bhizini priestin in the Pradishar?"

Aar'ryn nodded.

"Will you help us?" Roe asked.

Fin looked at Roe's eyes, at Aar'ryn's eyes. He studied their faces. He thought about Prissica, about Durq, about Milli Mor'n. He thought of their expressions, the way they looked at him. With hope and—with need. Bhea had told him to look, not listen, and he'd seen. And his heart had more than felt.

"Of course I will," he said. "Though I still don't know what it is you're looking for."

Later Fin'roq wondered what would have happened if he'd refused to help them. Would they have held him captive until the Pradishar returned, joined him with an imperialized crystal, swung him about like a puppet on a string? Would they have torn the secrets from his mind before executing him? They could do such things, once you were Joined, even from the other side of the world.

All crystals, Bhea said, meant bondage.

But Fin knew he would never have said no to them. He couldn't have refused the chance to prove his worth to the others. With this act, they'd be eternally grateful. And if there really was a Bhizini priestin—Aar'ryn and Roe had sworn again it was true—then that changed everything. His hopes and dreams for the future—they were possible again.

And so he'd determined to believe them.

When they told him they sought a Dyna'arin operations chamber, known to be accessible from the surface, he panicked. What was a Dyna'arin operations chamber? He'd heard the older villagers mention the Guild and their operations, and there were more than a few pieces of their maquina still in use on the island, including the cookery at Jock'imo's tavern and the glowbes which lit the village every night. There had been an old lift on the edge of the eastern pier until a few years ago, when the dynamin that powered it began to overload, and before long the maquina, and most of the pier, were turned into rubble when it blew. The villagers had been dreading the day that Jock'imo's cookery, long bereft of maintenance, finally met the same fate.

Fin didn't know how much to tell them—how much to give away. Should he confess that the ruins of Old P'anorum, the capital with its plazas and temples, stood intact and accessible beneath the lava, the cobblestone streets and burnstone walls painted red by the light of the crystalline lava overhead? He thought of Aar'ryn and Roe traipsing through the ruins of the city—his quiet place, his sanctuary, *his* city.

"Old P'anorum is inaccessible," he lied.

"This chamber wasn't in the city, but far beneath it," Aar'ryn said. He pulled a scroll from his robe and handed it to Fin'roq. He unrolled it and saw that it was a map of the old city with the main avenues and plazas and landmarks noted.

"It's hard to believe something like this is here on this island, when all we know is this crater and the edges of the Swarthen Forest," Roe said.

"You youngsters don't remember like we old timers do," Aar'ryn said. "That's a blessing from Trevian, I assure you." He pointed to the map, to the northwestern edge of the city, up along the Flamewater, which once—and still—flowed from the gap between the Crag and P'anorum Peak, down through the heart of the city, it's waters hot to the touch and fragrant with minerals. Then his finger trailed the line between the two peaks.

"I know the area," Fin said. "A labyrinth of corridors and stairwells. But there's a bad smell to the air. I've never gone very deep."

"Just get us in the door," Roe said. "We have the schematics in here." He touched the crystal on his forehead, and Fin'roq wondered what it felt like to see two things at once, to be two places at once.

They set out early the next morning. Fin thought it took about four hours to get there, which gave them about five hours to explore and four to make it back before dark. A full day without sunlight would make most Verdillions tremble, but most could go a few days before they grew stiff and started to howl themselves to death.

The hike to the entrance was uneventful, a long and trudging climb, first up the stair to the rim, then a much more treacherous hike up a broken and crumbling stair along the edge of the Crag and the base of P'anorum Peak. The path led to a small lookout tower near the False Lip, a pseudo-crater on the Crag's eastern side. They took a moment to gaze northward, into the waters of the Swirling Sea, though they had to shield their eyes from the glare of the sun off the massive red peak in front of them, it's crystal-coated sides sparkling like hot magma.

"Now we go underground," Fin'roq said.

Aar'ryn passed out glowbes, small ones that fit in the palm of Fin's hand. Then they both nodded at him. Roe's eyes were twitching, and his face looked flushed.

Fin led them to a stair at the rear of the lookout tower, and they gave their glowbes a shake. They crackled like kindling in a flame, and warm light spread down the steps in front of them.

Down and down they went, on a narrow spiraling stair, down through the rock of the Crag. Fin'roq closed his eyes and counted silently, one hand on the outer wall, the other trailing the central column of the stairwell, til he took one final step and passed into a long, narrow, flat corridor. Fin knew it headed east, under the narrow valley between the Crag and P'anorum Peak, and under the edge of the city.

He set off without speaking to the others and debated whether or not he should count his way or rely on the glowbe instead. Not counting was a good way to get lost. But then again he'd always found his way out, and Aar'ryn and Roe had said they had access to a map of the place via crystal, so there wasn't any reason to act like he was in the dark.

He counted anyway.

The corridor ended at a large doorway. Fin'roq saw that a metal door had been torn away from it's hinges, blasted off the wall and folded up like a discarded page from one of Bhea's books. He'd never seen this before, only felt the rough edges of the door jam in the dark, and hadn't understood what had caused it. Now he saw what a powerful weapon it must have been.

"We are close now," Aar'ryn said. "Good work, Fin. I'll take over now. Follow me."

Aar'ryn and Roe started off down a corridor, turned into another, then headed down a staircase to a lower level and off down another corridor. They were practically running, which made counting paces impossible, and Fin had soon lost track of how to get back to the entrance. He tried not to panic. The others were moving so confidently, surely they'd know the way back.

But then he smelled it, and his stomach churned and he thought he might throw up the rhupan jerky he'd been chewing on during the hike. That foul air he'd warned them about, dry and sour, filled his nostrils and seemed to seep into his pores.

"We should go back," Fin said. "The air. It could be poisonous."

"It's not poison," Aar'ryn said. "It's petrification."

"And we're not turning back," Roe said.

Fin realized he had no choice but to stay with them, so he tried not to breathe through his nose and nodded at them.

They descended another long spiraling stair, and Fin'roq distracted himself by counting. At around 2,000 steps, he gave up, overwhelmed by the stench of petrification that had been steadily growing as they dropped down into the bowels of P'anorum. Fin thought they must be far below sea level by now, much deeper than he'd ever dared to go.

And then the steps ended. A short hallway led to a cavern so vast, the light of the glowbes seemed to vanish away into the black that sprawled out before them. In the far distance, a soft red glow fanned out of a flat black line, and Fin thought for a moment he was staring at dawn across the surface of the sea, until he realized he was seeing the glow of lava at the far end of the cave.

He took a few steps forward and saw that the floor was cobblestoned, like a city street. He looked at Aar'ryn and Roe, and they were both wide-eyed, looks of rapture on their faces. Both of their eyes were twitching wildly.

That was when he saw the wall behind them. It wasn't so much a wall of a cave as it was the wall of a building, the front of a great palace, etched with faded friezes and hieroglyphics, its porticos empty, it's windows gone, its vast doorway a gaping black hole that Fin was certain would swallow him.

"What is this place?" he whispered.

Aar'ryn turned to follow his gaze and he looked up and down the facade of the palace before them, his arms held wide, his eyes glowing. Roe was laughing, and he and Aar'ryn gave each other a hug.

"This is what we've been seeking!" Aar'ryn said. "The lost temple of Trevian."

"So we can go back now?" Fin asked.

"Don't be ridiculous," Roe said. "We've only just arrived."

"And we've rituals to perform," Aar'ryn said. "Prayers to recite. Blessings to procure."

"We should go," Fin said, but they ignored him and headed for the door of the temple. "Don't—" But they were already inside. He looked around in desperation. The smell was too much, and the stuffy hot air seemed to choke him. But he couldn't leave without them, because he didn't know the way back. He thought he might cry, but no—if they were brave, he would be brave.

Swallowing his fear, he forced his legs to move, and he passed through the threshold, one slow pace at a time. Aar'ryn and Roe were just inside the entrance. Roe held up his glowbe while Aar'ryn fiddled with an open panel on the wall.

"The dynamin should still work," Aar'ryn was saying. "Just need to make the connection again. That should do it."

Fin'roq heard a slow humming that rose to a high-pitched whine and he could feel his back teeth clenching. Glowbes overhead began to crackle and come to life, and Fin'roq saw a large chandelier hanging down from a vaulted ceiling, in what looked to be a long, wide chamber stretching back into the darkness. A portion of the ceiling in the front right corner had collapsed and partially crushed a large maquina, some sort of metal chamber, like the oven in Jock'imo's cookery, only taller and wider. The door was ajar, and next to it were two dead Verdillions, face down on the ground and long petrified, their skin shiny and gray like wet stone.

Behind the maquina, row after row of statues, arrayed in lines like an army ready for battle, stretched back into the dark depths of the chamber. Only they weren't statues, but corpses, their mouths agape and twisted into misshapen holes, and for a moment Fin'roq swore he could hear them screaming.

He tried to move, tried to look at the others, but he couldn't. Someone was pulling on his arms, pulling on his legs, tugging at his hair fibers, but he couldn't respond, couldn't move. He was trapped, held fast, tranquilized.

No, he was being torn apart! Ripped into two pieces. Shredded.

Aar'ryn and Roe saw Fin's look of horror, his face frozen in a soundless scream, and they stood on either side of him and began to pray. Their eyes were twitching as they recited words long forgotten. Aar'ryn sang and wept and beat his breast. But Fin'roq stood still, rigid, broken.

"It's not working," Aar'ryn said. "He won't wake up."

"Fin'roq," Roe said, shaking him. "Fin'roq!" He slapped him across the face. No reaction. Roe made a fist, shrugged to Aar'ryn, and popped Fin in the jaw. "Maybe it's not him," he said.

"Maybe," Aar'ryn said. "I guess that's good news. But what do we do with him? I don't want to carry him back up."

"Worthless Bhizini scum," Roe said. "Let's just leave him here with the others. We got what we needed. Let's get the fuck off this rock already."

Aar'ryn stood. "Pity," he said. "I was sure...but oh well."

"Farewell, Fin'roq," Roe said, and he took one last swipe at him, a hard punch into Fin's belly, crushing his flower.

And Fin'roq awoke from his stupor.

He could hear someone speaking to him, laughing. Friendly laughter, warm and joyful. Welcoming. He followed the laughter, and felt an embrace, branches wrapping him up in a hug not unlike the hugs Bhea Bell gave him, making him feel so safe, so loved, so special.

But the warmth vanished, the voice faded, and the pain—the tearing, crushing pain—was all he knew. He staggered backward, felt himself falling over, but something stood him upright again. Roe's face filled his mind, and he groped for him, leapt for him, and grasped him—a warm, pulsing flame, filled with words, with emotions, with images—and he devoured them all, pulling Roe's memories into himself.

Roe struggled, tried to fight, to close his mind to him. He staggered backwards, thrashing his head from side to side, swinging wildly at the air. But Fin, eyes rolled back in his head, stared with empty pits at his own hands. And as he slowly turned them, Roe's head began to twist around. Fibers popped and Roe's screams turned into gurgles. His head kept turning, round and round until it snapped free. The body collapsed away under it, while the head hung there for a moment longer before exploding, spraying Fin and Aar'ryn with sap and brain, with bits of skull and shards of crystal.

Aar'ryn watched a moment longer, his eyes twitching, a mixture of horror and wonder on his face. But when Fin'roq turned to him, his eyes two cloudy white pits narrowed with fury, Aar'ryn turned and ran.

Fin'roq's skin faded and his eyes rolled forward and closed, and he dropped to the ground, screaming, certain he was being torn in two. He screamed and screamed, but found no relief. He was still screaming when the glowbes began to flicker and fail, still screaming when the room fell into darkness.

It wasn't long before he was sure he'd always been there, in that chamber, in the darkness, torn apart, locked away, screaming, screaming forever.

Chapter 2

The Terrible Blossom

BRYN ANDRI'N SAT IN her study long after the sun had set and her parents had gone to sleep, an enormous book in her lap, piles of scrolls and larger volumes stacked around her on the floor. The tome she held was ancient, and the leaves looked like they might crumble at any moment. Little whorls of dust spread out on either side of her with each turn of the page. Bryn didn't notice. Her eyes were too busy scanning the old words, occasionally twitching as she archived relevant passages through her crystal. She turned the last page and then placed the book with the other useless texts and sighed when she realized that it was by far the largest stack of them all.

She yawned, then poked the glowbes at her side to rekindle them, their warm flickering light wanting to fade out and sleep, just like her eyes. But she resisted the urge and kept scanning.

As much as Bryn loved research, and loved these dusty old books and scrolls, tonight she found no pleasure in her perusal. The issue was just too great, too worrisome—and her progress had been too slow—to bring her the usual joy she should have been experiencing from so much research.

She was running out of time.

Bryn took her hand and placed it gently on her navel and rubbed it in slow circles. Even through her robe, she could feel the hard little nob protruding from her belly button. She gulped when she realized it had gotten bigger since earlier in the evening. Now wide awake again, she grabbed another scroll from the pile—*The Blossoming of Power*, by Dalian Rorh—but when she untied the lace and began to unroll it, she realized it was about volcanic eruptions and not flowering. She retied the scroll and placed it in the useless pile, thought about going for a fresh pot of jha'ala, but reached for another text instead.

Bryn didn't know what time sleep won out, only that she had slumped over in her chair, her legs crossed under her, and thus her feet far from the soil. She woke with an ache in her side, cramps in her shins, and a heavy feeling in her bowels, and she was horrified when she realized she'd drooled on a page in Darth'n's *Exhibitions of the Dynamics of Pollination on Grand Gardenia in the Third Millenia C.O.B.* Fortunately the ink hadn't bled, but she felt like a fool.

At least it wasn't a first edition, she thought.

"I was just about to wake you," her mother said, coming into the study.

Bryn groaned and stretched her thick arms and carefully untangled her long legs from under her. She closed Darth'n's book and went to place it in the pile for further consideration when the hard cover swiped her belly and she gasped.

"Brynnie, love, are you okay?" Mama Andri'n asked.

Bryn looked up at her mother, her eyes wide, and shook her head no. She looked down at her abdomen for a moment, then grabbed her robe and lifted it up to her chest. There at her navel, covering a third of the width of her belly, was a fully-bloomed flower, creamy white on the edges with little swirls of yellow and pink near the middle.

Mama Andri'n smiled, a sparkle of moisture in her eyes. "A beautiful flower for my beautiful Bryn," she said, but her smiled faded when she saw Bryn's face. "Oh love, it's okay. Come here." Mama Andri'n hobbled over to Bryn, wincing as she stepped on her bad leg, and put her arms around her. Bryn let out a sob. "We all bloom eventually. It's nothing to be ashamed of. Just means you're an adult now. My little Brynnie, all grown up."

"You know what it means," she said, struggling to get her breath under control.

"Don't you worry about that," Mama Andri'n said. "I'm sure the committee will see the beautiful female you are. You'll see."

Bryn gave her mother an incredulous look. "With this body, these shoulders, these hands? With this voice!?"

"Assignment is something we all gotta do. No choice about it, love. But it'll be okay. You'll see."

"Not all of us," Bryn corrected her mother. "Bhizini aren't assigned. They get to choose."

"Well, everyone under Balance Authority at least. Unless you wanna go spend your life on the sea? Somehow I don't think you could go a day without your library or your mountain of scrolls and books." She was smiling but Bryn was unappeased.

"I've spent weeks trying to find something—*anything*—that would explain why gender has to be assigned. But there's no historical evidence anywhere for the practice. It's all just anecdotes by priestins and bishrops, trying to explain things morally but not rationally. I want evidence, arguments, facts! I can't even find out when or where the first assignments took place, but somehow I doubt they were already well-established when Balance was formed."

"I don't know about any of that," Mama Andri'n said. "But the Pradishar aren't blind. They'll see the female you are. I promise. Now, dry that lovely face of yours and come with me. I've got something for you."

Bryn wiped her eyes and followed her mother into the bathing room.

"Now then, your very first cumberdome," Mama Andri'n said, pulling out a piece of underwear from a chest in the corner. "Now you've got a flower, you gotta keep it safe. Don't want it gettin' smooshed. Also don't want it gettin' rubbed at the wrong time neither. I bought these for you just a few weeks ago when you got your first bud. Aren't they nice?"

Bryn took one of them in her hands. The garment had a reinforced half-sphere with straps on either side, and a rim of soft fibers along the edges.

A hideous thing, she thought.

"The fabric is lovely, Mama," she said. "Is this squorkwood on the edge?"

Mama Andri'n beamed. "It is indeed. And the fabric is silk all the way from Filamon. Isn't it soft? Won't chafe ya like some of 'em will. Now then, go on and wet your finger and run it along the squorkwood, then place the dome square over your flower, making sure you don't pinch none of the petals. You'll sure feel it if you do! Now press it down good on your belly and it should stick there, keepin' it from sliding about. Now then, wrap the strap around your back side, and these around your legs there, and fasten 'em up right here. Good good." She unstrapped it and took it off Bryn. "It takes a bit of gettin' used to, but it ain't so bad. Now then, you practice putting it on yourself while I go get breakfast ready."

When Bryn was alone, she threw the cumberdome on the ground, sat down on the edge of the fountain, and went back to weeping. She felt for her friends Ginjy and Rhingus through her crystal.

<<Well my lovelies, it's official. I've got a flower.>>

<<Keep your head up,>> Rhingus said. <<Welcome to adulthood.>>

<<Strength, dear one,>> Ginjy said.

Bryn felt a wave of love and warmth and support from her friends through the crystal, and she found the courage to lift her head and face the day. She rinsed off her tears in the fountain, then picked up the cumberdome and looked at it warily. But before she put it on, she decided to have a closer look at her flower. As much as she didn't want to have it, she had to admit it was beautiful. She'd seen plenty of streams on the weavryn with Verdillions coupling. She'd even tried a few sense streams, but without a flower of her own, she hadn't felt anything, and hadn't understood what all the fuss was about.

Now her curiosity got the better of her. She bent over as close as she could get her face to her torso and breathed deep. The flower had a sweet, tangy scent, like spun sugar clouds at the Riverwalk. She took her finger and stroked some of the outer petals. They were so soft, softer even than the silk cumberdome. And they were sensitive too, each stroke making her shoulders tingle. Then she stuck her finger down in between the petals, down in the heart of the flower, and she screamed, a high, short outburst.

"You okay in there?" Mama Andri'n called from outside.

"Mmm-hmm," Bryn said, blushing. "Just pinched a petal."

"Takes some gettin' used to is all. You'll get it," she said through the door.

Bryn put the cumberdome on, strapped it up, slipped a clean robe over her head, retied her hair fibers into a bun on the back of her head, and walked out into the heart of her family's garden. Her father, Doc Andri'n, was sitting at the round stone table in the middle of the terrace, his eyes barely twitching, a scroll unrolled in front of him, a mug of steaming jha'ala in one hand.

"Ah Bryndax, good," he said, his eyes falling still and crinkling when he smiled. He patted the table next to him. "Come, sit, sit. I have a surprise for you. And perfect timing too, what with this being a very special day—the day you are no longer my little scamp." His eyes misted over but he was still smiling warmly.

Bryn forced a smile and sat down at the table. "Thanks Papa. What do you have for me?"

"You've seen the stream of the Bhizini?" he asked.

She gave him a look. "You'll need to be more specific than that."

"I wouldn't if you'd seen it. The Pradishar are trying their best to suppress it, but its spreading faster than they can contain it. I was sure you would have seen it already."

"I've been distracted."

Doc Andri'n's eyes twitched and Bryn's did too. In her mind, she saw an old temple, a chandelier of glowbes, a large maquina that looked like an oven. She was looking through someone's eyes, seeing and hearing what they'd experienced. Two Verdillions were standing face to face, an Andrasian with typically pale skin, and a Bhizini, a patchwork of bright and dull greens on their face and arms, mouth ajar, face twisted in pain, yet catatonic, frozen in place. The Andrasian approached, screamed, poked, slapped, and punched the Bhizini, but the Bhizini didn't budge. Bryn watched the Andrasian jam his palm into the Bhizini's flower. The Bhizini's eyes rolled back in their head and their skin seemed to shimmer like wet stone, and the Andrasian's head began to twist around.

Bryn saw the entire thing in a instant, though it felt like real time to her.

She looked at her father. "A fake," she said, analyzing the stream and its data. "A ploy by one of the studios to promote a new melodrama, perhaps. It's stripped of its original metadata, so we can't trace its origin. Low lighting makes it harder to see the artifice they've created. That said, they've done a marvelous job. Any idea who made it?"

"What if I told you that I don't believe it to be a fake?"

Bryn stared at her father for a moment. "Not even an imperious crystamin could make someone's head spin around like that," she said.

"I have the metadata," Doc Andri'n said. "The source is a Pradishar monkin, recently recruited, by the name of Aar'ryn Ruu'n."

"Any relation to the Gran Pradesh?"

"His nephew. The Andrasian was also recently recruited. And by recently, I mean within the last week. See for yourself." His eyes twitched and Bryn received the stream's original metadata. "What do you make of it, Bryndax?"

She scanned the information. She could tell her father was excited, perhaps disturbed. And he wasn't telling her something. If real, the stream was unexplainable, a fascinating puzzle to solve, the kind Bryn and her father both loved. But she just couldn't focus, couldn't even make herself care. All she could think about was her flower and what it meant.

"Papa," she said, and started to cry. Doc Andri'n looked confused for a second, then quickly wrapped his arms around Bryn's shoulders and held her.

"Don't worry, Bryndax, dear. You know I don't give two hoots what the Pradishar think. Whatever they decide, whatever they proclaim, you'll always be my beautiful daughter."

Mama Andri'n came in with the breakfast and hastily sat the food down so she could join in the hug.

Once the food was served, Doc Andri'n couldn't help himself.

"I'm sorry to push, Bryndax. Not only are you my daughter, you're my best student. I need your insights on that metadata, when you can bear to have a good look at it."

"What are you talking about?" Mama Andri'n said. She had a furious look on her face. "Bryncent, I told you already, it's too risky sharing that kind of information. You might be the brightest mind on this blessed island—after Brynnie, of course—but Sweet Trevian, you're a fool sometimes. Don't you know the Cul'tavin are sniffing around everywhere, looking for Ren'fallow conspirators? And here you go sharing classified information, putting Brynnie at risk of the dungeons!" Her dull green face had darkened, and tears were in her eyes.

"Easy Mama," Doc Andri'n said. "I know you're scared, but we've discussed this many times before, and the facts haven't changed. The life of a scholar is always risky, regardless of what you study, because nobody fears facts like an authoritarian regime, and no society needs scholars more than one like ours. And Bryndax here isn't some fool, she's an Andri'n! My little archivist knows how to keep secrets."

"Don't worry, Mama," Bryn said.

Mama Andri'n hissed softly but said nothing.

"I'll have a look at the data when I get to library," Bryn said to her father. "I promise."

"Not today you won't," Mama Andri'n said. "We got to go and register. Get you evaluated."

"Can't it wait a few days?" Bryn said. "I'm close to finding something. I think."

"Have you checked Darth'n's *Exhibitions of the Dynamics of Pollination on Grand Gardenia in the Third Millenia C.O.B.*?" Doc Andri'n said. "I remember she mentioned courtship rituals that included selective—"

"A bust," Bryn said. "I'm at my wit's end. I can't find a single thing to explain where Balance's gender laws come from. Everyone just assumes they were laid down by Trevian himself. But if that were the case, it should be in the Pruu'log. But Trevian says nothing about gender. How can we, as a society, be actively doing something, the purpose of which is utterly lost, and continue to do that thing, adamantly and obstinately, as if the very fabric and structure of the civilization depended on it? It's madness!"

Doc Andri'n clapped his hands together. "There's my little professor," he said. "You tell 'em!"

Bryn smiled. "Speaking of which—now that I'm, well, flowered. I wanted to talk to you again about enrolling with the Dyna'arin."

Doc Andri'n frowned. "Wouldn't you rather complete your annual as a monkin first? You're already taking classes at the Academicon. I don't see the need to rush your enrollment."

Bryn felt the anger rising in her chest. They'd had this conversation several times before, always with the same result.

"But I can't become a tinker if I don't join the Guild," Bryn said. "And if you're worried about me being an adult and keeping my research safe, what is safer than a Guild servryn? Even the Cul'tavin can't touch them."

Doc Andri'n sighed. "You can join the Dyna'arin after you complete your basic studies. And if you wait and get your annual done first—and maybe even receive a priestin rank with the Pradishar—you'll have more of a say in where you get placed. You could stay here in Andramere, work at the Academicon, close to your mother and me."

"Is that what this is about?" Bryn felt embarrassed at her anger. "You don't want me to leave? But I don't want to leave Andramere either! You think the Dyna'arin would send me away if I enlisted?"

Doc Andri'n didn't answer at first, then said, "I know you're an adult now, and I can't stop you from doing what you think is best. But I think the Dyna'arin would want you on Callo Baton, to train you themselves. Once you're already educated, they won't care so much."

"Okay, Papa," Bryn said. "If you think that's best, I'll wait."

But the thought of a whole year at the Pruu'patch, taking orders from priestins and bishrops, and performing various rituals in the sharlum, sounded absolutely awful to Bryn. She wasn't sure she'd make it through her annual without telling one of them off. Then again, she did already have a Pradishar crystamin, and that had benefitted her research far more than she liked to admit. Since she was opposed to so many of the Pradishar policies, perhaps joining them, and rising up in the ranks, would give her the chance to one day change those policies from within. Bryn Andri'n, Sui Pradesh on the Council of Nine—that was nearly as appealing to her as becoming a Dyna'arin tinker.

Nearly, but not quite.

"Thank you, Bryndax," Doc Andri'n said. "I've got to get to work, but I am sorry. I'd hoped to accompany you for registration, which your mother tells me is already scheduled for midday today."

Bryn looked at her mother with an exaggerated look of horror. "So it can't wait then," she said.

"Afraid not," Mama Andri'n said. "Don't need you sitting and worrying for days anyhow. Better to take the plunge and get the thing over with. Sorry, love. We gotta take the tram too. I don't think my leg can make it up the hill today. So we gotta get a move on soon."

Bryn scrambled to think of an excuse, any excuse, but the look on Mama Andri'n's face said nothing was going to get her out of this. So she nodded, and swallowed hard, and tried to remember to breathe, but that was easier said than done.

❧❦

Bryn and her mother walked down the hill along the winding pathways through their residential neighborhood of Stone Garden to the tram station, rode across New Town down the 'Mirri River, then back from the Inner Harbor to Old Town, up the lift station to the royal plateau, and through the crumbling structures of the Forum to a small door in the mossy rock labeled "Gendering Analysis and Assignment," but Bryn didn't remember the trip. When her mother touched her arm, Bryn jumped, her awareness snapping back to Andramere, back to her body, back to what awaited her inside the door.

She blinked hard and long, her eyes weary from twitching, her mind weary from searching for answers, and stepped through the door.

Inside was a small waiting room with dirt patches on one side and chairs on the other, so you could perch or sit as you pleased. There was a window on the back wall, foggy glass, shut, with a small bell in front. Mama Andri'n nodded to Bryn and took a seat with a sigh of relief, her hand reaching down to rub her bad leg with her eyes closed. Bryn stepped up to the window, tapped the bell on the counter, and jumped when it squeaked like a branta bird.

The window slid open and a petite Andrasian, looking bored, locked eyes with Bryn but said nothing. Her eyelids were fluttering.

"I'm here to register," Bryn said.

The Andrasian continued to stare.

"Bryn Andri'n," Bryn said, "Here to register for Gender Assignment."

The Andrasian blinked. "Be with you in a moment," she said, and slammed the window.

Bryn sat down by her mother and dove into the weavryn to distract herself. Jaun von Andron, the actor-extraordinaire and crown-prince of Andramere, was currently streaming his weekly melodrama, *The Tides of Fate*, and at least half of Andramere, and maybe the world, was spellbound by it.

Maybe that's why the receptionist was ignoring me, Bryn thought, and she decided to give it a try. But it was too ridiculous, too overacted, to distract her. She crinkled her nose and slipped into a notestream discussing another Bhizini raid on the Great Sea Lanes, this time near Spy'rin.

"Bryn Andri'n," the Andrasian behind the window called, and Bryn's eyes stopped twitching as she jumped to her feet. "Through the door." The Andrasian slammed the window again.

Mama Andri'n took her hand and squeezed it. "Just be yourself, love."

Bryn took a slow, deep breath. The receptionist led her down a dimly lit corridor that smelled vaguely like vinegar and into a small room that looked like a consultorium one of the Me'dicant healers might use for diagnosing. A number of metal contraptions sat on a shelf along one wall, and there was a scale in the corner and some measuring sticks and bands on hooks.

"A committee member will be with you shortly," the Andrasian said, already walking out of the room.

Bryn looked around carefully, her eyes twitching as she catalogued each and every thing she could see, labeling the data while storing it on the servryn with her crystal. She was about to open one of the drawers when three Pradishar priestins walked in, their long gray and purple robes dragging the floor, their hoods up and over their heads to block their faces. One was short, one tall, and one fat.

"You're Bryn Andri'n?" the tall one asked.

"Mmm-hmm."

"Yes or no," the short one snapped.

"Yes," she said quickly.

"You're here because you've flowered?" The tall one again.

"Mmm—yes!"

"Show us." The short one.

Bryn hesitated.

"Undress. Now." The fat one this time.

Bryn blushed but did as she was told. She lifted her robe over her head and then unclasped her cumberdome, fumbling with the latch which didn't want to release, and finally lifted it off her navel. She stood, her arms feeling awkward and heavy, fully exposed to the priestins.

The fat one stepped forward, grabbed a measuring vine from the hook on the wall, and dangled it from the top of Bryn's head down to her feet, holding the tip of it on the ground with his toe. They said nothing, but Bryn knew they were sharing the data with the others through their crystamins, and adding it to her docket. Next the priestin stretched the tape between Bryn's shoulders, then around her biceps, then around her thighs, then around her waist. Then they pulled out a smaller tape and measured her nose, her ears, the distance between her eyes.

While the priestin took the measurements, Bryn was busy archiving the experience on her servryn, careful not to let them know what she was doing. She was an expert at using her crystamins without the tell-tale sign of twitching eyes, though she still allowed the twitch to happen whenever others expected her eyes to twitch—a rare skill, and one that had allowed her to archive almost every experience she had to a servryn without anyone knowing she was doing so. She was afraid now of what the Pradishar might do if they found out, but her desire to store and later analyze every detail of the experience won out. With great concentration, she watched them measuring her body, each moment carefully recorded, her eyes never once giving her away. Archiving the experience helped keep her mind off the situation, although Bryn recognized the paradox and noted it for later consideration.

When the priestin was done with the measuring tape, the fat one pointed to the scale and Bryn stepped on it. The metal bar swung up the half-circle, nearly four-fifths of the way across the arc, and Bryn archived the image, trying not to let tears emerge and blur her vision. Again the priestin said nothing. They indicated for her to step off, and she obeyed. The tall priestin produced a scroll from his robe and handed it to Bryn.

"Recite this to us."

Bryn unrolled the scroll and began to read, her voice wavering.

"Without intonation," the short one snapped. Bryn tried to keep her voice flat, even though she realized how deep it sounded, how gravelly, and so she tried her best to make it seem higher without sounding like she was faking it. When she finished, the tall one took the scroll from her and tucked it away.

The three priestins stood silently then, staring at her, slowly walking in circles around her, occasionally poking at her skin, squeezing an arm, touching her hair fibers, sniffing at her. She squirmed under the attention but never once stopped archiving. And then they walked from the room without another word to her, and Bryn didn't know what she was supposed to do. Moments later, the Andrasian from the front desk arrived, and when she saw Bryn was naked, she made a face and looked away.

"The Pradishar remind you that assignment is obligatory," the Andrasian drawled, while Bryn grabbed her clothes and started to dress herself. "Your docket has been updated to show that you're now an unassigned adult. You're no longer permitted to access scamp-only facilities, and you're not permitted to access gender-specific facilities until the ceremony is complete. Failure to appear for the designated Floronation will result in fugitive status on your docket and imprisonment when you're captured. Do you understand these obligations, Bryn Andri'n?"

"Yes," she said, while she archived the conversation.

"The Floronation will be held the day after tomorrow, at mid-afternoon, at the shar-lum in Old Town."

"So soon?" Bryn said, but the Andrasian was already walking out of the room.

Bryn found Mama Andri'n dozing in her chair and woke her with a hand on her shoulder.

"Brynnie love, how'd it go?"

"Fine," she said. "Let's go."

Mama Andri'n gave her a look. "How about we stop at the Riverwalk and have a slurpan on the way home?" she said as Bryn helped her to her feet.

"Only if I can have two," Bryn said.

On the lift down to the station, and then on the tram into New Town, Bryn sifted through the weavryn, looking for the names and background information on the contraptions she'd seen that day and the processes used to test her. Once she found them, she appended the names and the data to each entry on the servryn. Satisfied that everything had been labelled, she used the rest of the time on the tram to re-experience the events of the examination, drawing on the memories of her crystamin and the data on the servryn to look for anything she might have missed herself.

When the tram had passed over the canal and down Grand Avenue to the heart of New Town, Bryn and her mother got off and walked the short pathway to the Riverwalk, a long shopping and entertainment district along the north bank of the 'Mirri River, on the stretch between the Bay of Bliss and the Inner Harbor. It was busy that afternoon, with Andrasians and Raccorin from all around Balance Territories out and about, shopping and eating and watching the performers in the plaza. They walked until they found their favorite vendor, ordered three slurpans, then found a patch of grass near the water's edge to perch and eat.

While Mama Andri'n chattered on about the many different plants milling around, and how crowded it already was with Zenithra and the summer months still so far off, Bryn suppressed the twitch of her eyes, carefully licked one slurpan and then the other, and was even able to respond to Mama Andri'n now and again. But all the while, inside her mind, she was busy slipping through the streams of the weavryn, right into the Pradishar servryn. There in front of thousands of Verdillions, Bryn plundered the data centers of the world government, looking for what the priestins had decided.

And her worst fears were confirmed, two words that ruined her day, her week, maybe even the rest of her life. Recommendation: male.

❧❧❧❧❧ ❦❦❦❦❦

Bryn worked feverishly to find a way to remain female, the gender she'd felt for as long as she could remember feeling anything about it, the gender she always imagined she'd be assigned one day. Even as she'd grown taller and broader, so tall and so broad that people thought she must be Raccorin if not for her unmistakably dull Andrasian skin—and even as her voice deepened and her muscles hardened and her shoulders grew wider and wider—she still couldn't imagine that anyone would really think she was male. The thought of being associated with a group of loud, aggressive alphas made her wish her taprin never been cut in the first place.

She left the library that next afternoon, just one more day until her Floronation, one more day until assignment, and her despair seemed to grow exponentially as the minutes passed. Worse, her friends had discovered the stream her father had shown her, the one with the Bhizini attacking the Andrasian, and they wanted to meet and discuss how they should approach it on their notestream. Bryn knew she should care, knew she should be excited, but she found herself angry at her friends for calling her away from her research.

Didn't they understand what was at stake?

The library where Bryn worked was on the edge of the Forum closest to the Academicon, and she headed down the long narrow park, once an avenue between the two sections of the royal plateau but now a green space full of grassy knolls and dipping ponds. Access to the plateau where the Forum, Academicon, and palace were located was restricted to those with credentials, meaning they either worked or studied there, or had official business in the area. Andramere was always crowded with travelers and tourists hoping to glimpse one of the many famous troupers who lived there—most of the major studios that produced weavryn entertainment were located in the Valley Wood section of the city, and many of the stars of the melodramas had luxurious homes along the seashore—but the Forum remained tranquil, regal, respected. Bryn loved it, the old stone buildings, mossy in the shadows of the eves, their walls carved with friezes worn down by rain and wind and time til some were hardly visible anymore. History seemed alive in the Forum, more than anywhere else in the city.

When she reached the edge of the plateau, she took the lift to the bottom, then walked over the Clear Water and took a moment to stop in the middle of the arched stone bridge and watch the crystalline water tumble down the rocks to the Bay of Bliss. Springing forth from the western hills on the edge of town, the short but spirited creek never changed, always running at the same pace, the water level at the same height, purring along day after day, year after year. The little creek provided all the fresh water for the city, as the Andramirri River—the 'Mirri to residents—was loaded with sediment and difficult to clean. Bryn always took a moment to appreciate the stream when she crossed it, to listen to its song over the rocks, and to admire the view of the bay and the Shimmering Sea beyond.

Bryn finished her prayer to the Clear Water and crossed into Old Town, onto much busier streets bustling with people from all around the world, many in groups with colored badges on their robes and spirited leaders waving palm fronds in the air, herding them to and fro. She felt like she remembered a time, as a little scamp, when the city had an off-season, when the streets were quiet and life simpler. But as public crystamins spread to all the cities of Balance Territories, and Andramere became truly world-renowned, there was no longer any down time. Each year the building authorities laid out new neighborhoods to the north, nearly into Sink'rin province. And each year the condos and towers in Eden Side, along Aquastafar Beach, and in New Town, seemed to grow taller and taller.

The narrow streets running flat across the slope of the hill opened up into the Gran Plaza at the heart of the neighborhood, a long open space which rose in terraces up from the Bay of Bliss to the crown of the hill where the old sharlum stood, the site of tomorrow's dreaded Floronation. The plaza here was always full of Verdillions, and Bryn couldn't help but notice that some of them were staring at her. A few scamps were even pointing. Old folks were whispering to one another. She was used to it—well, not really, but she liked to think she was. Bryn had never met another Andrasian who even came close to her height, or her girth, and indeed she was taller than most Raccorin she'd met as well. Even though she tried to hunch down and fold in her shoulders, there was no going about unseen.

She lowered her head, her face burning, and hurried across the width of the plaza, onto the east side of Old Town, and up the stairs into the alleyway where the Sweet Treat was located. The cafe was famous to the intellectuals of the world as the place where Grumion wrote part of his *Discontent,* and free thinkers and youth who imagined themselves to be free thinkers—and others who imagined themselves to be young—liked to gather to sip hot drinks, eat fresh baked sweets, and ponder the mysteries of the universe. The owner was a friend of Doc Andri'n, like an old uncle to Bryn, and he'd let her rent a small room upstairs, with a wide balcony and a view of the city, river, bay, and sea, so Bryn never had to worry about finding a table to work. Best of all, her and her friends could conspire in private.

When Bryn rounded the corner, she saw Ginjy sitting on the stone bench in front of the cafe, a large book open on her lap, which made her look even tinier than she already was. Bryn could see that her glasses were about to fall off her nose, and Ginjy pushed them up only to have them slip back down again.

"Hey Gin Gin," Bryn said when she was in front of her but still hadn't been noticed, and Ginjy jumped.

"Oh, Bryndax. Didn't hear you approaching," she said, almost whispering. Her moist eyes darted back and forth nervously. Then she looked at Bryn for a moment. "You okay?"

"Yeah, just the normal tourist gawking session on the way here," she said.

<<Fuck 'em!>> Ginjy shouted in her mind. <<Stupid yokels, spent their whole life on the farm, don't know how to treat anyone with courtesy. You know who you are.>> She closed her book, stuck it in her satchel, and stood up.

Bryn wanted to give her a hug but knew Ginjy might freak, so instead she sent warmth and love and affection through the crystal, though Ginjy didn't acknowledge it.

<<My parents want me to attend their pre-streaming party this evening,>> Ginjy said. <<I tried to feign illness but to no avail. So we gotta make this meeting quick.>>

"You have your piece ready to share?"

Ginjy nodded.

They went inside the Sweet Treat and it was crowded that afternoon, even though the alleyway had been empty. Mostly tourists, but a few regulars waved at Bryn and

Ginjy when they entered. The newbies stared curiously at this pair of shockingly tall and unusually diminutive Andrasians. They got in line and waited to order when Rhingus walked in.

"Sorry I'm late!" she said. Her wide Raccorin face was flushed with amber patches and she was breathing heavily. She spoke in their minds. <<So busy today! I couldn't get a seat on the tram, so I had to walk over the hill.>>

"You aren't late," Ginjy whispered.

"Figures Trexbo isn't here yet," Rhingus said. "Anyway, order me two rhingamis and a fizz water." She handed Bryn two merits. "I'll be upstairs."

Ginjy handed Bryn two more merits. <<The usual. I'll be upstairs too.>>

<<I only have two hands!>> she said to them both, but she knew they'd give her a tray and her friends ignored her anyway.

"Bryndax!" Trexbo had just entered the Sweet Treat, and he half-walked, half-slid across the floor, one of his favorite *flourishes*, as he liked to called them. He put out his hand for a back and forth bump, then patted Bryn on the head in his awkward way.

"I didn't know if you would show," Bryn said. "You didn't confirm with any of us."

"Oh yeah. Oops." He grinned, and Bryn rolled her eyes. "But don't be mad!" he sang. "I promise you'll soon be glad, glad, *glad*!" He laughed, and Bryn rolled her eyes again.

<<How much bhiza did you eat today?>> she said.

<<Just a smidge, Miss Cul'tavin, officer, priestin, your highness.>> He was still grinning though.

<<Just be careful, Trexy. Didn't you see Prop-Sector's latest streams? Malisha Andra'asnia's raised the fine for bhiza intoxication. And you're a repeat offender.>>

<<I never stream that Pradishar shit, and that fucking pollen-smacker can stick her face in my flower,>> Trexbo hissed. <<She wants to ruin everything that makes Andramere great. This city is what it is because people here are relaxed and thoughtful and accepting. A little disobedience is good for society, right Bryndax?>>

<<I was just worried about you.>>

"Ahh, I'm touched," he said aloud. "Hug?"

"Sweet Trevian no, you smell like garbage!" Bryn pushed him away gently when he stepped forward. It was true, after all. Trexbo smelled a bit funky. His robes were always a little soiled, his skin grimy, his hair fibers disheveled. What with his wandering eye, his penchant for bhiza, and his theatrical manner of walking and talking, he didn't exactly blend in with the crowd. In fact, many Verdillions alerted the Cul'tavin just because he walked down the street, thinking he must be up to no good. Bryn would admit he sometimes was up to no good, but always for a good reason, and never anything that would hurt anyone. He had the biggest heart of anyone Bryn had ever met, stinky and weird as he was.

<<Treats are on me,>> Bryn said, knowing Trexbo was probably broke. <<Now get upstairs already.>>

He grinned, put one arm across his torso and the other up in the air, and bowed twice, deeply, toward Bryn.

<<Go!>> she hissed, swatting at him, and he scampered off up the stairs. Bryn saw a few patrons sneering at him as he went by, and crinkling their noses in disgust.

"Mmmm, food! I'm starving!" Rhingus said when Bryn entered. She patted the table next to her. Ginjy was at the small desk in the corner, her nose back in the book she'd been reading earlier, her glasses about to fall off. Trexbo was pacing in front of the door to the balcony, his eyes twitching wildly.

"Shall we call to order?" Rhingus said, after she'd swallowed a few bites. The others nodded. "Alright then, I declare this meeting officially open. Respect for one and all. Thanks for coming today. Ginjy and I—we thought we needed to stream something. I'm assuming you've had time to watch—and rewatch—the stream?"

"Mmm-hmm," Bryn said, trying to focus. She rewatched it in her mind, the Bhizini grabbing the Andrasian's head, twisting it around.

<<Craziness!>> Ginjy said. She turned to face them, her eyes darting back and forth. <<Never seen anything like it in my life. Not even in a melodrama.>>

"So you think it's real?" Rhingus asked. "One minute I'm certain it's fake and greatly relieved to think that way. Then the next minute I'm certain it's real, and I'm horrified by it."

<<Even Raccorin masters, who have complete control over their slaves, can't twist their heads around or fling them about like that,>> Ginjy said.

"And Bhizini aren't given crystals," Trexbo said. "Known a lot of Bhizini but I've never met one in my life who had one."

"Roman Anthem has one," Ginjy said aloud.

"I didn't see a crystal on the Bhizini," Rhingus said. "Did I miss something?"

"No visible crystal," Trexbo said. "Could be on the chest or back. And don't get me started on Roman Anthem." Just why the Bhizini warrior had become a Pradishar priestin and the Gran Pradesh's most trusted servant was one of Trexbo's favorite mystery-conspiracies.

"Has anyone figured out who streamed it yet?" Rhingus said. "Every version I've found so far has no metadata."

The others shook their heads.

"I have it," Bryn said. "Got it yesterday morning." Her eyes twitched.

"Yesterday?" Ginjy whispered. "And you're just sharing it with us?"

She looked at the others, and they were all staring at her, not with anger but with uncertainty, and concern.

"Sorry," she said, blushing. "I've been—"

"Sweet Trevian!" Trexbo said, his eyes twitching. "Is this metadata legit? Pradishar—on P'anorum?!"

"Yeah," Bryn said. "It's legit. My father gave it to me."

"Well if Doc Andri'n supplied it, then it's the real thing. But damn Bryn, not cool holding out," Trexbo said.

"I'm sorry, I just—"

"I thought the Far Archipelago was abandoned, even uninhabitable?" Rhingus said.

"Pradishar lies," Trexbo said.

<<Have we decided this is legitimate?>> Ginjy said. <<I can't—even begin to comprehend the consequences if it is.>>

"Well, since the censors are wiping every version of it they can find, it's probably legit," Rhingus said.

"Perhaps," Trexbo said. "But it also seems like every time it's shared, a bunch of chatter about the Ren'fallow and the Harvest immediately follow. And we know the Pradishar censors don't tolerate any mention of such things, aloud or on the weavryn."

"So what's our take?" Rhingus asked. "Does the Bhizini have a crystal? And if so, is it some kind of new class, able to manipulate people in that horrible way? And what about the glow, the shimmer? A Mund'umbrian?"

Ginjy actually laughed aloud, then realized what she'd done and stopped, blushing lightly, her eyes darting around. <<Sorry Rhin,>> she said. <<I wasn't laughing at you. Well—not entirely. Just surprised to hear someone as smart as you talking about Mund'umbrians, as if it were a legit possibility.>>

"You don't believe?" Trexbo said. He wasn't smiling.

"Are you saying you do?" Ginjy said aloud, surprise on her dull green face. <<Why am I not surprised?>> she added through the crystal.

"Look, Mund'umbrians have been talked about in books and scrolls for thousands of years," Rhingus said. "So while I don't know if they actually exist, plenty of people across many, many years have been believers. That at least makes it possible, right?"

<<Wrong,>> Ginjy said. <<Mermaids have been talked about for just as long, and yet for thousands of years, even when Balance Authority ruled the entire world and sailed all the seas, not a single mermaid was ever seen.>>

"What about the Three Goddesses?" Trexbo said. "Nobody in Balance believes in them, but every Bhizini does. And I've seen them with my own eyes."

<<And how much bhiza had you consumed beforehand?>> Ginjy chuckled but wouldn't look at Trexbo.

"Not enough to hallucinate. But I swear on Sweet Trevian's spirit, I saw the Goddesses. They swam through the ocean like seastallions, leapt above the water like dolphins, and floated through the sky like birds in wisps of fog. They were—" he sighed. "They were the most beautiful creatures I've ever seen."

Everyone was laughing now, even Bryn. "Oh Trexie," Rhingus said. "I'm not sure you're helping this conversation."

<<He is,>> Ginjy said. <<He's made it clear we aren't going to have a consensus on what we've seen—or believe. Unless you have something to add, Bryn? You're awfully quiet today. We thought you'd be the most excited one here. But you've hardly spoken. Anything you wanna talk about?>>

"I—" Bryn said, but her throat had closed up, and tears started to pour out. "I'm sorry. I'm so sorry, I'm trying. I'm trying to care, trying to focus, trying to—be myself. But I can't. All I can think about is the assignment. That's all I can research, all I can argue, all that matters at all to me right now!"

"We're here for you," Rhingus said. "We know how scary it is."

"No, you don't," Bryn said. "None of you do. All of you—you're all the way everyone else thinks you are. But I'm the way only I think I am. And the government is about to make that difference official. My life will be over. I—can't live as a male. I can't. I won't."

"We don't think you're a male," Trexbo said. "Nobody who knows you does. You're our sister! Right everyone?"

They all agreed.

Bryn took Trexbo's hand and squeezed it.

<<About the assignment,>> Ginjy said. <<Rhingus and I—we might be on to something. We just don't want to get your hopes up.>>

Bryn wiped her eyes. "Really?" she said. "What could I have missed? I thought I'd checked every avenue, twice. What have you found?"

"Darth'n's *Exhibitions of the Dynamics of Pollination on Grand Gardenia in the Third Millenia C.O.B.*," Rhingus said.

Bryn's face fell. "I checked it. No good."

<<You've checked the first edition?>> Ginjy said.

Bryn opened her mouth, then closed it, and blushed.

Ginjy tsked in Bryn's mind. <<You know a stream is only trustworthy once you've vetted the metadata. It's no different with books and scrolls, they are just harder to extract that information from. Not only must you learn who made it, in what form, when, where, who produced the medium, and why it was produced at all, but how it changed over time. How many versions, how many translations, how do they all differ. I know it's easily the most tedious aspect of research, but without it, you risk misunderstanding. Or in this case, you miss the fact that the first edition contained a thirteenth chapter removed from all later versions.>>

"The only remaining first editions are all held in private collections," Rhingus said. "And there aren't any versions of it on the weavryn."

<<But Po'stillian references the chapter in his treatise on the Purgation,>> Ginjy said.

"You're right, Gin," Bryn said. "I was sloppy. Won't happen again."

"You just overworked yourself," Rhingus said. "Sometimes the best thing you can do is nothing."

"Just tell me what the chapter contains already!" she snapped.

"That's why we didn't want to get your hopes up," Rhingus said. "We haven't read it yet. But we know who has a copy. And we should get to look at it tomorrow morning."

Bryn groaned. "That's hardly enough time to prepare an argument. My assignment is at midday!"

"I told you we shouldn't have said anything," Rhingus said, looking at Ginjy, but Ginjy just shrugged. "Either way, we'll let you know when we know anything."

"Thanks," Bryn said. "I guess we should get back to work then. Sorry I messed up the meeting. We have a notestream to prepare, after all. We can't keep our fans waiting."

"That's our Bryndax," Trexbo said, and Bryn forced a smile.

Mama Andri'n poured a large dram of rum into Bryn's jha'ala. In spite of her size, she was a lightweight when it came to spirits, and Bryn slept more than she had in weeks. She woke to ruddy light streaming through the window and the sounds of leaves rustling in the garden. The north wind blew briskly every morning before sunrise, cool from the snows of Mun'maximo, dusty from the plateaus of Ru'canyon, floral from the forests of Shad'n'grove, and fragrant with the ripe smells of the marshes of Sof'soil just outside the city.

Bryn breathed deep of the smells of Andramere and closed her eyes again, and for a moment she and her home were one. Like the great 'Mirri flowing through the heart of the island, she too stretched from icy peak to the Bay of Bliss, feeding and cleansing and connecting everything she passed, the life-sap of the dogedom.

But when she opened her eyes, she was Bryn Andri'n again, and the terror of the last few weeks flooded in upon her, like a wave from the sea overflowing the bay and surging up the river, making it flow in the wrong direction. She let it carry her off, allowed herself one last breakdown, then she dried her tears and got ready for the day ahead.

Bryn tried to eat breakfast and managed to get down a few swallows. Mama Andri'n noticed but didn't push. Doc Andri'n asked her if she'd had any luck analyzing the stream from P'anorum, and she promised she'd focus on it after today was over.

Just let me get through today, she thought.

"Of course, dear," Doc Andri'n said. "But not to worry. I put in a word with some of the local bishrops, one of whom is on the assignment committee, and I expressed my deepest desire to have a daughter." He beamed at Bryn.

She blinked back the tears. "Do you think that'll help?"

"Perhaps. There are one hundred on the committee, but the word of a bishrop does carry weight. We'll just have to see." He winked.

"Thanks Papa," she said, wiping away her tears and eating a few more bites.

After breakfast they played a game of Tiles and Coins together, all three of them. Bryn was grateful that they were trying so hard to distract her, even if it wasn't working. The morning crawled by, each hour making Bryn feel more and more like she might lose her breakfast.

When midday approached, they left early and traveled together to the old sharlum, taking the long route again on the tram down the river and through New Town so Mama Andri'n didn't have to climb the hill. When they got to the sharlum, the monkin at the door directed Bryn to a nook on the east side of the building while her parents went to find somewhere to sit with the other family members. There were several dozen others her age, recently flowered, waiting to be assigned a gender, all milling about in the nook, some looking excited, others nervous. Bryn recognized a few of them from her days at the nursery and suddenly her legs felt stiff and awkward. Bryn had been top of her class every year, and also nearly twice as big as everyone else, but she was so timid that she'd been bullied mercilessly. Seeing her peers made the torment feel like it had happened yesterday.

"Well, well, if it isn't the barge!" a tall, stocky Andrasian said, looking at Bryn with a smirk on his face. "Still calling yourself a female?"

"That's right. And I'm about to be assigned one too," Bryn said, trying to sound confident. "And you, Aerid? Still pretending to have a brain?"

Aerid scowled, then looked at his group of friends. "Isn't this the ugliest fuck you've ever seen? Hey E'mo, you remember Bryn the Big, don'cha?"

E'mo nodded. "You sure that isn't dull green paint? I think you're a Raccorin in disguise. No true Andrasian is so broad." He swiped his hand down Bryn's cheek and held it up.

Bryn shrank from his touch.

"Guess not," he said. "Just the biggest, ugliest Andrasian in all of Balance."

"In the world," Aerid said. "The ugliest Andrasian *male* in the world." He laughed.

Bryn walked away without responding, her hands shaking, but they didn't follow her. She found an empty corner and slumped against it, and tried to distract herself, to forget the way they made her feel. But the only thing she could think to do was slip back inside the Pradishar servryn, see if her father's friend had had any influence on her assignment. When she checked her docket, and knew she'd lost, she didn't cry or scream or lose her mind. She just sat there, feeling exhausted, like there was no energy left in her to do anything at all.

<<It's too late,>> she said to Ginjy and Rhingus. <<In a few minutes, I'll officially be a male.>> But there was no response. She wrapped her arms around her legs and hugged them tightly, gently rocking back and forth, awaiting her fate with a rising panic in her heart.

Should I pray to Trevian? she thought. *Could that work? Am I that desperate, to abandon all reason in hopes of a miracle from a myth? Sweet Trevian...*

But her group was called to assemble on the stage, and Bryn stood warily and followed the others out. E'mo and Aerid looked at her with narrowed eyes but said nothing.

The bishrop of Andramere began the service, praising Trevian, saluting Balance Authority, reciting the requirements to uphold Balance in all aspects of life—between races, between continents, between genders. Then the first of the group was summoned forward and given a chance to speak a few words before assignment. When Aerid was called, he thanked the committee, thanked the Pradishar, thanked the high doge of Andramere, and thanked his parents. The committee named him a male, and the crowd cheered. Aerid threw his arms in the air, gloating, triumphant. E'mo was next and was also named a male.

The assignees went one after another, speaking a few words and then receiving their assignment with enormous smiles and cheering. Bryn had never felt so alone, so different. The group dwindled down, until all that was left was Bryn. The bishrop called her name and she shuffled forward on the stage.

And then she felt her friends with her.

<<We've got this,>> Rhingus said. <<And just in time too.>>

<<You found something?>> Bryn asked, and she went ahead and prayed to Trevian they had.

<<Here it is,>> they said together, and Bryn had the data in her mind.

She took a deep breath, then spoke.

"Esteemed Pradishar, loyal subjects of Andramere, citizens of Balance Authority. I stand before you as something special—something different. I'm sure I don't have to argue that point. I'm tall and wide, with big shoulders and big hands, and all these make me look like a Raccorin. These make me look like a male. But I'm one hundred percent Andrasian, one hundred percent Andramerian. And I'm one hundred percent female.

"I'm also a student of history, and a monkin of the Pradishar. And I have learned that there is a precedent for those like me, here on Andramere in particular, and in the cities of Balance Territories as well, for allowing the assignee to declare their own gender at their Floronation."

Bryn paused as the audience began to murmur.

She cleared her throat and continued, "A von Andron, third princeling of the doge of Andramere, in 174 C.O.B., was the first recorded case where the assignment committee failed to reach a unanimous decision. At the time, the Gran Pradesh himself was summoned to cast the vote. But he deferred to the high doge of Andramere, who in turn deferred to the assignee. This precedent for undecided committees was followed until at least the 7500s C.O.B., though in the last two thousand years, it has fallen out of practice and been largely overlooked. And yet it fell out of practice not from being overturned by the Council, but from the turmoil of the Purgation, when the great libraries were sacked and so many records were edited or lost. And so, I beseech the assignment committee, in following the advice of the Gran Pradesh and high doge of Andramere, and in adhering to a solid tradition of Balance Authority and the Pradishar, to allow me, Bryn Andri'n, to decide my own gender."

The murmurs in the audience increased, and there were calls to let her decide and calls to silence her.

<<There you go,>> Rhingus said.

<<How will I ever thank you both for this?>> Bryn said.

<<Consider it a coming of age gift,>> Ginjy said.

The bishrop of Andramere stepped forward, signaling for silence from the audience, and the murmurs died down.

"Bryn Andri'n, you are truly your father's offspring," the bishrop said. "For those of you who don't know, Bryn's father is our own Academicon's esteemed professor, Doc Bryncent Andri'n. It's then no surprise that his offspring would be so well-informed, even better informed than our own assignment committee. I have just conferred with a representative for the Council of Nine in Balan Su, and they have given a final ruling on this matter. Bryn Andri'n, what would you have us assign you today?"

"Female, bishrop," she said, unable to keep a grin off her face.

"So it shall be. Subjects of Andramere and citizens of Balance Authority, join me in welcoming Bryn Andri'n, female, to our community, as a full adult, full subject of the dogedom of Andramere, liege-member of the Andrasian Republic, and full citizen of Balance Authority. May Sweet Trevian bless your days, and may your fruit grow strong and true."

Bryn wept. She could feel her parents cheering for her, sending her love, and Ginjy, Rhingus, and Trexbo were congratulating her via crystal too, and some in the crowd were cheering and welcoming her. But a good portion were also glaring at her, shaking their heads in disapproval, and murmuring to each other about the end of Balance.

"Obviously a male," she heard one shout, but today she didn't care at all. She'd been named female, and that was all that mattered.

She joined the other assignees on the dais. Aerid and E'mo were scowling at her, a dark look in their eyes. She ignored them. Nothing was going to ruin her day. Nothing.

And despite what they had said, she'd have to find a way to make it up to Ginjy and Rhingus, if she ever could return such a favor. What would she have done without them? She didn't deserve the praise the bishrop had showered on her.

Without her friends, she would have failed.

The bishrop closed the ceremony with prayers and songs, and Bryn sang praises to Trevian at the top of her lungs. Her parents gave her hugs and kisses, and Doc Andri'n even did a little dance, twirling around in circles while flailing his arms. Bryn laughed and cried, happier than she'd been in a very long time. Ginjy, Rhingus, and Trexbo suggested they meet her at the Sweet Treat to celebrate, so she accompanied her parents to the tram and told them she'd be home by dinnertime.

Bryn left the station and the crowds and started down the twisting alleyways of Old Town for the Sweet Treat. Many of the shops were closed for the weekend and the back alleys felt like they were in a sleepy little hamlet in the countryside and not in the middle of the city. Bryn appreciated the quiet, but then she thought she heard her name being called, and she stopped to look behind her but nobody was there.

When she turned back around, Aerid and E'mo had emerged from a side alley with a group of friends behind them.

"Bryn the Big," Aerid said. His face was flushed, making his pale green skin look like mud. "Don't you know it isn't safe for a *female* to go unaccompanied in the back alleys of Old Town?"

"What do you want?" she said, taking a step backward. She turned to run but the group had circled around her. When she turned back to Aerid, he had a scytherin in his hand and a feral look in his eyes.

"Scream, or call for help on the weavryn, and I'll slit your crystals, maybe your throat too," he said. "Bryn the Big, the male who always wanted to be a female, right guys? Well, you got what you wanted. Now it's time to show you what that really means."

One of Aerid's friends slipped his arm around her neck while another kicked out her legs from behind. She fell backward to the ground, grabbing with both hands at the arm around her neck and scratching, but it wouldn't budge. Aerid held up the knife and moved it close to her forehead, hovering over her crystals, and she stopped fighting.

Bryn was too scared to send for help on the crystal, too scared to fight back. Instead she started running through the stack of books she knew were piled up in her study, reciting their names in her mind, reciting their authors, over and over again, until she heard one of the men warning that someone was coming, and they scattered. She couldn't feel her arms or legs. Breathing hurt, and her stomach throbbed. She was afraid to move, afraid to uncover her head, afraid to look at herself. So she just lay there, continuing to count books in her mind.

And that was how Trexbo found her, sprawled on her back on the cobblestone alleyway, her robe over her face, her flower badly crushed, the petals sticky with pollen, as she softly mumbled the names of books and their authors, one after another, to no one in particular.

Chapter 3

A Cruelly Crafted Cage

ELLEX ANDRIA COULD STILL hear his voice when she woke from the old dream. Her father's face lingered in the air in front of her, slowly fading as she reminded herself, like she did every other morning, that her father was dead—had been dead for over thirty years now. The twinkle in his eye flickered for a moment longer and was gone.

Time would make sense of things, they'd said. Just as her body had healed, just as she'd been made whole again, so too would her mind. And yet each morning felt just like the first day, when she woke up from the accident remembering nothing, an entire year gone from her life, along with her father, her mother, so much. Half the world had been lost.

She rubbed her temples in slow circles, the dull ache in her head sharpening, the migraine she'd fought off since yesterday threatening to return. But once she withdrew her rootpads, threw on a silk robe, and walked out into her sprawling rim-side garden, she began to feel better. The stars were still twinkling overhead and the glowbes of Balan Su City flickered on the far side of the caldera. A faint hint of dawn barely blemished the horizon to the east. Ellex breathed deeply of the cool, wet air, heavy with mildew and the smell of the sea, and she put the past away again.

What does it matter now? she thought. *No lost memories will bring Father back. I'm needed, here and now, and that's enough.*

Her aide, Pander, scurried into the garden from the cookery, wiping one hand on his apron and carrying a steaming clay mug in the other. "Good morning, Sui Pradesh," he said, bowing his head.

Ellex smiled at the old Andrasian, with his crinkled nose and watery eyes, always scurrying about with a harried look on his face. She took the mug of jha'ala and breathed deeply of the scent. Pander always had the water bubbling hot, ready to drop in the leaves and stir in the honey just as soon as he heard her. And although he looked old enough for planting in the gruynfeld any day now, he had yet to slow down, and Ellex couldn't bring herself to look for a replacement. The last time she'd mentioned him retiring, he'd wept.

"Sui Pradesh is up early for her day off," Pander said.

"Surely you know me better than that?" She gave him an annoyed look.

Pander wrung his hands, his nose twitching slightly, his eyes darting to and fro. "Of course, Sui Pradesh, of course I do. I remember the day your taprin was cut," he said, lifting his head for a moment with pride. But he let it fall again and resumed his nervous tick. "One can change though, yes?" He looked at her expectantly.

"No," she said, "at least not intentionally. I've never been able to sleep in. And you know I don't take days off. I'd go out of my mind if I had to sit here all day, doing nothing, when there's so much to be done."

"I meant no offense," he said.

"Unless..." Ellex said. "Are you trying to ask for time off yourself?"

Pander looked up wide-eyed, shaking his head back and forth but saying nothing, and Ellex thought he might cry.

"It was only a question," she said. "You're welcome to take the weekend off, you know. I can manage a few days without you."

Pander's pale green face turned a dull gray.

"Sui Pradesh is too kind, but my place is here with you. If you're working, I'm working."

Ellex smiled but then her face grew serious and she stared at Pander. He shrunk under her gaze.

"What is it, Sui Pradesh?" he squeaked.

"Why did you suggest I was up early today?"

"Just making conversation," he said, wringing his hands.

Ellex narrowed her eyes. "Out with it."

"I—Sui Pradesh is mistaken—she—" Pander said.

"Don't make me scan you."

Pander looked defeated and began to weep. "Forgive me, Sui Pradesh, forgive me! He—*scares* me! I am loyal to you, only to you, I swear it. I swear it! Scan me! Scan me and you'll see I'm loyal."

Ellex hissed. "What is my brother hiding now? No, don't tell me."

"He—"

"That's enough, Pander," Ellex said. "I've told you before not to take his threats seriously. Now go and prepare my breakfast. Pack it up for me. I have somewhere I need to be."

She took another swig of her jha'ala, handed Pander the mug, and hurried for her dressing chamber. Her eyes twitched as she scanned the notestreams and checked the servryns. She looked over the Pradishar docket for the latest updates, contacted the squad leaders of her Cul'tavin peacekeepers, and began to solicit information from her advisors. She had to confront her brother as soon as possible, but she wanted to know what he was hiding first. He might be the head of intelligence for the Andrasian Republic, but he was a fool if he thought he could keep secrets from her. She was, after all, the highest ranking Andrasian in Balance Authority.

The stars had vanished and the sky was streaked with pink and orange pastels when she emerged from her garden estate, her long pradeshan robe, dark gray streaked with purple, flowing around her as she headed for the citadel. With her hood up over her head and her face in shadow, she was safely anonymous, just another of the pradeshan faithful milling about the upper rim of Balan Su, where many thousands of Pradishar—whether lay, monkins, priestins, bishrops, Me'dicants, or Cul'tavin—lived and studied and worshipped. Nobody seemed to pay her any attention.

And yet Ellex was being watched, and she knew it. She could feel it, a soft flutter on the edge of her awareness, as the Cul'tavin peacekeepers, strategically situated along the streets of the city, on balconies, in the plazas, at the lift and tram stations, kept their eyes on those who passed and kept their crystamins scanning for trouble. No more than a surface scan, nothing intrusive, or so PropSector ensured the public on their notestreams. That was true most of the time, and it kept the public appeased to think so. The crystamins remained sufficiently mysterious that nobody had any choice but to trust the Pradishar, since they and they alone could produce them. But even Ellex, second in the Pradishar to only the Gran Pradesh himself, didn't know their origins, even though she had long been familiar with their power. Her bishrop crystal did have some perks—she was only able to sense that she was being scanned because of it.

Ellex took a moment to feel out the peacekeepers, to sense their location, and to greet them each in turn. Most of them were her own troops—she commanded the largest squadron in the capital—but some were here brother's and a few belonged to Cort Andramon, the city's manager. She was warm and kind to all of them, even the few Raccorin in the bunch. There were more Raccorin in the Pradishar than ever before, and Ellex wanted to do all she could to encourage the integration. She thanked them for their hard work and loyalty, and she sent them her confidence and her trust, and she could feel them feeling it, and she let herself revel in it for a moment.

But no—she had to pull back. Such emotional looping could be dangerous, could draw you in too far if you let it, so she drew her awareness back into herself and focused on her surroundings, with her own senses to ground her. She was at the edge of Grand Plaza. Off to the north, the Pruu'patch and sharlum peaked up above the walls of the Pradishar citadel, flanked by the evergreens of Corda'mere. And in the midst of the thicket rose the obsidian spire of the citadel, like burnished metal in the twilight, wide at the base but soon tapering off and thrusting high up into the heavens a thousand feet above the island, like a misshapen sword waiting to slice the crescent in two.

She crossed the plaza, past the Weeping Wilvryn with its curtain of hanging branches, and up to the gates of the citadel. The sky was bright with twilight, the horizon in the east nearly ready to burst with sunshine. With luck she'd make it before sunrise. Once through the gates and past the lush gardens of Corda'mere, Ellex approached the great spire and entered through the arched passage into its interior. The main hall was a massive domed chapel, the walls and ceiling carved right into the obsidian, with narrow slits to allow sunlight to reflect off the floor and light up the surfaces. And yet the black walls seemed to suck up the light, and the chamber always felt dark and mysterious, yet comforting. Dank and dreary, but safe. Timeless, like the sun, always there and always the same.

She headed for a lift on the right side of the chapel, back down a corridor cut into the stone. She signaled for it with her crystamin, her eyes twitching briefly, and the door opened with a soft whoosh. Once inside, her eyes twitched again and the lift rose, the high pitched whine of the maquina making Ellex want to grind her teeth. The whining faded and the door opened and she stepped out into a black corridor barely lit with glowbes, little more than greasy brown smudges of light.

Every corridor in the citadel looked nearly the same as this one, black walls and floor hardly lit. Some with shiny walls and floors, some with opaque ones. Some running straight, others turning gradually, others sharply at right angles. Some were flat, some angled downward or upward. Some led out of the obsidian and into the bedrock of the island itself. But mostly they looked alike. Ellex always thought it had been intentional, to make it impossible to make sense of the place or to get a feel of the layout and thus to know where you were within the spire, or beneath it. She had spent many decades coming and going through these halls and chambers, but she doubted she had seen more than ten percent of them. There were stories of various groups over the millennia who had tried to seize the citadel, tried to reach the bowels of the castle where the secrets of the crystals were kept, only to be found many years later, petrified. She shuddered at the thought of such a death, of slowing growing stiff, howling mad in the black.

How could anyone come back from that? she thought. *How did I?*

But a migraine raised it's claws and started to pinch at her temples, so she put the thought out of her mind. She reached the end of the corridor and signaled another lift. The maquina whined as it rose, and rose, and rose some more. Ellex had to pop her ears before it stopped. On the way up, she reached out to her brother and asked him to meet her, making sure to send him a feeling of urgency and panic—that should bring him running—along with the coordinates for their meeting and the winding pathway through the citadel to reach it. Then she broke the connection and refused to respond when he tried to contact her.

When she stepped out of the lift and into the alcove just below the top of the spire, the sun had just peeked out from the horizon. The doors closed and the whine of maquina grew fainter as the lift dropped back down.

Ellex had discovered this lookout decades ago while lost in the citadel. The lift that came here had only a single balcony as a destination, a small circular notch carved into the stone and wrapping completely around it, just below the glassy black tip, which protruded overhead like a massive teardrop or the flame of a candle.

She stepped out of the alcove and onto the balcony, and she looked down at the city over the edge, a thousand feet below her. She could see the tiny green clumps of Corda'mere at the base of the spire, the marble flagstones of Grand Plaza on the edge of the rim, all shiny with dew, and the buildings of the eastern and western arms of the crescent, still dark in shadow, like a slivered gray moon floating atop the fog. The city covered the entire island, a once great volcano whose rim now stuck only some eight hundred feet above the surface of the Threshinveld Sea. The south wall of the crater had long ago collapsed onto itself, forming a separate island in the gap, and Ellex could see the tips of the great fortress that sat atop the rubble and guarded the two gates which stood on either side. Far in the distance, away from the mists of the city, the waters of the Threshinveld blended into the blue overhead, completing the illusion that the city had indeed been cast adrift in a cloud, lost somewhere in the sky.

Ellex didn't know why, but the view always made her feel grounded, and the solitude of the place always helped clear her head of whatever was troubling her. She took a moment to watch the sun inch upward, breathing deep of the salty sea air, just a hint of the wet and moldy stench of Balan Su reaching her from down below. And she waited for her brother to arrive.

❧ ❧

The whine of maquina as the lift returned to the top of the citadel made Ellex's jaw clench. Sweet Trevian, she hated that sound, like a insect after your ear in the stillness of the night. She took one last look at the city down below, then turned toward the lift and hardened her face. Her brother had deceived her, again, and she was prepared to make him pay for it. He wasn't getting out of it this time.

The door opened with a whoosh and Uthyr Andria stepped out into the alcove, looking panicked. His dark brown eyes were wide with concern, his pale green cheeks even paler than normal. His pradeshan robe, dark gray streaked with purple, looked rumpled and there were stains on the sleeves.

"Are you alright?" he said. "I came as quickly as I could—"

"Damnit Utte, did you think I wouldn't find out?"

His mouth hung open there for a moment, gaping, before he slowly closed it. Ellex watched his look of concern vanish, and a blush of shame painted the tops of his cheeks a muddy brown. For a moment, Ellex felt she was a little scamp again, and Uthyr her younger sibling, always needing to be looked after and protected. He had eventually grown taller than her, and wider and stronger, and more than capable of taking care of himself. But even now, more than four decades after they'd come of age, he still seemed like her little sib sometimes.

Ellex could feel a pang of nostalgia in her heart and it threatened to break her anger, so she pushed the memories aside and glared at him. "How dare you."

Uthyr smirked at her then. "You'll need to be more specific," he said. "I've dared many things."

"You're not smiling your way out of this one," she said.

He stepped out of the alcove by the lift and onto the overhanging balcony next to her. "Ell—" he started, but he exhaled sharply and grabbed the stone railing with both hands. "Sweet Trevian!" His knuckles were white.

Ellex suppressed a smile. "I forgot you were afraid of heights," she said.

"No, you didn't," he said, taking short breaths, looking straight ahead. He looked back over his shoulder at the tear-shaped stone overhead, then took a peek downward and made a small whimper. "Sweet Trevian, this is the *top* of the spire?!" He chuckled. "Great spot you discovered. Can we finish this conversation elsewhere. Anywhere else? Please."

Ellex laughed. "How in Trevian's name did you ever qualify for the Cul'tavin?"

He ignored her. "You must be really angry with me to bring me up here. This—this is it, your secret spot! All these years and you finally reveal it to me." He looked at her with a wary look. "Why today?"

Ellex looked down at the bushy green smear of Corda'mere at the base of the spire and at the buildings of the upper rim peeking above the fog, now bright white in the morning sun. Then she looked back at her brother. "I figure a fall from this high, you probably won't be recognizable. Just a puddle of green goo."

Uthyr chuckled again, then swallowed hard. "Come on, Ell, what did I do this time?"

She sighed. "You ordered Pander to lie to me."

"What?" he said, looking relieved. "You really ought to fire that bumbling fool and hire yourself a competent keeper. I *asked* him not to mention anything so I could tell you face to face. I wanted it to be a surprise. I knew how excited you'd be."

Now Ellex was the one with her mouth open.

Uthyr laughed. "I was going to tell you at brunch today, I swear it." But then his smile vanished, and he looked away. "You know, I really thought something was wrong with you. I mean, look at me, I didn't even have a chance to clean up. You shouldn't play like that."

Ellex closed her mouth, and now it was her turn to blush, the tops of her cheeks turning a ruddy brown. But no—something still didn't feel right. She gave her brother a thin smile.

"I'm sorry to spoil your surprise," she said. "But I'm not sure why you thought I'd be excited about some silly stream floating around the weavryn." She watched his face for his reaction, knowing he wouldn't be able to hide his feelings from her.

Gotcha, she thought.

Uthyr laughed nervously. "Oh, *that*!" he said.

"That," she said. "You tried to make me feel guilty for accusing you. But you *are* guilty! Damnit Utte, we talked about this. And you promised. You promised you wouldn't keep stuff from me. I always find out—and more importantly, *I need to know*! For Trevian's sake, I outrank you. I could have you executed for this, though I'd have a hell of time justifying it back home. There's just no excuse. None!"

Uthyr looked defeated. He finally let go of the railing, took a small step back, and turned to face her. He exhaled. "Believe it or not, I was going to share it with you. I was! I just—I wanted to prepare you first, is all."

Ellex suppressed a hiss and sighed instead. "Must I have you scan me? I'm healed! I don't need you looking out for me."

"You know the Me'dicants say otherwise," he said.

"Nonsense," she said. "I've been in perfect health for years now."

"Shall we consult your docket?" His eyes were twitching.

Her head was pounding again and this time she let out a hiss. "If you throw that in my face, I swear you're going over the edge."

He put his hands up in the air in a gesture of surrender and his eyes fell still. "Come on Ell, you're making me look like the aggressor here. I'm just trying to protect you. You don't know—" He paused and looked away. "You don't know what it was like, seeing you like that. I thought you were gone. I thought you'd never stop howling—that you'd be stuck in that terrible pose for the rest of your life."

Ellex blushed again with shame, and this time when her anger broke, she let it.

"I'm okay, Utte, I am. I really am. I'm not going to relapse. I promise." She wanted to take his hand but didn't.

He looked at her and there were tears in his eyes. "Alright big sib, but I'm going to hold you to that promise."

"You better," she said, and gave him a smile. "And for what it's worth—I'm sorry I made such a fuss."

"So I'm not going over the edge today?" He grinned.

"Not today," she said. "But do it again—"

"I won't. I shouldn't have been dodgy about things. I just worry too much, I guess."

"What were you afraid would happen?" she asked. "I watched the stream already, and see, I'm fine. Besides, it's obviously a hoax. Some Bhizini savage having a fit in a cavern? An exploding monkin? Looked like something from *Dampiron Visits the Deep*."

"You think this comes from Andramere?" he asked. "Free publicity for a new melodrama?"

"Without the original metadata, we can't conclude anything, can we?"

Utte looked abashed. "No more secrets," he said. "I promised. Here, I have it." His eyes twitched and Ellex's fluttered as she scanned the information. He watched her face for her reaction.

"P'anorum," she said, but the word seemed to come out in slow motion, like her mouth didn't want to speak the name. Worse, the migraine was definitely back now, not just scratching but digging into her brow. She shook her head. "This stream—there are Verdillions still living on—" she paused, "still living there?"

Ellex swallowed, her mouth dry. Why did she feel so out of breath?

"Easy, Ell," Uthyr said. "This is why I didn't—"

"Just answer the question," she snapped.

"Yes, there are still inhabitants on P'anorum," he said.

She winced.

"But we only just discovered them. About a dozen survivors. Well, one less, now."

"So this stream is real? I wasn't expecting that." She paused for a moment, feeling foolish, and scanned it again. She clenched her teeth, realizing what this meant. "Who the fuck gave that Bhizini a crystal? And how did it wrench that monkin's head off?"

"Unknown, and unknown," Uthyr said. "I've been told Roman Anthem sailed to P'anorum, and enlisted the two monkins—the one killed and the witness. But the information is classified."

"By whom?"

"The Octa'vin."

"Damn," Ellex said. The guards of the citadel were servants of the Gran Pradesh and answerable to him and him alone. "How? How are people still living—there?"

Ellex couldn't make any kind of sense of it. Verdillions on P'anorum? The island, the entire Far Archipelago, had been evacuated, abandoned. Destroyed! She thought of the cobblestoned streets of the old city, the open-air theaters with their tinkling fountains and fragrant gardens, and all the seasons she'd spent there as a scamp—but the pain in her head grew so intense, her vision seemed to flash and fade, and she moaned. She closed her eyes and clutched the railing, dizzy.

"Ell—" Uthyr said. He touched her shoulder and Ellex could feel him soothing her through the crystal. <<Deep breaths,>> he said in her mind. <<Come back to the present. Hear my voice and follow it. I'm here. You're safe.>>

Ellex breathed deeply, in and out, as she shut the door on the past for the third time that morning. Her headache began to subside as her breathing returned to normal. When she opened her eyes, Uthyr was watching her.

She looked away. "I just needed a moment." But then she looked at him again. "Maybe—maybe you could handle this one?" The top of her cheeks were brown again. "And you don't need to say I told you so."

Uthyr smiled. "Never dreamed of it."

"Uh-huh," Ellex said. "Anyway, if this stream wasn't what you were hoping to surprise me with—" She was desperate to change the subject.

Uthyr clapped his hands together. "It's a doozy, too."

"Well, don't keep me waiting," Ellex said, and she managed a smile.

"A burrow of Bhizini," he said, "a big one. Several dozen holed up on the lower rim."

She frowned. "There's no way so many could get past security."

"Not at once, maybe. But if they came in slowly, over time?"

Ellex's eyes twitched as she checked the docket on the servryn. "Nearly five years since the last unauthorized Bhizini was captured in the capital. So you might be right. But we've never arrested more than two at once." She scanned the rest of the data. "And you don't have much to go on. Eastport is a big place."

"So—you down for a little beat work?" Uthyr said. "A bit of espionage? Some light interrogation? Maybe some breaking and entering?"

Ellex grinned. "You know me too well," she said, her migraine already forgotten.

❧ ☙

Ellex spent the morning doing research, looking over her brother's notes on the servryn to learn all she could about this burrow of Bhizini on the lower rim. Eastport ran along nearly one-third of the harbor-front—an assortment of piers and wharfs, public docking houses and private ones, even a number of structures held by the Guild. Some of the records she wanted to look over were old—the titles on some of the warehouses in Eastport were nearly as old as Balance, almost ten thousand years—and Ellex knew there was a good chance that the information she needed was languishing somewhere in a dusty book or scroll, in the library at the Academicon or in the bowels of the citadel, perhaps lost, perhaps waiting in a seemingly endless line to be carved onto a datamin with the other ancient documents, added to the servryn and made accessible with only a thought.

She sighed, and for a moment she wished every day were a work day, that those she needed could always be available, whenever she needed them. But this research would have to wait til the weekend was over and the monkins were back at their perches, ready to serve.

Back in her garden by midday, Ellex dressed in her Cul'tavin fatigues, tight fitting with a built-in, reinforced cumberdome, light and breathable like cotton but woven through with metal fibers designed to stop a blade. She stuck a club in the belt on her left hip, an enflamer on her right, and a dagger on her ankle, then pulled her pradeshan robe over her head to hide her uniform. Once her hair fibers were pulled back in a low, tight bun, she sent word to Uthyr and headed back to the citadel.

The city had gotten busy since that morning, and Grand Plaza was filled with Balan Susians out enjoying the sunshine. Scamps ran about laughing while their parents perched with their branches out, leaftips open to the sky. Along the inner rim of the plaza, the fog rose a dozen feet higher than the edge, a wispy white wall that drifted inward and faded away as it inched forward.

Uthyr was waiting for her by the Weeping Wilvryn at the heart of the plaza, standing alongside the curtain of hanging branches, the feathery leaves like velvet on vines of hardened leather. He was peeking in through the vines, and he jumped when she touched his shoulder.

"What's wrong?" Ellex said, taking a peek through the branches. The space within the canopy was cool and wet, with a rich earthy scent. There were large tangled roots on the ground and a gnarled, massive trunk rose into the foliage overhead. Nothing out of the ordinary.

Uthyr blushed lightly on the tops of his cheeks. "Would you think less of me if I told you I was streaming *The Tides of Fate*?"

Ellex crinkled her nose. "Jaun von Andron? Oh please, since when were you a fan of that trash?"

His cheeks turned a dark shade of brown. "Well, since you shared a secret with me, I thought I'd share a secret with you."

Ellex raised her eyebrows. "At least my secret wasn't embarrassing! But I suppose you never did have any taste. Remember when you used to quote Grumion all the time?"

"I think you're the only scamp in all of Balance who never had a pro-Grumion phase," he said. "Reading his *Discontent* is practically a rite of passage."

"Perhaps I grew up too fast," she said. "I always had duties to perform, responsibilities—even at a young age. You, on the other hand, were Mother's precious little cottontail, who got to do whatever he pleased, whenever he fancied it."

"Is that how you remember it?" he said. He wasn't smiling anymore. "For Trevian's sake, Ell, she only spoiled me so I'd leave her alone. Her only real interest was you."

"Making me miserable, perhaps," Ellex said.

"Making us both miserable," he said. "Give me that at least."

Ellex said nothing.

"Oh well," he continued, "what's it matter anyway now that she's dead and gone, right?"

"I'm not taking accounts, Utte," Ellex said, "but damnit, how many times must I fight off the past today? We have enough to deal with already without bringing up old grievances." She rubbed her temples.

"You're right," Uthyr said. "Look, we can have our peacekeepers handle this if you aren't feeling up to it."

Ellex narrowed her eyes at her brother. "No way in Mund'umbria are you taking this away from me," she said. "This is too big to let others handle. If we really do have a Bhizini burrow, right here in the capital—"

"I know," he said, "but you know what it says in the Pruu'log, when you're facing an unknown—"

Ellex put up her hand to cut him off. "Do I look like I care what scripture says?"

"Spoken by a Pradishar bishrop," Uthyr said, grinning now. "Damn Ell, that sounds like Ren'fallow talk. Now I'm the one who could have you executed." He winked at her.

She opened her mouth to respond but then closed it and smiled. "Détente?" she said.

"As always," he said. "And I was going to say, make no assumptions until the facts are clear."

"It says that in the Pruu'log?" She shook her head. "Who knew scripture could be so practical."

Uthyr laughed.

"So what's the plan?" she asked.

"Let's start along Flatlands. We can browse the vendors, have a snack, listen to some music, get a scope of things. I have an informant at a tavern on Memorial Square who might have a lead for us. But he's unJoined, so we need to talk to him face to face."

"Why wasn't he mentioned on the docket?"

Uthyr's eyes twitched. "He is now."

"There aren't many unJoined left in Balance. Are you sure he can be trusted?"

"Of course not, but I have some leverage that will keep him cooperative." Uthyr grinned, a wild gleam in his eye.

"I see why Pander tells me you scare him," Ellex said. "Good work. Let's hope it pays off. Shall we?"

The lift traveled down through the rock of Balan Su, the whine of the maquina making Ellex's teeth clench together. Down they dropped, through the obsidian of the spire and the bedrock of the island, nearly to sea level. These lifts were the only way to get between the upper and lower sections of Balan Su, and were accessible only to those with permission to use them. For most of the residents of the upper rim, the lower rim hardly seemed to exist, forgotten down in the fog.

With good reason, Ellex thought, as she stepped out of the lift station and into the mist. The air was so thick around her, cold and wet on her skin, that she could hardly see the promenade across the street, and the sharply rising buildings disappeared overhead, their damp gray walls spotted with moss. She squinted to see the ancient sharlum at the back of the promenade, but the terraced plazas that rose in stacks above it were completely obscured by the milky air. Only the glowbes were visible, an ever-fainter progression of muddy brown light rising nearly to the cliffs below the upper rim.

If it weren't for rhupan imports, and the meager nutrition one could glean from the glowbes inside the buildings, this place would be uninhabitable, she thought.

They followed Flatlands to the east as it arched around the crescent, wedged between the wharfs and warehouses of Eastside at the harbor's edge and the towering jumble of buildings in East'fall'n that were stacked up the face of the crater overhead. As one of the only continuous thoroughfares across the inner section of the lower rim, Flatlands was always crowded. Peddlers sold crafts and goods along the edges of the avenue, some from elaborate stands of polished wood, others from a blanket spread on the ground. Some of the finest herbs and spices were to be found from these traders—lovely pottery and woven fabrics, and some of the best tinctures around—and Ellex regularly sent Pander down for supplies.

As she browsed the goods on offer, she noticed that many of the vendors wore prade-shan robes like hers, with the hoods pulled low over their faces. Ellex reached out for the hunched figure sitting in front of her, feeling for them with her crystamin, and could sense their presence. An Andrasian female, with one of the public crystamins freely dispensed to citizens of Balance Authority for the last century. Ellex easily cross-referenced the Andrasian's crystal with her docket on the servryn.

Permissions all in order. Importations cleared with the Guild. No need to worry with this one.

But she looked down the avenue in both directions, at the vendors fading away into the fog in the distance, and realized how easy it would be for a Bhizini to buy and sell goods here. Perhaps her Cul'tavin could perform a stall-by-stall scan on a regular basis? She appended a note to the servryn for later consideration.

When they reached Memorial Plaza, they turned into the square and made their way through the crowd, Uthyr leading the way. The fog had lifted from the ground level, leaving the air in the square clear, and Ellex could see the gray buildings of the lower rim rising up into the cloud above her. A band with horns, bells, and whistles were playing a song from *The Tides of Fate* and the crowd was loving it, dancing and cheering. Nearby, vendors sold frosted buns and hot drinks, and when Ellex caught a whiff of chocolate and cinnamon, her stomach growled.

"Should we get a bite to eat?" Uthyr asked.

"You read my mind," Ellex said.

Uthyr chuckled. "Not this time. I just smelled those buns and realized I forgot to eat today."

"No wonder you're so thin. I'm surprised you aren't shaking. You spend too much time in the Dankburn and don't eat enough to compensate for the lack of light."

"Thanks, Mama," Uthyr said, giving Ellex a hug.

She pushed him away. "Where's this tavern of yours?"

"This way." He led her away from Flatlands and toward the back of the square, where the warehouses along the harbor's edge loomed upward, their gray stone walls spotted black with lichen, in a speckled pattern that made Ellex think of Bhizini skin. She couldn't help but shudder at the similarity. The tavern was at the base of the warehouse, along the back edge of the plaza. Wooden panelling over the stone wall had long ago weathered and cracked, and the boards were warped and mossy.

"Why are harbor-side taverns the world over always decorated this way?" Ellex asked. Then, via crystamin, she said to Uthyr, <<Guild Enforcers. Two of them.>>

"Hearkening back to the golden age of sailing," he said. <<I see them. Not too surprising, given the warehouses in the area.>>

"Ha! More like the dark age of sailing. Do we really want to cruise the Great Sea Lanes in a leaky wine barrel, completely dependent on, of all things, the moods of the winds in order to move around? Bhizini savages travel that way." And via crystamin, she said <<I'm surprised the Bhizini would want to live in a neighborhood patrolled by Enforcers. Maybe your information is wrong. Something doesn't feel right. They shouldn't be here.>>

"Would you prefer they decorate with gurgitators? Metal plates from a cata'rin, perhaps?" Uthyr opened the door and held it for her. <<Perhaps the Guild is helping hide the Bhizini? They do allow them partial membership, after all.>>

"I just don't understand the nostalgia factor," she said, stepping inside. <<Nonsense. They'd never take such a risk.>>

"Don't blame nostalgia, blame the weavryn. Blame Andramere and their melodramas. Blame Jaun von Andron. If you had streamed *The Tides of Fate*, you'd know it takes place before Trevian, so no crystals. No maquina at all." In her mind, he said, <<Not as a group, but an individual Dyna'arin might. Though I'm not sure I see the benefit. Unless it's family members. Bhizini are born all the time, after all.>>

"Jaun von Andron? No thanks," she said. <<You have a lead you aren't sharing?>>

She looked around the tavern. A long bar ran the length of the right wall. Booths lined the back and the sides, while long tables filled the open space in the middle of the room. The place was decorated much as she thought it would be, with weathered wood, rusty anchors, nets, and sails. But unlike most seaside taverns, this one had a number of distinctly Bhizini features—lilypads on hooks on the walls, a cano'rin hanging from the rafters, and mounted over the bar, the full dress of a Pal'meran leaf-strider. The palm fronds were in remarkable condition.

"Who owns this place?" Ellex asked. "The archives I searched for Eastport were spotty at best. Dismally spotty. I can't find anything on the servryn. And yet there's something familiar about it."

"The tavern belongs to my associate, the one I mentioned," Uthyr said. <<But the building belongs to Lithuigi Von'nDrino.>>

"Are you sure?"

"Positive," he said. <<Only thing is, he's leased parts of the building to different parties. Some are privately held, like this place. But others are leased directly by the Guild.>>

"Who'd he get it from?"

"Unknown," Uthyr said. <<The records were archived on datamins, but they were lost in the Andramere Crisis.>>

<<A hundred years later and Balance Authority still hasn't cleaned up that mess,>> she said. "Have we been here before? Why does this place seem so familiar?"

Uthyr slid into the seat of a booth in the back and Ellex sat down across from him.

"I wondered if you would recognize it," he said, handing her a menu. "We came here—me, you, Father, and Mother. We'd come to the lower rim to check the vendors on Flatlands. Mother wanted to mix a tincture for the trip to P'anorum." Ellex winced at the word but Uthyr didn't seem to notice. "Do you remember?"

She looked down at her hands and thought of her mother, could see her in her memories, but they were hazy, fogged over like the streets of Balan Su. She remembered her mother always needing something—attention, sympathy, obedience—and never being happy with how much Ellex could afford to give her.

"I don't," she said, barely more than a whisper. "I don't remember. Just a feeling, like I know the place." She blinked back tears and cleared her throat.

But when she looked back at her brother, he was no longer alone.

Seated beside him in the booth was their father, Luthyr Andria. His hands were folded on the table, a small smile on his thin lips, the faintest hint of a blush on the tops of his cheeks—like an older version of her brother, of her too. Just like in her dreams. Just like when she woke that morning—every morning—still hearing his voice.

She closed her eyes and put her hands flat on the table. The wood was cool and smooth on her palms, and she let her awareness linger there, trying to slow her breathing, trying to keep herself from screaming. Exhaling hard, she opened her eyes, opened her mouth—but her father was gone.

"Are you alright, Ell?" Uthyr was staring at her. "You're shaking."

Ellex closed her mouth. "Uhh," she said. She took a breath. "I mean, of course. Yeah, totally alright. Just thinking about coming here with everyone and not remembering it, made my mind run away with itself. Got a little choked up, is all. That, or I just need some food! I need to go freshen up. Do you mind ordering something? Whatever you're having is fine."

Uthyr nodded. "Sure thing," he said, looking skeptical.

"Where is it?" She looked around.

"You really don't remember then. I'm sorry, Ell. I thought maybe—it's out the back door. Next door on the left."

Ellex stepped out into a small alleyway that ran along the rear of the tavern. Even in this narrow space, the fog still managed to make the walls look hazy, farther away than they were. The air smelled like salt and rotten wood and seaweed, but she was glad for the sharp coolness of it.

Am I losing my mind? she thought.

The wash room was down the alley, at the first door she came to on the left. A hooded figure emerged as she approached the door, and Ellex caught a glimpse of their lips, their chin, as they passed.

Patchy blotches of bright and dull green.

Bhizini skin!

All thoughts of her father, of her flashbacks, all of it, were immediately gone from her mind.

"Halt!" Ellex called. "By order of the Cul'tavin—"

The figure bolted.

Ellex hissed. With one swift duck and a quick whirl, she had her pradeshan robes off her head and her baton in hand, and she was sprinting down the alleyway. She shared her eyes with Uthyr while she felt out for her Cul'tavin troops, for any nearby in the city, but there were none in Eastport.

Where were they all?

<<Ell, wait for me!>>

She scoffed and sent Uthyr her frustration but didn't respond.

The Bhizini reached the end of the alleyway and passed through a small door on the left. When Ellex reached it, she saw there was a stairwell inside leading underground.

<<Something isn't right here,>> Uthyr said. <<It feels like a trap. Just wait for me!>>

Ellex saw her brother enter the alleyway from the tavern. She turned and started down the stairs, taking them two at a time, her baton sheathed, her enflamer in her hand. Her peacekeepers in Westport were en route but would be awhile crossing the city. She felt her brother's anger, and pushing it aside, she continued downward.

Light flooded up the staircase but it fell dark again when Ellex reached the landing. She blinked to see. A long warehouse stretched out in front of her. And there were shapes, furniture or objects. The smell of death, of entrails, nearly overwhelmed her. And there was something else in the air. Bhiza.

Ellex reached out with her crystal but couldn't sense anybody in the building. She felt her brother coming down the stairs and he joined her, enflamer in hand, and they nodded to each other.

With a crackle like popping timber in a hot fire, the glowbes along the ceiling came to life. Ellex peered across the warehouse. What looked like set pieces for a weavryn melodrama were arrayed in the far end of the chamber. The scene had been designed to look like the Solarium, the holy chamber where the Council of Nine met to rule Balance Authority, where Ellex herself ruled in the name of the Andrasian Republic. There were Verdillions perched, four on each side and one on the great throne between them. Below, the nine advisors of the board were seated in their lower chamber. Something was written along the wall in what looked like sap.

"Sweet Trevian," Ellex whispered. "Who—are they Bhizini?"

But no, they weren't Bhizini. They were Raccorin and Andrasians, members of the Pradishar, Cul'tavin peacekeepers from Ellex's own troop, all of them, all eighteen of them. Only their faces were intact, pale and bloated, unmistakeable purple and gray Pradishar crystamins in their foreheads. Their bodies had been hacked apart, chopped into smaller pieces and crudely sewn back together with coarse twine, into a macabre medley of bright and dull green segments, a mock up version of a Bhizini.

On the wall, the words in sap were now clear.

True Balance.

Ellex looked at Uthyr, who still looked confused, uncomprehending—and in the midst of that carnage, Ellex found she couldn't help but think of herself, how she too must look when she gets confused, as she had done so often lately. She thought about how terrible it looks, how untrustworthy someone like that seems, how awful, how weak and pathetic they are. How weak and pathetic she was. How mortal.

"Not a trap," Uthyr was saying, but all she could think about was how she had to be strong, had to keep it together, had to not look back, not let go. Had to be present, in the moment, here and now. But when she looked at her brother, her father was there again, standing at his side, a look of shock and horror on his face.

Ellex looked back at her slaughtered troops while the tears flowed down her cheeks.

Chapter 4

Far Off But Not Far Gone

R AKK RAEDER'S EYES WERE closed but he wasn't sleeping.

Moments earlier, he'd stripped off his army fatigues, his golden armor, even removed his crown, and piled them all in a heap. Then he'd taken a quick dip in the sea and sprawled out on the hot sand, his legs spread wide, his arms outward at his sides, his bright Raccorin skin drinking up the midday sun, sighing with pleasure. He could hear ghu frogs ghurpling nearby, the small splashes of water on the edge of the coral-lined atoll where he was marooned, the clattering of palm leaves in the breeze.

It sounded like heaven.

I could stay here forever, he thought, and not for the first time. *There's rhupan growing on the rocks, enough rainfall for fresh water to gather in the nooks. I could build a fort with palm fronds—have a peaceful life, right here on the edge of the Carcaspian Sink.*

He stood up and looked around at the expanse of coral just below the surface, the colorful reef interspersed with tiny atolls topped with palms and sandy shoals which peaked out of the water for as far as his eyes could see.

A sailor's nightmare, but damn beautiful, Rakk thought.

The edge of his tiny atoll had a deep bathing pool ringed by coral, full of tropical fish and bright sponges on the rocks. The surface rippled gently in the breeze, and the sunshine was bright on the surface, but he could still make out his reflection there, peering up at him, squinting to see who was looking down.

"Who's that handsome guy?" he asked, grinning at the water. The ripples on the surface made his bright Raccorin skin looked mottled and patchy like a Bhizini, and he frowned. "Even my sea twin has me confused," he said, remembering the old story he'd loved so much as a little scamp, half a lifetime ago. Back when he lived with his family in the palace on P'anorum, with friends and freedom and a future.

Back when everything was different.

Rakk remembered being that scamp and how he'd tried to find his twin in the sea. Wherever he had searched, the surf had been too rough for Rakk to see anything, or else the light had cast only shadows on the surface of the water. He'd run into the palace, screaming that his twin was dead, lost at sea. There'd been a terrible uproar of sadness and grief, for Rakk had an actual twin, and he hadn't cared to specify that it was his sea-twin who had died and not the real one. When his father had summoned him to the throne room, his sibling had promised him that all sorts of humiliating public punishments would ensue. His prank had disrupted one of his father's famous pageants, and the king had been furious.

Rakk spat at the memory of the humiliation, and borderline torture, that had followed, and his mottle-faced twin disappeared momentarily in the spray. Then he dropped back onto the sand before it could return, cursing the memory of his father and wondering if he was dead yet. After the eruption had destroyed their capital in the Far Archipelago, King Rhakksees II had returned to their ancestral capital in Raccorum Rhazzat. His last act had been to name Rakk's sister, Raq'asha, as regent of the empire before disappearing entirely from public view. Rakk hadn't heard from him since.

He stood again and shook his head, determined not to ruin his day with old grievances. He had such little time left, he had to enjoy it. It might be months before he could get away again. Nearly a year had passed since he'd last snuck away from his troops. In fact, he was pretty sure this was the same atoll he'd visited last time.

I could get used to this, he thought.

Rakk clapped his hands, and the flamingoes on the reef stopped pecking to look up at him. "Distinguished guests," he said. "Dearest ghu frogs, branta birds. Noble flamingoes. Thank you all for coming. It is with great pleasure that I—Prince Rhakksees Raccorine Deri the Third—declare myself your king." He bowed, picking up his crown from the pile of clothes on the sand and placing it carefully on his head. "King of Nowhere Atoll. Emperor of Sand and Reef. Lord of the Sea Spray. Steward of Palm Trees." He looked around, beaming, but the flamingoes, unimpressed with their new sovereign, had gone back to pecking. A ghu frog ghurpled. "Thank you, kind one. I *will* do my best. At least—at least I have a kingdom. And I promise you, my humble subjects, to serve with honor, for as long as it is within my power to do so."

Take that, father, he thought. *Take that, sister.*

Take that, world.

But then he remembered the other reason why he'd snuck away to the atoll that morning, and he frowned. He took off his crown again and placed it back on the clothes pile, then sat cross-legged in the sand and took a deep breath. Yes, he'd wanted some alone time, to relax and be himself. But more than anything, he wanted a chance to quietly, and safely, look at affairs back home in the empire. And he wanted to do so without any disturbances, without anyone noticing, without the spies he knew were amongst his troops, tracking him and reporting on everything he did.

Rakk took a few deep breaths, then reached out for Raccorum Rhazzat, his mind racing across the sea, across the hundreds of miles between the Carcaspian Sink and the Raccorin mainland, over the Dagwoods, across the tip of Brinewater Bay, up the narrow waters of the Stretch, and into the capital at Rhen'zoran. He sought out his slaves—he had tens of thousands of them spread across the empire—though most of them were with his fleet at sea. He only had a few dozen in the capital and a handful in the palace, not counting the ones held by his family in general. Rakk felt for their presence, and focused in on one in particular, a servant he'd known for decades. He could sense that she was pouring a cup of jha'ala while standing next to his sister, Raq'asha, as she discussed affairs with the prime minister.

Rakk waited til the slave was finished pouring and had taken her place in the corner. <<Careful now,>> he said in her mind, and he could feel her surprise. <<I need an eye and an ear. And I need you to give no indication that I'm here. Understood?>>

<<Yes, my prince,>> the servant said, and Rakk saw through her eyes and heard through her ears, but left her in control of her body to avoid any signs of imperialization.

"You can understand why I hesitate to say anything," the prime minister said. Rakk recognized the Raccorin although he'd never met him face to face, given that he hadn't set foot in the empire since P'anorum was lost.

A cousin, perhaps? he thought.

Pretty much everyone in the palace was a relative of some sort or other.

I should really know that, he thought, while he queried the information on the weavryn.

Yes, a cousin, from the Deri side of the family.

"What is it you're saying?" Raq'asha asked.

Rakk thought she sounded bored, or maybe a little irritated.

"A good dozen or more have approached me about the noise. Some even claim to have seen him with their own eyes, walking about, muttering to himself."

Rakk's heart was pounding in his ears. <<Do you know what they're discussing?>> he asked the servant.

<<Yes, my prince. The king...your royal father...he's been seen in the palace. I saw him myself.>>

Rakk reached into her mind and pulled out the memory.

He could feel her fear—could hear the sound of moaning, low and sad. He felt himself running down the hallway of the palace, looking over the balcony into a small courtyard. A Verdillion was down below, pacing slowly back and forth, but his face was in shadow. Tall though, with massive shoulders. But thin, much thinner than his father had been.

Is that really him?

"I want a silence order for all palace staff," Raq'asha declared. "No discussion of King Rhakksees or these sightings, on pain of death."

"And the nobles?"

"Increase scans on the streets of Rhen'zoran. And I want a squad up here, imperialized, to sweep the palace," Raq'asha said. "I want the intruder found and detained."

The prime minister gasped. "Regent, Your Highness. You know the king cannot be seized by any authority."

"Then do it quietly," Raq'asha said. "If he's finally come out of seclusion, then I want to see him. Don't shackle him, for Trevian's sake, just make sure he can't escape. I'm to know the second he's found."

"You ask a lot, Regent," the prime minister said. "I could lose my head for this."

"Nonsense," Raq'asha said, laughing. "I'm the authority here. Your head is safe with me. Now leave me."

Rakk watched the prime minister give a curt bow. He scowled when Raq'asha wasn't looking and scampered out of the room like a dismissed servant.

Raq'asha beckoned to the servant and she approached the throne.

"How are you today, brother?" she asked, a smirk on her bright green face. "Enjoying a bit of sabotage on this lovely afternoon?"

"How did you know?" Rakk asked with the servant's voice.

"You're so subtle," Raq'asha said, rolling her eyes. "Why are you here? Don't you have Bhizini rebels to harangue? I, on the other hand, have important affairs of state to tend to and really can't be bothered right now." She took a bite of rhupan cookie and looked at him.

"Yes, you look so busy, stuffing your face," Rakk said. "I want to know what's going on with these sightings. How long has this been going on?"

Raq'asha tsked. "Now, now, brother, your jurisdiction is the open seas. I'm the regent here. The king is just fine. He's been fine. He's just old and tired and wants to be left alone. It's really no concern of yours."

"No concern?" Rakk hissed with the servant's mouth and Raq'asha's eyes grew wide.

"Careful, brother. Insulting the royal authority is punishable by death. Shall I lop the head off this brazen slave right here and now?"

Rakk ignored her. "Surely you've heard that the noble houses are discussing Rishar?"

Raq'asha almost choked on her cookie. "Don't tell me you're taking seriously the gossip on the streets of Rhen'zoran? Oh, that's rich. The nobles have been discussing Rishar since the dawn of the empire, if you believe what the Ordens and the Rhank have to say about it." She laughed again. "You really have no idea how politics work, do you brother? The nobles don't want revolution, only concessions. A lowered tariff here, a preferred passage through the Stretch there, their latest scamp in the royal palace, that sort of thing. Ten thousand years they've discussed Rishar, since the dawn of Balance, but it won't happen."

Rakk was fuming but didn't let the servant express it. "It could," he said.

"Not so long as the Pradishar support us. But that is more our brother's territory." Raq'asha narrowed her eyes. "Dear Rajj seems to have everything precisely where he wants it. So please, no more talk of Rishar."

He took a deep breath, then continued with the servant's voice, "I want to come home, to show my face in Raccorum Rhazzat again. It's been over three decades. My own people have forgotten me. I want our subjects to remember that I'm their crown prince, not just some slave-master fighting savages on the high seas."

Raq'asha scoffed. "Come home? But you're *needed* on the high seas. That's why you're there. You're keeping Balance Territories safe. Or, at least, you're suppose to be." Her eyes twitched. "Just what are you doing in the Carcaspian Sink?"

Rakk swallowed a hiss. He hated knowing she could track him so easily.

"I can deploy my armies from anywhere in the world, you know that."

She narrowed her eyes again and took a sip of her jha'ala. "I'll tell you what I know. I know that father ordered you to keep the Great Sea Lanes safe because he believed you were the only one who could do it. I know that Father named me regent of Raccorum Rhazzat, and that until his death, that means I have final authority, whether you're crown prince or not. I also know that if you step one foot on Raccorum Rhazzat without an invitation from me and me alone, I'll throw your bright green ass in the dungeon to petrify in the dark. Are we clear?"

Rakk withdrew his consciousness from the servant so abruptly she cried out, and he could feel her surprise and discomfort fading as his awareness returned to the tiny atoll a thousand miles away from the imperial palace. He was on his feet pacing, and he punched a palm tree, scattering the branta birds in the leaves and knocking down some coconuts, one of which smacked him hard on the top of the head. He sat down in the sand, rubbing his skull and then his knuckles, cursing Raq'asha, cursing his father, cursing the world.

In such times, Rakk didn't know what to do with himself, how to calm down and unwind. He paced, he yelled, he swore, but he couldn't relax, couldn't stop seeing Raq'asha's smirk—couldn't stop feeling he was about to lose his throne forever and was absolutely powerless to do anything about it. Even the beauty of the sea around him couldn't undo the clench in his chest.

And Raq'asha had lied to him. His father hadn't chosen him to keep the Great Sea Lanes safe because he trusted him, but to exile him as punishment for P'anorum. Rakk had been so furious that night, he'd sailed away from the island, vowing to never return. He had already turned back when the first cry for help came to him.

From his mother.

Rakk remembered racing back, gurgitator open wide, wind in his face, tears stinging his eyes, the three peaks of P'anorum in the distance, growing steadily larger, when it looked like the sun had risen into the night sky. He could feel the heat of the fire, the blinding light off the water, the steam billowing up around the island, the seas boiling—hot, too hot to get back to shore.

He never sat foot on P'anorum again. Never saw the palace again, the city, his mother or father, his sister or brother.

All gone, all of it, in an evening.

Rakk let out a cry of frustration and fled from himself into the crystal, passing through his slaves in rapid succession. He felt the ones in his fleet, not far away in the Threshinveld Sea, as well as those scattered across the Inner Archipelago. And he felt the ones on land, the ones in the capital and the ones in the cities of the empire. He could feel them all at once, and he singled out a troop engaged in hostilities with a group of Bhizini near the Tranquin Reef.

A dolph'rin, accompanied by a few dozen skiff'rins, had lobbed several boulders at a nearby Guild ferry, then fled. The Corkin had caught up to them as they made north for the Sargassian Sink. And even better, one of Rakk's favorite puppets was with the fleet—Rhannokti, a massive beast of a Raccorin that Rakk had long favored when partaking in battles from afar. His body was big like Rakk's, and his zeal for fighting, his delight in butchering Bhizini—even when under Rakk's control—made fighting a real pleasure. He leapt into Rhannokti's body just as the slave jumped onto the deck of the dolph'rin, and his senses came alive with the full rush of battle, with the trilling war cries of the Bhizini and the sounds of hacking and slashing and grunting. He could feel the damp wooden planks of the deck beneath Rhannokti's feet, and he could feel his excitement for the battle.

Rakk lunged into the fray, swinging with a sword in his right hand, down through a Bhizini's arm. He whirled around and took off their head with the next stroke. The oarsmen down below rushed up the stairs to the main deck, and Rakk pulled an enflamer from Rhannokti's belt with his left hand and fired it into the crowd, and he could hear the popping flesh and feel the surge of heat on his face. Soon the mast was aflame, the deck catching fire, and the Corkin scrambled to abandon ship, and as Rhannokti dove into the sea, Rakk slipped back to his atoll, breathless.

But it wasn't enough.

So he felt out again, this time for his slaves in the cities, for any of them who might be worth a quick ride. He felt a sudden surge of pleasure from a Corkin soldier stationed in Rheghanza, who was enjoying a late-afternoon dalliance with a lovely shopkeeper, and he snatched the soldier's body and took it over wholly.

He could feel the slave's surprise as always, then anger and shame, trapped inside himself, helpless to protest, helpless to act, knowing it would be instant death to him and his family if he tried to resist or speak out. Rakk ignored the soldier's presence and focused instead on the shopkeeper. He could feel the soldier's stamen deep inside her flower and her stamen deep inside his own flower, engorged, throbbing, and he relished the sensation. He could smell her, feel the warmth of her skin, her branches unfurled and clutching his back. She, of course, was unaware that it was Rakk and not her lover, and he kissed her, and she moaned and squirmed and rubbed against him and he forgot about his pain for a moment. He waited until their stamen's were spent and they lay exhausted in each other's arms before he returned to the atoll, to his own body, where his own stamen was sticking out of the petals of his flower, swollen and aching. He put his hand to it, hoping for release, but it wouldn't come.

So he went back through his slaves one more time, until he found another one in the throes of passion, seized his body and focused intently on getting his pleasure, until he finally released the slave, his petals sticky with pollen. He scooted down the beach and into the water, dunked himself under the surface and gently cleaned off his flower, feeling disgusting, his face burning, his chest tight with shame. Then he lay back on the surface of the water and looked up at the sky and wondered if he wasn't a slave himself.

He considered getting ahold of a scytherin, slitting his crystals with the edge of the blade, freeing himself from duties and obligations once and for all. Maybe he could even join the Bhizini, convince them he had abandoned Balance, help them in their fight against his own army.

I can't believe I'm even thinking it, he thought, as he climbed out of the water and spread himself out on the sand. *Is it better to just give up, admit my throne is lost, and spend the rest of my life free from doubt? Or to fight on for my inheritance?*

But he already knew the answer. It hadn't changed in thirty years of sailing in circles, hunting Bhizini, exiled in fact if not in word, slowly forgotten by his people, by his kingdom. He closed his eyes and wished he could cry, wished for tears to pour down his face, but none would come.

None ever came.

⚘

Q'orin arrived moments later. Too soon. Rakk heard the oar smacking the water long before he reached the atoll, and he rolled over onto his side and watched his friend navigating between the reefs in a small, narrow, shallow-bottomed skiff'rin. His rescue party, here to return him to the fleet.

"Sorry to disturb you, my prince," Q'orin said, stepping out of the skiff'rin onto the atoll. He looked down at Rakk, then at his pile of clothing, then quickly out to sea. "Your pet swims swiftly. I hope I left you enough time to finish whatever it is you came here to do."

"Hardly," Rakk said. "I told you to fetch me at sundown, but since you're here at mid-afternoon, I know you must have a good reason for it. Come, sit with me." He sat up and patted the sand next to him. "The bad news can wait another few minutes. Let's talk of happier times for awhile."

Q'orin looked at Rakk for a moment, not hiding a look of annoyance, and Rakk could feel him on the edge of his awareness, lightly touching him through the crystal. Not a scan, nothing intrusive—his crystamin wouldn't have allowed it—no, just a feeling out for what Rakk was sending out, like you might hold your hand over a frying pan to see if it's hot enough yet. He sat down then, the annoyed look gone.

"Remember that time in Old P'anorum," Rakk said, "when the Rhyantis clan had come to call on my father? It was the year that Big Gingeroo died, and the city was throwing a huge festival in her honor. The city was always celebrating something. My father had made an appearance in front of the theater, in a big long flowing gown, but you and I had tied the ends to the column while he prattled on and on, and when the king finally stepped forward into the square, his clothes didn't go with him, and the whole city got a glimpse of the royal flower." Rakk laughed. "Don't you remember?"

Q'orin ran his finger in circles through the sand, watching the grains bunch up and scatter off as he went. "I'm not sure, my prince," he said.

"Maybe I was—" Rakk trailed off and looked down at the sand for a moment, a pained look on his face.

"Maybe I just forgot," Q'orin said. "I don't remember much of when I was a scamp, truth be told."

Rakk sighed. "Fuck the past then. I've had enough of old memories today. Let's plan a better future instead. Q'orin, friend, I've decided to become the king of this atoll. In fact, I've already taken the oath of office. These ghu frogs here were my witnesses. What do you say you join me? I'll make you my prime minister. We can frolic about like the Bhizini, our flowers hanging out for everyone to enjoy. We'll weave baskets from palm fronds. We'll eat bhiza and make love all afternoon. We'll dig out rustic cano'rins from the stumps of palms, and then we'll tame seastallions to pull them. You and I will go atoll to atoll and claim them all for our growing kingdom. We can even make a litter of little ones and raise up a dynasty together." Q'orin was blushing fiercely, making his bright green cheeks look brown like mud, but Rakk kept on. "We'll give an atoll to every scamp we have, until the whole Sink is ours. First the Carcaspian, tomorrow the world. What do you say, old friend, old buddy, old pal? Join me, won't you?"

He was still blushing. "I am yours to command, my prince."

Rakk frowned. "I don't want to *command* you to join me, I want you to join me willingly! Be my friend, not my servant."

Q'orin paused. "I can only ever be both, my prince."

"You're too bold," Rakk said. "That's part of why I love you so. I suppose I could free you and then ask you to join me, but you'd probably run off and leave me."

"My life is at your side, my prince, crystal or not."

Now Rakk blushed and looked away. "Well, it was a pretty thought, wasn't it?" He stood up, grabbed his clothing, and began to dress. "Come, we should get back."

"Abandoning Rakkonia already?" Q'orin asked, and Rakk grinned. "What will your loyal ghu frogs think of such an abrupt abdication?" One ghurpled and they both laughed.

"Come, friend," Rakk said, and he put his hand on Q'orin's shoulder. "If I ever decide to abandon my throne, my family, my legacy, I won't do so without you by my side."

"Then I shall consider myself a lucky plant indeed," Q'orin said.

"Now, how about that bad news. That's why you're early, right? Let's get it over with."

"There are several things to report, I'm afraid," Q'orin said, holding the skiff'rin's edge while Rakk stepped in. "There's been an attack in Balan Su. More than a dozen Cul'tavin, butchered. The troops all belonged to Ellex Andria."

Rakk tripped when he heard her name and fell into the boat. "Is she alright?"

"She's fine," Q'orin said. "We've been ordered to patrol the area around the capital, and to monitor ships coming and going from Balan Su's waters."

"The Andrasians are allowing it?"

"Both Ellex Andria and Uthyr Andria have shown support, my prince."

"I'm surprised."

"You shouldn't be. There are more Raccorin in the Pradishar than ever before, even as Cul'tavin."

"I guess I'm a pessimist. There's a reason Balance Authority exists to keep the peace between us and the Andrasians. You start blurring the lines between the two sides, and the thing will start to wobble."

"Careful, my prince, not to repeat such things in front of others. Many of the men are on edge. They have heard whispers of the Harvest, my prince. And with the stream from P'anorum, they are—"

"What stream?" Rakk said, shaking the skiff'rin as he lurched to attention.

"That was the other thing I came to share. Forgive me, my prince, but I thought it was a hoax. PropSector dismissed it as a Ren'fallow conspiracy aimed at overthrowing Balance and vowed to catch the troupers who had staged it. But others—trustworthy sources—have acquired the metadata for the stream and shared it."

Q'orin's eyes twitched and Rakk saw the scene in his mind. There was a Bhizini, standing awkwardly, rigidly, in a darkened cavern. A large maquina of some sort, similar to a Guild oven, was partially crushed by rubble. There were corpses on the ground. And statues in the distance? Rakk couldn't tell. He watched the monkin beating the Bhizini, and the Bhizini—what were they doing? Rakk watched the monkin's head twisting around and he laughed, it looked so absurd.

"I see why you thought this was a hoax," he said, but his smile faded when he scanned the metadata. No doubt about it, the stream came from a Pradishar crystamin, on P'anorum, that belonged to a Raccorin named Aar'ryn Ruu'n.

"Any relation to Ra'shard Ruu'n?"

"His nephew," Q'orin said. "Thought to have died in the eruption. Only Joined with a crystal a week ago."

"What? And the victim?"

"A local named Roe."

Rakk hissed. "Impossible."

"Perhaps—" Q'orin started.

"No," Rakk said. "No way. The island was evacuated. Abandoned! The entire Far Archipelago was lost. The cities of our far empire, destroyed. Nothing but boiling seas and toxic fumes left. Nothing but treacherous seas filled with sap-thirsty Bhizini pirates—pirates who don't take prisoners. No reason to sail there, no reason to restore it, to reclaim it. A wasteland, fit only for savages."

"That's what we all believed," Q'orin said. "As far as I can find out from the notestreams, there's only about a dozen left on the island. They've been living in the harbor, at your family's dock, in the shadow of the palace."

Rakk felt like his head was going to explode. Verdillions living on P'anorum. The island—habitable. His home—he could still go there! He could go there right now! How could it be possible? How did he not know?

"You know we have to go to Balan Su," Q'orin said. "And that the Far Ocean is restricted."

Rakk hissed. "I just got my home back, and now you want to snatch it away from me."

Q'orin stopped rowing and put his hand on Rakk's shoulder, and he gently squeezed it. "I will go with you," he said. "We will see your home—our home—again one day. But my prince must be patient. This is the closest you've been to the capital in decades. And if it's true that Qardymion the Saltsap is responsible for the attack in Balan Su, it means the Pal'meran have gotten reckless. They'll soon be in your grasp. I can feel it. And you'll be the hero again, the prince I know you are, the king I know you'll be. You'll see."

Rakk looked away. "You truly believe the throne will be mine one day? Truly?"

"Take it from my mind," Q'orin said. "And you'll know I've always believed it to be so. And still do."

"It's never felt so unlikely," Rakk said. He sighed, and Q'orin went back to rowing, pushing here and there to steer them through the reefs and atolls, back out into the open waters of the Threshinveld Sea, where dozens of heavy cruisers awaited their arrival.

Rakk slipped into Q'orin's mind, felt the confidence he felt in him, sturdy and rooted down, springing from his core, and he was lifted by it, warmed by it, motivated and inspired by it. He lingered there a moment, feeling his friend thinking of him, and he felt so warm and so loved, he could have reached out and kissed him.

Instead he pulled out, back into his own dark thoughts, and wondered if anything a slave ever felt could truly be genuine.

Chapter 5

The Life and Lies of Lithuigi Von'nDrino

WHEN LITHUIGI VON'NDRINO RECEIVED the summons to Balan Su, he was on the docks at Callo Baton and already facing a difficult decision—which wife to sail to—and the request to return to the capital didn't make the choice any easier. For a moment, he was tempted to reach out for the servryn, to access the notestreams on the weavryn and see what had happened, but no, he'd avoided doing that for a century now, and he wasn't about to break his vow over something as insignificant as a subpoena from the Pradishar.

Lithuigi boarded his cata'rin and started to pilot the ship out of the harbor using his Guild crystal while he used his right hand to unclasp the small hooks that held his left arm—a prosthetic made of long thin rods of metal wrapped in fabric—and then to rub the stump, which itched and tickled and drove him mad. The arm was a poor substitute for the original, which he'd charred so badly in a laboratory accident that it was already turning to ash before it could be removed. At least he looked whole when he wore it. Over the years, he'd learned to tinker with maquina using just one hand, and also to rely overly much on the help of assistants. On this voyage, he had no intention to tinker, so he stored the prosthetic and then went up on the top deck to enjoy the view.

He piloted the cata'rin north through the narrow mouth of the harbor, the mangalar trees thick on either side, and out into the Threshinveld Sea. He'd have to go back to the capital and see what this was all about. He'd been planning to return anyway, until he'd boarded his cata'rin and the thought of the fog-strewn slopes of Balan Su, cold and wet and dreary, made him suddenly desperate, even despondent, and wishing he could go anywhere else.

But Lithuigi had classes to teach. He had a wife, and two sons, in Balan Su. He had important projects underway in his labs at the Academicon. He was needed there, summons or not.

There's just so little time, he thought. *So many years, and now so little time...*

Lithuigi locked the gurgitator at one-quarter, set his bearings to take him directly across the open ocean rather than following the Great Sea Lanes to the west and then north and then east again. The Threshinveld was known for treacherous weather and Bhizini raiders, and Balance Authority no longer risked maintaining a lane across it. But bad weather in the middle of the ocean didn't bother him. Indeed, if Lithuigi could be said to have only one true love, it wasn't either wife, or any of his offspring, or even the maquina that he tinkered with every day, but the sea.

Sometimes his loves overlapped, as was the case with sailing. Lithuigi had modified the old gurgitators used by Balance Authority for millennia, increasing spule efficiency several times over. Even at one quarter aperture, his cata'rin was speeding across the Threshinveld faster than the older model when fully open. The thrill of the achievement helped damper the growing unease in his heart. Soon he'd be able to test it fully open, and he looked forward to setting a new record for circling the globe. But if only he could share his achievement with others! He'd done his best to keep it a secret, if only from necessity. The Far Ocean was still restricted.

He looked across the azure waters—flat today and with full sunshine, just perfect—and he determined to make the most of his last few hours at sea. He didn't know when he'd get out of the capital again. Probably not for several months, which in Balan Su felt like forever.

These trips should cheer me up, he thought, *and yet as soon as I approach the capital, I feel as dreadful as ever.*

He perched on the upper deck for awhile to drink up the sunshine and try to clear his mind. When he finally stirred a few hours later, the blue skies overhead were slowly but surely giving way to wisps of cloud and soon to patches of fog as he approached Balan Su. The water, dark with streaks of bright turquoise and whorls of deep emerald, turned to shades of gray, and the wind, warm and moist, now sent a chill down his back.

Lithuigi knew he was coming in too fast, so he sent the signal via crystamin to dampen the gurgitator, and the cata'rin, not wanting to slow after such speed, continued to slice through the water. So he activated a reverse-gurgitation modification he'd been tinkering with, and he grabbed ahold of the rail and gripped the deck with his rootpads just as the craft braked suddenly. He heard a loud pop from the hull but the ship slowed to a crawl.

Not bad, he thought, *but I'll need to adjust the timing.*

He reopened the gurgitator, just barely, and piloted the ship onto the Great Sea Lanes. He signaled the nearest controllers—at the fortress on Nunan—and indicated his approach. The controller signaled for him to halt and await confirmation of his trajectory.

Out of the fog bank, a fleet of Corkin heavy cruisers appeared, and Lithuigi killed the gurgitator and signaled his compliance with the lane controller. The Corkin fleet stopped and a single cata'rin sailed out from behind the ships and approached Lithuigi's craft, pulling up alongside it. He could see the captain, a tall, broad Raccorin, with a wide, bright green face. On his forehead, there were two crystamins, one a deep and pulsating scarlet—a master Corkin crystal—the other a dull adobe with hints of orange, like burnstone—the royal crystal of Raccorum Rhazzat.

The captain raised his hand and Lithuigi returned the gesture.

"Well, isn't this an honor," Lithuigi said, smiling warmly and bowing slightly. "How do you do, Prince Rhakksees?" The resemblance of the prince to his kingly father was uncanny, and Lithuigi pushed down the nostalgia that swelled up inside of him, taking him off guard. "It's been many years."

"The honor is all mine, professor," the prince said, grinning. "And yes, it has been a long time. Not since P'anorum, I think." His smile faded.

"I'm surprised to see you so close to the capital," Lithuigi said. "Has there been trouble?"

"So it's true what they say about you," Rakk said.

Lithuigi laughed. "Many things are said about me, Prince Rhakksees."

"That you don't use the weavryn," Rakk said. "Some sort of vow to never access a servryn?"

"The good prince is well informed," Lithuigi said.

"Perhaps the good professor underestimates his own fame," he said. "That's a difficult vow you've taken. How's your cata'rin? Having any troubles today?"

"A beautiful crossing. Seas just the way you'd pray for them to be when setting sail."

"We heard a strange sound from your gurgitator," said another Raccorin, joining the prince at his side. He also had two crystamins, similar to the prince, though his Corkin crystal was not a master crystal, so it was red rimmed in black. He was dressed in Corkin fatigues, black with red and orange. A slave warrior—but the other crystal showed he belonged directly to the prince, property of the royal family. No slave would have been so bold otherwise. They couldn't have even if they'd wanted to be.

"You sure did," Lithuigi said, looking back at the prince. "The old bird isn't as smooth as she once was. She's old and feeble like me. Likes to holler when she doesn't get her way. Didn't like me closing her down hard like that. Should of eased her in, is all. I won't know what happened for sure til I take her in to my lab."

"Your trajectory appears to have taken you far off the Lanes," Rakk said.

"An unfortunate necessity," Lithuigi said, "when tending to affairs of the Guild."

"Any run-ins with the Bhizini you'd like to share?" Rakk looked at Lithuigi's stump then, barely sticking down from his shoulder. He remembered then that he'd forgotten to reattach the prosthetic, and his cheeks blushed slightly on the tops, but the prince didn't seem to notice.

"None at all, thank Trevian," he said. "Any luck chasing down Qardymion the Saltsap?"

"I've been drowning in leads for decades, none of them substantive, obviously," Rakk said with a grim smile. "But I won't keep you. Nice to see you again, professor. Farewell."

Lithuigi flashed a charming smile at the prince but he had already turned back to the bridge, the other Raccorin following at his heels. He swallowed the smile and frowned at the ship as it moved away from his cata'rin. Then he contacted the port authority for clearance to enter the harbor, and sent a message to his assistant Mha'arlo to meet him on the docks. The fog got so thick as he approached the crescent, he asked the port controllers to direct his ship through the narrow gate into the inner harbor for him. He watched as the cata'rin bypassed a long line of ships waiting to enter the city, then went and fetched his prosthetic and carefully reattached the clasps to his stump.

Once near the Guild docking facility in Westport, he took control of the ship once more and piloted it carefully through a narrow passageway and into a large hangar on the water's edge. He grabbed his satchel, lowered the ramp, and stepped down on to the pier.

Mha'arlo was waiting for him, a friendly smile on his bright Raccorin face.

"Welcome back, professor," he said. "I hope your trip was productive?"

"Indeed it was," Lithuigi said.

"Perhaps next time you'll remember to take me along," he said, his smile fading. "I came down to the docks all ready to set sail only to find you had left without me."

Lithuigi smiled. "Next time," he said.

Mha'arlo nodded. "Your scrolls," he said, handing him a silken pouch with a half dozen rolls of parchment. "You've two weeks worth to catch up on."

"I suppose they'll tell me what's going on with the Corkin patrols around the capital?"

"Of course, professor, in detail."

"Good, good. And what about this summons I've received from the Pradishar?"

Mha'arlo spoke to Lithuigi directly through the crystamin. <<I've confirmed with the Dyna'arin that you're under no obligation to appear, nor to speak.>>

<<I know that, but what is this about?>>

<<A Cul'tavin troop of both Andrasians and Raccorin, under the command of Ellex Andria, was found butchered, professor. Chopped into pieces and sewn back together. The words 'True Balance' were written on the wall in sap. They were arranged as if sitting in the Solarium, councilors and advisers both, conducting affairs of state.>>

"Sweet Trevian," Lithuigi said aloud. <<Here in Balan Su?>>

<<In a warehouse in Eastport,>> Mha'arlo said. <<And professor, the warehouse—it belongs to you.>>

Lithuigi hissed, and then he stood silently, staring at Mha'arlo for a moment, his mind spinning.

"I'm going to need more than a scroll today," he said. "I need everything you've gathered so far."

Mha'arlo reached in his satchel and pulled out a datamin, a short, stout hexagonal crystal embedded in a cube of metal, about the size of a die, the crystal clear like quartz with a cloudy core, the metal burnished bronze.

"Already done," he said, handing Lithuigi the datamin. <<I've also appended a stream you need to see. This hit the weavryn a few days ago. The Pradishar have struggled to keep it under wraps. A few have been arrested for sharing it. It's from P'anorum, professor.>>

<<What?! Are you sure?>>

<<I've confirmed the metadata.>>

Lithuigi closed his eyes for a moment and cursed himself for coming back to Balan Su.

"I'll watch it as soon as I get home. Thank you, son," he said. "What would I do without your help?"

Mha'arlo managed a small smile. "Learn to use the weavryn, I suppose."

Lithuigi wagged a finger at him. "One more thing before I forget. I need you to remove the gurgitators from my ship and bring them to my lab at the Academicon. Both the left and right ones, and their attachments. Make sure you use locked crates. Place them in secure storage."

"Right away."

"Very good then. And thanks again for the scrolls and the datamin. I'll get to them shortly. And I promise I won't leave you behind on my next trip."

"Thanks, professor. Oh, and one more thing. Your wife—she knows I didn't go with you this time. I tried to be subtle, but she's a force to be reckoned with."

Lithuigi sighed and looked longingly at his cata'rin, fighting off the urge to climb the ramp and head back out to sea.

"Don't I know it," he said, starting for the lift, not sure what he was dreading more—an interrogation from the Pradishar, or coming face to face with Rebesh'a's anger.

❧ ❧

The private Guild lift raced upward through the rock of Balan Su, the maquina whining as it went along, carrying Lithuigi from sea level to the upper rim. He fingered the datamin Mha'arlo had given him, reached out for it with his crystamin, and absorbed the information it contained into his mind. The images from the warehouse were ghastly, but what really had caught his attention was the stream from P'anorum.

He watched Fin'roq, eyes glazed and glowing. He saw the vast room he stood in, the large maquina partially crushed. He watched the monkin Roe, his head twisted round and round, then flung aside by a flick of Fin'roq's hand. The stream lasted only a moment, less than a minute. But Lithuigi knew what it meant. He knew, even as he wished he didn't.

Not yet, he thought. *Sweet Trevian, not yet.*

When the lift came to a stop on the upper rim, and the doors opened with a whoosh, he stepped out into a private corridor at the Academicon. The sight of his beloved school lifted his spirits, and he considered going straight to his lab, throwing himself into his work—that was the surest way he had for getting his mind off of uncomfortable topics and losing himself in space and in time for awhile—but he knew he'd only make things worse with Rebesh'a if he didn't go home first.

He took a moment to put on his heavy robe and pull his hood up over his head, then he stepped out into the alleyway along the edge of the Academicon and walked down the cobblestones to the Forum. The fog was thick that evening, even on the upper rim, rising in wispy clouds to hover over the ancient marble buildings of the Forum, making the city look abandoned, neglected, forgotten in the mist. But by the time he emerged into Grand Plaza in front of the citadel, there were peaks of soft orange sunshine breaking through. He passed the Weeping Wilvryn, the dew on its leaves and long-hanging vines glistening in the light, as if strung up with diamonds. And the great obsidian spire of the citadel shimmered like glass, a great black knife stabbing upward into the sky.

He crossed through the archways into the Old Stones district, with its winding alleys and narrow cobblestone streets. He liked the neighborhood, the only place on the upper rim that seemed to have any character of its own, but he pulled his hood farther down over his face, ignored the shopkeepers beckoning him to enter their stores, and kept walking. Soon enough he was at the gates of his exclusive residential community, Sunrise Ridge, where he pulled off his hood and smiled at the security guard, who nodded and opened the gate for him to enter.

As he stepped into the grassy pathways and lush foliage of the subdivision, he reached back to pull his hood over his head, but it was too late. He'd already been spotted by one of his neighbors.

"Welcome back, professor," Ellex Andria said. "I thought we'd need to send a patrol out to look for you."

"Ahh, Sui Pradesh," Lithuigi said, beaming. "How good to see you again. Looking absolutely radiant this evening, as always. Truly, you might be the only one in all of Balance Territories who can make those drab Cul'tavin fatigues look like a fashion statement."

She narrowed her eyes at him. "The good professor is too kind," she said. "Perhaps, as a gesture of your infamous generosity, you might tell me where you've been for the last week? A summons from the Pradishar is not usually dismissed so lightly."

"Dismissed? By Trevian, no! I came as soon as I could. We tinkers are often in our labs, hard at work, oblivious to the world around us. And no other Dyna'arin would dare disturb a tinker in the midst of working. Accidents with dynamins are almost always deadly, I'm afraid."

"And yet you lost only an arm," Ellex said.

"By the luck of Trevian," Lithuigi said, touching his prosthetic. "No, Sui Pradesh, I promise you, as soon as I heard, I came at onel. But Callo Baton is in the heart of Mon Mangalar, and my lab at Vergis is even farther away. In truth I didn't know what this was about until moments ago, when my aide informed me of it."

"Oh right, your vow," Ellex said, sounding unconvinced. "Only just heard of it, you say?"

"Indeed. And I am sickened by it. Truly sickened. Tell me, Sui Pradesh, what have the Cul'tavin learned? Who was behind this attack?"

She stared at him for a moment, a cold look on her face. "When we find out, they will pay. That much I can promise."

"I am at your disposal," he said. "How can I help?"

She sighed, almost a hiss. "I hope that's a sincere offer, professor. The Guild isn't known for being cooperative with the Cul'tavin."

"Well, I can't speak for the Dyna'arin as a whole, only for myself. Believe me when I say, I want to know who is responsible for this outrage, and I want them to pay for it too."

Lithuigi watched her face for any hint that she had been appeased.

Poor Ellex, he thought. *To go through all that she went through—to do all that she did—and not remember any of it. This hostility, though—where is it coming from?*

"You're the owner of the warehouse in question?" she said.

"Indeed I am. I acquired the property shortly after I moved to Balan Su, a century ago. I was a budding young tinker trying to make a name for myself in the capital, and I rented the space for my experiments. But once I became a professor, and rose in the ranks of the Dyna'arin, there was no longer any reason to use the space for lab work. I'm ashamed to admit it, but I used the building to store some of my older ships, ones I couldn't bear to part with but which I rarely take out anymore."

"There were no ships," she said. "Any idea why that warehouse in particular would be used for terrorism purposes, professor?"

"I'm utterly clueless," he said. "I'm sorry Sui Pradesh, but I'm just as shocked and confused as you are."

"Would you be willing to come to the citadel and make an official statement on the matter?" she said.

"Of course," he said. "Just as soon as the Dyna'arin request it of me. I'm afraid there are protocols to follow, after all. Until then, if you'll excuse me, I've had a long journey and I need to get home to my wife."

Ellex opened her mouth to respond but closed it.

"Be seeing you soon, professor," she said, turning to leave.

He watched her go, down the grassy pathway into the fog, which had blotted out the evening sun and turned everything around him a deepening gray. He wrapped his robe around himself but couldn't suppress a shiver as he headed for home.

Lithuigi's palatial garden estate was on the inside edge of the upper rim, a multi-level compound of wide-open terraces and lush green gardens, the buildings made with the soft pinks and blues of marble and the ruddy orange of burnstone. He hated it, but Rebesh'a loved it, had hired the designer and helped draft the plans to build it—had even renovated it at least a dozen times in the last seventy years that they had lived there together.

He sent the access signal via crystamin and the door to the estate slid open with a whoosh. He went straight to his office, deposited his things in the safe, then went to the bathing room to freshen up. He grabbed fresh robes from the chest in the corner, then spent some time carefully ladling the water over his dull green skin, scrubbing under his arms and along the base of his flower, and rinsing out his hair fibers. Then he dried off, splashed a bit of musk water on his front, and pulled a clean robe over his head. He took a comb and carefully arranged his gray hair fibers, and when he was satisfied that he'd washed away all vestiges of two weeks at sea, he emerged and headed for the patio on the inner rim.

But Rebesh'a wasn't there.

He found his wife in her studio, standing in front of her workstation, her hands in wet clay, molding and shaping a small mug. Her ebony hair fibers were pulled back in a ponytail, and she was humming a show-tune, carefully scouring the clay so she could attach the handle.

Lithuigi stopped and stared at her for a moment, her dull green skin shiny with coconut oil, her small hands white and ashy with dried clay, pressing the top of the handle to the body of the cup and caressing the curved edge as she brought the other end down to attach near the bottom of the mug.

Rebesh'a glanced his way and jumped when she saw him, her hand jolting forward and knocking the handle loose.

"Look what you've made me do," she said, turning her attention back to her mug and picking up the handle. "How long have you been standing there?"

"Sorry, love. I didn't want to disturb you. It's beautiful."

She made a sound of disapproval. "Didn't want to disturb me? Ha! Where have you been the last two weeks?"

"Working," he said.

"Liar," she said. She dropped the handle back on the workstation. "You always take Mha'arlo when you're working. He's been on Balan Su the whole time you were gone."

"Mha'arlo was busy with his studies, so I left him behind this time."

"I contacted Callo Baton but you weren't there."

"I was on Vergis," he said. "At my lab. Guild headquarters wouldn't know if I was there or not. You know that."

Rebesh'a shook her head, and there were tears in her eyes. "The Cul'tavin have been here every day, asking for you. Asking me if I knew where you were. Can you imagine how embarrassed I was, that I didn't know where you were, had no way to contact you, no idea when you'd be back, nothing! All because you're a damn stubborn old fool who refuses to get with the times."

"Easy, mama," Lithuigi said. "I came home as soon as I got the summons. But I had no idea how serious it was until I arrived and Mha'arlo filled me in."

"It's terrible," Rebesh'a said. "Those poor peacekeepers. The notestreams say they were drugged with bhiza beforehand—so their crystals were numb. They couldn't call for help, couldn't—" She looked away.

Lithuigi touched Rebesh'a's shoulder but she shrugged him off. "Fortunately the notestreams haven't mentioned you by name—yet. But the city is in a panic. The last thing we need is to appear like we have anything to hide—like, oh, say, vanishing for a week after the incident!"

"I told you, love, I was working," Lithuigi said.

Rebesh'a hissed. "Working? Or seeing your whore?"

He sighed. "Working," he said. "And she never speaks unkindly of you, you know."

She slapped him hard across the face, and Lithuigi considered whether or not he deserved it.

Rebesh'a opened her mouth to speak but stopped suddenly, and Lithuigi was surprised to see a warm smile on her face.

"Is that my lovelies I hear?" she said, pushing past him and giving him an elbow in the ribs as she passed.

He followed her out the door and saw her hurrying onto the terrace, where their grown sons, Vilder and Hesh'n, were coming in.

"You're early," she said. "Your father just got home and I was busy in my studio. Let me go get cleaned up. I'll be right back!" She smiled and started marching toward her quarters.

Lithuigi ducked into his office, got the scrolls that Mha'arlo had given him when he arrived, and sat down in a lounger in the garden to peruse them. He took them from the pouch and saw that Mha'arlo had numbered them along the outer edge, in his clean, clear print. Inside each scroll was a point by point account of the events of the day, culled from the notestreams and summarized with unusual clarity. Mha'arlo was an exceptional synthesizer of information, and Lithuigi knew he'd make a fine professor, although he dreaded the day he was no longer his assistant.

"No good news as always," he said aloud.

"Still getting your news from a scroll, father?" Vilder said, standing in the doorway, a sneer on his long, thin, sickly green face. He stepped inside and took a moment to carefully lift his pradeshan robes as he sat down on a lounger across from Lithuigi. "Seriously, a renowned professor of the Academicon and he doesn't even know how to access a notestream!"

"I know *how* to access notestreams," Lithuigi said. "I choose not to."

Vilder snorted. "I mean really, you can get information directly into your mind from the crystamin, and yet you make your poor assistant write out the day's news in longhand? I mean, who even reads these days?"

"Intelligent people," Lithuigi said flatly.

Vilder's thin upper lip curled into a sneer, but he seemed to push it down and replace it with a small smile. "I heard about your warehouse," he said. "Terrible."

Lithuigi looked at Vilder for a moment.

"What do you want, son?"

"To help," Vilder said. "I've always just wanted to help."

Lithuigi sighed. "Out with it already."

Vilder exhaled. "I—" he stopped, closed his eyes for a moment, then opened them and continued, "—need a recommendation."

Lithuigi laughed. "You? Joining the Guild?"

"Not the Dyna'arin," Vilder snapped. Then he softened his voice. "The Pradishar. I—know you're working for them, Father. I know you have contacts who can help me—who can help the bishrops to see my worth."

"Not happy being a lowly priestin but they haven't invited you into the ranks of the bishrops yet, eh? Tough luck, son. Even if I could help you, I wouldn't. A hundred years from now, when you've done the thing yourself, you'll thank me."

Vilder snorted. "But you could help me?"

Lithuigi bunched up his shoulders in a shrug.

Vilder's pale cheeks darkened. "Have I told you lately how exceedingly arrogant you are, Father?"

"Have I told you lately how little I care what you think of me?"

Vilder's eyes were shining with rage. He clenched his jaw. "Fine, disregard me, you know I don't like you anyway. But Mother, on the other hand—for Trevian's sake, you could at least learn how to stream a melodrama, even if you insist on reading your news like someone from a thousand years ago. No, not for Trevian's sake, but for our mother's! For her! I'll never know how she puts up with you ignoring her life's work like that. It wouldn't kill you to stream one, just one, for her."

"A thousand years? The weavryn is hardly an hundred years old. And I'm trying to read here," Lithuigi said. "Reading takes peace and quiet. The same as learning any skill. Perhaps that's why you never could master anything. You have to be able to reflect and absorb, not just parrot back what someone tells you."

Vilder jumped to his feet and strode stiffly from the room, his nose in the air. Lithuigi watched him go, thinking how much he disliked his son and how little he could seem to do to feel any differently. When Vilder had left, he looked at the scrolls again, then threw them back in his satchel and went outside. He walked to the edge of the rim and stared out at the fog, the city completely obscured by the mist.

"What a grouch you are," Rebesh'a said, standing next to him, her hair fibers combed and pulled up, a bit of color on her face, looking like a goddess in her silken violet robe. "Now isn't the time to spar with your son. He's here to celebrate your nameday after all."

"My...nameday?" Lithuigi groaned. "Is that today?"

"Silly professor," Rebesh'a said. "Vilder sweetie, don't pout, come, help Mother get the garden ready." Vilder shot his father a scowl then took his mother's arm and followed her to the cookery.

"Father," Hesh'n called. "Can you come here for a moment?"

Lithuigi found his other son in his old room, stooped over the workstation, making adjustments to something inside a long metal box. He was squinting as he worked, as he always did, low light or not. The warm orange glow from the glowbes made his wavy, tousled brown hair fibers look like copper.

"What is it, son?" Lithuigi asked.

"A special gift for you, Father," Hesh'n said. "I wanted it to be a surprise. Here, let me get the old one off."

"My arm?"

Hesh'n motioned for his father to sit, then carefully unstrapped the prosthetic from the stub on his left side and pulled off the vines that were attached to Lithuigi's skin.

He only had a few inches of arm dangling down from his shoulder, all that had made it through the blast that vaporized the rest of his arm many decades earlier.

"Your prototype is finished?" Lithuigi asked.

"You remember then." Hesh'n looked relieved.

"Of course I remember," he said. "You've been working on it for a decade now. How could I forget?"

Hesh'n shrugged. "You never mention it. Never ask me about it."

"I don't want to pressure you. I know how a tinker needs space to work."

Hesh'n reached into the metal box and pulled out the new prosthetic, and Lithuigi gasped when he saw it. The old one had been metal, with gears and pulleys, and with fabric pulled taut over it to make a semblance of an arm. But this one—this one looked like an actual arm.

Lithuigi's heart was racing. He reached out and touched it—definitely flesh. He looked at Hesh'n, but his son was beaming at him.

"Father, I present to you the very first organic/maquina prosthetic the world has ever seen," Hesh'n said. His eyes were crinkled up and he was grinning like a little scamp.

Lithuigi fought to calm his racing heart. He tried to swallow, his throat dry. "Where..." He took a deep breath. "Where'd you get this arm?"

Hesh'n's smile slipped a little. "Not to worry, Father. It's one hundred percent legitimate."

"Son," Lithuigi said, lowering his voice. "You know what I had to go through for you last time."

Hesh'n's smile faded completely. "I told you, it's legitimate. I got authorization through all the proper channels, to grow my own spratlyn and harvest the arm. Don't spoil this, Father."

"I'm not," he said.

So Hesh'n had been experimenting with flesh again, and someone in Management had given him the green light. Lithuigi didn't like it, but he had to admit the prosthetic looked amazing. And if it was just a spratlyn he used, maybe it was okay this time. He'd have to give it some more thought later.

"Well, what are you waiting for?" Lithuigi said. "Show me how it works."

Hesh'n's smile came back, and he nodded. He took the arm from the box and began to fit it to Lithuigi's stump. "The bonding agent will help the flesh fuse, but it might sting a little at first," he said, and for a moment Lithuigi thought his stump was on fire, and he clenched his teeth to keep from crying out. But the pain was gone as fast as it had appeared. "And now for the best part. The Pradishar have issued me a crystamin for the arm, even tied it to your own Dyna'arin crystal. It might take a bit of practice, but once you get the hang of it, the arm should function as if it were your very own." He stepped back and looked at it. "Well, how's it feel?"

Lithuigi looked down at the arm. Except for a band of metal just below where the prosthetic met his stump, the entire thing looked like flesh, like a real arm, dull green like his own. Like Hesh'n's. "It's heavier than the other one," he said. "How'd you get a spratlyn arm to grow so big so fast?"

"Try to move it."

Lithuigi tried to lift his arm, but the stump felt so heavy, dragged down by the weight of it. He looked at Hesh'n. "How do you keep it alive?"

"Use your crystal to help lift it," he said, nodding encouragingly. "Feel out for the crystamin in the prosthetic. It should be sensitive to the flesh."

Lithuigi took a deep breathe, then reached out through the crystal to his new arm. He could feel the crystamin there, and to his surprise, the arm responded to his mental touch. He picked up a pair of pincers from the workstation, opened and closed them, turned them to and fro, then sat them back down, just by willing it. He could even feel the coolness of the metal on his fingertips.

"Extraordinary," Lithuigi said, barely a whisper. "As if it were my own hand, doing what I want it to do."

Hesh'n was all grins. "I may need to make a few more adjustments but I didn't want to miss your nameday."

"Son, I—" He had tears in his eyes.

"You can thank Vilder, too," Hesh'n said, looking away. "He helped me get the authorization for the crystamin from the Pradishar."

Then why was he asking me for a recommendation? Lithuigi wondered.

"Well, as long as this is all above board. If I check with Management, I won't find anything amiss?"

"I already told you, it's all legitimate, all legal."

"Well, it had better be," Lithuigi said. "I'm taking a risk if it isn't."

"Can't you trust me?" Hesh'n asked.

"Well, alright," he said. "If Management approves. But what about Durbian's Line? You don't think we've crossed it?"

Hesh'n rolled his eyes and let out a soft hiss, but a sharp bell rang, someone calling at the door, and he turned away, closed up the box and put away his tools, not looking at his father. Rebesh'a called out to them both.

"Who is it?" Lithuigi asked. "Are you expecting company?"

"Of course I am," Rebesh'a said. "Gushyr Vaincorr's been badgering me for an interview for weeks now. What better time than with the family all here?"

Lithuigi hissed loudly, and Hesh'n laughed. "Oh, the joys of fame, eh Father?"

He took a moment to prepare himself, closing his eyes and taking a few slow, deep breaths. Then he emerged onto the terrace where Rebesh'a and Gushyr were discussing the azaleas in bloom and he was telling her what an amazing gardener she was.

"Professor L'uigi!" Gushyr said, all smiles, his eyes twitching. Several of Gushyr's crew were standing around the garden, eyes twitching as well, watching them all.

Lithuigi gave Gushyr a warm smile and placed his hand on his chest in greeting. "Welcome back, old chap," he said, patting him on the shoulder with his new prosthetic. "I heard you got a promotion? Well deserved, I'm certain of it!" He winked.

"Oh, you flatter me!" Gushyr said, blushing. Lithuigi put his arm around Rebesh'a and gave her a peck on the cheek, and when she smiled, she was glowing.

"I'm Gushyr Vaincorr, here with loveliest couple in Balan Su City," Gushyr said. "What do you think?" He took a moment to look at one of his crew—a stand-in for his audience—then turned back to Lithuigi and Rebesh'a. "Just look at you two! I think every couple in Balance Territories wishes they were you two."

Rebesh'a smiled. "We're just normal people, really," she said.

Gushyr laughed and gave a knowing smirk. "So production has finally wrapped on your next melodrama?" he asked. "The sneak preview makes it look like a real tear-jerker! Everyone can't wait to see you and Jaun von Andron together again." Gushyr fanned himself. "What about you, professor? How does it feel to see your wife in a melodrama with another male, one as comely as Jaun von Andron? Jealous?" He raised his eyebrows.

Lithuigi smiled and looked at his wife. "I met my Rebesh'a on Andramere at the playhouse in Stone Garden," he said, his cheeks flushed. "Her voice brought tears to my eyes and her laughter made me swoon. The way she danced—I've never seen anything so perfect. Gushyr, I mean it when I say this, I'd never deny the world the glory of her talents."

"Awwww!" Gushyr cried. "And the world thanks you for it! Today is something of a celebration for you anyway, right?"

"Indeed," Lithuigi said, "but shhh, don't tell. I can't afford to get any older!" He grinned.

"How many years is it?" Gushyr asked. "Come, come, don't make me look it up!" His eyes twitched. "What?! Not much on your younger years, is there? We need to remedy that! What do you say to a tell-all autobiography with yours truly?"

"You flatter me, Gushyr, you really do. But there's not much to tell. I'm much more boring than people assume. I'm 140 years old now, can you believe it? I'm practically ancient. No doubt I'll be planting myself soon enough."

"Oh, listen to him," Rebesh'a said. "He's still got a good fifty or sixty years in him, but you'd think he was already a tandavin on the gruynfeld. But I can assure you, he makes love like a Verdillion half his age! And I would know, we've been married that long!"

Lithuigi blushed and gave Rebesh'a another kiss.

"I just love you two," Gushyr said, wiping away a few tears. "Any nameday wishes?"

"No, truly," he said. "Here I am with my beautiful wife, with my amazing sons Vilder and Hesh'n, wonderful plants so smart and kind and hard-working. Here in our beautiful home, in this most amazing city. I have the best job in the world. I love my students so much, my work so much. No, there's nothing at all I could wish for, except for another year, another decade, for the rest of my life to go on as perfect as it is now!"

Lithuigi pulled Vilder and Hesh'n into hugs and together they all posed, all smiles and laughter, while Gushyr took some stills and Rebesh'a chatted about her upcoming melodrama. When Gushyr and his crew finally left, Vilder and Hesh'n left too, and Rebesh'a went and sat on the patio and stared out at the fog, a blank look on her face. Lithuigi watched her for a moment, then went into the bathing room and stripped, feeling the desperate need for another shower. And when he had dressed once again, he had to fight the urge to head for the lift, head for his cata'rin, and sail from Balan Su just as fast as he could—off to the Far Archipelago, off to the other life that waited for him on the backside of the world.

But he knew he couldn't go. He had classes to teach. He had a job to do. He had his name to clear. He had a family here, a famous one. And this wet, cold, dreary city he pretended to love, felt more like a prison than it ever had before.

Chapter 6

And So They Came For Him

Fin'roq's mouth was dry, his throat sore from screaming. His head hurt, his neck hurt, his arms and legs hurt, everything hurt. The sunlight through his eyelids, warm and red—even that made his eyes burn. A soft sea breeze on his skin felt like sandpaper, rubbing off the outer layers of his chest and shoulders, his knees and elbows, and grinding harshly across the wounds, again and again with each gust.

Only the dreams provided a respite—dreams in which he was anyone but himself. Dreams of distant lands full of adventures, with family and friends and even with lovers. But they always ended the same way, always with a double waking—first to silent darkness and the certainty that he was trapped somewhere, locked away in the void—and then a second waking, to the real world and the feeling of being torn apart, every limb and fiber crushed, overwhelmed by a desire to howl his lungs out.

At least the screaming had stopped. How long it went on, he didn't know. It felt like lifetimes had passed, that it had gone on and on until Fin'roq forgot who he was or where he was, or even if he was—only the pain had existed. But then he'd heard Bhea Bell—she sang to him, her voice low and husky, yet soft, cozy, like the sound of the sea at the bottom of a long hill, or the soft crackling of a fire, or the popping of rhupan on the grill—and he'd remembered who he was. He'd known her voice, known his Bhea—she'd always been there to soothe his fears. Even in his dreams, he saw her mottled face, dark patches like wings across her forehead, guiding him, reassuring him on the journey home.

Now he tried to open an eye, but the pain—how could light, delicious light, light that he loved to bask in, to drink up every hour of every day—how could it hurt so much?

"Don't force it, little sprout," Bhea said from nearby. "Here, easy now. Got some water for ya."

Fin felt the cup by his mouth, the fresh water on his lips, and he took a small sip, swallowing blades. But the cooling sensation as it went down was irresistible, and the more he drank, the better his throat felt. The water had a tangy taste, some tincture that Bhea had brewed no doubt. When he'd drained the cup, he started to drift off to sleep again, and he tried to open his eyes, but couldn't.

"Sleep now," Bhea said. "You just need a few more days. Don't you worry, soon you'll be back to your old self again. You'll see."

Fin slept. He woke, drank, and slept. Woke, drank, and slept. The pain in his joints, in his limbs, in his head and neck, in his skin, were fading away. And when he woke without the urge to cry out, the late morning sun warm on his shoulders and his back, he opened his eyes and blinked as the view off Bhea's cliffside came into focus. He carefully retracted his leaftips, folded his branches into his arms, and lowered them to his sides. His muscles were weak and moving felt like it took great effort, but he pulled his rootpads up out of the soil and into his feet and took a few small steps. His legs cramped and he had to extend his rootpads once again to steady himself.

"Look at you, moving around already," Bhea said from behind him. "I always knew you was a strong one."

"What happened to me, Bhea?"

"Too much darkness, my sprout. Started to petrify. But it weren't too late. Baboo gotcha out in time."

"Baboo? How?"

"Wasn't there myself."

"What about Aar'ryn and Roe? Are they okay?"

Bhea held her breath, then sighed. "What's the last thing you remember?"

Fin shook his head. "There was a smell. An awful smell. Aar'ryn said it was the smell of petrification. They wanted to go down, deeper underground than I'd ever been. We found something, a temple maybe. And then—I don't know."

"You don't remember?"

"I remember being scared. Very scared. And it felt like I was being pulled, like my limbs were being stretched. I remember reaching for Roe. I must have been dreaming, because I could see myself out of Roe's eyes. I could feel his body, and it was my own. I—Sweet Trevian, I still have his memories. All those times he tormented me—I can see myself being tormented! I can feel his hatred for me."

"And then?" Bhea said, her face calm, her eyes fixed on Fin'roq's.

"And then the pulling became a ripping. I screamed. I thought I was going to die. There was only pain. And dreams—dreams I can't remember now—and then I heard your voice, singing to me."

Bhea exhaled loudly. She took Fin's hand. "Ain't no way to sugarcoat this. Roe's dead, love."

Fin stared at Bhea, his mouth slowly opening and then closing. "What are you saying?"

"I know it were an accident," Bhea said. "I know you."

"Aar'ryn—what about Aar'ryn?"

"He's alive," Bhea said. "Been up to check on you a few times, but I haven't let him in."

"He can tell us what happened," Fin said. "He can explain—that it wasn't my fault."

"Not likely, my sprout," she said. "He's already told the villagers what you done."

Fin shook his head. "They wanted me to go under there. They begged me to go! I wouldn't—I couldn't—I didn't hurt anyone. I swear it. Bhea, they were finally accepting me! Why would I ruin my one chance—I can go and explain. I can tell them I'm innocent, that I would never—"

"They ain't gonna listen. I'm sorry, little sprout, but they already made up their minds."

Fin'roq knew that could mean only one thing—slowly simmered to death over a low burning fire.

In his mind, he saw Roe, handsome face contorted into a sneer, promising one day he'd tie him to the post himself, douse the flames with water to make sure he didn't die too quickly—a favorite threat of his. And then he saw his own face through Roe's eyes, skin a blotchy mess of greens, eyes looking down at the ground, so meek, so fucking timid it made him sick to look upon himself. And he didn't know if he was feeling what Roe had felt in that moment, or if this was something all his own.

He only knew the hatred felt richly deserved.

❧ ⸙ ❧

Days passed in a blur of sun and sleep. Fin'roq's young body grew supple and strong once again, but he still felt so tired. He didn't want to wake up in the mornings, didn't want to walk the pathways of Bhea's garden, didn't want to read anything, and didn't want to see anyone.

Grizmond was there during the days—perhaps at night too, though Fin'roq didn't know. The old Raccorin said little as usual, and Fin hadn't even felt like questioning him. Why bother? Besides, whenever they looked at him, Grizmond and Bhea both, he felt like they were judging him. He was a burden to them, a murderous halfbreed just like the villagers had always said.

Bhea insisted he go back to his normal routine—cleaning and tidying, studying and gardening. He'd gone through the motions, put in the effort, but with every sweep of the broom, every turn of the page, every herb picked or bug collected, he thought of Roe. He didn't want to have his memories, didn't want to have his feelings and sensations—he felt like a thief with stolen goods—and yet they played out in his mind, over and over again, like a waking dream. He could hear Roe's voice as Roe himself had heard it, almost unrecognizable. He could smell him, feel the sun on his skin, the sand on his toes. Fin'roq had never been kissed, but Roe had, and he could taste Milli Mor'n's lips on his, feel his heart fluttering as if the memory had been his own.

Only fear chased the thoughts away. Every evening, as twilight waned in the west, Fin'roq felt the shadows creeping into the garden, creeping inside him. Bhea lit glowbes around the patio and torches throughout the gardens and pathways, but there never seemed to be enough light. For the first time in his life, he understood why the other villagers had feared to venture under the island—why the thought of going down into the black was too much to handle.

Fin swore he'd never go underground again, not even down into Bhea's grotto.

He could sense that Bhea was nervous, on edge. Even Grizmond, who normally spent the day staring at the sea, couldn't stop pacing the estate and checking the perimeter. When he left for the afternoon, Fin assumed he'd gone to the village for news. Sure enough, he returned that evening, out of breath and looking haggard. Fin'roq found them talking by the hedges.

"Aar'ryn's done all he can," Grizmond said. "They'll be coming, sooner or later."

Fin crouched back into the shrub, hoping they hadn't noticed him.

"I'm not worried about the villagers," Bhea said.

"Grief's made them unpredictable," he said. "They won't let this go. He can't stay here."

"I know it, but we still got time."

Grizmond grunted. "You think so? Seems to me the Pradishar got what they came for. They know, Bhea. They must."

"We don't know who knows yet," she said.

"Those who matter do," Grizmond said. "Aar'ryn streamed Roe's death to the weavryn. Everyone in Balance is talking about it, if Aar'ryn can be believed. I don't think he understands enough to lie about it, either."

Bhea hissed. "You're just telling me this?"

"I just found out," he said.

She sighed. "Damnit. They'll be comin'."

"Probably already on their way," he said.

A loud knocking sounded from the front gate, three sharp raps, and Fin'roq jumped at the noise, rustling the bushes around him. He felt a hand on his arm, and he was pulled out onto the path. Grizmond scowled at him, an enflamer in his other hand, pointed directly at Fin's face, but when he saw who it was, he lowered the weapon.

"Stay close, Fin," he said.

Bhea had palmed an enflamer as well, and she led the way to the two towers at the front gate. When she looked through the peephole, she hissed.

"It's Aar'ryn Ruu'n," she said, looking at Grizmond.

"I think you should let him in," he said.

Bhea hissed again. She pocketed her weapon and went into the tower on the right side of the gate, and Fin'roq heard the whine of maquina and a loud clanging inside the metal door. A smaller door within the door opened and Aar'ryn stepped inside, a flurry of gray and purple robes, a look of relief on his bright jowls.

"I intended to knock until you let me in," he said, smiling at Bhea, but she pulled the enflamer back out of her pocket and pointed it at him.

"Try anything stupid, we'll be having barbecue priestin for dinner. You heard me?"

Aar'ryn swallowed, his large chin pulling up into his neck, puckered up like cracked leather. But when he saw Fin, his features relaxed, and his eyes took on a distant look, and he turned away from Bhea without giving her an answer.

With a whirl of her blue robes, Bhea pulled a dagger from her sleeve, wrapped her other arm around Aar'ryn's neck, and held the blade to his forehead. "Stream one word, one sound, one thought or feeling—give one tiny twitch of those pretty brown eyes of yours—and my scytherin will shatter your precious new crystal. I'm told it's the most painful thing one can endure, as the filaments that have grown deep inside your body start crackin' apart, and then slide through your flesh like you had glass in your veins, each tiny shard rippin' and tearin' as it passes. You hearing me now, priestin?"

Aar'ryn's eyes were bulging and he made a wet gurgling sound.

"I'm still not hearin' ya," Bhea said. She removed her arm from his neck and shoved him forward.

"My hand to Trevian," he said, coughing. "Not a word will be streamed. Please, I mean no harm. I've just come to talk. In private. I swear it."

Fin'roq found he was glad to see the kooky Raccorin again. Aar'ryn had pretended to be a priestin of the Pradishar for all those years, and had always been a source of optimism for the village, at times annoyingly so. Maybe he could offer some answers, since Bhea and Grizmond seemed intent on keeping things from him. Maybe he could find out why people were after him. Maybe Aar'ryn knew what had really happened in the cave.

"I'm glad to see you safe, priestin," Fin'roq said. "Why have you come? Why are you still here? Why are any of you still here? I thought the Pradishar were going to rescue you."

"Fin'roq, my good plant," Aar'ryn said, forcing a smile. His normally bright cheeks had gone so pale they were gray and chalky. "I'm glad to see you safe as well. I'm so, so terribly sorry about what happened, Fin. I truly am."

Fin could feel the emotion coming off the priestin—and he could tell he was lying to him. He wasn't sorry, but scared. Fin felt him in the same way he felt Roe, right before he seized him and devoured him. The lure to do the same to Ruu'n made his head spin, his legs wobble.

But then he remembered something Bhea had taught him long ago, when he was just a little scamp. She called it the cyclone, and she made Fin'roq practice it every time he started to let his mind wander. He imagined a strong wind, blowing in from off the ocean, swirling around his body but never quite touching him. Stronger and stronger the wind would swirl—in, around, and onward—carrying with it anything that came near him, making him impervious, calm in the middle of a raging storm.

Why didn't I try this earlier this week? he thought, as the surge of feelings he felt from Aar'ryn dropped away. Even the feeling of Roe in his mind seemed to fade.

"I want you to know," Aar'ryn continued, "that I don't blame you for what happened. Nobody in the village does."

Fin looked at him and was tempted to reach for his mind again, to see if it was true, but the thought of touching him like that, feeling himself inside him in that terrible way, was too much.

Sweet Trevian, he thought, *what am I?*

Bhea snorted at Aar'ryn.

"Honestly," he said. "I told them what happened. I told them you weren't yourself. That your eyes, your skin—Durq held out for awhile, sure that you were just another Bhizini savage. But I convinced him otherwise. I convinced him that you'd been possessed by a Mund'umbrian. That a shade had used your body as its own."

Grizmond shook his head, scowling. "The 'cure' for possession is the same as the punishment for murder," he said. "So how is that any better?"

"Is that what happened to me?" Fin said.

"The Pradishar are what matter," Aar'ryn said. "And the Pradishar don't believe in such nonsense. Fin'roq, you did as we asked of you. You took us under the island. We found what we were looking for." Aar'ryn looked at Bhea but she remained tight-lipped, her face blank. "And the Pradishar keep their promises. Your invitation to study in Balan Su still stands, should you choose to accept it."

Fin'roq stared at Aar'ryn as if he hadn't heard him.

Bhea hissed softly. "Are you telling me he has a choice?"

"Of course he does," Aar'ryn said. "You know the Pradishar are a voluntary organization. Anyone can join, or not join, as they so desire."

"I don't need you to explain anything to me, priestin," Bhea said. "You're telling me if he says no, he can just go on living here, no problem? Hmm?"

Aar'ryn sighed. "Well, no. You see, I've convinced the villagers that Balance Authority must be the one to carry out Fin's sentence. If he doesn't go with the Pradishar to Balan Su, then I'm afraid the villagers will take it upon themselves to—cleanse him."

"Over our dead bodies," Grizmond growled, and he trained the enflamer on Aar'ryn again.

"I'm just the messenger," he squealed, his eyes bulging.

Grizmond looked at Bhea. "Shall I?" he asked.

Bhea stared at Aar'ryn for a long time, her cheeks drawn and tight. He had tears in his eyes, a pitiful look on his face. He looked at Fin'roq.

"Fin, sweet Fin," he said. "I'm your only chance. Yes, your only chance to get off this rock. Your only chance to see the world. You won't let them hurt me!"

"Stop," Fin said. "Grizmond, don't!"

"This visit's over," Bhea said, opening the door and beckoning Aar'ryn to leave.

He sobbed with relief, his hands together in supplication, bowing to Bhea. "This weekend," he blubbered. "The ship will be here. If you want to go."

And then he was gone.

Bhea closed the door and Grizmond let out a hiss, a murderous look in his eyes. Bhea stared at the ground. They all stood there for a moment, not moving. Not saying anything.

Fin's head was spinning, and he struggled to focus on the cyclone, to calm his mind down, but he couldn't.

"Are you going to tell me what's going on?" he said, looking at Bhea. "What happened to me? What do the Pradishar want with me? What am I supposed to do?" He was crying now and he cursed himself for being so weak.

"I don't know what to say, my sprout," she said.

"Is his offer sincere? Will the Pradishar really let me enroll as a monkin?"

"I can't say for sure," Bhea said.

"Aar'ryn and Roe told me the Pradishar priestin who joined them with their crystals was a Bhizini," Fin said.

"I thought as much," Bhea said.

"You knew? But you always told me the Pradishar hunted and killed Bhizini."

"I know that much is true," she said.

"As do I," Grizmond growled. "Look Fin, Bhea and I need some time to talk things out—privately." He narrowed his eyes at him, but his hands lifted as if in apology.

Bhea put his hand on Fin's shoulder. "You got til the weekend to make a decision, little sprout. Be patient, and I promise, we'll talk about things real soon. You heard me?"

"I heard ya," Fin said. "I'll do my best." He gave her a hug.

"That's all any of us ever can do," she said. "That and nothing more."

᷿᷿᷿᷿᷿᷿ ᷿᷿᷿᷿᷿᷿

The week had only just begun, and Fin'roq felt, as he returned to his chores in the garden, that he couldn't possibly make it through the afternoon much less to the end of the week without getting some answers. He tried to relax, to pray, but his mind didn't want to stop. And every thought he had, every scenario he imagined, seemed to end in him being tied to a stake, a slow smoldering fire filling his lungs with smoke, the embers roasting his toes, his rootpads, his ankles, cooking him to death over many long hours.

For a moment he was Roe, laughing about it. But then he was his own miserable self again, and he was sure the panic would suffocate him.

Baboo returned that afternoon, marching down the pathways of the garden, singing a song in gibberish, waving his arms in tune to the beat, as if leading a grand procession through the streets of an unseen city. Fin heard him before he saw him and he ran to him, tears streaming down his face. Baboo gave him a big smile when he saw him, and gestured for him to join him, never missing a beat of his fanciful song.

Fin joined his parade and started to march, twirling his hands one over the other. He thought himself a terrible singer, so he accompanied Baboo's song with pure sound, with hums and whistles and hisses, doing his best to match his friend in rhythm and tone. Baboo pretended to wave at the imaginary crowds on either side, nodding and winking and grinning.

They marched past the main terrace near the entrance to Bhea's grotto, and Bhea and Grizmond came upstairs to watch them pass. Bhea clapped and cheered and even Grizmond looked mildly amused. Then they continued back past the herb gardens and up the terraces to the fruit orchards. Baboo finally stopped when they reached a round marble fountain in the middle of four different fields of fruit trees. He bowed in all four directions, then he took a drink out of the fountain and grabbed two apples from an overhanging branch.

"Good to see you, Fin'roq friend," he said, handing him one of the apples, a big smile on his small, speckled face. "A good day to celebrate, don't you think?"

Fin took a bite of the warm fruit, and tears burned his eyes as he chewed on it.

"Oh Baboo, thank Trevian you're here. I don't think I've ever needed a friend more than I need one now."

Baboo cocked his head to one side. "What has turned your smile around, Fin friend?" he said. "Tell me your troubles, so we can get rid of them."

"I wish it were so easy," Fin said.

"It might be," Baboo said. "You won't know 'til you tried."

Fin sat down on the edge of the fountain. "You know, a few days ago, I thought I was mad at you."

Baboo's eyes went wide and he put his hand on his chest, and he looked at Fin, mouthing 'me' at him with a look of total shock on his face.

Fin laughed. "Yes. I'm sorry, I should thank you. For saving my life. I'm still not sure you did me a favor, but I'm glad you tried. How'd you find me? How'd you get me out of there?"

Baboo just grinned.

"Please tell me," Fin said.

"Nothing to tell," Baboo said.

"Okay," he said. "Well, something bad happened down there, before you came and rescued me. I did something—unforgivable. And now I don't know what will happen to me. The villagers want to kill me, Baboo. But the Pradishar—they're still offering to fulfill my dreams. It's too good to be true. It's probably a trap. If I stay, the villagers will kill me. If I go, the Pradishar might kill me too. And if for some reason they're telling the truth, and they let me study with other monkins, I'd be going somewhere where they hate Bhizini. It was bad enough facing the scorn of a small village, but imagine the scorn of an entire city! Sweet Trevian, what should I do?"

Baboo took his hand and squeezed it. "Nothin', my sprout," he said, mimicking Bhea. "Ain't nothin' you can do 'cept go right along with whatever's goin' on. You gonna do that whether you wantin' to or not, whether you tryin' to or not. So just go with it, you heard me?"

"Wow, good impression," Fin said. "Only it isn't that easy. I'm a murderer, Baboo. I killed Roe."

Baboo raised his eyebrows. "You remember this?"

Fin shook his head no.

"Didn't think so," Baboo said. "Nope. It was your spirit, Fin friend, not you, that did the killing."

"The villagers think I was possessed by a Mund'umbrian shade."

Baboo chuckled and squeezed his hand. "Don't be scared, Fin friend."

Fin moaned. "But I don't want to die," he said, looking away from Baboo, a single tear running down his cheek.

"Death follows fruit," Baboo said.

"Meaning we live to die? How exactly is that supposed to cheer me up?"

But Baboo just stared at him, a serene look on his face.

❧ ⸻ ☙

They came for him that night.

Fin woke to the sound of shouting voices, the smell of smoke burning his nostrils, thin filaments of blue haze slowly expanding in the milky light of the moon. He heard a loud thudding, the crackle of flames nearby, and he pulled up his roots as quickly as he could.

Baboo was perched on the other side of the room, still sleeping, and Fin'roq tapped him on his chest. His eyes popped open and darted back and forth. Fin put his finger to his lips and Baboo nodded, folded up his branches, and stepped off the soil.

Fin peek his head through the doorway and looked around the garden. A palm-thatched roof on one of Bhea's storehouses was on fire, a few torches lay strewn about on the ground, smoldering. Another arched over the gate, between the two towers, and skidded across the flagstone pathway.

Another loud thud, and Fin realized the villagers were ramming the door.

He turned back to Baboo, panic rising in his chest, squeezing the air out of his lungs, making his legs cramp up, his mind stutter.

But Baboo grabbed his arm and pulled him through the door. Bhea came up the stairs from her grotto, her hair fibers a silver halo around her head, and she ran toward them. He heard the singe of water on flame and saw Grizmond, bucket in hand, trying to douse the fire on the roof.

"Give us Fin'roq!" the villagers screamed.

He recognized Durq's voice, and Prissica's.

Aar'ryn lied, he thought. *They hate me. They've all come for me. Even M'illi? Do they all want me dead?*

Bhea grabbed his arm, and Baboo's too.

"Careful, my sprouts," she said. "Stay back from the gate. I'm gonna have a little chat with the locals. See if old Bhea don't send 'em packin'.'"

She grinned but Fin'roq thought it looked forced.

He nodded at her.

Bhea spun around and ran for the tower on the right side of the gate, hair fibers bobbing with each step she took.

Fin looked around. "Grab those torches off the ground and dunk 'em in the fountains," he said, pointing. "Make sure nothing else catches."

Baboo nodded and scampered off, and with his friend out of the way, he ran after Bhea. Inside the tower, a narrow spiral stair led upward to a fortified lookout platform atop the structure. The stairwell was dark, with no light penetrating the thick stone walls, and Fin froze, suddenly gasping for air.

He turned back, out onto the flagstone pathway, back into the milky moonlight, and he leaned against the rough wall of the tower and tried to fill his lungs.

Another loud thud on the door and Fin jumped, feeling the vibration in his back.

"Quit that racket already, you damn fools, I heard 'ya," Bhea shouted from above.

"Give us the halfbreed," Durq said, "Give us Fin'roq and we'll stop. Refuse, and your life is forfeit."

Bhea laughed heartily. "Is that right? It looks to me like I'm the one looking down on y'all. Don't take but a squeeze of my finger to drop that bridge out from under ya'. 'Course, way that water's flowing thru the gorge, you ain't got a chance of gettin' out 'fore the Ka'Hala dumps you off the cliff."

"That—*creature*—killed my son!" Prissica screamed.

"The Bhizini must face justice," Durq said. "Open this gate or we'll break it down!"

"So it's a swim then," Bhea said.

Fin'roq could hear the panicked cries of the villagers as they fled from the bridge, shouting curses.

"You can't keep him in there forever, Bhea Bell," Durq screamed. "This isn't over."

Fin stood with his back to the wall of the tower, breathing heavily, when Bhea came back down the stairs and out the door.

"They're gone now, little sprout," she said, "but I s'pose you heard that yourself."

He blinked back the tears and nodded, struggling to swallow in a tight throat.

"Go back to your quarters and try to get some sleep," Bhea said. "I opened the bridge so they can't get across." She looked up at the sky. "And it's hardly past midnight. Grizmond and I can clean up."

"I can't sleep now," he said. "Let me help."

Bhea sighed. "Come on then."

Grizmond had put the flames out on the roof but not before it had spread to the nearby trees. Fin watched ropes of flame singe the leaves and curl the branches as a gusty breeze off the water carried the sparks farther up into the garden. A sharp smell that he didn't recognize burned his nostrils, and the heat off the blaze was the most intense warmth he could ever remember feeling.

"The villagers must've thrown pitch in here," Grizmond said. He coughed and tears streamed down his face. "We need more buckets."

"Pitch?" Bhea said. "Must be something else."

Someone grabbed Fin's arm. He jumped, but it was only Baboo.

"All the torches are out," he said. "Didn't help much though."

Bhea turned to Fin and Baboo. "Up in the shed, alongside the orchards, on the north side. There should be carrying rods and buckets. Bring two sets a piece. Hurry!"

"Come on, Baboo," Fin said. They started back toward the gate, then up along the flagstone pathway into the herb gardens. Fin's heart was racing and he sprinted along the winding walkway, past the fountains, then up the terraced hillside to the fruit orchards, his long green legs pumping, the familiar scenery passing by, dreamlike, enameled silver in the moonlight.

When he reached the shed, at the end of a long lane between mango orchards on the right and figs on the left, he stopped and turned back to wait for Baboo to catch up. But his friend wasn't behind him.

He could see the fountain at the heart of the orchards, down at the end of the lane, and he watched, squinting in the low light, waiting to see Baboo's diminutive form appear.

Fin could hear the crackle of the flames and so he turned back to the door of the shed and opened it. The moonlight crept a few feet in, trailing off into a deep black, and he felt his legs wobble. He took a deep breath, then reached inside the door, groping along the wall with his hand, and when he felt the coarse, veiny skin of the glowbe sitting on its pedestal, he grabbed it and gave it a shake.

Warm orange light spread into the shed, and Fin'roq hurried inside. He found the poles and the buckets and tried to carry Baboo's as well, but when he got outside, they slipped from his arms and clattered onto the pathway. Fin dropped to his knees to gather up the mess when he heard rustling in the leaves on both sides of him, and he froze, his face hot, his cheeks pulsing.

He looked to both sides, scanning the masses of long, narrow leaves on the mango trees, like thousands of fingers reaching downward, and the thicker leaves of the fig trees, like hands grasping for him. A gust of wind lifted the branches and made the fires below pop, and Fin sighed when he realized it was only the breeze through the trees he'd been hearing.

The fire popped again, a loud crack, closer this time, much closer, right on top of him. The sound was still ringing in his ears when the next crack rang out, and a long, coarse vine wrapped around his neck. He was on his feet, pulled upward into the air, and the flagstones were shrinking away below him, a blur of leaves all around him.

He tried to scream but the vine had cut off his air. Branches slashed at his face, caught in his hair fibers, tugged at his robe—but nothing slowed his ascent.

And then more pops, more vines, and his ankles and wrists were bound tightly together, drawn upward so that his knees pressed into his chest and his face dug into his shin bones, smashing his nose.

His stomach heaved and fell as the upward motion stalled out and turned into a downward plunge, leaves whipping past his arms and legs, his body in a free-fall, til he was sure he'd crunch into the ground at any moment, but instead he swung forward in a rush of open air.

Another loud pop, another drop, another swoop forward.

Fin struggled to push down the panic, to force himself not to try and breath. He knew he could go a few hours without air if he had a lungful, but he hadn't had time to think much less inhale. Still, something told him his captors wouldn't be fleeing with him through the trees if they'd wanted him dead, and so he stopped struggling, stopped pulling on the restraints on his wrists, and tried to see what was happening.

But there was no longer any moonlight overhead, and he seemed to swing forward through the darkness. He hadn't been expecting that, and he closed his eyes, his mouth gaping as he tried to scream.

And then he was on the ground, dropped on his back, his arms stretched over his head, his legs held fast by the ankles, but the vine around his neck slipped off. He sucked in the warm wet air, heavy with the smells of damp earth and the moldy undergrowth of the Swarthen Forest, and he coughed and spat and bile ran down his chin and tears dripped into his ears.

When he'd caught his breath, he looked around, straining into the darkness. Only a few beams of moonlight penetrated the canopy overhead, but all Fin could see were leaves and dark tangled branches and hanging vines.

Then he saw a glint amongst the leaves, and another and another, as four pairs of eyes came into view above him. He squinted to make out their faces, but they were cloaked by the leaves of the trees.

And then one descended toward Fin, slowly dropping down from the branches overhead, as if a branch of the tree had broken off and was falling in slow motion. Fin'roq realized then that their faces weren't blocked by the leaves, rather they were wearing them—wearing clumps over the hands and feet, long flowing palm fronds over their torsos, fans of them around their shoulders and over their heads, so that they blended into the jungle.

The figure above slid down a vine until he was hovering just over Fin'roq's face. He could feel their hot breath on his cheeks, briny like the smell of a sea sponge, and he could see the skin around their eyes, speckled with patches of light and dark, just like his own skin.

Bhizini pirates, he thought, his heart pounding. *Sweet Trevian, save me.*

He stared into the eyes of his captor, the panic swelling until he thought his chest would explode. He had to do something, anything. He saw Roe's face in his mind, he exhaled loudly, and he reached for the Bhizini with his will, clutching for him as he'd clutched for Roe.

But nothing happened. The Bhizini just stared at him, two dark holes between palm fronds, unmoved and unmoving.

One of the other Bhizini stirred and the figure hanging over Fin'roq slid back up into the branches. They were all looking around now, and they vanished into the darkness.

Fin looked around but saw nothing. What had they seen?

He held his breath and listened. The forest roared with sounds—the buzzing and chirping and trilling of insects, the ghurpling and groaning of frogs and toads, the squeaking of bats and the holler of monkeys—all normal sounds of the canopy. And there was something else, low and far off, rumbling like rocks in a landslide, then falling silent. Then again, closer, deeper.

Not a rumble, a hiss.

And not from a Verdillion.

Fin didn't know if he should laugh or weep.

Kidnapped, he thought, *only to be eaten by a jaguar.*

The sound was right on top of him now, the branches nearby whipping back and forth. He heard the popping of vines as the Bhizini went on the offensive, and he heard the crunching of fibers, the terrible howling of pain, as the jaguar, unfazed, made short work of Fin's captives.

And now I really am going to die, he thought, the tears filling his ears and dripping into the wet soil beneath him. *And what's it all been for? What's any of it been for?*

The leaves alongside him crunched underfoot, but Fin was too scared to look, and he kept his eyes squeezed tight, whispering prayers to Trevian, forgetting to breath. He heard the soft growling of the jaguar, felt its hot breath as it sniffed him, felt its fur on his legs, on his arms, as it climbed on top of him.

Fin opened his eyes, opened his mouth, moved to thrash and howl, but his bindings had been cut and he rolled onto his stomach and jumped to his feet and turned to face the beast.

But it was Baboo who stood by his side, hands in front of him, palms outward in a gesture of calm and peace, a small smile on his speckled face, sap running down his chin, the last tufts of patchy black and orange fur fading from his chest.

Chapter 7

The Restoration of Her Fascination

H ER FIRST WEEK AS a female passed in a blur of sleep and tears. Bryn spent her days perched in front of the window, staring out at the little courtyard in the back corner of her family's garden, listening to the water tinkling in the fountain. Mama Andri'n brought her jha'ala and rhupan throughout the day, knocking softly at the door, setting down the tray of food, picking up the old one—the food untouched—then looking at Bryn with tears in her eyes.

"You gotta eat, love," she said.

But Bryn put up her hand and waved her mother away, and she left, softly weeping. Bryn thought she'd die from the guilt, and she opened her mouth to call out to her mother, to beg for her to come and hold her, but she couldn't bear the thought of it—couldn't bear the thought of being touched.

Even just letting her mother into the room had been hard at first. Bryn still couldn't look at her, much less speak to her. She told herself she was content to stay in the room forever, to live out her life there, never having to deal with anyone ever again.

But then Bryn felt something was wrong. Something was very wrong.

She knew the moment she woke. She could feel it, hanging there, cool against her belly.

The pain in her flower had subsided sooner than she'd expected. She really thought she'd been torn open, grievously wounded, that it would never heal right, never look right again. Never feel right again, either. But the tenderness had subsided, much more quickly than the pain in her thighs, her wrists, her face.

Bryn withdrew her rootpads and stepped out of the soil patch, fumbling for the clasp on her cumberdome. She pulled the straps loose from around her legs and lifted the fabric off her midsection. The sweet, tangy aroma of a freshly bloomed flower filled her nostrils, and Bryn looked down to see a small green fruit, not much bigger than her thumb, dangling from a thin tendril and lying against her groin, just below her lower-most petals.

She stared at it for a moment, confused at what she was seeing. When she realized what it was, and what it meant, she screamed.

Mama Andri'n crashed through the door, stumbling on her bad leg and catching herself against the handle. She gripped it hard not to fall. Bryn screamed again in surprise, and dropped to her knees, curling over into a ball and cowering in the corner, trying her best to shrink out of existence.

"Get out, get out, get out!" she cried.

Mama Andri'n turned to look at her daughter when her leg gave out, and she gasped and dropped to the floor, falling facedown. She let out a sharp cry and twisted hard, trying to turn over and get her weight off her leg.

Bryn scrambled over to her mother, sobbing, and helped her turn over and get to her feet. She clutched Bryn's arms as she stood, breathing heavily, then grabbed her and hugged her tight. Bryn froze but didn't push her away.

"You okay, love? You scared me half to death!"

Bryn shook her head. "No, Mama, I'm not."

Mama Andri'n pulled back, her pale green cheeks wet with tears, and she took Bryn's hands in hers. She squeezed them, pulled them to her mouth and kissed the backs of them.

And then she saw the fruit.

Bryn watched her mother's eyes grow wide, her face turn gray. She pulled her hands away from her mother and reached for her robe.

"Oh Brynnie," Mama Andri'n said. "'It's nothing to be ashamed of."

Bryn wailed and Mama Andri'n hugged her again, but she pulled away.

"I can't," she said, looking down at the fruit again. "I think I might be sick."

"It's okay, love."

"Okay?" Bryn hissed but it broke into a sob. "It's theirs. It's one of theirs!"

Mama Andri'n looked at the fruit again. "It's not quite ready for picking but I can go ahead and pluck it, you want it gone."

Bryn nodded emphatically.

"Normally you'd wait til it gets a little color, a little blush of red, before you twist it off. Might sting a little."

"Do it," Bryn said, gritting her teeth.

Mama Andri'n gripped the fruit and twisted.

Bryn gasped, but more from surprise than pain.

"I'll go take it out for the branta birds can get it," Mama Andri'n said. "Be in their gut before you know it. Don't you worry."

Mama Andri'n turned to leave, limping heavily across the room.

"Wait, Mama," Bryn whispered. "I'll go with you."

Mama Andri'n nodded, a few tears sliding down her cheeks.

"You know Brynnie, sometimes when things get smooshed around down there, our own pollen gets pushed up inside there. We end up pollinating ourselves."

"You think I don't know that, Mama? I've seen everything on the weavryn. And I've known about replicants since I was a tiny scamp."

"Of course you did, love. Just letting you know it might not be one of theirs. Might be another one of you."

Bryn pulled a clean robe over her head, then offered her arm to her mother and helped her out into the open air of the garden, and she couldn't help but sigh with relief when the full sun hit her skin. They walked around back to a small courtyard with a tiered fountain in the center. The bottom level was much larger and wider than the top, and just behind the front edge of the bottom tier was a small round column, the top hollowed out into a bowl.

Mama Andri'n went to place the fruit on the pedestal but Bryn touched her arm and stopped her. She put out her other hand for the fruit, and Bryn closed her eyes, momentarily overcome with revulsion at the feel of it in her hand. Then she placed it in the bowl atop the column and dropped her hand to her side.

"Trevian take this fruit away," Mama Andri'n said.

"Send us scamps another day," Bryn added.

"This to you we humbly pray," they finished together.

Bryn helped her mother to the wooden bench on the far side of the courtyard, and they sat down in the sunshine and Bryn closed her eyes and let the tears fall silently.

She felt her mother touch her arm, gently, and she opened her eyes.

There on the pedestal, two branta birds were perching, their bald heads shiny with black scales, their dark gray wings and purple breast like a bruised storm cloud. One bird stared cautiously at Bryn and her mother, beady eye pulsing, while the other pecked at the fruit. As the bird that was eating began to lift it's head, the bird that was watching lowered her head and began pecking, the other staring at Bryn and her mother. They continued this dance, back and forth, swapping roles, til the fruit was gone, the tiny pit swallowed by one or the other of them, digested, gone from the world.

The birds took flight and Bryn watched them rise up from the garden, wide wings beating the air, which then spread out to catch the swells. They circled one another slowly, the warm sea air rising off the city, lifting them higher and higher, their forms shrinking smaller and smaller, til they blended into the blue and she lost sight of them.

Bryn put her head on her mother's lap, as she hadn't done in years, and silently wept while Mama Andri'n stroked her hair.

⁂

After another week, Bryn still wasn't ready to leave her family's garden, to face the city and the crowds and the leering faces, but the window to report her assault to the Cul'tavin was nearly closed. Justice, it seemed, had a time-limit.

Trexbo had gone straight to the Pradishar the night of the attack, but the Cul'tavin had refused to investigate. The victim had to come forth and corroborate the accusation before they'd help. The peacekeepers gave him two weeks to return before they'd drop the case. He'd been contacting Mama Andri'n every day, asking if Bryn was ready yet.

But for Bryn, the thought of recounting what had happened to her, in detail, to some random Pradishar, was unthinkable. She was trying her best *not* to think about it, to read scrolls, to play games with her parents, anything to give her a respite, no matter how brief, from her own thoughts.

She woke that morning out of breath, too anxious to stay still, her rootpads already withdrawn into her feet. The water in the bathing room was cool on her skin, and she ladled it over her shoulders and shuddered as it ran down her back. Once scrubbed and dry, she brushed oils through her hair fibers and pulled them low on her head, in a tight bun that sat against the back of her neck. She rubbed a few drops of rosewater behind her ears and under her arms, then grabbed a clean scholar's robe, maroon with cream, and pulled it over her head.

When Bryn got to the door, she took a long, slow breath, then headed out into the garden.

Doc Andri'n was already at the table, a scroll unrolled in front of him, his eyes gently twitching, sipping from a steaming mug of jha'ala while mumbling to himself.

Mama Andri'n came from the cookery carrying breakfast and when she saw Bryn, she stopped. Her mouth opened and then curled into a smile, and she had tears in her eyes.

"Morning, love," she said, setting down the tray.

Doc Andri'n looked up from his scroll, and he too paused and smiled when he saw that Bryn had bathed and dressed.

"Good morning, Bryndax, dear," he said. "You're looking absolutely beautiful this morning, right Mama?"

"Like a cherry tree in early spring," she said.

Bryn blushed and sat down.

"Anything new, Papa?" Bryn asked.

"Nothing to worry yourself with," he said.

"Good to see you all dressed up," Mama Andri'n said. "Maybe you were thinking of going somewhere today?"

Bryn nodded, her throat suddenly too dry and swollen to speak.

Doc Andri'n put his hand on Bryn's and gave it a soft squeeze.

"Bless you, Bryndax," he said. "I've been trying to figure out how to convince you to go, examining each angle rhetorically, the pros and cons of certain approaches, what kind of reaction I might get—Sweet Trevian," he chuckled, "what a relief."

Bryn took a sip of jha'ala to wet her throat. "Sorry Papa," she said. "I didn't think I was ready, but—I guess I have to be, don't I?"

"I think you're doing the right thing," he said.

"We all do," Mama Andri'n added.

❧ ☙

The trip to the security office in Old Town wasn't as bad as Bryn was expecting it to be. The area around Stone Garden where her family lived was quiet and peaceful, the cobblestoned roads and grassy pathways between the individual estates were lined with low-growing foliage and bright flowers, and the sounds of birdsong was more common than the noises usually associated with urban living.

Even the tram wasn't so bad. Bryn kept her hood up over her head and she was just another student, en route to her classes at the Academicon. She enjoyed the view of the 'Mirri, the skimp'rins plying the muddy water, the Verdillions coming and going along the riverfront, as the tram moved across the top of New Town to the station near the Inner Harbor, and she realized how much she missed being out and about in her city.

The next tram cut back to the west and crossed the canal into Old Town, where the buildings pressed close together overhead and the wide avenues gave way to narrow alleyways and staircases. They got off at the station at Port Royal, alongside the Bay of Bliss. The security office for the Old Town district was inside.

Trexbo was waiting for them. Mama Andri'n gave him a big hug and Doc Andri'n put his hand on his chest in greeting.

"Hey, little sis," he said.

"Hey, Trexie," she said, avoiding his eyes. She hadn't seen him since the attack, had refused to see any of her friends when they'd come to visit. She'd even given them the cold shoulder when they'd reached out to her through the crystal.

They walked inside and found their way through the crowded corridors. The port was busy with passengers coming and going on the great ferries that linked the cities of Balance Territories together, but when they entered the security office, it was empty. The layout was familiar to Bryn, as it looked identical to the "Gendering Analysis and Assignment" office where she'd been just a few days before the Floronation ceremony.

That was just two weeks ago, she thought. *It feels like a lifetime has passed—like it happened to someone else.*

Trexbo approached the frosted glass window and tapped the bell, but this time Bryn didn't jump when it squeaked like a branta bird, though the sound made her cringe.

A bored-looking peacekeeper in Cul'tavin fatigues opened the glass, and when he saw Trexbo's face, he sighed with frustration, but it came out more like a hiss. "You again," he said.

"Afternoon, good Cul'tavin," Trexbo said, grinning. "I'm back, and this time I'm not alone."

The peacekeeper looked at Bryn and crinkled his nose. "*This* is the victim you spoke of?"

Trexbo wasn't smiling anymore.

The peacekeeper's eyes twitched several times while he glared at her, and she looked away, knowing others were watching her through him, analyzing and judging her—rendering her worthless from afar.

"Are you here to make a formal accusation?" the Cul'tavin asked, giving Bryn an impatient look.

She nodded and the peacekeeper sighed, then slammed the window shut.

Three hours later, Bryn was ready to head home, feeling absolutely drained, when the door finally opened. The Cul'tavin stood there sighing and tapping his foot, as if they had been the ones to make him wait.

"Madam Andra'asnia will see you now," he said.

Bryn couldn't believe what she heard, and she looked at her parents and at Trexbo, and they all looked surprised and confused.

Why has the top ranking Cul'tavin on Andramere come to hear my deposition? she thought, trying not to panic.

They all stood together, Doc Andri'n helping Mama to her feet, but the peacekeeper grunted at them. "The victim only," he said.

"One of them punched me in the face," Trexbo said. "Makes me a victim too. I'm coming with her."

Bryn saw the peacekeeper's face harden. And she knew that Trexbo hated Malisha Andra'asnia more than anyone on Andramere. Who knew what he'd say, or do, if he had her face to face.

"It's okay, Trexie, I got this," she said, surprised at how calm she sounded.

"We love you, Brynnie,," Mama Andri'n said.

Bryn followed the Cul'tavin through the door and down a series of corridors dimly lit with glowbes. The air was heavy and smelled of mold, as much of the city did. The warm orange flickering of the glowbes gave the place a strangely cozy feeling, and made Bryn think of the library where she worked. Except here there were peacekeepers coming and going, clad in Cul'tavin fatigues or draped in long-flowing pradeshan robes. Each one stopped to gawk at her as she passed.

The Cul'tavin beckoned her through a door and into a small room, much more brightly lit, with a small table and a single chair on either side. A petite Andrasian sat at the table, a book open in front of her, a bun in her left hand, her right hand turning the pages, her eyes scanning quickly before going on to the next, twitching the whole time.

"Have a seat," the Andrasian said without looking up.

Bryn jumped when the door closed behind her, then she hurried over and sat at the table. She looked at the Andrasian sitting across from her and recognized Malisha Andra'asnia from the notestreams and the PropSector feeds, but was surprised at how little she was, how frail.

Malisha continued to munch on her bun, to scan the pages of the book in front of her, and Bryn shifted in her chair, unable to get comfortable. Unable to relax. Not until the food was finished did Malisha close the cover and fix her eyes on Bryn.

She might be pretty if she smiled, Bryn thought, looking at her narrow cheeks, her yellow eyes bright like daffodils, her hair fibers red like threads of saffron.

Malisha's lips pressed together into a thin green smile, and Bryn realized she'd been wrong.

"I've reviewed your docket, Bryn. Impressive recommendations for someone so young. You've only two weeks as an adult, and yet you have glowing praises from professors at the Academicon, even a few worthy mentions from Pradishar priestins. Indeed, you're something of a special case, aren't you?"

"I don't—"

"No need to be modest. How many scamps would die to have a crystamin at the young age you were given one? You must have made all the others in the sprouting patch pretty darn jealous, am I right?"

Bryn opened her mouth but Malisha cut her off.

"You were, after all, initiated as a Pradishar monkin when you got your crystal, even though you've yet to complete your annual. Is this correct?"

"I'm working on it now," Bryn said.

Malisha's smile faded. "The answer is yes, Bryn. Yes, you are a monkin. Yes, you are a member of the Pradishar. And yes, you are thus bound by our rules, and our obligations. So tell me, monkin—why have you brought an internal dispute to the Cul'tavin security office instead of taking up the problem with your priestin first?"

"I'm not sure I understand—"

"Perhaps you think you deserve special treatment? That the rules don't apply to you?"

"I don't—"

"Oh, but you do. You made that clear at your Floronation, when you sifted through the annals of history to find one tiny, one insignificant, one long-forgotten example of a gender freak as an excuse to disregard thousands of years of Balance traditions, all because it's what special, entitled Bryn Andri'n thinks they deserve—thinks *he* deserves. Isn't that right?"

Bryn shook her head no, blinking back the tears.

"If only it had stopped there, I might be able to ignore it. But you've sent a convicted criminal to this security office to harass my peacekeepers for upwards of two weeks, and now I've had to come down here—to take time out of my busy schedule—to deal with your falsehoods. Perhaps I'm a fool, but I look at you and I see a massive Andrasian, so tall and wide, so thick and bulging, that I simply can't believe I'm not looking at a Raccorin, and a Raccorin male at that. Then I look at your accusation, at the normal-sized

Andrasians you've accused of seizing your body and forcing their wills upon you, and I think, surely this Bryn Andri'n thinks me a fool. Do you think me a fool, Bryn?"

The tears ran hot down Bryn's face as she shook her head no.

"Have you anything else to offer me? Anything to convince me you haven't wasted my time?"

Bryn's mind was blank, her ears ringing, her eyes fixed on the sneer on Malisha Andra'asnia's thin green lips. She shook her head again.

Malisha sighed. "I'm going to be patient with you, Bryn. You've only recently flowered, and perhaps you don't yet know what's expected of you as an adult, as a subject of Andramere and as a citizen of Balance Authority. But I know you're a smart one. I know you'll drop this charade, you'll take the role you're meant to take in our society, and you'll stop provoking decent citizens to violent outrages. Cries for attention are expected when one is young. But now that you've flowered, it's time you acted as everyone expects you to act. I hope it's clear to you that there are consequences for not behaving. Is that clear now, Bryn?"

She slowly nodded, as more tears spilled out of her eyes.

Malisha sighed as if with great disappointment, and waved Bryn from the room.

She stood and walked out the door. The peacekeeper who had escorted her in was waiting for her in the corridor. He grinned when he saw her tears. She wiped her face with the sleeves of her robe on the walk back to the waiting room.

Her parents and Trexbo stood when she came through the door, and Doc Andri'n offered Mama a hand getting up. Trexbo opened his mouth to ask how it went, but when he saw her face, he closed it.

She walked out the front door without looking at them.

❧ ❧

Over the following week, Bryn tried to figure out how to get on with life. There was to be no justice, no catharsis, no one who could make right what seemed to have gone so very, very wrong with her. Each morning she looked at her body as she bathed and wished it were different, and all day, her thoughts were poisoned with doubt and self-hatred.

Ginjy and Rhingus came to see her at home. They were kind and patient, and told her to take her time, not to rush anything—but Bryn couldn't help but marvel at their insincerity, since it was them who had forced her to see them when she'd wanted more time, more space. She knew they were concerned for her, that they needed to see her, needed to help her, and the guilt she felt for rejecting their kindness—for feeling unable to accept it even as she longed for it—made Bryn wish she could just die and be done with it.

Mama Andri'n had done her best to go on with the normal daily routine, to chatter about the melodramas and the social notestreamers that she loved so much, but Bryn would catch her looking at her with tears in her eyes, like she was broken—pitiful—and it made her feel awful inside. Guilty that she didn't feel better.

As for her father, she'd find him sitting at the table in the heart of the garden, gripping a book in both hands, grinding his teeth together, looking like he was preparing to murder someone. As soon as he'd see Bryn, he'd smile warmly and call to her, but she found it hard to shake the image of him like that, so angry, so primal, so unlike the calm and collected professor he usually was. Seeing it made her feel like she had been rolled over by a wave on the beach, tossed about til she didn't know which way was up and which was down.

Bryn knew she needed to get out of the house, out of her head, and back into her work, but the thought of traveling across the city by herself was still too much to face. But by midweek, she'd given in to the pressure from her friends, and Trexbo's kind offer, and had agreed to return to normal life, whatever that was.

Mama agreed to accompany Bryn on the tram down to the Inner Harbor, where Trexbo would pick her up and take her the rest of the way on her journey, either to the Sweet Treat for their meetings or up to the royal plateau, where both the library and Academicon were located. At the end of the day, Trexbo would return to escort her home. A full week passed and the notoriously tardy Trexbo had yet to disappoint.

At mid-morning, Bryn and her mother stepped off the tram at the station at Inner Harbor. Trexbo stood leaning against a column, hands in his pockets, eyes twitching, a goofy grin on his face. When he saw them step off, he jumped to attention.

Mama Andri'n gave him a long hug.

"Thanks for always watching out for my little one," she said, then turned to Bryn, wincing as she pivoted on her bad leg. She hugged her daughter and Bryn leaned down so her mother could give her a kiss on her cheek. "Same time this evening?" she asked.

Bryn hated that her mother had to travel halfway across the city every time she wanted to go somewhere. Her leg wasn't getting any better, and she refused to let the Dyna'arin fit her with a prosthetic. But the thought of traveling alone was still too much, so Bryn had agreed in spite of the shame.

"Same time," she said. "I'm sorry, Mama." She looked at the ground, her bottom lip quivering.

Mama Andri'n hugged her again and let out a little sob. "Oh love, you've got nothing to apologize for," she said. "I'm just grateful we get to spend so much time together."

Bryn, feeling stupid, nodded and broke away from her mother. "Same time," she said. Her and Trexbo stepped onto the tram to Old Town and Mama Andri'n stood waving as they pulled away from the platform. Bryn shook off her shame and gave her a big smile, hoping to convince her mother that she was fine, and hoping to convince herself too.

Once the tram had left the station, they took a seat and Bryn stared out the window.

"You okay?" Trexbo said. "Awfully quiet over there."

"Sorry, Trexie," she said. "I'm fine. Really. I just—I'm sick of having to make everyone take care of me. My mom has a hurt leg and I make her go everywhere with me. And you—"

"I don't mind," Trexbo said. "I like being needed."

"I know. But I also know it's been hugely inconvenient to you. I'm interfering with your life so much now, and all because I'm as useless and pathetic."

"That's not true," he said, louder than he should have. A few heads turned. He lowered his voice. "Trauma takes time. I know that from experience. And it's been my own pleasure to help you out. What d'you think I spend all my time over in Feral Heights and Tear's End doing anyway?"

"Helping people out," she said. "You're right. But still. I know it's time I did this on my own. I just—can't."

"Don't rush it, little sis," Trexbo said. "When you're ready, you'll be ready. 'Til then, I'm here for you."

"What if I'm never ready?"

"Then I'll still be here for you."

Bryn looked out the window, but she took Trexbo's hand and gave it a squeeze.

The tram followed Grand Avenue through New Town, across the canal into Old Town, and stopped between the avenue and the Bay of Bliss. Bryn and Trexbo walked away from the bay, through the tiered plazas, up steps and across squares, up more steps and across more squares, as they climbed the hillside of the old city. The sun was shining, a soft, salty breeze was blowing in from the south, and the streets of Andramere smelled like jasmine and mildew and the sea. Troupers were putting on a mime show in one of the plazas, and little scamps were laughing and playing. In another plaza, musicians were singing and blowing horns while a few older folk and a handful of tourists danced. Two lovers held hands on the edge of one of the fountains, laughing and smiling.

Bryn really did love her city.

But when they left the open square and turned into the alleyway that led to the Sweet Treat, Bryn felt her heart pounding, felt her lungs empty and become too big to refill, like each inhale couldn't satisfy her needs. There was a group of young Verdillions talking and joking and they stopped and turned to look at her and Trexbo as they passed. Bryn felt like her legs weren't going to work, but they ignored her and went back to whatever it was they had been talking about, and she exhaled hard.

"You al—" Trexbo started, but Bryn cut him off.

"Please don't ask," she said. "Not anymore. Please."

He nodded and opened the door to the Sweet Treat, holding it for her to enter. Once inside, the panic started to fade as the smells of the cafe filled her nose and the cramped alley gave way to a familiar sight. Some of the regulars waved at them as usual, and a few of the tourists gawked.

It's only because of my size, Bryn reminded herself, *and not what happened to me.*

Ginjy and Rhingus were waiting in line. They offered to buy Bryn and Trexbo's treats and she gladly accepted. Her and Trexbo went upstairs and unlocked their office. When they arrived with the food and drinks and everyone was settled in their chairs, Rhingus called the meeting to order.

"Respect for one and all," she said. "I'd like to start today, if there aren't any objectio ns.".

Rhingus filled the group in on the latest in her investigation into Guild mischief on Andramere. Her parents were Dyna'arin—her father was an operator and her mother a tinker—but they were also activists pushing to reform the Guild from within. Rhingus had grown up in Dyna'arin communities in various Balance cities, on the front lines of the struggles between the operators and the managers, only to realize that what she experienced was never reported on the notestreams, never mentioned on the official PropSector streams, and never discussed openly outside of Guild-controlled areas.

Bryn tried to pay attention.

Ginjy went next. She'd prepared a scathing takedown of Ritty Rin Randal's latest melodrama, a period piece about the Andramere crisis 100 years earlier. Her own parents had starring roles, and Ginjy was employed in the records department by the studio that produced the drama, so she had inside access to all the goings-on in Valley Wood and had likely helped out in more ways than she would let on. Ginjy wasn't one to boast, and her widely-watched streams, full of juicy gossip about the thriving weavryn entertainment industry—which had practically become synonymous with Andramere in the last decade—were all produced and shared with a pseudonym.

Bryn hadn't heard of the melodrama, so she streamed some of the promo materials on the weavryn while Ginjy talked.

Another widely devoured piece of garbage, Bryn thought. *Looks pretty good, but I'll wait til it's on the public servryn.*

Trexbo followed Ginjy. He alone had his piece ready for sharing, an eloquent, if slightly ranting, defense of the Bhizini in general and of Qardymion the Saltsap in particular. Trexbo argued that Qardymion, rebel leader and enemy number one for Balance Authority—and the recently accused mass murderer of Cul'tavin troops in Balan Su—was simply a misunderstood and wrongly accused defender of life, doing his best to protect his people against a ruthless genocide carried out by the Corkin army and by Cul'tavin peacekeepers in the name of Balance Authority. Trexbo claimed Qardymion and their followers stuck to the old Bhizini ways, which meant that they were true creatures of the sea and never set foot on dry land, so how could they have orchestrated such a murder, or constructed such an elaborate crime scene, without touching ground in Balan Su? Something wasn't right, and it wasn't just the ire and malice of that fool Ellex Andria either. He urged all citizens of Balance to ignore the official streams and to demand an end to assaults on Bhizini ships in the Inner Archipelago.

When Trexbo finished, he sat down with a flourish, and everyone clapped. Even Bryn, though she wasn't feeling it.

"What about you? Anything to share today?" Rhingus asked, looking expectantly at her.

Bryn looked away.

"No worries if you aren't ready," Trexbo added.

<<Not up to it yet?>> Ginjy said.

"I guess I just need a little more time. To get my notes ready, and whatnot."

<<Anything to say about any of our stuff?>>

"No," Bryn said. "It's all great. Nothing to add."

Rhingus and Ginjy looked at each other and Bryn felt her face burning.

"I think I should get home," Bryn said. "Not feeling too well. Trexbo, do you mind?"

"Not at all, sis," he said. He grabbed one of the buns off the tray. "Ready when you are."

"See you," Bryn said, already walking out the door.

When she reached the exit from the Sweet Treat to the alleyway, she waited for Trexbo to catch up. He hurried down the stairs and grinned at her, still chewing the bun he'd hastily stuffed in his mouth.

"Sorry you aren't feeling well today," he said. "There's something going around I think, but you'll feel better soon."

"Yeah," Bryn said.

"Your fans can't wait to hear from you. They've all been wondering where the Mighty B*zzness has been," he said, using her pseudonym.

"I think the Mighty B*zzness is dead," Bryn said. "Gone. Fizzled out. Cold. I'm not sure she'll ever be back."

"You just need some time," he said.

"Oh, is that all?" Bryn said. "*Just* some time? *Just* that?"

"I didn't mean—"

"No, you didn't. But I did. I don't feel it anymore. The drive. The interest. I'm not sure I should be working with you guys. I don't think I have anything to say anymore."

Trexbo stopped walking. "How can you say such a thing?" he said, barely above a whisper. "You're the fiery heart of our project. You inspire us all! You motivate us to keep fighting for what we believe in, because we see you doing it every day."

Bryn blushed. "You're just saying that to make me feel better."

"No, I'm not. You have so much to offer—to our stream, to Andramere, and to the world."

She said nothing but her face was burning.

Trexbo watched her, hesitating. He took her hand.

"I know how it feels to suffer at the hands of others, to have nobody care that you've been hurt, even to delight in your pain. They singled you out to make you small and scared, but you know what that means, right Bryndax? You might not think you have anything worth saying, but they *know* you have something worth saying, and they've done their damndest to make sure you don't go on saying it. Isn't it comforting, in some twisted way, to know that they fear you? It means you have power over them. It means you can hurt them, should you decide to wield it."

Bryn started to cry again. "Please, Trexie, please, just shut up already. Just please shut up."

"I'm sorry," he said. "Not another word about it."

"Thank you."

"For today at least," he said, grinning.

But Bryn just glared at him.

The next morning, she had breakfast with her parents and did her best to act like everything was status quo, but Bryn could tell from their faces that they weren't convinced. They ate in silence, and she blamed herself for ruining the meal. What was wrong with her? Why couldn't she pretend that everything was okay, if only for her parent's sake?

"You nervous, love?" Mama Andri'n asked.

"I don't think so," Bryn said. "But yeah, I guess I am."

"Don't worry, Bryndax," Doc Andri'n said. "Your professors have all been very understanding. Classes have only been back in session for a few weeks, and we know nothing much happens when lessons are just getting underway. You'll catch up in no time."

Mama Andri'n tsked. "She's not worried about classwork," she said.

Doc Andri'n looked away for a moment. "I'm proud of you for returning to the Academicon," he said. "You always loved the campus. Once you step foot on those hallowed grounds, you'll feel back to your old self again. You'll see."

Bryn managed a small smile.

"Plus, I have a surprise for you," he said. "A good one, too."

She raised her eyebrows.

"What would you say to a little lab time this afternoon? One on one with my latest prototype?" Doc Andri'n watched Bryn's face, saw her mouth drop open a little bit, saw her recover and close it, saw the realization blossom in her eyes, the light seem to return to her cheeks for the first time in a month. He looked away again and swallowed hard. "Well, what do you say?"

"Are you serious, Papa? Finally?"

"Finally, my dear," he said.

"You sure everything's ready?" Mama Andri'n asked. She gave her husband a hard stare, but when she saw Bryn's face, she sighed. "Of course it is, if you say it is."

"You know what Papa's been working on?" Bryn said.

"Oh, you know your Papa only tells me what I can understand, and that ain't much. Just thought he still had a long old way to go before it was ready."

"Not to worry, love," Doc Andri'n said. His eyes twitched and he looked at Bryn. "I see your classes end at noon. Think Madam Madr'gin will mind if you're a few minutes late on your first day back?"

"I can squeeze in a lab visit," Bryn said. "And speaking of work, this—well, this has put me behind a bit. I've been thinking I might take on more hours, stop spending so much time studying with my friends. I'm an adult now after all, right?"

"I hate to bring it up," Doc Andri'n said, "but yes, that would be great. How much do you think is left on the project?"

Bryn's eyes twitched while she checked her notes on the servryn. "I should be done with the essential collection by the end of the year, if I double down."

"That's wonderful news," he said. "Then it's settled. And even better, my schedule syncs up nicely with yours today. Why don't you let Trexbo know that I'll be your escort and he can have the day off?"

Bryn's eyes twitched again. "Done," she said.

They left at mid-morning for the royal plateau, cutting up the hillside of Stone Garden and passing through the ancient wall into Old Town. The walk was much shorter than taking the tram down the river. Once in the old city, they followed the avenue along the crest of the hill, up and over the Clear Water, and into a lift station. The maquina whined as the lift carried them up to the surface of the plateau, where they emerged in the great hall of the Academicon.

"Thanks for walking me," Bryn said. "See you at noon." She gave him a quick hug and hurried off before he could reply.

The campus of the Academicon was one of Bryn's favorite places in the world, and also one of the safest. Since the institution was ultimately administered by the Dyna'arin, there were Guild Enforcers milling about at any given time, and there was maquina—much of it secret—observing the corridors and courtyards, the stairwells and auditoriums, that made up the largest and oldest Academicon in all of Balance, now that P'anorum was lost. There had never been a violent crime on the campus, or so it was claimed. And Bryn tended to believe it. One time she'd seen two students arguing, heatedly, and when it looked like the fight might escalate, Enforcers swooped in to break it up and cart them off to the disciplinary committee. Bryn still didn't know where they'd come from, or how they'd responded so quickly. At the time it had disturbed her, but now she felt grateful to know they were around, watching.

Her first lesson that morning, a survey on the miniaturization of maquina, had looked to be one of her favorite classes for the term. The professor seemed to genuinely love the subject, and he spoke with passion and with delight. But as she sat in her chair struggling to pay attention to what the professor was saying, she realized something must indeed be seriously wrong with her. If there was one thing Bryn loved, it was being in class, learning from masters in their field, absorbing insights on history and politics and technology—and archiving all the data diligently on the servryn. When the class was over, she slipped out the door before having to face her professor and discuss her absence.

Her other class that morning was a seminar on the history of Andramere since 8000 COB. Bryn normally spent a good deal of the time in seminars talking, asking questions, and challenging others to think and to solve problems. There were only a handful of students in the hall, and they all sat at a round table, with the professor taking a minimal role, guiding when guidance was needed, redirecting to the proper topic when the conversation went astray, and suggesting experiments and reviewing results for the lab portion of the class. The thought of having to engage intimately with the topic, to debate with her peers, was suddenly too much too soon, and she wondered why she'd ever agreed to come back to school in the first place. So she ducked into one of the cafes along the courtyard, ordered a hot jha'ala, and sat down to drink it.

One more skipped class won't hurt, she thought.

When midday finally came around, Bryn walked to her father's office and knocked at the door. When she entered, he was sitting at his desk, writing in a notebook.

"How was class, dear?" he asked.

"Fine," she said.

"Well, I know you need to get to work, so let's not delay. I do hope you're ready to have your mind completely shattered."

She gave her father a dubious look, and he laughed.

"You'll see for yourself," he said. "But Bryndax, I have a favor to ask. I was hoping you could do a demonstration for a colleague of mine? Show them your technique for slipping streams?"

Bryn shrugged. "I can do that. Is it someone I know?"

"First, I need you to swear to me that you'll keep this experiment, and everything you experience here, absolutely secret. You can't tell anyone, not even your friends. And especially not Trexbo!"

"Really Papa? You think I'm not trustworthy? Sheesh," she said, frowning, half-joking.

"Swear it, or you can leave," he said, his lips pressed together.

Bryn was shocked but did her best not to let him know. "I swear not to tell anyone," she said. "So help me Trevian."

"Good," her father said. "Now then, have a seat here and relax. I want you to join me at my lab space on the servryn. You should have access already."

Bryn put her bag by her father's desk and took a seat. Then she reached out with her mind, seeking the crystamin located in her father's private servryn. In an instant she had found it, and through the crystamin she was re-directed to her father's datamins stored within the servryn.

<<This way,>> her father said in her mind, and when Bryn followed him, she gasped aloud.

In her mind's eye, she was in a room that looked exactly like her father's lab, the one she was actually sitting in. Bryn had used her crystal to peer through the eyes of others, of course. Many, many times—practically on a daily basis. Notestreams were full of first-hand images and sounds and sensations, the same as when two people communicated through a crystamin—it had a strange sense of communion but without a physical referent. But here in this imaginary space, she could see her father standing in front of her—and with her real eyes, she could see him sitting behind his desk. The sensation gave her a sudden wave of vertigo, but she closed her eyes and it subsided.

<<Are you okay, Bryndax?>> her father said, and in her mind's eye, she could see her father speaking, see concern on his face. It even sounded like the voice came from his mouth.

<<You were right, Papa. My mind is officially shattered.>>

Doc Andri'n laughed. <<I've been waiting to share this with you for so long. It's been torture keeping it a secret.>>

<<This is your prototype?>>

<<One of them. A new incarnation of the weavryn, a third one, not yet available to the public, and in fact known to only a few people in the entire world.>>

Bryn was about to explode with giddy glee but instead she imagined herself walking about the room and was shocked at how easy it was to manipulate her body in that world.

She felt out for the datamins that contained the stream in the servryn, for the crystamin that linked the datamin to her own crystal, and realized how different it was from anything she'd analyzed before. The paths were all twisted around, circular, self-contained or cut off in some strange way. She couldn't quite describe what she was feeling. But before she could ask, her father began to speak in her mind.

<< I want you to imagine, as best you can, that you're getting dressed, pulling a robe over your head. But imagine that the robe is a costume, a full-body costume, head, face, everything. Whatever you want to put on. Whatever you want to *be*. Start with something easy. Try putting on a pradeshan robe.>>

Bryn imagined pulling a robe over her head, and when she looked down at herself with her inner eye, she indeed saw the purples and grays of a pradeshan garment. She rubbed her hand down the robe and was shocked that she could even feel the fabric.

<<I knew you'd have no trouble,>> he said. <<That took me a number of tries. Now for something different. Imagine again that you're getting dressed, but instead pull on a seastallion costume. Become one.>>

Bryn complied, and when she looked down this time, she was a sea creature, awkwardly flapping her fins in the air, her body shiny and gray and covered in scales. She laughed and immediately turned into a ghu frog, hopping around the lab, ghurpling.

Doc Andri'n clapped his hands. <<Marvelous! Now try something that isn't a creature. An object of some sort. Anything.>>

Bryn's ghu frog form melted into a bowl of rhupan on a small table.

<<Yes!>> he said. <<Amazing work, Bryndax. Now, try to speak.>>

<<Hello,>> the bowl of rhupan on a table said. The table began to walk around the room. <<Oh Papa, this is the most amazing thing I've ever seen in my life.>>

<<I knew you'd love it. I've hated keeping it from you. I—>> He paused. <<Oh good. Now then, let me introduce you to my colleague. Bryndax, this is Anorian Grain.>> Doc Andri'n stepped aside and next to him was a large tree, its leaves dappled with sunlight, and on its many branches were boughs of fruits of every color. <<Anorian, this is my daughter, Bryn Andri'n. We've been working together for a long time.>>

She wasn't sure if that last statement was about her or about Anorian.

Bryn started to transform into herself, but she decided against it, choosing instead to appear as a smaller, thinner, hooded figure clad in scholar's robes, her face well hidden in shadow.

If Anorian is cloaked, I'll be cloaked too, she told herself.

The tree slid forward and Bryn could see a face in the trunk. <<Pleased to meet you, Bryn. Your father has spoken very highly of you and of your prodigious talents.>> The tree slid even closer, leaned forward, and whispered, <<And I'm a big fan of your notestream.>>

Bryn couldn't believe it. She'd been so careful to keep her identity secret. Nobody knew but her friends.

<<Don't worry, your secret is safe with me,>> the tree said, and Bryn could feel an incredible warmth coming from Anorian. Warmth and safety and trustworthiness. She immediately relaxed but then wondered if she was being manipulated and put her guard back up.

How does Anorian know?

<<Do be careful, Bryn. I'm afraid your position on some of the issues of our times has captured the attention of PropSector and the Culture Bureau. That's part of the reason why I've been eager to meet you. I may be able to keep you safe from their spies, when the time is right.>>

<<Just what are you two discussing?>> Doc Andri'n said, feigning annoyance.

<<I was complimenting Bryn on her ability to slip streams, a truly remarkable skill,>> Anorian said, <<and asking if she'd be willing to share some details about that with me, and perhaps let me observe her in action.>>

<<Well?>> Doc Andri'n asked.

<<Of course,>> Bryn said. <<Anything I can do to help.>>

<<No doubt you've noticed something amiss about this servryn,>> Anorian said. <<I want you to try and pull some data from the Andramere public servryn into this one. I've created a restricted stream for you to slip inside. Once there, pull any data you find back to this servryn. If you don't mind, I'd like to watch, closely, from alongside your mind, while you work. Are you okay with that?>>

Bryn turned to her father and he nodded.

<<Sure,>> Bryn said, and she could feel Anorian inside her mind, seeing what she saw, feeling what she felt, sharing all of her thoughts. Bryn reached out for the Andramere public servryn and quickly found the crystamin, but was surprised that it didn't recognize her. None of her streams showed up, as if she were a new user accessing the servryn for the first time. She queried the private stream and tried to access it. When the servryn denied her permission, she let her focus grow fuzzy and allowed her attention to diffuse through the servryn, through each individual datamin that made up the servryn, til she found the

source of the stream and was able to access the restricted data it contained. She quickly pulled the data and brought it back to her father's private servryn, and she giggled when the data appeared as a stack of books in her hands.

<<Remarkable,>> Anorian said. <<How'd you learn to do that, Bryn?>>

She turned to her father and he nodded again.

<<I'm not sure exactly. When I was much younger, in fact when I was first Joined to the crystal, I saw something—strange. It was only there for a second and then it was gone, and I was back in my family's garden. But apparently I had been unconscious for several days. When I started to use the weavryn, I realized that my experience was different from everyone else's. There were pathways, routes, shortcuts, connecting everything. I told my father about it, and he helped me to discover, through experimentation, that I could use those pathways to slip between streams, to access data that shouldn't be publicly accessible.>>

<<You have quite the daughter,>> Anorian said. <<Thank you, Bryn, for sharing that with me. And for sharing your mind with me.>> Again, such warmth from Anorian that Bryn nearly swooned. <<We'll meet again soon. Good day, Bryn. Professor.>>

The tree vanished.

<<Gone already?>> Bryn said. <<Was that all?>>

<<Anorian is very busy, dear,>> Doc Andri'n said. <<Now, let's return to my real office.>>

Bryn put on a sad face. <<Can't I play here a little longer? There's so much I'd like to experiment with.>>

<<Indeed you can, but not now. You have a job to get to, right?>>

"I do," she said, opening her eyes and pulling her awareness back from the servryn. "Wow, Papa. Just wow. I don't know if I'll be able to concentrate on my work, or anything else! This is—huge! The biggest transformation of the weavryn in its hundred year history! I have about a thousand questions for you. Any chance you'll start answering them? Maybe fill me in on how you managed all this?"

"All in good time, dear," he said. "All in good time."

Bryn hugged her father and started across campus to the library, her step light, her mind whirling with excitement, the terrible burden of existing finally—if temporarily—forgotten. For the first time since the attack, Bryn felt happy to be alive.

Chapter 8
Stunted and Stumbling

ELLEX ANDRIA WAS ELECTED to public office within a year of first flowering, the youngest Andrasian ever to sit on the Camerooge in Andropolis. Five years later, she became the youngest member ever appointed to the Council of Nine in Balan Su. Some said that her father had gotten her elected, that her father had gotten her appointed, and that it was proof Andrasia's republic had been replaced by an oligarchy. But as far as Ellex could remember—and she'd admit her memories before the accident were spotty at times—her father never helped her in her political career, not directly at least. He was a warm, supportive, charming leader, and always encouraged her and cheered her on, but he was always willing to let her fail.

Her successes had always been her own.

But after the eruption, after the year she lost to darkness and confusion, when the world thought her dead and buried with the rest of the Far Archipelago, Ellex's return became something more than she ever could have imagined, ever could have planned for. In a world wracked with grief and loss, she came back with her head held high, seemingly uninjured, unaffected by the tragedy, a potent symbol of rebirth and renewal that, in some organic way, took root in the hearts of her people. She became something of a religious figure to Andrasians, a mender, a good-mother. And her people demanded she take up her father's position as their leader on the Council.

Called to serve, Ellex served. For over thirty years, she'd done all she could to honor the memory of her father, to serve Andrasia and defend Balance as he had done. And she had not doubted that she had done so, never once.

Until now.

The bodies of her butchered peacekeepers had hardly been properly identified, the investigators barely surveying the scene, the senseless horror of it all just managing to register in Ellex's mind, when someone leaked everything. The peacekeepers, Raccorin and Andrasian, sewn back together in a medley of parts. "True Balance" written in sap.

Snippets of her investigators working. The smell of the place. All of it, available on the weavryn and spreading like a brushfire.

Ellex didn't know what she'd do when she found the leaker, but it would be slow, that much she knew for sure. Only trusted members of the Pradishar had been in to survey the crime scene. They'd all sworn loyalty to the Gran Pradesh, loyalty to Balance Authority, and loyalty to her. She'd make sure they remembered that the good-mother of Andrasia was not one to cross. But she'd have to worry about that later. Uthyr had promised to deploy his seekers, and he assured her he'd find who was responsible and slow the spread of the leak in the meantime. She had to trust him, because she couldn't trust anyone else.

She peeked at a few of the notestreams to try and gauge the public's mood, but didn't like what she learned. Ellex thought the Bhizini would be the obvious target of everyone's ire, and there was a good deal of blame being lobbed on Qardymion the Saltsap—but more than a few were holding Ellex herself responsible. These peacekeepers were, after all, under her care. How had she not known they were under attack, or had been kidnapped? Wasn't she, as top-ranking Cul'tavin in Balan Su, the one responsible for the security of the entire city? How had Bhizini snuck into the capital, managed to chop apart and sew back together these Cul'tavin, then flee, without anyone ever knowing? Can Bhizini come and go as they please on the streets of Balan Su?

She hissed, furious at the conjecture, the theories being thrown about without any regard for their validity. Even the Council of Nine had contacted her, wanting to meet already, but she had succeeded in getting the meeting postponed, at least for now. For Trevian's sake, she needed a bit of time to find the answers. And damnit but there were a lot of questions to deal with, and few of them were the ones the public were demanding answers to.

Although she was sure the Bhizini were responsible, she had to admit there were circumstances that needed addressing. This wasn't just a random attack on a group of Cul'tavin. This was a targeted attack on a particular squad, one that Ellex had been carefully putting together over the last decade—the very first one composed of both Andrasians and Raccorin. Even though Raccorin had always been welcome to join the Pradishar, only the Andrasians had fully embraced the religion, while the Raccorin clung to the Loricean faith of the imperial family. But when the Far Archipelago erupted and P'anorum was abandoned, the Loricea collapsed as well, in all but name. And then a Raccorin, Ra'shard Ruu'n, had been elected Gran Pradesh. Since that time, more and more Raccorin had joined the Pradishar.

And not all the Andrasians—or the Raccorin—were happy about it.

After that first squad, more interracial groups began to spring up across the Inner Archipelago, also to controversy. The problem was that everyone—Raccorin, Andrasian, and Bhizini—could see this as a threat. Ellex knew that ten thousand years of Balance had not fully erased the idea that Andrasians and Raccorin were opposed and hostile to one another, and that only the force of long-held mutual agreements, cemented by the power of the crystals, kept the two sides at peace. And the Bhizini knew that if the two sides of Balance became one fighting force, their chances for survival on the fringes of civilization were over.

As for the Dyna'arin—well, the Guild would profit off of any conflict, since they made all the maquina, all the ships, even the weapons used to fight. But would the Guild really resort to staging violence in order to start a war? Ellex didn't think so.

What about the warehouse? It's owner, Lithuigi Von'nDrino, was a Dyna'arin tinker. Ellex knew him and didn't trust him for a second. Something on the edge of her memory, something she couldn't recall, made her suspicious of him. But was the good professor willing to butcher Cul'tavin? Ellex found the idea nearly impossible to consider. So was this a setup then—an attempt to smear Von'nDrino? He had single-handedly created the most destructive weapon in Balance history. And his ship designs, prized for their speed and maneuverability, had yet to become the standard ship issued by the Guild, not for the Corkin nor for the Pradishar. And it wasn't the first time he'd been accused of hoarding innovations. Someone like that was sure to have enemies within the Guild and without.

But the butcherers themselves—the sheer horror of the act—no civilized Raccorin nor Andrasian could ever do such a thing to their comrades, Ellex was certain of that much. In the era of Balance Authority, Verdillions rarely killed other Verdillions, and the few murders each year were from crimes of passion, outbursts that accidentally turned deadly, but never something premeditated. Never anything so savage. The only one Ellex could imagine capable of such a thing was Qardymion the Saltsap, and their band of Bhizini outlaws, who never hesitated to slaughter anyone they came across.

Did the Saltsap have some connection to Lithuigi Von'nDrino?

Too many questions, and zero answers. And until Uthyr had found the leak, she'd have to focus on the most pressing issues, then work down the list in order of descending urgency. Tomorrow was going to be hell, but she could face it. She had to face it. Her career, her future, depended on it.

By the time Ellex reached her upper rim estate and dropped her roots down into the soil of her sleeping patch, it was already well past midnight. Had it only been that afternoon that she'd headed to the lower rim to meet Uthyr? It didn't seem possible, and though dawn's first light steadily grew nearer, Ellex couldn't stop replaying the events of the evening in her mind.

Eventually she did drift off to sleep, though it was so brief, and so restless, that she might have sworn she'd never gotten any at all, had it not been for the sight of her father's face when she woke, the sound of his voice still in the air—and had she not struggled, as she did every morning, to remind herself that he was dead.

Pander had the jha'ala hot and steaming when she emerged from her bathing room dressed for the day. She'd donned long silk robes, black as the panthers in the Upper Fernclads, open in front to reveal her dressy Cul'tavin fatigues.

The morning sun beamed down into her garden, warm on the skin but soft on the eyes, and Ellex snacked where it fell on her cheeks and on her forehead while she sipped her jha'ala.

"I've overslept," she said. "It's been a long time. Perhaps I'll have to start setting alarms again."

"The body knows what it needs, Sui Pradesh," Pander said. When he saw the look on her face, he added, "Well rested is well prepared, after all."

"You stole that from my father," she said.

Pander smiled proudly. "By Trevian, I miss him."

Ellex nodded, tears in her eyes. "I wish we had time for nostalgia. I could use a reminder of Father's signature charisma. A little inspiration for my own troubles."

"Sui Pradesh underestimates herself," Pander said.

"Surely you've been following the latest?"

Pander nodded, a troubled look on his face. He glanced nervously to and fro and Ellex knew he had something to tell her—something he very much wished he didn't have to share.

"What's troubling you, old friend?" she said, touching him on the shoulder.

He exhaled loudly. "The summons came in early, just at first touch of dawn. Malisha Andra'asnia has called for a council meeting at noon today."

Ellex hissed. "I thought they'd agreed to postpone?"

"I'm afraid Andra'asnia has exercised her right as a member of the advisory board to summon the full council."

"Not if I have anything to say about it," Ellex said.

"I have already scheduled you a meeting with Prince Rajesh'n," Pander said. "For midmorning."

"Perfect," she said. "Now tell me, what are the notestreams saying about me this morning? I know I ought to look."

"Sui Pradesh, you mustn't listen to the rabble, at least not to the loudest and most obnoxious ones."

"But those are the ones most streamed, I'm afraid."

"Even still, they don't capture the pulse of the city, I can assure you. Nor do they speak for history. No, Sui Pradesh, the masses are not angry with you. But they are scared. Very scared. I am too. Such barbarism—I can't fathom it. Here in our city. Our *safe* city. Safest city in all of Balance." He looked like he might cry.

"That's what I was most afraid of, that everyone will panic and the Council will overreact. Malisha Andra'asnia is always trying to grab more power for herself. And charlatans on every side will be trying to claim the narrative."

Ellex knew what might work, what might ease the fear of the people, if she could pull it off. If she could convince him to help her. But first—

"You've had an idea," Pander said. "I can see if in your eyes, the way they just sparked to life."

"A prayer to Trevian might help it work," she said. "But I mustn't delay. Rajj should be at the citadel by now."

Ellex hurried for the Pradishar headquarters, down the grassy pathways of Sunrise Ridge and out through the security gate into Old Stones. She pulled her hood low over her face as she felt out for her Cul'tavin peacekeepers. She'd ordered patrols doubled on the upper rim, and gold priority to access the lifts. In a bold move, Cort Andramon, the manager of Balan Su, had declared a day of mourning after the attack, cancelling sessions at the sprouting patches, the Pruu'patch, and at the Academicon, while the Guild had ordered all non-essential operators in the capital to stay home. Meanwhile, the Culture Bureau had expressly prohibited all streaming of public spaces until further notice.

The streets were mostly empty, her troops in place, saluting her and sending her their support and affection—and grief—through the crystal. Ellex took in all their pain and sent back a mournful but motivated determination to avenge their fallen comrades and a confidence in her ability to protect them in the future. She nearly swooned at the emotion she felt from her peacekeepers. She may have lost the confidence of the notestreamers, but her Cul'tavin still trusted her.

She was grateful that the streets were quiet, the plaza nearly vacant as well, because the last thing she needed was a notestreamer cornering her and pestering her and making her look incompetent on the weavryn. But with the sun already rising in the sky, there should have been many more coming and going about their daily lives than there were, and the scene added to her unease, to the sense of panic gripping her city.

Once through the walls into the misty gardens of Corda'mere, the obsidian spire of the citadel towered high in the morning sunshine, the flagstones were cool and moist beneath her feet, and she let herself exhale and breathe deeply of the rich, earthy scent of the thicket.

Prince Rajesh'n was right where she expected him to be, hard at work in his neat little office, so unassuming and spartan for a prince of Raccorum Rhazzat. That was one of the things she admired so much about Rajj—he knew what was needed and saw no reason for anything more than that. His door was open and Ellex tapped lightly on it with her knuckle. He looked up and smiled when he saw her.

"Thought you'd be here early," she said.

Rajj stood and walked over to Ellex and gave her a hug. He towered over her, broad shouldered like most Raccorin, but his bright green face was narrow, his cheekbones high, his features fine and delicate.

"You doing okay?" he asked, in his soft, soothing voice.

Ellex pulled back from the hug and sighed. "That remains to be seen," she said.

"I'm so sorry about your troops, Ell," he said. "Good Verdillions, all of them, Raccorin and Andrasian."

"Grief will have to wait, I'm afraid."

"Of course. What can I do to help?"

Ellex sighed. "I was hoping you'd offer. If you didn't, I might have gotten on my knees and begged."

Rajj chuckled awkwardly. "I don't ever want to see that," he said. "You know you only have to ask."

She took Rajj's hand and squeezed it. She knew she could count on him. He was—well, he might have been her only real friend in the capital. Maybe anywhere. And he was just so—she hated to say it—so unlike a Raccorin. He was soft-spoken, sympathetic, kind, patient. So Andrasian. It had made her job that much easier—made keeping Balance that much easier.

"My troops—the ones that were butchered—they were the first multiracial group of Cul'tavin in Balance history. I need you to be frank with me. What are they saying about the attack in Raccorum Rhazzat? What's the chatter on the streets of Rhen'zoran?"

Rajj frowned. "You're not going to like it."

"Then I'm glad to hear it from you first. Don't go easy on me."

"I don't like it, either," he said. "You know it's practically a Raccorin pastime to hate on the Andrasians, especially among the Ordens but also, more secretly, among the nobles. They've always resented the special preference that Andrasians get in Balance Authority."

"Do they reject history outright?" she scoffed. "Surely they know that the Pradishar faith was adopted by Andrasia *after* Balance was formed and not the other way around?"

"I'm not sure that matters in their minds. All they see is that their ancient Loricean faith has been abandoned and the religion practiced by almost every Andrasian has taken it's place. They see the Pradishar ordering them to abandon half of their empire—and forbidding any attempts to reclaim it. Now they see the Cul'tavin trying to move into domains where the Corkin army once had sole jurisdiction—to have a fleet and an army of their own and, as they see it, no longer need the Raccorin. With the world's most famous anti-slavery crusader now the head of the Pradishar, they worry about the future of the Raccorin way of life, and blame Andrasia for it's decline."

"Any Clades in particular that might have had a hand in this attack?"

"I don't think so. Any noble who moved against the Pradishar would be moving against their own best interests. Their mandate relies on the crystals. They wouldn't risk the Pradishar revoking them."

"I didn't think it was the Raccorin," Ellex said. "My instincts tell me the Bhizini are responsible. That Qardymion the Saltsap is the architect."

Rajj raised his eyebrows. "That would be bold, indeed. And difficult to pull off, considering that they and their followers never set foot on land."

"So the stories go," Ellex said. "But I know there are Pal'meran leaf-striders who walk about on stilts, who move through the treetops and swing from the ends of whips, never touching soil and yet unhindered by being ashore."

"But to butcher—and sew back together—while suspended in the air?"

"There's no reason to think Qardymion couldn't enlist allies who weren't so strict with such customs. Besides, this hasn't come out on the notestreams yet so I'd appreciate your discretion, but I was led to the crime scene, Rajj. A Bhizini was waiting for me, knowing I'd follow. This whole thing was a present. If there's one Cul'tavin that the Saltsap must hate above all others, it's me. But I need more time to investigate. I have a feeling, a hunch, that Qardymion isn't finished yet. This was only the beginning. If I'm right, they're still close-by, if not within the city, then not far either. I was hoping you'd order the Corkin to step up patrols in the area between Aga'thyn and Princip'asia, and not less than 100 miles south of Nunan. I want the gaps in the Great Sea Lanes crisscrossed regularly. And I want the order to come from you, not a request from me nor from the Council."

"Done," Rajj said. "Raq'asha sent similar orders this morning. I'll request she amend them slightly to accommodate your requested coordinates."

Ellex sighed. "Thanks," she said. "But I have one more favor to ask. Together we can overrule Malisha Andra'asnia's request for a council meeting. Give me a week, max. If I don't have anything then, well, I'll deal with it then. But for now, if I can find something, a lead, an arrest—"

"We've been after the Saltsap for decades," Rajj said. "It's like trying to grasp the fog of Balan Su."

"Maybe we've been going about it the wrong way. Will you help me?"

"Issue the postponement and I'll add my authority alongside yours," he said. "But Ell—Andra'asnia has already made a public statement."

"What?" she said, her eyes twitching rapidly. The sneering face of Malisha Andra'asnia came into her mind and Ellex listened to her brief announcement in an instant, time seeming to slow as she absorbed the information and ran over it several times.

"Sweet Trevian, is Andra'asnia insane?" Ellex said, giving Rajj a look of disbelief. "Fools have been blaming the Ren'fallow for society's woes for all of ten thousand years—ten thousand years of unfounded conspiratorial crap. And now she puts the good Cul'tavin name behind it? This is unacceptable!"

"And yet she finds a rapt audience on the weavryn," Rajj said. "Perhaps we should hold the Council meeting after all, just to clear some of this nonsense out of the air."

"I have a better idea," she said. "And that's the next stop on my list this morning. I should get going, but—thank you, Rajj. I don't know what I'd do without your help. Truly."

"You would manage just fine, my friend," he said, "but I'm glad to be of service."

Ellex didn't have far to go for her next stop, just a short walk back to the main hall of the citadel, then down a narrow corridor behind the dais. The hallway looked as if it had been made for someone much smaller than her. The black obsidian walls seemed to swallow all the light, and she had the sense of descending deep underground, even though the floor was flat.

The corridor ended in a room too dark to see. A single glowbe crackled to life when Ellex entered, and in the warm orange light, she could see the cloudy eyes of an Octa'vin guard staring lifelessly at her, their gray waxy skin pulled tight, their lips pressed together in a thin dark line. As many times as she'd made that walk, as many times as she'd had to deal with the Gran Pradesh's guards, she still had to force herself not to shudder when she saw them.

"Good morning," she said, smiling and clasping her hands together in front of her. "I'm here to see the Gran Pradesh."

The Octa'vin's thin lips opened but didn't move as the reply came out. "His Worship is not seeing supplicants at this hour." The voice was breathy, and the breath was sour.

So this is how it's going to be.

"I'm Sui Pradesh Ellex Andria, here to see Gran Pradesh Ra'shard Ruu'n."

The thin gray lips opened again. "I'm afraid the Gran Pradesh is unavailable."

Ellex raised her clasped hands in a sign of supplication. "This is a matter of the utmost importance. If you could just let him know I need to speak with him?"

The Octa'vin raised a thin gray arm and beckoned her to leave.

She sighed and turned in a huff, just as more glowbes crackled to life, and she spun back around to see two more Octa'vin opening the metal doors at the back of the room. In the threshold stood Ra'shard Ruu'n, Gran Pradesh of the Pradishar, in his long ceremonial robes, his hands clasped in front of him in the same way Ellex had held hers before balling them into fists. He smiled when he saw her, his bright wrinkled skin looking like copper in the light of the glowbes. The red scar on the left side of his face—down his brow, over his eye, and partway across his cheek—looked almost black, and the glass marble that had replaced his crushed eyeball rolled around and fixed upon her. Ellex always thought the glass eye made him look quaint, giving a doll-like quality to the old Raccorin's face.

She gave the accustomed bow for her position—a half-one rather than a full prostration on the ground—and couldn't help but give a quick smirk at the Octa'vin who had sent her away, though their clouded eyes didn't seem to see her.

"Were you looking for me, Sui Pradesh?" the Gran Pradesh said. His smile said he knew she was.

"I'm sorry to bother you unannounced, your worship," Ellex said. "I know I've broken protocol by coming here."

Ra'shard Ruu'n waved his hand in the air. "There's no rule which says my Sui Pradesh can't call on me. And I'll not have Balance Authority be handicapped by clinging to protocols which came about by habit rather than by reason, and which continue through inertia rather than effort."

"The thesis of your second book," Ellex said.

The old Raccorin beamed at her, but then his face fell. "Oh, if only I could still speak like that, still fight for what I believe in. I've become a silent old fool. An utter failure, and with such little time to make things right."

Ellex would have taken his hand and squeezed it, had the penalty for touching the Gran Pradesh not been death. She knew the Octa'vin would strike before she could get near him. But he had been the closest thing to a father that Ellex had had in the last thirty years, and it was hard not to comfort him.

"Nonsense," she said. "You've spent your entire life fighting for justice. And you have plenty of years left to keep fighting. Just tell me your will, your worship, and I'll help you. The Council of Nine will help you. Everyone in Balance will help you."

The Gran Pradesh blushed. "You flatter me, my dear, and I thank you for it. But I'm old. Nearly two centuries, and with each passing cycle, I feel ready to set my roots down, to speak my last, and rest. Time to pass things off to the next generation." He gave her a long look.

Ellex felt her stomach clenching. "My lord is too kind, but you still have many years before becoming a tandavin. Balance still needs you. And I—well, I suppose—" She trailed off.

Ra'shard Ruu'n smiled. "You aren't ready to take my place."

"In truth, I'm not sure the citizens would have me," she said. "It seems my efforts to integrate the Cul'tavin have not been well-received." She looked at the Gran Pradesh for a moment, at the holes in his forehead where his crystals had once been. Did the Octa'vin keep him informed of what the notestreams were saying? Did he know of the attack? Surely he must.

"I'm dreadfully sorry about what's happened," he said, as if he'd read her mind. "Is that why you've come this morning?"

She nodded. "I know I'm asking a lot, but I hoped your worship could address the public today. Speak to them and calm their fears. Reassure them that everything is status quo—that the Pradishar are working to bring justice to those responsible for this atrocity."

"Do you have any leads?" he asked.

"Yes," she said.

"Qardymion the Saltsap?"

"Afraid so," Ellex said.

Ra'shard Ruu'n sighed. "You ask a lot, my dear, even if it seems like you ask very little. I want to help you, but I hesitate, and for two reasons. First, I worry about the precedent I would set. The Gran Pradesh only addresses the public on very specific occasions, as you well know. I'd hate to inspire these criminals to further acts of violence, in hope of getting a response from the highest positions in government. And second, I fear that, rather than calming fears, my sudden appearance will cause a panic throughout Balance Territories, that everyone will think this must indeed be grave for me to show my face. And so I ask you, Sui Pradesh, are the gains worth the risks?"

Ellex considered his words for a moment.

"We are fighting a war, your worship, a war for the survival of our civilization. And our enemy has struck the heart of our alliance, in the shadow of this citadel, in our inviolable capital. With all the strength of the crystals on our side, we are still vulnerable. And yet Trevian's power cannot be overwhelmed or defeated. And you are that power. Your words soothe and heal, but also inspire and motivate. Balance will receive them with joy, not fear, I promise you."

Ra'shard Ruu'n smiled. "Very well, I will honor your request, though I'm not convinced I should. But I feel I owe you a favor. You were kind to me in my first years here in the capital, in this dreary, dreadful city. You made it feel warm, as warm as the Fierrin Desert where I was born. It seems so long ago, and yet it seems like only yesterday. Those were difficult times for us all, and I don't believe I have ever told you what your kindness meant to me."

"It's been my honor to serve," she said, letting out a sigh. "And you don't know what this means to me. I think your worship is going to save my career with this speech."

"Nonsense," he said. "Your career was never in jeopardy. In fact, I'm certain you're due a promotion. I'm not getting any younger, after all."

Ellex thanked the Gran Pradesh again, politely deflected the conversation into other matters, and soon bid him farewell.

Gran Pradesh? she thought. *Me?*

But no, the thought would have to wait til later. There was too much to deal with right here and right now. And she was taking care of things, one at a time. She allowed herself to relax a little as she strolled back down the narrow corridor to the main hall of the citadel, checking another goal off her list as she went.

❧ ☙

Ra'shard Ruu'n addressed the citizens of Balance Authority that afternoon. Nearly everyone with a crystamin streamed it, and PropSector had been repeating it for anyone who somehow missed it. Like the old rhetorician who had railed against slavery, the Gran Pradesh elevated the people of Balance Authority, vilified the Bhizini threat, and roused the citizens to fearlessly face the challenges at hand. Everyone rallied around their leader, suddenly full of confidence instead of fear, and full of moral outrage toward the Bhizini for such a brutal attack—a moral outrage that Ellex knew would soon turn against her if she failed to deliver.

The council meeting was postponed, and Ellex used the time to investigate. Still no luck locating Lithuigi Von'nDrino but the summons to the capital had officially been sent. By the time the good professor returned to Balan Su a week later, Ellex was already sure that he wasn't the one responsible for the attack, though she couldn't put her finger on why she thought the old Andrasian was up to no good.

He'll bear closer watching, she thought.

Rather, as the week had progressed, and leads into potential aggressors from Andrasia, from Raccorum Rhazzat, even from a few islands in the Inner Archipelago, all failed to pan out, and the sheer brutality of the scene continued to weigh on her mind, she no longer had any doubt that Qardymion the Saltsap was responsible.

When word finally came that the Saltsap and their Pal'meran rebels had been spotted near the Sargassian Sink—and from a reliable source, no less—Ellex knew just the plant to ask for help. But it had been over thirty years.

Since P'anorum, she thought, wincing. *Will he be willing to help me after all these years?*

Does he remember the promise he made?

Did he mean what he said when we fought?

Ellex closed her eyes and reached for Rakk Raeder with her crystal.

Chapter 9

And Once Again There is a Future

RAKK STOOD ON THE bridge of his ship and stared into the fog. For nearly a week, he and his fleet had circled the waters around Balan Su, setting up checkpoints on the Great Sea Lanes, sending scouts across the gaps in between, stopping all the ships coming and going from the city. No Bhizini had been found, no ships attacked, no suspicious goings-on to report, nothing. With the fog so thick he couldn't even see his own ship from end to end, he doubted he could spot a tiny skiff'rin if it tried to slip past the blockade. He was beginning to feel like he'd been assigned guard duty, and his hopes of any kind of heroic capture of Qardymion the Saltsap were fading fast.

Even still, in over three decades, this was the closest Rakk had come to Balan Su. And yet he wasn't allowed to come ashore, wasn't allowed to enter the harbor, and with the damn fog, was unable to even look upon the city from afar. Not that he liked the capital. In fact, he hated it, quite passionately. The cold, damp streets, the dank tunnels, the buildings stacked one upon another up the rim-side—the perpetual mist that blotted out the sun and made you feel constantly weary, constantly hungry, constantly unsettled. No, he was not yearning for a stroll through those streets. Even being here alongside the place was miserable enough.

But it wasn't the city that Rakk was thinking of as he stared into the fog.

Q'orin touched his arm and he jumped.

"I'm sorry to startle you, my prince," he said, an amused look on his face.

Rakk chuckled. "I appreciate the distraction," he said. "Any word?"

Q'orin shook his head no.

Rakk looked back out at the fog. "I don't know what I expected, coming here. She hates me, I know it. She'll never speak to me again, and I deserve it."

Q'orin said nothing.

Rakk turned and looked at him. "No response?"

He frowned. "Not any that my prince hasn't already heard, and rejected."

Rakk sighed. "Damn your honesty, but you're right, aren't you? I never could think straight when it came to Ellex Andria. And now she's so close I can practically taste her in the air, and I'm about to lose my mind."

"Reach out to her," Q'orin said.

Rakk shook his head. "No. No! She doesn't want to speak to me, I already told you that. She could have reached out at any time, but she hasn't. She knows I'm here. She could call me ashore. So could Rajj, but he hasn't. He won't. Neither of them want to see me."

"If you insist," Q'orin said.

"Meanwhile, they have us out here playing door monitors, stopping cargo ships and passenger ferries, when we should be hunting the Bhizini in sink and in swamp. How am I to capture the Saltsap when I can't even see off the side of my ship? This is hopeless. Qardymion is long gone, and my crown with him."

Q'orin swallowed a sigh. "Perhaps we could patrol the area around Nunan? I've word the fog has cleared there this morning. Some sunshine would do you good, I'm sure of it. It would do all of us some good. My prince, the troops are as restless and anxious as you are."

Rakk felt for his Corkin soldiers, first the ones on his ship, then the ones in his fleet surrounding the capital. He didn't need to scan them to know they were agitated. Q'orin was right.

"Make sure every ship gets at least a few hours beyond the fog," Rakk said. "Move us into the light."

Q'orin grinned, his eyes twitching. "With pleasure."

Rakk looked back out at the fog and felt the despair rising up inside him again. He heard the gurgitator open and the ship began to rumble beneath him, and he clutched at the deck with his rootpads as the cruiser lurched forward. His troops really were eager to get out of the fog! Maybe that's all it was. Maybe sunshine would solve his malaise.

When the cruiser passed out of the mist and the sky blue waters of the Threshinveld Sea spread out before him, he unfurled his branches and moaned with pleasure, and he could feel the elation radiating outward from his crew and from Q'orin. He closed his eyes and felt the pulsing warmth on his skin, the nutritious rays on his leaftips chasing away his fatigue and loosening up his fibers.

After he'd eaten his fill and withdrawn his branches, he looked toward Balan Su, at the gray-white wall between the sea and sky, and he knew then that the sunshine would not help him feel better.

He debated with himself what to do. He thought of his brother Rajj, and he thought of Ellex Andria. What would she say if he reached out for her now, after so long? Would she even respond? Would silence be worse than a good cursing out?

Does she know what I did the night P'anorum erupted?

Rakk pulled off his robe, ran to the edge of the ship, filled his lungs full of air, and dove into the sea. The water was warm but refreshing, and he rose to the surface and laid back and felt the rays of the sun on his face and on his chest.

Q'orin stood by the railing looking down at him as he lowered a ladder, and several of his troops were gawking as they always did when he leapt overboard. It was said that even the ancient Bhizini feared to swim far from shore, but Rakk had never been afraid of the sea. He'd been swimming for as long as he could remember, and he was a master at keeping his lungs half-full. Verdillions were too dense to float, so he would sink to the bottom if he exhaled too much. And since Verdillions could go for several hours, if not longer, without air, this meant either a slow suffocation while trying to walk to the nearest shore, or being crushed to death in the deeps of the ocean. Few were willing to risk it.

Rakk pumped his long arms down toward his legs, propelling himself away from the ship, then dropped his head under the water and flipped around under the surface and back toward the ladder. He was in the middle of a stroke when Ellex Andria contacted him.

He gasped and sputtered and frantically drew in a breath as he felt himself start to slip downward. He hooked his arm through the bottom rung of the ladder and steadied himself, while in his mind, Ellex touched his crystamin through the weavryn, a few soft taps, like knocking at the door of his thoughts, beckoning him to open to her.

Had he drifted off to sleep on deck? Was this a sunshine reverie? He'd dreamt of this moment so many times, but in his dreams he'd never stopped to question if it was real, so he took that to mean it must be. What was he supposed to say? What *could* he say? So he said nothing, but sent her the surprise and joy he was feeling and indicated he was listening. He hoped that wouldn't make her angry.

Her response came through in characters and Rakk couldn't help but feel he'd been slapped in the face. She didn't even want to speak to him. He thought he'd been about to hear her voice in his mind, but no. Only glyphs, soundless, empty, un-alive. He absorbed them immediately into his thoughts, then ran back across them, finally really seeing what they said, and understanding what it meant.

Ellex Andria had asked a favor of him.

Rakk let go of the ladder and laid back on the water again, his eyes closed, a small smile on his bright green face. Then he climbed up to the deck and grinned at Q'orin, who was standing ready with a towel to dry him off.

"The sunshine has done wonders for you, my prince," Q'orin said. "Look how happy you are already. And your skin, so bright. If only we'd sailed out of that pestilence days ago!"

"It's not just the sun that did it, old friend," Rakk said. "I've just received a message from Ellex Andria herself."

Q'orin's eyes widened. "With good news, I imagine?"

"Indeed! She has asked me to capture Qardymion the Saltsap."

"They've been spotted?"

"By the Sargassian Sink," Rakk said.

"That's not much to go on, my prince. The sink is massive. And we've been hunting them, amongst other places, in the Sargassian Sink, for decades."

"And Ellex Andria wants them captured by the end of the week," Rakk said.

Q'orin's eyes looked like they would pop out of his head. "That's—a difficult request," he said, choosing his words carefully. "How exactly is this good news, my prince?"

Rakk looked at Q'orin and frowned. "It's good news because it's the first chance I've had to see Ellex again. The first chance in *half* my life, that's why. It might be slim, but slim is better than nothing. And—and it means she still trusts me."

Q'orin was speechless for a moment, his face blank. "Shall I set course for the Sargassian Sink? We have a Bhizini to catch."

Rakk put his hand on Q'orin's shoulder and smiled gratefully. "The eastern flank. Fully open. Leave the heavy cruisers on patrol here and bring the cata'rins with us."

"Understood," Q'orin said, his eyes twitching as the ship began to move out and the crew scrambled to take up their positions. As they picked up speed toward the west, Rakk watched as the gray smear on the horizon finally vanished away, and his initial elation slowly replaced itself with worry.

Q'orin is probably right, he thought, *there's no chance for success.*

But if he wasn't right, and the Saltsap could be captured—if he could be the one to bring them in—not only would he be back in Ellex Andria's favor, but he'd be back on the lips of his Raccorin, back in their praises. He'd no longer be forgotten. Raq'asha would have to let him come home.

And so he had to hope. There was no other choice.

Rakk worked late into the night, poring over maps, reading and re-reading the intelligence reports that Ellex had sent him, contacting the captains of his ships across the Inner Seas, and trying to draw up a plan for the morning. Q'orin had been right, they didn't have much to go on, and even narrowing down the Sargassian Sink to just the eastern flank still meant he was dealing with four hundred miles of border-seas and nearly 75,000 square miles of treacherous shoal and reef-infested waters, impossible to navigate in anything larger than a skiff'rin. The only confirmed land in the entire region was Aga'thyn, a large protruding rock on the northeastern tip of the sink, with sheer cliffs and no harbor, like a massive river stone in the middle of the sea.

His captains had all reported clusters of Bhizini ships hitting the Great Sea Lanes, down south near Thester, out west at the mouth of Brinewater Bay, in the east near Princip'asia, and up north near Rheganza, but Qardymion hadn't been seen with any of them. When Rakk ordered some of the ships patrolling near Balan Su to investigate these attacks, Raq'asha intervened, telling him Balance Authority feared this was an attempt to draw their forces away from the capital.

But something about it didn't feel right to him. Qardymion wasn't a fool. They wouldn't risk an attack they were sure to lose. No, their style was to strike when least expected and flee before a coordinated response could be mustered. Bhizini fleets were a ragtag assortment of mostly wooden ships, piloted by captains who fought amongst themselves as much as they did against Balance. True, the Saltsap had organized the Bhizini like few ever had, but a single Guild-equipped cruiser with Corkin troops aboard could easily take on dozens if not hundreds of Bhizini craft, no problem.

And yet the size and material of Bhizini boats did confer one benefit that made them nearly impossible to wipe out—they were extremely light, and thus could easily slip into the sinks and swamps and reefs where the larger, heavier ships of Balance Authority couldn't follow. Since the Inner Seas were plagued with such sinks and shoals, there were many places where the Great Sea Lanes had no choice but to pass close to them, and such spots were frequently targeted by raiders who were next to impossible to catch.

What are you up to now? Rakk thought. *There's nothing of value along the eastern flank.*

He returned to the intelligence report in his mind. A Guild cruiser had spotted a boat flying Qardymion's flag. The navigator had streamed the incident to Management, who had passed it on to the Council of Nine. The stream was scrubbed—the metadata had been stripped, the background speech garbled, and the forms of the others on the ship were fuzzy. Streaming it gave Rakk an uneasy feeling, like his ears were ringing and his eyes were blurry, and he rubbed his temples. The scrub had removed the location data, and there was nothing but vast waters and blue skies, so it could have been anywhere. Ellex had narrowed it down to the eastern flank—probably the only information the Guild had given the Council, those secretive bastards—and Rakk found himself suddenly so furious he felt like punching someone. He wanted to find one of his soldiers, preferably his favorite Rhannokti, and use his body to pick a fight, to crack some heads together, but he clenched his teeth and returned to his research instead.

There were a few sources on the weavryn that hadn't failed him before, though he was always wary of trusting information that came from some random stream. But as the night threatened to give way to morning, and he still didn't have a clue on what to do come daybreak, he found himself watching the stream from P'anorum again, seeing that monkin's head twisting around.

And then suddenly it seemed that the deck beneath him gave way, that he'd dropped down into the dark sea below the ship, although his body hadn't moved at all. In his mind's eye, the streams of the weavryn were severed and he landed somewhere dark and warm and so quiet he could hear his heart beating, hear the air slowly drifting in and out of his lungs. He could sense the weavryn again, but he couldn't locate himself within it, or tell for sure which servryn he was contacting. Wherever he was, he felt as if his own body were there, even though with his physical body he knew he still sat at his workstation aboard his ship, sailing fast across the Threshinveld Sea.

Wherever he was, he wasn't alone.

<<They say a friend in need is a friend indeed,>> Rakk heard in his mind. <<I'm not sure I understand why this would be true. Perhaps they mean a friend in need is a friend in *deed*—in that they are willing to do good things for you, favors and gifts and services and the like, in hopes that you'll help them. Like a prayer offered to some ancient, angry Mund'umbrian. What do you think?>>

The voice seemed to come from everywhere, without a telltale stream, without metadata to identify it.

<<Is that you, dear sister?>> Rakk said. <<Come to distract me from my work and ensure I fail in my mission?>>

The voice said nothing for a moment. <<Raq'asha is busy at the palace in Rhen'zo-ran,>> it said.

<<Who are you, then?>>

A sigh of exasperation. <<Haven't I told you already? I'm a friend in need, and a friend in deed.>>

<<A friend you say? So we've met then?>>

<<After a fashion. You can call me Anorian Grain. There'll be time for explanations later, Rakk Raeder. Right now, I need your help. And I know you need mine as well.>>

Rakk laughed in his mind and did his best to exude confidence, but his heart was pounding, like drumbeats in his head, announcing some terrible fate. <<How can you know what I need?>>

<<I'd rather show you,>> the voice said.

And Rakk saw the stream of the Guild navigator once more, but this time the metadata was intact, the audio-visuals in their original form, un-scrubbed. And the stream was longer—a full thirty seconds had been clipped from the end in the version Ellex had sent him—*in the version Ellex received from the Guild*, he reminded himself—and he hissed as he watched Qardymion the Saltsap through a spyglass, setting off from their boat in a small skiff'rin. The stream cut off and another began, this one from just an hour earlier, the same navigator peering again through a spyglass, the Saltsap still on the skiff'rin, Aga'thyn looming behind them like a gray dome in the moonlight.

<<What do you want?>> Rakk demanded.

<<There's a hidden stair on the southwestern side of Aga'thyn. Go. Climb it. Find—and capture—Qardymion the Saltsap.>>

Rakk felt the knowledge of the stair, and how to access it, come into his mind, along with what felt like a warm blast of confidence and encouragement, which hit him so hard and so unexpectedly that he pulled his awareness out of the weavryn, back to his ship, up from the strange dark hole in which he'd fallen. When he tried to return to Anorian Grain, he didn't even know where to look.

Damnit.

Q'orin was knocking at his door and he entered with a tray of rhupan buns and a mug of steaming jha'ala.

"Sorry to wake you, my prince, but it is first dawn."

"I wasn't asleep."

"The regent has sent new orders," Q'orin said, setting down the tray. "We are to sail south for the Tranquin Reefs immediately."

Rakk stared at Q'orin for a moment, as if he didn't hear him, and then he started to laugh. Did she know? Was Raq'asha testing him? Trying to provoke him into disobeying her, so she'd have a reason to take the Corkin away from him?

"My prince?" Q'orin said.

"Sorry," Rakk said. "Sometimes—sometimes laughter is all that keeps me sane." His eyes twitched as he sent Q'orin the unaltered streams and the conversation he'd had with Anorian.

"The Saltsap is an hour away from capture?" Q'orin said.

"Yes," Rakk said. "And right at the first moment of this terrible night that I've felt like maybe I have a chance of success—no, even just a direction to sail in—here comes Raq'asha to hack it all down. Like she knew."

"If you openly disobey the regent—" Q'orin said.

"But if I have the Saltsap in chains?" Rakk said. "She wouldn't dare move against me."

"Can you trust this Anorian Grain? It could be anyone. It could be Raq'asha. Or your brother." He took a rhupan bun off the tray and took a bite of it, then another bite. He held out the tray to Rakk, and he took one and had a few bites too. Then he took his jha'ala and had a few sips, breathing deeply of the spicy, earthy aroma.

"Send the fleet to the Tranquin Reefs," Rakk said, "as the regent ordered. You and I will take this cata'rin to the border-shores south of Aga'thyn, and proceed by skiff'rin to the stair. I can run my army from anywhere, so by the time anyone notices I'm not actually there, we should be back with the fleet. No big deal, right? Even if this is all a bust."

Q'orin said nothing, his eyes twitching as he sent out his prince's orders.

⁂

Q'orin waited until he and Rakk were aboard the cata'rin, anchored off the Sargassian Sink, ready to head off in a skiff'rin and make for Aga'thyn, before he said anything. Rakk knew it was coming. Q'orin only went catatonic when he had something he really didn't want to say.

"I have a bad feeling about this," Q'orin said.

Rakk had to grin.

Q'orin blushed in frustration, and Rakk looked at him for a moment. "What are you so worried about?"

"It's just—as far as we know, Qardymion practices the ancient Bhizini ways. They don't set foot on land. Ever."

"You saw the stream. You know it was them. Why do you doubt?"

"I doubt only that which seems too good to be true, my prince."

"Maybe the universe loves me after all," Rakk said, no longer grinning. He accessed the gurgitator via his crystamin and the skiff'rin lurched away from the cata'rin. Off to the west, a few patches of palms along the atolls at the edge of the sink were visible in the twilight, and Aga'thyn, to the northeast, looked like a bruised thumb. Rakk opened the gurgitator wide and the skiff'rin raced toward the sink, lurching like a horse in full stride, and slapping against the water in rhythmic claps. As Aga'thyn began to loom overhead, Rakk started to close the gurgitator, and when the palm-encrusted atolls along the border-shores of the Sargassian approached, he shut it entirely. Their momentum carried them nearly into a reef just below the surface, but Q'orin was ready with his oar to push them through the narrow channel and into the sink.

Rakk reached for Q'orin with his mind, and he could feel him waiting for him, ready and eager to open to him. He was in Q'orin's thoughts and Q'orin in his, and Rakk showed him the way to the stair, the knowledge shared with him by his mysterious informant Anorian Grain. Rakk could feel Q'orin's confidence boosted with this new information, like having a memory of the path to rely on, and he could feel Q'orin's body, the oars in hand, the smell of the sea in his nose. Q'orin could feel his body too, as if they were one will with two parts.

With incredible speed and coordination, they propelled the skiff'rin through the winding passages along the edge of the sink, past jagged coral that could have easily torn open the hull, and over shoals that could beach their craft and delay them. They did so in complete silence, not even needing to speak through the crystal or to look at one another, to debate on what to do in each particular circumstance. All that existed was the path and traversing it. And when the front of the skiff'rin bumped into the rocky cliff of Aga'thyn, and they severed their connection with one another, Rakk had to fight off the urge to leap back into him, it felt so good to be there, so safe and powerful. But he remembered where they were, and why, and he shook off the loneliness and closed off his mind.

"My prince," Q'orin said. "Look."

They had reached the western-facing side of the island, and its cliffs rose overhead like a great wall, still deep in shadow though the sun had already risen in the east. At the water's edge, just to the right of the skiff'rin, a small nook was set back into the wall.

Rakk stepped out into the water, which only came to his knees, and Q'orin followed. His heart racing, he stepped toward the alcove, peered round inside it, and exhaled loudly. A small passage led to a spiral staircase up into the rock.

"Right where you're supposed to be," he said, grinning. "Q'orin, grab our weapons."

The stair spun upward so narrowly that the inside surface was deceptively skinny. They had to take it much more slowly than he wanted to, gripping each step with their rootpads, since only the front part of their feet would even fit on the surface.

Worse, as soon as Rakk had completed the first turn, he was in pitch darkness. The whole world seemed swallowed up by it, and he laughed at himself when he realized he was panting. He closed his eyes and steadied himself. He tried to keep to the outside of the curve, where the stairs were larger, but his shoulders were so wide, he had little room to move left or right. He had to keep his head hunched forward in order to proceed. And he laughed again when he thought about what would happen if he were to run into Qardymion right now, while they were on their way down.

Rakk and Q'orin climbed and climbed and climbed, until finally there was light again, and Rakk smiled at the spontaneous burst of joy he felt in his heart. The stair ended on the upper portion of the island, atop the cliffs but not yet at the apex. Rakk turned and looked off to the west, at the chaotic landscape of the Sargassian Sink, a tangled patchwork of white and blue strips speckled with green spreading to the west and southwest, while off to the north, the flat, unbroken sapphire of the Threshinveld Sea stretched to the horizon.

Behind them, to the east, the rocky surface of the island continued to rise in a gentle slope. Rakk waved to Q'orin and they hurried up the incline, an uneasy feeling growing in Rakk's chest. So far, it didn't look like anything was up here on the top of the island, just a smooth rocky surface, more of the same the farther they went. When they approached the summit, Rakk ran to the top, and he motioned to Q'orin to hurry and look.

The island looked like a potter had taken a great ball of clay, fashioned it into a ball, and then sank a massive thumb into the middle of it, making a grooved interior while nonetheless conserving the outer, stone-like edges. The valley wasn't large, and it wasn't very deep, but it did descend far enough from the height of the surrounding rock to entirely conceal it from view, trees and all. Rakk felt like he was looking at a painting of an idyllic mountain pastoral, a small thicket of beech trees around a pond, with a log cabin amidst it all.

<<My apologies for doubting, my prince,>> Q'orin said in Rakk's mind. <<It seems your strange informant was reliable.>>

<<Don't jinx me now, old buddy,>> Rakk said. <<Come on. Quietly. I don't see the Saltsap, so if they're up here, they're probably inside that cabin. I just can't figure out what Qardymion would be doing here? What is this place? Aga'thyn is supposed to be uninhabited.>>

<<Only one way to find out,>> Q'orin said, clutching his fighting pike and nodding gravely at Rakk.

A small path led down through the trees and into the valley, but they kept to the thicket, ducking through the foliage but staying close enough to the path so Qardymion couldn't give them the slip. Rakk ran his fingers along the silvery gray bark of the tree trunks, relishing the texture, and he breathed deeply of the wholesome, nutty aroma. He didn't realize how much he missed walking through the woods, how much he missed the thick canopy and tangled undergrowth of the Swarthen Forest on P'anorum, where he'd spent so much of his free time as a youth.

Just having land underfoot felt like a blessing.

<<What's the plan, my prince?>> Q'orin said.

<<We know the Saltsap is here alone,>> Rakk said. <<If they hear us approach, or see us peeking in through the window, we risk being picked off before we can storm the place. If we just kick the door down, they could be expecting us, and we'd be walking right into an ambush. If we wait for them to leave the cabin before we make a move, we could lose a whole day and never even confirm they're here. So I say we walk in the front door like we own the place.>>

Q'orin nodded and Rakk grinned. Then they sprinted for the door and Q'orin barreled into it with his shoulder, dropping onto the ground as Rakk came in on his heels, leaping over him, enflamer in hand.

The cabin was large but simple, one massive room with a kitchen in one corner, a bed in another, a dining area in the third, and a small sitting area at the entrance.

Rakk was expecting the Saltsap to be—what did he expect? That they'd be brewing poisons, tinkering with illegal maquina, drinking the sap of the innocent? What did Bhizini rebel leaders do when they snuck away from everyone else to a secluded cabin atop a deserted island?

What Rakk didn't expect to find was Qardymion standing over the dining room table, scrolls spread out in front of them and books stacked up around them, small round spectacles on their mottled green face, a mug of steaming jha'ala in one hand, a quill in the other, like a scholar at the Academicon.

Qardymion didn't look surprised, but their eyes zeroed in on the enflamer in Rakk's hand, and they smiled. They sat their mug of jha'ala and their quill down on the table and raised their hands in the air.

"Well done, Prince Rhakksees," they said, and their voice was deep and low and purred like the surf from afar.

Rakk had never heard their voice, never seen Qardymion with their own eyes before, only glimpses from others over the years. He studied them now, surprised at how small they were. Their eyes were big and brown and warm, surprisingly soft, and the shape of their face was comely, their body toned and strong.

"I'm sorry if the accommodations aren't up to the standards of a prince, but you're both welcome to come in and stay awhile. I'm sure there's much we can discuss."

Rakk laughed as he pulled a restraining vine off his belt and handed it to Q'orin, never taking his eyes off of Qardymion's. "I'm afraid we have somewhere to be, so we'll have to save the small talk for the sea."

Q'orin grabbed the Saltsap by the arm and pulled them to their feet, twisted their arms together behind their back, and wrapped the vines around them. Any squirming would cause them to restrict. Q'orin ran his hands up and down the Saltsap's body, looking for weapons, but they had none. Then he wrapped a lead around the vines and handed it to Q'orin.

"Get them outside," Rakk said, "while I have a look around."

Rakk thought someone had lived in this place a long time ago, decades if not longer, if the trinkets on the shelves and the decorations were any indication. The place was in good shape considering its age, so it had been maintained over the years, even if not inhabited.

He looked over the books and scrolls, a mixture of histories, some old novels from Andramere, and a collection of journals, handwritten in a lovely script, at least twelve volumes of them. He found the first volume and opened to the first page. The date read 9901 COB, nearly one hundred years ago.

"So begins the account of Aga'thyn the Unnamed, Aga'thyn the Forgotten, Aga'thyn who should have died but here is forced to live on."

Rakk hissed. He needed to bring these journals, to bring this evidence with him, all of it, but how would he get dozens of books and a mound of scrolls down the stairs and into a skiff'rin, in the pitch dark spiral staircase, while also escorting the world's most dangerous prisoner?

No, he'd have to come back for them later.

All that mattered right now was the Saltsap. He'd done it. He had them in custody. Now the most important thing was to get them to the Pradishar.

And hope the Bhizini didn't find out they'd been taken first.

Chapter 10
The Hard Edge of Progress

LITHUIGI SAT ON THE terrace under the stars and looked out at Balan Su. The fog had dropped to sea level, a true rarity, and he could see the lower rim and harbor-front, the guard towers on the northern end of Nunan, the entire inside slope of the crescent, all aglow in orange light, the thousands of glowbes like tiny flames burning in the night. He'd awoken out of breath, his heart racing, sure his prosthetic had torn itself loose from the stump of his arm, but when he opened his eyes, he found it hanging peacefully at his side.

A mug of steaming jha'ala sat on the small stone table beside the lounger where he was reclining, and he reached for it with his right hand but stopped himself and grabbed it instead with his false arm. He sat up and lifted it toward his lips, still shocked he could feel the heat of the mug—that he could feel with the thing at all. He sat the mug back down and touched the prosthetic with his other hand and he could feel the caress. The arm felt warm, alive. He had to admit how much he liked it. After decades of doing most things with one hand and relying on his aides for more complicated tasks, he'd found his work had never been more productive, his self-reliance—he'd forgotten what it was like to be able to tinker for hours on his own, without a helper nearby.

And yet he also hated it, this hybrid monstrosity, this duplicate of his own son's arm. Something just wasn't right about it, he was certain. How had Hesh'n made it sensitive to touch, to heat? How was it adult-sized, if it came from a spratlyn? And why had the Pradishar, and the Dyna'arin, agreed to the breaking of so many laws in order to make this? He had no illusions it was for his benefit.

He couldn't fall back asleep, so he sat brooding til the stars began to vanish and the sky grew light, ignoring his jha'ala til it grew cold. Rebesh'a was on Princip'asia working and wouldn't be back for a few more days, so Lithuigi had the garden to himself. Usually he enjoyed such moments but not now. No, he needed to talk to Hesh'n again. He needed some answers. But first, he had classes to teach.

Before he left for the Academicon that morning, he fetched his old prosthetic, disassembled it, and took the canvas cover and fitted it as best he could to the new one, covering all the exposed flesh on the arm. Then he put a glove over the hand. He'd just have to remember to treat it like it wasn't a functioning arm and he should be able to pass without anyone noticing it had been upgraded. But then he remembered the interview with Gushyr Vaincorr. If anyone had been paying attention, they'd have noticed. As far as he knew, the notestreams could already be discussing it, though he wasn't about to break his vow to stay off the weavryn just to find out. He took off the glove and the canvas before he headed out the door.

Mha'arlo found him in the hallway after class.

"You wanted to see me, professor?" he said.

He nodded and Mha'arlo followed him. When they were in Lithuigi's lab, he turned to his assistant. "I have a very important assignment for you, and I'm afraid it can't wait til later. You're the best sailor I know. Can I count on you?"

Mha'arlo's eyes lit up and he lifted his head and held back his shoulders. "I won't let you down, professor," he said.

"You'll sail for Andramere. Immediately. Avoid the Great Sea Lanes while en route. If for some reason you're stopped by Balance, or if the port authorities in Andramere want to inspect the ship, you'll need to jettison the cargo."

"Understood, professor," he said. "I'm glad this is finally happening."

"Mha'arlo," Lithuigi said, a serious look on his face, "It pains me to put you at risk like this."

"You knew the day would come eventually."

"That doesn't make it easier," he said. "Stay off the Lanes to avoid the Pradishar and the Corkin. And if, Trevian forbid, you're captured by the Bhizini, you tell them you're on your way to see Bhea Bell. It might not secure your immediate release, but it will keep you alive until I can come for you."

"Don't worry about me, professor. I can outmaneuver the Bhizini any old day. I was practically raised on a ship after all. I've got more salt in my sap than the Saltsap!"

"I believe you do," Lithuigi said, laughing. "Now go. And sail safe, son. Sail safe."

As Mha'arlo hurried out of the lab, a bounce in his step, Lithuigi said a silent prayer to the sea, and to Gray'may'n the Unseen, to carry him to Andramere and back in one piece. How he wished Mha'arlo were his own son. How'd he go so wrong with his real ones?

Well, no matter, he thought, *you can't choose your family, but they remain family nonetheless*. He needed to see both his sons today, and realized he was dreading that more than anything he'd dreaded in a very long time. Maybe he'd just go to his lab and tinker for awhile instead.

But no, he at least needed to see Vilder. He needed to see if he'd give anything away in his malice. And Hesh'n too—he had to make sure this prosthetic of his was as legal, and moral, as he was claiming. Tinkering would have to wait.

❧❧❧❧❧ ❧❧❧❧❧

Lithuigi decided he'd save the worst for last and go see Hesh'n first. So he headed out of the Academicon and into the bright midday sunshine. The fog had returned, filling the caldera with mist, but the upper rim stuck up out of it, glowing brilliantly white, except for the spire of the Pradishar citadel, whose obsidian spire shimmered black in the light. He headed west, past the Industrial Quarter with it's assortment of Guild operations and massive maquina cloaked in marble, through the Regalia with its high-end shops and restaurants and entertainment venues, and into the Sunset Point residential district on the south-western tip of the crescent. Not as fancy as Sunrise Ridge where Lithuigi lived, Sunset Point was nonetheless a premier neighborhood, younger with more families, a lot of smaller and more affordable gardens, and far more public spaces, recreation halls, sporting venues, and other shared facilities.

Hesh'n had a small garden on the western side of the district which, on the rare days when the fog lifted, offered a stunning view of the Threshinveld Sea and the colorful sunsets for which the area was named. Lithuigi hadn't been to his son's garden in many months—maybe years—and he was half-surprised that his crystamin still granted him access through the gate. Once inside, he was shocked at the conditions. The plants were all untrimmed, many of them brown and crusty with neglect. The grasses were uncut and un-raked, the cookery stank of moldy rhupan and swarmed with flies. There was dust on everything, and piles of dirty robes laying about in the sleeping quarters.

Hesh'n needs a partner, a family of his own, to force him to stop living like a bachelor or a lazy scamp. Heck, even just a keeper to clean up the mess once a week. I know he can more than afford it!

He knocked at the door of Hesh'n's lab, which he knew led to a stair down to a secure basement, but there was no answer. He knocked harder, but again there was no response. So he reached out for his son via his crystal and told him he was at his garden to visit him.

The response came, short and abrupt. <<At the Academicon. Busy.>>

Lithuigi sighed and began the walk back to where he'd come from, frustrated he'd gone so far for nothing, but decided to stop off in the Regalia for a bite to eat first. When he got to the Academicon, he checked the time—just enough to meet with Hesh'n before he had to meet his students to oversee their lab sessions. So he headed to the building where his son's lab was located and knocked at the door.

Hesh'n worked as a technical coordinator and adjunct professor at the Academicon, mostly giving introductory lessons on Guild operations to first-years while helping maintain the servryns and tinkering in his lab. He was, needless to say, not nearly as popular of a professor as his father, and many students complained that he was boring, strange, and bumbling—basically, a bad teacher. But Hesh'n had a true gift in working with the servryns, and was a fine tinker in his own right.

Maybe one day he'll learn some people skills, Lithuigi thought.

The door finally opened and Hesh'n stood there, an annoyed look on his pale green face, his brown eyes crinkled up, like he was confused. "Oh, it's you," he said. "Just a minute." He shut the door and Lithuigi waited, to the point he was about to knock again, when the door re-opened and Hesh'n invited him inside.

The lab reeked, a smell that sent chills down Lithuigi's back. It was the smell of death, of sap and innards. He could see a few smears on the floor, a glisten from the quick mopping Hesh'n had tried to give the place while his father waited outside. His son had returned to his workstation and was busy with a pair of pliers, manipulating something inside a metal box. Lithuigi was afraid to approach, afraid to speak. But he took a deep breath, the smell almost gagging him, and then turned to Hesh'n.

"What's that smell? Why is the floor so sticky? And this mess?"

"What mess?" Hesh'n said, not looking up from his work. "What smell?"

"Don't fool with me, son. I can smell the sap, smell the death in this room. You've been experimenting with flesh again, haven't you?"

Hesh'n put his pincers down and sighed loudly. "I told you, I have permission to do this. I haven't killed anyone, or raided the morgue again. This is my own flesh, my own sap."

Lithuigi touched his prosthetic with his good hand. "Spratlyns, you said. But you never told me how. And you know Balance Authority prohibits self-reproduction."

"I don't cut the taprin. It's not a crime to grow one. They're insentient, just a shrub and nothing more. They don't feel anything. It's like saying it's a crime to prune your garden, which is nonsense."

"How do you get the spratlyn so big—adult sized—if you don't cut the taprin?"

Hesh'n paused for a moment. "As one tinker to another, I'm not willing to share that yet. Although—if you were to tell me about your prototype—"

Lithuigi cut him off. "Damnit son, have you thought about the consequences? About the laws you're breaking? About how far you've crossed Durbian's Line?"

Hesh'n glared at his father. "Not the line again!" he snapped. "Sweet Trevian, what a hypocrite you are! I've told you, again and again, this work is legitimate. I've run everything by Management. I've broken no taboos, no laws. My hands are clean, figuratively at least. Which is more than I can say for you."

Lithuigi ignored the jab. "Management? Who gave you permission?"

Hesh'n hissed and opened his mouth to say something when there was a knock at his lab door. He hissed again and started for the door. Lithuigi took the chance to peek at what Hesh'n was working on. He saw that it was some type of prosthetic similar to his arm but was surprised to see both a dynamin and a datamin inside the apparatus embedded in the arm. On the workstation, Lithuigi could see a sheath with a crystamin inside.

"What do you want?" Hesh'n said when he opened the door, but his brother stepped into the lab without saying anything.

Vilder crinkled his nose. "Sweet Trevian, what a stench. Seriously, this is positively unsanitary. You're going to get sick working in these conditions. I could bring over some monkins to tidy up in here?"

"Stop acting like you care about my health," he said. "And if you bring a monkin in here, I swear I'll vaporize them."

Vilder snorted. "The Dyna'arin can't vaporize anyone. I'm not a scamp anymore to believe such nonsense."

"Send a monkin over and find out for yourself," Hesh'n said, returning to his workstation.

"Father," Vilder said, his voice flat.

"Son," Lithuigi said back, then turned to Hesh'n. "What are you working on here? Why do you have a dynamin and a datamin in the control box? And what is the crystamin for?"

Hesh'n's eyes lit up, suddenly wild with excitement. "I'm hoping I can store a set of instructions in the datamin, power the prosthetic with the dynamin, and allow a remote user to control it when needed with the crystamin." Hesh'n looked proudly at his father, but Lithuigi kept his face blank.

"Don't you even care why I've come by?" Vilder asked.

"No," Lithuigi and Hesh'n said together. Vilder hissed softly, then sat down in one of the chairs along the wall, folded his arms, and sat pouting, his eyes twitching.

"I think I've got it," Hesh'n said, after placing the crystamin inside the apparatus with the pliers. He closed the box, whose lid was already integrated with the flesh. Then he picked up the arm and placed it on a hanging wrack, fastening the upper end to a hook so that it hung like an arm would hang at one's side. He pulled a zapren out of his drawer and placed it on the workstation, then he positioned the hand of the prosthetic, palm open and downward, on the handle of the zapren. "Step back, Father."

They both took a step back and Hesh'n sent a command via crystal to activate the prosthetic. The arm twitched and then, with incredible speed, the hand clutched the zapren, flicked it on, and began to move it about menacingly. Hesh'n howled with laughter. Lithuigi couldn't help but be impressed, even though he felt himself struggling to breath.

"Absolutely incredible," he managed to get out. "How did you get the three crystals to communicate like that?"

"I used the basic idea behind a servryn," Hesh'n said.

No, he thought. *Sweet Trevian, no!*

Lithuigi began to examine the arm, hoping Hesh'n couldn't see his face, couldn't tell that his hands were shaking. He saw some scorching on the flesh, and he swallowed in a dry throat.

"Are you sure this is safe?" he said. "The console box looks too small to be properly sheathed."

"You're right, it is too small," Hesh'n said, looking slightly abashed. "There's been a lot of scorching." Hesh'n lowered his voice. "Maybe we can make a deal. I'll tell you how I got the spratlyn's to grow so large so quickly, if you'll tell me how you shrunk a dynamin."

"Absolutely not," Lithuigi said. "Out of the question."

"But this is my last obstacle. Your prototype is the only thing that can make that possible. Please, Father, this is important."

Lithuigi eyed Vilder across the room, then spoke directly to Hesh'n through their Dyna'arin crystals. <<Tell me the Pradishar don't know about my prototype. Tell me you haven't told them!>>

<<I haven't,>> Hesh'n said. <<And I won't. You have my word.>>

Lithuigi was regretting having told him in the first place.

Vilder came over, a suspicious look on his pale face. "What are you two whispering about?" he said.

"About how much we hate interruptions," Lithuigi said.

Vilder sneered. "Charming," he said. "You always were a terrible liar, Father."

"Just drop it," Hesh'n said.

Vilder looked surprised but then let his face go blank. He looked at the prosthetic, touched it, and pulled his arm back in disgust when he felt the flesh. "I'm glad to see you are making progress on the project," he said, wiping his hand on his robe.

"You knew about this?" Lithuigi said.

"Of course I knew about it. The Pradishar are very interested in Hesh'n's work. How else do you think he was able to get all three types of crystal for this project?" Vilder looked positively delighted.

"The Pradishar?" he said, turning to Hesh'n. "What kind of deal have you made with them?"

Hesh'n said nothing, but Vilder spoke up. "This is a very important project, Father," he said. " The Pradishar care deeply about security. About order. These are what matter most to the keepers of the crystals."

"Is it now?" he said. "I've been around a lot longer than you have, son, and you only make a fool of yourself when you spout such nonsense. Don't you ever think for yourself? Power is what matters most to the Pradishar. Keeping it, exerting it, growing it. When is enough enough!"

"We need all the power we can get, what with the Harvest approaching," Vilder said, but the look on his face showed he realized he'd said too much.

"A Pradishar priestin speaking like a Ren'fallow conspirator?" Lithuigi said. "Why am I not surprised you'd be fool enough to join those idiots?"

Vilder took a step forward, as if he wanted to physically attack his father, but instead he turned around and left the lab without saying another word. Hesh'n, who had gone back to tinkering with the arm, looked up at his father. "You know, it's far worse when he says nothing than when he whines or complains or hurls insults."

He snorted. "I'm not afraid of my son, I'm not afraid of a Pradishar thug, and I'm certainly not afraid of a Ren'fallow conspirator. How many apocalyptic cults have there been throughout the history of Balance and the Age of the Incarnate, and yet here we are, still growing, still fruiting, still spinning round and round beneath the sun."

"The Age of the Incarnate?" Hesh'n said, his eyebrows raised. "Now who sounds like a Ren'fallow?" Then he laughed. "My brother just needs something to belong to, a hobby, since he's not an intellectual like you and me, not a manager, not a tinker, not a trouper, not a merchant, not even a very decent plant to be around. He deserves our sympathy, I think."

"Was he serious? Is this—a Pradishar project?"

"Is there a difference between working for the Guild and working for the Pradishar? Aren't they one and the same, part and parcel of Balance Authority?"

"Not yet," Lithuigi said. "Hopefully not ever. The Pradishar are religious fanatics, control freaks—both. They only maintain power because of their monopoly on the crystals. But the Dyna'arin are a group of talented individuals working together for the common good."

Hesh'n laughed. "Do you really believe that? Seriously Father, you might be as foolish as Vilder!"

Lithuigi hissed softly. "I may be wrong about the Guild, but I'm not wrong about the Pradishar. Don't trust them, son. Don't ever let them have any power over you or over your tinkering. They already have enough as it is. And it's our special privilege as Dyna'arin tinkers to be largely free of their dominance. Don't give them what they don't deserve!" Lithuigi paused for a moment to catch his breathe. "And while I'm giving advice, why not abandon this project altogether? Management approval or not, I have a bad feeling about it. There's so many other projects you could work on. I know you have dozens, hundreds, *thousands* of ideas. Will you at least consider it?"

Hesh'n sighed. "I will, Father."

"That's my son," he said. "Brightest tinker I've ever known."

"A rare thing indeed, a compliment from the good professor. At least for his sons."

"Why would you say that? I've always supported your work—always tried to make sure—"

Hesh'n put up his hand and cut him off. "Just forget it. And thank you. I appreciate it."

Lithuigi didn't know what else to say, and after a long and awkward pause, he told Hesh'n he had better get to class and that he'd see him again soon. "I'd like you to look at my prosthetic later," he said. "I think it was acting up in my sleep."

He left the lab, wanting to cry, to scream, to get in his ship and sail away from it all, back to the far side of the world where he could be free. But instead he walked across campus, showed up at the student's lab, a smile on his face, ready to teach, to perform, as he always did.

Afterward, he made his way back to his own lab. He opened his walk-in safe, stored his things, and shut himself inside. Then he activated the panel which allowed access to the hidden door that went down to a secret lab far beneath his normal lab, through various locked doors and a variety of stairwells and corridors, all the way into the subterranean innards of the obsidian spire of the Pradishar citadel.

He went through the last door and closed it behind him. His aide Rhyntysha was sitting at a workstation looking over some scrolls. "Good afternoon, professor. I wasn't expecting you until this evening."

"Yes," he said. "I had a bit of spare time, so I thought I'd drop in and give you a break. Go get some rhupan and a bit of sun. You've got an hour."

"I appreciate it, professor," she said.

He waited til she had left and locked the door behind her, then he turned and walked over to the enormous stasis chamber, a maquina which took up well over half of the lab. It was humming away, a soft purr that was the only sound in the room. The chamber was large and metal, almost identical to the half-crushed one in the ancient temple in the bowels on P'anorum, the one everyone in Balance had now seen on that stream that Aar'ryn Ruu'n had shared.

He walked over to the door and peered inside. Glowbes lit the interior a soft orange. Strapped in the middle of the chamber, covered in tubes, with maquina of various sizes sticking out of its skin, was a tiny Bhizini, eyes closed, body deep in stasis.

Lithuigi sighed, pressing his forehead against the glass.

He knew what it meant to work for the Pradishar. He knew indeed.

Chapter 11

And All That Was Left Was Nothing

AFTER THE BHIZINI TRIED to kidnap Fin'roq, Bhea Bell refused to let him out of her sight. Either she or Grizmond had to stay with him, and they rotated night shifts so someone was always awake. So far the villagers hadn't returned, nor had the Bhizini. And after several days of constant vigilance, Fin'roq was starting to feel like a prisoner in Bhea's garden, though he wasn't sure he would have gone anywhere else even if she'd let him leave. He couldn't bear the darkness anymore, so the thought of setting foot in one of the tunnels under the island, once his favorite place to roam, was unthinkable. His neighbors wanted to spill his sap, or worse, burn him alive, so he couldn't go home to his village. The Bhizini wanted to kidnap him, so the Swarthen Forest was off limits. They'd nearly succeeded, and would have if it hadn't been for Baboo.

Fin still didn't know what he'd seen in the woods that night, and Baboo was gone the next morning before he could ask him about it. He'd planned to bring it up in front of Bhea, hoping to draw an answer out of one of them, but with Baboo gone, Bhea just plain refused to answer. She deflected question after question before finally putting her foot down.

"Baboo will explain it one day, when he's good and ready," she said, and Fin'roq knew any more questions would be futile. He also knew Baboo would never explain anything.

"Fine, Baboo may or may not be a Mund'umbrian," he said. "My best friend, a beast of the underworld, who tore through those Bhizini warriors with his teeth and claws and then smiled afterward. I really am as wretched as the villagers say I am."

"Baboo wasn't taking pleasure in the killing, little sprout, if that's what you're thinking," Bhea said.

"I don't know what I'm thinking, or feeling. Or anything, Bhea. Sweet Trevian, how did everything go so wrong? That ship appeared on the horizon, and my world fell apart."

"I'm sorry, my sprout. It's as much my fault as anyone's. The truth is, you was always gonna suffer. I knew it from the time you was just a fruit on your mama's belly. It's my fault for keeping so much from ya. I just—well, I just wanted you to have a little time of your own, is all."

"What do you mean?"

Bhea sighed. "Have you made up your mind on Aar'ryn's offer? It's nearly the weekend and the ship'll be arriving any day now. You best decide whether you're gonna be on it or not when it leaves."

Fin'roq groaned. "I hate making decisions. I don't know what to do. What should I do?"

Bhea shrugged.

"If I stay here on P'anorum, the villagers won't rest until I'm dead. Which means I'd have to stay here in your garden. But even here in your garden, I'm vulnerable to the Bhizini without constant supervision, so you and Grizmond would have to be with me all day, every day. If the Bhizini capture me, I'd be forced to follow their ways, to join a clan, to fight for my survival. Or they might just enslave me. If I go to Balan Su, I'll be in a city of a million Verdillions, a million Andrasians and Raccorin, and no Bhizini. No one like me. I could be beaten to death on the street and nobody would care. Does that about sum up my choices?" He laughed, then looked at Bhea and started to cry.

She wrapped his arm around his shoulders and pulled him into a hug.

He sniffed and rubbed his face against her robe, drying his eyes. "I want to go, Bhea. To Balan Su. I think it's the best choice, because even if everyone there hates me, at least I'll get the chance, the only chance I'll ever have, to do something I've always dreamed of doing. I'll get to wear the purple and gray, to pray in the sharlum, to sit in the Academicon. I'll get to learn about the faith and study lore with others who find that stuff interesting like I do. I think I have to try. Do you think I should?"

"Oh my sprout, I wish I had the answers. But I don't know what's best any more. I wish I could cheer you up like I did when you was just a scamp. You'd come to me with your woes and I'd sing 'em and dance 'em away, and you'd leave here laughing and singing and dancing too. You remember, don't ya, little sprout?"

"Of course I do," he sniffed.

"Well, maybe this will cheer you up. There's another option than the one's you've listed."

Fin'roq just looked at her expectantly.

"I can get you to the Bhizini—not to those that captured you, my sprout. I'm talking about my allies. It won't be an easy journey. And you'll find their ways strange and, well, tough. But you're a fast learner, Fin. And you'll be around others who look like you."

Fin'roq exhaled hard, and took a few deep breaths, surprised at the anger tightening his chest. When he spoke, it was barely a whisper.

"You have a way off P'anorum," he said.

It wasn't a question and Bhea didn't answer.

"All this time, all these decades that we were all trapped here—you've been able to leave. Those times when your drawbridge was up, when weeks passed without sending for me, my lessons neglected—you were off sailing the world?"

"Fin, I—"

But he put up his hand and she stopped talking. And when he walked off into the garden, she didn't follow. Once he was out of sight, Bhea put her hands over her face and wept.

Fin'roq did the same.

On the morning that Fin was to depart for Balan Su, Baboo returned, dancing and tumbling and laughing. Fin could hardly manage a smile. Bhea had cooked a large breakfast for everyone, and she was doing her best to act chipper, to show support for Fin'roq's decision.

He could hardly look at her.

Was this really the last morning he'd wake up on P'anorum? The last time he'd see Bhea or Grizmond—ever? Who knew if or when he'd be back. And they were getting old. He knew that deciding to leave meant having to say goodbye, but since he'd never left before, he hadn't known just how painful that would be.

Was he really going to leave while still so angry with Bhea?

But she'd betrayed him, lied to him, lied to them all, for so long. When he looked at her, it was like seeing someone different, a stranger. Someone cruel, and cunning. The feeling made him think his chest would crack open and all his sap would drain out.

He walked to the edge of the garden and looked down the cliffs at the water splashing against the rocks, at the little tufts of white across the surface of the sea, and at the frothy line along the edge of the reef to the north. He was about to head out into those waters, away from this island, the only island he'd ever known, his entire world. It didn't feel real.

Off to the southwest, he could see a Pradishar cata'rin, just like the one he'd spotted a month earlier—the very same one in fact—racing toward P'anorum, coming for him, coming to take him away.

"The ship is incoming," he said.

Grizmond joined him at the edge. "You about ready?" he growled.

"I guess so." Fin sighed and went to turn back when something caught his eye, up along the reef. He could see several dozen brown and gray shapes just to the south of the breakers, and many more amidst the scattered chunks of coral that made up the barrier. Beyond it, in the distant waters of the Swirling Sea, a mass of objects were splashing the water.

"Seastallions on the move," Fin said, pointing to the northwest. "A massive herd."

Grizmond followed his gaze, squinting. Then his eyes widened and he hissed.

"Bhea!" he screamed, and she came scrambling up the steps from her grotto, wiping her hands on her robe, looking around in a panic. When she looked out to sea, she too gave a loud hiss.

"Not seastallions," Grizmond said. "Bhizini ships. Heading here, no doubt."

Bhea looked to the south at the approaching cata'rin, then back at the Bhizini fleet. "Might be we'll beat 'em to the harbor. I gotta seal up the grotto, then we can get out of here."

Fin looked around the garden while they waited for her return, and he remembered that he might never visit this place again, this beloved strip of land he'd spent so much of his life on, and he was weeping before he realized what was happening.

What was he thinking? He couldn't leave P'anorum—couldn't abandon Bhea, his home. And where had Baboo gone to? He couldn't leave without saying goodbye. No, he'd stay.

But when Bhea returned, he wiped his eyes, gulped down his sobs, and said nothing. She was carrying a bundle wrapped in a blanket, slung over her shoulder. "Let's go," she said, and he followed, Grizmond coming up behind him.

"Baboo, where are you?" he called, but his friend didn't show. And Fin blinked back the tears as he left the garden.

The three of them marched toward the village in silence, over the Ka'Hala and through the dark shadows of the Swarthen Forest. Bhea took the lead while Grizmond followed, his sword unsheathed. Fin felt like he was sleepwalking, his vision a bit blurry from crying, and with each step, he wondered if he'd made a terrible mistake. But his legs kept moving, onward through the forest, then up the ridge along the back of the crater. When Bhea reached the edge, she put up her hand for them to stop, and she was scowling and hissing, and Fin and Grizmond both ran to see what she'd seen down below.

The opening of the harbor came into view first, just as a sleek gray and purple cata'rin drifted through the gap between the walls of the crater, the ship that would carry him away from P'anorum for the first time in his life. But as his view expanded across the water toward the beach as he came over the summit of the rim, he saw more gray and purple ships, a half dozen of them, anchored just offshore. The villagers were amassed on the sand by the pier, and there were others too, a few hundred at least, positioned around the beach.

"Cul'tavin peacekeepers," Grizmond said, whispering a curse.

The wind carried up the sounds of angry voices, and cries of anguish, and Fin shrank back from the edge.

Bhea shook her head, her lips pressed together, her eyes narrowed.

"I don't understand," Fin said. "Why are they here? What's going on?"

But Bhea had pulled out her enflamer and was pointing it down the stairs, where the path turned sharply and cut back into the foliage. A purple and gray robe emerged, and when the figure turned to face them, Fin saw Aar'ryn Ruu'n, looking startled and then pleased and then nervous. He stared at the enflamer.

"I was just coming to find you," Ruu'n said, putting his hands together as if praying. "Fin'roq, my friend, you've come. You'll join us, then? I'd so hoped you would."

"What're you playing at, priestin?" Bhea said, indicating the harbor below with her head. "Thought Fin'roq had a choice?"

Ruu'n looked down at the beach below. "I didn't want this," he said. "But the Cul'tavin—they've affixed the villagers with restraining crystals. For their safety."

Bhea snorted. "What else have you not been telling me, priestin?"

"You know I had nothing to do with this."

Fin felt himself starting to panic, hot tears threatening to spill from his eyes. He clenched his teeth. "Stop, both of you. Just stop."

Bhea and Ruu'n looked at him, saying nothing, and Fin sighed. "Does the offer stand or not?"

Aar'ryn Ruu'n's eyes brightened while Bhea's fell.

"Of course it stands," he said, starting to smile. "Fin'roq, my friend, these Cul'tavin are your future comrades. They've come to make sure the villagers never hurt you again. And they'll keep you safe until you've reached Balan Su and we get you enrolled in the Pruu'patch. Everything is ready, if you're still ready."

He looked at Bhea but she wouldn't look at him. Grizmond just stared at Ruu'n, still holding his sword at the ready.

"I'm ready," Fin said, hardly believing the words had come out.

"Then allow me to escort you to the ship," Ruu'n said.

Fin nodded. "Just give me a minute."

"Of course. I'll meet you at the bottom of the stair." Ruu'n glanced at Bhea and Grizmond, but he started down the steps without saying anything else.

"I guess this is it," Fin said. He turned to Bhea. Tears were running down her face. She wrapped him in a hug, and his anger with her was momentarily forgotten. He took a long deep draw of her scent, and he wept into her robe. Neither said goodbye, as neither wanted to, and his throat was too tight to speak.

When he turned to Grizmond, the old Raccorin actually dropped to his knees and bowed his head, and he grabbed Fin's hand and squeezed it, but refused to look at him. Fin didn't know what to say, so he squeezed his hand too. When he started down the steps, he didn't turn back.

Aar'ryn Ruu'n was waiting for Fin at the bottom of the steps, on the landing where the pathway met the sand, and Fin stepped out of the thick foliage and looked up the beach, a sudden surge of panic rising up in his chest when he saw the Cul'tavin up close. Some part of him knew it was a trap, had been a trap all along, and he knew the peacekeepers would move on him as soon as they saw him. But as he followed Ruu'n up the beach and through clusters of Cul'tavin, none of them appeared intent on stopping him, and most didn't even look at him as he passed.

Fin'roq saw the villagers up ahead, a small cluster of eight figures standing in a line, where the pier met the beach. They looked like statues, completely still.

The incoming Pradishar ship had docked and it lowered a gangplank onto the end of the pier. A large Verdillion in long purple and gray robes stepped out and started for the beach. Fin'roq watched the stranger approaching, and when he saw the speckled pattern of bright and dull greens on the peacekeeper's face—a Bhizini face—his panic broke. His despair, too.

So it's true, he thought. *It's really true.*

The Bhizini raised a hand in greeting, even flashed a smile, and Fin thought it was a genuine one. A beautiful one. One that said, welcome home. One that said, this could be you one day.

"Fin'roq," he said. "Roman Anthem, Cul'tavin peacekeeper, at your service. Are you ready to depart?"

"Yes, I am," he said, as loud as he could muster, but his voice was shaking.

Anthem nodded, grinning. Then he turned and, with long strides, crossed back toward the dock. Fin had to hurry to keep up with him.

"Good luck, Fin'roq," Ruu'n called after him. "Trevian go with you."

He waved to the priestin, then looked up the beach at the village, at the makeshift sharlum on the western edge, at the huts huddled together at the back of the sand, and he said goodbye forever, just in case.

When he looked back at the pier, he realized that he was going to have to pass by the villagers to reach the cata'rin. As he approached them, he saw they all had crystals on their foreheads. When they saw who he was, their faces twisted up with scowls of anger, their eyes darted around and rolled toward him, and stared with hatred and with rage and with disgust, but their bodies stayed frozen in place.

He found Milli's face, full of fear and sadness, and when he looked into her eyes, he saw disgust there too, and it felt like he'd been punched, the air knocked out of him. Milli, who had always smiled at him, always been kind to him when nobody was around. Milli, whose lips he remembered in Roe's memories, as if he had known them himself. He stopped and stared at her, his bottom lip quivering.

"Don't worry, Fin'roq, they can't harm you," Anthem said, looking back from the pier.

"What's going to happen to them?"

"They'll be taken to East'whaling for debriefing," Anthem said.

Fin nodded and turned away from Milli, the tears streaming hot down his face. He took a few steps toward the pier, into Durq and Prissica's line of sight, where they stood behind Whisk and Whenton and Milder. Prissica began to screech through clenched teeth and closed lips, a muffled shriek that would have been deafening otherwise. Durq's body began to shake, slowly at first, and then faster. His face was moving, contorting, as if something under his skin was trying to dig its way out, squirming beneath the surface. Then he too started to howl behind closed lips, and the rest of the villagers took up the chorus.

Fin could hardly stand it. He put his hands to his ears, the muffled screams filling his head, as if they were inside of it.

Anthem took his arm and Fin jumped, and the intensity of the screams dropped away.

"Let's go," he said, just as a loud horn echoed off the walls of the crater in rising and falling tones, bouncing back and forth so that it seemed to be three calls instead of one.

Across the harbor, pouring through the narrow opening, the wooden ships of the Bhizini fleet came into view. The beach exploded with a frenzy of activity. The Cul'tavin had enflamers in their hands and were lining up on the sand in formation. Anthem and Fin'roq sprinted up the plank and onto the cata'rin, and the ship lurched and began to turn about. Fin followed Anthem upstairs to the bridge, which afforded him a full view in every direction, and he realized the ship was moving farther into the harbor, toward the northwest corner, not out of it.

"We're going the wrong way!" he said, but Anthem ignored him. On the beach, Fin could see the villagers were beginning to move again, their restraints lifted, and they were looking about wildly, panicking.

The cata'rin stopped drifting and Fin'roq heard the gurgitators open wide.

"Ramming speed," Anthem said. "Over here. Brace yourself."

Once the ship began to move, it picked up speed quickly, darting south across the middle of the harbor, right toward the gap in the crater that would get them out to open ocean. Bhizini boats were still coming in, but Fin could see that they were all small, even the dolph'rins which led the assault were low and flat and wooden. He watched as the Bhizini faced down their approach with defiance, even as the cata'rin slid across their boats and crushed them.

Fin looked back at the village and saw that some of the Bhizini had reached the shore. They were fighting with the Cul'tavin, while others were running up the docks. Flames were shooting out of the other Pradishar ships in the harbor, and a few of the Bhizini boats were on fire. Before long, the village itself had been ignited, the dry, thatched huts sparking quickly, the palms along the shore like candles on a cake, even Jockimo's tavern was engulfed. The Cul'tavin and the Bhizini were cutting each other down, as more and more Bhizini swarmed ashore.

The peacekeepers were already overwhelmed.

Anthem piloted the cata'rin through the gap and into the open ocean, plowing across some of the smaller Bhizini craft that continued to sail around the western side of the island and into the harbor. Fin'roq watched the village vanish into the distance, there between the gap in the crater wall, covered in smoke and flame, all lost. The villagers, all dead. His home, destroyed. And he threw back his head and opened his mouth and he screamed at the heavens overhead, howling in anguish, and his voice was wild and feral and thunderous. The sound knocked Anthem onto his back, and the Bhizini in their ships fell to their knees, hands over their heads, weeping.

But all Fin'roq knew was pain, ancient and terrible. A pain that he knew could tear the world apart.

When he closed his mouth, the cry ended, the light shrank. He swayed back and forth, his eyes vacant. Anthem, dazed, sat up and looked around in a panic, just in time to see Fin'roq falling, head first, over the rail and into the sea.

Chapter 12

Vanishing Into Everything

THE SCREAMING STOPPED WHEN Ellex woke from sleep, as it always did. The old dream, dark and featureless, faded away again. The pain, the sensation of her every fiber stretching and straining upward, desperate for light, was now nearly forgotten. Only the face of her father remained, full of pity, hanging in the air.

"You're dead," Ellex said, closing her eyes, and when she opened them, his face had vanished.

She took a few deep breaths to calm her racing heart, and wondered again if she shouldn't tell her healer that the visions were back, that they'd never gone away in the first place, that all this time she'd needed help—Sweet Trevian, how she needed help—but the pounding in her head forced her to shake off her thoughts, and she pulled her rootpads out of the soil and took a few awkward paces around the room, reaching for the servryn with her crystamin and looking over her schedule for the day, desperate for a distraction.

As the information flowed across her mind, she started to feel like herself again.

The council meeting that Ellex had been putting off for the last week had finally been scheduled for midmorning, and she knew it would be pointless to try and delay it again. She didn't want to test Rajj's friendship, either. He'd bought her a whole week to prepare, and though she would have liked to have had Qardymion the Saltsap in chains already, she had just asked Rakk the day before to track them down.

When Ellex emerged from her quarters, Pander brought her a mug of steaming jha'ala and she took it out onto the terrace and stood at the edge. The sun had yet to rise but the sky was light in the east, and the bowl of fog filling the caldera of Balan Su, the old white stones of the city's upper rim, even the towering obsidian spire of the citadel, were all aglow with pinks and oranges. But Ellex hardly saw them. Her eyes were busy twitching as she took in a notestream.

The Bhizini were on the attack this morning, and not the ambush-and-scatter tactics they normally employed, but coordinated and sustained assaults on the Great Sea Lanes, in all four directions from the capital. The news certainly wouldn't hurt her arguments with the council today, but what was their motive? And why change up their tactics?

She found another stream, this one a particularly loud and obnoxious notestreamer, whose latest diatribe called for the cancellation of the upcoming Balancing Act, and insisted on a Corkin soldier on every corner of the capital. Ellex didn't know why she watched this crap, though she told herself it was important to know what the loudest and most awful of the opposition were thinking, even if it made her jaw hurt from all the clenched teeth and swallowed hisses.

When she found whomever had streamed the crime scene to the weavryn, whomever had broken their vows to her and to the Pradishar—she clenched her fist and imagined the pleasure she'd feel in making them regret the decision to cross her. Such images should never have been seen by the public, and only helped Qardymion's goal of terrifying her city. She'd make sure the leaker was charged with treason and executed as an example to any others who might get ideas.

After she drank her jha'ala, she went into the bathing room and began to prepare for the day. Most in her position had servants to dress them and do their hair fibers but Ellex's mother had taught her that such tasks were always better done herself. Better to be self-reliant, at least on tasks that didn't require help.

Perhaps the only good advice that tyrant ever gave me, she thought.

She pushed the memories from her mind while she carefully cleaned and scrubbed and perfumed herself, then she dressed in her finest ceremonial garb, in silken pradeshan robes of dark gray with long streaks of purple. She tied the sash of office across her shoulder and combed her hair fibers into an old style popular when she was a scamp and which she always thought looked regal and serious. Finally, she applied a little bit of oil to her skin, right under her eyes, which made her look not quite so exhausted. Ellex knew the power of an outfit, the power of presentation, and as she reviewed her dress in the mirror, she nodded, satisfied that her look said, "Serious, strong, faithful, no nonsense."

The sun had risen and the orange and pink sky had given way to a bright white glare, nearly blinding off the fog bank, which sat thick and heavy in the caldera of the city when Ellex emerged from her estate and headed for the Pradishar citadel. When she left her upscale Sunrise Ridge neighborhood, she headed left, down to the edge of the rim, and followed the broad overhanging pathway that skirted the edge of Old Stones and led right to Grand Plaza in front of the citadel. The Weeping Wilvryn's long canopy of ropy branches still sparkled with dew.

Once through the walls, she relaxed a bit. The great obsidian spire loomed overhead, the garden forests of Corda'mere were moist and delicious in the air, and Ellex felt the awe and reverence she always felt when she entered this hallowed space. She remembered the first time she'd visited the citadel, and how wondrous it seemed, so special, so different from the sacred spaces where she'd worshipped in Andrasia. And that obsidian spire, wavy and contorted yet smooth and elegant, a frozen eruption pouring forth out of the white crescent city, like something magical and awe-inspiring.

Ellex had a small office next to the Solarium, where the Council of Nine met, and she sat down to work, pouring over books and scrolls and absorbing datamins, all the while preparing her notes on the servryn. She took a moment to look at the docket of one of her peacekeepers whom the Bhizini had butchered. She studied the facts of their life—the images, their remaining family members, all the tiny details that the Pradishar had meticulously gathered over their lifetime.

She had known all of them who had died, though not as well as she would have liked—it was in fact impossible to maintain a relationship with the tens of thousands of Cul'tavin under her charge—but she owed it to them, to their families and their friends and their memories, not to let this brutal act go unpunished.

There was just so little precedent for this. Bhizini raiders had always harassed Balance, but the attack on her peacekeepers, the brutality of their murder, was new terrain. Ellex took a moment to empathize with the notestreamers and the public, to recognize that their fears weren't without some merit, and that what they were saying in their panic didn't speak to their true character, at least not all of them. She recognized that her citizens lived a really sheltered life, a safe and secure life, and that they did so thanks to the power of her government and it's long reign of peace and prosperity. If everyone acted like such butchery was normal, just no big deal, just another blurb on the notestreams, then she really would be failing as a leader.

No wonder PropSector can't keep this under wraps, she thought. *Nobody has seen such horrors, not in many thousands of years.*

Damnit, she had to find that leaker.

And Rakk had to find the Saltsap.

<<Utte,>> she said, reaching out with the crystal. She could sense her brother was nearby, in the citadel somewhere.

<<Whoa,>> Uthyr said. <<I was just on the verge of contacting you. Funny how that works. Do you think our crystals were communicating without us knowing, giving us

both the urge to contact one another in order to make sense of the fact that they already were?>>

<<What?>> Ellex said, flooding her brother's mind with her confusion and frustration.

<<Just thinking aloud. Are you in the citadel?>>

<<In my office. I want an update on the leaker.>>

<<That's why I was reaching out! Get down here. I think I've found them.>>

<<You think, or you have?>>

<<Just get down here!>>

Ellex was already on her way out the door.

Maquina whined in Ellex's ears as the lift dropped down through the rock of Balan Su, down into the bowels of the citadel, to the wet, dark, pestilent dungeon known as the Dankburn. Few who went into the Dankburn ever came back out.

Her brother's office was surprisingly bright and warm with the light of a half-dozen glowbes, the furniture gaudy and old-fashioned, a thick rug spread across the floor in front of a massive oak desk, a chair wrapped in velvet—everything out of time, as if the whole scene had been taken from the early years of Balance and placed here in the year 9999.

"What do you have for me?" she said without greeting.

Uthyr had a half-eaten bun in his hand, and he swallowed before speaking, gesturing at a chair, but Ellex just stood and stared at him, eyebrows raised, foot starting to tap.

"That was fast. Did you sprint to the lift?"

"You're damn right, now what have you got?"

"To tell you the truth, I'm not sure. Have a seat will you?"

She hissed softly and sat down, crossing her arms and glaring at her brother.

"Notice anything strange?" he said, and his eyes twitched.

Ellex saw the crime scene through someone's eyes—a Me'dicant healer. An Andrasian male, fifteen years with the Pradishar. Docket full of praise. He'd spent about three hours at the scene, and Ellex scanned through the visual data several times in a few seconds, but none of it matched the sequence that had been leaked to the weavryn.

"I don't," she said. "Care to enlighten me?"

<<Here,>> Uthyr said in her mind, showing her a several minute long stretch where the healer seemed to be looking for something amongst the medical supplies. Finally finding it, he turned to one of the other healers and began to assist them. <<Look closely. See anything strange?>>

"Yeah," she said aloud, "he's checked the same spot for supplies at least four times now. Wait—he's checked every time in exactly the same way. It's a loop!"

"And nearly seamless."

"How'd you find it?"

"I narrowed down the potential leaker to three who had been at the scene, based on the angles of streaming and the time it had to have occurred. Then I scanned the suspects, pulling in the entire morning, and going over it moment by moment. I might not have noticed anything was amiss with that scene in particular, except that the motion of the healer's head, the way it swooped in a large circle to one side and then back in a large circle to the other—it made the symbol of infinity."

"I'm impressed," Ellex said.

"A rare thing," Uthyr said, looking pleased.

"I want to see him," she said.

"I thought you would."

When they got to the cell, she found the healer perched in the middle of the floor, a tiny slit in the damp stone wall letting a single shaft of light into the room.

"Are you Rhuzan Rhyndimar?" she asked.

"I was," the healer said. He laughed as a few tears fell. "But I'm nobody now."

"Why's that?" Ellex asked.

"Because nobody comes out of the Dankburn."

"Why'd you do it?" she said. "We're your family. We've taken care of you, taught you, clothed you, fed you, given you purpose in life. You took an oath, and you've lived by that oath for so many years. And with honor. What changed?"

Rhuzan smiled through his tears, which ran freely now down his bright green cheeks and dripped off his chin to the greasy stone floor, but he said nothing.

Ellex lunged with her mind, grasping for his crystal, planning to thrust herself into his thoughts and to tear his memories out, one by one, til she found the answers she sought. Even if it damaged him—even if it shredded his mind.

But he wasn't there.

She widened her senses, confused. But no Rhuzan. She looked at his face, at the purple and gray crystamin glistening like an eyeball on his forehead, but couldn't sense it with her own. Uncomprehending, she reached again and again, but it was as if the cell were empty—as if someone un-Joined stood before her.

"He's taken bhiza," she said. "Numbed his crystal."

"No," Uthyr said. "He's clean. And I've had him in lockdown for two days, so it would have faded by now."

"Two days? And you're just telling me?!"

"He submitted to the original scan, so I didn't know anything was amiss. And you told me to contact you when I had answers. I just found the loop in his memories this morning, right before I reached out to you. My hand to Trevian. Scan me if you'd like."

Ellex turned back to Rhuzan, who had closed his eyes and stood in the beam of light, breathing slowly.

"You know the penalty for leaking classified information," she said.

Rhuzan opened his eyes and stared calmly at Ellex. "You can't touch me," he said. "I'm safe in here." He touched his temple, then spoke directly in her mind. <<And what of you, Sui Pradesh? Do you know what happened to you on P'anorum?>>

P'anorum.

Ellex winced at the word, her head throbbing. Rhuzan's voice had seemed to come from nowhere, from nothingness, without a path to travel, without a connection across the weavryn or directly between crystamins. She looked at Rhuzan, and he was grinning.

She ignored the approaching migraine and turned to her brother, feeling for him with her crystal, using his presence to anchor herself. Then she stared into Rhuzan's smirking face and narrowed her eyes.

"Have you tried a restraining crystal?" she asked Uthyr without looking away. "Perhaps he'd be unable to block us if his crystamin were imperialized. In the meantime, he won't be sharing anything else with anyone else but us."

Ellex slid her hand down to her ankle and pulled out a small dagger she kept hidden there, a Bhizini scytherin. She held up the blade. Rhuzan's eyes had barely begun to widen, his wry smile to fade, when she flicked it across his forehead, the tip of the scytherin passing over the face of his crystal, which shattered beneath it.

Rhuzan's knees buckled under him, and he reached for his forehead, screeching at the top of his lungs, thrashing about on the ground as if he were on fire, as the crystal filaments throughout his body shattered and the crushed remnants were pumped through his muscles.

Ellex looked at Uthyr, her lips pressed tightly together, her pale green face a sickly gray in the low light of the Dankburn.

<<What the hell is going on, Utte?>> she said in his mind. <<Nobody can just shut off their crystal and vanish from our senses like that. It's not possible!>>

He said nothing, but she could feel his panic too, the same panic she felt.

Damnit, and only a few hours til the council meeting.

All her prep work, all the arguments she'd planned to bring up, were beginning to pale in comparison to what she'd just seen.

She grabbed her brother's arm.

<<Tell me we're the only ones who've witnessed this? None of your scanners are nearby watching in the shadows? I think I'd sense them, but—>>

<<There's nobody here but us.>>

<<This can't get out until we know more. Surely there's a logical explanation for this. There *must* be. Some sort of slow-release bhiza intoxication? Me'dicant healers are always brewing tinctures and experimenting on themselves.>>

<<Let's not jump to conclusions,>> Uthyr said, <<but I agree that nobody else should know.>> He looked at Rhuzan still writhing and moaning on the floor. <<I just doubt Rhuzan learned how to do this himself. So who's helping him, and how many are involved?>>

<<It's one thing after another, it seems,>> Ellex said. <<I'll have to leave the restraining crystal to you. Let me know if he still resists. I've got to get upstairs and finish my prep work for the council meeting. And you could use a bath.>>

<<Have I ever showed up in council looking like I'd just strolled out of the torture chamber, mother?>> he said.

She gave him a side-eyed glare as she walked back to the lift, the sound of Rhuzan's whimpering fading into the heavy silence of the Dankburn.

⁂

Ellex spent the rest of the morning dreading the council meeting, her mind searching for answers about what had happened in the dungeon, and questioning her own plans for the city's response to the Bhizini attack on her troops.

When midday approached, she took a few bites of a rhupan bun that Pander had stuck in her bag that morning, knowing she should eat something before the meeting started, but she wasn't hungry. She forced down a few bites, and then very nearly choked when Pander touched her mind, a sharp poking rather than the soft tapping he usually used. She could feel his excitement through the crystal and knew it must be good news.

She exhaled sharply and opened her awareness to him.

<<They have him, Sui Pradesh. Prince Rhakksees. They have the Saltsap!>>

<<Tell me everything!>> she said, as calmly as she could manage.

<<I'm afraid there's little to report.>> She could almost hear Pander squeaking with nervousness. <<Q'orin Grievenson tells me they have Qardymion bound, but they are not yet held in irons. And—well, it seems the Bhizini are in pursuit of the prince and his captive as we speak.>>

<<If Rakk has them, Rakk won't lose them,>> she said, hoping that was true. <<Any visuals? Anything I can share as proof the Saltsap's in custody? Something to boost morale?>>

<<I'm afraid not. You could try contacting Prince Rhakksees directly. He may be willing to share—>>

<<Keep me informed the instant you hear anything,>> she cut him off. <<But a little softer on the approach next time?>>

Ellex could feel his embarrassment as she severed the connection. She left the bun unfinished, went to the wash room to freshen up, then headed back by her office and down the corridor to the Solarium, refusing to celebrate just yet, even though her heart felt full to bursting.

Not until that monster is marching through my city in chains, she thought. *Then I'll celebrate.*

The Solarium was surprisingly small for being the center of the world government, as the public was not allowed to enter, nor were any notestreamers, so the space was built only for those who needed to be there. That meant only the eight members of the Council of Nine and the nine members of the advisory board were allowed to attend, along with a single Octa'vin acolyte who served as record keeper and ballot box and streamed the meeting to a private servryn accessible only by the members of the Council of Nine.

The room was arranged into two sides with two levels. On the upper level, a half-circle table for the Andrasian delegation on one side, a half-circle table for the Raccorin delegation on the other side, and in between, a large vacant seat flanked by two smaller ones, the largest held symbolically by the Gran Pradesh, the ninth member of the Council, who appeared only as a tie-breaker when needed. On the lower level, between the two sides, was a round table where the nine advisors sat in a half circle. And above them all, in a small alcove, sat the Octa'vin record keeper, silent, shrouded, watching and listening, largely ignored, their presence forgotten.

Next to the vacant throne of the Gran Pradesh, a bit lower on either side, were the raised seats for the heads of the delegations, and Ellex took her place there. On the Raccorin side, Rajj was already seated, and Ellex smiled at him and he returned the smile. Down below, the advisory board members were all in place. Uthyr entered with the head of intelligence for Raccorum Rhazzat, and the two heads of homeland affairs followed and took their respective seats. The two representatives for the Dyna'arin were the last to enter, and once seated, Ellex looked at Rajj and they stood together.

As she looked around the chamber, she pulled up the scene at the warehouse in her mind, and she saw that the re-creation of this room for that sick display was surprisingly accurate. She looked at the faces of her fellow council-members, at those on the advisory board, at their skin—at the lovely pale green of her Andrasian compatriots, and at the bright, exuberant hue of the Raccorin—and when she thought of the mottled disaster that was Bhizini skin, at those sick half-breeds mocking this holy chamber, her bottom lip quivered with rage.

"Thank you all for your patience," Rajj said. "My fellow Sui Pradesh and I both thought it unwise to rush into any kind of decision making, fearing that panic would prevail over reason, and that one needed time to gather facts and take inventory of the situation before offering solutions."

Ellex looked for Malisha Andra'asnia down among the advisors, but she had sent a double. Of course she had. She spent practically the entire legislative term on Andramere, only deigning to appear herself a few times each year. Ellex knew her power base was on Andramere, where she oversaw the largest group of Cul'tavin peacekeepers on the island, and where she had the ear, and the pocketbook, of its ruler, high doge Amalia von Andron. And she had achieved some success in Balance Authority as well, as the advisor for the Culture Bureau was no small position. Malisha had done her best to expand and strengthen her responsibilities as well as her hold over them. Ellex admired her ambition, she really did, but failed to see her as anything more than another overly zealous, power hungry bureaucrat, misunderstanding that what it takes to rule has nothing to do with administrative or technical capacity, or the coercive power one can achieve in such a position, but with one's nature. You had it, or you didn't. And as far as Ellex was concerned, Malisha didn't.

And yet Malisha had presumed to publicly accuse the Ren'fallow of the attack on Ellex's troops rather than the Bhizini, a move that Ellex found alarming, not because Malisha thought it was true—conspiracy nuts had been foreseeing the end of Balance since it was founded—but because it opened the door to public frenzy. By sowing distrust of the government, by suggesting that shadowy agents are moving about behind the scenes working against the common good, everyone becomes a suspect, while the real villains are allowed to continue their work. Ellex didn't think this was Malisha's intention, only that she was naive to the consequences of her actions.

Rajj summarized the events leading up to the attack, the evidence gathered in the last week, the answers they'd obtained and the questions that still remained, and Ellex watched him speak, listened to him carefully laying out the facts, drawing on all the resources she'd added to the servryn as well as information he'd gathered on his own. He was a calm and collected problem-solver, and Ellex was grateful that they'd been able to rule Balance together for all these years. She didn't know if she would have been able to do it without him, and she needed to let him know how much that mattered to her.

When he finished, Rajj turned to Ellex and nodded.

"Thank you, Prince Rajesh'n," she said. "I know that what you've all heard here today, and what you've seen over the last week, is truly shocking. Many of us feel like things are no longer what they seem, and that perhaps the long-held assumptions about the power of this alliance are also suspect. If Balan Su isn't safe, then nowhere is safe.

"We asked for some time to prepare our response. I know there are some, not least in this chamber, who disagreed with that decision. I want to thank the Culture Bureau and their allies in PropSector for their remarkable coverage of his holiness the Gran Pradesh and his unprecedented speech to our citizens. This helped assuage the fears of the public and gave us time for due diligence."

The double for Malisha Andra'asnia stood, in that stiff and awkward way that doubles moved, and Ellex could see the vacant, waxy eyes staring lifelessly ahead. The double opened it's mouth and a voice that sounded vaguely like Malisha's came out. "Sui Pradesh honors me," it said.

"Indeed," Ellex said. "I call for the Council to commend the culture minister."

She looked at Rajj, at the Raccorin delegation, and at her own Andrasian delegation. "Shall we?"

The votes were sent by crystal to the Octa'vin above, who received and tallied them.

"Yea," he announced in a dull monotone.

"Congratulations on your service," she said to Malisha's double. "And now I call for the Council to censure the culture minister."

Ellex wished she could have seen Malisha's face.

"On what grounds?" said Trip Anders, the representative for the Dyna'arin on the Andrasian delegation.

"For rumormongering."

The advisory board, even the members of the Council itself, began to whisper to one another, and Ellex put her hand down flat and hard against the table.

The room fell silent.

"In the midst of a tragedy, and in the face of the most severe leak of Pradishar intelligence in known history, the culture minister spread unsubstantiated rumors rather than following the protocol of waiting for the intelligence commission on this council to issue a proclamation."

"And your defense?" Trip Anders said, looking at Malisha's double.

"Sui Pradesh has erred in her understanding of several words," Malisha said. "Two to be exact. 'Unsubstantiated rumors.' Rather, 'accepted facts' would be more precise. The intelligence commission's annual report on threats to Balance Authority lists the Ren'fallow as, and I quote, 'a continual threat to the long-term stability of Balance's institutions.'"

Ellex had the report in her mind, scanned it, and gave Malisha's double a thin smile. "The report also states, and I'll quote, 'the Ren'fallow remain more of an idea than any kind of coherent entity, a catchall for anyone or any group who intends to challenge the Accords of Balance. Having endured for millennia, there is little chance the Ren'fallow as an idea will ever be entirely wiped out, though it will remain a continual threat to the long-term stability of Balance's institutions.'" She glared at Malisha's double. "Context, minister."

"Surely you can see—" the double began, but Rajj tapped his desk and the chamber fell silent.

"We'll have the vote," he said.

"Yea," the Octa'vin droned.

Ellex suppressed a smiled.

"Let the record show the culture minister has been censured for rumor-mongering," Rajj said.

"I apologize to the Council of Nine, and to the Pradishar, and to Balance Authority," Malisha's double said, it's waxy eyes staring at Ellex. "My intent was never to undermine anyone's authority. I hereby petition the Council that I might enter into record the very statement I made to the notestreamers, and put my full confidence behind it, that the Culture Bureau communicates the sincerest concern about the Ren'fallow conspiracy and the threat it poses to our way of life."

"What evidence do you present?" Uthyr said.

"The evidence that you presented," Malisha's double said. "The very same evidence. You said yourself that the leaker of the crime scene had stripped the metadata from the stream before sharing it. Not only that, they'd muffled voices, distorted faces, seemed to warp the passing of time. Only a member of the Pradishar could have leaked that information, and if you still haven't found their identity, it's because there are conspirators on the weavryn that are so many steps ahead of us, so many steps ahead of this government, that we can hardly be said to be in the race. So I ask this council, I beg them, to tell me what is being done to find the conspirator Anorian Grain."

"Surely you aren't suggesting that Qardymion the Saltsap isn't our priority?" Rajj said. "You think someone who can erase metadata is responsible for butchering Cul'tavin?"

"Of course not," Malisha's double said. "Qardymion is a brutal savage, there's no doubt about it. If they weren't the one who killed the peacekeepers, they would have done so if they'd had the chance. And if they did, they couldn't have done it without help. The leak only confirms that there are those in the Pradishar who don't serve the ends of the Pradishar. And from what I've seen of what Anorian Grain can do—we need to take this seriously."

Cort Andramon, Balan Su's manager and a member of the advisory board, stood up. "I hate to cut in like this, and with respect to the culture minister, but I have a city full of Verdillions who are afraid to go out of their houses, who look over their shoulders with fear, who see Cul'tavin peacekeepers who are their family and friends and neighbors, and they wonder if they won't be the next to be butchered. I beg this council to address our city, not with platitudes but with plans. How are you going to keep us safe from the Saltsap, now that we know they can hit us inside our city? We need guidance, and we need it now."

"Here, here," Rameen Rutar, the Guild representative for the Raccorin delegation and head manager of the Dyna'arin, said, standing to his feet, his giant gut sagging out over the table, his bright, wide jowls shaking as he looked around. "My Dyna'arin are under constant threat from these savages, and as you all probably know, the snakes are hitting a half dozen points on the Lanes as we speak. This isn't on the notestreams yet, but I'll share it here for the first time, that they've sunk a passenger ferry near Princip'asia. Travel has been down the last week after the attack, so thank Trevian the ship wasn't full, but there were still several hundred aboard."

There were murmurs of horror amongst the council-members.

"I may have a silver lining to your bad news," Ellex said. "The Bhizini assaults are a deliberate diversion, meant to draw our forces away from the eastern flank of the Sargassian Sink, where I can report here for the first time that Prince Rhakksees Raccorine Deri the Third has captured Qardymion the Saltsap and they are en route to Pradishar custody. We're only waiting to hear they've been clad with iron before making the announcement public."

"Truly, he's done it?" Rajj said, looking dubious.

Ellex gave him a look.

"This news shouldn't wait," Cort Andramon said. "Let the city know the threat has passed! Let's us make the announcement now, and declare a celebration in the capital, if not all of Balance Territories!"

"Now is *not* the time to let down our guard," Malisha's double said. "Right now, we have a rapt public, scared yes but also attentive, eager to do what is necessary to face this threat. If you relieve that tension, you'll miss the opportunity that such a situation affords us. Besides, cutting off the head of the snake doesn't mean it's body won't continue to thrash about, to wrap around and strangle whatever it encounters. If anything, we should press forward by making sure a similar situation never happens again, and we do that by allowing the Cul'tavin to have stronger methods of investigation and more secure tethering of peacekeepers with their superiors. Had these troops been thoroughly looked after, their disappearance would have been noticed long before they'd been cut apart and sewn back together, don't you think?"

Ellex stared at Malisha's double, her mouth open, shocked at the presumption.

"Is the minister suggesting we use imperial crystals on our peacekeepers—pull them around like puppets on a string—turn our Cul'tavin into nothing more than a depraved slave army like the damnable Corkin?" Ellex sputtered.

"Those are your words, not mine, Sui Pradesh," Malisha's double said. "I'm merely suggesting that more oversight of our peacekeepers, and greater investigative authority for public crystamins, is in order, to make sure something like this never happens again. I already have PropSector prepared to sell the idea."

"Citizens of Balance are not the threat," Ellex said, "and snatching away the privacy of our people when they've done nothing to deserve our mistrust is against the Pradishar ethic of honorable service. Until you show me a Ren'fallow conspiracy that involves a significant chunk of our people, the Andrasian delegation will stand against any alteration to the current investigative regimen. Must we vote?"

"The Raccorin delegation concurs. No vote needed," Rajj said.

Malisha's double took a seat and never stood nor spoke again for the remainder of the meeting, and Ellex wondered if she was even listening anymore. The Council approved Cort Andramon's request unanimously, and a jubilee was declared. The citizens of Balan Su poured onto the streets to celebrate the capture of Qardymion, and Ellex could only pray that Rakk wouldn't let her down.

Things were suddenly looking up, and better than she ever could have hoped. What a difference a moment could make—how one bit of information could turn everything around.

❧◈◈◈◈◈ ◈◈◈◈◈❧

That night, when Ellex finally returned to her upper rim garden, it was late. She washed up in the bathing room, then went into the cookery and steamed herself some jha'ala. She took the mug to the verandah and sat on a lounger, carefully sipping while she looked up at the stars. Then she went into her sleeping quarters and was soon rooted in her patch. It was nearly midnight.

Once asleep, Ellex dreamed, but it wasn't the old dream this time.

She was somewhere she didn't know but thought she should know. Raccorin architecture—flame-colored burnstone walls, figurines of Verdimers in the alcoves. The whine was there—that high-pitched whirring of maquina, an insect buzzing in her ear. It wouldn't go away, even as she paced the corridors. One after another, hallway after hallway, they all looked the same to her, and she realized she was hopelessly lost.

So she started peeking in doors.

In one room, there was a small Bhizini, one she didn't recognize, looking at her. Others stood nearby, staring as well. She looked past the crowd and saw a maquina she'd never seen before—was that where the whine came from? It looked familiar, some sort of compartment with a door, a small window in the middle, glowing. Ellex wanted to go and look inside but she couldn't. She just knew whatever was in there was too awful to look at. But finally she got the courage and she approached the maquina, peered through the window, and saw a small Bhizini, just a scamp, in deep stasis, various tubes and small maquina with vines attached to its body. Filled with terror, and a sadness that felt like it would swallow her up, she ran out of the room and slammed the door behind her, and when she turned back, the door was gone. Only a wall remained.

She checked the next door down. Room after room after room, she looked for an exit, for an escape. Each room was filled with people and places she didn't know. Someone was crying over a body as someone watched. A tree, gnarled and twisted, its bark the color of scabs and bruises, and right in its middle, a withered flower growing into a fruit. A grove of old Verdillions, long since planted, one by one bursting into flames, til the room was an inferno.

The hallway ran out of doors save for one at its end, and Ellex ran for it. Once through the threshold, she recognized the throne room of King Rhakksees II, who sat looking down upon everyone from his burnstone perch. Below stood a long line of Raccorin, slowly shuffling toward the king, a scattering of headless corpses and severed heads growing at the king's feet. There was a group in shadow, watching—and someone with a sword, hacking. It was too awful to watch, but she had to, even wanted to. The blade fell again, and for a moment, it was her hand holding it. She strained to see—she wanted to take in every detail, certain it was important, but everything had fallen into shadow, blurry. Nothing was clear but King Rhakksees's face. And the delight on it was unmistakeable.

Now she couldn't look away from the king's gaze, as his broad, intimidating, even curiously handsome face seemed to grow larger and larger, to fill everything in front of her. The whine of maquina grew louder and louder. There was laughter. She looked around and saw her father.

Papa! she cried, but he was laughing. She looked down and saw that she was naked. She was naked and everyone was standing around watching her. She could see her whole self for a moment, as if she were out of her own body, but the sharp sensation of pain pulled her back. The room was shaking. The king was pressing against her, into her flower. Someone at her side took her hand. The maquina whirred and whined, and Ellex screamed, sure her entire body was being ripped in two.

She woke still screaming, sitting up from the lounger on the verandah where she'd fallen asleep, confused about where she was, the images and sounds of the dream still in her senses. Hadn't she gone to her quarters?

It was just a dream, she told herself. *Just a dream.*

<<I'll be right there,>> Uthyr said in her mind, and she shouted in surprise.

<<What? Why?>> She could feel that he was panicking, and so she didn't persist, and waited til he arrived, bracing herself for some terrible news, while the dream replayed itself in her mind.

"If the Saltsap has escaped, I'll kill Rakk Raeder myself," she said when her brother came into the garden, out of breath.

"I got here as soon as I could. Are you okay? Are you alone?"

"I'm fine. With the jubilee, I told Pander to take the night off, so it's just me here. But why have you come? Is it the Saltsap?"

"It's not the Saltsap." He looked down at the lounger. "Were you sleeping out here?"

"I just dozed off for a few minutes."

"A few minutes? It's almost first light."

"No," Ellex said. "It was barely midnight. I sat down with some jha'ala—and then I had the most peculiar dream."

"That's why I'm here," Uthyr said, and he was blushing.

"I don't—understand. How'd you know I had a dream? Did I share it with you somehow?" She put her hand over her mouth when she thought of what the dream had contained.

"I'm afraid it's much worse," he said.

"Oh Sweet Trevian, with my entire troop?"

Uthyr shook his head. "With the entire world."

Chapter 13
The Unexpected and the Consequential

BRYN SPRANG TO HER feet from the depths of sleep, books and scrolls flying across her den as she stood, her mouth open, a scream still on her lips, sure she'd just been ripped apart. *What the hell was that?* She swore she'd drifted out of her own body, only to see that she was Ellex Andria, Sui Pradesh of the Council of Nine, getting pollinated by the king of the Raccorin.

And that Bhizini inside that maquina, Bryn thought. *Those eyes, staring at me.*

The memory made Bryn's heart race.

She was prepared to shake it all off as just a strange nightmare, head to her quarters and go back to sleep, but she found her mother and father outside her den, having just woken up screaming themselves from the exact same dream. Bryn's mind momentarily seemed to freeze up with the impossibility of it, before she dove into the weavryn for answers. The streams were going wild, with everyone voicing their confusion and terror and excitement, and a good deal of lewd remarks about the good-mother of Andrasia's flower.

And then scenes of death and devastation began to hit the streams, and Bryn was shocked at what she saw. The dream had affected everyone with a crystal, regardless of what they were doing, or even whether or not they were sleeping. The docks at Balan Su were in flames, a heavy cruiser crossing the harbor had plowed into the pier, rupturing its gurgitator and exploding. Footage from other cities showed Verdillions that had tumbled down stairs, that had been hard at work on a delicate operation only to end up overloading the dynamins when they lost consciousness. Trams had overrun their stations and crashed. Some areas of Balance Territories looked like a war zone, and Bryn wept at the death and destruction. She also knew the official order to cease all discussion of the event would go out from Balan Su any moment, so she archived as many sources as she could on the servryn while she cleaned up and put on a fresh robe, drying her eyes as she emerged.

Mama Andri'n brought a tray of rhupan cookies and mugs of steaming jha'ala to the round table in the middle of the garden where Doc Andri'n was already sitting, scrolls unraveled in front of him, his eyes busily twitching away. Bryn sat down by her father and he looked at her, surprised.

"Ah Bryndax, good. I need your expertise on an issue with the servryns."

Bryn nodded, just as the order went out from PropSector to all Joined in Balance Authority—discussion of the "incident" was strictly prohibited, on pain of seizure and interrogation by the Cul'tavin for crimes against information. She knew they'd never be able to follow through with that threat, at least not in the immediate future—everyone in Balance Territories would *only* be discussing the dream, and there wasn't enough space in the dungeons for that many people, nor Cul'tavin to arrest them.

Her and her father ignored it.

"My associates and I agree that the dream originated with Ellex Andria, but my colleagues in Balan Su assure me that they can't trace it through their servryns, nor to any particular stream in the weavryn. It seems to be a sort of non-localized phenomenon that left no trail, as if it were a one-to-one communication between crystamins and yet on a massive scale. Stranger still is that the dream went to *all* crystamins everywhere in Balance, all types, not just to the ones Ellex Andria holds—Pradishar, Balan Su, Council of Nine, and Andropolis public. Only those crystals should have been affected by a direct transfer. And yet it went everywhere, even to Corkin slaves, which makes me think it must have taken advantage of a servryn, and thus the weavryn. Thoughts?"

Bryn stopped munching on the cookie in her hand and took a moment to swallow. She always imagined she had many arms and at least three eyes—one in the real world, one in the weavryn, and one in her own mind. But no matter how well she multi-tasked, nobody could yet talk and swallow at the same time. Communicate, yes. But talk, no. And Doc Andri'n had insisted that all conversations in the home take place aloud, face to face. He'd lectured her for half an hour when she'd called to him across the garden through the crystal.

"Definitely not localized in Ellex Andria herself, no," Bryn said once she could speak. "She oversees just over thirty thousand with her Pradishar crystal, but it's an organizational one not an imperious one so she can't directly compel the actions of her peacekeepers unless invited to do so. None of her crystals are imperious, and she has spoken against imperious crystals on many occasions. And I don't see her putting such—intimate moments—out for public consumption. The Pradishar wouldn't want scenes of interracial pollination to be associated with a Sui Pradesh. And unless she's secretly a Dyna'arin tinker and I don't know about it, I doubt she could manipulate a servryn in order to create the experience we all had on her own."

"She's not a tinker," Doc Andri'n said. "And I agree that she didn't do it directly. But the Pradishar would have had access to tinkers, if they wanted to arrange something like—whatever this is."

"See, we don't even know what to call it, much less how it might be done. And who would want to share Ellex Andria's dreams with the world? They were mostly gibberish as far as I can tell. Someone wanting to embarrass her? The same ones who plotted to kill her troops and frame the Bhizini?"

"It's still too early for those answers," Doc Andri'n said. "We're in unprecedented territory here. I don't know how Balance and the Pradishar will take this. But I do know you need to lay low for awhile. No mentioning this dream on your stream."

Bryn looked at her father, eyes wide.

How does he know?

She blushed and stammered. "I—uh—"

"Honestly Bryndax, an archivist like you who is unwilling to share everything they discover? Impossible! I'm a professor, I know all about wanting to share information. I also know how dangerous that can be, and you should too."

"But we're careful. Nobody on the weavryn has ever identified us. Except for Anorian Grain. Is that how you found out?"

"No, but all the same, that's two of us who have discovered your identity. There could be others. Please Bryndax, promise me you'll follow the Pradishar mandate. Lay low, just til we see how this plays out."

"But Papa—"

Mama Andri'n came back into the garden with another tray of cookies and placed them on the table.

"I must be going soon," Doc Andri'n said. "I need to get to the lab."

"But it's hardly two in the morning," Mama Andri'n said. "And tomorrow is meant to be a holiday for the capture of the Saltsap. You're tired, and you deserve a day in the sunshine. Or at least a full night's sleep!"

"Sorry, Mama," Doc Andri'n said. "The sun's already up in Balan Su, and I'm too excited to sleep. I have work that needs doing and it can't wait."

"I can go help," Bryn said.

"Not now," he said. "You should get some sleep." He chuckled when he saw her face. "I know. Not possible. But at least try to rest. I need you at the library today, and I need you to redouble your efforts, as we discussed."

Bryn sighed and nodded. "I need another datamin for the carver."

"I'll send one over later. Your mother can take you to work after the sun rises."

"Whenever you need to go, love," Mama Andri'n said.

"No," she said.

Her parents looked at her, then at each other, unsure what to say.

"What I mean to say is, thank you Mama, for accompanying me everywhere I've needed to go. But today—" she took a deep breath. "Today, I'm going to go out by myself."

"Are you sure?" Mama Andri'n asked, tears welling up in her eyes.

"Mhh-hmm," Bryn said. "It's time. It is. I know it is."

Doc Andri'n put his hand on Bryn's. "I'm proud of you," he said.

She nodded, unable to speak.

Bryn couldn't sleep so she spent the early morning hours in her den, reorganizing the mess she made when she woke from the dream, taking the time to put her rootpads into some proper soil before she had to leave for work so her body could clear out its wastes, and to scour the data she'd archived on the servryn about the dream.

Mama Andri'n knocked at the door. "Time to go soon, Brynnie," she said. "Sun's up. Come have some breakfast before you head out."

After Bryn ate and gathered her things, her mother offered to walk her to the tram station, but she refused. "You need to take it easy and get off that leg. I'll be fine, I promise. Besides"—she touched the crystals on her forehead—"I'm never really alone anyway."

Mama Andri'n gave her a hug, then turned and shuffled back into the garden to sit down and prop her bad leg up. Bryn opened the door and stepped out into the city, her head held high, her heart pounding, terrified but ready at the same time.

She closed the door, felt the panic start to rise up, and thought she would have to turn back for her mother after all. But she focused instead on the sunlight falling on her face, on the blue sky overhead, and the terror started to fade.

❧❧❧❧❧❧ ❦❦❦❦❦

Bryn started down the grassy pathways and cobbled streets of Stone Garden for the station when she realized she didn't have to take the tram anymore. The climb up the hill had been too hard on Mama Andri'n's leg, so they'd gone the long way around, down the river instead of over the ridge. Now Bryn could walk up the hill and through the gates into Old Town, and from there it wasn't far up and over the Clear Water to the royal plateau. That would save her nearly an hour roundtrip. For a moment, it seemed foolish to her that she'd ever gone the long way around.

When Bryn reached the top of the ridge, she passed through the stone archway into the old city, there on its gentle slope down to the Bay of Bliss. The neighborhood was buzzing with activity and the plazas were brimming with Verdillions, but Bryn noticed most of them seemed concerned, spooked. Yesterday it had been festivals everywhere, a jubilee for the capture of Qardymion the Saltsap, but today nobody was celebrating. It felt more like nervous commiseration. And the sight of so many people frightened Bryn more than she expected, so she hurried up the avenue toward the bridge and stair that led to the Forum. Once over the Clear Water, with Old Town below her awash in morning sunshine, she could see several columns of smoke in the west, near the Inner Harbor, where boats on the 'Mirri had piled up during the dream and several dynamins in the industrial quarter had overloaded.

Once out of the lift and onto the royal plateau, Bryn took a moment to congratulate herself on making it there without even feeling panicky.

Well, not too panicky.

When she got to work, the old librarian Madr'gin gave her a big smile.

"Bright and early today, Bryn dear," she said. "I hope you have a wonderful day." Bryn looked at the old Andrasian's forehead, wrinkly and dull and so noticeably empty of crystals. She wondered if she'd even heard the news, and had no intention of spoiling her day.

"My father should be sending over a datamin later. Let me know when it arrives?"

"Of course I will." She winked.

Once Bryn was in her office, she set up her workstation, put a scroll in the carver, and started archiving. She really did love where she worked. She could shut the doors to the world outside and retreat into the old sanctuary. The hushed atmosphere, the soft light, the musty smell of old paper and fall foliage—it was better than the Academicon's great hall. Nothing had happened since you were last there, a timeless space, a place to relax, reflect, and grow. A temple. A garden, full of leaves.

What the sharlum of the Pradishar used to be, she thought sadly, *before the Pradishar became the government, and the holy temple became little more than a place to worship bureaucrats.*

She spent the next few hours in constant contact with Ginjy, Rhingus, and Trexbo as they poured over the evidence they had gathered so far about what was going on with the dream. And she lamented her father's decision not to take her to work with him today. She could imagine being with all the other professors, many of them Dyna'arin tinkers, in contact with top officials around the world, getting the really juicy information on what had happened.

Her and her friends were forced to sneak around the weavryn trying to glean what they could. And yet Bryn and her friends were all consummate researchers, and they had soon gathered an impressive number of sources and archived them on the servryn, and had already drawn some conclusions, even if primitive ones.

<<I've cross-referenced with the chamber from the stream of the attack under P'anorum, and while similar, the two maquina are different,>> Bryn said. <<Perhaps one is an older model and the other newer.>>

<<And what about the Bhizini scamp inside it?>> Trexbo asked. <<Looked like it was sleeping. Is this the stasis chamber the conspiracy nuts are always mentioning?>>

<<Sleeping?>> Bryn said. <<The scamp was staring right at me!>>

<<No,>> Rhingus said. <<The eyes were definitely closed.>>

<<Confirmed,>> Ginjy said.

<<Then consider this,>> Bryn said, and shared her memory of the dream scene with the Bhizini scamp to her friends.

<<No way!>> Trexbo said. <<What the fuck?>>

<<This changes everything,>> Ginjy said. <<This means there could be multiple versions of the dream out there—not one simultaneous dream, but who knows how many. Are the rest of our dreams all the same?>>

They compared one to the next and only Bryn's was different, and only that one part.

<<This needs more research,>> Bryn said. <<I'll work on it.>>

<<Are we going to stream something soon?>> Rhingus asked.

<<About that—my father made me promise not to.>>

<<Doc Andri'n isn't a part of this,>> Trexbo said. <<We have to decide on this together.>>

<<Agreed,>> Ginjy and Rhingus said. <<Let's vote.>>

Bryn was the lone opposer.

<<Damnit,>> she said, jumping when someone knocked at her office door. She opened it and her father was standing there, along with Madam Madr'gin. <<My father just showed up. I'll get back to you.>>

"I wasn't expecting you so soon," she said.

"It's already mid-afternoon, Bryndax. You've lost track of time while working."

"I thought you'd send someone over."

"I sent myself. Where's the full one?"

Bryn pulled the datamin from the carver and handed it to her father. "I'll come with you," she said.

"Not today," he said.

"Oh come on, Papa. I wanna help. I've been down there a dozen times already. I could probably install it myself."

"I don't doubt it. But not today, and that's final."

Bryn suppressed the urge to hiss, and balled up her fists instead. She waited til he had left before contacting her friends. <<We're streaming tonight.>>

<<What happened?>> Rhingus said. <<Did Doc Andri'n change his mind?>>

<<I changed my mind,>> Bryn said. <<My father's not infallible. And we have the ideals of our stream to uphold.>>

<<That our sister!>> Trexbo said.

<<I'll meet you all at the Sweet Treat after I finish up here,>> she said. <<And we'll see what we can find on the Pradishar servryns.>>

When she finished her work for the day, she headed back out of the Forum the same way she'd come that morning, back over the Clear Water and down into Old Town. When she rounded the corner into the alley that led to the Sweet Treat, she froze, overwhelmed for a moment that she was all alone. She stuck her hands in her robe and hurried along, looking down at the ground, and soon enough she was inside, with the smell of sugar and buns and hot drinks in the air, and her friends were waving to her from the line.

"I'm proud of you, lil' sis," Trexbo said. "I knew you'd do it."

<<Bryn the Brave,>> Ginjy said, and she was smiling, a truly rare sight.

"It was time," Bryn said. "That's all."

Once they had their treats and drinks, they went upstairs to their office, and Bryn, quickly and without batting an eye, began to slip streams, one after the another, until she had effectively obscured her presence in the weavryn. Then she cloaked herself in her father's credentials, which were enough to get her into the restricted part of the Pradishar servryn. From there she could get to any datamin linked to it, given enough time to look around. But she knew she shouldn't linger long. She reached out for the docket on today's events, copied the data to her own datamins on the public servryn, and then severed her link.

"Not much new to share," she said, running through the data in her mind.

"You're already in?" Trexbo said.

"And out," she said.

"Impressive, Bryndax. Damn impressive!" He stood and bowed.

"Thanks. And like I said, not much new to share. I'll look through it some more later, and you all are welcome to it. From what I can tell, they have no information on the dream being different for different people. So that's what I'm going to cover."

They each took turns going over their plans for the stream, questioning and defending their positions to one another. When they had finished, Bryn clapped her hands together.

"To work then," she said. "Double time if you can."

Now she was sounding like her father.

❧❧❧❧❧ ❦❦❦❦❦

Bryn contacted her mother to tell her she'd be late, but that she'd be home soon. And no, she didn't need an escort. Yes, she was sure.

The sun had set and the stars were twinkling by the time they shared their stream. Trexbo accompanied her to the arched gateway at the top of Old Town, asking twice if she didn't want him to walk her all the way to her garden. But Bryn insisted she was fine.

And she was. Stone Garden was one of the nicest neighborhoods in all of Andramere, even if one of the oldest areas in the city. When she turned into the grassy lane that led to her family's modest garden, she saw her father coming along from the other end of the path, returning from an extremely long day at the Academicon. But he still had a smile on his face.

"Ah Bryndax, good," he said. "I hope you had a productive afternoon at the library?"

"Mmm-hmm," she said.

"It's been an incredible day. I have much I'd like to share with you over dinner, my dear. Come, your mother is worried. It's quite late."

She sent the signal to open the door to their garden and gestured to her father. "After you, Papa."

"You were okay on your walk today?" he asked, stepping inside. Bryn followed. "I was wor—"

Bryn crashed into her father, who had suddenly stopped in front of her, and she knocked him over onto the ground and landed on top of him. A row of Cul'tavin peacekeepers appeared outside the door, and several more were already inside their garden. She struggled to get off of him.

"That worked better than I'd hoped," Malisha Andra'asnia said as she marched into their garden, her long Pradishar robes trailing behind her. "He surely won't move under that beast, even without an active restraint signal."

Bryn heard her mother scream from the cookery, and she rolled off her father and sat on the ground. There were Cul'tavin peacekeepers all around her, brandishing blades and zaprens, even a few enflamers, and Bryn froze, suddenly on the ground in the alleyway again, and she bit down on her lip so it wouldn't shake.

Doc Andri'n made no attempt to move—he couldn't. And Bryn wanted to go to his side, but she was too scared to move.

"By order of the Cul'tavin and the Culture Bureau, you are hereby seized for interrogation on suspicion of espionage, treason, and crimes against information." Malisha used her foot to flip Doc Andri'n over onto his back. He looked up at Bryn and seemed to plead with her, but when he saw Malisha Andra'asnia, his eyes narrowed and he sneered at her.

"I'm a member of the Dyna'arin," he said, "I have rights."

"Oh yes, yes. The pesky Guild. But fortunately for us, you hold a priestin crystal with the Pradishar, if I'm not mistaken—and I'm not, of course. In cases where the safety of the Pradishar is at stake, all who hold Pradishar crystamins must respect the chain of command. It's a part of your crystal, you see. And the Guild knows that. And so we'll have the information from you now."

Doc Andri'n began to thrash and whimper, his limbs alternately shaking and then relaxing, his eyes bugging out of his face, his pale green skin turning a dull gray.

Bryn cried out but couldn't bring herself to stand, to move, to help him.

Malisha turned to her. "You also hold a Pradishar crystamin," she said. "And that makes me your superior. Now silence your tongue, monkin, or we'll have your memories too."

"It's...no good," said one of Malisha's peacekeepers. "His entire day...it's blank. He's blocking us somehow."

"Impossible!" she said. "Tear it out if you must!"

Doc Andri'n screeched, a horrible sound. Bryn was sobbing, shaking, unable to move. She stared at the ground, and she started counting—counting the rocks between the step-stones, counting the time between each scream. She didn't know how long she counted. But her father had quit screaming.

"Take him to the dungeon," Malisha shouted. "A few days in the dark will loosen his resolve."

Two peacekeepers grabbed Doc Andri'n under the arms and began to drag him off, but Malisha stopped them. "Wait," she said, then turned to Bryn. "Up." But Bryn didn't move. "Up!" Bryn looked up. "Hello again." Malisha waved with two fingers. "Sweet Trevian, you really are the size of a Raccorin farknuckle player, and yet with the beautiful pale tones of an Andrasian. Fascinating. You deserve to be on one of those streams, you know the ones, where they show all kinds of freaks and half-breeds from Mon Mang'alar? Would you like that, Bryn? A special expose for our special, precious, entitled Bryn Andri'n?"

Bryn just stared at Malisha, unable to respond, her body trembling.

"We could call you the Raccorin with Andrasian skin. A most unusual Bhizini. A true half-breed. Or maybe—maybe you'd prefer to be left alone, hmm? Is that what you'd like? Your father has committed terrible crimes, Bryn. Crimes against information. You know the consequences. And they'll only be worse if you try to interfere in any way. You be good and stay out of our way, won't you?"

Malisha smirked, and Bryn watched her turn and march out of the garden, her purple and gray robe swirling as she went. She watched the two Cul'tavin peacekeepers drag her father out the door and out of sight, and Bryn could only stare after them. And when they had left, and Mama Andri'n had slumped down next to her on the grass and wrapped her in her arms, Bryn still just sat there, powerless to hug, powerless to respond.

Powerless to do anything at all.

Chapter 14

If Only the Sea Was Forever

WHEN BALANCE AUTHORITY ANNOUNCED an impromptu jubilee on the day that Qardymion the Saltsap was captured, all classes at the Academicon were cancelled, Mha'arlo was on his way back from Andramere having safely delivered the cargo to Doc Andri'n, and Rebesh'a was busy with one of her social clubs. Lithuigi had nothing to do, and so—after confirming with Rhyntysha that she could manage the stasis chamber for a few days—he went to sea.

This was partly a pleasure cruise, partly a work cruise, and partly a matter of survival. It was said a Bhizini would eventually go insane if forced to live on land for too long, that they were truly an aquatic plant, happy only if bobbing on their lilypads or rowing in their cano'rins or gliding across the open ocean on a great wooden dolph'rin. And yet of the people who lived in Balance Territories, very few could be said to really love the sea. Verdillions feared its dark depths, knowing how easy it was to slip under, to plunge down and down and down, all the way to the bottom. Since Verdillions could go for so long without air, they would be crushed by the pressure long before they drowned. But many of the stretches of sea between Andrasia and Raccorum Rhazzat that wrapped around the archipelagoes of Balance Territories were shallow. Greet reefs and atolls and other treacherous sinks were scattered across the Threshinveld and Mesh'apo'tamian Seas, and both the Stillwater and Shimmering Seas weren't very deep either, which meant that many shipwreck victims had at least an hour or more to ponder their fate on the bottom of the ocean.

But Lithuigi didn't fear the sea, nor did he think it was a gateway to a higher existence. It was something much more profound than that, which words often failed to explain. He only knew that the longer he spent in Balan Su, or tucked away in his labs on Callo Baton or on Vergis, the more neurotic he became. He'd lose himself in his work, to the point that his good hand would shake from a lack of sunlight, and he'd forget to eat or sleep or bathe. But when he'd try to relax, he couldn't—the only way to relax was to stay busy, to keep working—he'd be utterly convinced of it. Finally, he'd have a chance to go to sea again, and as soon as he saw open water around him, felt the mist on his face, tasted the salt on his lips—only then would he realize how empty he'd been before. He'd know that he'd been completely wrong about so many things, maybe everything.

He piloted the cata'rin through the narrow passage out of the harbor and into the Threshinveld, sending warm regards to the gatekeeper through the crystal. The fog was low, barely above the water's surface, and the city looked magnificent from afar. He went south past Nunan, then headed due south for an hour before trailing west. That would take him off the Great Sea Lanes and into an area where he was pretty confident he wouldn't be bothered. He spent the journey on the deck, rootpads clutching the wood, the branches of his good arm unfurled, taking in the sunshine and feeling like a real Verdillion again.

Once he reached his destination, he decided it was time to get to work—which meant having fun with his prototype gurgitator. He'd only been running it at a quarter of the output of a normal gurgitator and yet the ship had moved as fast as any other in the fleet. His goal was to raise the speed of any ship by four-fold—a revolutionary achievement if he could pull it off. And he was Lithuigi Von'nDrino, so of course he could pull it off! The real challenge would be designing a hull that could take the added strain.

He folded up his branches and pulled his rootpads out of the wood and went inside to the bridge. Rubbing his hands with excitement, he sent a signal to the gurgitator via crystamin. He opened the aperture to half capacity and had to grab on to the rail in surprise as the ship lunged ahead. Once at cruising speed, he walked along the deck and looked around, even letting out a whoop of pleasure—he'd never traveled so fast in his life and it felt absolutely exhilarating. But the cata'rin was definitely starting to skim the surface a little. Was the ship too light for so much speed?

He walked back onto the bridge and sent a signal to open the aperture to seventy-five percent of capacity. The ship sped up again, surprisingly peppy, but as it continued to gain speed, the cata'rin began to slide and then slap, slide and then slap, against the surface. And as it lurched up and then fell down, Lithuigi found himself launched toward the ceiling and then the ceiling launched toward him, and he slammed his head before crashing back down onto the deck. He landed on his prosthetic and it twisted around and tore free from his stub.

Wincing, he sent the signal to close the gurgitator and the lurching eventually stopped but the ship continued to travel at a high speed for a very long time—something that would need careful consideration before these gurgitators were in widespread use, he thought. Once he could stand, he got out his repair kit and reattached the prosthetic as best he could, then he spent an hour going over the cata'rin, looking for damage. The hull had cracked in several places but wasn't taking on any water. But if he'd gone on any longer at that speed—he'd have to work on reinforcing the hull and increasing the weight of the ship, though that would slow both acceleration and braking considerably. Just the type of problem he loved solving.

He opened the gurgitator to only five percent of capacity and gently steered the ship around, back toward Balan Su.

Nice and slow, he thought. *I want as much time out here as I can squeeze in.*

After he watched the sun set into the water and the sky fall dark, he closed the gurgitator, went to the captain's quarters, and got ready to call it a night. Once his feet were on the soil patch, he was asleep.

He woke thrashing about, trying to walk but held fast by his rootpads, screaming in pain and then awash in confusion. The strangest dream he'd ever dreamt, and he'd had some crazy ones over the years. He laughed at how absurd it was—at the notion of him getting pollinated by King Rhakksees—and was greatly amused. Then he fell back asleep.

When the sun rose, Lithuigi woke feeling great—he always felt great when he woke up on a ship. He went to the deck, surveyed the sea, and then opened the gurgitator. He steamed some jha'ala and stood sipping it while he stared across the water. The hours passed as he glided along, his mind quiet, his focus on the air, the sunshine, the sensation of motion. Up north, on the horizon, a gray smear appeared, wedged between two endless blues, like a smudge of ash, a flaw in an otherwise perfect painting—the fog of Balan Su—and Lithuigi couldn't help but feel disappointed.

He felt Mha'arlo reaching out to him through his Dyna'arin crystal. <<I'm docked in the capital, professor. Just arrived. Everything's perfect—well, with me at least. You probably haven't heard about the dream, but I have a scroll ready and waiting to fill you in when you arrive.>>

<<The dream?>> Lithuigi felt all the anxiety of his life in Balan Su scratching at his skin, wanting back inside.

<<Ellex Andria's. Surely you had it too? Everyone did.>>

<<What do you mean, son? Explain yourself.>>

<<Everyone with a crystamin had a strange dream this morning—well, its was about 5 AM in Balan Su, mid-morning in Eastwhaling and the Three Pearls, just past midnight on

Andramere. The same dream. Ellex Andria's nightmare. Are you saying you didn't have it?>>

Lithuigi's mind was spinning. <<Indeed I did,>> he said, <<but I thought it was my own.>>

<<The rumor is that she did too, til she realized she'd somehow shared it with the world. Nobody knows how it happened, so far as I can tell from the streams that are still reporting anything. Any thoughts?>>

<<Not yet,>> he said.

Sweet Trevian! he thought. *The entire world saw the inside of my lab, saw the stasis chamber—saw the prisoner!*

He risked opening the gurgitator to twenty-five percent and raced north into the fog. When he passed through the gates into the Inner Harbor, the mist was so dense he could hardly see in front of him. The harbor authorities warned Lithuigi to go slowly and to watch for debris.

Debris?

Mha'arlo was waiting for him in the Guild port when he brought in the cata'rin.

"She's taken some damage," he said. "The hull, and the integrity of the seams through-out the ship, need inspecting."

"Too much for the new gurgitator?" Mha'arlo said.

"Unfortunately, and I didn't even have the darn thing open all the way. We'll need to make some adjustments before we try it again."

"We?" Mha'arlo said.

"Sorry son, time constraints, and you weren't back yet. But I'll share all my data with you, I promise."

Mha'arlo grinned, but then his face fell. "Professor, your lab. The dream."

"I know," he said. "But I went over it again, and I don't think there was anything in it to identify us. I'm confident the project is safe."

"So far you're right," Mha'arlo said. "A message from Balance Authority went out on the public crystamins—no discussing the incident. Of course, that's all everyone is discussing, everywhere. The weavryn is lit up, there's destruction in every major city, accidents and dynamin meltdowns, trams not stopping, people having accidents or drowning. Just terrible. Some streams estimate ten thousand have died."

Lithuigi felt terribly ashamed that he'd been so worried about himself. And as much as he wanted to get to the lab, he decided he should go home first. He wanted to check on his family. And he needed to gather some information before he made an appearance at the Academicon, just in case.

Mha'arlo handed him several scrolls. "This will fill you in with what I've gathered so far," he said. "But information is still coming out fast, so there's a short shelf-life for these. I've been adding information to a datamin, but I'm not finished yet."

"I'll get right to reading," Lithuigi said.

"Welcome home, professor."

"And to you," he said, thinking he hadn't been home in a hundred years.

He headed for the upper rim—barely sticking up from the fog-bank into the sunshine—and reached his garden in Sunrise Ridge, where he found his wife Rebesh'a on the terrace, in a lounger, sipping a fizz water while her eyes twitched.

"Isn't it horrible?" she said when she saw him. "I just saw that a cata'rin carrying monkins from Angard's Pruu'patch were en route to Andramere City, but didn't manage to turn while passing through the Narrows. They plowed right into the cliffside of Mount Mun'maximo. All dead."

"Are our sons alright?" Lithuigi said. "Hesh'n's work—I know he's been using dynamins. Though I suppose you wouldn't be sitting here checking notestreams for more tragedy if our sons weren't alright."

Rebesh'a glared at him. "You could have asked Hesh'n yourself! Honestly, your communication skills are legendary in the classroom, so why is it so hard to talk to us?"

"Please not today," he said. "I don't want to fight with you, honest. I'm just happy that you're okay. I came here as soon as I got home, to check on you."

Rebesh'a didn't say anything.

"So what are these notestreamers saying about the dream?" he asked.

"Nothing at all! They're only covering some of the fallout, not the cause of the fallout. Official streams won't even use the word dream, nor have any mentioned Ellex Andria."

"And the unofficial streams?"

"What are you implying? That I disobey the law and commit crimes against information? I've never broken a law in my life."

"Oh?" he said, grinning. "And what about that time you were just a trouper on stage in Andramere, just a small-town player who'd come to the city for the chance to perform. You remember the night, the one that we ate far too many bhiza cookies and then snuck onto the roof of the sharlum to make love in the moonlight."

Rebesh'a blushed. "I've—not thought of that in a long time."

"I have. You had a small part as the great moon spirit Astra'bel, swooping down from the heavens to bless the lovers at the end of the play. And yet your small part stole the show and the hearts of the audience. I met you at the gala after the play and we spent the evening laughing and dancing. I miss those days. I miss—you."

"You hardly show it," she said. "You act like you can't stand being around me. It's you who's changed, not me."

"That's not true," he said, a pout on his lips. "I just get so wrapped up in my work. I can't think about anything else. I didn't mean to cause offense."

"It still hurts," she said.

He took her hand and kissed it, then wrapped his good arm around her and pulled her close.

Rebesh'a started to pull away. "You reek of the sea," she said.

"You used to like that," he said, pulling her in for a kiss. She squirmed away, slapped him, and then sealed it with a hiss.

"And I'm the one who's changed?" he said.

"Oh, don't act all humble now. You come in here smelling like fish, probably out meeting that Bhizini whore of yours, and then you want to be all flirty and lovey? Who do you think you are?"

"Your husband, or a damn fool, one!" Lithuigi yelled, and Rebesh'a swung to smack him but he ducked under it and scampered away.

She didn't follow him.

Damn it, I knew he should have gone to the lab first, he thought.

Or not come home at all.

⁂

After Lithuigi had washed off the sea, he grabbed his things and headed for the Academicon. He didn't see Rebesh'a when he left.

He walked around the upper rim as quickly as he could without running. Except for the lifts between levels and a single tram across the inner arc of the lower rim, Balan Su had no system of public transportation like the other major cities of Balance, mostly because of its strange geography on the crescent, trapped in a small space with nowhere to expand or grow except on top of buildings that were already there. This kept the city extremely conservative, unwilling to make any kind of major change, certain it would destroy the delicate balance of the island.

On the plus side of things, he got plenty of exercise because of it.

The jubilee for the capture of Qardymion the Saltsap meant the campus of the Academicon was largely empty of students, but the faculty hall was filled with excited professors working feverishly to understand and describe what had happened and then share it with everyone else, each one jockeying for a chance to talk and not have to listen to their colleagues. Lithuigi made some small talk, deflected their questions, and headed for his lab, through the hidden door in the back of the vault, down the stairwells and long corridors, to his other lab inside the black obsidian of the Pradishar citadel.

"You're back early," Rhyntysha said when he shut the door. "I think I know why."

"Any word?"

"No mention of it by any of the colleagues. They all think it's the stasis chamber on P'anorum, the one from Aar'ryn Ruu'n's stream."

"What about the prisoner?"

"Just fine. Body in healthy stasis. Vitals are strong."

Lithuigi looked in through the glass door at the Bhizini scamp, tubes and maquina piled on skin and connected to the device by hanging vines—this monstrous thing Lithuigi tended and which the whole Joined world had looked upon in Ellex Andria's dream.

"I fear this phase of the project will soon be over," he said. "I keep thinking the Pradishar are going to tell me to empty the chamber, to prepare it for the next subject, the next prisoner."

"The next one?" Rhyntysha said.

"I shouldn't have said anything," he said. "It's still an unsubstantiated suspicion, and therefore not something to worry about."

He looked through the glass again. "It's so strange, of all the things in the dream, the one I can't get out of my mind are the eyes—the eyes staring at me, fathomless and penetrating."

"The eyes? But they were closed in the dream, professor."

Lithuigi opened his mouth to reply, but instead checked his memories of the dream using his crystals, and indeed the eyes were open.

"I must have misremembered it," he said.

But Rhyntysha saw through his lie. "So they were right, and there are different versions of the dream," she said. "You know what this means."

"Perhaps—" but a warning bell chimed in Lithuigi's mind. Someone was calling at his upstairs lab. He reached out with his crystamin and felt Hesh'n at his door.

<<Give me a moment,>> he said to him.

<<Is this payback for making you wait the other day?>>

<<Me? Vengeful? Nonsense. Just give me a minute.>> He was already on his way up the corridors and stairs to his lab. Once the vault door was closed, he sent the signal to let Hesh'n inside. He came in smiling, and Lithuigi immediately felt something must be wrong.

"How are you, Father? Glad to see you're well after Ellex Andria's nightmare."

"Is that what it was? Isn't that still conjecture?"

"Perhaps. Regardless, I wanted—well—I came over to apologize. You were right. I want you to know, I contacted the Guild about my project. I let them know I intend to substitute bhrubean stalks for uncut spratlyns. The fibers are similar to Verdillion flesh, and I think I can make them work with a little shaping. Plus they grow faster than spratlyns, so I'll have a more regular supply to tinker with. If I wrap them around metal, it should give me the infrastructure I'm looking for."

Lithuigi exhaled. "I'm glad to hear this," he said.

"Yes," Hesh'n said, "my only problem is, the bhrubean stalks don't handle heat quite as well as spratlyn flesh."

So that's why he's playing nice.

"I'm sorry son, I know you want one of my prototypes to tinker with, but if the Pradishar ever found you with one of my them—they'd have you executed."

"Executed?" Hesh'n said. "But surely they'd want…" He paused for a moment. "What exactly is it you've made?"

"Please drop it."

Hesh'n looked at the ground, a distant look in his eyes, and Lithuigi found himself holding his breath again, suddenly nervous. If he wasn't careful, he'd lose him for sure.

"Maybe you could help me," Lithuigi said. "I had an accident in the lab—sort of. Got a bit tossed around, and when I fell, I wrenched my arm off. It's still working fine, but the seam on my stump—maybe you can have a look, see if you can't reattach it better?"

"Sure thing," Hesh'n said, grabbing some tools from the workstation. When he looked at the connection, he grimaced. "Did you put this back on yourself?"

"I was alone."

Hesh'n shook his head. "You should have left it off." He took the tools and set to work removing it, carefully disconnecting the fibers and using drops of tincture as he worked, numbing the nerve tips and slowing the sap flow. Once it was removed, he cleaned up the stump, then turned to the prosthetic. He lifted the skin-grafted lid which hid the innards of the device, then grabbed some pliers and slowly lifted out the dynamin. Lithuigi saw there was scorching on the edges of the compartment. The sheathe was so thin—there was so little room to cram one inside and still fit the dynamin—which was why so much heat was leaking. With his prototype dynamin, which was much smaller, Hesh'n would be able to thicken the sheathe and keep the prosthetic safe.

"Let us compromise, son," he said, and Hesh'n looked at him hesitantly. "I'll let you put one of my prototypes in my arm. You can observe it and tinker with it, here with me. And we can see how they do together."

"It's a deal," Hesh'n said, a wide grin on his face, and Lithuigi went into his vault to retrieve one. When he placed a full-sized dynamin casing on the workstation, Hesh'n looked at him with a blank stare.

Lithuigi held up his invention and turned it back and forth. "Behold," he said, beaming. "A normal dynamin to the untrained eye. It even functions in the space inside maquina made to hold a dynamin. And yet..." he paused and whirled his hand over the object for effect, "this one has a secret inside." The casing around the dynamin fell open on all four sides, to reveal a small cube the size of a die. Lithuigi placed it in Hesh'n's hands.

Hesh'n held the object reverently, bringing it up close to his eyes and examining it on all sides. "But how did you shrink the core?" he said.

"I didn't shrink anything. It's not from the usual source."

Hesh'n whistled, his eyes wide. "Now I understand your concern," he whispered. And then he laughed, incredulous. "Just what *are* you up to, Father?"

"I hope I can still trust you."

"That's not an answer. And of course you can. I don't give a fuck about the Pradishar and their holier-than-thou purity. I only want the freedom to tinker, and I want the freedom to use the best resources to perform my work. I think the dependence of the Guild on the Pradishar is a travesty, and this dynamin—this could free the Guild from the Pradishar entirely."

"No," Lithuigi said. "The crystals are not one, but three. And the way you're talking scares the hell out of me. Balance depends on the Guild and the Pradishar keeping each other in check, just as Balance depends on the Raccorin and the Andrasians keeping each other in check. No one group should have such power."

"That is exactly the problem—the Pradishar have too much power. This could be the start of making it equitable again."

"You forget how many in Management are fanatical followers of the Pradishar, bishrops even, and they have no intention of declaring independence. What you're suggesting would tear the Guild apart. We must always, always be cautious before we release a new technology on the world. It's nearly impossible to predict all the outcomes."

"Why didn't you think of that before you released the enflamer?" Hesh'n said. "Your little weapon changed the nature of combat overnight. And even though they started in the hands of the Pradishar and the Corkin, they were soon in the hands of some Bhizini too. We went from hand-to-hand combat to the ability to cook a Verdillion from head to foot with the press of a button."

"That is why you should listen to me," he said. "Let me be the only one to sin. Don't make my mistakes. Don't live with my regrets. And please—please—don't follow in our family's footsteps."

"Easy, Father, or you'll say too much. Enough politics for today. Let's get to work on your prosthetic. I'm dying to tinker with this little miracle of yours."

He nodded and then watched as Hesh'n spent the next few hours adapting the arm to work with a much smaller dynamin and adding a larger sheathe to absorb the heat. Lithuigi was so excited to have someone to talk to about his prototype, and the time passed quickly. When Hesh'n finished, he carefully re-attached the device to Lithuigi's shoulder. "How's it feel?"

"Like it's my arm," he said. "And a bit lighter than before. Good work."

They cleaned and stored the tools and put the lab back in order.

"How's your brother," Lithuigi asked, with a sigh.

"Power-hungry. Narcissistic. Ugly as sin. Oh, you mean with the dream?" Hesh'n grinned. "He's fine, I guess. No injuries or anything. I'm sure."

"So you haven't talked to him."

Hesh'n shook his head. "I was only thinking of my lab, and then of your lab."

"Me too, son, me too."

An alarm sounded in his head, someone at the door to the lab. He sent the signal to open it and Vilder stepped inside, taking large strides into the room, trying to make a grand entrance as he always did.

"There you are," Vilder said, looking at Hesh'n. He narrowed his eyes but didn't look at Lithuigi. "Hello, Father. I see you survived the incident."

"What a wild dream," Hesh'n said. "What do the Pradishar think of it?"

"Dream? What dream? What in Sweet Trevian's name are you talking about?"

"Did I miss something?" Hesh'n said.

"No, you didn't," Lithuigi said. "Pradishar, like your brother, are just so good at being anti-intellectual."

Vilder smiled. "Indeed. And I have all kinds of information about the *incident*, but its confidential. Only important figures can know."

"I'd really like to hit you sometimes," Hesh'n said. "Or maybe poke you with a zapren, make you thrash about on the floor for a bit. That would really get that smug look off your ugly mug. Important figures? Weren't you just begging Father for a recommendation not that long ago?"

"Oh—?" Vilder said, his eyes wide, his hand on his chest in a gesture of shock. "I came here to help you, brother! And you're attacking me? Very well, I'll still be the better plant. I came to tell you that there's smoke coming from a residence in Sunset Point. A lot of smoke. Sounds like it's coming from your lab."

Hesh'n dull green face turned an ashen white, and he sprinted from the room without another word, his eyes twitching as he went. Vilder waited til the door had closed before he turned to his father, laughing as his eyes twitched. "Did you see his face? Oh, I'll have to stream that later."

"His lab is fine I assume?" Lithuigi said.

"Of course, but the evidence I prepared is convincing. We'll have enough time to chat before he figures out it's a false alarm."

"It's not a false alarm. It's a lie from a brother."

"And hilarious," Vilder said flatly.

"I don't have time to talk today," Lithuigi said. "I'm very busy."

Vilder looked around at the clean, tidy lab. "Yes, consumed with work I see."

"The real work often goes on in the mind, not with the hands," he said.

"Well good then, because you'll be using your hands far less now. You see, I came with terrible news, Father. I'm afraid your stasis project has been cancelled."

"Nonsense," Lithuigi said, but he felt like he'd been jabbed in the chest with a zapren.

Vilder pressed his lips together. "You really should be more grateful, Father. You see, I made sure that those who needed to know, knew. A special project, you see. You love those most of all, don't you Father?"

"What special project?"

Vilder tsked. "I'm not a messenger," he said. "You'll have to wait til you're summoned to find out."

"They didn't trust you with the details, then?" Lithuigi said, smirking in spite of the panic in his chest.

Vilder hissed. "Just keep the chamber active until you're told otherwise."

"So nothing has changed," he said. "Did you come only to waste my time?"

Vilder opened his mouth to reply but closed it, his nostrils flaring. "You think you're so smart, don't you? I came to warn you, Father, but since you're the most ungrateful wretch in all of Balance Territories—"

"You must really be moving up in the world," Lithuigi said, cutting him off. "But you can tell your master—"

"What?" Vilder snapped. "That you'll defy him? That he can't order you around like a puppet on a string, as he has for all these years? That you aren't his slave any longer? Oh please, Father, please defy him. Do it! I'd love that so much. And so would he. I'm sure there's all manner of things he could do with your face."

"Get out!" Lithuigi snapped, a dark look in his eyes.

Vilder laughed. "Scared, Father? You should be."

"The Pradishar can't do anything to me," he said. "I'm a member of the Dyna'arin. We have rights to privacy, and freedom of thought and action. His threats are insubstantial. You must know that."

"Those rights might have protected you yesterday," Vilder said. "But today is a new day. Haven't you heard? Didn't your little servant, Marius, or Marwin, or whatever his name is—didn't he give you your little scroll today? Didn't he tell you that the emergency powers passed by the Council in response to the *incident* give the Pradishar the right to detain and interrogate anyone accused of threatening Balance?"

Lithuigi had forgotten to read the scroll Mha'arlo had given him, but later he found that indeed it was there, duly noted by his assistant. He really needed to stay up with things.

"And we already have our first catch," Vilder continued. "As we speak, Doc Bryncent Andri'n has been arrested, and I'm told the Cul'tavin on Andramere are starting a very thorough picking apart of his mind. Any minute now he'll break open like a ripe grape, and then they'll squeeze every last bit of information right out of him." He clenched his teeth and laughed through them.

But Lithuigi could hardly breathe.

"On what charge?" he managed to whisper.

"Oh, many charges, Father, many indeed. He was *quite* the suspicious character. Let's see…there's tampering with the Pradishar servryn. A big no-no, as you know." He giggled. "Then there's stealing secrets and leaking them to the notestreamers. Vandalism against Pradishar property. Illegal smuggling. Working with the Bhizini to undermine Balance. Crimes against information. In other words, treason."

Lithuigi slammed his fist on the table. "Out," he said.

"I assure you—" Vilder said.

"Out!" He stepped toward his son, pulling a zapren from his robe with his prosthetic, and he held it in front of his son's chest. Vilder's eyes went wide, and Lithuigi could see the fear in them, though his cheeks had drawn up into a proud sneer. With his nose in the air, and a side-eyed scowl at his father, Vilder turned and left the lab without another word.

Lithuigi scrambled to contact Management with his Dyna'arin crystal, certain the Pradishar must have thought they could keep this a secret from the Guild. Vilder's malice in sharing the news just might save Doc Andri'n.

But no, even stopping the interrogation wouldn't be enough, not with all the evidence.

Oh, my poor brother, he thought, weeping, as the guilt threatened to break his heart. *Mha'arlo's delivery sealed your fate.*

Chapter 15

The Captor, the Captive, and the Slave

R AKK R AEDER KNEW HE was almost out of time.

Qardymion the Saltsap was in the holding cell. Somehow they'd gotten them down that treacherous staircase, through the labyrinthine atolls of the Sargassian Sink, and out into the Threshinveld without incident. But then his captains had begun reporting in from the battles taking place near Princip'asia, near the Tranquin reefs, by the mouth of the Brinewater, and off the coast of Rheganza, letting him know the Bhizini had broken off their attacks.

Their diversion has failed, and they know it, he thought.

Moments later, ships appeared along the border-shores of the sink, amongst the breaks in the palms that clustered in bunches along the atolls, passing through the narrow channels into the open ocean, first a few and then more—hundreds, thousands, to the north and south along the eastern flank, pouring out and spreading in a growing wave across the surface of the sea.

Rakk knew he needed to move out, to get Qardymion to land, to the Pradishar and Ellex Andria. Now he knew he was out of time, but he still couldn't decide where to go. This was the most important captive of his life, and while he was confident he could stay ahead of the Bhizini fleet, he knew they'd follow him, in a broken line strewn across hundreds of miles if they had to. If he took the Saltsap to Balan Su, he was sure the Corkin and the city's defenses could stop an assault, but he could already imagine what the notestreamers would say if he led a Bhizini fleet to the doorstep of the capital.

He turned the cata'rin toward the south with his crystamin and opened the gurgitator wide. Rakk had to grip the deck with his rootpads as the maquina whined and the ship lurched forward, picking up speed across the Threshinveld.

"You've decided on a destination, my prince?" Q'orin asked.

"More like I accepted an inevitability," Rakk said, his eyes twitching. "Look at all those ships! Maybe the rumors are true and the Bhizini do have a city somewhere, deep in the Sargassian."

"Their courage is commendable," Q'orin said. "But most won't keep up with us."

"No, but they'll be enough that do, and they'll be able to track us. We need to lose them before that happens."

"You intend to confront them?"

Rakk grinned. "To entrap them."

Q'orin raised his eyebrows.

"Part of the fleet is already near the Middle Passage, so I'm redirecting them to the Eastern Passage. They're to move south through the reef, toward the Tranquin Sea, and set up for an ambush in the lagoon in the heart of the passage. We'll lead the fastest of the Bhizini ships into the channel, and once we're clear of the lagoon, we'll blockade the exits. Then we can slip away into the Tranquin, with the pursuing Bhizini trapped to the north of the reef."

"A bold plan, but with great risk. If the Bhizini get across the reef, we'll have few options in the Tranquin. She's small and hemmed in."

"But if we can buy enough time to get away from them, we can head east to Thester, and back into the Threshinveld. We could be to Balan Su by the time they knew we'd left the Tranquin. And if we can't lose them, there's always Andrasia. We could sail for Andropolis."

"Sail a Corkin ship into the Bay of Ani? The Andrasians would have our heads."

"Yours, maybe," Rakk said, grinning. "But a prince of Raccorum Rhazzat? Unlikely."

Q'orin ignored him. "We should avoid Andrasia at all costs, my prince. And I don't say so only to save my own skin."

"Easy, soldier," Rakk said. "I have no intention of sailing to the Andrasian capital. Now take the helm. I need to prepare."

Rakk spent the next several hours closed up in his study, perched in the corner, his eyes closed, his awareness in the minds and bodies of his troops, as the first of his fleet arrived at the Eastern Passage and he helped them set up for the ambush. It felt good to be inside his men again, digging trenches on the sandy atolls that lined the laguna, or setting out the rows of pikes on the bottom of the channel, the water warm on their skin and salty on their lips.

And then Rakk felt Q'orin's hand on his shoulder—his own shoulder—and he opened his eyes, pulling his awareness back to the cata'rin.

"What is it?" he said.

"The Council of Nine," Q'orin said. "They've just declared a three day jubilee, in celebration of the capture of Qardymion the Saltsap."

Rakk hissed and slammed his hand against the wall. "Damnit, what did you tell them?"

"Only that Qardymion was bound but not yet in irons," Q'orin said, speaking quickly, "and that we were under pursuit from the Bhizini."

"Well, this is either one hell of a vote of confidence from Ellex Andria, or someone is setting me up for the worst failure of my career." His face darkened and he added, "Well, second worst."

"Your plan is a solid one, my prince. Take it as a show of support from Balance Authority. You're the hero. They are singing your name on the streets of every city in Balance Territories right now. Take a look a the notestreams."

Rakk looked at Q'orin. "Really?" he said.

Q'orin's eyes twitched and Rakk could see it in his mind, hear the songs being sung on the streets of Rhen'zoran, the prayers being said for him, and his heart swelled up with pride, only to clench tight with a terror so profound, he didn't have a word for it—couldn't even comprehend it. Everything he wanted had never been closer, and yet his hopes had never been so fragile.

He looked at Q'orin again, a somber look on his face. "If the Saltsap somehow gets away from us—just promise I won't have to ask you to kill me—that you'll just do it, as a service to Balance and to all of Raccorum Rhazzat. Can you do that for me?"

"No," Q'orin said. "You know I can't."

"Why not?" Rakk said. "Don't be obstinate. Must I order it?"

"A slave can't harm their master, my prince. Even if ordered to. The crystamin won't allow it."

Rakk turned away, looking at the deck, forgetting to breath.

"Then I'll do it myself," he whispered.

"How about we make sure the Saltsap doesn't escape?" Q'orin said, and when Rakk looked at him, he was grinning.

Rakk exhaled. "Thanks buddy. I'm just so close—" He clenched his fist in a ball.

"But now you must be patient, my prince," Q'orin said. "By the time you wake, we'll be at the Eastern Passage."

"Sleep? You must be joking."

Q'orin gave him a stern look. "You didn't sleep at all on the crossing to Aga'thyn." His eyes twitched. "You're at 40 hours and counting. I estimate peak performance in battle will have dropped...30 percent by the time we reach the passage, if you continue this way."

Rakk laughed. "You sound like a scholar. Have you been on the medical streams again?"

"A bit," Q'orin said, blushing. "I—well, I've been auditing a class at the Academicon."

Rakk raised his eyebrows.

"I hope I haven't overstepped my bounds. My prince told me not to ask his permission for every small thing."

"Small thing?" Rakk said.

"I shall withdraw from the course immediately, if you so desire it," Q'orin said.

Rakk grabbed his arm. "Please don't," he said, and he smiled. "I'm glad of it."

Q'orin nodded. "The course is on the Verdillion body in warfare. Fascinating stuff. The latest session was all about sleep, how important it is, how it clears your wastes and strengthens your fibers, and how depriving the enemy can crush their morale, slow their decision making, warp their sense of reality. The professor—"

Rakk put up his hand, laughing. "I'll go to sleep already. Sheesh. I swear you're more my wife than my friend sometimes."

Q'orin had an uncomfortable look on his face and Rakk swallowed a pang of guilt. He clapped him on the shoulder. "Thanks for looking out for me, old friend. I mean it. Good night then."

"Good night, my prince," Q'orin said. "Sweet dreams."

⁂

When Rakk woke, the early morning sunshine was on his face and chest, his back was on the sand, the sound of water lapping and bird-wings flapping were in his ears—and an excruciating pain was in his head, which seemed to stab him every time he heard his name. He opened his eyes, hoping it would take the pain away, but the glare from the sun was worse than the sound.

"My prince is finally awake," Q'orin said.

"Am I?" Rakk said.

"Yes. The dream's over now. You were knocked unconscious when our ship crashed into the edge of the Tranquin Reef."

"The dream—wait—what!?" Rakk stuttered.

"Everyone in Balance with a crystal experienced the incident," Q'orin said. "No word on why, or how, or what it means. I'm—sorry you had to endure it."

Rakk went over the scenes in his mind, re-experiencing it all in a flash. Ellex Andria—his father—Sweet Trevian. He shuddered.

"And now I've made you re-live it," Q'orin said. "Forgive me."

"No, it's just—wow. Disturbing. It's not every day you have a dream where you become the one you love most in this world and then climb in bed with your father."

Q'orin tried hard to contain a laugh, knowing he risked punishment, but he couldn't help it. Rakk looked at him wide-eyed, then joined. He stopped as quickly as he had started, and struggled to sit up, looking around in panic.

"The Saltsap!" he cried.

Q'orin helped him to his feet. "He is still restrained, my prince. This way."

He led Rakk to a chunk of what was once the back half of a cata'rin, pitched over onto it's side on the edge of the reef, wobbling precariously, it's front half shattered and strewn on the craggy coral. Rakk noticed the mangalar trees growing in sporadic patches off to the east, palms off to the west, and he knew they must be near the great Mon Mang'alar swamp, a vast wilderness spreading nearly a quarter of the way around the globe.

We're too close to dangerous and unpredictable territory, he thought. *Pal'meran territory.*

"We need to move fast."

Qardymion was still inside the holding cell, although it had been busted open by the impact. The door had fallen over on top of the Bhizini, wedging them in place.

"This is what you meant by restrained?"

Q'orin blushed and handed Rakk a fighting pike, then grabbed one of his own. They used them to hoist the door off the Saltsap, then they dragged them out onto the reef.

"Careful, they could be faking it," Q'orin said. "Let me find something to restrain them properly." When he returned with a vine, they tied their hands and feet together, then carried them to a nearby mangalar tree and fastened them to one of the thicker roots.

"That should hold them until we figure out how to get out of here," Rakk said.

"Let me see to your wounds," Q'orin said, and Rakk sat down on the reef. He closed his eyes and sent his awareness out for his troops.

What the fuck happened? he thought. *How did everyone dream the same thing at the same time?*

But no, he needed to focus on the moment. Answers would come later. Right now, he had to know where the Bhizini were. They'd been following them toward the Eastern Passage, but the seas were clear in every direction.

He found his troops in the middle of the lagoon, still arranged in formation to ambush the Bhizini and blockade the channel, and he could feel their confusion, their anxiety at what had happened, at what they'd seen in the dream. He used their eyes to look around, but the Bhizini weren't in the lagoon. He opened to all his captains, brought them all together to fill him in, and he took in their updates at once.

Chaos had been strewn across Balance Territories by the dream. But the Bhizini had vanished. No attacks on the Great Sea Lanes. The fleet that had chased him across the Threshinveld never reached the Tranquin. They had slipped back into sink and swamp.

But the Bhizini don't have crystals, he thought. *So how would they know what had happened? And why would they abandon Qardymion?*

Rakk looked around again at his surroundings, and he put their location about sixty miles east of the passage, maybe forty miles from Thester. And nobody—not his men, not the Pradishar, and not the Bhizini—knew where they were.

He could work with that.

When Q'orin finished tending Rakk's wounds, he stood and walked over to the Saltsap and began to bind and seal their injuries. Rakk looked around the wreckage for something they could salvage, but there wasn't much left of the cata'rin. When Q'orin put a particularly acidic salve on one of Qardymion's wounds, they winced and opened their eyes, squinting in the bright light off the sea.

"What—happened?" Qardymion said, their voice parched. They coughed, and Q'orin put a satchel of fresh water to their lips, and they drank.

"Oh, I just thought we'd take a detour," Rakk said.

Qardymion laughed, then winced when Q'orin put more salve on their leg.

"You're healing me?" they said.

Q'orin nodded. "Prisoners are treated with respect by the Corkin. It's part of our mandate."

"Lucky you," Qardymion said. "And lucky me today, I suppose."

"Rest up awhile," Rakk said. "We'll be leaving shortly."

"Will we?" Qardymion looked around. "On what?"

"Still working on that," Rakk said and walked off.

But Rakk wasn't sure what to do. The Bhizini might have scattered but they'd be back. And if they saw his troops massing along the reef, they'd know where to find them. No, better to keep the fleet in the Eastern Passage, while they walked down the reef to Thester. It would be slow going, but it wasn't that far.

He thought of Ellex Andria and wanted to ask her if she was okay—to tell her that he still had the Saltsap, that he was shipwrecked but hadn't abandoned his post, and that he's not sure he can trust anyone anywhere right now. He wanted to tell her that seeing P'anorum in the dream, walking the halls of his old home, seeing her, *being* her—that he was about to go out of his mind thinking about her.

Instead he turned back to the others and sat down by Q'orin. He touched him on the shoulder. "You doing alright, old friend? I'm sorry I didn't ask."

"I'm fine. Uninjured from the crash."

<<And from the dream?>> He didn't want Qardymion hearing.

Q'orin shrugged.

<<What do you think it means,>> Rakk asked.

<<You ask the wrong Corkin, my prince. I'm a simple plant. I don't understand such things.>>

<<Simple? Ha! But surely you have a feeling about it?>>

Q'orin shrugged again.

<<You recognized the royal palace on P'anorum?>>

He nodded.

Rakk sat for a moment, lost in thought. <<How great it was to see that place again, even if the rest of the dream was...chilling. Awful. Such butchery. I can still smell the sap.>>

<<From the dream?>>

<<From the event itself.>> He looked at Q'orin but his face was blank. <<That really happened. I had barely flowered. One of the noble families defied my father and the head of the family was sent to the dungeon. The heir tried to free him, and in doing so, made an attempt on my life. As punishment, they were made to watch while their entire family was executed.>>

<<I'm sorry you had to experience that, my prince,>> Q'orin said.

Qardymion had been leaning against the trunk of the mangalar tree, watching them. When the two men turned away from one another, they smiled. "Well, is it good news or bad?" they said. "Looks like a little of both. You know, I might not be able to overhear your conversation, but body language speaks louder than words."

Rakk turned to the Saltsap and chuckled. "No news, just one hell of a dream," he said. "It seems our little crash here was all because of a nightmare."

"I don't understand," said Qardymion, "or am I not meant to?"

"We don't either," Rakk said. "It seems that early this morning, Balan Su time, everyone in Balance Territories, everyone with a crystamin, had a very vivid, very real feeling nightmare—even those who weren't asleep at the time. As if the world weren't mad enough already."

Qardymion stared at Rakk, a smile spreading on their face, their eyes aglow with a sense of shock and wonder.

"Why do you smile?" Q'orin demanded. He pulled a zapren from his robe, and it crackled when he ignited it. "Speak, snake, or I'll jam this in your neck. What do you know?"

"Easy, Q'orin, easy," Rakk said.

"This is a special day," Qardymion said. "A special day, indeed. And not only because I get to spend the morning with such lovely company. Today, the great sea has given us a sign. The Harvest approaches."

Q'orin jabbed the Saltsap with the zapren, and their body jerked hard against the restraints, their eyes bulging.

"Stop!" Rakk yelled, and Q'orin pulled the zapren away. Qardymion moaned and slumped over, unconscious.

"Forgive me, my prince. They spoke crimes against information. Ren'fallow conspiracies. It is my mandate to silence them."

"They're just a fanatical savage," he said. "They'll probably spout a lot of nonsense before we get them to Balan Su. The Bhizini have been prophesying the fall of Balance since the beginning of Balance, and every generation sees the rise of the one who will wipe everything out. This isn't a new song they're singing, trust me. Besides, they're unarmed and tied up. You won't mistreat them again, understood?"

"My mandate requires I silence Ren'fallow conspirators," Q'orin said, a pained look on his face.

Rakk narrowed his eyes. "I order you not to harm them. Is that understood?"

Q'orin nodded.

"Good. Now go and look around for any rhupan or fresh water in the wreckage. And weapons. And quickly, too—I can hear the dynamin in the gurgitator starting to whine. It'll probably blow before we could get a tinker out here to fix it, so we should get away from the ship as soon as we can."

Q'orin nodded and walked away, a blank look on his face. Rakk watched him go, then turned to the Saltsap.

Just what do you know, you old pirate, he thought. *What were you after on Aga'thyn? And what do Ren'fallow conspiracies have to do with the dream?*

Q'orin returned after a while with several weapons, a few satchels of fresh water, and a sack of dried rhupan. That would do well. He told Rakk that one of the lifeboats, a cano'rin, was still mostly intact and might be repairable. Rakk went with him and helped him get it loose from the wreckage.

When they had dragged it back to their base by the mangalar tree, Qardymion was awake but very groggy. They stayed quiet but sat and watched them while they carefully examined the cano'rin. Rakk thought it was beyond hope to fix, but they tried anyway. On the first attempt to float it, the boat sank. They dragged it out, flipped it and drained it, then tried again to patch the holes. It sank again. They were dragging it out a third time when Qardymion laughed.

"You're wasting your time," they said.

"I suppose you could do better?" Rakk said.

"A Bhizini scamp of five years could do better than you, mighty Corkin master," Qardymion said, grinning. "You Balance types depend far too much on the inventions of your Guild and not nearly enough on the abilities of your own hands. And you royals have others do everything for you, so you never learn anything yourself. But we Bhizini keep the essential knowledge with us, and we treasure our skills and practice them. Come, untie me, I'll have us a boat—" they paused to look around, then up at the sky, "—by midday, if you two do the heavy lifting."

Rakk laughed. "Untie you? So you can help us get you to prison?"

Q'orin brandished the zapren again and scowled at Qardymion.

"We'll find another way, or else we'll walk," Rakk said. "Q'orin, watch them." He returned to the cano'rin and then to the heap of debris they'd collected to try and patch it, and began to rummage for anything salvageable, anything he could use. But the task seemed pretty much pointless. Then he heard Qardymion talking to Q'orin, and he snuck around behind the mangalar to have a listen.

"There's a great deal I can offer you, Q'orin Grievenson," Qardymion said. "That's right, I know who you are. I've watched you for a long time, with admiration. I thought—that is the kind of plant we need. That is the kind of plant who should become a Pal'meran warrior."

Q'orin held up the zapren and stared at the Saltsap with hard eyes.

"You'd be welcome among my people. You'd be able to build your own ship, be the captain of it, take it wherever you wished, king of your own kingdom. Slit these bindings, friend, and I will slit your crystals in return."

Q'orin ignited the zapren and it popped, a spark of lightning flashing on its tip.

"I've liberated thousands of slaves over the decades," Qardymion said. "My first when I was not yet ten years old. Sure, some of the tribes won't accept a pure-sap like you, but most warmly accept them and consider them Bhizini. I make sure everyone I free finds their way to friendly tribes, who teach them our ways and help them to build a ship of their own. And on a Bhizini ship, they are perfectly free. And every single one of them thanks me."

Q'orin snorted. "No one is perfectly free. We all sacrifice some freedom in order to enjoy the benefits of the community. My prince has never once used an imperial mandate on me. I serve him, I do as he asks, but he never seizes my body, never seizes my mind, never forces me to do his will. With him, I travel the world. I command armies. I keep Balance and all of civilization safe. I protect the subjects of my nation and the citizens of Balance Authority from the brutality of barbarians like you. I would rather die a servant than live as a savage king. And if you somehow managed to slit my crystals, I'd petition my prince for replacements."

"Well spoken," Qardymion said. "Beautiful nonsense. But perhaps your mandate won't let you see it? Have you considered that, Q'orin Grievenson? That your own thoughts—your own *feelings*—are not your own but come from the crystal?"

Q'orin hissed and bared his fangs, but lowered the zapren.

"I really do admire your loyalty," Qardymion said. "Truly. I just have to wonder how genuine it is. Crystals don't only compel service, they also distort truth. So how can I ever know, when I speak to a slave—which is *anyone* with a crystal, not just the Corkin or Rhank—how can I know that they're being their honest selves? I can't. It's a dilemma for anyone who interacts with them. But I suppose it's no matter. If you're content, then Prince Rhakksees is lucky to have you. But should you find yourself free from his tyranny one day, come and find me."

"You assume a lot in thinking you'll ever return to your Pal'merans," Q'orin said.

"I suppose we are all fools then, aren't we?" Qardymion said, their eyes laughing.

Rakk walked back around to the rubble and then returned to the others, and he stared at Qardymion for a moment. "You don't speak like a Bhizini from Mon Mang'alar," he said. "And I'm not sure anyone in Balance would believe me if I told them you were hunched over a table, spectacles on your face, reading books and scrolls on Aga'thyn. Who are you, really?"

"Who am I, *really*? What a silly question, Prince Rhaksees, but very well. I'm a plant, Verdillion technically. I have the sap of Andramere and Raccorum Rhazzat, and the sap of the ancient Bhizini, and certainly all sorts of other saps mixed in from across the millennia. I'm a body that drinks up water, that eats of rhupan, that soaks in the sunlight, and that craps out my feet while I sleep, like you do. I'm the mind that brings me pleasure and the occasional regret. And I'm the desires, for life, for safety, for a family, for my scamps to be able to sail the seas without being butchered by Balance Authority, as both my parents and grandparents were. I am a restless hatred of your government and the spirit of death that rules over it, and I will never stop fighting til all vestiges of its poison—all aspects of Trevian that pollute this world—are gone from it forever."

"Let me spill their sap on the reef, my lord," Q'orin said.

Rakk ignored him and stared at the Saltsap, at their soft brown eyes with their lilting laughter. "I appreciate your honesty. But I also know the Bhizini are anything but united in their hatred of Balance. No, many, if not most, simply want to be left alone. They want a homeland of their own, do they not? Isn't that the oldest Bhizini dream? Those Bhizini don't raid shipping lanes and pillage seaside communities, as you and your Pal'merans do. And they don't butcher Cul'tavin in the heart of Balan Su. They want a peaceful solution. Why must you insist on a violent one?"

"Because death is what rules Balance. And death is the only present and only future, so long as Balance endures."

"But you spoke of the Harvest. You must think the end of Balance is near, right?"

Qardymion smiled.

"I've watched you and your people fighting for decades," Rakk said. "I've seen the loyalty you command, even if you don't have all the Bhizini on your side. I have half a million Corkin beneath me, I'm supposed to be a crown prince, the future king of Raccorum Rhazzat, and yet I wonder sometimes how many of my soldiers would rally to my side of their own free will."

"More than you imagine," Qardymion said. They looked at Rakk, a twinkle in their eyes. "And there is hope for you yet. I've watched you for decades as our forces have scuffled around the Inner Seas. You're an exceptional fighter, and should you try to amass a volunteer army, I know serious warriors would respect your intelligence, your loyalty, and your willingness to throw yourself into the battle. It's too bad you aren't a Bhizini."

Rakk turned back to Q'orin. "Cut their binds," he said, and Q'orin scowled fiercely and narrowed his eyes, but did as he was told. Then he turned to Qardymion. "Now you can show us how to make a cano'rin that doesn't leak?"

"It would be an honor," Qardymion said, stretching their limbs. "Though there are some of my people who would not take kindly to this knowledge getting out. But you seem an honorable plant, Rakk Raeder. And I know your throne hinges upon my capture, does it not? So I'll help you now, in hopes you'll return the favor one day. And who knows, maybe you'll take me someplace where I can actually escape from." They looked around. "Anywhere is better than here. Now then, you see this spot where the joints between these roots come together?" They were looking at the base of the trunk they'd been tied to. "See the ridge? Slice it open, but not too deep."

Q'orin sliced into the root and a thick sap oozed out.

"Good," Qardymion said. "This one's rich. Now, gather some leaves from the palms, and use them to rub this sap all over the bottom of your cano'rin. Try to keep it off your hands."

"And here I was thinking you were going to build one from scratch," Rakk said.

"Next time," Qardymion said, grinning.

They set to work applying the sap, spreading it out, letting it seep into the cracks between the branches. Already it had begun to harden. Qardymion instructed them to layer in palm fronds with the sap in a crisscross pattern, wait for it to harden, then add another layer, and finally one more.

"That should do it," Qardymion said, surveying their work. "Flip it over and we'll see if there's any leaks."

Q'orin pushed the boat into the sea and they waited to see if it sank, but it stayed afloat.

Rakk clapped the Saltsap on the shoulder. "You're pretty handy to have around," he said. "Very well, into the front. Q'orin, you behind them. I'll take the rear." He handed Q'orin an oar. Once in the boat, Rakk pushed off the bottom of the reef with the oar, and they headed north, away from the craggy edge and into deeper water but still close enough to get back into the trees if they needed to hide. As they drifted slowly east, the mangalar grew larger and the foliage thicker and closer together, and the palms were noticeably thinning out. Before long they could see Thester in the distance, wedged in between the Tranquin Reefs, Mon Mang'alar, the sea, and the Andrasian mainland. They were closer than he thought.

As the island and its signature fortress rose up into view, Rakk grew nervous about bringing the Saltsap into Corkin custody. Q'orin might have resisted their offer to free him, but would the other soldiers? And what would Raq'asha do when she found out he was there? Seize the Saltsap, throw Rakk in the dungeon, and take credit for the capture? He *had* disobeyed her orders, after all. So he veered to the south, back into the thickets of mangalar, and navigated between them til they were as close to the island as they could get.

"Restrain them, and tie them to a tree again," Rakk said, then reached for Q'orin through the crystal. <<I'm slipping into Thester alone. It'll be easier that way. I'm familiar with this fortress, so it shouldn't be a problem. When I send the signal, be ready to get the Saltsap back in the cano'rin and move north to rendezvous with me.>>

<<We aren't staying here then?>> Q'orin asked.

<<We can't. I'll get a ship, and you watch the Saltsap. If for some reason I don't return, head south across the reef, and try to get to the Andrasian mainland. Make for Angard at the mouth of the Norian. And don't torture Qardymion or kill them if you can avoid it, but don't let your guard down either. They're a dangerous one.>>

Q'orin nodded at Rakk and Rakk headed for the edge of the thicket, back to the sea. He closed his eyes and scanned the area. While the fortress normally held several thousand Corkin, most were at sea, and he could only sense a few dozen troops inside.

Rakk felt a single soldier in the guard-tower by the docks. He knew it was a gamble—if he was tethered with anyone, they'd soon know of his presence—but he seized the Corkin's mind and body anyway. He could feel the slave's surprise but there was no resistance, no protest, and no one else streaming in. Rakk ran with the soldier's body as if it were his own, down to a small cata'rin, sleek and fast like the one they'd crashed. He saw through the soldier's eyes as he boarded the ship, opened the gurgitator, and began to pilot it out of the harbor. An alarm began to whoop nearby—or was it sounding in his head?—and Rakk felt for the one who set it off and used his hands to shut it down. He scanned the area again. So far nobody was coming to investigate, but they would soon enough.

Once out of the harbor, he used the slave to pilot the ship slowly past his own physical location, and he dove into the water, swam to the ship, climbed the small footholds, grabbed the rail, and flipped himself up and over onto it. He had the slave direct the ship to Q'orin's location and he lowered the winch to pull the cano'rin up onto the deck of the cata'rin. Then he made the Corkin slave run and leap into the sea, swim to the nearby mangalar, and climb up onto the roots of the tree. Then he wiped the slave's mind of the memory and rendered him unconscious. He felt for the gurgitator, turned the cata'rin to the north, and opened the valve to full aperture.

When he returned to the deck, Q'orin was getting Qardymion out of the cano'rin.

"The first good luck we've had," he said. "I'll take the Saltsap to the holding cell, then I'll meet you on the bridge."

Q'orin nodded, and Rakk led Qardymion down to the lower deck, to one of the two holding cells on the cata'rin.

"My people won't stop, you know," Qardymion said. "They won't stop fighting. They won't stop trying to rescue me. And they won't stop coming for you. Balance is doomed, Prince Rhakksees. The sooner you see that, the better off everything will be. And when you do see that—and you will, eventually—come find me. I'll embrace you as a friend and ally."

Rakk stared at Qardymion for a moment, and he couldn't help but feel a pang of regret, a moment of doubt, and a strange desire to free the prisoner—to sail away with them and join the Bhizini with Q'orin, as they'd offered him. As much as he hated to admit it, he liked Qardymion, and turning them in, even though it meant he'd save his throne, gave him a bad taste in his mouth.

But no. He had a civilization to defend, and a throne to win. He had people who expected things from him. He had services to render, duties and obligations to perform. And he wanted to fulfill those obligations more than he wanted to be free. He would never abandon his post again. Not after what had happened at P'anorum. Never.

That's the problem with the Bhizini, he thought, as he turned away from Qardymion, saying nothing. *Q'orin is right. Nobody is perfectly free. Even a prince—especially a prince—must serve his people and serve his government, despite how appealing the alternative might seem. Balance Authority is still the prevailing force in the world, and that force helps keep the world peaceful and its citizens able to pursue their dreams. And that's worth something.*

No, it was worth a lot. Besides, he had the Saltsap in custody. And in spite of how he felt about them, Qardymion was still a pirate who hadn't hesitated to use violence against peaceful citizens for many decades. But no more, thanks to him. And now they were heading for Balan Su, not to circle it's shores in the pestilent fog, but to walk the streets of the capital, to see his brother again after so many years.

And—Sweet Trevian—he was about to be face to face with Ellex Andria again.

He looked at the horizon and smiled.

Chapter 16

Three at Sea, Where the Miracles Be

F IN'ROQ WOKE WITH HIS eyes closed, afraid to open them. His throat hurt, his head hurt, everything hurt. He could hear the purr of a gurgitator open wide, and the soft slap of a ship against the water.

Roman Anthem's ship, he remembered.

He listened awhile longer, opening his senses, trying to get his bearing. He was flat on the deck, the wind cool on his skin. His robe was wet and he could taste the sea in his mouth.

The Bhizini. The villagers.

He thought about leaving his eyes closed, and trying his best to fall back to sleep—perhaps this would all be a dream and he'd wake up in Bhea's garden, on familiar ground, doing familiar things with familiar people—but Fin'roq had the suspicion that someone was watching him, someone close by, and his curiosity got the better of him. He opened one eye, hoping to be subtle about it, just to grab a quick look, but when he saw the Andrasian sitting next to him, he opened both his eyes and he turned his head and stared.

"Thank Trevian you're awake," the Andrasian said, his brown eyes twinkling, and he smiled at Fin'roq. "You gave us quite a scare."

"I—" Fin started. "Uh—-" but words failed him.

His felt like his face had caught fire.

The Andrasian chuckled. "Not to worry, Fin'roq, I get that all the time."

Fin coughed and the stranger helped him to sit up, then held a cup to his lips and gently tipped it back. The water tasted like it had been in a barrel for weeks, but it felt good going down.

"Thank you," he whispered, then struggled to clear his throat. "It hurts to talk."

"Indeed it would. That was quite a scream you gave us."

"Scream?" he said. "Why am I wet?"

"You don't remember? You fell overboard. You're lucky to be alive."

"What happened?"

"I rescued you, of course." He was grinning, a wide smile on his pale Andrasian face. "I'm quite the swimmer!"

Fin blushed again. "Thank you," he said. "You seem to know my name. And you are?"

The grin vanished and the Andrasian stared at him, his head turning slowly toward one side, his mouth falling open. "Come again?"

Fin swallowed, wondering what he'd said wrong. "I'd very much appreciate the name of the one who saved my life."

The Andrasian broke out in an enormous smile and he clapped his hands together. "Sweet Trevian, you're serious, aren't you!" Then he composed himself and gave a small bow. "I'm Jaun von Andron," he said. "I have a feeling we're going to be fast friends."

"Should I—know you?" Fin said.

"Should? Absolutely not! Yet most do." He looked at Fin'roq, glancing at his forehead. "No crystamin, so you wouldn't have seen any melodramas, or any streams at all for that matter. Hmm...have you heard of Andramere?"

Fin nodded. "The Jewel of the Shimmering Sea," he said. "I know the songs and some of the histories."

Jaun's eyes seemed to dance with excitement. "Where'd you hear them? From your fellow villagers?"

"Well, they—" Fin stopped for a moment, not sure what to say. "No. I was taught by another Bhizini."

"You're Bhizini?" Jaun asked.

Fin looked down at himself, held up his splotchy bright and dull green hands, and then looked at Jaun, who was still smiling. "Definitely Bhizini," Fin said.

"If you say so," Jaun said. "Bhizini Fin'roq, it's a pleasure." He bowed again. "Now come on, let's get you to your quarters and out of those wet robes. You can freshen up and rest for awhile. We have a long trip to Balan Su, so we'll have plenty of time to chat later."

He reached out his hand and helped Fin to his feet.

"Good plant," Jaun said. "This way."

Fin steadied himself with his arms, feeling woozy and not used to such a large ship moving so quickly. He held on to the rails and looked out at the sea.

So much water, he thought. *So, so much water.*

He'd never seen so much before, all around him, in every direction, with no land anywhere to be seen.

"How far are we from P'anorum?"

Jaun's eyes twitched. "Not far yet," he said.

"Far enough," Fin said. "The peaks of P'anorum. They're gone."

"Not to worry," Jaun said. "I guarantee they're still there, even if you can't see them."

Fin looked at Jaun, then back at the sea. "I've always been able to see them."

"You've never left P'anorum before?"

Fin'roq shook his head. "And the peaks might be there," he said. "But my village, the villagers, my home…" Tears began to fall from his eyes, and he turned away so Jaun wouldn't see.

Jaun said nothing for a moment, politely ignoring Fin while he pulled himself together, then he took his arm and gave it a tug, and Fin reluctantly followed him. They descended to the lower levels of the ship, to an area reserved for the crew, except there didn't seem to be any crew aboard. Jaun showed him a room lined with cubbies in the wall and opened one of them for him. Inside was a stack of clean pradeshan robes and cumberdomes. On the other side of the room were a series of small dipping pots with ladles for bathing.

"Easy on the fresh water usage," Jaun said. "Bathing at sea can't be like bathing on land. You'll get used to the sailor stench eventually. This way to the sleeping chamber." The room was small with a low ceiling and the floor was completely covered in a thick layer of firm, sturdy soil from wall to wall. "You can sleep anywhere in here," he said. "Or, if you'd prefer to perch outside for awhile, there's a number of lovely spots. The captain said we're guests aboard his ship until we reach the capital and our recruitment officially begins. So relax and rest up. You'll need it for Balan Su."

"You're joining the Pradishar too?"

Jaun nodded, and Fin wondered if they'd be studying together at the Pruu'patch.

"Thanks again," Fin said. "For everything."

"Don't mention it," Jaun said, waving his hand in the air as if saving someone's life were nothing. "Anything else you need before I head back up?"

Fin shook his head. "How long til Balan Su?"

"Well, it's hard to predict the duration of sea travel," Jaun said. "Balan Su is halfway around the world from P'anorum, but we can't sail in a straight line, nor can we maintain a steady speed the entire way. From here to Eastwhaling, we'll have the gurgitator wide open. But then we'll be slowed by the passage into Balance Territories, and once in the

Inner Seas, weather in the Threshinveld is notoriously hard to predict. Storms can spring up unexpectedly, causing delays."

Fin was looking at Jaun with wide eyes.

He laughed when he saw Fin's face. "Not the time for a lecture, is it!" He chuckled and shook his head. "At least four days to Balan Su. It's been done in two and a half days, but the circumstances were different when that record was set. More likely we're looking at a week. Plenty of time to tell you everything you absolutely must know before setting foot in the capital!"

"I'd appreciate that," Fin said. "I've heard a little about it, through songs mostly. And from our pretend priestin. It seems so beautiful, the great crescent that rules the world, the obsidian spire towering over it all."

"It's beautiful until you look too closely," Jaun said. "But I suppose that can be said about most cities."

"I wouldn't know," Fin'roq said. "The only city I've ever seen is Old P'anorum, and it's not really a happening place."

Jaun paused. "Old P'anorum? But how old are you?" He looked at him askance.

"Thirty three," Fin said.

"Then you were cut after the eruption."

"Yes," Fin said, "But the city is still there, even if you can't see it." He grinned. "It's all there, perfectly preserved under the lava. And I'm the only one who knows the way in."

"Incredible!" Jaun said. "One day you'll have to show me."

He blushed and Jaun grinned. "Then to rest, friend. Tonight we dine with the captain. I'll make sure you're awake by then. Or if you wake before, come find me upstairs." He bowed slightly, a serene look on his face.

Fin watched him leave, his cheeks still burning.

⁂

After Jaun left, Fin stripped out of his soiled robes, did his best to clean himself using as little water as possible, then donned a fresh robe from the cubby. He went back into the sleeping quarters, rooted his pads, and spent a few hours refreshing himself in the soil, feeling weepy again. He saw the Bhizini in his mind, pouring across the sand, hacking down the villagers. Were they all dead? Was Milli? Were Bhea and Grizmond?

No, it was too much to consider.

So he dried his eyes and went upstairs and found a spot in the sunshine, and he unfurled his branches from his arms and closed his eyes and spent the afternoon drinking up the delicious energy, thinking about P'anorum getting farther and farther away from him. And thinking about Jaun, too.

When the sun had set and twilight had faded away, Jaun found Fin'roq on the main deck and waved for him to come up the stairs. They climbed to the top deck and into the captain's quarters. He was expecting to find great opulence, incredible maquina, something wondrous—but Roman Anthem's quarters were spartan. The room was nearly bare, stripped of any frivolity, without a single item that didn't have a use. There was a long table which doubled as a meeting space and a dining space, a study space in one corner, a sleeping patch in another, with a bathing area alongside it.

The table was set for three at one end. Roman Anthem sat at the head and he beckoned them to either side of him, a smile on his weather-beaten face, the dull and bright patches on his cheeks curling together in waves, like the line between the sea and the sky, melting into one another.

"Glad to see you've recovered, Fin'roq," he said.

"Thank you, Captain. I feel better. Thanks to Jaun."

"Yes, quite the hero, that one," Anthem said. "Of course, had I been closer, I would have been the one who saved you. Jaun just happened to beat me to it. Isn't that right, von Andron?"

Jaun laughed and wagged his finger at him. "You've just gotten old, I think."

"Old! Me? Impossible!" Anthem laughed and his whole body shook. Then he turned to Fin'roq. "But seriously, I would have gone in after you. The Pradishar are your family now, so you can think of me as a big brother. I'll be looking after you."

Fin looked at Anthem and felt the sense of anticipation and wonder that he'd felt when he first learned there was a Cul'tavin peacekeeper who was also Bhizini—one with his own ship, no less. Fin imagined that one day that could be him. But it felt too good, and he felt too happy about it, that he couldn't trust it, not after what happened with Roe and Aar'ryn. He wanted a friend in Anthem, but he also felt like it was entirely possible that Anthem would just as soon imprison him as protect him, if it was in Anthem's best interest to do so. And that made him scary.

"I appreciate your support, Captain," Fin said. "I—greatly admire you."

"Really?" Anthem said. "You knew I existed? Way out on P'anorum?"

"Well, no." Fin blushed. "But when I learned of you, and then when I saw you—when I saw your skin—when I saw that you looked kind of like me. But were also in pradeshan robes. With your own ship!" He was rambling and he knew it, and his face burned.

"And yet for so many, my face is a source of fear," Anthem said. "And anger." He stared at Fin for a moment, a fierce look in his eyes, and Fin'roq seemed to wither and crumple beneath it. Then Anthem grinned and Fin gulped. The smile might have been worse than the scowl, if only because both had seemed so genuine.

Jaun had been watching the interaction with an amused look on his face. "And I'm the world famous performer?" he said. "Perhaps you're in the wrong role?"

Anthem laughed again, a hearty laugh, a warm laugh that made Fin'roq want to laugh with him.

"I'm sure you're both hungry," Anthem said, standing up. "We're a bit short of staff on this cruise, I'm afraid. I did my best to whip something up for us tonight, but for the rest of the crossing, there's dried rhupan in the crew's cookery." He left the room briefly, and Jaun looked over at Fin.

"You okay?" he asked.

"Just nervous," Fin said, exhaling loudly. "Anthem—he's—"

"Yes," Jaun said. "A hard one to crack."

"He scares me," Fin whispered. "But I want him to be my friend, too."

"I'm not sure a plant like him can have any friends," Jaun said, a sad look on his face. He lowered his voice. "And he scares me a little, too."

"Really? But you were just teasing him."

"I do that to everyone, I'm afraid. A terrible affliction of mine, leaping into every role that presents itself. Dreadful." He grinned, and Fin wondered for the first time what it would be like to kiss those lips.

Don't even imagine, he told himself, remembering Milli Mor'n. *Just don't even go there.*

Anthem came back into the room carrying a tray with a huge clay pot full of stringed rhupan and clovins, as well as a pitcher of rhu'berry juice. "This is my favorite dish," Anthem said. "But I'm afraid nobody makes it as good as my old mum. I did my best though. I hope you enjoy it."

"You have a 'mum'?" Jaun said. "Here I was thinking you sprang up out of the sea, fully formed."

Anthem laughed warmly. "Clever plant," he said. "I like you. One day you'll say too much. I just hope I'm not around when you do!"

"One day?" Jaun said, and Anthem laughed again.

The soup smelled delicious and Fin'roq realized how hungry he was. Anthem ladled a large scoop into his bowl, then one for Jaun, then one for himself. Then he poured them each a full glass of rhu'berry juice, and Fin saw that it was fizzy. Then he sat down and offered a hand, palm upward to Jaun, palm downward to Fin, and they both took it. Jaun reached across the table and Fin reached out for his hand and grasped it. He gripped the floor with his rootpads.

"Sweet Trevian," Anthem said. "Thank you for your sacrifice. What a long and terrible one it has been. May it end. May it never happen again."

Fin had never heard that prayer before. And it definitely wasn't in line with the teachings of the Pradishar. He looked at Anthem, but his eyes were closed. Then Anthem laughed.

"That's not the right prayer!" he said. "You two *are* recruits for the Pradishar, right?"

Jaun laughed. "We're here to learn."

"I thought you were here for a role," Anthem said. "An upcoming melodrama of some sort?"

"Indeed, I'm here to learn *for* a role. But still here to learn."

"Fair enough," Anthem said. "If a bit despicable. Nobody likes a trouper, right? Too hard to trust."

"What?" Jaun said, looking horrified. "I thought people loved troupers. Everywhere I go, it's 'Marry me Jaun, I love you Jaun, oh Jaun, oh oh OH.'"

Anthem nearly howled with laughter. "You performers are great for entertainment but little else."

"On the contrary," Jaun said. "I have everyone's rapt attention, so I make it a point to only take roles that I can be sure are in some way educational for my streamers. I consider myself a professor of sorts."

Anthem groaned. "Nobody streams melodramas to learn anything," he said. "It's to see beautiful fools doing exciting things, like fighting and fucking, laughing and crying. Not bettering themselves."

"That's brilliant!" Jaun said. "That'll be the name of my exclusive behind-the-stream look at the making of this entire project! 'Fighting and fucking, laughing and crying, with Jaun von Andron, Prince of Andramere. Creative consultant: Roman Anthem.' What do you say? I'll give you—ten percent? Twenty?"

"It's a deal," Anthem cried.

"You're not here to be a monkin?" Fin finally asked, looking at Jaun, wondering for the first time who this plant he'd met really was. And if it had been a good idea to trust him so suddenly and so thoroughly.

"Of course I am," Jaun said. "I need to be a convincing Pradishar, and I've only got til the end of the year to get it down. So I'll go through orientation and spend a few months doing the rituals in the Pruu'patch, and then I'll transition right into the role, so everything is natural and graceful and true."

"True?" Anthem said.

"True in the sense that I'll know what it feels like to be a monkin, because I will have truly become one."

"True enough," Anthem said, and he grinned.

"But you don't care about the teachings of the Pradishar or the Pruu'log?" Fin asked. "And—you're a prince?"

Jaun looked at Fin, feigning a look of deep confusion. "Of course I care," he said, reverently. "You see these three crystals on my forehead? The blue one belongs to my family as rulers of Andramere. The black one is a public crystamin from Andramere City, through which I perform on the weavryn and take part in popular society. And the red and orange one is a Dyna'arin crystamin, as I have a small role in Management with the Guild and can perform a few dozen operations. I can even tinker a few things on a good day! These crystamins connect me to the entire world. Well, very nearly. In Balance, almost everyone has one. We can speak together instantly, share memories, share eyes and ears and taste and smell and touch. And there are datamins in great servryns around the world, holding the information of the ages on them, and I can access that information anytime, anywhere, right inside my mind. This ship that carries us around the world at incredible speeds moves because of a dynamin in the core of its gurgitator. These three crystals—crystamin, datamin, and dynamin—come from the Pradishar. They are the literal power of Trevian, uniting our world and holding it together, and giving each individual who holds one the potential for tremendous power. Trevian's gift to the world is magical and mysterious and mind-blowing, and I am in awe and wonder of it, truly. And so yes, I do care about the teachings of the Pradishar, and about what is contained in the Pruu'log, very much so. Don't be concerned, my friend," he said, nodding at Fin'roq, "I know you're taking this seriously, and I am too. I have no intention of disrespecting the faithful in the process."

Fin nodded, feeling relieved. But then he wondered if Jaun hadn't just told him what he wanted to hear, and used his skills as a performer to make it convincing.

Roman Anthem seemed to read his mind. "The consummate trouper," he said. "Award-winning even. Of course, it seems much more likely to me that you're the type who believes the crystals are naturally occurring and the Pradishar's only power is keeping the source a secret. Whether or not Trevian ever existed is irrelevant to the issue, and there's no magic here, nothing spiritual. The crystamins link together. Just a fact. The dynamins? They emit energy. Just a fact. Just like the fact we all stay stuck to this planet instead of floating up toward the stars. Right, von Andron?"

"As far as I'm concerned, the two points of view are just two ways of talking about the same thing," Jaun said. "The crystals can seem mundane, just like any other thing that's always around. But when you really ponder them, they are wonderful, mystical, mind-shattering. Can't more than one reality co-exist at any one point, in any one thing? Doesn't every unity contain multitudes?"

"Jaun the philosopher," Anthem said. "A plant of many faces."

Jaun stared at Anthem for a moment, and Fin thought he spotted a crack in his facade for the first time. But Jaun quickly recovered, flashing a grin and bowing to Anthem, then to Fin'roq.

"It's nice to have company," Anthem said. "A toast!" He lifted his glass of rhu'berry juice. "To a safe voyage from here to there."

"And back again," Jaun said, looking at Fin as he drank.

"Well, now that we've had some fun, it's time for the bad news," Anthem said. "The ambush at P'anorum wasn't all the Bhizini had planned. The Pal'merans know we're heading for East'whaling, and their ships are on the move, heading north out of Mon Mang'alar into the Gulf of F'aryndon, hoping to cut off our approach."

"How far are we from the gulf?" Jaun asked.

"We're halfway across it now. I expect they'll come on us in the northern narrows, an ambush from both the northern reef and from Mon Mang'alar. I'm confident we can outrun their ships, and I've notified Eastwhaling to be ready to open the gates when we approach. But it could get rough again. I'd like both of you in a safe place this time. We can't afford anyone falling over. Stay below deck and root yourselves down, until I come to fetch you both."

That was not what Fin'roq expected to hear. "I thought we were safe," he said. "Why do they pursue us?"

"I don't think they like me very much," Anthem said.

"They aren't after me?" Fin asked.

"They're after all of us," Jaun said.

Fin tried to sleep but couldn't. Jaun was soon out though, so he perched quietly, feeling the motion of the cata'rin, listening to the gurgitator purring, and trying not to stare at him. He dozed for a while, then woke, but nothing had changed. So he slept some more. When he woke, there were streams of sunlight coming through the slats and the room was empty. He pulled his roots out of the soil, quickly cleaned up, and headed upstairs.

Jaun was standing on the main deck looking out at the sea. "Good morning, Fin," he said. "Beautiful day, isn't it? The sun is shining, the sea is calm, and we weren't ambushed, kidnapped, dissected, and then potentially eaten last night. So it's a nice morning! Hungry? Let's go find that stash of dried rhupan, shall we?"

But Jaun stopped when he heard the gurgitator close. He looked around the horizon, alarm in his eyes. And then Fin'roq watched Jaun's legs give out, and he collapsed to the deck. His eyes rolled back in his head, his eyelids started twitching wildly, and his mouth hung open.

Fin'roq screamed.

"Jaun!" he managed, and he ran to his side, dropping next to him and turning him over onto his back. "Jaun, can you hear me?!" He looked up the stairs at the bridge. "Captain! Captain Anthem! Help!" But there was no answer. Fin ran up the stairs, taking them three at a time with his long legs. He pushed open the door to the bridge and found Roman Anthem, also collapsed on the ground, eyes agape and twitching, his body still. Fin turned him over onto his back too, groaning with the weight of him, far heavier than the short, slender Jaun. Anthem had landed on his left arm and Fin'roq had to roll him one way, lift his arm around, and then roll him back. Then he ran back to Jaun.

Fin's head was pounding. He felt sick, like he was sinking, melting into the deck. But he shook his head and let the tears flow. Then he took Jaun's hand and held it. And he waited next to him, weeping, with no idea what to do, no idea what was happening.

Is he imperialized? he wondered. *Did someone imperialize both of them? So that the Bhizini can nab me without any resistance?*

Minutes went by, little eternities, but still Jaun didn't move, though his eyes were still twitching. And then Fin heard something else, and he realized things were about to get far worse for him. The horn of the Bhizini echoed across the gulf, rising and falling in trills that sent chills down his back.

"Wake up, Jaun, wake up!" he screamed, but Jaun didn't move.

Fin sat up on his knees to peer over the railing and he could see ships, dozens in both directions, hundreds—little wooden ships like the ones that had stormed the harbor at P'anorum. Even if he'd wanted to, Fin couldn't pilot a ship without a crystal, so there was nothing to be done. He sat, squeezing Jaun's hand, whispering for him to wake up, while the Bhizini drew closer and closer.

When Jaun leapt to his feet, screaming, Fin'roq screamed too. They both stood, screaming at each other, until they realized what they were doing and they stopped.

"Sweet Trevian, what a dream," Jaun whispered, his face lighting up with wonder. Fin noticed his eyes were twitching wildly again.

"I thought you were gone! But it doesn't matter, because we're all about to die," Fin said, pointing.

Jaun looked around and saw the fleet surrounding the ship. "Oh no," he whispered.

The gurgitator opened wide and the cata'rin lurched forward, and Fin and Jaun fell over onto the deck as the ship began to accelerate and turn hard to the right.

"Looks like Anthem woke up," Jaun said.

"What happened to you two?"

"Something incredible," he said, his eyes still twitching. "Yes, something incredible indeed."

"Well, good for you two," Fin said. "It was horrible for me! Don't ever do that again!"

"I had no choice, Fin," Jaun said. "But I promise it won't happen again."

Fin rolled his eyes and hissed, then fell away from Jaun as the ship lurched to the left.

"Come on," he said, getting up one foot at a time and clutching the deck with his rootpads. "Let's get downstairs before we take our final swim."

But then the gurgitator closed again, and they looked at each other with alarm.

"Were we hit?" Fin said.

"Maybe. But the gurgitator wasn't. The sound. Anthem closed it."

They looked around and it seemed like the ship was starting to pitch to one side. Fin heard the noise first—a gurgling and smacking sound—and turned to look at the water, but he wasn't sure what he was seeing. Jaun came and stood next to him, his mouth hanging open, dumbfounded. One by one, the Bhizini ships were sinking under the surface, in a wave moving from right to left. The ocean on the leftmost side of the fleet rippled and the tip of a seastallion fin erupted into the sky, long and scaled and glistening dark and gray—the longest fin that Fin'roq had ever seen—and when he thought of the size of the seastallion that would support such an appendage, he wondered if it wasn't time to scream.

"We're saved," Jaun said.

Fin looked at him like he'd lost his mind.

"But I don't understand," Jaun said. He looked confused but there was a sense of wonder in his eyes. "Why would he help us?"

"Who?" Fin said.

"Gray'may'n, the Unseen. The lord of the deep. The old spirit of the seastallions. The largest beast in the world. The Bhizini revere him. He's—" Jaun paused.

"A Mund'umbrian?" Fin said.

Jaun nodded. "Many doubt that Gray'may'n even exists. But once people see him—well, there are those who worship him, and those who think he's just a really big, really pesky fish. Especially since he almost always aids the Bhizini. What do you think, Fin?"

"I don't know what to think," he said. "Is he killing them all? The ships are gone, will he eat them?"

"Eat them? I doubt it. No. Besides, the sea isn't deep here. And look, Mon Mang'alar is not far. Most of them will walk out of here. No, for some reason, Gray'may'n wants us to get through here. He's given us a great gift today. I wonder what it means. Or if he'll want anything in return."

"The beast can talk?" Fin said. "I mean, Gray'may'n?" He blushed.

"Who knows. He definitely *wills*, whether he speaks or not. And he is cunning on top of that. Consider yourself lucky to have seen him, and survived."

The gurgitator whined as it opened wide and the ship began to lurch forward. Anthem came up the stairs. "What have you two been doing up here? I looked for you in your quarters, where I told you to stay! A projectile busted a hole the size of my head in the hull. We had water in the lower level, but thanks to yours truly, I plugged the leak." He wrung out his robe. "She'll stay afloat, don't you worry about that, though we'll need to dock in East'whaling to drain her out. Anyway..." he looked around at the disturbed water sloshing about but absent any ship. "Where's the fleet?"

"It seems they called off the attack," Jaun said. "Maybe they thought we were sunk and they fled? They all headed toward the swamps, best speed. We watched them leaving, wondering what the hell was going on."

Anthem reduced the gurgitator to a light purr. He shook his head. "Well, I suppose I should go steer this thing, if we hope to make it into port in one piece. And I'll pick up some fresh food from East'whaling. We deserve a proper meal after such a close call with death."

"Definitely a day to long remember," Jaun said.

For Fin'roq, it was a day he'd never forget.

Chapter 17

Counsels on the Abyss

ELLEX ANDRIA LEARNED AT a young age that a politician must put aside private issues, must postpone outrage or grief, fear or anxiety, or risk being considered unfit to rule—at least by sensible citizens. Balance was not a republic, so her authority didn't depend on public support, but Andrasia was. Her family's fame and fortune were the result of years, and generations, of loyal service. And her father had put aside his private beliefs and ambitions, his grievances, his sadness and frustration, in order to appear worthy of leadership. In order to *be* worthy of leadership. Her own life in the public sphere was no different. Calm, level-headed, rational. That was what a leader should be. And that was how Ellex Andria planned to act that day. Once the confusion and horror and fear and outrage had been properly tucked away.

She'd sent Uthyr home that morning. He'd bombarded her with information, with the rising toll of devastation that the incident had caused—with questions, assumptions, predictions, possibilities. She'd listened for as long as she could, occasionally streaming something he sent her, saying nothing. And then she'd snapped, screamed at him to shut up, to leave, to just leave her alone. When he left, a pained look on his face, she promised herself she'd apologize later.

Everyone in the world had seen her naked, seen the Raccorin king, Rhakksees the Second, on top of her. And her father had been there, in the room with them. She shook her head, feeling like she might vomit.

What happened to me on—she hesitated even to think the name, fearing her head would start throbbing again, her vision would crackle along the edges, and she'd feel like she might pass out—but she pulled up her memories of the island and said the word aloud, "P'anorum."

Nothing. No headache.

And then it hit her—for the first time in thirty-four years, it hit her.

"What happened to me on P'anorum?" she said slowly.

Her lungs seemed empty and she took one deep breath after another, but her chest had clenched up tight and her legs felt like they wanted to twitch. She stood and paced but it was too much, and she still couldn't breath and thought she might pass out, so she sat back down and rocked back and forth, hugging herself. She turned and looked around the room, her shoulders drawn up, her eyes wide, but her head seemed to spin and she struggled to remember who she was or where she was.

She almost reached for Uthyr, cried out for help, but she closed her eyes and whispered prayers to Trevian, repeating the words aloud over and over, until the need to escape from her skin had calmed down, and she knew herself again.

How—how had she gone all these years, through three whole decades, and never asked what had happened to her on P'anorum? Never read a report from the Me'dicant healers? Never tried to piece together the events leading up to the eruption? Never once, when Ellex prided herself on being someone who always got to the bottom of things, who worked to understand them from the ground up—someone who knew her own thoughts and intentions and motivations thoroughly and intimately.

She wept, and as the tears fell, she realized it was the first time since P'anorum that she'd really cried. The first time in three decades. And she finally knew—she *really* knew—that her father was dead.

But who was he? she thought, while she hated herself for doubting him. She didn't want to think about it any longer, but she couldn't stop, and she spent a long hour alone, delirious with grief.

She didn't snap out of it until Uthyr contacted her to let her know the Council of Nine had called a meeting for midday. She replied in characters, careful not to send him any of her emotions, then severed the connection and stood up from the floor, and she tried to hold her head high as she walked to the bathing room.

The cool water ran down her hair fibers and over her face and shoulders as she ladled it over her head, and the streams tickled her back as it fell across her skin. She focused on the feel of each cupful as the freshness spread from her forehead down her core to her legs and feet. And as she brushed out her hair fibers, she went slowly, feeling the motion, the sound, relishing the sensation, fully present. But then her thoughts returned unbidden to the dream, to her father, to P'anorum, to her confusion—and it was like she'd been punched in the stomach, all the air forced out of her lungs again, and her mind raced for an anchor, for a shield, for an explanation to calm the panic.

She prayed to Trevian, singing the words aloud, and she scrubbed herself again from head to toe, and ladled more water over herself, but she couldn't get rid of the feeling that she'd been violated, touched in some loathsome way, without warning and without permission.

Ellex reached for the servryn and brought up her notes, and she added the council meeting to her schedule. Midday gave her a few hours to prepare, but the only way that could happen was if she could stop the surge of questions that kept flooding her mind. Whatever had happened, had happened *to* her, not *by* her. She was as much a victim as everyone else who had suffered from this strange occurrence. Maybe the Council of Nine would have some answers for her.

In the meantime, she needed more immediate advice from someone older and wiser. Someone who remembered what had happened on P'anorum because they had been there too. Someone she trusted, and there were so few of those in the world. The Gran Pradesh, Ra'shard Ruu'n.

That is, if the Octa'vin would let her in to see him.

⁂

When Ellex reached the citadel, the sun had risen low in the sky, a shimmery white disc in the mire of the fog, which swallowed up the entire upper rim that morning. She passed through the gates and into the misty gardens of Corda'mere, then entered the obsidian spire and followed the squat corridor behind the main hall to the entrance to the Gran Pradesh's chambers. An Octa'vin stood on either side of the door, waxy skin looking gray in the dim light, vacant eyes staring straight ahead.

"I'm Sui Pradesh Ellex Andria. I have urgent business with the Gran Pradesh."

"I'm afraid the Gran Pradesh is unavailable."

Ellex suppressed the urge to hiss. "I have assurances from the Gran Pradesh that he would see me."

The Octa'vin said nothing for a moment. "He is currently unavailable," they said.

Ellex really did hiss this time, though she knew it wouldn't do any good. The Octa'vin couldn't be bribed, and would never budge. And since the Gran Pradesh had no crystal, there was no way she could contact him—no way she could let him know she needed to see him.

She fumed as she walked back through the corridors, her anger a welcome replacement to the anxiety she'd been trying to suppress. She decided to head to her office and work until midmorning, but as she approached the chambers of the Council of Nine, she heard a voice. No, voices. A meeting was already in session.

Her anger exploded.

Rameen Rutar was speaking when she entered the Solarium, and he faltered when he saw her but quickly recovered and continued. "And thus the servryns can't give us any data on the incident."

"Isn't it unprecedented?" Ellex asked.

Rutar looked around, his jowls swaying, then he looked back to Ellex. "Indeed it is. Servryns are, after all, full of datamins."

"Indeed," Ellex said, "but I was referring to starting a meeting of the Nine with only seven present."

Rutar scowled. "Your summons was for mid-morning, Sui Pradesh, so it's you who are breaking protocol here."

"Don't jerk my stem, Rutar," she said. "This is unheard of, it's unacceptable, and it's a grave insult to myself and to the Andrasian delegation."

Uthyr stood up. "Ellex, forgive us," he said. "We only wanted to ascertain the threat before you arrived."

"The threat?" She laughed. "You're referring to me?" She laughed again.

"This isn't a laughing matter," Malisha Andra'asnia's double said, standing in that awkward way that doubles moved, the eyes vacant and lifeless, like an Octa'vin. "Until we understand what has happened, you must necessarily be considered a threat to security, and to the privacy of this council." The double's voice remained flat but Ellex imagined Malisha Andra'asnia was all smiles as she said it.

"Easy, minister," Rajj said, standing up and putting out his hands, in what seemed more of a gesture of surrender than anything else. "As leader of the Raccorin delegation, I vouch for the loyalty and patriotism of Ellex Andria. I know she would never willfully break Balance, nor compromise this sacred body we represent. Until we know otherwise, we have to assume this incident could have happened to any one of us." He looked at Ellex and nodded, his eyes smiling.

"While such testimony might have carried a great deal of power in older days," Malisha's double said, "the current situation is unlike anything we've ever faced before. And in times that are unique, one must have unique solutions to complicated problems. Until we know for sure whether her thoughts are private and the secrets of this council secure, the Sui Pradesh should excuse herself for an extended leave of absence. If she refuses, then I call for the Council of Nine to vote no confidence in Ellex Andria's leadership."

Ellex couldn't believe what she was hearing, and all her preparation for this meeting, all her decades of experience, her notoriously quick wit, everything escaped her. The Council seemed dumbfounded as well, looking at one another, unsure of how to proceed. But then Rajj raised his hand and spoke.

"With reluctance I call for a vote," he said, scowling. "When an advisory member requests a vote, the Council votes, regardless of how impertinent the suggestion might be. So let us have the vote and be done with it."

"Surely those who want to end my career should have the courage to do so while I watch," Ellex said. "Let's have an open vote."

"Sorry Ellex, there's precedence for no confidence votes being anonymous," Rajj said, a pained look on his face.

"And is there a precedent for the accused having a vote in their own trial? I am, after all, still a full member of this council." Her eyes twitched rapidly as she queried Council of Nine protocol on the Pradishar servryn and found a pertinent case. "There is," she said, sharing it with the group. She walked from the door to her seat on the dais and sat down. "Shall we?" she said, acting more confident than she felt.

The eight members sent their votes to the Octa'vin record keeper, who sat over their heads on his tiny ledge, streaming the session to the Pradishar servryn.

"Tie," the Octa'vin said.

Ellex's heart sank but she didn't let her face show it.

"Summon the Gran Pradesh," Rajj said.

Ellex pored over the possibilities of the vote in her mind. A tie? She had expected the full support of the Council. Only four votes out of eight! She knew she had her own vote, Utte's vote, and Rajj's vote. Right? That meant at least one of the other two delegates for Andrasia didn't vote for her—most likely Trip Anders, the Dyna'arin representative for the Andrasians. That meant the entire Raccorin delegation except Rajj wanted her out. And so did the Guild. Not good.

<<Ell—>> Uthyr said in her mind, but she cut him off and cast him a look that made him wither, and he turned away and didn't try to contact her again.

When the Gran Pradesh Ra'shard Ruu'n arrived in the Solarium, slowly padding in on his bare feet, everyone stood and bowed. He shuffled silently across the floor, then carefully and with some effort climbed the dais and sat down on his throne between the two delegations. "How may I serve today?" he asked, short of breath.

Rajj informed the Gran Pradesh of the issue and his need to cast the deciding vote on whether or not to suspend Ellex Andria from the Council of Nine.

"Oh, this is an easy one. I vote nay."

Ellex felt like she could breathe again, and she inhaled slowly and carefully.

"I'm surprised such a vote was called," the Gran Pradesh continued. "I have tried to remain distant from this council, to let you decide how best to administer Balance, but perhaps my silence has allowed you to go astray. Balance is about union, after all. With grave threats from the sea, with strange occurrences with the crystals, with high profile arrests and accusations of treason—surely you see why this council must remain together in times like these? If the very top of Balance cracks, what is to stop the rest of it from splitting apart? Do you understand?"

"We do, your worship," the Council said together, bowing.

"Then forget this bickering and these pointless theatrics." He stood with great effort while the councilors bowed to him. When he reached the door, he turned back. "Sweet Trevian bless us all," he said. "And Ellex, dear, I'm available anytime today to speak with you. I assure you, the Octa'vin won't hinder you."

She'd heard that before.

"Thank you, your worship," she said gratefully, knowing the Gran Pradesh didn't normally show any favor for particular members.

"Then let us proceed," Rajj said, "with the full Council present."

Ellex sat back on her throne and allowed herself to really breath for the first time since she'd come into the chamber, enraged and then scared and then enraged again. This morning had turned into the closest she'd ever come in her life to losing her career, and it had taken her entirely by surprise.

Later, she thought. *I'll deal with that later, when I deal with everything else. Focus, focus.*

The meeting droned on for hours, with little progress and fewer answers. The Guild blamed the Pradishar for the dream—which the Council had deemed the "incident"—and the Pradishar blamed the Guild, claiming only a malfunctioning servryn could possibly reach everyone with a crystal. But nobody had proof of anything, not even educated guesses, just speculation and accusation. The Council decided to adjourn without issuing an official statement on the incident, except to prohibit any direct discussion of it, and they determined that the Cul'tavin would increase arrests and start targeting some higher-profile citizens in hopes it would cool the chatter on the weavryn.

"Before we adjourn, I have one last request," Rajj said. "The Gran Pradesh was right. We need to present a united face, in perfect Balance. Our petty divisiveness mustn't leave these chambers, not in decree and not in public displays of animosity. And so, in the spirit of such an endeavor, I suggest we invite my brother, Prince Rhakksees Raccorine Deri the Third, to oversee security in the capital."

Valden Andron, representative of Homeland Affairs for the Andrasian delegation, looking half asleep, shook his head and leap to his feet. "Corkin soldiers in Balan Su? Slaves! Here? I mean, really. Have you lost your mind, Prince Rajesh'n?"

Rajj seemed amused by the outburst. "Perhaps," he said. "But imagine, the Corkin and the Pradishar, working together to protect the heart of Balance Territories. Our subjects, and your citizens, rising above the old differences that divide us. And before I hear any more dissent from Andrasia, this is a direct request from the royal family, on behalf of my sister the regent. Per Balance protocol, the royal ruler of Raccorum Rhazzat can petition the Council of Nine at any time, and their request must be met, unless there are *extreme and convincing* circumstances that negate such a response. Given that Prince Rhakksees is currently the most beloved hero in Balance Territories for his daring capture of the violent terrorist Qardymion Saltsap, I can hardly imagine an extreme and convincing circumstance that could negate such a request." He looked at Valden Andron. "Can you?"

Valden cleared his throat and sat down.

Ellex decided she needed to get involved. Surely everyone had noticed her conspicuous silence. Better that they not know how grievously they'd wounded her pride.

"As we are all well aware, I've been working hard to integrate Raccorin and Andrasians into my Cul'tavin, and I was the first to put such squads on the streets of the capital and around the Inner Archipelago. The attack on my troops was directly related to our efforts to integrate the Cul'tavin, so don't imagine that I don't know the importance of this work. I know Prince Rhakksees is a competent leader and would be a great asset to our city, but do you really think we can bring a Corkin slave master to the capital and just expect that our Cul'tavin peacekeepers will work with him? Besides, would Prince Rhakksees even accept such a role?"

Rajj smiled thinly. "My brother will recognize that this is a rare opportunity for a nearly-exiled prince whose star had lost it's luster until late. He'll know that capturing the Saltsap was temporary glory, but the chance to put together a new squadron of elite peacekeepers would have enduring merit, and grant lasting political power. He'll accept the role, and he'll accept our conditions as well."

"Conditions?" Ellex said.

"Only a Pradishar of bishrop rank or higher can command Cul'tavin," Malisha's double said, "so Prince Rhakksees will need to be ordained first."

Ellex laughed, loudly and unexpectedly. Rameen Rutar and Trip Anders both glared at her, while Malisha's double stared with that vacant look on their face.

"Rakk Raeder, a bishrop of the Pradishar?" She laughed again. "He'll never accept, no matter what you bribe him with."

"It's not what we bribe him with," Uthyr said, avoiding her eyes. "It's who."

❧❧❧❧❧ ❧❧❧❧❧

Ellex left the Solarium when the meeting adjourned, furious with the Council, feeling like the entire thing had been a setup. They'd started without her, they'd questioned her fitness to rule, and before she'd even had a chance to defend herself, they'd been plotting behind her back. In case they failed to vote her out, they had an impossible task lined up, just for her—making a Pradishar bishrop out of a rowdy Raccorin prince who often thumbed his nose at authority and had been sailing the seas for thirty four years, practically a pirate himself.

And she hadn't seen him—hadn't heard his voice—since P'anorum.

P'anorum again. Always P'anorum.

And yet no headache. Just a feeling of panic and shame, confusion and regret.

It was all too much, all of it, everything. P'anorum. The dream. The vote of no confidence. Now Rakk would be coming to the capital, and not just to visit, but to live and work. And she had to oversee his training to become a bishrop. Which meant they'd be spending—what, every day together, for months? How was that even possible? She had never expected to see him again.

None of it made any sense to her.

So she hurried away from the Solarium, through the shiny black corridors of the citadel, til she once again reached the Octa'vin guards outside the Gran Pradesh's chamber.

"He said I could come in this time," she said. "Just a few hours ago."

"Name?"

Ellex looked at the Octa'vin. She swore this one had been there when she'd come that morning, though they did look so much alike that it was hard to tell them apart. And with those empty eyes and revolting, waxy skin, she did avoid looking at them as much as possible, so maybe it was a different one.

Still, she thought, *they all know me.*

"Sui Pradesh Ellex Andria to see Gran Pradesh Ra'shard Ruu'n, at his request," she said.

The Octa'vin paused.

"I'm sorry, he's unavailable at the moment."

Ellex Andria's shoulders slumped and she turned to go, feeling suddenly drained, not even able to manage a snappy insult.

"You may enter now," the Octa'vin said.

She looked back and blinked. "Really?"

The Octa'vin said nothing but the door opened behind them. Ellex entered and ascended a large curving black staircase that led to a small audience chamber lined with glowbes, but the room felt cold in spite of the light. The ceiling and floor were so shiny, so polished, they reflected each other back and forth across the gap, til you didn't know what was up and what was down anymore. She felt that she was floating there amidst it all.

Ra'shard Ruu'n sat perched on a small grassy mound at the end of the chamber, a beam of light shining down from the darkness above, four Octa'vin guards around him. When they saw Ellex approaching, they dispersed and Ra'shard yawned.

"I'm sorry to wake you, my lord," Ellex said, bowing.

"Not at all, not at all. At my age, all one wants to do is sleep. But life is in the waking, is it not?"

"It is."

"Best to let bad dreams be forgot," he said.

"A harder task than it sounds, your worship."

"Oh indeed, indeed. Nothing like a pesky thought to spoil, well, everything. Now, tell me my dear, how can I help?"

Ellex took a deep breath. "I hoped to break protocol," she said.

Ra'shard's eyes widened, his face a bright sea of concerned wrinkles.

"I want to ask about the nature of the crystals," she said.

"Oh, that," he said, a bit of disappointment in his voice. "Surely the Pruu'log told you they come from Trevian? And that we Pradishar are stewards of his spirit."

"My question isn't doctrinal. I suppose it isn't even metaphysical. I want to know about possibilities. The incident—this nightmare I've gone and shared with the entire Joined world—is there a precedent for such an occurrence? Or is this a result of Guild maquina streaming through servryns to the entire world? Can you at least tell me that?"

The Gran Pradesh sighed. "I can, but you won't like my answer. There is no precedent in any of the archives for such an occurrence. But you know Ellex, when Trevian sacrificed himself to create Balance, nobody knew his spirit could transform—could shatter apart as it did. There was no precedent for it, and yet it happened."

"But Trevian wanted to be sacrificed. I didn't want this to happen to me."

"Wanted to be sacrificed?" the Gran Pradesh said. "Do you know anyone like that?"

Ellex paused. "Who willingly wants to die, or doesn't feel the panic when it approaches, or horrors at the thought of it? No."

"If you hold a flame to someone's hand, they'll pull away, even if they don't want to. There's no question of choice, no morality involved, just a reaction to a specific action. And so, if Trevian didn't want to be sacrificed, why would he do it? What was he reacting to?"

Ellex swallowed hard, feeling like a scamp at the sprouting patch. "I wish I'd paid closer attention to the lore," she said, blushing.

The Gran Pradesh chuckled. "I'm not a taskmaster today, Ellex. There's no test to pass. I'm not sure there's an answer, or that I'm looking for a particular one. I just want to know what you think about when you ponder why Trevian had to die. I want you to remember that unprecedented things do happen. Our traditions in Balance Authority go back for ten thousand years, and the Pradishar for even longer. Sometimes we think that means everything that could happen has happened. Don't let the rarity of the event make you assume the worst."

"And what about the guilt?" she said. "What do I do about that? I—my dream—they say ten thousand citizens were killed as a direct result. What do I do about that?"

"You do your best and play your part," the Gran Pradesh said in his wizened old voice, though Ellex swore she heard her father. "The people need you. All across Balance tonight, our citizens are worried about you. They know what you endured and they hurt with you."

"What did I endure?" Ellex said. "Not just this dream, but—I'd like to ask another question. Again, I'll be breaking protocol here. I'd like to ask a private question."

"Anything that will help," the Gran Pradesh said.

"You must know I have no memory of the eruption—no memory of the year that followed. There is, as it were, a giant gap in my mind."

The Gran Pradesh nodded. "It's a cruel thing that happened to you. And yet the eruption is a very painful event for anyone to remember. And so, in a very, very small and strange way, you've been blessed to forget it." He sighed.

"I have so many questions," she said. "I didn't. I thought I knew everything I needed to know. I thought—I knew who I was. But suddenly all I have are doubts."

"Digging can cause an unexpected avalanche, sweeping you away when you least expect it to, and taking you somewhere you never intended to go. Sometimes it's best to leave the past in the past, although I know this is a great thing to ask. When I was chosen to be the next Gran Pradesh, I had to give up my crusade against slavery, to abandon what I had fought against for a century, for longer than that. I could either look back and consider my life a failure—or I could look forward with hope to a greater future. The world had called me to serve, and I had to take the call. Your time is now, and tomorrow. Not then. And it is here on Balan Su, not on P'anorum."

"I know you're surely right, my lord," she said.

"But you don't feel it," he said, smiling sadly.

She shook her head and lowered her eyes.

"I was raised with the Loricean faith," the Gran Pradesh said. "Back when all Raccorin were. The faith was tied to the royal family, as you know, and so it was obligatory to believe. But I really did believe. When I came of age, and read the Pruu'log for the first time, I joined the Pradishar instead—a big scandal in my village. I became a monkin, and the more I studied the lore and the Pruu'log, the more convinced I became that slavery was an abomination in the eyes of Trevian. Well, you can imagine how popular that made me in my Clade. I fought against the Loricea, and I fought against slavery, but I never could have predicted that the eruption would wipe out the Far Archipelago and would take down the Loricea with it. Or that I would end up chosen to lead the Pradishar in the wake of such tragedy."

"Your worship was born to lead," she said.

"As were you, Ellex," he said. "And I hope I haven't undershot my point as I've prattled on here like the old fool I am. When I joined the Pradishar and spoke against slavery, I alienated myself from my community, from my family, and from my ancestors, and they all made sure to let me know I had committed a very grave sin every time they saw me. This scar across my face that crushed my eyeball was a gift from my father. There are others you can't see, but which hurt just as much, or more, because they left no physical wounds. At any one point in my life, had I stopped to look back, to consider what others thought I should do—what my ancestors would have done, what my parents would have done, what my society insisted I do—I would have been lost. I would have driven myself mad with doubt. Only now do I wonder if all those sacrifices were in vain, seeing as how I'll soon be planted in the gruynfeld and slavery shows no sign of waning in Raccorum Rhazzat. I have to believe that I've always done what I *had* to do—like the hand in the flame, I reacted as I must, and am what I am. And the direction I go is always forward. Onward, and never backward. Never down into the darkness of doubt and despair."

Ellex nodded, but said nothing.

"I know what you've endured is a burden to you," the Gran Pradesh said. "But you must know that it is also your strength. Your ability to survive great tragedy, to keep your head up and soldier on—to be injured but not broken, challenged but not defeated—this has made you the idol of our citizens. They look up to you for guidance, and they turn to you for strength. Turn to them now. Speak to them. Share with them. Guide them through this crisis. Let them know you are okay, and let them know you are still looking out for them."

That was something Ellex could do, something that made sense when little else did. Yes, she'd close off the fear, and close off the doubt. She'd do her best at playing her part, at being the good-mother. And she'd let all of Balance know that she was busy on the job—busy working for them, serving them, and keeping them safe from threats near and far. The past could wait. Maybe it could wait forever. The present would only be fixed right now, in the present.

She thanked the Gran Pradesh profusely, and returned to her estate that evening feeling confident again, ready to face this crisis—all these crises—one day at a time. But when she accessed the weavryn, and reached out to see what her people were saying, what they were sharing, what had happened to them—when she saw the scenes of accidents and dynamin meltdowns and ferry boats crashed on rocky shores—the real horror of what had happened, not just to her but to her citizens, to Balance as a whole—her confidence slipped away and the tears from that morning, the first tears in decades, returned in full force.

Chapter 18

Strength in the Depths

B RYN DIDN'T KNOW HOW she'd gotten into her sleeping quarters, or when she'd fallen asleep, but she woke in the darkness of her room already sobbing. She slept a bit more, then woke again sobbing. Slept, and sobbed some more. She didn't know how long this went on, but eventually she heard drums banging, the sap in her ears pulsing. They wouldn't go away, but only got louder. Bang—bang—bang, as if they were inside her head, thumping at her skull, trying to get out.

"Can I come in?" Mama Andri'n said, hitting the door now with her walking stick. "You alive in there?" She pushed the door open and peeked in. Bryn squinted at her with swollen red eyes but didn't say anything. So Mama Andri'n hobbled on into the room and stood beside her, a bit wobbly on her bad leg. "You gotta come out, Bryndax," she said.

Bryn sobbed and screamed at her mother, "No! Only Papa can call me that!"

Her mother nodded. "Brynnie, then. That's what I always called you when you were just a scamp. You were always so curious, always asking, asking, asking. Thought you'd grow out of that—hoped you would, I guess—but you're just like your father."

"Are you trying to make me miserable?" Bryn said.

"Just sharing with you. Brynnie, you can't stay in here forever. I'm doing everything I can to keep going, but—well, it feels like I lost you both. You're here, but...you're not."

Bryn looked away.

"I don't pretend to know what's in your head. I never could know. I never could understand your father's mind either. But his passion—that I could. That I still can."

"Mama..."

"Let me finish. I know your Papa was more than your father—he was your mentor and best friend."

"You talk about him like he's not coming back," Bryn said. "Like you've given up on him!"

Mama Andri'n looked at her hands, trying to control her face.

"I know you don't think I'm bright, but I see what's going on. I see it, and it scares the wits out of me. The Pradishar have me feeling like—well, like having this conversation with you is somehow gonna get me in trouble. Right here in our own home, having a talk with my daughter. How can that be dangerous? So you know what, Brynnie? Fuck 'em."

Bryn looked at her mother with wide eyes.

"I don't know if your Papa is coming home or not. We can't know yet, so it doesn't help thinking about it. I pray he will, but I don't know for sure. Right now, what matters is what we do. We're still free. They're trying to make us afraid to remember that. But you got to remember that. You got to remember that *right now*! You got to go on doing whatever it is your Papa had you doing at the library. You know what I'm talking about. If he wanted you to do it, it was important. And you need to keep at it."

Bryn was sobbing now. "Oh Mama, it's all my fault! It's my fault they arrested him! Tortured him! I looked up information I wasn't supposed to. I used his credential—I—"

"Shh, Brynnie, shh. Honey, I know your father didn't do anything with bad intentions, and I know you didn't either. I also know your Papa has a lot of friends, powerful ones, good ones, honorable ones, all over the world. They won't sit around and watch Balance fall apart. This'll get fixed up. And you got a part to do in fixing it. Now get your bum outta this dark little cell and out into that sunshine! Come on now, you got this."

"Mama, I—how—" she gulped. "How are you so strong?"

"Strong? I'm in pieces. I don't know where I am or what I'm doing half the time, I'm so lost. But that's what routines are for. That what rituals are for. You just do 'em. You don't even have to think about it, you just do 'em. Get you through anything, you got a routine to follow."

"I guess I'd better get to the library then," she whispered.

"Now that's the spirit," Mama Andri'n said. "But first you need to eat."

Her mother hurried off to fix lunch while Bryn went into the washing room to clean up. When she came out into the garden, Mama Andri'n had set a tray down on the table and was using tongs to put the fried rhupan chunks on Bryn's plate.

She sat down and Mama Andri'n spooned a large scoop of ghugurt over the rhupan. Bryn looked at her platter and began to sob.

"I know, love, I know. Just eat what you can."

She ate her food in silence, desperately wanting to contact Trexbo, Ginjy, or Rhingus—all of them at once—to warn them. But she didn't dare—not today, not with the

Cul'tavin watching. Her friends hadn't contacted her either, so she thought they must know the danger they were all in. But still—she needed to share with them, and to know what they'd figured out. She'd pass by the Sweet Treat later and see if they were there—no, then she'd be leading the Pradishar to their office. Damn it, what was she to do? And with no one to ask for help. Was it worth it?

Bryn clenched her teeth together, gripped the soil with her rootpads, took a deep breath, and then gave herself a much needed pep talk. Her father needed her help, and she was going to help him. She might be scared, and if the Pradishar did arrest her, it would truly be awful—no, it was too awful to think about—but if her father had to go through it, then she could too. If there was a chance to help him, she would.

Even if I can't breathe, she thought. *Even if my hands shake and my voice squeaks like a mouse. Even if the panic, the urge to run and hide, seems too much to handle. I will face this. I will!*

And so, pushing down the panic, she reached out for the servryn and began to scan the streams, archiving data as quickly as she could, her eyes not even twitching, as she munched on her rhupan.

"You want me to go with you today?" Mama Andri'n said. "I don't mind. Be good to get out of the house."

Bryn nodded, then shook her head. "No. I'm fine. I'm okay. I'm good. Really."

❧❦

When Bryn left for work, she gave her mom a long hug and let the tears flow freely again, though she held back the sobs. After a deep breath, she lifted her head and exhaled hard, then walked out through the gate and headed up the sloped paths of Stone Garden toward the old wall. The Council of Nine had changed the celebration jubilee for the capture of Qardymion into a week-long 'gathering—a holiday to mourn our losses and celebrate our future'. Bryn was suspicious. When she came into the old city, she saw the plazas were full of locals and tourists, a strange mixture of groups clearly in mourning and others clearly on vacation. Bryn thought it a strange sort of balance.

Before long, she noticed that everyone on the streets of Old Town were staring at her. This was nothing new, except that instead of the surprise and mockery she usually saw in their eyes, she saw sneers and accusations and threats. Traitor. Anarchist. Lab experiment. Ren'fallow. Gender offender. They said them all, on the weavryn if not to her face. By the time she crossed the Clear Water to the royal plateau, away from the gaze of the public, clips of her walk were already being torn to pieces on the gossip streams—the daughter of today's most infamous traitor, finally showing her hideous face in public. Off to commit more mischief for her treacherous father, no doubt.

When she entered the building, the old librarian Madr'gin flashed her a big smile, her face wrinkled up like an old grape. Bryn wondered if she even knew what had happened to her father and decided she didn't. Once in her office, she wiped away a few more tears, then set up her workstation, placed a scroll in the carver, and set the maquina a'whining.

Then she sat down and started sobbing again.

How had public morale turned against her father? From admired to reviled, so suddenly, and without reason.

How dare the Pradishar turn everyone against him, and how dare the public so easily eat up their lies!

Bryn smacked the workstation and knocked the scroll off it's holster. She gasped and grabbed it, tenderly, and returned it.

"Sorry," she said to it. "Didn't mean to threaten you like that. Just had a rough day." She laughed through the tears. "I've been saying that for so long now, haven't I? Just had a rough day. Ha!"

How was she going to do anything with the Cul'tavin watching? They'd probably followed her here. She wouldn't have noticed if they had. But what would they find if they busted in? Scrolls? A carver? These were standard things in a library.

If only she could contact Anorian Grain, her father's colleague. That was her best bet at finding any kind of answer about what was going on. And maybe she could find out if—it was too awful to think about—if Bryn was the reason her father had been arrested. But where to start? Anorian had come to her father's lab in some kind of cloak, so Bryn wasn't sure a normal query would work.

Bryn wouldn't be deterred. As the hours wore on and the carver continued to whine the day away, she scanned through her archives on the servryn. Over the years, she'd collected an impressive amount of sources about the creation and development of the weavryn. She could have taught a course at the Academicon on it—and thanks to her work in her father's lab as a scamp, she'd had first-hand experience with much of weavryn technology for most of her life. She had a feeling that Anorian, in helping her father with a new incarnation of the weavryn, would still be active on the first incarnation, though few now were. It was worth a shot.

The world's very first servryn was still active, a short walk from where Bryn sat, somewhere in Andramere's Academicon. When it was invented one hundred years ago, the servryn created a seamless blend of all three crystals—communication, energy, and information—that could unite the crystamins of all classes, and allow immediate access to datamins from anywhere in the world instead of requiring close proximity to them. This first servryn was very basic, more about data storage and sharing, and communications were only through characters, no emotions, no mental or sensual streaming.

When the second incarnation came about, any two non-imperialized crystal holders anywhere in the world could connect and share their thoughts and feelings and sensations, regardless of crystamin class, so that an operator could stream to a Pradishar monkin, or a Guild Manager on Callo Baton to an Orden in the wastes of the Fierrin Desert. This sharing, once restricted to two people with the same class of crystamin, was now available for everyone, and the rise in popularity of Andramere's weavryn entertainment industry spoke to the hunger among Balance citizens for such an experience. It was no surprise that the first incarnation of the weavryn was soon forgotten.

And yet the servryn remained, and Bryn had spent a lot of time as a scamp playing around on the old system, communicating with other enthusiasts who shared a penchant for relics while learning to manipulate the data and archive it onto more modern servryns. Interacting with others entirely with characters was quaint and fun for a young Bryn, and she still liked to poke around the old servryn from time to time, if only for nostalgia's sake. She figured the likelihood of it being actively monitored by Cul'tavin scanners was slim to none.

But what to say? I need to speak to Anorian Grain?

No, it would have to be more subtle than that. Damnit—she always had people to ask, sources that could explain what to do. Allies willing to help her. She was worthless on her own.

"Anorian help." That was what she sent, all in caps. ANORIAN HELP. Might as well make it a shout. There was no response, but she didn't expect one right away. When the workday ended and Bryn needed to head home, there was still nothing at all.

Frustrated, Bryn stored her carver inside the workstation, made sure everything was in its proper place, and locked up. Madam Madr'gin nodded at Bryn as she left. "Working late today, Bryn dear?"

"Is it late? I lost track of the time."

"Twilight is fast fading."

She stepped outside and saw the old librarian was right—the sun had set, the sky was still bright, but the streets of the Forum had fallen dark, and the glowbes were casting orange smudges of dull but warm light on the stones.

She cursed herself for not paying attention to the time, and for not wanting to admit how scared she was. She thought about going back inside, reaching out for Trexbo, pleading with him to come escort her—but the last thing she wanted to do was risk Trexbo getting arrested. He had long been a target of the Cul'tavin, and Malisha Andra'asnia already knew they were friends. If she ran to him so soon after her father was arrested, she was afraid it would look suspicious. They hardly needed a reason to take him in.

So she took a deep breath and started for home.

When she had descended from the plateau into the old city, and was walking along the walls at the top of the ridge, she heard a commotion coming from the plaza—a crowd chanting—and while the thought of a large group made her stomach rumble, her curiosity got the better of her. As she approached, she heard her father's name, and she froze, in a sudden panic, ready to turn and run.

But she realized they were demanding his immediate release. She stopped at the edge of the square and watched, blinking back the tears, which fell hot but happily down her face.

That's what I get for focusing on PropSector streams, Bryn thought. *They're always the loudest, most visible streams on the weavryn, and also the most fallacious.*

Not everyone has abandoned Papa.

She leaned against the brick wall and cried softly, watching the crowd grow larger and start to get rowdy. When she saw swarms of Cul'tavin peacekeepers coming into the plaza, she turned and started down into an alley, her joy forgotten, replaced by an overwhelming sense of panic, of blind terror, at the sight of so many of them.

She'd barely taken a few steps when two dark shadows stepped out into the alley in front of her, and she realized she was just around the corner from the Sweet Treat, right where she'd been attacked that night.

"Bryn Andri'n, by the authority of the high doge of Andramere, please step over here for questioning."

Two Cul'tavin peacekeepers, brandishing zaprens, stood in the alleyway.

Bryn's hands were shaking and her legs seemed attached to the pavement, and though she desperately wanted to run, she couldn't.

"Over here. Now."

Somehow her legs began to move, but awkwardly, like they'd been drained of sap—like they weren't really hers. She could see Malisha in her mind, her father writhing on the ground. She tripped, fell toward them, and took down the peacekeeper on the left. The other one kicked Bryn in the stomach, and she rolled off the Cul'tavin, unable to breath—no, she'd already been unable to breath. Now she was sure she'd black out.

The Cul'tavin she'd squashed rolled over on top of her, dug his knee into her belly—crushing her cumberdome into her flower—and put his hand around her throat.

"Now this looks familiar," he said, shaking off his hood.

Bryn stared up into Aerid's face, and she was back in that terrible moment again, and she started to jerk and thrash and flail. But then her body went rigid, and she felt like her limbs were no longer her own. She lay back against the ground and put her arms out to the sides. Aerid stood up, digging his knee harder into her flower, sending knives through her gut and making her vision crackle and flash, but she couldn't scream, couldn't move.

"Bryn the Barge, you just don't take a hint, do you? Nothing to say? No? Well, you don't need to talk to reveal your secrets to me. Let's see what you were doing in there all day." He reached for Bryn's mind. "What shall we peak at first?"

"We don't have authorization to probe and you know it," the other peacekeeper said. "Our orders were to follow and question only."

"That was before I was attacked," Aerid said. "You saw it happen. The freak lunged at me. She endangered a Pradishar. Anyone threatening Balance is subject to enhanced interrogation techniques."

"Nah, she tripped. Let's just get outta here. You saw her doing busy work the entire day. Malisha's got the internal stuff covered. Besides, this freak does anything, we'll come back and nab her later."

"You don't get it, do you," Aerid said. "Her type can't be left alone. You gotta make sure they know they're freaks, or they start thinking they're your equals. You gotta make sure they *feel* your authority, or it's not real." He turned back to Bryn. "How's this feel?"

Bryn had never been probed before. It was like reliving a moment of her life, in a long and drawn out flash—as if she were forced to perform the same way she had in memory but with the full knowledge that she was being watched, every detail inspected, the entire time. She tried to scream, to do something different, to attack the intruder who had come uninvited into her memories—but everything happened, just as she remembered it.

Aerid started with the morning. It was over in a second, but not for Bryn. She had to re-live several hours, perched in her sleeping quarters, sobbing quietly so her Mama wouldn't hear, ashamed and guilty. Aerid got to feel everything she felt, looking down on her from the edge of memory, hanging over her from the shadows, laughing at her pain, mocking her shame, pointing at her and screaming obscenities, waving his flower in her face.

Bryn was trying to fill her lungs, trying to sob, and trying to retch, all at the same time. She writhed and moaned and gasped on the ground, straining against the restraints in her mind.

"Enough Aerid, I'm serious," the other peacekeeper said. "No more twisted shit. Just scan her and let's go. You're gonna get us in trouble again. Come on."

But Aerid couldn't resist. And so Bryn lay there, twitching on the ground, while she re-lived the last five hours at the library, but every few minutes, Aerid's face appeared, mocking her, making faces at her, and then vanishing again. When she got to the time when she searched for Anorian on the old weavryn, Aerid was inside her head, using her eyes, watching her send out the post, and waiting patiently—and then impatiently—for a response.

"Let's go!" the other peacekeeper said, grabbing Aerid's arm.

But Aerid pulled a dagger from his waist and held it up to the other peacekeeper's throat. "Never, *ever* touch me like that. Or I swear to Holy Trevian, you'll never bloom again. Understood?"

The peacekeeper looked at the ground and nodded. "Clear."

"I'm gonna have a bit more fun here, is that a problem?"

He shook his head no.

"Is it?" Aerid said.

"No."

"Good," Aerid said. "She needs to know what happens when she disobeys and attacks a Cul'tavin peacekeeper. And what happens when she calls out to help from Ren'fallow conspirators plotting to take down Balance. Isn't that right?"

"That's right," the other one said.

"Hmm...Let's say we take a trip through...what do you say...old papa's arrest? How'd you like to relive that? Hmm?"

"Please no!" Bryn cried. "No!"

"Let me have it!" Aerid said, reaching for her mind again. He leered at her, his eyes twitching.

Bryn braced herself, trying to turn her mind away from what was coming, to close herself off. But nothing happened.

Aerid's face turned from malicious to confused to enraged. "How?" he spat the word out. "She's blocking me. She's blocking me!"

The door to the Sweet Treat creaked loudly as it opened.

"What's going on out here?" someone said.

"Let's go," the peacekeeper said.

"Damnit," Aerid said, hissing. Then he looked at Bryn. "Be seeing you soon."

Bryn tried to rise but lay back and closed her eyes and wished for the ground to swallow her whole instead.

That night, Mama Andri'n cleaned her wounds and dabbed a tincture on all of them. Then she served her hot jha'ala with rum and a squeeze of citrin, to help her sleep. Mama Andri'n climbed into the patch beside her, unfurled her long branches from under her arms, and held her through the night. But Bryn never slept, even though she'd lived that day twice already.

She couldn't even cry anymore.

Chapter 19

Deceit, Desperation, Disgust

WHEN BALANCE AUTHORITY ANNOUNCED that the jubilee for the capture of Qardymion the Saltsap would be expanded to a weeklong 'gathering' to bring the citizens together, Lithuigi's first thought was on the sea, and getting far away from everything else. His cata'rin was still being repaired, but there were other ships. They could carry him away from Balan Su.

He'd come down to the docks, satchel in his good hand, intent on leaving, but knowing he couldn't.

Mha'arlo was waiting for him.

"I'm afraid today's scroll is all bad news," he said, handing it to Lithuigi. "I hate to share this at all. Professor, I'd rather you hear this from me than from a piece of parchment. Doc Andri'n's been arrested and charged with crimes against information."

"Oh Mha'arlo, thank you, I wish I'd heard it from you first," Lithuigi said. "But my vile elder son informed me of it last night."

"Doc Andri'n was so nice and so kind," Mha'arlo said. "Brilliant, but warm. Approachable. Professor, was this my fault?"

"Your fault? Goodness no! If anything, it was mine. The good Doc knew the risk, and I suppose I did too. But don't worry too much about it. The Pradishar have made an unprecedented move—they must be desperate after Ellex Andria's dream—and I think the Guild is scrambling to understand how to react to it. When they do, Doc Andri'n will be released and all will be fine. Not to worry."

"I don't know," Mha'arlo said. "I don't know of anyone who's come out of a Pradishar dungeon once they go in. At least not for crimes against information."

"But Doc Andri'n isn't just some rogue from the streets burning Pruu'logs and dreaming of revolution. He's a priestin, a professor, and a Dyna'arin tinker, one of the finest in the world. The Pradishar will see his worth and treat him differently than the common criminal. He's too valuable to just toss aside."

"I hope you're right," Mha'arlo said.

Lithuigi did too.

Mha'arlo eyed his satchel. "Going somewhere, professor?"

Lithuigi looked out at the harbor but all he could see was gray and white. The fog seemed darker than usual today, wet and cold and stifling. Even the upper rim was covered, and that kind of gloom across the entire city settled into one's core, making everything slow—making every movement a monumental effort that hardly seemed worth the effort. On such days, you just wanted to perch in a corner under a glowbe and wait for a better day.

"I wish I was leaving," he said. "But I can't. Not yet."

"Zenithra is only a few months off with the new year. And then you can travel all summer long. And hopefully take me along!"

"It'll be here before we know it," he said. "But first, you should take the rest of the jubilee-mourning-whatever this holiday is—take it off. Go be a normal student and have some fun."

"Thank you, but in this weather, and with these tidings, I think I'll just find a glowbe in a cozy corner and hope tomorrow looks better. Good day, professor."

"Good day to you too, Mha'arlo. Farewell. And thanks again for the scroll."

Later Lithuigi took the lift back to the upper rim, still deep in the fog, and carefully followed safe walkways far from the edge back to Sunrise Ridge and his garden estate. Rebesh'a was in the study, glowbes glowing brightly, perched while reading a book. She put it down when she saw Lithuigi, then walked over and gave him a hug.

"I'm so sorry to hear about Doc Andri'n," she said. "Truly L'uigi, it's not right, not right at all. Everyone on Andramere is up in arms about it, and the Pradishar are struggling to keep down a popular uprising in Andramere City—though not a peep of that on the official notestreams. Nobody believes the charge of treason. Your brother has many allies." She touched his face and then hugged him again. "Have you petitioned the Guild for his release?"

He looked away.

"They've said nothing so far," she said. "Make them speak in his defense! Speak to Management. Go to the citadel, to the Council of Nine, and ask to be heard. Ask for an audience with the Gran Pradesh. Do whatever you can to save him! He's your brother!"

"Yes, but nobody can know that," he said. "Even you shouldn't know that. We would risk our lives, our sons' lives, Bryn Andri'n's life, if that information got out."

"Then speak to Rameen Rutar."

He suppressed a hiss and frowned at Rebesh'a.

"I know you despise him," she said. "But he's head manager. He's powerful."

"Why would he help me? I haven't exactly been supportive of his faction over the years."

"It's not about helping you. In this case, helping you means helping the Dyna'arin, and that means helping himself. He's probably like you are—hesitant to speak out, wanting to feel the pulse of things first, to make sure he doesn't do something he'll regret. The Pradishar have been amassing new authority and demonstrating it. That alone could upset Balance. Speak to him, L'uigi. Do it for me, if you won't do it for Doc Andri'n."

"I'll try," he said. "But please—this is all I've thought about all night. And it's too terrible of a day outside to make it worse by thinking of futilities."

"Yes," she said. "No more news, no more notestreams. Let them wait til tomorrow."

"Thank you," he said.

"I have just the thing to distract you," she said. "Let's stream one of my melodramas. The Winds of West'whaling, the one you promised to watch with me."

"I made no such promise," Lithuigi said. "I said I'd read the summaries and reviews. I always do that."

"But with the premiere gala coming up this Zenithra—you remember, right? That you *must* attend, right? Good. It would help your conversations at the gala if you'd stream it first. What do you say?"

"Oh, don't worry about me," he said. "When have I ever failed to impress that boozy director and his fey flunkies?"

"Only every time you've met them," she said. "Even if you don't realize it! And would it kill you to watch it for my sake? Just because I want you to and for no other reason? Do you know how much it hurts to have to keep secret from my colleagues—from *everyone*—that my esteemed husband, beloved professor Lithuigi, has never once streamed a single one of my melodramas! I'm world famous, and yet my own husband can't be bothered to care."

"I was always your biggest fan when you were on stage," he said. "And stage work is real work, real art, real storytelling, and real performance. Weavryn melodramas are all about sensation and emotion, so contrived as to be revolting to anyone with a modicum of finer feelings. Besides, you know it's a matter of principle to me that I not use the servryns that make up the weavryn."

Rebesh'a scowled at him. "No public servryns. Right. Okay. Then how about I get a copy placed on a datamin. Would that be okay? You could stream from there? No weavryn, just a good old fashioned crystal intel grab. I'd have to ask Ritty, but what do you say to that?"

He desperately wanted to say no way, that he would rather sit in silence for two hours than waste that time on a melodrama—at least he'd get something out of the silence—but he could see how eager she was, how hopeful, and it broke his heart.

"I would love that," he said. "But only if we can stream it together."

Rebesh'a cheered and whooped and danced about the room, then grabbed Lithuigi and pulled him into her dance. "My dear L'uigi," she said. "My cranky, curmudgeonly—" She kissed him. And then she kissed him again. Their dance slowed, and they unfurled their branches and wrapped them around one another. Before long they were naked, moaning softly between kisses, their robes on the floor, their flowers pressed against one another, the stamens in the tight buds of soft petals, sticky with pollen, swollen up and held together, one into the other, as they swayed away the hours of the fog-swept afternoon, forgetting entirely how miserable the world outside was, at least for a little while.

❧ ❦

That evening, Lithuigi felt rejuvenated and with a renewed determination to save Doc Andri'n from execution. He contacted Rameen Rutar's secretary, but she was dismissive, refusing to guarantee a meeting until summertime, and only on Callo Baton, where Rutar would spend the break. That wasn't nearly good enough. Who else did he know who was on a friendly basis with the old bastard?

<<Do you have a minute, son?>> he asked.

<<Perhaps,>> Hesh'n said. <<How's the arm?>>

<<Oh, just perfect,>> he said. <<I forget I ever lost one. Strange, like that entire period of my life didn't happen.>>

<<What do you need?>>

<<Rameen Rutar. I need to speak with him.>>

<<He'll be on Callo Baton all summer. He's easy enough to find there.>>

<<I need to talk to him today, not three months from now. You heard about Doc Andri'n's arrest last night?>>

<<Yes, and I'm outraged the Guild hasn't spoken up—oh, I see. Okay. Well. Let's see, the day is growing late, and it's technically a holiday today. So I can guess where he'll be tonight.>>

Nunan, he repeated to himself. *Not far, but a little out of the way. Oh well.*

<<I owe you one,>> Lithuigi said to his son in his mind, then he found Rebesh'a on the veranda.

"I'm off to get answers," he said. "I have an unofficial meeting with Rameen Rutar. So don't wait up for me."

Rebesh'a was beaming and gave him a long kiss. "You're doing the right thing," she said. "Make him listen to you."

"I'll do my best," he said. "Of course, there's a significant chance that Doc Andri'n is guilty of what he's been accused. Just so you know."

He left her there with her mouth hanging open, but she didn't call after him. As he walked toward the lift in Grand Plaza, he contacted the dock and asked for a skiff'rin. When he reached the Guild wharf, the skiff'rin was ready to go, and Mha'arlo was in the pilot seat.

"Where are we off to tonight, professor?" he asked, grinning.

"Nunan," he said, "*I'm* off to Nunan. *You're* just watching after the skiff'rin so it doesn't get stolen while docked."

"Ahh, but professor," Mha'arlo said, and his bright green face seemed to grow fainter with disappointment. "I'm not a scamp, you know. I've been to Nunan before. I know what goes on there. And I know I can help you, if you'd trust me."

Lithuigi realized he was being selfish, not wanting to endanger Mha'arlo—not wanting him to be another victim of his foolish plots. But he knew it was too late for that, he was already in danger, and knew way too much to ever be safe again. Besides, he'd risked Mha'arlo's safety before. And it's true, he wasn't a scamp anymore. He could decide things for himself. "You can come along," he said.

Mha'arlo cheered, but the fog seemed to swallow up the sound.

"So what's the plan, professor?" he asked, once they had navigated through the western gate and out into the Threshinveld Sea. The air was too thick to even see the towers on the northern tip of Nunan. There were no directions discernible, just shadows all around. But Mha'arlo could use the crystamin to navigate, feeling out for the beacons on the buoys around the island, and he opened the gurgitator, steering the ship toward the south.

"Dock on the east side of the island," Lithuigi said. "We're early, so that's good. Hopefully we'll beat Rutar to the tavern, and we can hide out in back and wait for him. He—has some unusual tastes. I just need to stream a brief glimpse of them to a datamin before I confront him about his silence over Doc Andri'n. And hopefully I won't need the blackmail."

Mha'arlo whistled. "You could be expelled from the Guild for that. Or arrested by the Pradishar."

"If I'd tried this on the crescent, perhaps. But there aren't Cul'tavin lurking around waiting to arrest people here. So we'll at least have a shot at escaping."

"You haven't really thought this one through, have you, professor?"

Lithuigi laughed. "Clever plant. You don't think me a criminal mastermind? Very well, but these are desperate times."

They rounded the southern tip of Nunan and Mha'arlo killed the gurgitator, allowing them to float gently into the lagoon that served as a shallow harbor for smaller craft. He anchored the boat alongside the dock and paid the attendant double the normal fee.

"That should keep the boat safe," Mha'arlo said. "Unless there's a shift-change before we're back."

"Look at you," Lithuigi said. "How'd you figure that out?"

"I watch a lot of melodramas," he said.

"Melodramas aren't real life."

"No, but real life is like the melodramas."

"If you say so, son. But enough of this. People don't come to Nunan to debate philosophy. Surely we're going to stand out."

Mha'arlo just laughed. "Are we heading to the Rusty Fin?"

"How'd—you know that?"

"Rutar comes for their Bhizini whores," Mha'arlo said.

"How do you know that?"

"Everyone knows that?" Mha'arlo said hesitantly.

"I didn't know until today. It's never been in one of my scrolls, I'll tell you that much. Perhaps you've not being doing them thoroughly enough?"

Mha'arlo laughed again. "Oh no professor, it definitely wasn't in one of your scrolls. No, you insisted that I post the stories from reputable streams. You were very strict about the sources, if you remember correctly? Well, no such stream would ever discuss Rutar's perverse fantasies. But the gossip streams? The ones where people can share information and comment on it? They discuss it all the time. It's kind of a running joke to many in Balan Su."

"So he won't be blackmailed, is that what you're saying?"

"That I don't know. As far as I'm aware, nobody has been foo—er—brave enough to get any proof."

He sighed. "I feel old, and out of touch."

"It's never too late to learn new things," Mha'arlo said. "That's one of your favorite maxims, no?"

"Very clever," he said. "You probably know the way around here better than I do. Fine, lead on then. To the Rusty Fin."

He felt like a fool. What if he'd come alone? He'd have only made a mess of things.

Most of Nunan, save for the rocky northern tip, was a long grassy sandbar interspersed with lagoons, over which had been built an assortment of wooden huts with thatched roofs, some several stories tall. Boardwalks and roped bridges connected the huts in an eclectic arrangement of rows and circles. The Rusty Fin was wedged on a slender strip between the lagoon and the open sea, and thus right between the docks for the small boats and the piers for the larger ships.

Glowbes were out on the boardwalks but spaced so far apart they were like hazy blobs in the fog. You couldn't see anything til you were right upon it. So when they stepped into the Rusty Fin, even though it wasn't a large place, it seemed cavernous inside, long and wide and fog free. The bar was busy and a band played in one corner, with people dancing in front of them. Mha'arlo saw a booth in the back corner open up and pulled on Lithuigi's arm, dragging him over to it, and just in time before someone else claimed it.

"I'll go get some drinks," Mha'arlo said. "Any suggestions?"

"So long as it doesn't poison us, I suppose anything is fine."

Lithuigi settled back against the wood of the booth, keeping his cloak on and his hood up, and he folded his arms over his chest and sat brooding. He glanced around the room—nothing spectacular, that was certain. He thought it looked like whoever made the bar had been trying to mimic the Captain's Table on Grand Gardenia, only running out of money early on in the construction and settling for a far shabbier design. An A for effort, but still a flunking grade overall.

Rutar wasn't in the bar yet. But Hesh'n promised him he would be here, and Mha'arlo seemed to concur. He looked around again, scarcely able to believe he was really on Nunan again. Surely it had been decades.

Mha'arlo sat two cups down on the table, tin ones with looping handles. The one he gave to Lithuigi was only a third of the way filled with a thick amber liquid. Mha'arlo's drink, on the other hand, came nearly to the brim, filled with a black, bubbling concoction that he was looking on with wonder.

"It's a Swamp Gas," he said. "Some sort of sugar-filled fizzy delight. Don't worry, no spirits."

"And mine?"

"I asked for their second best rum, a dark spicy one. The bartender said I picked well, that it's a specialty here in this bar, and many sail around the world to have a sip of one."

"Really?" Lithuigi said, amused. "He sold you more than a drink, no? And this for the second best one? What about the best? What story could top that one?"

"He says the best one really is the worst one, the cheapest one, and that he makes it himself in a bucket under the bar. Only he's convinced the tourists that it's the really premo stuff, and he charges them whatever he wants for it. He says if you charge a lot, people will think it's good regardless—that you could give them sea water and they wouldn't know the difference."

"What a charming character," Lithuigi said. "He told you all this just now?"

Mha'arlo smiled.

Lithuigi sniffed the drink, then thought what the hell and took a sip of it. The flavors were rich, and the liquid was warm as it went down, sweet and strong on his tongue.

"A fine pick," he said.

Mha'arlo took a swig of his Swamp Gas and grinned at him. "Cheers," he said, holding up his cup. "To such an unexpected night."

Lithuigi lifted his cup and tapped it on Mha'arlo's. "I hope we don't have long to wait," he said.

"We don't," Mha'arlo said, and pointed with his eyes. Lithuigi turned to see that Rutar had entered the bar, but he wasn't alone. Two large Raccorin accompanied him, and he had little doubt they were Guild Enforcers without their uniforms or masks on.

"That might complicate things."

Rutar ordered a drink at the bar and downed it. Then he ordered one more and downed it. His guards took a seat by the door, and Lithuigi was surprised to see them pull out a set of tiles and coins and begin to lay them on the table. Clearly they were used to this and had found a way to pass the time.

"Good," he said. "His henchmen are starting up a game of Sailors and Snakes. Rutar should be alone for awhile. Now, how do we get upstairs?"

"I arranged for that," Mha'arlo said, "when I ordered our drinks. And right on time too."

A Bhizini had approach the table, wrapped in fine silks, whirling around, smiling and laughing at Lithuigi, taking his hand, pulling him to his feet.

Lithuigi made to protest.

"Play along, professor," Mha'arlo whispered, "and you'll be able to go upstairs without being noticed."

So he let the Bhizini drag him off to the dance floor, whirl him around a few times, hold him and rub close to him, and then pull him toward the stairs and up to the second floor. He took a quick glance around, but nobody was paying them any attention. They went down a short hallway and to the left, and into another room. The Bhizini leaned close. "Down this hall, third door on the left. Go inside. He will be through the next door. Go now."

Lithuigi nodded and started off in the direction the Bhizini had pointed, down the hall to the third door on the left. He took a deep breath, carefully turned the knob, and entered. The room was small and he did his best to walk slowly and avoid making the floor creak. He could hear noises in the room beyond, and he approached the door.

He readied himself to stream everything he saw and heard to the datamin in his pocket, then he ever so slowly turned the knob on the inside door, just wide enough to get a peek inside. He almost slammed the door when he got a glimpse, but steadied himself, then opened it a bit further for a full view.

And he began to archive.

Rutar was naked, perched on a small dirt mound in the middle of the room, his legs wide apart, his branches unfurled from his arms and stretched out to grip the ceiling. His eyes were closed, his jowls swaying as he huffed and heaved. His massive gut hung down over his waist, glistening bright green, his flower drooping off of it, the stamen engorged and protruding downward toward the ground. Beneath his belly, cross-legged on the floor in a circle, were three Bhizini, barely flowered themselves, each taking a turn. And all the while, Rutar threatened them, mocked them, said blasphemous things to them—things that made Lithuigi want to vomit up his drink.

He had seen enough. He closed the door carefully, took a deep breath, and then banged loudly on the door. "Cul'tavin peacekeepers. Open the door!" he shouted.

"How dare you interrupt me!" Rutar screamed. "I'm a bishrop, you fools."

Lithuigi didn't know what to do so he banged on the door again. "Open up!" He opened the door and saw Rutar pulling on a robe, a look of exasperation and annoyance, even a bit of panic, on his face. The Bhizini were nowhere to be seen.

"Your expression will make a nice cap to the stream of you violating Bhizini and promising to bear scamps with them. The notestreams are going to love this."

Rutar reached behind him and turned back holding a Vintrani blade, the metal nearly brown in the light of the glowbes.

"It's already archived," Lithuigi said. "And will stream to the weavryn in the event of my death."

Rutar stared at him for a moment and then sighed, looking defeated, his shoulders dropping. "What do you want, Von'nDrino? Why the fuck have you followed me here tonight, to do something so very, very stupid?"

"I needed to get your attention," he said. "And I wasn't about to wait three months for a damn interview."

"You couldn't have thought of a better way?"

"You're quite busy, apparently. But this can't wait. I need to know, right now, why Doc Andri'n was arrested! He's a Dyna'arin tinker! Why hasn't the Guild protested? Why haven't you spoken in his defense?"

"Because he's guilty," Rutar said. "And I have assurances from the Pradishar that no Guild material has been accessed during their probes. Since I'm a bishrop and a member of the Council of Nine, I'd know if they'd broken their agreement. Doc Andri'n has been working with the saboteur Anorian Grain to damage the servryns on Andramere and perhaps elsewhere. And he's been sneaking out classified information from the Pradishar servryn and leaking it to the notestreams for several years. They just finally caught him."

Now it was Lithuigi's turn to look defeated.

"So you see, Von'nDrino? I'm in a terrible position. The Guild is in a terrible position. If we speak up to defend him, we risk the flow of dynamins and datamins that only the Pradishar can supply. And since the Pradishar have damning evidence of Andri'n's complicity, we couldn't possibly convince them to let him go. We have nothing to bargain with. But if we don't speak up, we risk allowing the Pradishar to become even bolder in the future, to start demanding more access to Guild servryns, and thereby risk the sanctity of our knowledge. I represent the Guild and I represent the Pradishar, and when the two are at odds, it's best for someone in the middle like me to stay silent and let the storm pass, then see about cleaning up the mess later. I might have taken that from your playbook, considering you know something about playing both sides against the middle."

"What are you implying?"

"Implying? Nothing. Just saying I make a point of knowing what my most famous tinkers are up to."

Lithuigi tried really hard to keep a straight face.

Could he really know?

"I'd hate for Hesh'n's little experiments to become public knowledge, wouldn't you?" Rutar said.

Lithuigi felt relief and terror at the same time.

"I see we both have secrets we want kept," he said, looking away from Rutar.

"You're a good Dyna'arin, Von'nDrino. I always liked you. Not like so many of these other tinkers, who might be geniuses with maquina but don't have a lick of sense about anything else. You've got technical skill and you've got social skill. Political skill, too, I'd guess, if you wanted to use it." He sighed. "But it was damn foolish of you to come here tonight, Von'ndrino. Damn foolish. But what do you say we let it slide? Just this once."

Lithuigi swallowed his pride. "Forgive me, minister. I had only what was best for the Guild in mind."

He knew Rutar had no intention of letting it slide.

"I'm no fool, Von'nDrino," Rutar said. "My wealth and influence, even my position on the Council of Nine, depend on the power, prestige, and privacy afforded the Dyna'arin by the Accords of Balance. You can count on me defending those til my last. I also know the Pradishar. I know how this government works. In time, this will blow over."

"How about I buy you a drink?" Lithuigi said.

Rutar waved him off. "I have more important matters to attend to," he said, gesturing at the door.

Lithuigi turned to leave, feeling sick to his stomach.

"I'm a failure and fool," Lithuigi said, slumping into the booth across from Mha'arlo.

"Nonsense," Mha'arlo said. "You just—"

But Lithuigi put up his hand to silence him.

"Let's go home, son. Let's just go home."

Chapter 20

Throne of Dreams, Throne of Ash

RAKK RAEDER HAD NOT gotten far on his stolen ship before the slave he'd used to steal it woke up and informed the command staff that something was wrong. He got the alert via crystal, from the top general on Thester, though the warning had gone to all Corkin in the region.

<<Cancel the alert, General Rhyantis,>> Rakk said to him through the crystal.

<<Are you sure, my prince?>> Rhyantis said, and Rakk could feel his surprise and his anger.

<<I am.>>

Rhyantis cancelled the alert. <<Now can you tell me what the hell is going on?>> he said. <<Who stole my ship?!>>

<<I did,>> Rakk said. <<Don't blame the soldier. I imperialized him. I'll take full responsibility for it.>>

<<Why'd you steal a ship from me—me of all people,>> Rhyantis said, and Rakk could feel he'd deeply wounded the old general's pride. <<You've always trusted me. You had but to give the order, my prince, and it would have been fulfilled. Now—>> He trailed off. << Have I done something to offend you?>>

<<On the contrary,>> Rakk said. <<I was trying to keep you from any unnecessary involvement. Of course, I didn't realize the hold would be practically empty, only a single guard in the western tower. Hell, General, a Bhizini scamp could have stolen a ship.>>

Rakk could feel Rhyantis's shame, even as he fought to control it, to stop it from oozing through the crystal. But he could also tell Rhyantis was angry—not with him, but with his family. With Raq'asha, his sister. And Rakk felt something else too, a small tremor that grew into a wave of anguish, one that that took his breath away with the speed that it hit him and with the depth of the pain he felt from the old general.

It was the feeling of someone giving up.

The experience was so terrible, and yet so enticing, that Rakk panicked without knowing he was panicking. He flooded the crystal with a mixture of righteous indignation and infallible confidence so profound, the old general's pain momentarily subsided, replaced with a sudden shock of elation, a spark where moments before there had been only darkness.

<<My prince, I have tried to warn the crown—tried to remedy the situation—but nobody in Rhen'zoran is listening.>>

Rakk pulled the general's docket off the servryn, and saw that in the last decade, he'd put in more than a dozen requests to the crown, each one explaining in increasingly dire terms the lack of upkeep at the fortress on Thester, the paucity of soldiers to fill the positions, and the increasingly bold movements of Bhizini into and out of the Tranquin Sea from the swamps of Mon Mang'alar.

He'd heard nothing of this, in part because the requests had been earmarked by the royal palace as requests for political donations, rather than for military supplies or funding. While Rakk wasn't the one to oversee bureaucratic proceedings in the Corkin, he still had access to detailed reports on such matters on the servryn. But if someone in Rhen'zoran was redirecting requests from his generals to the political office, then his reports were incomplete. And if this could happen on Thester, where his ally Rhyantis was in charge, it was probably happening elsewhere.

<<General, why didn't you come to me with this, when Rhen'zoran failed to respond?>>

Rakk was hit with a surge of fear so intense, chills passed over his shoulders and down his arms. There was something Rhyantis didn't want to share, because he knew the consequences would be dire. Rakk hoped he wouldn't have to pull it from the general's mind himself.

When Rhyantis failed to respond, Rakk pushed with his crystamin, not a seizure or a scan, but a heavy presence, his own presence, ready to respond if Rhyantis wouldn't.

<<I'm not afraid to die,>> Rhyantis said, <<only to die in vain. My prince, we generals haven't been allowed to contact you. We haven't been allowed to share what's going on. Our supplies are spent. Our numbers have shrunk away to nothing. Thester, Rumesh, the Whalings, Bru'nord—none are being maintained as they should. And no new recruits are being sent to the archipelago.>>

<<Are you telling me—>> but Rakk was interrupted by an urgent contact from one of his allies in Raccorum Rhazzat.

<<My prince, I am sorry to bother you,>> said Rhyntak Rorh, sending a wave of apologetic deference through the crystal. <<I have urgent news. Your sister—that is, the high regent—has summoned the noble houses for a meeting. I'm afraid there was no warning, and well, it's about to begin.>>

Rakk hissed.

Damn that Raq'asha, could she have picked a worst time? Or a more perfect one? But Rakk stopped himself, thinking maybe he was being too paranoid. Then he sent his gratitude washing over his friend. Thank Trevian for Rhyntak Rorh! He was the second son of the lord of the Barrens and had been a close friend of Rakk in the olden days on P'anorum. His family had spent a month of every year at the royal palace, and in Rakk's decades of exile at sea, Rhyntak had remained his closest ally in Raccorum Rhazzat.

<<Bless you,>> he said as he began to see through Rhyntak's eyes, hear through his ears, and his mind's eye filled with the council chamber of the palace at Rhen'zoran. In his mind's ears, he could hear the quiet chatter of the other noble families, all wondering why this meeting had been called on such short notice.

Raq'asha entered the room surrounded by a swarm of attendants and, notably, a small cadre of palace guards and at least two dozen scamps ranging in age from a few years to several decades, just shy of flowering. She was smiling and laughing with the little ones, and was still chuckling when she took her seat on the throne. The attendants kneeled at her side and the scamps sat in several rows in front of her. The guards arranged themselves in a half circle on either side of the group. Rakk didn't have to scan those in the room to know they were surprised, and confused, by these theatrics.

Raq'asha waited until her servants were all seated, by which time the smile had faded from her face, to be replaced by a look of annoyance, even a bit of anger.

"You've all come," she said. "I've called this meeting at the request of Chief Rhingoven, whom I trust has a serious and pressing matter to address, given the magnitude of this disturbance to protocol." She crossed her hands on her lap and then looked directly at the old Noble and narrowed her eyes. "What is it you'd like to discuss?"

Chief Rhingoven stood and looked around at the others. The rulers of the Clades, or their representatives, were seated at a semi-circular table in front of the dais, and they all turned their attention to the short, wide, and very old Chief Rhingoven, whose wrinkly jowls were scowling and whose eyes were narrowed in barely concealed anger.

"Thank you, high regent," he said, without the slightest gratitude in his voice. "I have requested this meeting with the consent and approval of many of my fellow chiefs from all around the empire—"

"Whom?" Raq'asha interrupted.

Chief Rhingoven paused and cleared his throat. "Well, none of them would *officially* join me in my request," he paused to give a side-eyed scowl at several of the others, "but they have given their support privately."

"Don't speak for others," Raq'asha said. "Out with it already. My patience is nearly spent, old one."

Chief Rhingoven narrowed his eyes further. "We demand—"

Raq'asha laughed and turned her head to the side. "You mean, *you* demand," she said.

Rakk thought Chief Rhingoven was about to hiss at the regent, though he knew such a slip of decorum would be fatal.

"*I* demand to see King Rhakksees Raccorine Deri the Second," Chief Rhingoven said. "Rumors have spread all across the empire that our sovereign is deranged, rambling on and mumbling to himself in the gardens and terraces of the royal palace at night, sulking in the bowels of the castle by day. And we chiefs of Raccorum Rhazzat deserve to know if our beloved king is indeed well and capable of rule."

Raq'asha was on her feet now, her upper lip curled into a snarl. "How dare you question my mandate," she said. "The king gave *me* the authority to administer the empire in his stead. Are you threatening Rishar, Chief Rhingoven? You wish to question my ability to rule—the ability of my family to rule?"

The color had drained from Chief Rhingoven's face.

"Not at all, your highness," he said. "No, no, no."

Raq'asha looked unconvinced.

"Perhaps I should contact the Pradishar at Balan Su, petition them to destroy the Rhingoven family's crystals? It is my right as ruler of the Raccorin, and the Pradishar won't deny such a request."

Chief Rhingoven's eyes briefly widened before he got himself under control. "No, no, no, your highness," he said, "I'm an old fool, your worship, a stupid old fool. I'd never dream of questioning your authority, no, never. Rishar? Why, I'd be the first to assassinate any noble who suggested it! I am ever your ally, and the ally of your family. No, I am only concerned about my king, whom I love deeply. Concerned about rumors, not about your rule, my regent."

Raq'asha relaxed her face but said nothing, fixing Chief Rhingoven with a curious stare, a stare that said, *Go on you old coward, I'm enjoying this.*

"I'm concerned about an increase in raids in the Dagmar, not only Bhizini pirates hitting our towns and ports but raids from out of the Dagwoods, down into the lowlands, right on the doorstep of the Primelands. I'm concerned that the Corkin numbers grow thin while the Bhizini grow bolder in their attacks. I'd hoped to help with this problem by raiding the Dagwoods themselves, to gather fugitives for slaves. I had hoped the breeding programs might increase output, to make up for the lack of soldiers in the Empire. And I'd hoped you'd consider using captured Bhizini as Rhank instead of executing them."

Raq'asha sighed wearily. "Qardymion the Saltsap is in custody. When the Bhizini see their beloved leader in chains, their morale will be broken and the attacks on our shipping lanes and coastal villages will cease. When that happens, we'll no longer have a shortage of Corkin in the homeland, because we'll be able to recall our legions from the Inner Seas. We'll even be able to bring home Prince Rhakksees and thank him, face to face, for his achievements." Raq'asha looked directly at Rhyntak, as if she knew he was watching through his eyes.

"Prince who?" said Chief Rhegan, smirking at the other nobles.

Rakk resisted the urge to use Rhyntak's hands to grab Chief Rhegan by the throat. Instead, Rhyntak stood of his own accord and slammed his hand on the table. "How dare you insult the crown prince?" he said. "Prince Rhakksees has spent decades keeping our empire safe from the Bhizini scourge, always sailing, always fighting, sacrificing his happiness and his freedom to defend our world, and you *dare* to insult him, you who sit on your fat ass sipping wine and fucking your Rhank?"

Rakk noticed that several of the other chiefs cheered for Rhyntak, while others were noticeably silent.

Chief Rhegan leapt to his feet. "I will not be insulted like this!"

"And yet you insult a member of the royal family, which is punishable by death," Rhyntak said.

Chief Rhegan opened his mouth to reply but then closed it when he realized that Rhyntak was right. He dropped to his knees and bowed before Raq'asha. "Forgive me, your highness, for insulting your royal brother," he said. "It was in poor taste. I merely mentioned it because it has been so long since we've seen Prince Rhakksees, and because we are so happy with you as ruler, we wonder why you are not given the crown yourself."

Rakk's heart dropped when there were cheers from some of the other nobles and attendants, and a few began to chant, "Crown her now, crown her now."

"Prince Rhakksees is the heir," Rhyntak said, "directly named by King Rhakksees, even over his first cut. He's spent his entire life serving our empire! How could you abandon him so easily?"

Rakk's heart lifted a little when he heard cheering and some in the crowd began to chant his name.

<<Enjoying the show, brother?>> Raq'asha said in his mind, and Rakk nearly fell overboard. He could see her smirk at Rhyntak—at him through Rhyntak's eyes—then she stood and put her hand in the air, and the room fell silent.

"Prince Rhakksees is ever your loyal prince," she said, "fighting hard to defend the homeland and all of Balance Territories. Chief Rhegan, in lieu of your head, you'll make a donation of ten million merits to the royal family, and no less than five thousand Rhank." Rakk could see Chief Rhegan's face blanch and he relished the moment.

"Chief Rhingoven," Raq'asha continued. "You have wasted my time and the time of the nobles with a request that could have come in private quarters and without rancor. Two million merits to our coffers, and no less than five hundred Rhank. Now leave my sight, all of you, before I stop feeling so generous."

The lords bowed and, along with their attendants, practically ran to get out of the council chamber.

<<Thank you, Rhyntak,>> Rakk said, <<for defending me. I miss you, old friend. Perhaps our paths will cross again soon.>>

He waited until Rhyntak had left the chamber before he addressed Raq'asha directly.

<<You let your nobles act far too boldly,>> he said through the crystal. <<Father would have had their heads for such treason.>>

<<Father abandoned his throne, which to me is far worse than letting nobles vent. And let's be honest—Father only really ruled a city on a tiny island, while the Deri side of our family handled the homeland. Besides, before P'anorum was lost, times were peaceful, the nobles were pacified, and the Raccorin had a grand purpose in this world. But the eruption took that away from us. Now we're dividing amongst ourselves. The Bhizini have grown bolder on our borders. The Andrasians are gaining more and more power in Balance Authority, so it can hardly be called a Balance anymore, and our nobles are noticing and wondering why we remain in the alliance at all. So don't tell me what Father

did. You have no idea what it's like to rule this blasted continent, with these treasonous nobles. You have no idea at all.>>

And Rakk suddenly realized why Raq'asha had shown up with so many attendants, many of them scamps. She'd been scared. Scared they were going to call for Rishar. Scared they might overthrow her.

<<It's all talk,>> he said. <<The noble families will never truly want to abandon Balance, because that would mean abandoning the power of the crystals, and nobody will give up that kind of power.>>

<<That doesn't mean the nobles can't decide our family shouldn't have the Empire's mandate anymore. Rishar doesn't mean getting rid of Balance, only our authority. An authority you don't seem to respect much anymore.>>

<<Me? I've spent my entire life following orders.>>

<<Yeah, we all know how you followed orders the night P'anorum blew.>>

<<Always so pleasant to speak with you,>> Rakk said, replacing the shame in his chest with anger and indignation.

<<The feeling's mutual. You have a lot of explaining to do. Perhaps you've forgotten that I ordered you to the Middle Passage of the Tranquin Reef? And yet somehow you abandoned your men, ended up on Aga'thyn, then at the Eastern Passage, all before stealing a ship from your own general! Great Sower in the Sky, what were you thinking?>>

<<So you'd rather I went and wasted my time on a pointless diversion rather than pursuing and capturing Qardymion the Saltsap? Is that what you're saying?>>

<<You know it isn't,>> she snapped. <<And you know you got lucky. If you'd failed to capture the Saltsap, I could have had your head for insubordination. I'm still tempted to throw you in the brig for awhile, after your little stunt on Thester.>>

<<You should be angry at how easy it was for me to infiltrate the fortress and commandeer a cata'rin. I could have done it without my crystals, security was such a joke. My reports show occupancy at 85%, but there weren't more than a few dozen on the entire island.>>

Raq'asha scoffed. <<That's only because Rhyantis has three-quarters of his men out on patrol at any one time, so obviously you wouldn't have sensed them on Thester.>>

<<Rhyantis has been asking for more resources for years. Maybe you can explain why his requests have been redirected to the political office?>>

<<Did you actually read what he asked for?>>

<<I read every request,>> Rakk said.

<<But the resources? He requested more men in the text, sure. Made it sound like the border-shores of Mon Mang'alar and the Tranquin Sea were about to burst open if we didn't send urgent help. But the Tranquin is the safest sea in the world, after the Stillwater, so he's obviously handling the situation just fine. And he was asking for luxuries, Rakk, not for military equipment. He wanted a new farknuckle pitch, a renovation of his quarters with silks from Avalon and jewels from Grand Gardenia and the Three Pearls. That's why it was reclassified as requests for donations.>>

<<That doesn't explain how easy it was for me to break into the fortress and steal a ship!>>

<<Are you not listening? That fool Rhyantis is to blame! I'm ordering him home to answer for his incompetence.>>

<<Not so fast. I promised him I'd take full responsibility. It was me who stole the ship.>>

Raq'asha laughed. <<You easily piloted a ship out of a harbor at a military fortress, right out into the sea, with nobody stopping you, and you're okay with his command? Have you suddenly become a fool, or were you always one? It's been so long since I've seen you, I honestly can't remember.>>

Rakk hissed, but she did have a point. <<He's been a friend of our family for over a century.>>

<<If you haven't noticed, nobody in our family has any friends.>>

<<That's not true,>> Rakk said.

<<No?>> She laughed again. <<Your only friend is a slave who doesn't have a choice in the matter. Tell me I'm wrong.>>

Rakk could feel his face burning.

<<You were such a sweet little scamp,>> he said. <<Always with a kind word.>>

<You deserved that,>> she said. <<And you won't convince me otherwise.>>

Rakk refused to let her know she was right.

<<What happened to make you like this?>> he said. <<When did you become so brutal?>>

Raq'asha laughed again, but it was full of sadness and grief. <<Me? Really, brother? Very well, then. How about when my home was destroyed? When my father went insane? When my mother killed herself? No, I think it was when my brothers abandoned me in a crumbling old castle in the middle of a strange, dry, miserable land that was suddenly

supposed to be my home. Do you know that, in thirty years, I haven't once—>> She trailed off.

<<Don't talk to me about sacrifice,>> Rakk said, clenching his teeth, suddenly enraged. <<This conversation's over.>> He sent anger, disappointment, and disgust through the crystal and severed the connection with his sister.

As Rakk's awareness returned to where he was, he heard the whine of the gurgitator, the sound of the air whipping past his ears, the feel of it on his face and in his hair fibers. He felt the warm deck of the cata'rin on his rootpads, the taste of the sea on his lips, and the smell of the rich salty air in his nostrils—and he did his best to exist only where he was, right in that moment, without thought of Raq'asha, or Rhen'zoran, or Thester—without past or present or future. Only now. Only within that tiny quiet space he reserved for moments when the pain and shame and regret and fear of failure were too much to handle, and he could tuck them away and pretend they weren't tearing at him any longer.

Why did his family always make him feel so miserable?

◈◈◈◈◈　◈◈◈◈◈

Rakk was still standing on the deck, staring at the horizon, when Q'orin found him.

"Is everything alright, my prince?" he said. "I heard you hissing."

He flashed him a big smile. "I'm great, now that my conversation is over. Families," he said. "What can you do but deal with them?"

"I have to admit, I had my doubts you'd pull it off," Q'orin said. "But here we are, with the Saltsap in our hold, heading for Balan Su City. I can hardly contain my excitement."

"Balan Su? Pah!" Rakk spit. "Balan Su hates me. I swear that city has it out for me, wishes me dead or something. Cold, wet, dreary, miserable, wretched—"

"You aren't thinking of defying the Council's orders?"

"They said it was a request," Rakk said. "And no, I'm not. Balan Su, here we come. Yippie."

"I do understand your distaste for the capital," Q'orin said, "but surely my prince can admit there's something special about the place? The food, at the very least. And the art, the galleries, the theater. Do you suppose they still have live performances, now that nearly everything is streamed?"

"I'm sure they do somewhere," he said. "And you aren't wrong about the food or the entertainment. I guess it will be nice to be in a city again. Thirty years socializing only with warriors, hardly setting foot on shore—I guess it's enough to make even Balan Su seem appealing."

"I hope we can stay awhile," Q'orin said.

Rakk clapped him on the shoulder. "I'm glad you're excited. You've made the inevitable look much more appealing now."

"I live to serve," he said.

"Good, because I have a favor to ask of you. I need you to deliver Qardymion to the city yourself."

"I—my prince?"

"Don't worry, I'll be along soon after. I need to meet a friend first. He'll get me into the capital."

"You mean he'll sneak you into the capital."

Rakk nodded.

"Be careful. Your friend is a dangerous one."

"He is, and yet I trust him. I need to arrive quietly, to scope things out with my own eyes, before everyone in Balance knows I'm there. He'll be able to get me in without the Pradishar knowing."

"You wish to speak with your brother first," Q'orin said. "Face to face. In private."

"You know me too well, old friend."

"Better than I know myself, it seems."

"Meaning?"

"Nothing important, my prince. You can count on me."

"Good," Rakk said. "I want you to take the Saltsap to the Pradishar fortress on Nunan, then head to the crescent. But lay low. I don't want any notestreamers recognizing you and wondering where I am. And I don't want Rajj tipped off that I'm in the capital. If the Cul'tavin ask you about me when you deliver Qardymion, tell them I'm on my ship awaiting orders from the Council. Understood?"

"Of course."

"Good. Then when we approach the capital, you'll drop me off near the southern tip of Nunan, and then head straight for the harbor."

"Understood."

They reached Balan Su in the middle of the night, the fog wrapping tightly around the ship and making the air cool and stale and terrible, and Rakk thought that it didn't matter how many amazing things there were to do in the city, in that kind of weather, it was an awful place.

He closed the gurgitator and started preparing the cano'rin, the one they'd patched up on the reef after the shipwreck. Q'orin came up from the lower deck when he heard the gurgitator fall silent, and he stood and watched while Rakk climbed into the boat and gave him a grin.

"Ready!" he said, and Q'orin began to lower the boat to the sea. Once on the water, Rakk used the oar to push off from the ship, heading north toward the sandy shoals at the south end of Nunan. Rakk could hear the small splashes on the outer bank and knew he didn't have far to go.

Once clear of the ship, he heard Q'orin open the gurgitator, but the cata'rin had already vanished in the fog. Rakk looked down at the cano'rin and touched the wood, rubbing his fingers along the patching he'd placed on the hull. He realized that what Qardymion had shown them, the wisdom they'd shared, was something special, precious even—a piece of knowledge that so few, almost no one in Balance Territories, even knew about. The thought made him want to weep, though he couldn't say why. And as he heard his ship fading away in the fog, he wanted to call Q'orin back, to set the Saltsap free. He'd been hunting Qardymion for decades, the great terror of the Inner Seas, but Rakk had expected them to be different—wild like an animal, brutal and sap-thirsty. What Rakk saw was a determined warrior and a cunning intellectual, and perhaps a better leader than himself. And a believer, too.

The thought of Qardymion in chains, marching through the foggy streets of Balan Su, was a tragic thought indeed.

But he shook it off and started rowing again. If he let Qardymion go, he'd be a traitor to Raccorum Rhazzat, to Balance, to the Corkin—to everyone. He'd be executed, and a headless prince can't wear a crown. And Rakk wanted to be king more than he wanted to honor a Bhizini rebel, no matter how much he liked them.

When Rakk's cano'rin slid up onto the edge of Nunan, on a long bar of sand and grass, he stepped out, pushed the boat back into the water, and then with great reluctance, he took his oars and began to knock off the repairs he'd made on the hull. Then he took some handfuls of sand and shoveled it into the boat, and it slowly sank beneath the surface and finally disappeared under the water.

Rakk thought he might cry, but then he laughed at the absurdity of such a thing. Crying, over a badly damaged boat that was hardly seaworthy. Great Sower in the Sky, he hadn't even cried when P'anorum blew.

⁕⁎⁕

Rakk stuck to the western side of Nunan and crossed the grassy marshlands on foot. When he reached the long boardwalks and clusters of huts that made up the village, all built on stilts across the middle of the island, he kept to the shadows and stayed down on the sand. The going was slow and the air thick and wet and too damn foggy to see anything, but he couldn't complain. He was on his way to see Ellex Andria, to see his brother too. Things were looking up.

After the last of the huts, he continued north along the edge of the lagoon, on a thin spit of land that connected the rocky northern tip of Nunan with the sandy marshes south of the lagoon. Rakk stayed low in the tall grass, though he doubted anyone in the fortress could see through the fog.

When he approached the steep granite cliffs—rubble of what was once the southern wall of the crater many millennia ago—he felt the rocky surface with his hands, cool and gnarled and slick with moss. Then he approached the lagoon and stepped in, hoping not to make a splash. The bottom dropped away quickly and Rakk filled his lungs with air, then took small paddles into the water, staying next to the wall. When he neared the middle, he looked around for the small notch on the face of the cliff, three small indentations and two raised lines in a row—the marker his friend had described.

But was the passage really there? The edges of the lagoon might be too steep to climb out if it wasn't.

Raq'asha said nobody in our family has any friends, he thought. *But he's my friend, he's never let me down, and so I have to trust him.*

He exhaled hard and plunged into the still, brackish waters of the lagoon, falling faster and longer than he expected to, the tips of his fingers trailing the granite edge of the cliff, the outer edge of Balan Su's crater. The pressure grew on his ears as he dropped.

And then he wasn't falling anymore, but had landed—with surprising softness—on the muddy sand deep below the surface. But his hands had left the wall and it was total darkness around him, so he groped blindly, struggling to lift his legs, as if moving in slow motion.

He took a dozen steps and started to worry he'd gone the wrong way—he'd only lost contact with the wall moments ago. He couldn't have fallen that far away from it. So he stumbled back in the other direction, moving in big slow steps, waving his arms around, feeling increasingly desperate and increasingly foolish.

Why had he done this? Why couldn't he just sail into port like any other prince would? Why did he always have to make things so complicated?

But then he felt the wall and he leapt against it, spread his arms out and leaned on it as if hugging it. He slid left and right, and felt the grooves his friend had described, long striations leading either downward to the left or downward to the right, which would eventually center one on the door.

And his doubts from moments earlier were forgotten. Of course he could trust his friend. He'd saved his life once. No, he'd done more than that.

When Rakk pulled the small lever on the cliff face, he could hear maquina whining and the sounds of rock rumbling, and a long narrow slit of orange light tore into the darkness and quickly grew into a gaping doorway lit with glowbes. He stepped forward into the chamber, found the lever on the inside wall, and pulled it. The maquina whined again as the door slid shut, then a loud gurgle and hiss made Rakk cover his ears as the water began to drain out of the room.

It was good to have friends in high places.

The corridor led, as promised, straight through the rock of Nunan and into another chamber similar to the one he'd first entered—an exit into the harbor. He continued down the corridor on the far side of the room, a much longer one than the first had been, somewhere deep under the island, under the harbor even. The corridor ended at a single spiral stair cut into the rock.

Right into the roots of the city, and nobody the wiser, he thought.

At the top of the stairs, a locked metal door with one of those old fashioned three-turn locking mechanisms blocked his way. Rakk lined up the ticks to the right, then to the left, then to the right again, and the door opened as normal. He stepped through to what looked like a storage basement for some kind of shop, and the door, with an attached shelf, swung back over the threshold, hiding its existence.

He went up the stairs and out into the main room of the shop on the ground level, glad that his clothing had finally stopped dripping. There were a number of long narrow stacks on either side of him, covered in books and scrolls. And to his right, there was a desk with a small Bhizini, dressed in a simple brown robe, reading a scroll.

"I wasn't expecting to see one of your kind here," Rakk said.

"I wasn't expecting to welcome a prince," they said, as if they couldn't care less. "I have permission to be here, if you care." Finally they looked up from their scroll. "That satchel is yours."

Rakk opened the bag and found a Pradeshan robe inside, large enough to fit his wide, thick, tall Raccorin body. Perfect! He'd look like one of the many thousands of faithful in the city who wore the purple and gray.

"Leave your soiled clothes behind and I'll see they get laundered," the old Bhizini said. "You can change downstairs. Or right here, if you'd like." They gave him a toothless grin and winked. "Don't worry, nobody comes in print shops these days. Its just you and me."

Rakk laughed.

"There's a bathing room downstairs. You best rinse up. Can't go out smelling like you do. Go on now."

Rakk did as he was told. Once downstairs, he stripped off his Corkin uniform and ladled the cool fresh water over his skin, then rinsed the brine out of his hair fibers. There was no way he'd get them looking good so he pulled them into a low bun and tied it up, then pulled the Pradeshan robe over his head and fastened it around his waist. He looked down at himself. There was no hiding that he was Raccorin, but with the hood up, nobody should know it was him.

He went back upstairs. The Bhizini was holding a tray. "Here. Fresh water, and a bhiza cookie. Eat it."

He sniffed the cookie. "Bhiza? This early?"

"A special blend. The robes are to hide your face," they said. "This cookie'll hide your crystal. Cul'tavin scanners are everywhere, checking who's who, trying to see what they're up to. Don't worry now, you won't get a funky head from this kind, and it'll wear off in a day or so."

Rakk nodded. "I need to find my—servant first. Before I take this."

"You mean your slave?" They snorted and scowled at him.

The door to the store opened and a pradeshan pilgrim walked in. Rakk looked at the Bhizini as if to say, 'I thought you said this place was private.' But the pilgrim pulled down their hood and it was Q'orin. Rakk flashed him a smile, then popped the bhiza cookie in his mouth.

"Your turn," the Bhizini said, pushing a cookie toward Q'orin.

"Are you sure?" he said, gesturing toward the old Bhizini. "They're a—friend of a friend?"

Rakk nodded.

"Understood," Q'orin said, and he ate the cookie. "How long until it takes effect?"

The old Bhizini stood and gestured at the shop. "Have a look at my books and scrolls. There's even some grimoires lying around, if you believe in that stuff. Just buy somethin'! Then you'll be good to go."

Rakk looked at Q'orin and nodded, then turned to the stacks and began to browse. Where to even start? He hadn't read a book in decades, and the only scrolls he'd perused had to do with battles and troops. He sniffed deeply, the smell of old leaves filling his nose and taking him back to P'anorum. His father, King Rhakksees II, had been a devout reader, and the library on P'anorum, both the one in the heart of the city and the one in the heart of the palace, had been spectacular.

He steered himself away from the military histories, perused the plays, then spent a while flipping through texts in the philosophy section. Finally he found Q'orin who nodded to him, and they walked up to the old Bhizini at the front desk. Rakk glanced at Q'orin's selection.

"'The Affairs of Astra'bel, Volume 9'?" he said, laughing. "I didn't peg you as a romantic."

Q'orin blushed. "They're much more than that. I—remember reading them when I was young. Before the accident."

"That's great," Rakk said.

"I had volumes one through eight. That's all there were at the time, I'm sure of it. Who knew there was another volume! This is very exciting."

"And here I thought I knew everything about you," he said.

Q'orin blushed again, then looked at what Rakk had in his hands. "Grumion's 'Discontent'? Required reading for angsty youth, maybe, but for an ambitious prince?"

Rakk laughed. "Look at you, all worried about what I'm reading."

"What else is here? 'A Case Against Slavery,' by Ra'shard Ruu'n. Do you plan on meeting with his worship the Gran Pradesh? Hope to impress him by quoting his treatise?"

Rakk laughed. "You're in a good mood. I haven't seen you this feisty in ages!"

Q'orin ignored him. "And finally we have Gilly Gilder's Gummy Gumsters." He raised an eyebrow.

"Hey, I like the sound of the rhymes, okay? It's like music on the page. And you have no room to judge!"

"Ah good, you find some stuff to read then? Good, you buy them and leave. They're twenty five merits each. But I give you all of them for seventy five. Coin only." She pointed at her crystal-free forehead.

"Merits?" Rakk said, looking abashed.

Rakk tried to contact Q'orin through the crystal but it wouldn't work. The crystamin had been numbed by the bhiza.

"Er...Q'orin—?" he said.

Q'orin pulled a small bag out of his robe and began to count out some coins. Rakk leaned close. "Throw in something extra for the owner."

He looked confused as he tried to respond through the crystal, then nodded in understanding. "How much extra?" he whispered.

"How much is a lot?"

Q'orin passed the old Bhizini a handful of coin. They nodded their head but didn't say anything, then went back to reading a scroll, ignoring them.

Rakk and Q'orin looked at each other, pulled up their hoods, and stepped out onto the street.

The sun had risen but the fog was well up over the upper rim, so the alleyway, narrow as it was, still seemed misty and fuzzy on the far end. The air was cool, and Rakk could smell mold and rot in the alleyway—and also the smell of steamed jha'ala and fried rhingamis—an assault on the senses like only a city can cause.

He looked around and squinted through the mist. "Great, I have no problem getting into Balan Su, but now that I'm in, I'm completely lost."

"This way, my prince," Q'orin said, heading left down the alleyway. "What would you do without me?"

"Retire to my little island paradise and lord it over the ghu frogs and branta birds. And not have to deal with this miserable, smelly, cold, awful place."

"It was a rhetorical question," Q'orin said dryly.

They left the alley and stepped onto a larger cross-street, and Rakk realized he did recognize the neighborhood after all. They were in Old Stones, a densely packed quadrant between the high-end residential area Sunrise Ridge on the tip of the eastern arm of the crescent and the ceremonial center of the city in the middle of the crescent. The neighborhood had older courtyard apartments on the backside, shops and bars and restaurants peppered throughout, lots of character and even a bit of sleaze, if you knew where to look. Rakk thought it was the only part of the upper rim that didn't feel phony.

"I know where we are," he announced. "We need to head left, toward Sunrise Ridge."

"I'm afraid we need to head right, to the western arm," Q'orin said. "I assume you want to visit Prince Rajesh'n? He lives in the Sunset Point residential area."

"Not in the family compound?" What was it his father had called it—the tiny house? It looked almost exactly like the palace on P'anorum, at least on the outside, but a fraction of its size. Still massive, of course. His father loved being ironic.

"Prince Rajesh'n prefers the Sunset Point area. It's a younger neighborhood, and not quite so exclusive, in theory at least. Small private gardens with sprawling communal spaces, shared dining and recreation. Lots of students, Dyna'arin managers, young bureaucrats, even some of the less successful weavryn stream stars who can't afford Sunrise Ridge."

"My brother always was a weird one," he said. "He turns down a miniature palace all to himself for a tiny apartment surrounded by, what, second rate citizens? Rajj always did seem ashamed to be royal—ashamed of his family and his status. Maybe he felt lonely in that big space. I'm sure he could have filled it with hordes of pandering family members and nobility from across the Empire if he'd wanted to. Though I suppose pageants and parties, and anything entertaining in general, never interested him much."

Q'orin didn't say anything.

They crossed Grand Plaza, the fog making it impossible to see the Pradishar citadel but Rakk looked up anyway, knowing it was there, stretching above him a thousand feet into the sky. He hoped the fog would clear soon so he could get a proper gaze at it. They continued through the Forum along the outer edge of the upper rim, and through the fringes of the Regalia shopping district to the boundary of Sunset Point.

"So what's the plan for getting in?" Rakk asked.

"We're fortunate the fog is so high today," Q'orin said. "We should have no trouble climbing over the barrier."

"Perhaps the only time I'll ever be grateful for fog in my life," Rakk said. "Let's go."

They climbed in, scaling the wall with their rootpads, one step at a time, hidden in the fog from anyone who wasn't nearly upon them, and nobody was. Once inside, they walked more comfortably, trying not to look suspicious. Rakk was relieved to feel grass on his feet—he'd missed the sensation. Nearly all of Balan Su was cold and damp stone, but Sunset Point had earthen pathways. Not exactly a forest, the neighborhood was much greener than most of the upper rim—outside of Corda'mere with its lush groves—but the plants were shrublike. No trees were taller than the height of the walls between the gardens, probably to keep them from ruining the view—when there was one. Regardless, it looked wrong to Rakk. Contrived and barren. Shorn.

"We are here, my prince," Q'orin whispered.

Rakk nodded, took a deep breath, and knocked on the door.

There was no answer.

He knocked again.

Q'orin touched his shoulder and he turned. He was brandishing a zapren is his other hand, his eyes scanning the fog behind them.

Cul'tavin peacekeepers appeared in the mist, leaping headlong at Rakk and Q'orin, knocking them to the ground. The door to Rajj's garden opened and Rakk saw his brother there, looking down at him, a disappointed look on his face.

"By the authority of the Pradishar, the Council of Nine, and High Regent Raq'asha Raccorine Deri, I hereby declare you bound and detained for disobedience to the crown, dereliction of duty, illegal entry, theft, identity theft, and failure to answer a summons of Balance Authority. Don't resist, brother. If you do, I'm not sure I'll be able to keep this off the notestreams."

"Rajj, you fucking fool, I snuck in here for that very reason!" He tried to heave the Cul'tavin off of himself but another peacekeeper jabbed him with a zapren and he collapsed on the grass, twitching. Q'orin had fallen next to him, shuddering from a zap.

Rajj smirked down at him. "Welcome to Balan Su City," he said. "Take them to the Dankburn."

He squirmed to rise but one last zap made him see darkness and stars, and his last thought was what a fool he had been for ever expecting any better from this city, much less from his family.

Chapter 21

A Strange Welcome in the Capital of the World

THE ARRIVAL IN BALANCE Territories was not what Fin'roq had expected. East'whaling rose from the sea as a wall of rock and sharp metal, not a speck of grass on its craggy surface, only row upon row of mounted enflamers and barbed barricades amidst scorched stone. The dread he felt in his stomach turned to panic when he saw gates at the base of the island slowly lifting into the air, opening to a deep cave like the gullet of some earthen beast, waiting to devour him whole. The thought of all that darkness pressing in on him drove the air from his lungs, and he knew he should go below deck, hide out until they had passed through, but he couldn't move, and his rootpads clutched the deck in a death-grip.

When the glowbes inside the passage crackled to life, and warm orange light spread outward from the mouth of the tunnel, Fin thought he might cry, feeling relieved and foolish at the same time. After the cata'rin passed through the opening, the gate dropped shut behind them with a loud thudding splash, and as the ship advanced through the passage, more glowbes lit up in front of them while the ones behind faded back to darkness, as if they sailed in a bubble of light through an endless black void.

Soon a large gate in the distance opened to the whine of maquina and the cata'rin sailed out into a harbor, wide and broad and filled with ships of all sizes. Fin turned and looked at the island, and saw that nearly all the land on this side was covered in buildings, from the shore to the rim of the crescent, and his mouth fell open as he took in the scene absolutely bustling with life.

Jaun von Andron joined him, grinning. "Welcome to East'whaling. A miserable dive these days, but once a bustling waypoint between the near and far sides of the world. See Fin—" Jaun touched his shoulder and pointed at the island, "—there's the heart of the city, right near the top. A grand open plaza, with the sharlum, Academicon, and Forum all clustered nearby. Nearly every city in Balance, even most in the heartlands of Andrasia and Raccorum Rhazzat, are arranged in a similar way."

"Just like Old P'anorum," he said.

"Right! See Fin, you already know more about the world than you realize."

But Fin knew that wasn't true. He knew that his only experience with Balance had been secondary, through the books and scrolls in Bhea's library, or the mournful nostalgia of the villagers when they talked of the olden days, before the eruption destroyed their lives. More recently, he'd had the word of Aar'ryn Ruu'n and Roe, who had seen through the crystal and had promised Fin'roq that Balance Authority, and their Pradishar, wanted to help him. Anthem seemed to think it was true, and Jaun hadn't questioned it, so he had to have faith. It was too late to change his mind anyway.

P'anorum is on the other side of the world now, he thought, *and the only way left to me is onward.*

The cata'rin docked at East'whaling but Fin and Jaun stayed in their quarters while the repairs were made to the ship. The hole in the hull would need to be repaired by tinkers from the Guild, but Anthem thought a patch would hold til Balan Su, provided they didn't go too fast.

Fin tried to relax and enjoy the trip. The next three days were pleasant and the weather was perfect. He spent the days perched in the sunshine, watching the sea go by, water and water and more water everywhere he looked. How did it go on so long in every direction? How could he ever learn to find his way around such a nondescript emptiness?

What would it be like to have his own ship, to sail off in any direction, the entire world his to explore?

Could that really be possible for him one day?

Anthem had his own ship, after all.

Jaun would join Fin in the afternoons, bringing him some dried rhupan he'd soaked and some bhru'berry juice he'd stolen from Anthem's cookery. They'd snack slowly, savoring the food and sipping the juice while relishing the sunshine. The first day this happened, Fin was so flustered he said practically nothing, just listened to Jaun's stories, hanging on every word but somehow hardly hearing them. But on the second day, he realized he needed to start asking questions. Balan Su was almost upon him and he had little idea what to expect. He was already going to stand out for his skin. If he could act like a Balance citizen acted, maybe it wouldn't be so bad.

So he starting asking Jaun about Balance society, about how people spent their time, what they talked about, the games they played. Fin'roq found that most of Jaun's answers made little sense to him, and required that more questions be asked to explain them, and he wondered if he'd ever understand or fit in.

"I know you're knowledgeable of the Pruu'log," Jaun said, "but I'm afraid knowing Pradishar scripture won't help you much with Balance society. Not unless you can balance it out with knowledge of our history and popular culture."

Fin'roq sighed. "How am I to learn ten thousand years of history in two days?"

"Especially without a crystamin," Jaun said. "But you don't need to know everything that far back. Just moments, and maybe the last hundred years or so. That'll give you enough to talk to people without sounding like a complete outsider. Besides, you don't actually have to know, just to sound like you know. Trust me on that. And if you don't know something, just stay silent. People will make their own assumptions."

"So what do I tell people when they ask me where I'm from and how I'm able to join the Pruu'patch? Just say hi, I'm that Bhizini savage from P'anorum who killed his monkin friend, but instead of being punished, I was asked to join the Pradishar."

"Is that what happened?" Jaun said, a carefully blank look on his face.

"Haven't you watched the stream? I know Aar'ryn Ruu'n shared what happened, and that everyone in Balance was talking about it."

"I'm sorry, Fin. That's how I knew who you were when I met you, but I didn't want to bring it up until you'd mentioned it yourself. Out of respect. Look, I know what it's like to be famous. I was famous first as the crown prince of Andramere, from the day my taprin was cut, before that even. But then on the weavryn I became famous for reasons other than the accident of my birth. Both types of fame have the same consequence—everyone else believes you exist only for them, only for their enjoyment. You become their court fool, the jester they can order about and insult."

"My village wanted to burn me alive," he said.

"Wow," Jaun said. "And here I've been feeling sorry for those we left behind."

"Are you sure everyone in Balan Su won't want to do the same?"

"Oh, some of them will, surely," Jaun said. "But unlike the rest of the Bhizini in the world, you'll have a chance to prove yourself to them."

"I had my whole life to prove myself to my village, and a lot of good it did me."

"Your village doesn't represent the wider world, Fin. Take Roman Anthem. He might be reviled by some, sure, but he's greatly respected by many Andrasians and Raccorin all across Balance Territories. I know that for a fact. Your pradeshan robe, and your status as a monkin, will open doors for you. And so will the fame you already have from that stream, if you'll allow me to be cynical. People will want to use you for their own benefits."

"So I've been warned." He looked at Jaun warily, and noticing, Jaun laughed.

"Here's the best advice I can think to give you. Cities are where you can be anyone you want to be. Just pull up your hood and lower it over your forehead, so your face is in shadow. Then walk as if you have somewhere to be and with a feeling that nobody had better get in your way, 'cause you ain't movin' for no one. Show me the walk, come on."

Fin blushed, then took a few paces across the deck.

"No, no, no. You're too meek, too timid. Here, shoulders back, head high, face forward, big long strides, brisk pace. Now show me again. Yes, like that. You're getting it. That's how people walk in a city like Balan Su. You go about like that, you'll be nothing more than another pilgrim on the streets, another bureaucrat in the great maquina of civilization, just one in a million, and nobody will notice that you're different, I promise. It works for me all the time."

Fin grinned at him, but then his face fell. "I didn't kill my friend," he said. "I just—want you to know that."

"I never thought you did," Jaun said. "I saw the stream. You weren't yourself. You're kind and sweet, Fin. I know you came to Balan Su, at least in part, because you want answers. I'll help you find them, if you want my help. And if you don't, I'll still be there on Balan Su with you, so either way, you won't be alone. Alright?"

Fin nodded, tears in his eyes, but his throat was clenched too tightly to speak.

❧ ☙

The night before they arrived in Balan Su, Fin'roq woke with a sick feeling in his stomach. He pulled out his rootpads and paced the sleeping chamber, dropped them back in the soil, then pulled them out again to pace. Shortly before sunrise, he nodded off, and when he woke, the ship had stopped moving and the air had grown cool and moist. He freshened up with ladles of water and put on the last set of crisp clean pradeshan robes from the cubby. When he climbed onto the deck, it was like stepping into a cloud, and Fin'roq ran to both sides of the ship, looking about at the white wall glowing around him, and wishing Baboo was there with him to see it.

What a marvelous thing, this fog, he thought.

"Dreadful, isn't it," Jaun said, coming down from the captain's deck in pradeshan robes, carrying a small satchel. "Puts a chill in my fibers."

"It's lovely," Fin said. "Like I'm thousands of feet high, drifting about in the sky."

"Wait until you've gone several days in it—or several months—and you'll curse it for making you feel so weary and blue. But fortunately for us, we'll be living on the upper rim, and up there we'll have a much better chance of sticking up above it, right out into the sunshine. At least on good days."

Roman Anthem came down the stairs wearing a full Cul'tavin outfit, a grin on his speckled face. He handed Fin a scroll. "Make sure you keep this on you at all times. Since you don't have a crystal, you may be stopped by peacekeepers on patrol. This scroll should keep you from having any problems."

"Should?" Fin said.

Anthem laughed, but then his eyes twitched and his face grew tight and he started to clench his teeth.

"I'm afraid I won't be able to escort you to the upper rim after all. Head straight for the Pruu'patch, both of you. Best of luck in the capital, Fin'roq. And stay out of trouble, von Andron."

He had disappeared into the fog before Fin could get out a thank you, and he hoped he'd get to see the grizzled old Bhizini again some day. He exhaled hard and Jaun took his arm.

"Nothing to worry about, Fin friend," he said. "Just pretend you're on one of those tour groups, where everyone has a little badge and the guide is always waving a palm frond in the air and herding them to and fro."

"I don't know what that is," Fin said.

"Oh, right. Well—what it means is that you're about to see a new place, full of exciting things you've never seen before, and you're about to do so with a friend who is looking forward to sharing with you the best parts of Balan Su, whenever we have a chance to get away from our training in the 'patch. How's that sound?"

Fin blushed in spite of the panic in his chest. "Sounds good," he said.

Jaun pulled him by the arm toward the ramp down to the pier. The fog was so thick, Fin couldn't see the city, couldn't even see where the cata'rin had docked. So he followed Jaun blindly through the mist, down onto land, the first time he'd set foot anywhere but P'anorum.

Balan Su, he thought. *I'm here. I'm really here.*

He followed Jaun through a door into a massive building, and they entered into a long, narrow room, with vines strung up on posts to make a winding queue along the length of the floor. At the other end of the room, Fin could see several figures in Cul'tavin fatigues watching them approach.

Fin's chest tightened under their gaze, and when they were about halfway across the room, he looked into their faces, into their eyes fixated on him, and it was hatred, and disgust, that he saw there.

"Jaun," he whispered.

"Not to worry, Fin, nobody in the world feels at ease with immigration officials. Just smile and hand them the scroll Anthem gave you. Everything will be fine, and if it isn't, I'm here, and I'm Jaun von Andron." He grinned at Fin. "You'll be fine."

But the panic wouldn't go away, and as Fin continued to walk toward the Cul'tavin, he had to blink to try and stop the tears from falling.

They don't even know me, he thought, *and yet somehow they hate me. How is that even possible?*

When they reached the Cul'tavin, Jaun smiled. "Good morning, I'm Jaun von Andron, and this is my friend Fin'roq. We're reporting for enrollment at the Pruu'patch."

The peacekeepers stood and stared at them, their eyes twitching, and Fin'roq felt his head pulsing, saw his vision flash and go dark—watched it happen before it happened, the intention of the Cul'tavin in his mind, as if it were his own will—but all he could manage to get out was a squeaky "Jaun" before the zapren jabbed him in the chest and his knees gave out from under him.

⊱ ━━━━ ⊰

Fin'roq felt heavy and light at the same time, a strange mix of inertia and effortlessness, as the Cul'tavin peacekeepers dragged him by each arm, his chin bouncing against his chest, his eyes too heavy to open, hardly aware of who he was. When they dropped him onto the floor, he did his best not to move, not to cry out, to pretend he was still unconscious. His heart was racing so fast he couldn't hear anything but the beating in his ears, and though the darkness all around him made him desperately want to open his eyes, to cry out for the light, he kept them shut, preferring the panic he was familiar with, the enemy he knew, to the one he didn't.

He stayed sprawled out on the floor like that, his cheek against the cold stone, for a small eternity, a few minutes at the most, or was it a few days? A voice broke through the darkness, even pushed away the panic—a soft and warm voice, firm but gentle.

"On your feet," the voice said.

Fin moaned and pushed himself up onto his side, his chest aching where the zapren had jabbed him, and he opened his eyes but kept them on his feet as he stood.

"Lower your hood," the voice said, and he reached up for his pradeshan robe and pulled the gray and purple fabric off of his head, and he stared into the face of his jailer through the metal bars of his cell, a petite Andrasian dressed in Cul'tavin fatigues. Her eyes grew wide, just for a moment, before they narrowed into a glare, and her pale green face turned an ashen gray. She rubbed her temples in slow circles, then dropped her hands and stared at him again.

She recognizes me, Fin thought.

"You're the snake from the stream," she said, sounding haughty, but Fin'roq could feel her fear, and he could see the hatred in her eyes. She hardened her gaze. "Who are you. Speak!" Her soft, warm voice had turned cold and sharp as a scytherin.

"Fin'roq," he said.

"And who do you serve? What tribe?"

"I'm—sorry, I'm—not sure what you mean."

The woman moved so fast, Fin'roq didn't have time to clench his teeth. In a single motion, she had a zapren in her hand and was driving it into Fin's stomach, too low to knock him out. Instead, the tip jabbed down into his flower, and when the electricity coursed outward, the jolt seemed to pull in all the skin, all the fibers, all the soft petals, and twist them up around a hot coal. It only lasted for a second, the zap, but it was enough to leave Fin on his knees, screeching and moaning and gasping for air.

"I will not tolerate lies, Fin'roq. You must know, by stepping foot in Balance Territories, you've forfeited your life. I'm doing you a courtesy by not roasting you whole right now. So you *will* answer my questions. You *will* tell me who you're working for, who helped you to get into the city, and why. Do you understand?"

Fin didn't know what to do, what to say, so he nodded and stood up again and faced her, trying not to let her know how scared he was, how hard he had to fight not to let any tears slip out.

"Who do you serve? What tribe?"

I don't know the names of any Bhizini tribes, he thought. *Can I make one up?*

"I—Bhea Bell," he said.

"Bheabel? I've never heard of that tribe." She lifted the zapren in a threatening gesture.

"Bhea Bell's a Bhizini, not a tribe. We were the only Bhizini on P'anorum."

The Andrasian gasped when he said the name of his island home, and he braced himself for a jab with the zapren but it never came. He looked at her uneasily, but she had a distant look on her face, and her body had gone rigid. Finally she exhaled sharply, fixed her gaze on his eyes, and Fin'roq watched as her brow furrowed, her cheeks flushed dark brown with sap, and her upper lip started to curl into a sneer of complete contempt.

"You think me a fool, don't you, snake?" she said, nearly spitting the words in his face. "I know it's no coincidence, your arrival today, just as Qardymion the Saltsap is set to arrive in chains. Enrolling as a monkin at the Pruu'patch? Who told you such a thing was even possible? Was it that beast Roman Anthem?" She tsked. "He's a savage himself, hardly trustworthy." She looked at Fin and gave him a mocking grin. "Someone's made a fool of you, Fin'roq." Her smile faded. "And now you've tried to make one of me. But enough is enough. Tell me what you know of the plan to free Qardymion, and I might let you live. Otherwise, I'll affix you with a restraining crystal and I'll have those plans myself. And afterward, I'll leave you in the Dankburn til you petrify. Now are you listening, snake?"

"Please," Fin'roq whispered. "I told you the truth. I don't know who Qardymion is. I'm here to enroll as a monkin. I was invited by the Gran Pradesh."

Fin saw the fury blossom in the Andrasian's face, and this time the zapren jabbed against his neck, and it felt like it had torn through his artery and allowed the sap to pump out through the wound, but when he shook himself out of his stupor and grabbed his neck, the skin was still intact.

He looked up at his tormenter through his tears, and he let out a sob.

"So you've chosen death then," she said.

"No!" Fin screamed, and he leapt for the Andrasian as he had leapt for Roe in the cavern under P'anorum, clutching at her and trying to pull her mind into his own. But this was different—something was wrong—and the more he fumbled to grab hold, the more he realized he couldn't. And then it felt as if someone or something had taken control of his assault, had taken that imaginary hand that reached out and turned it back upon himself, so that he clutched only at himself.

When he looked up at the bars of his cell, the Andrasian was still staring at him, but her eyes were twitching. When they fell still, she continue to stare, to wordlessly judge, and

Fin'roq had to turn away from her gaze. He stared at his feet, at the stone floor behind them, a green and gray smear through his tears.

Fin'roq heard the sound of a commotion in the distance—a slamming door, a muffled scream. He looked at the Andrasian, and she was looking down the hallway, her eyes twitching.

"What's the meaning of this?" she said, as a figure in Cul'tavin fatigues approached the cell.

Fin looked at them in the low light. Another Andrasian.

"Sweet Trevian, Elle, what are you doing?" the man said.

"Why have you come?" she said.

The man looked at Fin'roq and then back at the woman, and his eyes started to twitch.

Both of them stood in silence for a moment, eyes twitching, while Fin'roq tried to swallow in a dry throat, whispering prayers to Trevian, praying that the woman had been wrong, that he hadn't been duped, that this wasn't all his worst nightmare coming true.

"No way, Utte, no way!" she screamed suddenly, and Fin jumped. "Is Ra'shard Ruu'n completely insane? A monkin? A savage recruit in our own ranks, after what those monsters did to my Cul'tavin! After what he did to that monkin on P'anorum!"

"Easy, Elle—" but he stopped when he saw the look she gave him. She pushed past the man, knocking him against the bars of the cell, and he glared but said nothing.

The Andrasian man sighed and turned to Fin. "My apologies, Fin'roq, for this misunderstanding. I'm bishrop Uthyr Andria, of the Council of Nine. My sister—I'm sorry for what happened—I'm afraid her fears get the better of her. She is still on the mend." He unlocked the cell door and opened it.

"So I'm—not under arrest?" Fin asked.

"On the contrary, Fin'roq. You've an enrollment ceremony to attend at the Pruu'patch. Your companion is waiting for you just outside." Uthyr handed Fin a scroll. "I've amended your transit papers. You shouldn't have any other problems in the city. Welcome to Balan Su, monkin. Good day." He gestured for Fin to leave, and Fin didn't have to be told twice.

He walked slowly but deliberately toward the exit, his head up, his mind full of questions, barely able to hope that things were going to work out, but desperately wanting to. When he emerged from the holding cells into the lobby of the port building, Jaun was waiting for him. When he saw Fin, he leapt to his feet and ran to him, pulling him into a tight hug.

Fin put his arms around him and let the tears fall, and Jaun rubbed his back with one hand and ran his hand down his long woven hair fibers with the other.

"Are you alright?" he said in his ear. "Did they hurt you?"

"Yes," Fin said, "but I'm okay. I think. I guess. I don't know. Sweet Trevian, what have I done? Why have I come here? I was a fool to leave Bhea's, to leave P'anorum."

"You're not a fool, Fin," Jaun said. "You told me yourself, you always dreamed of being a monkin of the Pradishar. And you know what? The hateful ones just failed in their attempt to stop that from happening. So what do you say?" He took his arm. "Shall we go take up the purple and gray together?"

Fin wiped his tears on his sleeve and nodded at Jaun, but Jaun just stood and stared at him, a sweet smile on his face, his brown eyes twinkling, til Fin couldn't help but smile too.

⚜

Jaun led Fin'roq by the arm through the lobby of the port building and down a long corridor to a room with a set of doors. One of them opened with a whoosh. They stepped into a small room and when the doors closed, the entire room began to rise upward, and Fin looked around, alarmed at the sensation.

"A lift," Jaun said. "One of the most convenient maquina the Guild ever made. Great for long vertical spaces. Otherwise imagine the climb!"

Fin'roq could imagine it. He had climbed out of the crater on P'anorum where his little village sat countless times, up the path to the Swarthen Forest, off to Bhea Bell's garden. And he'd climbed up through the forest too, through caves and on vines, to reach the old lookout on the False Lip of the Crag at least a few hundred times, and it was much higher than the upper rim of Balan Su. Didn't climbing to a place make it special, for the climber and for the place? Did reaching it too easily take something away from it?

They exited the lift in the station near Grand Plaza. Once out on the street, Jaun led the way north to the Pruu'patch grounds, along the edge of Corda'mere near the great citadel and its spire.

"If the fog were clear, right above us would stand one of the most magnificent structures on the entire planet," Jaun said, "but it will have to wait for better weather."

A single Cul'tavin stood guard at the door when they reached the Pruu'patch, and he nodded to them. "We were informed of your arrival," he said. "Inside with the other recruits."

Jaun entered first with Fin'roq trailing behind him, looking around with anticipation. They were in small room, arranged like the welcoming hall in a typical garden—fully enclosed and sealed off from the main space, with flagstone floors instead of soft grass. Verdillions in older times, and still many in rural places, would keep this room as a means of screening visitors without being rude. They were technically invited in, so no protocol was breached, but then they could decide who merited the real invitation into the inner sanctuary.

I'm really here, Fin thought. *At the Pruu'patch! Am I dreaming?*

Fin and Jaun kept their hoods up, their faces in shadow, and Fin at least was glad of it, for when they stepped into the hall, a half dozen other young Andrasians, and one Raccorin, turned to look at them, expressions of annoyance and frustration on their faces.

"Finally," one of them said, and they all glared in their direction.

"We apologize profusely for our late arrival," Jaun said, lowering his hood.

Several of the recruits gasped and started laughing nervously. A few looked unimpressed.

The sole Raccorin narrowed his eyes. "Out of work?" he said. "Did the masses finally realize that a pretty face does not a talent make?"

"On the contrary," Jaun said, flashing a toothy grin. "I've never been busier. This is preparation for the role of a lifetime."

"Be nice, Uryn," a pudgy Andrasian said. "He doesn't speak for all of us," she said, turning to Jaun.

"I never imagined he did," Jaun said, winking at her.

A bishrop entered from the inner door and everyone snapped to attention, heads bowed. Fin'roq did his best to mimic. He'd have to remember to thank Jaun for keeping the attention off of him. Or maybe that was just the way Jaun was?

"You're all here," the bishrop said. "And I'm a very busy servant of Trevian. So let's be quick today, shall we? Your local priestins have all vouched for you. When you walk through this next door, into the heart of this Patch, you are officially monkins of the Pradishar. If you later decide to leave us, if you fail to complete your training and fail to be rewarded with a crystamin, you will still be able to call yourself a monkin and to appreciate the privileges that affords. Others of you will go on to be full-time monkins with a variety of important responsibilities in your community. Or perhaps you'll become brave Cul'tavin peacekeepers, kind Me'dicant healers, wise priestins, or bishrop leaders. Perhaps even Sui Pradesh one day, or Gran Pradesh. It all begins here, and now."

The inner door of the welcoming hall opened and the bishrop beckoned them all to enter. As the recruits walked past, the bishrop stared at Fin'roq, ignoring everyone else, his eyes following him into the next room. Fin'roq gulped but didn't remove his hood.

The door led to a vast garden, with grassy paths and plots, with large thickets of trees, with old stone buildings covered in moss, the bricks worn down by moisture over the millennia. The bishrop ushered them into a flagstone clearing in the heart of the sanctuary and put up his hands to speak. "In this space, in here, we are all siblings, all family. We treat other monkins with respect, with patience, and with kindness. Regardless of who they are or how we feel about them. Is this understood by all?"

The monkins affirmed.

"Fin'roq," the bishrop said. "Please lower your hood."

Fin gulped but did as he was told. Several of the Andrasians gasped and the Raccorin hissed. The bishrop turned to the Raccorin. "Kneel," he said, and the Raccorin dropped to his knees obediently. The bishrop pulled a zapren from his robe and jabbed it in the Raccorin's neck. He flopped around and fell to the ground, moaning.

"You have disobeyed me only moments after lying to me," the bishrop said. "We have no patience for such behavior. I mentioned earlier that some might fail to pass the training of the Pruu'patch but will still be a monkin. I didn't mention that there might be some who fail so utterly as to warrant removal from the Pradishar entirely. Of course, the monkin will have seen a lot, will know a lot, and can't be allowed to take that information out of the family, now, can they? Let me be clear, you don't want to become one of those monkins. Am I understood?"

They all affirmed with soft murmurs.

"Fin'roq here is a Bhizini, yes. And we are not used to having a Bhizini in our Pruu'patch. Only one wore our robes, until today. And I will not tolerate any disorder in my 'patch on account of this. Are we clear?"

The monkins nodded meekly.

"Now for your housing assignments. You'll be two to a room," he said, and he began to call names.

Fin looked around, and the thought of having to live with one of these strangers, possibly one of the ones who had looked at him with revulsion, made the panic rise up in his chest.

"Fin'roq with Von Andron," the bishrop announced, and Fin thanked Trevian as he exhaled.

Jaun turned to Fin. "Looks like you aren't getting rid of me yet," he said, and Fin blushed.

The bishrop passed out scrolls with schedules for each of the monkins, with the hours for feeding, for prayers, for sunshine, for the library, for recreation. Everything tightly routinized, Fin saw. Training sessions, even a few classes at the Academicon, began tomorrow.

"Now I want to—" but the bishrop stopped when someone approached. They were wearing a gray robe similar to a Pradeshan robe but without the purple, and their face was wrapped so only the eyes could be seen. But Fin'roq thought their skin looked gray, and their eyes were empty, vacant, lifeless and terrible things, wide open, seeming to look everywhere and nowhere at once.

"The Gran Pradesh, his holiness Ra'shard Ruu'n, requests the monkin Fin'roq attend him in the citadel," the messenger said in a flat voice.

The bishrop had a shocked look on his face. "The monkin was just getting settled," he said.

"The Gran Pradesh will see him now," the messenger said, and the bishrop slowly turned to Fin'roq and nodded.

Fin looked at Jaun and Fin thought he saw a crack in his facade again—was it jealousy?—but he flashed him a grin and winked. "You lucky guy," he said. "Already getting in good with the boss."

"Real lucky," Fin whispered. "Now everyone in the whole Pruu'patch will hate me for sure."

He followed the messenger across the inner sanctuary, down a set of stairs, and into a series of tunnels with shiny black walls and glowbes that struggled to light them. Eventually they reached a set of doors which opened with a whoosh. Fin didn't speak and the messenger said nothing. When the lift doors opened again, Fin was beckoned to exit. He stepped out into a black room, its walls so polished and shiny that they reflected back upon themselves time and time again, making it hard to tell what was up and down, or right and left, or back and forth. He had to close his eyes and take a deep breath and focus on how his body felt in order to proceed.

Fin saw an old Raccorin in the distance, perched on a small mound of soil, a beam of light shining down from somewhere above. He was old, as old as Bhea Bell, maybe older. Fin thought he needed to plant himself soon. He had a kindly look on his face and he spread his arms wide as Fin approached him.

"Welcome Fin'roq," the Raccorin said. "I'm Ra'shard Ruu'n, Gran Pradesh of Balance Authority. I've been waiting for you."

"I'm sorry to have kept you," he said.

"You misunderstand," he said. "My nephew has watched you for many years and it was him who told us about you. He said you showed great promise for the Pradishar."

"Aar'ryn Ruu'n," Fin said. "I had no idea."

"I'm terribly sorry about what you've endured," the Gran Pradesh said. "But I want you to know that you're safe now that you're in the capital. I assure you, no Cul'tavin will raise a hand against you again, and I do hope you'll forgive me for the circumstances of your arrival."

"Thank you, your worship," Fin'roq said, though the words felt strange to say aloud.

"You've taken a real risk to come here, to leave your home behind. And after such stressful occurrences, and the wretched treatment by those who were meant to take care of you—yes, you are indeed brave."

"I've always wanted to join the Pradishar," Fin said. "I'm grateful to be here. I never thought—this could happen."

The Gran Pradesh nodded. "I'm terribly sorry Fin'roq, but I was hoping I could ask some uncomfortable questions of you."

Fin bowed. "Of course, your worship." His face felt flushed.

"I hoped you could tell me what happened in the tunnels under P'anorum?"

Fin looked at the Gran Pradesh's forehead and saw the pits where his crystamins once were. Then he stared at the long scar down his face, at the shiny marble where his eye had once been.

"That's right," he said, touching his brow then letting his hand fall. "Only holes remain now. A Gran Pradesh has to remain separate from the crystals, Fin, separate from the world within them, master of none and no one's master. When one is selected as the new ruler, their crystals are all removed. So I have not seen the stream of what happened to you on P'anorum myself, only what my advisors have told me. That is why I'd like to hear it from you. In your own words."

"I'm afraid I can't help you, your worship," Fin said. "I have no memory of what happened."

"I'm sorry to hear that," the Gran Pradesh said. "Is there nothing at all you recall?"

"Well, I remember going underneath the island. Aar'ryn and Roe, they were looking for something. They asked me to guide them, because I've spent a lot of time exploring the island. We reached an old stair. There was a smell. I remember going inside, going down steps and not wanting to, but they insisted we continue. I remember a room, and I remember panicking, reaching for Roe, trying to grab hold of him, but it was like I'd become him. And then I remember suddenly being pinched and squeezed and torn, crushed by something, sliced apart. I screamed, for a long time it seems, for ages—but when I stopped screaming, I was in Bhea Bell's garden, and it had only been a few days. She told me what happened, what I was accused of doing. But I didn't. I wouldn't have hurt Roe. I swear it." Fin'roq was ranting and he knew it. He dropped his eyes in shame.

"Thank you for sharing, Fin'roq. I know that was hard on you. But I can tell you're being honest. Strange things have been happening with the crystals lately. Your case is one of many that we don't fully understand. I wanted to bring you here, to the capital, to the Pruu'patch, to keep you safe. I brought you here so you could help us, and we in return can help you. Are you willing to help us, Fin'roq? To help me?"

Fin'roq bowed, still not looking at the old Raccorin. "I'm your faithful servant," he said, his heart racing.

"I can tell you have a great future here with the Pradishar," the Gran Pradesh said. "I'd like to ask a favor of you. You're going to stand out here in the city, and in the Pruu'patch. This may be tough, but it could potentially be a great benefit. You see Fin, there are factions in the Pradishar. There are some who speak treasonous things, who plot against Balance Authority, under the protection of our pradeshan robes. They even operate here in our holy citadel. There is no doubt they will try to recruit you. Therein lies the opportunity, Fin'roq, to expose their plots. I hope I can count on you to report to me on any suspicious activity you might notice?"

"I—"

"I know, Fin, everything seems strange to you now. But soon you'll get a feel for life here, and then you'll be able to distinguish when something seems off. Don't worry, I have faith in you." He smiled, and Fin'roq bowed again.

"I will do my best," he said, and as Fin walked back to the lift, he didn't need the illusion of the reflective floor to feel like he was floating.

When the lift came to a stop and Fin'roq stepped out, he looked around, expecting to find the messenger who had brought him, but the corridor was empty. The lift door slid shut behind him, and Fin tapped on the door but it didn't open. When he turned back to the corridor, he saw a familiar face approaching.

"Left you here, did they?" Roman Anthem said. "Those nasty Octa'vin wouldn't have cared if you got lost in the hallways of the citadel. Some of them—they seem to go on forever, and they all look the same! Let me show you the way out, but just this time. Take care you memorize the route."

"I'm grateful, Captain," Fin said.

"I trust the Gran Pradesh was happy to see you?" Anthem said.

"I—don't know if happy is the word I'd choose. He was very friendly to me."

"He can make you feel incredibly large," Anthem said. "He can also make you feel incredibly small. You've been given a tremendous favor, being given an audience like that. I hope you don't squander it."

"I wouldn't dream of it," Fin said reverently, and Anthem laughed.

"You're all right," he said, clapping him on the shoulder.

They followed the tunnel that lead to the Pruu'patch, out of the obsidian tunnels of the citadel and back through soil, and when they reached the threshold of the 'patch, Anthem beckoned Fin'roq onward.

"Good luck," he said. "We'll meet again."

Fin'roq bowed as Anthem turned and walked back toward the citadel, then he half-ran into the inner sanctum. A priestin frowned at him, then pointed the way to his quarters, and he hurried inside, hoping to tell Jaun what had happened, but the sleeping chamber was empty. There were two patches of soil on either side of the room and two small workstations next to them, with shelves in between. On either side of the door were two chests containing robes and study materials. These were to be Fin and Jaun's only possessions while in the Pruu'patch. Pradishar recruits could only bring with them what they could carry—the intention being that they'd bring only themselves—but most brought a few trinkets in the pockets of their robe.

Jaun had placed a few scrolls and some robes on the workstation to the right so Fin took the one to the left. Then he unbundled the small satchel Bhea had given him. He'd forgotten it on the ship, so Anthem must have brought it up. Inside were a few objects from his youth, stones and sticks and shells and other treasures he'd gathered from his explorations of P'anorum over the years. His eyes teared up as he fingered them, and he gave a kiss to each object as he placed them on the shelves. One was a small mollusk shell no larger than the tip of his finger that he had found on a morning swim in the harbor. So many of them looked alike, the same fine line spiraling out from the center, but this one was different. On this shell, there was not one line but many lines, many circles instead of one spiral, all running together at one point in the center.

Fin'roq climbed onto the sleeping patch and let his rootpads down into the soil. It felt good to be back on land again, after so many days at sea. He couldn't believe he was halfway around the world from P'anorum, and he tried to imagine that Bhea and Grizmond were walking around beneath his feet, flipped upside down on the backside of the planet, but the image was too absurd.

If they're even still alive, he thought, swallowing down a sudden surge of terror and homesickness and confusion and loss that took his breath away.

Jaun came into the room and shut the door behind him. "How did it go?" he asked, as he walked over to his workstation and began to put his few belongings in order.

"I don't know," he said. "I think it went well. Ra'shard Ruu'n was kind to me. Didn't you tell me he tried to overthrow slavery before he became the Gran Pradesh?"

"I have one of his books you can borrow," Jaun said. "But what was he like? Did you trust him?" He looked at Fin'roq with anticipation, like a professor awaiting a reply from an anxious student during an exam.

"I—think so," he said. "I liked him. He was kind to me. I'm glad I chose to come here."

Jaun's eyes twitched and Fin'roq felt a stab of betrayal.

"When you're eyes twitch," he said, looking at the crystals on Jaun's forehead, "are you sharing our conversation with someone?"

"Of course not," Jaun said. "It's my damn director, nagging at me as always. I—sort of told him that Pradishar basic training would only take one week, not several months. He's just found out, and he's not too happy about it. Not too happy at all."

"Oh, I'm sorry, I thought—"

"No, I'm sorry, I should have given you my full attention," Jaun said. "And now I have an excuse to get out of this. Hang on." His eyes twitched a moment longer and then they stopped. "Just you and me," he said. "What do you think of this place? Think it'll feel like home for awhile?"

"Maybe," Fin said.

Jaun unrolled his scroll and glanced at his upcoming schedule. "Ooof," he said. "This isn't a day in the sunshine, is it? We're really expected to do all this, on the first day?"

Fin smiled. "We'll get used to it soon enough. My teacher always said that a routine, while it seems boring and stale, is actually how the really wonderful things of life manage to get done." He pulled out his roots, grabbed his own schedule, and unrolled it on Jaun's workstation, side by side with his own. "Looks like we're together in the mornings, apart in the afternoons. You're—" he looked at Jaun, "—studying to follow the Cul'tavin?"

Juan took Fin's hands in his own and turned them both palm up. Fin froze.

"Do you see how your hands are?" he said, running his fingers across them. "The palms are rough and coarse and strong. You've gardened with them your whole life, no?"

Fin nodded, blushing.

Juan turned his own hands palm upward. "Now feel mine."

Fin thought his hands would shake but they didn't.

"Soft as silk, no?" Jaun said. He sighed, dropping his hands and turning away. "It's funny, since I play a hero in so many melodramas. I've played a warrior so many times, it's ridiculous. I've been amongst thousands of ships in mock battle, in what are truly impressive works of art, the arrangement, the design of it all, like a real battle laid out on the sea. And yet the truth is, I'm worthless with my hands—worthless with my fists. I need my body to be quick, to respond. I want such skills for myself, and not just to pretend I have them. It's not about power either—not about being a bully like so many who join the Cul'tavin. It's not even about some role for a fantasy stream. It's a private goal of mine. A deeply important one." He turned and looked at Fin, a serious expression on his face. "Thank you for letting me share it with you, Fin'roq friend."

"I wasn't judging," Fin said, turning away, afraid he'd fall into Jaun's eyes. "I was just surprised. I thought you'd follow the Me'dicants and learn to heal. You bring so much joy to people already with your work. You'd be a natural at it."

He had inadvertently discovered the one topic sure to have Jaun von Andron's attention: the wonderful ways in which his art was helping the world, not harming it.

Jaun smiled from ear to ear. "Tell me more about this healing business," he said. "And take your time. We have all night."

Chapter 22

Sui Pradesh and the Prince

ELLEX ANDRIA WAS STILL fuming over the release of Fin'roq from her custody—she'd given Uthyr more than an earful about it, and wished she could give the Gran Pradesh an earful too—so when she learned that Rakk had been apprehended after sneaking into the city, she was furious but unsurprised. Arriving on a ship, registering with port authority, greeting the notestreamers, indulging in a bit of pomp and circumstance—that wasn't Rakk Raeder's style, Ellex knew. But damnit, why did he have to make them all look like fools? Now the one meant to take over the security of the city was himself in the Dankburn. And Ellex had a mind to make him wait there as long as she possibly could.

Rajj, and the Council of Nine, were on her side. This had been a grave insult. A few days in the dark would surely make him repentant, they said. Ellex knew they were wrong, but this way, she'd have time to prepare. The Council was counting on her to convince the prince to accept the position they'd offered—a position Ellex knew Rakk would reject once she revealed the price for taking it, i.e. a Pradishar crystamin on his forehead. She also knew why the council had picked her to do the negotiating, which only infuriated her even more. But no, she refused to stoop to that level. She'd just have to convince Rakk with logic, and maybe a few threats for good measure. And if that didn't work—she'd figure that out later.

But as the next few days passed, Ellex didn't have much time to prepare. The fallout from the dream—the incident, as she had to call it—had all of Balance Authority busy. Ellex had called another meeting, much to the frustration of some of the council members, and insisted that the government step up and start remedying the chaos the incident had caused. She suggested generous benefit packages for the victims of major accidents and grants for cities to rebuild damaged infrastructure. The Guild would get a brand new fleet of top of the line skimp'rins, faster and with better armor, to protect against Bhizini assaults on the Great Sea Lanes.

As for Ellex, she was done hiding out and done being a victim. It was time to make herself seen—everywhere, often—comforting victims and reassuring operators and making clear she was busy finding answers. She knew she needed some herself—in particular, why had Ra'shard Ruu'n let the Bhizini Fin'roq come to the capital? There was something about that one—something Ellex didn't trust—but there were other issues to deal with first.

Later, she thought. *One thing at a time.*

On the third morning after Rakk had been imprisoned, she woke early, donned her Cul'tavin uniform and pradeshan robe, strapped up her boots, and hurried through the glowbe-lit streets of the capital to the citadel. When she reached the tiny balcony far atop the spire, the faintest hint of light had just touched the eastern horizon, where fog-swept sea met twilit sky.

Ten weeks, she thought. *Just ten weeks til Zenithra begins. And just two more after that til the Balancing Act and the beginning of a new year.*

Ellex knew that pilgrims and patriots from around Balance Territories were already making their plans, booking passage to Balan Su, securing rooms in inns. Many would travel by skimp'rin, which could carry a large number of people at once but topped out at a fraction of the speed of a well-equipped cata'rin. For some, the voyage would take nearly a month, and they would begin by walking from their villages and towns, down the paths through forest and field to the nearest river, where they'd wait for a passing ship to take them down to the port for passage across the Inner Seas. By the time Zenithra peaked, the population of Balan Su would triple. And with this being the 10,000[th] anniversary of Balance Authority—and thanks to the recent capture of Qardymion the Saltsap—Ellex expected far more to come than ever before.

We'll be ready, she thought. *We will.*

The sky turned from backlit black to a dull purple gray, like faded pradeshan robes, before lighting into soft oranges with streaks of rosy red. And when the first ray of light shot skyward, Ellex exhaled for as long as she could.

But it didn't help with the jitters.

She returned to the lift and dropped back down the spire to the main levels of the citadel, then walked to the other lift, the one which would drop her down into the guts of the island, to the damp, foul chambers of the Dankburn. When she emerged, the air was very cool and the stones under her feet were slick. Mold seemed to coat everything.

Maybe I shouldn't have left Rakk here for so long, she thought, but pushed it from her mind.

The guard leapt to his feet when she emerged from the lift. "Sui Pradesh—" he said, bleary eyed. "I—well, I wasn't expecting you, is all. Your brother's not in, I'm afraid. Unless…"

Ellex waved her hand at him. "As you were. Sleeping, I think? I know the way."

The guard blushed, a dark brown in the light of the glowbes.

"Won't happen again, Sui Pradesh," he said, but Ellex was already walking down the corridor, her eyes twitching as she appended his docket with a flag to review his performance.

Rakk was being held in a small cell at the far end of the hallway, in one of the nicer chambers, the description being relative to the surroundings, of course. Nothing about the Dankburn was nice. The cell had a tiny series of windows, no more than slits along the back wall, that opened out through the sheer face of the spire on the backside of the island, not far above sea level. Light trickled in through them, but not nearly enough to nourish anyone, diluted as it already was from the fog. Nonetheless, Rakk was doing his best to stand under the meager beams and soak them up. Ellex stood in the shadows and watched him as he struggled to position his unfurled branches, trying to maximize their exposure. But eventually he gave up, withdrew them into his arms, and sank to the ground.

"Starving for light, Raeder?" Ellex said, stepping up to the bars of the cell.

Rakk nearly fell over, but he did his best to recover quickly. "Nah, just doing some stretches," he said, feigning exercise.

"You always were a terrible liar."

"Was I? My father was a brilliant one, a true performer at heart. My brother and sister, my aunt, my mother, my grandfather—I thought it ran in the family. Guess not. Maybe that makes me lucky?"

Ellex crossed her arms and looked at him for a moment. He was shaking slightly in his hands from the lack of light, and his eyes were red and puffy. Thirty four years had passed since she'd seen him face to face—seen him at all—and it seemed to her that he hadn't changed a bit, except maybe in the shoulders, which seemed wider and thicker than before, if that was even possible. Still the same broad face though, the same strong chin. The same eyes. He looked so much like his father, why had Ellex never noticed that before?

"I never thought I'd see you in the Dankburn," she said.

"I never thought I'd see you again, period." He stepped up to the bars, and Ellex remembered how he towered over her, how he filled her view with his presence—how safe she always felt when he was with her.

"I thought for sure I'd spend the rest of my life sailing the seas," he said, "fighting Bhizini, doing the grunt work of Balance Authority. Until you contacted me. And until I was summoned here, of course." He looked around. "Fabulous hospitality, truly. If I'd have known, I'd have come earlier. Honest."

"If you'd arrived as a proper prince, with forewarning and due ceremony, you wouldn't be in this predicament."

Rakk laughed. "Just walk right in? Just stroll into a city that hates me? Just trust that the Pradishar are telling the truth?"

"We invited you here to help us, not to set a trap for you. Instead you decided to embarrass us by undermining the security apparatus that you were meant to come and bolster! Seriously, Raeder, what were you thinking?"

He sighed. "Oh, come on Ell, I haven't seen you in three decades. Let my brother chastise me. Please, just talk to me—small talk—anything! Tell me how you've been. It's like a dream seeing you."

"Charming," she said. "Are you *trying* to make me angry? You were always so good at it."

"Oh—I didn't mean it like that, honestly. I wasn't even thinking about the incident. I just meant—forget it." He looked away.

She paused for a moment to swallow and catch her breath. "It's good to see you too, Prince Rhakksees," she said.

"Oh, all formal now, is it? Very well, princess, if that's how you want it."

She hissed softly. "Not that nonsense again. I'm no princess! You know Andrasia abandoned royalty long before Balance Authority existed."

"Did they now? What's that you call yourselves? A republic? And yet only those with land and titles can participate? Doesn't sound too different from the Raccorin Empire, if you ask me."

"Oh? Tell that to the millions of slaves you parade around your homeland like puppets on strings!"

"You mean the puppets who keep Balance safe—and delivered the Saltsap to your door?"

Ellex opened her mouth to reply but said nothing, and Rakk looked away again.

"Why are we fighting? I don't want to fight. I don't. I'm overwhelmed with joy."

"I don't want to either. You just make it so easy sometimes."

"I know," Rakk said. "I snuck into the city because I wanted a chance to see my brother before the whole world was watching. I haven't seen him since P'anorum. I wanted to smooth things over before the big public show. I never expected him to be waiting to arrest me!"

"But why did you run off with the Saltsap? I heard you defied orders from the regent, stole a ship from Thester, wouldn't tell anyone where you were! You know how bureaucracies work. You can't just break the rules because you're royalty. If anything, you have a bigger obligation to keep them!"

"I didn't break the rules because I'm a prince. I did it because I don't know who I can trust right now. Look, as much as I wish I could take credit for capturing Qardymion, the truth is I only found them because of an anonymous tipoff. Someone wanted them captured. Someone who was able to—I don't know how to explain it—to take me somewhere in the weavryn that didn't seem to exist anywhere. There was no way to sense or track the informant. I know this sounds crazy, but it was as if they were within the realm of the crystal but didn't have one themselves."

Ellex exhaled in what almost sounded like a hiss.

Rakk looked at her face. "What is it?"

"You know we had a leak within the Pradishar after my peacekeepers were attacked? Someone streamed the crime scene to the weavryn and expunged the metadata from the stream, so we couldn't track it. Uthyr found the perp, a Me'dicant, but rather than getting answers, things got even stranger. He'd altered the memory on his crystamin, looping a different memory over the part where he'd streamed the crime scene. We'd never seen anything like it, and when we tried to probe his crystal and extract the real memory, he vanished away from our senses, as if he'd taken bhiza to numb his crystamin. I've never seen anything like it. But now you're telling me someone with the knowledge of Qardymion's whereabouts, and the ability to cloak themselves, is the only reason we have the Saltsap in custody? Damn it, I'm starting to think Malisha Andra'asnia might be on to something."

"Who?"

"She's the head of the Culture Bureau, an advisor on the Council. She's also the top Cul'tavin on Andramere, and a major pain in my you-know-where. She's obsessed with the Ren'fallow, convinced there's a conspiracy within the Pradishar to disrupt Balance, though she's never gone so far as to mention the Harvest, at least not yet. She's convinced there's some shadowy threat on the weavryn, intent on sabotaging the servryns, alias Anorian Grain. Malisha had Doc Bryncent Andri'n arrested on suspicion of helping Grain. And his resistance to any kind of probing means she's probably right."

Rakk's face turned paler in the dull light, his bright green skin taking on a waxy tone. "Any leads on who they are?"

"That's the question, isn't it?" Ellex said, not noticing his face. "So far there's no evidence Anorian Grain exists, which is why the Council of Nine has been dismissing Andra'asnia's warnings. It's probably some disgruntled tinker mucking up the servryns, but she's using it as an excuse to persecute the Dyna'arin and unravel their long-held exceptions to Balance norms. So far, the Guild has cautiously been going along with it, since Doc Andri'n does hold a Pradishar crystal with priestin rank."

"Anorian Grain told me where to find the Saltsap," Rakk blurted.

"What!? You spoke to them?"

He nodded. "The conversation I told you about, with the cloaked informant. I could have been talking to anyone."

"Why would Anorian Grain help you, and Balance Authority? The Bhizini are the biggest threat to our mandate. Why hand-deliver us our enemy? It doesn't make any sense."

"Worse, the information was given as a quid pro quo. I—might owe them a favor." He gave Ellex a sheepish look.

"That's perfect actually. When you make contact again, I want to know about it." She sighed. "Speaking of which—I came down here expecting to convince you to take a job, not find even more reasons to doubt..."

He watched her for a moment, saying nothing. "You can see how this has all been too good to be true, right?" he said. "Capturing the Saltsap, seeing you, being offered a job in the capital—you see why I wasn't keen to just come strolling in the front door?"

Ellex said nothing for a moment. Her eyes twitched and the guard arrived, running, eager to please. "Release him at once," she said, appending the authorization for his release to his docket. The guard unlocked the cell and bowed to her.

"Follow me," she said. "And don't get any ideas. You aren't off the hook yet. Just—let me check on some things."

Rakk nodded and followed at her heels, saying nothing. They took the lift up to the surface, then walked the narrow, dark corridors to the lift to the top of the spire. Ellex's eyes twitched as she added the new information she'd learned from Rakk to her notes on the servryn, along with a list of the many questions his information had brought up. He stared at Ellex the whole way, though she did her best to ignore him. Finally, she'd had enough.

"Please stop looking at me like that," she said.

"I'm sorry. I just can't believe this is really happening," he said. "I feel like maybe I'm still in my cell, in the darkness, imagining all this. I was being serious when I said I never thought I'd see you again. When you contacted me—"

"Come on Raeder, we're only in our 70s. We've got another 130 years to go before we set down our roots. How would we go all that time without a reunion?"

"You forget I'm not living the pampered life in the palace anymore. I'm *always* at sea—fighting Bhizini, driving off raiders, risking my sap, keeping the Great Sea Lanes safe. Any day a scytherin could slit my throat, an enflamer cook me to a crisp, or a storm send me to the bottom of the ocean."

"Surely you have generals to direct, and Corkin to do the fighting, while you stay safely distant from the combat? Oh right, you're Rakk Raeder, of course you're more bold than that."

"I'll consider that a compliment," he said, grinning.

Ellex smiled in spite of herself. The lift came to a stop and the doors opened with a whoosh. They stepped out onto the tiny balcony atop the spire, the sun in front of them, bright and warm. Rakk unfurled his branches as fast as he could and flung them wide, drinking up the light. He moaned with pleasure, and Ellex felt bad she'd left him in the dark for so long.

When Rakk had had a nice drink of light, he opened his eyes and whistled. "What a view, princess," he said. "And this sunlight! I bet the fog never rises this high, am I right? Hey—did you bring me up here to impress me? This looks like the perfect spot for a date." He grinned.

"You're high on sunshine," she said. "Try anything and I'll throw you over the edge."

Rakk laughed. His hands weren't shaking anymore, and the patches under his eyes were beginning to fade.

"Don't worry, I'll be the perfect prince," he said. "Hands to myself."

"Good," she said. "Now let's get to the point. I want to talk about why you're here."

Rakk looked pensive. "Why I'm here on Balan Su? Why I'm here on this spire? Or why I'm here on this planet?" He smiled.

"Don't get smart, Raeder. Are you here to take the job or not?"

He looked out at the horizon and down at the hazy crescent of Balan Su, barely visible in the fog, his smile fading.

"This city hates me," he said, "has it out for me. The people hate me too. All of the offshore territories despise the Corkin. They don't want me here."

"You're wrong," Ellex said. "They see the hero who captured the Saltsap, the future ruler of the Raccorin Empire. Come on Raeder, you know how public opinion works. You might be the damn dirty slaveholder one day, the savior of freedom the next day, and they aren't any wiser to their own hypocrisy. They love you now, and one day they'll hate you again. You can't expect reason from the mob. That's why we have strong institutions that can outlast the moods of the masses. That's why we need strong leaders to keep those institutions strong—and strengthen them. And right now, you're considered the strongest, most capable warrior in the world. Who better to provide security for the capital of all of Balance?"

"You flatter me, princess, you really do. But I'm afraid I have to decline."

"Oh? Why's that?"

"I have seas to patrol. Villages to protect from Bhizini looters. The Lanes to keep safe. And if I have to spend months—or years—in this cold, wet, dreadful pit of despair, I'll lose my mind."

"Careful," Ellex said. "This is my home you're insulting."

"No, it's not. Avalon is your home. Andropolis, too, maybe. You only call Balan Su home because you have to."

"Don't assume you know how I think or feel, Rakk Raeder. You might have known me long ago, but I'm not that young fool anymore."

"You were never a fool. You were kind, and sweet, and tender. Now you act hard and tough, but I wonder."

"So it's back to the dungeon, then?" she said.

Rakk dropped his head. "Is that how it's gonna be? I play along, or you imprison me?"

"I could throw you over the edge?"

He made a pouting face but she didn't budge.

"I didn't want to have to do this," she said. "Look, right now, nobody knows you've been arrested. The city is holding it's breath waiting to welcome you. But defy this request, and we'll make a big show of throwing you back in the Dankburn, complete with an expose on the notestreams about how you defied orders from your empire and from

Balance Authority, stole a ship, and tried to help the Saltsap escape justice. The reckless prince, intent on destroying Balance. We'll parade you through the streets along with the Saltsap, and you'll see first hand how quickly public opinion can change. Then we'll send you home to Raq'asha, in chains."

"Damn Ell, you really have changed."

"You're one to talk. The Rakk Raeder I knew would've contacted me. I lost my father, my mother, my memories, *everything* on P'anorum. And never a word from you. I thought we would have at least remained friends."

He turned away and stared out at the horizon again.

"So what will it be?" she said after awhile. "The dungeon or the promotion?"

"Promotion? You're asking me to bring Corkin soldiers into a major city, full of peaceful civilians, when these soldiers are machines of war, not urban peacekeepers—and this is meant to be a promotion?"

Ellex sighed. "That's not all of it, either."

Rakk raised his eyebrows.

"This security force will be a joint one between Cul'tavin peacekeepers and Corkin soldiers."

He laughed. "You're joking."

Ellex shook her head and he stopped smiling.

"But Corkin generals can't command Pradishar."

She shook her head again. "No, they can't. In order to take over security, you must become ordained."

He stared at her like she'd lost her mind. "The Raccorin crown prince becoming a Pradishar bishrop? My nobles would have my head. They'd never—" He paused and looked at Ellex. "This was Raq'asha's idea, wasn't it?"

"No," Ellex said. "The Council of Nine decided this, and the eight spoke as one. And I think you're wrong about your nobles. You aren't looking at the bigger picture. This is the 10,000th anniversary of peace between our two races. I know there's concern on Raccorum Rhazzat about the incursion of the Cul'tavin into areas once dominated by the Corkin. So imagine when your nobles learn that their own crown prince has, to use the jargon, infiltrated the opposition and even assumed a place of authority in its power structure. You can sell this as an undermining of the Pradishar effort to create an Andrasian-led army."

"You admit the Andrasians seek an army of their own?" Rakk looked shocked.

"Absolutely not," she said. "Don't be absurd. Only misinformed Raccorin believe such nonsense. Andrasians are peace-loving. And the Corkin have kept us safe for ten millennia. Why change what works?"

He shook his head. "There's still too much risk. There's too many ways this could turn out terribly wrong for me."

Ellex hissed softly. "Always thinking of yourself, Raeder, aren't you?"

The look he gave her nearly broke her heart, and she wondered why he'd taken it so harshly.

"Back to the dungeon, then," he said, avoiding her eyes.

Damn the Council, she thought. She'd wanted to avoid this. And she hated when others found her predictable.

"Do you remember the promise you made me, all those years ago?" she said. "When we walked up to the old lookout on the Crag when you thought your mother was about to die? The place was ancient and the forest had reclaimed most of the path. We had to climb over tangled roots and swing about on vines. But we made it to the top. We stood staring down at the city, down at the palace, at the harbor far beneath us, at the ships coming and going, and the crowds along the shore, high above it all. Do you remember what you said to me?"

Rakk's eyes were shining but his face was stern. "Of course I do."

"Then keep it. Don't be Rakk Raeder. I need you to be Prince Rhakksees Raccorine Deri the Third, future king. I need you to convince this city and all of Balance that you're the hero and savior of the day, and that you'll keep us safe. I need you to do it for me, and I need you to do it for yourself. Your star may have been waning in Raccorum Rhazzat, but with the capture of the Saltsap, you're wildly popular again, the heroic prince that everyone loves. They're singing your name on the streets of Rhen'zoran, if you haven't watched the streams for yourself. Raeder, if you play this right, your people will love you for it. All of Balance will. Prove you deserve to be king by playing the part as perfect prince, and the crown will surely be yours."

"You sound like my father," he said.

Ellex sighed. The topic she'd been avoiding all morning had a chance to come out, and she had to take it. "Raeder, I want you to know something. The dream. Your father. I have no memory of that. I don't think it happened. I don't think—I did anything with him. Ever."

"Does it matter?" he said, looking away again. "Dreams are just dreams. They don't mean anything."

"You're probably right," she said. "But I just wanted you to know. I've—been struggling. To remember. To even think. I don't know how it happened, but after the dream—I realized I've never questioned my life before the accident. I've never questioned my life *since* the accident. I don't even know what happened to me on P'anorum. I couldn't even bear to think about it without feeling like my head might explode. I just—I've just been so worried that I've changed. That I'm not who I'm supposed to be. Does that make any sense?"

"No, it doesn't," Rakk said. "And yes, it does." He started to reach out, to touch her hair, but he pulled away before she noticed. "You seem the same to me."

"You said I'd changed."

"Well, of course you have, it's been three decades! But not where it matters. That's what I meant to say. I was worried about it too. I knew you'd been injured. I didn't know what to expect. But seeing you—I'll keep my promise, Ell. I'll take the job."

"Thank you, Raeder." Ellex could feel the relief spreading from her chest down her arms and legs and up her neck.

"Great Sower in the sky, I'm about to become a Pradishar bishrop! My great grandfather will likely burst into flames and fell the entire gruynfeld with him. Trevian help me!"

"Rajj will be happy to know you've accepted, and so will the Council."

"Rajj—?" Rakk's eyes grew wide. "Wait—he—you—you two planned this all along, didn't you? You knew I wouldn't agree to the job, so you arrested me instead and tricked me into agreeing. Damn you both!" But he was smiling. "I'm going to kill him. After I hug him."

"Come," she said. "You could use a change of robes and good long bath. Your family quarters await your arrival."

"Ah, the tiny house," Rakk said.

"Tiny? I don't know about that. Q'orin's already there, though I'm sure he kept you informed while you were in the cell? He's been petitioning for your release, oh, just about every hour. I'm about to kill him."

Rakk smiled.

Ellex signaled for the lift and the doors opened with a whoosh.

"Once you're settled and sunned up, Rajj will come by. I want you two to make peace, understand? Only hugs. I want a smiling, happy family when the notestreamers arrive. Can you do that for me?"

"It seems I'd do anything for you, princess."

"Then you can start by not calling me princess anymore."

"I can do anything for you but that, princess."

Ellex hit him lightly on the arm, and tried her best not to smile, but couldn't help herself.

Chapter 23

Cruel Uncertainties

MORNING CAME BUT BRYN Andri'n had not slept. She hadn't even thought, hadn't streamed the weavryn, hadn't considered the future, hadn't formulated a plan. Instead, she'd spent the night feeling. Whenever she closed her eyes, she saw her father thrashing on the ground, Malisha Andra'asnia leering down at her. She saw Aerid and E'mo in the alleyway, their faces twisted up, a terrible pain in her belly. She saw Aerid probing her mind, making her re-live her entire day, peering in and mocking her incessantly, for what felt like hours on end but was really only a few seconds. It was more than she could take. So she kept her eyes open, feeling Mama Andri'n next to her, feeling the soil under her feet, trying not to think, terrified her thoughts might be read the next time the Pradishar came for her.

When the sun finally rose, she went to the bathing room and ladled water over her shoulders, wincing as it ran down her back. She ladled and ladled, scrubbed and scrubbed, but never felt clean. She dried off and put on an Academicon uniform—maroon with streaks of gold—and a pradeshan robe on top of that. When she came out into the garden, she could hear her mother talking to someone, and her heart started to thud in her chest. She could see a figure seated at the table in the center of the garden—a Cul'tavin peacekeeper, sipping from a mug of steaming jha'ala.

Bryn's legs froze when she saw Malisha Andra'asnia's face, and she wondered for a moment if she hadn't been imperialized.

"Bryn, good," Malisha said, and she smiled at her, a ghastly grin that she probably intended to look warm and caring but which made Bryn's skin tingle. She stood. "I came to sincerely apologize for the way my peacekeepers treated you last night. They were *not* acting on my authority, I assure you. I'm afraid that's the way it goes when you have a massive organization—there are always bad ones in the bunch, and those few examples can make an otherwise noble organization look positively awful. Such it is with all governments. Even the Guild, too. That's why the enemy within is always more dangerous than the enemy without, and why a regular pruning keeps the tree healthy, right?"

Bryn didn't know what to say. She only knew she felt an overwhelming urge to grab the culture minister around the throat and squeeze—this Andrasian who had dragged off her father and threatened to rip his mind apart—but the thought of moving against her was too much for Bryn to handle. Not even words would come out, and when she thought that Malisha might scan her—might know her intentions—she started to panic.

"Regardless," Malisha said, "as an act of good faith, I came to share some news. We believe your father, while guilty of performing the crimes he's been accused of, may have acted without the knowledge that what he was doing was in fact a crime. If that is the case—that his intention was pure—that may mitigate his punishment. That's where I need your help, Bryn. We believe your father was working under the influence of the saboteur Anorian Grain, whose ability to disrupt servryns and avoid detection in the weavryn has become our number one concern following the incident. Furthermore, we suspect you may have had contact with this Grain before." Malisha looked sharply at Bryn. "If Grain could manipulate a brilliant professor like your father—well, surely you can see the danger you're in. Help us, Bryn. Help us set a trap for Grain. Once we have this villain in Pradishar custody, your father can be freed. This nightmare will be over. And Balance will be safe. You can forget this whole misunderstanding ever happened. Wouldn't that be wonderful, Bryn."

She swallowed and tried to hide the fact that she was out of breath. "I don't know any Anorian Grain."

<<I know you sent a message to Grain from the library yesterday,>> Malisha said to Bryn in her mind. <<Don't forget, I know everything Aerid knows. Everything he saw. Everything.>> She waved her hand. "Not to worry about that," she said aloud. "Anorian Grain will reach out to you, we're sure of it. And when that happens, I hope you'll think about your father. Think about his freedom. Think about it, Bryn, and then do the right thing. His liberty—even his life—are in your hands."

Bryn just stared at her, saying nothing.

"Well, I must be off. Perhaps I'll be seeing you both soon," Malisha said. "Thanks for the jha'ala. It was delicious."

Mama Andri'n just nodded.

"You'll release him if I help?" Bryn said. "I have your word?"

Malisha turned back and nodded gravely. "You have my word. Bryncent Andri'n will be free."

"And all charges dropped."

"Every one of them," Malisha said.

Bryn archived the conversation on the servryn, careful not to let her eyes twitch, not even once, while she nodded to Malisha. When she had left their garden, Bryn turned to Mama Andri'n, tears in her eyes. Her mother hugged her and they cried together for a moment.

"Don't you help her," Mama Andri'n said. "Don't you turn in Anorian Grain. Don't you dare!"

"Why not?" Bryn said. "We could save Papa. He could come home!"

Mama Andri'n sighed. "Brynnie—talk to Anorian first. Then decide. But promise yourself you'll wait til afterward to make a decision."

The door chimed and Bryn looked at Mama. "No one else," Bryn said. "I can't—I'll be in my quarters."

"No," Mama Andri'n said. "You've been hiding in there too much lately. Now go get the door. I'll heat some more jha'ala."

She suppressed a hiss, then reached out with her crystal to see who was calling. She sent the signal to open the door, shaking her head in relief and in anger as Trexbo, Ginjy, and Rhingus walked into the garden.

"No, no, no," she said. "You can't be here. The Pradishar—" She started to cry. "They'll interrogate you."

But Bryn's friends gathered around her and gave her a hug, everyone interlocking arms and swaying together in silence. Bryn calmed down but her tears still fell.

"We're so sorry, sis," Trexbo said. "We should have come earlier."

"You were following protocol," she said. "And you should have stuck to it. The Pradishar will know you've come. They'll interrogate you! Don't you understand what that means? They'll rip into your mind and expose everything!"

"We know," Ginjy whispered.

"We were all visited by the Cul'tavin on the night your father was arrested," Rhingus said. "Ginjy and I were only lightly scanned, but Trexbo, as a repeat offender—"

"It's no big deal," Trexbo said. "I've been probed loads of times. I'm used to it by now."

"Liar," Ginjy whispered, but Trexbo just grinned.

"They let us go, but we know we're being monitored," Rhingus said. "So we knew the risk before we came here."

"There's no way to not take risks anymore," Mama Andri'n said.

"Why was Andra'asnia here?" Trexbo said. "We saw her leaving before we arrived."

"Offering a deal," Bryn said. "Anorian Grain for my father's freedom."

"I hope you don't believe that wretch," Ginjy whispered.

"I want to," she said. "This is the first time since the arrest that I haven't felt hopeless. I want to believe my father can be saved, released—healed."

"If they can't get anything from your father about Anorian, that means he's resisting their probe," Ginjy whispered. "They'll never let him go knowing he has an ability like that, even if Anorian is captured."

"Ginjy's right," Trexbo said. "And if you aren't careful—if you actually contact Grain, or if the Pradishar discover you have the ability to cloak yourself in the weavryn—you'll never leave the dungeon again either. This might not be the bravest choice, but I can get you out of Andramere City. We can slit your crystals, sail north up the 'Mirri, find the Bhizini on the cliffs of Mun'maximo."

"The Bhizini? Why would they help me?"

"They help all who flee Balance. At least, some of them do. The ones I'll take you to."

"I'm not leaving the city, and I'm not slitting my crystals. But I'm glad to know I have a last resort option. Thanks, Trexie."

"We need to keep up with our stream," Ginjy whispered. "Now more than ever."

"Agreed," Rhingus and Trexbo said. "Bryn?"

"I don't know," Bryn said, feeling the panic rising in her chest. "The Pradishar are watching so closely." She saw Aerid's face again, his flower, stamen engorged, spraying her with pollen. "It's too risky."

"We talked about this, Brynnie," Mama Andri'n said, returning from the cookery with a tray of mugs full of steaming jha'ala. She took Bryn's hands in her own. "You have to go on with your life, day by day, as you would live it if you weren't afraid, even when you're terribly afraid. We're all afraid, love. But the time to avoid risk is over now. You need to go on with the work you've always done. Back to the library to finish those carvings, and then get your stream ready for sharing."

"You know about our stream too, Mama?" Bryn said.

"I'm your number one fan," she said. "Even if I don't always understand what you're talking about—still, don't you dare stop now. 'Cause then the Pradishar will know for sure who streams it. Like I said, we've got to go on, day by day, as if nothing happened."

Trexbo bowed to Mama Andri'n. "Bryn may get her intelligence from her father, but I see she gets her wisdom from you."

She patted Trexbo on the cheek and he blushed.

"How are you all so strong?" Bryn said. "I'm not wise, and I'm not brave. I feel like I can't do anything to stop the shivers. I can't do anything to save Papa. I can't even stand up to his torturer in my own garden!"

She took a few deep breaths to calm herself, but the tremors continued.

Rhingus touched her shoulder. "You're Bryn the Brave. Bryn the Strong. We all know that. Time for you to know it too. You can do this."

"Thanks, everyone." She gave them each a hug in turn. "A normal day it is, then. As if nothing happened," she said. "Right. Normal. Whatever that was."

"To the library, then," Mama Andri'n said. "But a bite to eat first? All y'all." She smiled when everyone sat around the table. "How's the carving coming, dear?"

"I should be done by the end of the year," Bryn said, "if I work through Zenithra. And if I don't have any other disturbances."

"From now on, I'll be your escort, everywhere," Trexbo said. "You won't be alone again. And it isn't because you *can't* be. It's because we want to protect you. I want to protect you."

Bryn blushed and nodded. "Thanks."

After they ate and finished their jha'ala, Ginjy and Rhingus gave Bryn another hug and promised they'd meet her at the library in the afternoon to discuss their next stream. They both had some research to do in the meantime and were taking the tram through New Town to the Inner Harbor.

Trexbo and Bryn said good-bye to Mama Andri'n and headed up the hill, through the walls into Old Town, and up the streets toward the Forum on the royal plateau. Bryn clenched her stomach every time they came to a group of people on the street, but nobody seemed interested in them that morning. She soon learned why on the weavryn—the Pradishar had cleared her of all suspicion of collusion with Anorian Grain. If that wasn't a message to Anorian from Malisha Andra'asnia, she didn't know what was.

When they reached the library, Trexbo opened the door for Bryn and stepped inside with her to greet the old librarian, Madr'gin, at the front desk.

"I have a bit of research of my own to do," he said. "I'll be next door at the Academicon. Give a holler if you need me. Otherwise, I'll come back when the others get here."

Bryn thanked him for the escort, smiled at Madam Madr'gin, and scurried off to her den, her lovely little nook, where she set up her workstation, put a scroll in the carver, flipped open a book, and pondered what she might work on for their stream while she began scanning the notestreams and archiving data.

But Bryn felt a presence on the edge of her awareness—a flutter as she passed her mind along through the servryns of the world—a beckoning which Bryn recognized and followed. Someone was using her own technique to slip streams.

Anorian Grain.

That didn't take long, she thought.

<<I'm so sorry, Bryn,>> Anorian said. <<I wanted to reach out to you earlier, but I didn't want to endanger you. But now I must speak with you, privately. Will you join me?>>

<<Yes,>> Bryn said, and she followed Anorian across streams, one after another, through every servryn in the world, leaping across the servryns and across datamins, and Bryn felt as if she'd stumbled, but there'd been no ground to hit, only a plunge, down into a darkness that had no bottom and soon had no top.

<<Don't be afraid,>> Anorian said.

<<I'm not,>> she said. <<I know I screamed but I'm okay now. Really.>> Bryn felt strangely warm and safe.

<<Can you forgive me, Bryn? I should have shown you this before, but I had strict orders from your father not to share it with you. Not until it was ready, and not until you were ready. Both of those are now true. So here it is. Welcome to the hollow.>>

A spacious lounge appeared around her as if from out of the fog of Balan Su, growing clearer, sharper, becoming real. A fire burned in the hearth and she could feel the heat, the power of its light on her skin. Anorian was in front of her, a tree with fruit of every color, a gentle face on a gnarled trunk.

<<You recognize the effect from your father's lab?>> Anorian said. <<I have perfected the technique and expanded it. I have wed it with your technique at cloaking to enter private servryns, and made sure it integrated seamlessly with the weavryn architecture that is already in place in Balance Territories. In here Bryn, you're completely safe from the power of the crystals, and any who might wield them against you.>>

<<Is this how my father is resisting the probe?>>

<<Yes. He is here with us right now, Bryn, but he is using all his strength to fend off the Cul'tavin.>>

<<Where is he?>> Bryn materialized a body, a branta bird, and she opened her wings and soared around the lounge. But no one else was in the room.

<<It doesn't work like that,>> Anorian said. <<Imagine this lounge as one bean amongst a vast stalk. If the beanstalk is the weavryn, then the pods that protect the bean are the hollow.>>

<<Why didn't my father want me to know this? If I'd had this ability yesterday, I could have resisted. I could have shut that Cul'tavin out of my head. Why did you wait so long to show me this?!>>

<<Forgive me, Bryn,>> Anorian said. <<I reached out to you as soon as I could.>>

<<As soon as the Pradishar announced I wasn't a suspect.>>

<<No,>> Anorian said. <<As soon as your father asked me to.>>

Bryn didn't know what to say, and she felt like a fool. Her form vanished though her presence remained.

<<Why did he keep this from me?>>

<<If the Pradishar knew you could resist a probe, you'd be in the dungeon like him. You're free today because you didn't know of the hollow yesterday. Consider that for a moment, and perhaps you'll understand what this place can signify.>>

Bryn looked around the lounge with her inner eye, feeling around with her awareness.

<<I can still stream from here?>> Bryn said.

<<Yes. There is no here. Think of it as a point in between. In the weavryn, when you step from one point to another, you leave prints. You can be tracked, and you can be identified. But the hollow exists between the steps, and its pathway leaves no prints. Bryn, you can stream on the weavryn, you can communicate with anyone else, in absolute privacy, and with absolute anonymity, anytime, anywhere.>>

<<No wonder the Pradishar want your head,>> Bryn said. <<And if my father's been helping you to establish this—then he really did tamper with the servryns.>>

<<Not to sabotage them, as the Pradishar report, but to enhance them. This is the weavryn of the future, Bryn. It is your father's life work. But it is still an infant, and still fragile. It lacks a few essentials to guarantee its survival. More than anything, it needs your help. I need your help.>>

<<What kind of help?>>

<<I need you to sneak into your father's office and recover the datamins he has hidden there.>>

<<What? Are you crazy? His office is Guild property. The Dyna'arin have zero tolerance for thieves. They might vaporize me.>>

<<The Guild can't vaporize,>> Anorian said.

<<You never know!>> she said. <<And the Pradishar are bound to have his office guarded.>>

<<I can help you with the guards,>> Anorian said. <<And the hollow will help you move unseen. The Cult'avin seekers will not be able to sense your presence, if you stay in here. But it must be done, Bryn. His datamins must be placed in the servryn in the basement beneath your feet.>>

<<The—servryn I've been working on. It's—part of this new weavryn?>>

<<Yes,>> Anorian said. <<You've been helping to make this possible for many years now, without knowing it.>>

<<Malisha Andra'asnia wants me to help the Pradishar arrest you,>> she blurted out, <<in exchange for my father's life.>>

<<I know,>> Anorian said. <<Is that what you want to do?>>

<<What if it is?>> Bryn said.

<<I'm afraid it wouldn't do you any good, Bryn. I'm already in Pradishar custody, and have been for some time now.>>

What? Could this be true?

<<Then why do they need me to help find you?>> Bryn said cautiously.

<<Because they don't know who I am,>> Anorian said.

<<So I have no hope then. There can be no deal.>>

<<I'm sorry, Bryn. I really am.>>

She said nothing for a moment. <<Fine. You want a favor from me? Then I want one from you.>>

<<Of course. There is always an exchange. What would you have of me?>>

<<Teach me what I need to know about the hollow, about the servryns, about what the hell is really going on here, and then I'll do what I can to get those datamins.>>

<<Deal.>>

Bryn felt a surge of gratitude from Anorian so powerful, and so warm, it flooded her heart and took her breath away. There was no doubting it was genuine relief. And for a moment—a very, very brief one—Bryn thought maybe she'd been wrong about losing hope after all.

Chapter 24
Something Like a Normal Life

Fin'roq had assumed, when he'd boarded Roman Anthem's ship in the harbor at P'anorum, that he would spend every day of the rest of his life thinking about his island home—about Bhea and Grizmond, and Milli Mor'n and Aar'ryn Ruu'n—about the Swarthen Forest and the Ka'Hala, even the ghu frogs on the shore. And he had thought about P'anorum every day on the crossing to Balan Su—he'd imagined he could still see the three peaks on the horizon, all in a line, like a footstool for the sky, still growing tinier as he went farther and farther away. But once in the capital, once in the routine of the Pruu'patch, he'd stopped remembering without even noticing that he had. Now it felt like he'd always been in Balan Su, always been a Pradishar monkin. What else could he ever have been? He ignored the past entirely, and was happy for it.

All except for Baboo. He missed him terribly. Every day he hoped to see his tiny friend, tumbling about, all smiles. Balan Su felt cold all the time—cold air, cold stones, cold people. But Baboo carried with him all the warmth of the Far Archipelago, and just the memory of him chased away the chill.

In truth, Fin'roq had seen little of Balan Su proper since he'd arrived, and he'd been too busy to think of much else. If he wasn't in the Academicon taking lessons, he was in the Pruu'patch learning prayers and methods. And since the two places were so close together, on either side of the Pradishar citadel, Fin saw only the very center of the upper rim. On the first day that the fog cleared and he could see the great obsidian spire towering over his head, he'd looked upward and stared until, woozy, he had to clutch the cobblestones with his rootpads not to fall over. And when he'd looked out, the fog had been sitting just below the level of the rim, as if the great crescent city were floating in the sky, riding a cloud across the ocean. It was hard not to swoon.

Besides, he was content within the walls of the Pruu'patch, where everyone except Jaun mostly ignored him. And he enjoyed visiting the Academicon for lessons, where Guild students were curious about him, some even warm to him. Not all, of course, but more than Fin expected. And his professors were so friendly. He was studying the Me'dicant lore, learning about Verdillion anatomy—how it functions, and how to heal and repair it. The material was tough and made him all the more aware of his own ignorance. He sensed an enormous world he knew next to nothing about, and that filled him with excitement and anticipation and wonder, rather than dread. Some days he'd find himself looking around at the great halls and plazas of the Academicon, at the thousands of students coming and going across the campus, and marvel at all the motion, all the chattering, an ordered swarm that seemed to have one mind but really had many. He'd seen the architecture of the Academicon's great halls and plazas in Old P'anorum, but there they'd sat in silence, forgotten. Here they were alive. Here, he could be a part of it all.

After two weeks in the capital, one of Fin'roq's professors announced that they'd be taking a trip to one of Balan Su's sprouting patches to study spratlyn's and their growth. Fin was excited to see more of the city. When the morning prayers and methods ended, he told Jaun not to work too hard that afternoon, then headed to meet his classmates at the Weeping Wilvryn in front of the citadel. He arrived early, and only his professor was there waiting.

"Ah, good afternoon, Fin," he said. "It's a small group today. Just waiting on a few others."

"Good afternoon, Professor Von'nDrino," Fin said.

"No, no," he said. "That's my father. I'll only tolerate being called that in the classroom. Call me Hesh'n out here."

"Okay," Fin said, and Hesh'n smiled.

"So how are you liking our fine city?"

"I haven't seen much of it yet, I'm afraid. But what I've seen so far is lovely. Lively too."

"Where do you come from, Fin?"

Fin thought he must surely already know who he was, and thus where he'd come from. But some professors did seem like they were in their own world.

"P'anorum," Fin said.

"You spent your whole life there?"

He nodded.

"Never left it before?"

"Never."

"Curious."

Fin said nothing, feeling awkward as Hesh'n looked at him while his eyes twitched. But the tension broke when two other students from Fin's class arrived—Cordi Kain, an Andrasian from Balan Su, friendly to Fin, and Mind'i Andra'asnia, an Andrasian from Andramere, who always acted like Fin didn't exist.

"Would it kill you to be on time?" Hesh'n said. "There's no excuse when you have a clock in your head. Now, we're going to the sprouting patch today. There's one in Sunset Point, and I've procured you access passes to the development. Cordi and Mind'i will be verified by crystal. Fin'roq, here's your permission." He handed Fin a scroll. "Let's be off. I walk fast. Believe me when I say, there is always something you could be doing other than traveling. So let's waste as little time as possible on this walk, what do you say?" He didn't wait for them to answer.

Mind'i rolled her eyes at Cordi and she chuckled.

"Hi Fin," Cordi said. "You can walk with us."

Mind'i made a noise that sounded like a swallowed hiss and Fin'roq hesitated.

"It's fine Fin, isn't it Mind'i?" Cordi said.

"Mmm—"

"That's a yes. Come on. Don't look so scared."

They started to cross Grand Plaza in front of the citadel, heading west toward the Academicon and the Forum. Mind'i leaned around Cordi and looked at Fin'roq. "How are you here?" she said.

"Uh—" Fin didn't know what to say.

"You heard me. How are you here? How is a Bhizini in Balan Su? In pradeshan robes? A monkin! I wanna know. We *all* wanna know!"

"Mind'i!" Cordi said. "Leave him alone. Fin, forget it. You don't have to tell us anything you don't want to share."

Should he drop the Gran Pradesh's name, and tell them he invited him to join the Pradishar?

"I mean, we recognize you," Mind'i said. "You're the Bhizini from the stream. The one that killed that Andrasian monkin. And now suddenly you're in Balan Su, becoming a part of the government! What the fuck?"

"Mind'i!" Cordi snapped. "Let's not have this conversation right in front of the citadel. They have scanners everywhere."

"I don't remember," Fin said. "I don't remember killing him."

"Wow, really? Is that supposed to make me feel better?" Mind'i scoffed.

Fin didn't know what to say.

"So why are you here?" Mind'i said, softer this time.

"The Gran Pradesh invited me," he said. "My villagers wanted me dead but he offered me life, in exchange for service to the Pradishar. I took the offer. That's the whole story."

"Ra'shard Ruu'n himself invited you?" Mind'i said.

"Through his nephew, initially. But he confirmed it with me when I arrived."

"You spoke to the Gran Pradesh?" Mind'i said, her eyes wide, a genuine look of shock on her pale green face. "Wow. You must be—some kind of super freak, right? For the government to just dismiss a murder charge like that, and then immediately invite you into their inner circle? They want you nice and wrapped around their fingers, don't they?"

Fin'roq blushed. "I—suppose that might be so—"

"Might be?" Mindi' said. "Fuck the Pradishar. Don't *ever* trust them!"

"Mind'i!" Cordi said. "Not here. Please!"

She rolled her eyes and took his arm. "Come on, Fin," Mind'i said. "Ms. Cul'tavin here wants us to move along. Do what the nice peacekeeper says."

"Me? You're the one whose mom is the head Cul'tavin on Andramere!" Cordi said.

"Why do you think I came to the Academicon in Balan Su?" Mind'i said. "And now I won't be speaking to you at all this afternoon, for reminding me of her." She made a pouty face.

Fin'roq allowed himself a silent sigh, feeling like he'd passed a test only after the test was over. And that maybe he'd made a new friend, though he still wasn't sure.

Mind'i and Cordi gossiped with one another as they walked to Sunset Point, while Fin mostly kept quiet, listening and looking around and admiring the new parts of the city. Once they passed the Academicon, he was in new terrain. The Forum ended when the Academicon ended, and past them both was a large plaza with an assortment of Guild maquina and large operation towers on one end. Across the plaza was the glitzy shopping, dining, and entertainment district known as the Regalia. Fin'roq could smell it before they arrived—sizzled rhupan, grilled rhupan, fried rhupan, candied rhupan—so much delightful food. They walked down wide streets where cafes were interspersed with shops and galleries, and Verdillions were wearing fine robes, their skin well oiled, their hair fibers in elaborate patterns and decorated with clips and pins of metal and stone.

At the far boundary of the Regalia lay Sunset Point, an exclusive community for younger elites. The guard welcomed Hesh'n home, verified Cordi and Mind'i with a twitch of the eye, then glared at Fin'roq, his eyes narrowed. Fin handed him the scroll. He looked at him a moment longer before unrolling it.

"I'm afraid the Bhizini will have to stay out here," the guard said, smirking at Hesh'n. "You see, the time on the permission slip for entry has passed."

Hesh'n looked at the scroll. "By one minute."

"That's a minute too late," the guard said. "Afraid you'll need to get a new one."

Hesh'n looked at Fin, then at Cordi and Mind'i.

"Another day then, Fin," he said. "You can find your way back to the Pruu'patch?"

Fin fought back the tears and nodded.

"See you tomorrow in class, Fin," Cordi said.

"Yeah," Mind'i said. "We will."

He nodded, and watched them walk through the gates into Sunset Point. The guard waited till they passed, then stepped in front of the gate and leered at Fin'roq.

"If you have no business here, you'll need to leave. Or I'll throw you in the dungeon for loitering. Seeing as you have no crystal, I'm sure it'll take awhile for the Pradishar to dig you out. Now scram!"

Fin didn't have to be told twice.

꙳꙳꙳ ꙳꙳꙳

When he was out of sight of the guard, Fin'roq started to run, his heart racing. When he was out of breath, he stopped at a corner and leaned against it, wiping away his tears. He looked around, then behind him, then around again. Soon all directions looked the same to him. He'd have to pick one and start walking. The upper rim wasn't that big. Eventually he'd find his way home.

He started off, his hood low over his face, nobody the wiser who was under it. The avenue he was on opened into a large circular plaza at the heart of the Regalia. Most of the plaza was checkered with patches of low cut grass and areas of hard, sturdy soil. There was a large perennial oak in the middle of the circle, flanked with square fountains inside concrete ponds and small circular depressions with steps. Fin saw a group of troupers, their tent pitched near the tree, a backdrop hung between two branches, performing for a crowd of onlookers. He wanted to go and see the show, but the size of the group scared him. He couldn't shake the feeling that he didn't belong.

So he walked on, down the wide avenues, past the diners at tables along the street-side and vendors in the doors and windows of their shops.

"Halt!" a loud voice shouted nearby, and Fin knew immediately that they were yelling at him. Worse, he recognized the voice. For a moment, he debated sprinting into the crowd, trying to lose them, but he was too scared to move.

"You will submit to scanning. Lower your hood." He reached up to pull his hood down. "I think he's blocking me."

When his hood came down, he looked at the Cul'tavin who had stopped him. He recognized the Andrasian who had interrogated—and tortured—him when he'd arrived in the capital, Ellex Andria. The bright patches of green on his face seemed to lose their luster, the dull ones to turn gray and waxy. He tried to swallow, but couldn't.

"No crystamins," said a deep voice beside the Andrasian, "so no way to block you."

Fin looked up into the broad, smiling face of an enormous Raccorin, shoulders as wide as two Andrasians, and one of the tallest Verdillions Fin had ever seen. He was wearing a purple and gray pradeshan robe over Corkin fatigues, and when he chuckled, Ellex narrowed her eyes at him.

"I assume you have a scroll to show us?" the Raccorin said.

Fin nodded and handed him the document.

"Much appreciated," he said, unrolling the scroll and then nodding. "Everything's in order. Carry on."

"Everything's in order," he said. "Carry on."

"Hold it!" Ellex said. She grabbed the scroll from the Raccorin's hand. Her left eye was twitching. The Raccorin looked amused, a smirk on his handsome face.

"You're a little far from the Pruu'patch, Fin'roq. A little far from the Academicon even. Just what is it you're doing slinking around the Regalia? Up to no good, are we?"

"Fin'roq," the Raccorin said before he could answer. "You look familiar."

"I'm told all Bhizini look alike, to non-Bhizini," Fin said, feeling bold.

"That's true to some but not to me," he said. "I've known many Bhizini, and I remember every one of their faces. The patterns of pigmentation can be quite distinctive, much more so than bland Raccorin or Andrasian faces. Why might I know yours?"

Fin's face was burning, and he blinked back the tears.

"It doesn't matter," Ellex Andria snapped. "Ra'shard Ruu'n has vouched for him, even in spite of my protests." She handed Fin'roq the scroll. "That said, you have no business in the Regalia. You're to stay confined to the Pruu'patch or the Academicon, and don't go wandering about as if this were your home. It isn't, and it never will be. Is that understood?"

Fin nodded, a single tear overflowing from each eye.

"Leave him alone, Ell," the Raccorin said. "I'm in charge of security, am I not?"

"Raeder—" Ellex said. "Are you pulling rank with me? You're still in training!"

"It's already pulled." He turned to Fin and smiled. "Sui Pradesh here is having a bad day, is all. It's my fault, you see. I'm a terrible student, and she's taking out her aggression on you. If Balan Su is currently my home, then Balan Su is currently your home, too. On your way, Fin'roq." The Raccorin winked at him, and Fin nodded, scurrying off down the street, thinking that that Raccorin had been the friendliest Pradishar he'd ever met. But Ellex Andria—*why does she hate me so much? Why does she try so hard to make me feel so miserable?*

When Fin'roq was safely back inside the walls of the Pruu'patch, he began to feel better. He loved the fragrant gardens, the tinkling fountains, the birds that came to perch and sing. He loved the old stones worn from caressing. He loved the hall where they rooted and prayed. He felt at home there, he really did, and home felt safe.

But is it any different than when I was on P'anorum? he thought, as he sat at his workstation, trying to read a book while he waited for Jaun to return for the evening. *I loved Bhea's garden, but I was basically confined there at the end. Now I love the Pruu'patch, but if I'm not supposed to wander the city, and never get to know it, then how am I anything but a prisoner within these walls? Will I ever be anything else, no matter where I go?*

❧ ～～～ ❧

The next few months passed in a blur of routines and learning, til Zenithra approached at last. The sun would reach it's highest point in the northern sky in just a few weeks, and Zenithra celebrated this occasion. A new year would follow with the anniversary of Balance Authority on the first day of summer. Classes at the Academicon were dismissed until fall, and the Pruu'patch had replaced the afternoon lessons with time for contemplation. They were even given permission to venture out, so long as they stayed on the upper rim.

"The next two weeks will be the biggest party in a thousand years," Jaun said, looking like he had the inside scoop on the greatest secret in the world. "Every day they pour into the city from all around Balance Territories. There's festivals, pageants, music and dancing, theater, fine food and drink—oh, just marvelous stuff. I know a wonderful place down on the lower rim, mostly locals. You'll like it."

"Sounds—well, I don't know how it sounds," Fin said.

"Surely you'll accompany me?" Jaun said.

"Right now? You mean—out? To a crowded place? On the lower rim?!"

Jaun laughed. "You sound so alarmed! It's a party. What's to worry about?"

Fin wanted to say yes—to say yes to whatever Jaun said—but the thought of going across the city, at night, where he wasn't supposed to go—when the city was full of people, many of whom came specifically to see a Bhizini in chains paraded through the streets—Fin didn't know.

"Don't make me beg," Jaun said.

"Okay, but how will we get to the lower rim? We don't have permission."

"You don't," Jaun said. "But you forget I'm Jaun von Andron! I not only have permission, I can bring along any guests I want, anywhere I go."

"Lucky you," Fin said, narrowing his eyes at him.

"Sorry Fin, I didn't mean it like that. Really. I just meant—forget it. Just say you'll come with me?"

"I guess," he said, as if he'd ever have said no.

"And don't worry, we'll pull our hoods low over our faces and travel incognito. I don't want to be seen either. At least half the travelers in the city will be pradeshan faithful. We'll go unnoticed, I promise."

Fin nodded and Jaun beamed.

They left the Pruu'patch and crossed Grand Plaza to the lift station. The door opened for them without any problem and the lift rapidly dropped them to the lower rim. They exited when they were halfway to sea level, and after a walk down a long, narrow, dimly lit tunnel, they emerged into the long, open plaza that ran down the slopes at the center of the crescent, from upper cliff to the shores of the harbor, in terraced squares interspersed with stairs. The fog had retreated to the water level, sitting atop the harbor like frosting on a cake. Fin looked up at the great crescent, all a-twinkle with the light of thousands of glowbes from end to end, like long arms hugging a cloud in its wide embrace.

"Jaun," Fin whispered. "It's beautiful, isn't it?"

"On days like this, indeed it is," he said.

They walked to the tram station and boarded the city's only tram. Jaun again had no problem entering the station, nor bringing a guest along. Nobody had looked twice at them. The tram took them down the center of the lower rim, hugging the slope of the island, traveling east and then south across East'fall'n, all the way to the end of the line, where the lower rim pinched down into a narrow strip. Next to the station was a large tapering square, the cliff sides of the upper rim and Sunrise Ridge just overhead, the wharfs of Eastport down below. The plaza was full of Verdillions, many in pradeshan robes, others dressed in skirts or shorts, cumberdomes in place, the tops of their torsos exposed. A band was playing and some were dancing, talking and laughing together in the warm light of the glowbes.

"Wait here," Jaun said. "I'll grab us some slurpans." He didn't wait for Fin to answer, but ducked off into the crowd, just another purple and gray robe among so many others.

Fin looked around at the scene. Even though there really were a lot of people, for some reason it didn't seem as lively to him as it should. On P'anorum, whenever he and Bhea and Baboo had partied, the dancing was always so fun and so spirited. They'd sway and howl with joy, and spin and twirl about, but these dancers were content to lean back and forth, stiffly. To jump a bit, randomly. Fin was amused.

But when Jaun didn't return, his amusement faded. The friendly faces around him were suddenly the faces of complete strangers, and complete strangers were unpredictable. After half an hour had passed, Fin started to panic. He pulled his hood low and clutched the cobblestones with his rootpads, looking for support, for an anchor, for protection. He thought he could board the tram back to the center of the city without a crystamin, but what if some transaction had taken place that he'd not seen? Would he have to walk back along the line? But then how would he board a lift? Could he run in when someone else was using it? Probably not. He had no way to contact the Pruu'patch. No way to contact Jaun. Everyone he knew in Balan Su was on the upper rim.

When an hour had gone by, the tears began to fall before Fin'roq could stop them. With his hood over his head and his arms at his side, he gently swayed back and forth, quietly sobbing.

"Here you go," Jaun said, handing him a frosty slurpan, fresh from the ice box. "Sorry, there was a long line."

"A long line?" Fin said. "You've been gone forever!"

"Oh, I'm—sorry," he said.

"Why did you abandon me? Where'd you go? What the—fuck Jaun!" He struggled to catch his breath.

"I had to meet someone. Real quick, I thought. It—I guess it went a little longer than I expected. But it's over now. I'm here now."

"You could have told me! Is that—is that why we came here tonight? Just so you could sneak off for some shady dealings?"

"Fin—no—I—"

"Forget it," Fin said. "Just take me home."

"Of course," Jaun said. He turned and started toward the tram. "This way."

They rode the tram across East'fall'n in silence, then walked through the plaza and down the tunnel to the lift station without a word. Fin sulked in the corner of the lift during the ride to the upper rim. When they got to the Pruu'patch, Fin climbed onto his sleeping mound and closed his eyes.

"I'm sorry," Jaun said. "I really am."

But Fin ignored him.

"Please don't be mad at me," he said. "I know what I did was wrong. I should have told you what was up. I—really did want to go with you, to show you the city and help you relax."

Fin opened an eye, and Jaun had a wounded look on his face.

"You don't get to be the victim here," Fin said. "You left me for an hour amongst strangers in a crowd—in a crowd on the lower rim, where I was essentially trapped. I'm the one who should have the wounded look." He tried to sound angry, but the sight of Jaun, the thought of him sad, distracted Fin from his pride, and disturbed him in a way he hadn't felt disturbed before.

"At least let me make it up to you?" Jaun said.

Fin waited a moment before he replied. "How?" he said.

"On the last day of Zenithra, on the Eve of the Balancing Act, at Corda'mere after sundown. There's a new melodrama streaming with the new year. I have a starring role in it, of course. The gala is to celebrate its release—a big deal in Balance Territories. Lots of big names from around the world will be there. I wondered—well, would you like to go with me?"

Fin laughed sardonically. "Why in Trevian's name would I want to attend a gala of the rich and famous? So you can show off your friend the freak? So they can scream in disgust at the feral Bhizini in their midst?"

Jaun's wounded look returned. "That isn't it at all. Not at all! Just—forget it then."

Fin sighed. "No," he said, his face burning. "I'm sorry. I just don't know why you'd want me to come along to something like that. And how can I trust you wouldn't abandon me again?"

Jaun smiled. "Not to worry, Fin. Jaun von Andron would never abandon a date."

Fin's blush spread down his neck and he felt like the city had vanished from beneath his feet.

"But if you don't want to go with me—" Jaun said.

"I do," Fin said. "Of course I do."

Jaun's wounded look had turned into a wide grin.

Chapter 25

In the Fog of Balan Su

N O TIME WAS WASTED in making Rakk Raeder a Pradishar recruit, and as he stood in front of a mess of dignitaries and notestreamers, the citadel's great chapel filled to overflowing—with Rajj at his side, all smiles, full of praise—he struggled to believe that just hours earlier, he'd been down in the Dankburn, in that cold, damp pit from which so few ever returned, and now he was standing here, with all of Balance watching, taking his brother's hands, reciting the oath to the Pradishar, about to undertake a project that he didn't have the first idea how he was going to pull off.

He felt exhausted, but somehow he grinned through it all and played the part of an eager but humble prince, one who recognized the gravity of the task while also showing his willingness to rise to the occasion. When the ceremony ended and the guests began to head for the door, Rakk turned to Rajj, eager to spend some time with him and really catch up after so many decades, but he had already left.

"This way," Ellex said, gesturing with her head. She started off without waiting for him.

Rakk swallowed his disappointment and followed her, out of the chapel and down the narrow, dark hallways of the citadel, barely lit by glowbe, to her office near the Solarium.

"You aren't exactly a normal recruit," she said, "so things can't be done in the normal way. With Zenithra only a few months away, we have to—" She looked at him. "Raeder? Are you even listening?"

"I—yes," he said. "Not a normal recruit. Have to make double time. Got it."

"More than double time. You'll need to complete your annual in a month."

He whistled. "Can it be done?"

"It better be," she said. "The Pradishar won't name you priestin, then bishrop, if you don't prove yourself a competent monkin first."

"Me, a monkin. It's just so absurd."

"Is it?" she said. "You used to talk of becoming one."

Rakk felt his ears burning and his chest clench up, and he looked away, desperate to change the topic, but his mind filled with memories of long ago and no words would come.

"I'm sorry," she said. "I didn't mean—"

"No," he said. "No. It's fine. Just another casualty of the eruption, I guess."

Ellex said nothing for a moment. "Raeder—"

"I'm looking forward to it," he said. "You know how much I love Balan Su, with it's warm sunny days, it's come-one-come-all attitude of friendliness and acceptance and—"

"Alright," she said. "I get it. This isn't what you want. But all opportunities have hardships, and risks. And you won't be doing this alone. I'm here to make sure you succeed. I may be Sui Pradesh, but I'm also a bishrop, so I can train you. I've arranged for you to study at the Academicon in the mornings, in Corda'mere during the afternoons, and on patrol of the city every evening—the last part with yours truly."

Rakk was all smiles.

Ellex saw his face and narrowed her eyes. "Don't think this will be a lovely stroll through the Regalia. These aren't dates. And I don't plan on going easy on you."

"I wouldn't dream of it," he said. "I promise to be the perfect monkin."

Things were looking up already, and Rakk felt like he was floating as he and Q'orin walked the cobblestoned streets of Old Stones, en route to Sunrise Ridge where his family's estate was located, later that afternoon.

Every evening with Ellex Andria, he thought. *And for the foreseeable! Is Trevian blessing me already?*

Even the cold air and the fog, which threatened to overwhelm the upper rim of the city, didn't dampen his spirits.

"Can you believe we'll be living in Balan Su for who knows how long?" he said, clapping Q'orin on the shoulder. "How I hate this place!" He laughed.

Q'orin gave him a hopeful look. "My prince has changed his tune. Perhaps he's finally recognized the opportunity he's been given?"

"Indeed I have," Rakk said.

"You have a busy schedule," Q'orin said. "What would my prince have me do while he is off training?"

"I'd hoped you'd spend the mornings and afternoons at my side."

"I'm not sure the Pradishar will permit that."

"They will if I tell them to," Rakk said.

"I'm not so sure," Q'orin said. "Forgive me for saying, but as a monkin, you'll have to follow orders. And I wouldn't want you making a diplomatic incident on my behalf. Besides, I'm always with you in here." He touched the crystals on his forehead.

Rakk could feel him on the edge of his awareness, a flutter in his crystamin, the strength and warmth of his presence like beams of sunshine on his skin.

<<What would I do without you?>> Rakk said.

<<Miss your appointments, forget to bathe, maybe escape to your island getaway and never return?>>

Q'orin rarely teased, and Rakk realized he was happy to be in the city, and Rakk was happy that he was happy, and he opened his mouth and laughed at the sky. "You know me too well," he said aloud. "How about this? You've been so excited about coming to the capital, why not spend the next month getting to know the place, walking its streets and tunnels, talking to locals on the upper and lower rim, getting Balan Su's pulse. And of course you'll have to check out the theaters and the markets, and sample the local cuisine while you're at it."

Rakk could feel Q'orin's joy flooding his crystal, and he wasn't sure he'd ever felt him that pleased.

He deserves it, he thought. *And it may be the last time he gets to relax and enjoy himself for a very long time.*

When they reached Sunrise Ridge and followed the grassy pathways to the tiny house, his family's ironically named estate, Rakk wasn't expecting the surge of nostalgia that rose up suddenly within him, and he stopped walking and stared, his heart aching, the happiness he'd felt before already draining away, leaving an empty feeling inside. The tiny house had been built as a way to try and make one forget where they were by mimicking the burnstone palace on P'anorum, warm and spacious and lively, in a city that felt so dead. As a scamp, it had seemed almost magical, as if walking through the threshold had actually transported them to the other side of the world. But now all Rakk saw was everything he'd lost. The halls that once echoed with the sounds of the court and the booming voice of his father now sat as silent as his ruined home on P'anorum.

Now I understand why Rajj can't bear to live here, he thought, stepping inside and feeling himself wither— feeling dried out and old.

Q'orin was at his side, his hand on Rakk's shoulder, his soothing vibes pulsing through his crystal, and he felt like he could breath again.

"Shall I find us somewhere else to stay?" he said. "Prince Rajesh'n warned me this was a sad, haunted old place."

"Those times here were always so awkward, so unpleasant," Rakk said. "Father's temper was always short, Mother weepy. Being here always made us scamps anxious. But that's over now. Father and Mother are gone. And with my training, we'll hardly be here. We can see it through. It'll be okay. I think. So long as you're here with me."

"There's nowhere else I'd rather be," Q'orin said, and Rakk felt his reassurance through the crystal again, and he let it wash away the doubt and the uncertainty. He tried to reclaim the excitement he'd felt just moments ago, the thrill at getting to spend so much time with Ellex Andria, but it just wouldn't come.

"You've had a long day—a long week," Q'orin said. "And you could use some more light after so much time in the Dankburn. I can feel your exhaustion, my prince. Come to the terrace and relax. We have to get you rested up if you're to become a bishrop in no time at all."

"What would I—" Rakk started.

But Q'orin cut him off. "You're quite capable of managing on your own," he said. "But I'm still honored to help."

❧ ☙

The tiny house didn't feel any more pleasant as the days and then the weeks began to pass. Rakk returned every night, exhausted from his long day of studying and training, and though elated from his evenings with Ellex Andria, the sad, empty halls of his family's estate seemed to crush him, to defeat him, to make him question why he'd ever taken on such a foolhardy mission—why he hadn't just given up decades ago, when everything else was lost.

It didn't help that he wasn't sleeping very well. He'd pass from dream to dream, waking with panic in his chest, his mind blank, the nightmares forgotten, the sounds of voices—of crying—fading away into the ground, as he struggled to remember where he was, *when* he was. Sometimes he was sure he was on P'anorum, just a scamp still, and he had to remind himself that no, all that was gone, had been gone, for decades.

But instead of grief, there was only more emptiness inside.

Rajj wasn't making it any easier for him. He'd tried, and tried, and tried again to meet up with his brother. There was so much he wanted to tell him and ask him. He needed his advice, and he needed his help. But Rajj wouldn't see him, and his ability to slip away whenever Rakk thought he'd finally cornered him was remarkable. Then again, Balan Su was crisscrossed by so many tunnels, not just within the citadel but connecting the inside of the lower rim to the outside. There were miles and miles of such passages, even more when one considered all the clandestine ones, like the path he'd taken to sneak into the city. It was a miracle the crescent didn't collapse in on itself.

Regardless, it was obvious Rajj didn't want to see him, and he wasn't sure why. Ellex told him his brother had been very busy with his work on the Council of Nine, but Rakk knew there must be more. She was on the Council and still had time to see him, even to train him. But when Ellex insisted he contact him directly via crystamin, he dismissed the suggestion with a wave of his hand. "He's busy," Rakk said. "So I'll leave him alone for now."

He couldn't help but feel punished.

At least Rakk was so busy himself that he had little time for self-pity. His day started early, at first light, and mornings were spent learning Pradishar history and lore at the Academicon. In the afternoons, he studied prayers and methods in Corda'mere, including Cul'tavin combat methods, and he welcomed the chance to get a first-hand look at how the Pradishar trained their fighters.

Not that Cul'tavin peacekeepers were soldiers, although Rakk knew that some in the Pradishar hoped for more, and envisioned a Cul'tavin force of both Andrasians and Raccorin capable of replacing the Corkin, but this depended on the Guild building them a fleet—and approval from both Raccorum Rhazzat and Andrasia. Such a thing seemed unlikely any time in the near future, but Rakk knew this was a trial run of sorts, a chance to show the potential benefits that might come from adjusting the Accords of Balance. And while he wanted to impress Ellex Andria, and wanted to demonstrate to the residents of Balan Su that he wasn't some barbaric slave master from the high seas, he knew more than anything that he had to serve the Raccorin first and foremost. They were his people and he their prince and future king. Their interests had to be protected.

Besides, this new security force of his wasn't just Cul'tavin peacekeepers, albeit from both civilizations. That would have been too easy. And as the month wore on, and his familiarity with Cul'tavin practices grew, he become increasingly despondent about the task before him. Just how was he going to manage integrating the highly skilled and well-refined war machine that were his Corkin slaves and their imperialized crystals with a group of city-dwelling Cul'tavin whom he couldn't even bodily control unless they gave him permission to do so? These peacekeepers were even allowed to choose their superior officer, as if they were a tinker deciding which operation to join, a truly baffling (and infuriating) concept to a slave-owning prince used to absolute command over his underlings.

But Ellex was helping him to see how capable, disciplined, and hard-working these Cul'tavin peacekeepers could be, even without imperialization. Ellex's followers practically revered her, and Rakk knew that she had earned that respect.

I will have to earn their respect too, he thought. *And their trust.*

Ellex was also helping him to forget his misery, the potential loss of his throne, the nights of tossing and turning in the tiny house, haunted by the memories of his ancestors. Each evening, weary from the hard work of the day, his brain feeling foggy and his muscles sore, he'd nevertheless find himself full of energy, a big smile on his face as soon as Ellex Andria appeared, renewed by her presence. They'd walk the streets and tunnels of the city, through its alleys and plazas, through factories and wharfs, through the fortresses at the great gates to the harbor, even the stronghold on the rocky northern tip of Nunan. On such walks, Rakk didn't mind the fog. He didn't mind the cold cobblestones slick with moss, the smell of mold and rot, the long dreary tunnels barely lit by glowbe.

"What a terrible place," he said to Ellex Andria one night, as they walked through the Regalia.

"What now?" she said. "If I've heard it before, I don't want to hear it again."

"The color," Rakk said. "Not enough blues or browns. The sky here, on the upper rim at least, when the death mist hasn't swallowed the island whole—it's never blue, but always white from the glare. And the stones of the streets and plazas and the buildings stacked upon one another—nearly all the soil is tucked away behind stone. And so the brown—the brown and blue are missed."

Ellex rolled her eyes. "And you say only your father was a trouper?"

"Why do we always bring him up?" Rakk said.

"Halt!" Ellex shouted, pointing at a tall figure in a long Pradeshan robe. The pilgrim pulled down their hood, their eyes wide with fear. They were a Bhizini, and Rakk asked for their permission to be in the city. He looked at the scroll and it was legitimate. Ellex was unappeased, but Rakk insisted there was no problem.

As the Bhizini scurried off, having pulled their hood far down over their face, Rakk turned to Ellex, who was glaring at him.

"Fin'roq," Rakk said. "I never forget a face. Who are they?"

"A Bhizini," she said. "I just don't get it, Raeder. How could Ra'shard Ruu'n let a Bhizini join the Pradishar? And how could you be okay with them being here in the capital, with Qardymion in the dungeon and the city on alert? You can't trust Bhizini. They should all be expelled from the city. No good will come of this. You'll see."

Rakk laughed. "You know, if you were on Raccorum Rhazzat, the phrase would be 'you can't trust Andrasians.' And if on Andrasia, it would be 'you can't trust Raccorin.' Here in the archipelago, it's 'you can't trust Bhizini.' It's all nonsense. Besides, I've seen the figures. There are fewer than half a dozen Bhizini in the entire city, and you're worried about an uprising?"

"These are special circumstances," Ellex said. "It only takes one to slit a crystal. Don't forget what happened to my troops—troops who were part of a joint Raccorin-Andrasian force, just like the one you're putting together. I'd say it's better to over-reach than to under-reach. Any Bhizini in this city is a security threat, even with Ra'shard Ruu'n's permission to be here. The eyes of my Cul'tavin are on Fin'roq now." Her eyes were twitching.

"I don't know what you're so concerned about," Rakk said. "Pilgrims are pouring into the capital, merchants are happy, the Bhizini aren't on the move, the Saltsap is in chains. We'll have the Cul'tavin in one hand and the Corkin in another. Who would dare attack such a force? The city is safe, Ell. And I'll keep it that way, as long as I have to."

Her eyes fell still, and she looked at him and forced a small smile.

"Thank you, Prin—er—Raeder."

"Prin'er Raeder, I like that," Rakk said, winking, and Ellex turned away from him, trying to hide a blush.

❧ ☙

Rakk passed his initiation into the Pradishar with honors, becoming the first bishrop ever ordained in such a short amount of time. Rajj was at the Joining ceremony in the citadel, all smiles in front of the notestreamers, warmly praising him and his accomplishments. The words stung, considering how he'd been ignoring him all this time, but Rakk looked at Ellex Andria, focused on her eyes, her face, her hair, and forgot about his brother.

More than three decades had gone by since his last joining, and Rakk had forgotten how painful the experience was. He spent a day recovering at the tiny house, agitated and weary from the uncomfortable sensations inside his body. That night, he tossed and turned, waking out of breath and struggling to remember where he was, a thudding and thumping and a moaning in his ears—no, coming from under his feet.

He screamed for Q'orin, and he was at his side, his hand in his, his presence in his crystal, soothing him.

"The basement," he whispered. "I heard something."

Was it Father? Could he be here?

Q'orin returned a few minutes later, shaking his head.

"The sound can echo through these burnstone halls like nowhere else," he said. "There's no one in the tiny house but us. Rest now, my prince. I will wait, and watch, and keep you safe."

"Promise?" he whispered, squeezing his hand and feeling like a fool, but not caring.

Only with Q'orin could he ever let himself be so weak.

"I won't move from this spot," he said. "Now rest. You've earned it."

Rakk lay silently, holding his breathe, listening. But Q'orin's smell, the feel of his hand, the warmth of his presence in the crystal, drew him away from his fears. And he closed his eyes and slept like a spratlyn, dead to the world.

The next morning, he woke to Q'orin's face looking down at him, his hand gently shaking his shoulder, his voice calling to him in his mind.

Rakk sat up, feeling refreshed, and grinned.

"My prince seems back to his full strength," he said, giving him a long look. "It will take some getting used to, seeing a purple crystal with the orange, yellow, and red ones."

Rakk peered through Q'orin's eyes and saw himself through them. "There's no going back now," he said. "And no time to lose." He got to his feet and started to stretch. "When does the ship arrive?"

"They arrived in the night, and only await your orders to disembark. Shall I greet them for you?"

"You'll greet them *with* me. But I'll meet you there. I have somewhere I need to be first."

"My prince? You've nothing on your schedule."

Rakk waved his hand. "Later," he said, heading for the bathing room.

He could feel Q'orin's annoyance through the crystal and couldn't help but grin.

A few minutes later, he was out the door and off down the grassy pathways of Sunrise Ridge, headed for the misty groves of Corda'mere, the sky overhead growing light with the approach of dawn, the brightest stars yet to fade entirely away. The fog had dropped well below the rim of the crater, and the spire of the Pradishar citadel rose a thousand feet into the air, it's glassy contours streaked with bronze. The sight of the great stone tower, when the weather permitted it, was one of Rakk's favorite things about Balan Su, and one that could still take his breath away. He marveled at the thought of the tiny balcony where Ellex Andria had taken him, so impossibly high above it all.

When Rakk passed through the gates into the foliage of Corda'mere, the air heavy with the smell of wet soil and sweet with jasmine, he felt for the timekeeper on the weavryn, and once he was sure he wouldn't be late, he darted inside the citadel and headed for the chambers of the Council of Nine and its members. Rajj always came to work early, before first light, or so it was said. He'd catch him in his office, force him to talk to him, brother-to-brother. But he didn't have permission to access that part of the citadel. And he wasn't about to make a scene trying to sneak in.

So instead he slumped his shoulders in defeat, but then physically shook it off, and put on a smile, and walked through the dark corridors back out to Corda'mere. He followed the path that wound around the citadel into the heart of the thicket on the west side of the spire, the smell of the evergreens making the city seem miles away.

Ellex was waiting where she promised she'd be, dressed in her Cul'tavin fatigues, a pleased look on her face.

"How are you feeling this morning?" she asked.

"Like new," he said, then exhaled hard and tried to grin. "Now the fun part begins. The real test of my leadership."

"Test?" she said. "Nonsense. You were chosen for that very skill. Why doubt yourself? Besides, I have something to show you. This way."

He followed her to a long, flat green in the middle of the western flank of Corda'mere, in what looked like a meadow but which Rakk could tell was actually a large plaza. It was empty this early in the morning, save for a few birds which had come to peck at the grass.

"Do you know that this is the original mustering ground for Balan Su's very first security force? They were a group of Andrasians and Raccorin who ensured that the capital stayed safe during the early years of Balance, when the Accords were new and peace was still fragile. Eventually they were disbanded, replaced by Cul'tavin, when their reason for being, well, ceased to be."

"The Defenders," Rakk said. "I remember the story from when I was a scamp. I thought it was only a legend."

"Mostly it is," she said. "But that doesn't stop the story, or it's associated relics, from having power." Her eyes twitched and Rakk saw movement out of the corner of his eye. On either side of the plaza, a stream of Cul'tavin peacekeepers marched in, lining up to fill in the open space before him. And when they had all taken up position, they stood to attention, facing him.

"A sample," Ellex said, "of those who have already pledged to serve you."

Rakk could see Raccorin and Andrasians in the group, young monkins fresh from the Pruu'patch and older ones with years or decades of service to a different bishrop, and he knew they had not made such a choice lightly. It was up to him to honor their decision by turning this team into a coordinated, reliable force that everyone could be proud of. And this symbolic start, where the Defenders of old had once gathered, was a wonderful touch.

"They've come from all over," Ellex said. "More arrive every day, hoping to make history with you. They're ready to work with the Corkin, and keep the capital safe."

"I—Ell—this—" The words didn't want to come. "How do I—?"

"Thank me?" she finished for him. "By seeing this through to the end."

He nodded. "It's a deal."

"Good. I have one more thing for you, in my office."

"Another surprise? I'm honored, but I don't know how much more I want to be in your debt."

She rolled her eyes. "It's not a gift. And it's not from me. Just come along."

Ellex started for the front of the citadel and Rakk hurried to catch up. Once inside, they followed the corridors to the chambers of the Council of Nine, and Rakk couldn't help but take a peek and see if Rajj was in his office.

"What do you think you're doing?" Ellex said from behind him, as he opened the door and walked into Rajj's small workspace.

The room was empty.

"You can't just walk into the office of a member of the Council of Nine! Out, now, before I call security!"

Rakk looked at Ellex and wasn't sure if she was joking or not. He didn't want to find out.

He threw up his hands in surrender. "Leaving already," he said, walking back out into the hallway.

Another near-miss, Rakk thought, tasting Rajj in the air. *Always leaving just before I arrive.*

"Rajj still avoiding you?" Ellex said, the anger gone from her voice.

He nodded, avoiding her gaze.

"I'm trying to sympathize," she said. "But for Trevian's sake, you two are impossible. Just reach out for him! He's literally a thought away."

"So what's this present you have for me?" he said.

Ellex swallowed a hiss and started for her office, shaking her head as she went, and Rakk followed, clenching his teeth, his face burning.

⋙⋙⋙ ⋘⋘⋘

Rakk tugged on the cape of his new uniform, a thick but silky black trimmed in silver, that hung over his shoulders and down his back. His fatigues were also black and silver, fashioned like the ones the Cul'tavin wore but without the traditional colors. Etched across the chest, and on his cape, was the symbol of Balan Su, a modification of the insignia used by Balance Authority, an idealized form of Balan Su's shape with the great spire of the citadel pointing upward, and a crystal between the tips of the crescent. There were no symbols to represent the Corkin nor the Pradishar anywhere on the outfit, only the city itself, and Balance Territories more generally. And though the craftsmanship was superb, the tailoring precise, the materials the finest that could be found anywhere in the world, Rakk still felt like he shouldn't be wearing it.

He adjusted his waistline and shifted on his feet.

"You don't like them," Ellex said. She was standing next to him in the lift, as it dropped through the rock and soil of Balan Su, down to sea level. A faint whine of maquina was in the air.

"No—I mean, it's not that. They're lovely, really. Thank you."

"I told you, they aren't from me, they're from the Council of Nine. And new uniforms always feel funny, like putting on a new skin, or a new face. There are new roles to perform, new expectations to meet, and you don't know all the moves yet."

"I've always worn the reds and oranges of the Raccorin," he said. "This feels drab and dark and bitter. Appropriate for this city, but what will my people think, to see me in the colors of Balan Su, and not of Raccorum Rhazzat—not in the royal red? Will they think I've abandoned the crown? Abandoned my subjects?"

"Your subjects are citizens of Balance Authority as well. Maybe you can make them see that being loyal to Balance doesn't mean being disloyal to the Raccorin, like some in Raccorum Rhazzat like to think."

"And some in Andrasia, too," Rakk said. "Anti-Balance sentiment isn't only a Raccorin problem, as Andrasians would like to think."

"Fair enough," she said. "But you need to stop worrying about what others are thinking of you. You need to be able to perform right now, to get up there and dance even if you don't know all the moves, and that won't happen if you keep giving yourself stage fright."

"You're right," he said. He took a deep breath and exhaled hard, then another.

Ellex said nothing for a moment, and he stopped tugging on his clothes and let his hand fall. The lift slowed and the maquina whined and the doors opened with a whoosh.

"You may not like the clothes," she said, adjusting the cape on his shoulders, "but you sure look handsome in black." She smiled and Rakk blushed, the color spreading across his bright green cheeks.

They walked the long corridor in silence, and when they emerged from the royal port building onto the pier, it was like stepping into a cloud. The air was heavy and wet and cool, and he could only see about twenty feet in any direction. He could hear the gulls screeching over the harbor, the sloshing of water against the seawall, and the chatter of a crowd nearby. And he could smell the wet, moldy wood and the thick briny stew of the ocean, and realized he'd been longing for a good swim ever since he'd arrived in the capital.

Rakk took a deep breath and then stepped on stage. He greeted the notestreamers who'd been given exclusive access to the event. Then he welcomed the Corkin soldiers to the city—the first troop of slave warriors to ever set foot in the capital—and introduced them to the Cul'tavin peacekeepers who had already pledged themselves to his service. The image of Corkin warriors and Cul'tavin peacekeepers, their hands on one another's chests, their eyes locked, smiling in friendly greeting and then embracing in friendship, was streamed to the entire joined world, while PropSector declared a new age of prosperity and cooperation between Andrasians and Raccorin after 10,000 years of Balance Authority.

And all the while, Rakk drank up the attention.

When the event finally concluded, and when all the new recruits from both Corkin and Cul'tavin had been assigned quarters—when all training schedules were dispensed, and when some of the logistics had been reviewed with Cort Andramon from Balan Su's local government—Rakk asked Q'orin if he'd accompany him to the barracks. He had one more piece to put in place, and the sooner he did so, the better. With Zenithra only a month away, there really was no time to spare.

Rakk found his favorite Corkin warrior, Rhannokti, sparring with a Cul'tavin peacekeeper in the training room of one of the barracks in Lower West'fall'n, and he and Q'orin stood back in the shadows and watched them fight. He hadn't seen the slave face-to-face in decades, and rarely through the eyes of anyone else either. The size of Rhannokti's body, his thick shoulders and massive hands, the power in his swing and the delight in his eyes at the thrill of the fight—that was what Rakk liked the most about him. He relished combat and never had that barely-concealed anger that so many others had when he used their bodies as his own. He would make the perfect puppet to have at hand, should Rakk need someone near the harbor.

When the fight ended, Rhannokti approached, bowed to Rakk, then fixed Q'orin with a stare that seemed meant to both intimidate and mock.

"I'm glad you came," Rakk said. He'd given all Corkin a choice on whether or not to join him in the capital—a stipulation of the Council of Nine—and he hadn't been sure that Rhannokti would want to enlist in an urban security force, since the likelihood of battle was so low. Perhaps the slave had other ambitions. Surely being nose to nose with Cul'tavin peacekeepers for the foreseeable future was an opportunity like no other for a Corkin soldier born and raised in bondage. Maybe that had been the Council's—and the Andrasian Republic's—plan all along. Many in Balance Authority had been trying to break the Raccorin's slave system for centuries.

"You honor me with your presence," Rhannokti said, staring at his feet. "I'm a humble slave who came only for a chance to glimpse my prince."

"Then be welcome," Rakk said.

Rhannokti glanced at his face, briefly, before returning his eyes to the ground.

"Thank you. I can die in peace now."

Q'orin could hardly contain a scoff, and Rakk could feel the contempt emanating off of him through the crystal.

<<Be nice,>> Rakk said in Q'orin's mind.

<<His empty praise hides a vile intent, my prince. This one is dangerous.>>

"I'd have you live," Rakk said to Rhannokti. "In fact, I'd hoped you'd spend the next month getting to know the harbor, and as much of the inside of the lower rim as you can. I want you on standby during the Balancing Act, in case I need you."

"I am yours to command," Rhannokti said, bowing again.

"I'll make sure you lack for nothing."

"My prince is kind to one so undeserving," Rhannokti said.

"Then prove that you deserve it," Rakk said.

"It will be so, my prince," Rhannokti said.

Q'orin swallowed a hiss and started for the door, but Rakk didn't stop him. When he emerged from the barracks onto the streets of Lower West'fall'n, Q'orin was standing in the fog, under the light of a glowbe, its halo a sooty orange in the mist. He joined him at his side but he said nothing on the journey back to the tiny house, and Rakk didn't bother him.

All in all, it had been a good day.

❧❧❧❧❧ ❧❧❧❧❧

The next month went by so fast, Rakk could hardly believe Zenithra had come at last. The festival that capped the last two weeks of the year had gotten underway without a hitch, and the days rolled onward toward the Balancing Act as the city swelled to capacity. All long-distance ships and pleasure craft were ordered to anchor at Nunan, in special floating docks erected by the city to handle the crowds. From there, ferries brought them into the harbor and onto the crescent. On the morning of the eve of Balance, the last day of the year, Rakk ordered the great gates of the harbor closed and locked. Until the Balancing Act was over, no ship would come or go from the crescent.

The Balan Su Defenders were in place throughout the city, and the Corkin were arranged in concentric circles around the islands of the capital and along the Great Sea Lanes, with reinforcements on standby near Aga'thyn and Princip'asia. The tram that crossed the lower rim was ordered to stop running, and maquina in the industrial quarter and along the harbor were powered down, all but the essential systems. All the main thoroughfares, all the entry and exit points, were under the watch of his Defenders. Balan Su was as ready as it could ever be. And Rakk felt confident. Like a good manager, he'd delegated to the right people. And he'd be there, ready to help if anything happened. And so now he planned to relax, to enjoy a lovely evening at the biggest party in Balance Territories—the Opening Gala in Corda'mere Park—and then find a sunny spot to watch the Balancing Act in the morning. Everything status quo, and he was feeling great.

But then he decided to go see Ellex Andria. They were both going to the Gala, so why not go together?

Only she didn't see it that way.

As he walked the grassy pathways of Sunrise Ridge back to the tiny house, he tried to focus on the afternoon sunshine on his skin, a warm and rare treat in most of the city. But he felt like a fool. He didn't even want to go to the Gala anymore.

No, that wasn't true. He did. Of course he did. He'd dreamed of dancing the night away with Ellex, laughing and kissing as they once had, not caring who was watching.

But it was a fantasy. And a stupid one. Maybe he just needed a drink. Or some flower. It had been—a long time. Too long. So, so long. At least since he'd had sex using his own body. Maybe bhiza would calm his nerves? But no, he didn't want calm nerves. He wanted energy, reckless energy. He wanted friction. He thought of finding a slave somewhere, but the thought sickened him.

The tiny house was empty and lonely. Q'orin was on patrol on Bleakside, on the back of the crescent. Rakk had stationed him there when Zenithra started. With Rhannokti on the inner arm of the lower rim, Q'orin on the outer, and Rakk on the upper rim, the three main sections of the city were covered. But it had been tough to pass the nights all alone. His sleep was never restful, and the noises never stopped, the thumping and thudding, the crying and the moaning. He'd dream of running, fleeing, his ancestors in pursuit, wanting to spill his sap in the sea, and he'd wake screaming and not knowing why, not remembering. And it seemed the shadows in the great hall were flickering and moving about, falling still just as soon as he opened his eyes.

Sunset came that evening and the estate grew dark, as Rakk paced through the halls of the tiny house, beneath the burnstone columns, his rootpads gripping at the cool stone, the soft padding of flesh on rock the only sound in the twilit chamber. The gala was meant to start at dusk, though he knew nobody would show til a few hours later. He should go. The notestreamers would be expecting him. All of Balance would be watching. The stage beckoned, and he had to take it. He wanted to. Right?

Did he want that? Did he want the crown? Did he want to be what his father wanted him to be?

A scraping sound rumbled beneath his feet, and he looked behind him, his senses open, feeling out with his crystal, but nobody was around. He sprinted for the stairs, down into the basement, where he grabbed a glowbe from the nook on the wall and flicked it. Warm light spread down the hallway. Rakk went room to room, checking each one, his heart beating in his ears. He knew he'd been hearing things in the night, and this confirmed it for him.

But Q'orin had checked and re-checked the basement.

Rakk looked in the last room at the end of the hall, a storage room, but it was empty. Nothing seemed out of place or disturbed. But he knew the estate must have secret passageways, like the palace on P'anorum, at the very least an escape route. And the sound he'd heard, the scraping of stone on stone—he felt along the back wall, and held the glowbe up to the corner. Down on the ground, a small heap of dust—finely powdered stone. He looked around the room, felt along the empty shelves, under them, looking for the latch, but he couldn't find it. He was about to give up when the wall rumbled and started to slide open.

It was too late to put out the glowbe.

Rakk held it up and looked through the doorway, into a narrow tunnel cut into the earth, disappearing into the darkness ahead.

And on the edge of the light stood Rakk's father, a dusky blur in the shadow of the cave, not moving.

Rakk stared, unable to move or speak, his mind flooding with questions, with doubts. The figure looked like his father, but it also looked like his grandfather, tall and broad and imposing. Was it him?

He finally breathed, and he could smell perfume on the air, a scent always worn by his father, and Rakk couldn't have doubted it was him if he'd wanted to, like his body knew it was him, with certainty, from smell alone.

But it was not his father—his body, his senses, had been deceived. Rakk took a step forward and the light of the glowbe lit up the face in front of him, and Rakk saw that it was his slave Rhannokti, tall and broad as the king had been, but with an ugly, sneering face that scowled at him with hatred.

Rakk reached for his crystal, grasped at his mind, went to seize hold of his body as he always had, only to feel Rhannokti slipping from his mental awareness, like slick skin through a tight grip, popping free suddenly. A blast of contempt and mocking laughter filled Rakk's head before Rhannokti turned and ran. Rakk reached for him again with the crystal, but he could no longer sense him.

Rakk shouted and started after him, his long thick legs pumping, his hand out in front of him, holding the glowbe aloft, still feeling out for his slave, his mind struggling to comprehend what was happening. Should he call for help? He knew how strong, how brutal, Rhannokti was. But if he could defy his mandate, others might be able to as well. He couldn't risk it.

He ran onward until the sides of the passage grew farther apart, the ceiling higher, and he slowed, stopping just before he crashed into the wall. He took a deep breath and noticed the air had changed, heavy with the sweet smell of bhiza, and he panicked.

<<Q'orin—>> he tried to call, but his crystal was already numb. His legs felt hollow and stretchy, and he collapsed onto his back, his eyes open wide, staring at the ceiling of the cave, unable to move. Unable to contact anyone, as his vision slowly blurred and fell dark.

He drifted in and out of consciousness, the minutes blending into hours. Rakk didn't know how long he dreamt. He wasn't screaming yet from the darkness, so maybe it hadn't been too long. Maybe it had only been a few moments.

He tried to move again, but couldn't. He tried to reach out, to touch anything with his crystal.

<<Q'orin,>> he thought. <<Q'orin, help.>> But it was no use, and he drifted back into a restless sleep.

When he woke again, someone was walking toward him. He could hear the footsteps echoing off the damp walls of the tunnel but couldn't tell who it was until the figure was standing next to him, leaning down and glowering at him.

Rhannokti.

"Good morning, brother," he said. "Mind if I call you that? Since I'll no longer be calling you master." He narrowed his eyes.

Rakk tried to speak but couldn't.

Rhannokti tsked. "Damn, I'd hoped you'd be awake enough for a comeback. Oh well. Next time."

Rakk gurgled.

"Oh, what's that? Why, you ask? Why, because of our dear father. You thought I was him, didn't you?"

Rakk exhaled hard through his nose.

"Enough chit chat," Rhannokti said. "I have things to do, places to be. Plans to enact. This has gone on long enough."

Rakk groaned.

"How long, you ask? For three days. Oh yeah, Happy New Year. It's too bad you had to miss the Balancing Act. It was really...explosive."

Rhannokti's laughter echoed in Rakk's ears as he walked away.

It took another five hours before he could start to squirm around, his eyes burning with tears, his limbs shaking from so much darkness, utterly convinced that everything he ever cared about must surely be lost, and wondering why he even bothered to crawl on out of this hole and see what had happened.

Chapter 26

Toward the End of the Year, Toward the End of Many Things

A S THE WEEKS ROLLED on toward Zenithra, Lithuigi tried to distract himself with his classes at the Academicon. The term would be ending soon, the students returning to their distant homes or heading somewhere sunny for the summer, so there was a lot to get done, exams to give, lab work to finish up, dissertations to read. When he could, he'd go down to the Guild wharf and work on restoring his cata'rin, strengthening the hull and making sure the joints were firmly latched, or he'd tinker with his special gurgitators. Sometimes he'd work half the night, til his normal hand shook so hard he couldn't use it. Only the prosthetic stayed steady.

He tried his best not to think about Doc Andri'n. Every time he did, he felt how truly weak and powerless he was. The guilt and the shame and the fear were too much—such thoughts kept him from focusing, kept him from working—so he worked harder to keep himself from thinking. Rameen Rutar, and the Dyna'arin, had said nothing about the arrest. Lithuigi had contacted every colleague, associate, and friend he could think of, many of them tinkers, some in Management, even a few Pradishar bishrops—but nobody would help him. They were afraid, he knew, but he was angry with them anyway.

He'd reached out to Vilder several times, asking him to stop by his lab, but his son still hadn't said a word to him since Lithuigi had last insulted him. Normally he would have been grateful for the space, but he needed information from the Pradishar, and Vilder, in his arrogant, boasting way, was always giving it away for free. He was desperate to know what was happening with the stasis project. Was it on hold indefinitely or was it outright cancelled? What was going to happen to the subject? And—he tried not to think about this problem either, but it wouldn't leave his mind—what was going to happen when they woke up?

When Zenithra came at last, Lithuigi wasn't sure he could stand to be in Balan Su anymore. He needed to go to sea, at least before the Balancing Act. That would give him two weeks, which was the perfect amount of time to test his gurgitators. What better way to distract himself from his woes than to race around the world in the fastest ship ever to sail the seas?

Plus, Lithuigi needed to see his other wife. He had a terrible decision to make, and he needed her wisdom.

His assistant Rhyntysha promised to look after the stasis project in his absence, as she had for many years—what would he do without such helpers. And Mha'arlo, dear Mha'arlo. He'd take him with him this time. He knew it would mean a lot to him. And they had important things to discuss.

Lithuigi was gathering some supplies in the den at his garden on the eve of Zenithra when Rebesh'a knocked softly and entered.

"You're leaving?" she said.

"A bit of work," Lithuigi said. "Won't take long."

Rebesh'a narrowed her eyes. "How long? It's Zenithra! We need to make appearances. And the gala! You promised."

"And I intend to keep my promise," he said.

"If only that damn Ritty Rin Rhandal had let you stream the melodrama from a datamin. Now you won't even be able to talk about it with anyone."

"Not to worry, love," Lithuigi said. "I can talk to anyone about anything and impress them."

"In your dreams, maybe," Rebesh'a said, smiling, and Lithuigi gave her a kiss.

"I'll be back before Zenithra ends," he said. "And I promise to 'make appearances' with you."

"You better. Are you taking Mha'arlo with you?"

"Yes," he said, and Rebesh'a seemed relieved by the answer. She grabbed Lithuigi and wrapped him in a tight hug. He held her and they softly swayed together around the room, unfurling their branches and caressing one another.

The next morning, Lithuigi woke well before first light and made his way across the upper rim to the lifts, then down to the harbor where Mha'arlo already had the cata'rin waiting, ready for departure.

"Someone's excited," Lithuigi said when he saw Mha'arlo's face.

"I hardly slept last night," he said. "I'm greatly honored, professor, to test your new gurgitators with you." He had a huge smile on his bright green face.

Lithuigi laughed. "I'm glad you could be convinced to work during the holidays."

"This isn't work," Mha'arlo said. He looked like he wanted to say something else, but he hesitated.

Lithuigi smiled. "The helm is yours today, captain."

Mha'arlo cheered. His eyes twitched, and the cata'rin lurched off the pier and into the harbor.

"Easy now," Lithuigi said.

"Sorry professor, these gurgitators are really something."

"Indeed they are. Set the aperture at one quarter of normal, for now."

"Understood," Mha'arlo said.

The cata'rin inched through the fog toward the gates, following the beacons on the buoys strewn across the harbor. When they reached the narrow passage through the guard towers, the Cul'tavin hailed them, reminding them the inner harbor would close the day before the Balancing Act.

"Get us out of this foggy deathtrap," Lithuigi said. "Drop southwest, then set a course due west. Once the fog lifts and the way is clear, we'll see about getting the gurgitator to full aperture. And hope this old fish stays together for the journey."

Lithuigi stood on the prow and stared out at the fog, smelling the sea, feeling the mist on his face, and sighing deeply with pleasure. The haze around them grew white and then patchy, and when they broke free of it, the world was suddenly warm and bright, the sun was already out of the sea and climbing into the heavens, the open ocean was spread out before them, serene and twinkling, in perfect balance with the blue sky overhead. He felt alive again.

Mha'arlo followed Lithuigi upstairs and into the enclosed bridge, where they could see far and wide in every direction. The deck upstairs was different—not wood as it usually was—and Mha'arlo admired the feel of it on his feet.

"Is this rhee stone?" Mha'arlo asked.

"Right you are. One of the shipments you brought back from Andramere when you visited Doc Andri'n. The durability of the stone, and it's light weight, meant I could cover the floor with it. I girded it underneath on metal hinges, to withstand the pressure of sharp turns and sudden accelerations. And the stone is very difficult to crack. We can set our roots deep inside it. No more tumbling about like marbles in a bag."

"Brilliant," Mha'arlo said.

"Let's open the gurgitator and see how she handles. Set your roots, and open her up to half capacity. What is this equivalent to on a standard gurgitator?"

"Twice of full speed," Mha'arlo said.

"Open it slowly."

Mha'arlo sent the signal to the gurgitator and brought it to half aperture over half a minute. The cata'rin was soon surpassing the normal top speed for a ship that size.

The improvements to the weight and to the material of the hull have made a big difference, Lithuigi thought. He could have walked around without needing to clutch the deck with his rootpads.

"Open to three-quarters."

The cata'rin began lurching and plunging, but was still manageable.

"Now fully open," Lithuigi said. "Use your judgement if you need to close it some."

The cata'rin hit top speed, and Lithuigi was thankful his rootpads were now deep in the rhee stone, because the deck was bucking hard. Getting any work done at this speed would be impossible. And the noise! But the ship seemed to be holding together just fine.

"Give her a turn, gently to the right," Lithuigi said. The gurgitators began to groan and the ship shuddered, but finally the cata'rin began to veer to one side. Steering at this speed would be a serious problem.

"Brace yourself well. Hard close."

Mha'arlo shut the gurgitator and the ship lurched as it stalled but still continued to rush forward, racing onward across the Threshinveld Sea at enormous speeds. They waited til it had spent it's energy and began to flounder, and both were amazed at how long, and how far, the ship had continued to travel. Stopping and turning would be tough. Maybe his new reverse gurgitator would be able to handle it?

"Let's do three-quarters aperture when we're in open ocean, especially in the Far Ocean. But in the Inner Seas, we should stick to three-eights aperture. A modest increase in top speed with minimal risk to ships on the Lanes," Mha'arlo said. "What do you think, professor?"

Lithuigi smiled. "I think I'll be calling you professor soon."

Mha'arlo beamed and his eyes twitched. "What is our course, then? At my calculations, if we travel all night, we can likely get around the world and back to Balan Su in—wow—three days! Professor, that smashes the old record!"

"Indeed it does. Too bad we can't share it with anyone."

Mha'arlo sighed. "All in good time. But professor, if we can circle the globe in three days—what are we going to do for two weeks?"

"We're going to take the scenic route," he said. "And include a few extended stopovers along the way."

"I was hoping you were going to say that," Mha'arlo said.

"You were?"

Mha'arlo nodded again. "Could we—I thought, if it's not too far—"

Lithuigi chuckled. "Nothing is too far in this ship. And I'd be glad to stop at F'aryndon."

Mha'arlo grinned and looked at the deck.

"In fact," Lithuigi said, "you should think about staying there."

His smile faded, and Lithuigi saw the hard look in his eyes, the way he set his brow, his bright cheeks pulling in and turning dark with anger. He had known his pupil his entire life and this was a rare sight indeed—and yet he also knew Mha'arlo's family. They were slow to anger, cool and collected and charismatic, but get on their bad side and Sweet Trevian, you best watch out.

Besides, Lithuigi knew he didn't have the authority to make Mha'arlo stay if he didn't want to.

"With respect, professor," Mha'arlo said, "there's much to get done before Gru'hallia blooms again. And I'm to stay at your side until Anorian joins us."

Lithuigi swallowed in a dry throat. "I just want you safe, son."

"Where can one go to stay safe from death?" Mha'arlo said.

"Our Guild privileges don't protect us anymore. The Cul'tavin took Doc Andri'n from his own home and the Dyna'arin said nothing. Right now the Pradishar still need me. But the stasis project is nearly over, and then I'll be expendable again. If they come for me, they'll come for you, too."

"I ask again, professor, where can one go to stay safe from death? Does the king not take all our faces in the end?"

"You don't understand," Lithuigi said, raising his voice.

"But I do. Your concern isn't about me. No—I know you're concerned about my safety, but you're also willing to risk it when necessary."

Lithuigi suddenly felt very old and very tired. He looked at Mha'arlo, and he sighed.

"You know me too well, damnit."

"Professor, we're too far into this to lose hope now. It has to be full gurgitator ahead, or surrender."

"And what if we're wrong? I know it's hard to imagine such a thing when you're still so young."

"What could we be wrong about?" Mha'arlo said. "We've lived the truth our entire lives."

Lithuigi sighed and shook his head. "I see I won't convince you otherwise. Very well. We'll let time be the teacher of us both. Let's be underway. I'm sure you're anxious to see your family, and I'm anxious to see mine. It's been many months since I could get away."

Mha'arlo's eyes twitched and the cata'rin picked up speed. Lithuigi looked across the water, felt the wind on his face, the sun on his skin, and he tried his best to shake off the gloom that overshadowed what should have been his favorite pastime, sailing the ocean blue, as each minute took him farther away from Balan Su.

❦

Two weeks later, Lithuigi and Mha'arlo sailed into the fog around the capital on the last day of the year, and the last day that the great gates of the harbor would be open til the Balancing Act had concluded. Their journey had passed quickly and neither were ready to return to the city. Lithuigi steeled himself for it, trying to talk himself into staying upbeat and optimistic, keeping the relaxed feeling of the sea with him at all times—but when he stepped off the cata'rin onto the cold wet stones of Balan Su, he shuddered, the weight of ages falling back on his shoulders.

Mha'arlo came down the gangplank behind him.

"These are for you, professor," he said, handing him a bundle of scrolls. "I prepared them on the crossing from East'whaling, so they're recent. I included anything important from the past two weeks. Plus, there's a very thorough summary and review of Rebesh'a's latest melodrama, for talking points at the gala."

"The day you are no longer my apprentice will be a sad day indeed," Lithuigi said. "I'd be hopeless without your help."

"Enjoy the gala," he said.

"How will you be ringing in the new year?"

"With study and with prayers," Mha'arlo said, "that the terrible feeling I have will pass with the old decamillennium."

"The decamillennium," Lithuigi said. "How ghastly. I feel it too, son."

"But everything is prepared," Mha'arlo said. "Should the need arise."

"Then go and enjoy yourself," Lithuigi said. "I intend to."

But he had no such intention whatsoever. And as he left the port and began the trek to his upper rim garden, he thought about the gala that night, how much it meant to Rebesh'a for him to be there, and how much it was the very last place in all the world that he wanted to be.

Rebesh'a exhaled sharply when Lithuigi joined her on the terrace. "You returned. At the very end of Zenithra. At the last possible day to come back."

"I promised I'd be here for the gala," Lithuigi said.

"I suppose you did," she said. "I missed you these last two weeks. I've been so busy, being everywhere, talking to everyone. It's been absolutely exhausting."

"But you're loving every moment of it," Lithuigi said.

"Yes." She grinned. "And the gala, that will be wonderful too—and the Balancing Act tomorrow, always fun—and then it's over. Everything back to normal. Just plain old summertime, the city empty and sad and cold."

"The city is always sad and cold," he said.

"But not always empty," she said. "And you'll be gone too, spending the summer with the Guild as you always do."

"I'll miss you," Lithuigi said.

"Andramere in the summer is a dream," she said. "Let's go together."

"Andramere," he said, and closed his eyes for a moment. "You know I can't."

"It's been an hundred years. Nobody remembers anyway. Can't that silly prohibition end already?"

"Let's go somewhere else this summer," he said. "Somewhere new."

"But I always go to Andramere," Rebesh'a said. "And you love working on Vergis when classes are out. You do your best tinkering there."

"We've always done it that way," he said. "Let's do something different. What do you say?"

"I don't know," she said, looking nervous.

"Let's go now," he said, taking her hands. "Let's go to my cata'rin. It's the fastest ever built. We can go anywhere. Nobody could catch up to us. We can find an island somewhere and slit our crystals. Live in a small village. I could teach the local scamps, and you could be a trouper, on stage again." He was out of breath.

"Have you left your wits at sea or what, you silly old plant?" Rebesh'a said. "I don't want to give up our life. I love our life. I love my job. I love our garden. I love this city! You think I want to go live in some village, in a hut, and be a nobody? Sweet Trevian, I know you don't want that either. What's gotten into you?"

"I don't know," Lithuigi said. "The sea, I suppose. I think I'm a Bhizini underneath, trapped in Andrasian skin. I only feel right when I have water under me. I feel like I could scrub at this wretched dull green and it would reveal my bright splotches. And then I wouldn't have to decide to leave Balance, I'd be exiled like all the others. I'd be free."

"Maybe you need a nap before the party," Rebesh'a said, giving him a sideways glance. "For my sake. Imagine if you started saying this nonsense in public! Come along, a nap." Then she sighed. "Look L'uigi, I'm flattered you want to run away with me. I—know I haven't always made things easy for you. But I feel closer to you lately than I have in a long time. Don't—please don't mess that up."

He held Rebesh'a that afternoon in his branches while they made love and napped in the sunshine on the terrace. When the sun had sank in front of them, down behind the western arm of the city across the fog-filled crater, Lithuigi rested his face on Rebesh'a's hair fibers, well oiled with coco and lavender, and breathed deeply. "Are you sure you won't sail away with me? B'esh B'esh."

"Enough of that," she said. "I thought I'd distracted you from that nonsense."

"Fine, fine," he said, trying to act like it was nothing, but his heart was breaking inside.

"I need to go," Rebesh'a said. "Gu'ger Ghandis is making me beautiful. But I'll be back so we can go to the gala together. Don't you sneak off." She gave him a kiss and hurried off.

Lithuigi went to his den and began to read the scrolls Mha'arlo had prepared for him. Still no word on Doc Andri'n. And Sweet Trevian but the melodrama sounded terrible—Lithuigi was glad he'd only had to read a summary and not stream the whole damn thing. Some critics were raving while others were panning it, but anything with Jaun von Andron was an instant hit already, regardless of quality.

When he was sure Rebesh'a was gone, he started to pack.

She returned wrapped in the ocean, dressed in teals with white crystals, like sunbeams on the sandy shores of Aquastafar where they'd gotten married. He gasped when he saw her, and she beamed. He realized the melodramas weren't only a success because of Jaun von Andron but also because of his wife. Because of her beauty, her spirit, her grace.

Lithuigi had donned his best formal suit, and he walked over to Rebesh'a. "You're the most beautiful creature in all three realms." He offered her his arm. "Ready, my love?"

She took his arm and gave him a peck on the cheek. "I am. Are you?"

Time to put on his best face. Time to be the beloved professor. Time to be an upstanding citizen. Time to be the charismatic and loving partner of a world famous super star. He could do this. He could perform. One last time.

"So long as I'm at your side, where else could I want to be tonight?" he said.

On the walk to the party, Vilder finally contacted his father.

<<The stasis chamber will be opened tomorrow,>> he said.

<What? When tomorrow? Why? The subject?>> Lithuigi said, but Vilder wouldn't respond, though he could sense his malicious delight through the crystamin.

He did that just to ruin my evening, he thought, his heart racing, his face turning pale. *And damnit, he succeeded.*

Chapter 27

From One Moment to the Next

FIN'ROQ COUNTED THE DAYS as the rest of Zenithra passed and the new year approached, his mind on the upcoming gala with Jaun. He'd seen little of him since they'd visited the lower rim together. Jaun returned late every evening, exhausted and saying little, only that he was being tutored while classes were out so he could become a Cul'tavin peacekeeper as soon as possible.

Jaun woke Fin early in the morning on the twelfth day of Zenithra. The sky was still dark and full of stars when he shook the glowbes in their sleeping quarters.

"Morning," he said. "I have a favor to ask of you."

Fin pulled his branches back down into his arms and stretched his neck. "I sure could use a morning swim," he said. "I wake as stiff as a petrified tandavin here. The air's too cold, maybe. On P'anorum, every morning that I could, I went to the harbor for a dip, before anyone else was awake. The water was always gentle inside the crater, no currents that would drag me out, and not too deep to be unable to walk out of, if I accidentally let my air out. I'd float about on the surface, my head back in the water, imagining I was swimming through the stars."

"That sounds beautiful," Jaun said. "When I'm on Andramere, I get up early and travel to the far eastern tip of Aquastafar, where the surf rolls in over the point. There are a few others there but I usually know them. We take flat-boards and try to swim with the waves. Mostly we crash over and get flipped about, but sometimes we stay right on the side of the wave, pushed along there, down the beach, til the wave ends at the shore and we glide off the back, never falling."

"That sounds beautiful, too," Fin'roq said.

"I'll take you some day," Jaun said.

"So what's this favor you need?"

"I'm getting joined with a Pradishar crystal today, in a private ceremony," Jaun said. "I hoped you'd be my second. I meant to ask you earlier. Getting a new crystal isn't a pleasant experience. As it grows into my body, I'll need to rest. My other crystals took a day and a half for recovery."

"You'll be okay before the gala?" Fin asked.

"Of course. You can look after me until then?"

Fin'roq nodded, feeling honored to be asked. Once dressed, he followed Jaun out of the Pruu'patch and along the edge of Grand Plaza to the Pradishar citadel. The sun had yet to rise, and the air was wet and cold, the stones slick, the fog well up over their heads, making even the ground difficult to see. They went slowly, using their rootpads on the stones so they wouldn't slip.

Once through the gates and past the lush groves of Corda'mere, they entered the spire itself. Jaun led the way through a series of corridors twisting about through the obsidian to a chamber decorated like a tiny sharlum, with room for a dozen or so Verdillions at most. But there were only two in the chapel, two bishrops with their hoods pulled low over their faces. There was a chair with straps and pads, a terrible looking thing. The bishrops said nothing while they strapped Jaun in the chair and restrained him. No prayers were said, no oaths were taken—something didn't feel right. Fin'roq didn't like this at all.

The bishrop opened a large chest and, pliers in hand, carefully lifted a tiny purple and silver Pradishar crystamin from inside its sheathe. He slowly but deliberately pressed it onto Jaun's forehead. Fin'roq watched the crystal react when it touched Jaun's skin, lighting up and sinking down into the flesh, while Jaun thrashed against the restraints, his eyes bugging and rolling about in circles.

Fin'roq gasped, his hand over his mouth, holding in a scream, his own forehead on fire, his skin feeling like it was ripping apart. He couldn't hold it in any longer, and he opened his mouth and howled. Darkness rose up around him and threatened to overtake him but he could see Jaun's face—he was inside Jaun, he *was* Jaun, and he could feel the filaments of the crystal growing under his skin, slicing through his flesh, tearing into his insides. And he could feel the crystal, he *was* the crystal—rabid for flesh, for nerves—lusting to insert himself into every part of Jaun's existence, to make his body his own, his mind his own. All three crashed together in his mind—himself, Jaun, and the crystal—and he dropped to the ground, not sure which way was up or which way was down—not sure who he was anymore.

And then he was Fin'roq again, scared and confused and alone.

Slowly he remembered where he was, and what had happened. He knew where Jaun was, even with his eyes closed. He could still feel him, the way he could feel sunlight on his skin, warm and nourishing. He used Jaun's presence to ground himself, and he opened his eyes and tried to look around the room. The pain made his vision blur but he squinted through it. He saw one of the bishrops stuffing his tools back in his satchel while the other urged him out the door.

"Wait," Fin gasped, and when he opened his mouth, he had to swallow down the vomit that rose up with a stab of pain. "Wait, please. Help us."

But the bishrops were gone.

Fin wasn't sure how long he crouched there by Jaun, whispering prayers to Trevian through bouts of pain. But eventually the agony subsided and he stood, shakily. He pulled loose the restraints from the chair, and sat Jaun up. But Jaun's eyes were closed and he slumped over to the side. The purple and silver crystamin was still glowing on his forehead, like an ember, and there was sap running out from the wound. Was that normal?

He held fast to the obsidian floor with his rootpads and hoisted Jaun up and across his shoulders, then began to take careful steps, as fast as he could, back the way they came, surprised he was able to find familiar ground. Rather than exit through the entrance and risk being seen by the Cul'tavin guards and half the city, he went through the shortcut Roman Anthem had shown him on his first day in Balan Su.

Once back in the Pruu'patch, he sat Jaun down on his sleeping mound and placed his feet against the soil. He checked to make sure Jaun had clutched it with his rootpads. He had, but Fin still propped him against the wall, afraid he might slump over again. Then he got a wet cloth from the bathing room, and he wept as he wiped the sap off Jaun's face, wondering if he'd ever wake up again.

He didn't fully wake that entire day or that night, but he did wake enough to have a few sips of water, to shift about lightly before returning to his slumber. Fin debated all day whether he should find someone to help him, but he didn't know who he'd ask and he was sure Jaun wouldn't want this story getting out to the notestreams. So he stayed silent and continued his prayers to Trevian, and hoped Jaun would be alright, and not at all sure what he'd do if he wasn't.

The next morning, Jaun opened his eyes and stretched, but didn't unroot from his sleeping patch. He had dark patches under his eyes and his normally pale green skin looked white.

"Thank Trevian you're awake," Fin said. "How are you feeling?"

Jaun managed a small smile. "Different than the other times," he said. "Much faster movement of the filaments into my body." He reached for the crystal on his forehead and winced when he touched the irritated skin around it. "And what happened to you? You were screaming."

"I'm okay," he said. "I don't know what happened. I felt—"

He looked at Jaun, but Jaun looked away and said nothing.

"Who were those bishrops?" Fin said. "They left us. Abandoned us, when we needed their help. That wasn't a normal Joining ceremony, was it?"

Jaun waved his hand at him. "I'm tired, Fin. Exhausted. Please, ask me anything, but later."

Fin blushed. "Sorry," he said.

"No, Fin, I know why you ask. You were scared, and I haven't been awake to make you feel better about it."

Fin looked at Jaun's forehead, at the Pradishar crystal that no longer glowed, and the three other crystals that before had formed a triangle but now formed a diamond with the fourth. "That will take some getting used to," he said. "I liked your triangle."

"Indeed," Jaun said, gingerly fingering his forehead.

"I know the orange one that shimmers like a candle is from the Dyna'arin. I see those at the Academicon all the time. And the black one is the public crystal. Everyone in Balan Su has one."

"Almost everyone in every Balance city or village has a public crystal," Jaun said.

"What's the one that looks like a blue ring? It's nearly the color of your skin on the inside, the color of the sky on the outside."

"That one is the crystal of the Von Andron family. Only royal members of our house have one. Not many of those left these days."

He looked so sad Fin thought his heart was breaking—or was he still feeling what Jaun felt?

"And now you have a purple and gray Pradishar one," he said. "You're a fully enlisted monkin now."

"A Cul'tavin peacekeeper," Jaun said.

"You've worked hard for it. I noticed how much you've bulked up. You were much heavier than when I lifted you on Anthem's cata'rin."

"You carried me here? From the citadel? I'm impressed. You're so thin—and yet your shoulders are so broad, your legs and arms and torso so long—you know, you could be a farknuckle player if you wanted to!" Jaun laughed. "It's nice to see you standing so tall lately."

"I feel—happy," Fin said. "I think that's what this is. Even if that sounds crazy. Maybe 'content' is a better word. I had a lot of happy times as a scamp on P'anorum, even if—but this feels different. I mean—I feel like I live in Balan Su now," he said. "Like I'm a Balan Susian. I have friends here—well, acquaintances from school, but some of them are really nice to me. They seem genuinely happy to see me when I get to class. My teachers are training me, talking to me with respect, even though I'm a Bhizini. I know I still hide my face in public, and keep my hood low most of the time. I know it's not perfect here, by a long shot, but—I don't know, I guess I want to say, I love this city. I want to finish my studies here. Become someone, you know? Someone that matters."

"You already matter," Jaun said. "But I'm glad you're happy here. Truly. I just wish that your first visit to a metropolis had been Andramere City, with it's year-round sunshine and soft breezes, not Balan Su of all places." He yawned. "I'll take you there one day and you'll see what I mean."

Fin blushed and Jaun yawned again.

"We'll talk about this later," Fin said. "Right now, you need to close those pretty eyes of yours. I want you well-rested before the gala tomorrow night."

Now Jaun blushed. "I like the happy Fin'roq," he said, closing his eyes. "I like him a lot."

❧❦

Fin'roq spent the day studying in their quarters while Jaun slept. By the next morning, the last day of Zenithra, Jaun felt refreshed and ready to emerge, and he came out into the gardens of the Pruu'patch, all grins, looking up at the sky and taking in the sunshine. His skin was his normal pale green and the patches under his eyes had faded entirely. Fin'roq, on the other hand, had hardly slept that night, thinking only of the gala, the biggest party in the greatest city in the world, and knowing that he was going to be a part of it, Jaun's date even. How wonderful was life? The world made no sense.

But when he emerged from his sleeping quarters that morning, his mood on the party had flipped upside down, and the very thought of it filled him with horror.

"I don't feel very well," he told Jaun, scowling. "I think I'll just go back to sleep. Wake me tomorrow."

Jaun laughed. "On a beautiful day like this? You've just got a bit of what the old-timey troupers call stage fright. Don't worry, it'll pass. And I've got something to distract you."

"Oh?"

"Get cleaned up. We're taking a trip."

"To?"

"The Regalia. We're going shopping!"

"What?" Fin scowled again. "Everything's closed anyway."

"I have a friend who has a shop there with the finest fabrics anywhere but Grand Gardenia. He knows I tend to wait to the last minute for things." He blushed slightly and grinned. "Don't worry Fin, the shop's closed, so it will only be us. Now go get cleaned up."

When they left the Pruu'patch, Fin'roq saw that barriers were being erected along the edges of Grand Plaza, and they'd cordoned off the large earthen mound and the Weeping Wilvryn tree in preparation for the Balancing Act festivities. The plaza was filled with tourists and pilgrims, and the excitement and reverie of the crowd was intoxicating. Fin found he was smiling in spite of himself, the dread from earlier nearly forgotten.

When they reached the Forum on the western side of the plaza, Jaun grabbed Fin's arm and pulled him down into the neighborhood along a wide processional avenue between pink and blue marble buildings bedecked with columns and little nooks with statues, the porticos along the top and the base of the porches all intricately carved with scenes from Balan Su's long and storied history. The avenue led to an oval plaza at the heart of the Forum, where double rows of columns arched wide and came back on the far side, not quite connecting but leaving a gap at the edge of the rim. The effect was of two massive arms hugging the plaza.

In the gap between the columns, a large promenade had been erected, and Jaun pointed.

"Tomorrow I'll be master of ceremonies right there on that stage," Jaun said, "streaming the event to the entire world."

Fin'roq didn't know what to say so he said nothing. He knew he couldn't take part in that part of Jaun's life, at least not until he had a crystal of his own. If the Pradishar would ever give him one. He looked at Jaun and thought he looked troubled.

"Now who has stage fright?" Fin teased, and Jaun gave him a half smile.

"This way," he said, grabbing his arm again and pulling him toward the Regalia. They crossed from the Forum to the wide, clean, tiled streets of the city's premiere commercial district, and Fin took in the sights while Jaun led him to the square where he'd had a run-in with Ellex Andria. The streets were busy, the restaurants overflowing, though most of the shops were closed.

Jaun pulled his hood lower over his face as they entered the plaza and kept ahold of Fin's arm. When they reached a storefront, the door opened and they stepped inside. Jaun immediately lowered his hood and wrapped the Raccorin shopkeeper in a big hug.

"Jauny, oh Jauny, I just knew I'd hear from you today! I thought, maybe my Jauny went with someone else this time. Maybe he thinks my fabrics are old and moth-eaten, hmm? My styles outdated?"

"Never!" Jaun cried.

"No," the Raccorin said, "I knew you'd come see me. The gala, I suppose? Sleek and sexy but not scene-stealing, right?"

"You know me so well. And I'll need garments for two today." He turned to Fin'roq. "You can lower your hood, Fin."

When Fin pulled back his hood, Jaun smiled. "Fin'roq, may I present the legendary designer, Gu'ger Ghandis."

"Hello," Fin said, bowing slightly.

Gu'ger was staring at him with wide eyes, a slight blush on his wide, bright Raccorin cheeks. He hurried forward to Fin'roq and picked up his hand, lifted it slowly, then bent over and kissed the back of it. "Oh Jauny, you didn't tell me how handsome he was! Those shoulders, that face, why, you've brought a prince to me, a prince from the high seas!"

Fin squirmed under Gu'ger's hungry gaze.

"Enough, you old lech," Jaun said, laughing. He took Fin's hand from out of Gu'ger's and pulled him away. "We're going to browse while you go behave yourself."

Gu'ger tsked. "You know me better than that, Jauny. But very well. I'll set a few aside for you both to peruse. Those shoulders are so wide, and the waist so trim, and his—oh, where was I?—yes. I'll have to adjust them, but you know me. Quick as lightning with a needle."

"Of course you are," Jaun said with a dramatic flare and a wink at Gu'ger.

When they went into the dressing room and Jaun saw what Gu'ger had picked out for them, he nodded with approval. "He may be a lech, but he's a damn fine artist too. Here, get out of those robes. Let's try this one first."

Fin blushed but let his robe fall to the ground, then stepped out of it. This was the first time in his adult life that he was thankful to be wearing a cumberdome. The robes Jaun held up for him weren't pull-overs, so he slipped his arms through the openings and Jaun buttoned him up. The sleeves were short, barely past his shoulders, so that his entire arms hung free. The fabric was gorgeous, shimmering black with a feathery padding for chilly Balan Su evenings and sheer silk for comfort. He'd never touched anything so fine before. He reached up to pull down the hood when he realized there wasn't one.

Jaun whistled. "Stunning," he said.

"No hood?" Fin asked, blushing hard even as he felt the panic rising.

"Don't get me wrong, I like you in Pradishar robes. But damn, Fin, you can really clean up."

"No hood?" Fin said again. "Jaun, I can't—"

"Everything will be alright. I'll be right there with you. Nothing to worry about."

But Fin didn't think he'd be alright. In fact, he knew he would absolutely not be alright. What had he thought this gala would entail? That he could stay hidden throughout it, a shadowy monkin that wouldn't have to speak to anyone? No, he was going to have to do more than speak. He was going to have to face the world.

He shook his head back and forth, his mouth open. "I think I might be sick."

Jaun took his hand again. "It's just nerves," he said. "That's all it is. All troupers get that at one time or another. Some troupers feel like that every single time they perform. Can you imagine? But I promise, you don't need to worry. It's just a performance, not the end of the world. And I'll be right there to speak if you forget your lines."

⁂

Fin'roq spent the walk back from the Regalia and the rest of the day worrying, feeling sick, even getting sick briefly, all while trying to pray. Finally the sun set and the sky fell dark and the glowbes of the Pruu'patch crackled as they came to life. Their light threw an orange glow on the foliage and the stone walls and the colorful murals.

Jaun found Fin pacing in their sleeping quarters.

"Stop that," he said. "It doesn't help, just makes you dizzy. I have something better." He held out his hand, and in his palm was a small bhiza cookie wrapped in mint. "It's within legal limits, though there'll be much more potent stuff going around at the gala, if you're interested. This is a recipe my family has used for millennia. Clarity. Motivation. No anxiety. You'll like it."

"Did you just bake this?" Fin gave him a sideways glance.

"My cook did."

"You have a cook?!"

"At my house in Sunset Point."

"You have a house in Balan Su?! But of course you do. You probably have houses all over the world, right?"

Jaun blushed. "Try the cookie," he said.

Fin'roq did love bhiza cookies. He and Bhea Bell and Baboo used to eat them on special occasions. So he bit into the soft, fluffy dough, relishing the tendrils of bhiza whipped with sugar, and he moaned with delight.

"Right?" Jaun said. "There's more, but let's see how you feel after you get cleaned up."

Fin went to the bathing room to wash up and put on his new robes, feeling like he'd be okay after all.

The gala wasn't far from the Pruu'patch, since the Pruu'patch itself was along the eastern edge of Corda'mere, the largest green space on Balan Su, which encircled the great Pradishar citadel's spire and stretched east and west along the northern edge of the upper rim of the crescent. The park was not open to the public, but walled and guarded by the Cul'tavin. Ritty Rin Rhandal, the director of the melodrama that the gala was celebrating, had ordered all notestreamers to remain just inside the park walls, cordoned off by the entrance, where they might interview those coming and going but couldn't mingle with the crowd up close. But Fin'roq and Jaun took the pathway through the Pruu'patch so they could avoid the notestreamers all together, and Fin was glad for it.

Though the party was said to start at sundown, they didn't walk over until three hours after twilight had faded completely, since Jaun said that was when nearly everyone but Ritty and maybe Rebesh'a would have arrived. They descended to the lower levels of the Pruu'patch, into a corridor which led to a small stair that resurfaced within the grounds of the park. Fin could hear the sounds of music and laughter coming from nearby but couldn't see anyone through the foliage.

Jaun turned to Fin and touched his shoulders. "Thank you for joining me tonight. I should have told you earlier. You look absolutely stunning."

"You're quite the trouper," Fin said, looking down at his arms, at his robe. "I look like a splotchy disaster tied up inside a beautiful garment."

"Nonsense," Jaun said, "and I won't hear otherwise." He offered his arm and Fin'roq took it. They found the path and walked toward the party, and Fin felt like he was floating above the ground, effortlessly, carried along by the moment.

The party was centered around a large clearing flanked with long fountains on either side, a broad dance floor and raised stage at one end and an open tavern at the other end. There were four solitary arches that bordered the clearing, around which grew dense evergreens, like jagged black towers in the light of the glowbes. Torches were lit all along the arches, and there was some sort of ice sculpture near the tavern. A band was playing and the tavern was pumping out food and drinks. Fin thought there were at least a thousand Verdillions there. Maybe more.

When Jaun came into the central plaza, Fin'roq on his arm, everyone nearby cut off their conversations to turn and stare, some with surprise, some laughing, some with crinkled noses, some with glares, their eyes all a'twitching. The effects of the bhiza cookie were immediately forgotten, and Fin was sure he had no air, no strength even to move, and yet somehow he continued to walk.

But everywhere he looked, the faces, the eyes. Judging. Finding him unworthy.

Jaun had found someone to speak to and he stopped walking. Everyone promptly returned to their own conversations, though Fin'roq thought the volume of the chatter in the park had doubled. When he looked up to see whom Jaun was speaking with, he saw it was Roman Anthem, and he let himself exhale.

"Welcome, Fin'roq," Anthem said.

"Good to see you again, captain."

"Brave of you to come tonight," Anthem said.

"Or foolish," Fin said, his voice breaking. "I'm not sure which."

Anthem laughed and looked around. "They're all watching us, listening. Every word they overhear, immediately shared across the weavryn, to be looked at, inspected, mocked, ridiculed. Isn't it a good thing that we have better things to do? Like celebrating your performance, for one," he said to Jaun, "and your uh, promotion is it?" He was looking at Jaun's Pradishar crystal.

"I'm a Cul'tavin peacekeeper now, just like you," he said.

"Congratulations," Anthem said, a mischievous look in his eyes.

"Enjoy the party, captain," Jaun said, smiling and nodding as he led Fin'roq away from him. Then he turned to Fin, still grinning. "And now we can enjoy the party too. Come, let's go to the VIP platform. We can get a nice perch there, and someone to serve us. I'm starving!"

Fin accompanied Jaun through the crowd, clutching at his arm, still unable to get used to the reactions of the guests, wondering with each Verdillion they passed if it would be fear, amusement, contempt, or even disgust he'd see in their eyes. The cold hard sneers made his chest feel pinched, his air supply closed off. And the amusement made him feel ashamed, made his ears burn. But the fear? He wasn't sure.

Even on the VIP platform, everyone couldn't help but gawk for awhile.

"Jaun!" someone cried out, and Jaun ran over to an Andrasian female in a sparkling blue dress and gave her a big hug.

"You look stunning," he said, "like Astra'bel on the eve of apotheosis."

She beamed. "See darling, he knows how to compliment," she said, turning to an older Andrasian who stood at her side, looking distracted. The Andrasian's eyes grew wide when he saw Fin, but then he caught himself, and he gave Fin a warm smile.

"I'm quite sure Professor L'uigi knows how to compliment," Jaun said. "He's given me more than my fair share over the years. Isn't that right, professor?"

"Indeed, indeed," Lithuigi said. "And most surely deserved, every one of them."

"See," she said. "He compliments his students all the time, yes, everyone knows it, friendly Professor Von'nDrino, so warm, so nice. If only he were so kind to his own family!"

"Rebesh'a, Lithuigi, this is Fin'roq of P'anorum," Jaun said. He stepped aside to present Fin, and Fin blushed from head to toe, his bright and dull splotchy skin turning dark brown.

"Ahh-ahhhh," Rebesh'a said. What had begun as a cry of surprise was quickly corrected into a cry of sympathy. "Look how shy he is," she said, smiling warmly. "Don't worry, we don't bite."

"Rebesh'a is the star of the melodrama," Jaun said. "You can surely see why? Have you ever seen anyone more lovely?"

"The star?!" Rebesh'a said, laughing. "Tell that to Ritty! He only has eyes for you!"

"Yes, I am easy on them," Jaun said, grinning.

"Oh, look at you," Rebesh'a said, waving her hand at him. "You're so bad."

"You're so bad," Jaun said, growling at her.

"You are!" Rebesh'a barked at the sky and they both howled with laughter.

"That's from a melodrama they were both in," Lithuigi said to Fin. "An inside joke of theirs, only they insist on doing it louder and more obnoxiously every time they perform it."

"You're—Professor Hesh'n's father?" Fin asked.

"I am," Lithuigi said. "You've come a long way from P'anorum, son. How are you liking Balan Su?"

"I love it," Fin said.

Lithuigi raised his eyebrows. "Really?"

"What's this about P'anorum?" said a soft but sharp voice behind Fin'roq.

He turned, recognizing the voice. Somehow he was able to speak.

"P'anorum is where I'm from, Sui Pradesh, your holiness," he said, bowing as a proper monkin ought to.

Ellex Andria glared at him with narrowed eyes. "I thought you might have left the city when we called for all registered Bhizini to leave."

Fin tried to swallow in a dry throat. "I have permission to remain," he said, struggling to keep his voice from wavering.

"Ahh, if it isn't Ellex Andria, the dear sweet good-mother of the Andrasian Republic," Jaun said, stepping to Fin's side and giving him a small nod. "Fin'roq is my guest tonight. And his permission to be in our fair city comes all the way from the Gran Pradesh himself. And I think, if you'd been able to overturn it, you'd have done so by now."

Ellex Andria looked at Jaun von Andron, at the square of crystals on his forehead. "A Pradishar crystal?" she said, trying to keep her voice flat. Her eyes twitched but she turned away, not waiting for him to answer.

Jaun offered Fin his arm again. "Come, have a dance with me," he said, winking. And Fin'roq gratefully followed him out to the dance floor. "Sorry about that," he said.

"No, it wasn't your fault. I just—why does she hate me so much? She looks at me like I'm diseased. A lot of them do. I'm either a joke to them, or a threat to them. Take your pick, none of them are accepting that I should be here." There were tears in his eyes but they didn't fall.

Jaun wrapped his arms around Fin and held him against him, and gently swayed to the music. Fin sniffled and tried to get his tears to dry, but they dropped down his face instead. But his heart was pounding, the proximity to Jaun making his head feel light, like he was floating. Jaun leaned back, looked at Fin's tears, and kissed both cheeks, capturing them as they fell. Then he kissed his lips.

When Fin looked around, everyone on the dance floor had stopped to stare at them with looks of revulsion. Even the music began to taper off.

But then Ritty Rin Rhandal arrived with a flourish of horns and the band struck back up again, and suddenly everyone was in a tizzy as the famous director walked onto the stage. The crowd cheered and whistled and shouted, waving their arms about. And while they did so, Jaun led Fin back to the VIP platform.

Ellex Andria approached Jaun and Fin with her hands shaking. "You've got some nerve, von Andron. With my authority on the Council and with the Cul'tavin, I should drag you off to the Dankburn for violating purity laws. You are a monkin—both of you."

"The law states 'No Andrasian nor Raccorin shall knowingly have offspring one with the other, nor with any Bhizini,'" Jaun said. "It says nothing about dancing, hugging, kissing, or love-making."

"Not in the letter of the law, but by tradition it has meant exactly that. No mixing whatsoever. Obviously the law is flaunted, as why else would we continue to have more and more Bhizini, in spite of our campaigns to keep the population in check? The Guild has been far too lax in their cities as well, I think. People look to you for an example, and you've just encouraged the world to flaunt the law. Don't think Balance Authority will continue to tolerate such behavior. And you—" she turned to Fin'roq. "You must know that nobody here at this party wants you here, save for von Andron, and that is more than likely because he's pulling one of his infamous publicity stunts. Your presence is making everyone uncomfortable, and worse, you've stolen the show. The party isn't about the troupers anymore. It isn't about the accomplishment of creating this melodrama that was supposed to be the center of everyone's attention. It's about how in the hell did a halfbreed savage end up attending the most exclusive party in the capital, on the biggest night of the year, on the arm of the most famous entertainer in the world. If you have any respect for the people who worked on this project, or for the citizens of this city and all of Balance Territories, you'll leave this gala right now. And never again presume to enter a world that isn't for you."

"That's enough!" Jaun said. Fin'roq had never seen him looking so angry.

"No," Fin said, the tears streaming down his face. "I should go."

"You should," Ellex Andria said.

"I said that's enough!" Jaun screamed.

Heads were starting to turn. Fin moved to leave.

"Wait," Jaun said. "I'm coming with you."

"No," Fin'roq said. "You belong here. You're a natural here. This is your world. It isn't mine. Just—just leave me alone!"

And Fin ran, off through the evergreens, back into the shadows of Corda'mere and down the hidden stair to the Pruu'patch, stumbling in the darkness, his eyes burning, his skin on fire, his ears pulsing in his head. When he got to his sleeping quarters, he sank his roots down into the soil, unfurled his branches, wrapped them around his own mouth as tightly as he could, and then let out a scream. He screamed and cried and shook.

And then he felt arms on his sides and he stopped. His branches unwrapped themselves and he turned. Jaun was looking at him, tears running down his face, and he wrapped Fin in his arms and held him. "I'm so sorry," he whispered. "I didn't—I never thought—"

"I don't want to talk about it," Fin said. "I don't ever want to talk about it. Never again." He couldn't look at him.

"Of course," Jaun said. "But—at least let me say, I had a wonderful time with you, while it lasted."

Fin nodded but couldn't speak.

"Dance with me again now?" Jaun asked, and Fin nodded again.

Fin rested his cheek on the top of Jaun's head and closed his eyes. They slowly circled, gently swaying.

"Why?" Fin said after awhile. "Why do I have to have this rotten, ugly, blotchy, terrible skin?"

Jaun unfurled his branches and wrapped them around Fin, surprising him with the speed and the intensity of the embrace. Then he used his hands to hold Fin's face in his. "There's nothing rotten, ugly, terrible, or blotchy about you! Sweet Trevian, Fin, if only you could see yourself the way I see you. You'd see that you're—"

"Shh," Fin said, and silenced him with his lips. Jaun was surprised but returned the kiss. He held Fin with his branches and used his arms to unbutton Fin's clothes, which dropped to the floor, and then he unclasped his cumberdome and threw it away from them. Fin fumbled with the buttons on Jaun's clothes, groping blindly, not wanting to stop kissing him. Then he unclasped Jaun's cumberdome and ran his hands up Jaun's back, felt the muscles in his shoulders and his arms and admired their grooves. Jaun kissed his chest, back and forth in zig-zags, down to his flower, which was wide open, the petals unfurled, the stamen up in the air, oozing pollen.

Then Juan pulled him close and guided them together, til both stamens had slipped deep down into the petals of the other's flower, into the heart of the bulb, enclosed in the soft, moist flesh, where they engorged and throbbed and pulsed. Fin had never felt something so wonderful in his life, a center of such extreme pleasure in his navel, radiating outward through all his fibers to his fingers and toes, nearly paralyzing him. He and Jaun held each other like that, gently shifting, rocking together, breathing on one another's necks with soft sighs and moans of pleasure, through the hours of the night, til sleep overtook them both.

Fin woke the next morning still wrapped up in Jaun's branches and he kissed his cheek, breathing deeply of his hair fibers, looking at his face, his beautiful face, and not being able to believe he was there, holding him, smelling him, tasting him, feeling him. Jaun woke and grinned at him, and they pulled one another tightly together once more.

"I wish I could stay here all day long," Jaun said, softly nibbling at Fin's neck, "but I have a role in the Balancing Act to perform."

"I forgot that was today," Fin said. "I forgot today was a day at all."

Jaun sighed. "Fin, I have to tell you something. And I don't want to, and I wish I could have earlier, but now there's only right now to tell it, so here goes." He took a deep breathe. "You know I'm the master of ceremonies for the main event this afternoon," he said. "Qardymion the Saltsap will be marched through the streets of the capital. Everyone in Balance will be watching. And I intend to take that moment to denounce the Pradishar and call for the resignation of the Council of Nine."

Fin looked at Jaun, uncomprehending. "Is this a joke?"

"Yes, the joke that is world politics, the melodrama of our time. And I'm about to assume a very risky role. Honestly, I'm not sure I can pull it off. But I have to try."

"What are you talking about?" Fin felt like he'd just fallen into the ocean without taking a breathe and was quickly plunging to the bottom.

"I'm so sorry. I never intended—I didn't know I'd meet you. I didn't know how I'd feel about you. When I made this plan, I mean. And now I'm bumbling like a fool."

"You've been intending to denounce the Pradishar this whole time? This—this training—it was all a hoax?"

"No, I—well—yes, I guess, kind of." Jaun looked so ashamed, Fin thought his heart would break, but he closed it off before it could. "I needed a Pradishar crystal."

Fin shut his eyes for a moment. "Are you one of the conspirators the Gran Pradesh warned me about? A Ren'fallow?"

Jaun looked at Fin without smiling. "That word can mean many things, Fin. I suppose I fit some of it's meanings, but not the others, if you understand?"

"I understand well enough. He told me they'd try to get close to me, to recruit me. To overthrow the Pradishar from within. I never imagined how close—"

Fin thought he might be sick.

"Fin, I—"

"Not another word," he said. "You've used me all along, haven't you? In every possible way you could think to use me."

"No, Fin, I—"

"Get out of here, Jaun. Leave. I'm—" Jaun's left eye started twitching, and when Fin saw it, his lips curled back and he screamed, "Who are you talking to? Who!" He lunged toward Jaun, looming up over him, hissing.

But Jaun ducked and spun out from under him, and the motion left Fin stumbling into the wall. "Don't challenge me, Fin. With my Cul'tavin training, I could hurt you."

"Oh?" Fin said, turning back to face him. "You could hurt me? I killed someone in my sleep. I could pass out right now and crush you with my thoughts."

Jaun looked at Fin and Fin thought he saw another crack in his mask—a bit of fear slipping through his performance—and that felt like a victory and also a terrible and incomprehensible loss.

"Get out of here, Jaun. Get out!"

Jaun nodded and turned, slowly walking out of their quarters. Fin wanted to scream his name and tell him to stay, but he didn't. Instead he slumped over to the ground and sobbed, beating the walls, the floor, howling with pain.

Bit by bit, hour by hour, the pain replaced itself with anger, and then with rage. Before long, he was hungry for revenge.

How could Jaun want to denounce the Pradishar? They'd given Fin everything he had. They'd taken him in and trained him, sent him to the Academicon to learn, treated him like anyone else. They were offering him a future, and Jaun wanted to take that away.

He went into the bathing room and scrubbed his skin til it hurt, trying to get the smell of Jaun off of him. Then he put on clean robes and took the underground passage to the citadel, walking as fast as he could toward the Gran Pradesh's quarters.

"I have important information about the Ren'fallow," he said to the Octa'vin guard. "It can't wait."

The Octa'vin nodded and the door opened.

Chapter 28

The Balance of the World

ELLEX ANDRIA SPENT THE months leading up to Zenithra working harder than she'd ever worked in her life, or so it seemed at least. She couldn't be sure—there were so many things she couldn't be sure about anymore—but she had no doubt that if she stayed busy, there'd be no time for her to brood over the past. There'd be no time for uncertainty. No time to question what had happened to her on P'anorum, or how she'd spent three decades without even bothering to find out. It never occurred to her that she was unwittingly continuing to put off asking these most important questions right now, but no—there was too much that needed doing, too much that needed her focus and concentration.

Rakk Raeder was living in the capital, just down the pathway from Ellex's own estate in Sunrise Ridge, and Ellex spent most of her evenings helping him learn the ways of the Cul'tavin, the politics of Balan Su, and to assemble the world's very first joint Corkin-Cul'tavin security team, the Balan Su Defenders. Some days she was sure it was a fool's errand, that both of them had been set up to fail by their enemies. Half of the eight on the Council of Nine had voted to remove her, after all. And so many of the peacekeepers were too self-righteous to fight alongside slaves, while many of the Corkin struggled to coordinate with the Cul'tavin, even when ordered to.

Yet by the time Zenithra arrived, Rakk had done it. He'd been ordained as a Pradishar priestin, received the purple and silver crystamin in a ceremony at the citadel, and he'd brought together the two largest peacekeeping forces in Balance Territories under a common banner. With Qardymion in the Dankburn awaiting execution, their rebels had scattered, losing their nerve to threaten the Great Sea Lanes, as Ellex had thought they would.

Cut off the head and the whole snake dies, she told herself, as she relished the thought of seeing the Saltsap marched through the streets of Balan Su, knowing their life's work to topple Balance Authority had failed—that their assault on her troops, her poor butchered peacekeepers, was not going unpunished.

Rakk found her on the afternoon of the last day of the year on her terrace, where she sat sunning herself, her eyes twitching as she went over the schedule for the Balancing Act and checked in with her people to confirm everything was in place.

"Finally taking a much needed break?" he said, and she jumped and let out a small cry. She reached for her gown and threw it over her midriff as her face blushed brown. "Sorry, Pander let me in."

And without asking me first? Bold, she thought. *Very bold.*

"Wait in the salon for a moment while I dress," she said.

"Of course, Sui Pradesh," he said, and Ellex imagined he was smirking.

She slipped her arms through her gown and fastened the buttons, careful not to smoosh her flower. She'd left her cumberdome in her quarters and didn't want to go and fetch it.

"Enter," she called, and Rakk came onto the terrace and sat down in one of the loungers.

"A lovely place when it's sunny like this," he said, looking out across the rim. "Even the fog has dropped down nearly to sea level."

"A good sign for the new year," she said. "Why have you come?"

"Ouch," he said. "Not glad to see me then?"

"It's not that."

"Alright. I just came to let you know that everything's status quo."

"And you felt the need to tell me that face to face rather than via crystamin?"

Rakk gave her a pained look, then grinned it off. "I came to thank you."

"For what?"

"Don't be so modest. I didn't have half a chance of making this work. I couldn't have done it without you."

Ellex blushed, even as she tried not to, and she sighed. Working with him these last months had been—Ellex wasn't sure how it had been, as she hadn't let herself stop to think about it. Everything had been about the business at hand, and they'd hardly had any time to talk about, well, anything. Any time Rakk had tried to get nostalgic, Ellex had cut him off and redirected him to Pradishar methods.

"You don't have to thank me," she said. "I swore to serve Balance Authority. And in this case, your success means our city is kept safe. So I should be thanking you."

"What do you say we have dinner tonight? We'll be all dressed up for the gala anyway, and then we can go together afterward."

Ellex looked at Rakk and she knew from his eyes that this would surely be a date in his mind. And what would the notestreams say if they showed up at the gala together? She'd been down that road with him before. An Andrasian Sui Pradesh with a prince of Raccorum Rhazzat? It could never happen. She'd lose her position on the Council, and Rakk would lose his throne. And he knew that.

How stupid, she thought, *to flirt with something you know you can't have.*

"That won't be necessary," she said.

"Who said anything about necessary?"

"Raeder, you know that we—"

"Forget it," Rakk said, standing from the lounger. "I'll see you at the gala."

"Raeder, wait—"

But he was already gone.

※※※※ ※※※※

The gala was a bust.

Rakk never showed—*probably my fault*, Ellex thought—and she was too proud to reach out to him and see if he was okay. Plus, seeing that damn Bhizini freak Fin'roq had given her the horrors, and it felt like all her efforts, all of Rakk's efforts, to keep the city safe were being undermined by his presence.

How could the Gran Pradesh allow him to stay? she thought. *Is Ra'shard Ruu'n a fool? No. Did it have something to do with that stream from P'anorum all those months ago?*

She'd asked Uthyr to take care of it, and then she never followed up.

Why haven't I been investigating? No—not yet. Wait til the Balancing Act is over. There's time for answers later. I have all summer to get to the bottom of things.

She spent the night dozing on the verandah, her feet on a soil patch. She woke and slept, woke and slept, until finally, when twilight was scarcely an hour away, she rose to her feet and stretched. No ghosts had haunted her that night. No image of her father fading as she woke.

Ellex took that as an auspicious sign for the day.

Now that the Balancing Act was finally here, her excitement blossomed like a morning glory in the first rays of light. This was her favorite day of the year, the anniversary of

Balance Authority, and this looked to be the biggest celebration in ten thousand years. It hardly seemed possible that there had been talk of cancelling the festival just a few months earlier.

Rajj and Ellex would spend the day at the Weeping Wilvryn as partakers in the key rituals of the day, while citizens would fill the squares and plazas all around Balance Territories with revelers. Bhiza limits were relaxed and modesty rules were briefly overlooked, and everyone would be feasting and celebrating from sunrise til sundown and beyond.

The gates of Balan Su were closed and firmly locked, and the city had filled to overflowing with visitors and pilgrims. Ellex thought of them now, of how far they had traveled, some taking more than a month to arrive from their distant villages. She knew a great many had come to see her—her loyalists across Andrasia and the Inner Archipelago, of course, but also a great many who wanted to see the Andrasian from the incident. Even months later, and in spite of the prohibitions on mentioning it, the sheer volume of chatter on the dream had proven impossible to suppress.

But she didn't think that mattered much anymore. What mattered was that she'd spent her time reaching out to the citizens, being present everywhere, active, connecting with the people—and her popularity, at least in Balan Su, had soared. In Andrasia, on the other hand—she'd been so busy with affairs in the capital that she'd largely ignored the homeland, leaving her aides to deal with fallout from the dream. She'd overlooked the problem for too long, she knew.

That will have to join the other list of things I've put off, she thought. *Me, who never puts anything off. No—later!*

She went to her bathing room and began to prepare for the day, cleaning and oiling her skin, dressing in her ceremonial robes, and assembling the props she'd need for the various rituals throughout the day. Then she headed out into the cool, dark morning, out of Sunrise Ridge and down to the edge of the rim, and from there past Old Stones to Grand Plaza. She looked down at the harbor from the edge, surprised to see that the fog was nearly gone, just sitting atop the water, and thrilled at what it meant for the day.

Even Balan Su itself wants to celebrate properly, she thought.

When she reached the plaza, she could see it was filled with plants waiting to welcome the new year, which officially began at sunrise. The Cul'tavin had barriers around the plaza, and when the peacekeepers saw her, they directed her to the front. Two guards escorted her through the crowd, as everyone nearby cheered and called her name and reached out hoping to touch her. She smiled and waved and blew kisses to the crowd.

When she reached the perch by the Weeping Wilvryn tree, a soft round mound of dirt that made her visible to nearly the entire plaza and even to many down below on the lower rim, she set up her things on the dais and waited for Rajj.

He arrived shortly thereafter, a look of panic on his face.

"Rakk isn't at his post. And nobody can contact him. That, or nobody will tell me."

So much for omens.

Ellex's eye flickered and twitched. "All the Cul'tavin are accounted for. Joint commander Rhurski assures me the Defenders are in place and that everything in Balan Su is status quo." Her eyes continued to twitch. "And yet no Raeder."

Sweet Trevian, Ellex thought, *did I upset him that much? Is he doing this to punish me? No. He wouldn't. Right?*

"He told me he was assembling a force that could run itself without him, since he planned to leave Balan Su once the Act is over. So maybe he's just testing that out, pretending to be absent so his troop leaders don't rely on him? It wouldn't be entirely out of character."

"If he's abandoned his post—" Rajj started.

Ellex sighed. "You might have been a little nicer to him. At least spoken to him. And I guess I could have been nicer too. But I don't know what else to say. There's no way we're cancelling. I think he'll show up as the day gets underway."

Rajj sighed. "I thought you'd want to go on with it."

"Do we have a choice? If Rhurski says everything is okay with city security, then what else can we do?"

"I don't know, but I don't like it."

"Have you tried asking Q'orin? He's always keeping tabs on Rakk."

"I have, but he's no help. He's Rakk's private slave, which trumps the Corkin hierarchy. He only obeys him. I can't compel him to speak. And he won't speak, unless Rakk specifically tells him to. Very loyal."

"You mean very well controlled. That's not the same as loyalty."

"Are we to debate slavery on this special day? If Ra'shard Ruu'n couldn't convince the Raccorin to change their ways, I'm afraid you won't either. But come, twilight is breaking. The year is nearly new. Let us welcome the sun."

"Fine, but when the ritual is over, I want to talk about why you've been ignoring your brother."

"Ahh, do we have to?" Rajj said, pouting.

"He doesn't deserve to be ignored like that," Ellex said. "When the day's over, I hope you'll talk to him. And thank him, for coming here. And for working so hard."

"I will," Rajj said, "if you promise to stop making me feel bad."

"Agreed," Ellex said, smiling.

The day was filled with sunshine and the air was actually warm. Ellex felt herself filling with energy and strength and a sense of lazy, euphoric delight.

When the sun rose, the crowd cheered and danced and sang and prayed, the ten thousandth Cycle of Balance had begun. At midmorning, Ellex danced the Raccorin Trot while Rajj did his best to do the Andrasian Andar, difficult though it was with his height. At noon they feasted on rhupan and bhiza. Ellex ate Raccorin preparations while Rajj ate the Andrasian ones. At mid-afternoon, Ellex sang the hymn of the Raccorin Empire and Rajj did a stirring rendition of Ahu A' Andra that had Ellex in tears.

When the afternoon grew old and shadows began to fill the inner harbor, Ellex and Rajj took turns swearing allegiance to Balance while the other held a copy of the Accords. The city cheered when they embraced, and everyone began to dance and sing, to feast and to kiss. They could hear the music and the laughter from atop the island where they perched watching the city celebrate.

And then they brought forth the Saltsap, Qardymion, from the great gates of the citadel, he was flanked by masses of Cul'tavin and his body was clad in metal casings that made every step an effort. The Bhizini still stood tall as they were paraded out across the plaza and around the great tree. Ellex had yet to look upon the rebel leader up close, and she ordered them to stop that she might stare a moment. They didn't look as she had imagined. Indeed, if their skin had been the soft greens of an Andrasian rather than the blotchy mottled mess that it was, Ellex might have found them handsome. They were proud like Rakk, but with a nobility that reminded Ellex of her father. Now she understood why Rakk had admitted it was hard to turn them in.

Or maybe she'd had too much bhiza today. The city wanted to see the Saltsap marched about in chains, hit with refuse, forced to degrade themself for their entertainment, and she had no intention of stopping it. So Ellex nodded and the parade moved onward, cutting back across the upper rim toward the Regalia. Ellex looked at Rajj and smiled.

"Let us unite our people once more," Ellex said.

"Peace through Balance, forevermore," Rajj said on cue.

They stepped off their perch to cheers from the crowd and passed through the hanging branches of the Weeping Wilvryn tree, into the cool interior, the stones moist with moss, the smell of old rotten leaves and the richest of soils, hearty and verdant. It was time for the final ritual of the Balancing Act, the symbolic union of Raccorin and Andrasian.

They slipped out of their robes and stood facing each other, as they'd done over thirty times before. Then they bowed at the same time and stepped toward one another.

Rajj hesitated. "Is this—is this okay tonight? I mean, what with—you know—the incident."

"Yes. I told you, I don't remember those things. They don't feel real to me. And besides, you're not your father. You've proved that to me time and time again, as we've ruled the world together these past three decades. I respect you as a Verdillion, as a leader, and as a friend. Now stop talking."

Ellex always enjoyed Rajj's lovemaking, though in all these years they'd only ever had sex at the Balancing Act. Rajj was slow and gentle and unenthusiastic. There was no doubt that for him, as well as for Ellex, this was a ritual of state that happened to feel nice but was nothing like a romantic encounter. Ellex rooted her feet in the rich soil and then gently swayed there, holding Rajj lightly with her branches.

A memory came to her then of being much younger, barely flowered, a rare glimpse from a hazy past. Her family used to vacation in the redwyn trees outside Andurst, in those magical, moist hollows. She remembered that she'd gone out by herself on a hike, and she'd found a grassy clearing with a small brook. She'd brought along a scroll with a series of sketches, an erotic story told in images that had made her heart race, and she'd explored her own flower for the first time.

Ellex was wondering what had happened to that young plant when, amidst the sounds of music and of revelry coming from all around them, a different noise could be heard, low at first, then higher and sharper and more pronounced. Rajj and Ellex looked at each other, not moving now, listening.

"It sounds like a swarm of bees," she said.

"Maquina going awry," Rajj said, an alarmed look in his eyes. "Overloading dynamins, I'd guess."

Rajj was right. An explosion shook the Weeping Wilvryn, and Ellex gasped as they pulled out of each other. Then another explosion farther away, then many at once, in every direction, near and far. The sounds of revelry had been replaced with the shrieks of terror and there were sounds of a battle right outside the long-hanging branches of the tree. A Cul'tavin, on fire, crashed through the vines and onto the ground next to them, falling still.

"Come on!" Ellex screamed, grabbing Rajj's hand. They stepped out of the curtain of branches and saw the city in chaos, smoke rising in large plumes in every direction, as the glowbes winked out across the crescent. Her eyes flickered as she called for help from her Cul'tavin, but most of her troops around the plaza were not responding.

A cloaked figure came out of the crowd, a long Vintrani blade in hand, marching toward them. Rajj screamed and grabbed Ellex, pushing her back toward the tree, as the blade sliced downward through the air. It passed cleanly through Rajj's bicep and out the other side, sending a stream of sap shooting into Ellex's face, hot, sticky, and pungent, as his arm fell to the ground. Rajj's bright green face had turned the color of ash, and his knees buckled under him.

The figure whirled toward Ellex, Vintrani blade coming down in a wide arc, but Ellex rolled to the side and let her momentum carry her backward through the branches of the Weeping Wilvryn. She backed up against the trunk, grabbing a nearby stick for defense, and waited. But the branches were pulled aside by a cadre of Cul'tavin peacekeepers.

"We came as quickly as we could, Sui Pradesh," one said.

Ellex left the stick and ran out of the canopy, dropping down to Rajj's side and grabbing his stump.

"We need to stop the sap," she said. She reached for her robe but realized then that she was naked and Rajj was too, so she grabbed the robe of the peacekeeper nearest to her, tore into it with her teeth, then ripped a strip from the garment and tied it around Rajj's stump. "We need to get him to the Me'dicants inside the citadel, now!"

Two Cul'tavin lifted Rajj and carried him through the plaza while Ellex followed at their side. The square had largely cleared out though there was sporadic fighting, and the ground was strewn about with corpses, some of them still burning. A few huddled around the fires, weeping over the dead. Ellex looked at Rajj's pale face and tried to focus. When they entered the citadel, several healers scurried to their side and directed them to their laboratory.

"We'll keep you posted, Sui Pradesh," one said after inspecting his arm. "Verdillions are tough. You did well tying it off. It might help if we had some sap for him though."

"His brother..." Ellex said, remembering then that she didn't know where Rakk was.

We were feasting and drinking, and we forgot he was missing.

"Thank Trevian," Uthyr said, entering the lab and rushing to Ellex's side. He cried out and pulled back when he saw her face covered in sap. He looked down at Rajj and cried out again. "Rajj! Is he okay??"

"He should be, but he's lost a lot of sap. It would help if we could find Rakk. What's going on out there?"

"Dynamin overloads in nearly every maquina in Balan Su. And in the chaos that followed, cloaked Bhizini took to the streets, attacking citizens with Vintrani blades. The Cul'tavin rushed to fight the attackers, but the Corkin...they wouldn't engage. We haven't ascertained who struck first, but the Corkin joined the battle against...well, everyone. There's still fighting on the lower rim and sporadically on the upper."

Ellex was in tears. "Where's the Saltsap?"

"Unknown. There's more, though. Much more. There was some kind of attack in the Forum. Jaun von Andron—" Uthyr's eyes were twitching as he trailed off.

"How'd the Bhizini get in the city?"

"The locking mechanisms on the gates failed. Or were sabotaged along with the other dynamins. The servryns seem to have been tampered with, too."

"Are you suggesting the Dyna'arin had a hand in this? But it would be suicide!"

"I've got a lock on a signal. The entire city's dark but there's still power in an underground lab near the Academicon. Deep under the island. And—potentially within the Pradishar spire."

Ellex's eyes twitched as she reviewed the docket Uthyr sent her, and she hissed aloud when she saw who the lab belonged to.

"Lithuigi Von'nDrino," she said. "Coincidence?"

"Unlikely," Uthyr said. "I'm going to summon the Council. We need to move, quickly. Let's get you a robe while we see what they decide."

Ellex dressed in Cul'tavin fatigues with a pradeshan robe thrown over the top while the Council meeting happened via crystamin. The Pradishar were granted emergency powers of investigation, effective immediately. Only the Dyna'arin had opposed the ordinance, so there was no need to summon the Gran Pradesh to cast Rajj's vote for him. Rameen Rutar was furious and promised there would be consequences from the Guild for this overstep of authority, and Ellex retorted that the Guild would do well to remain silent until they got to the bottom of this.

Ellex finished strapping up her boots and turned to her brother. "Let's go see what Lithuigi Von'nDrino is hiding," she said.

"We haven't been able to locate him," Uthyr said. "But his son Vilder is a member of the Pradishar and agreed to show us where his labs are located."

"Then let's get going. No time to waste."

Ellex and Uthyr took one of the tunnels beneath the citadel to the entrance of the Academicon, emerging in a locked corridor in the basement of the great hall. The campus was quiet and empty. Most of the students were gone until the fall, and the chaos that had ensued earlier had not greatly affected the area. They went to the lab building and found their contact. Ellex had never seen the Andrasian before, but the gray and purple crystal of the Pradishar on his forehead was unmistakeable. He was tall and thin, too pale even for an Andrasian. His forehead was too big, his face sunken in, like an old face on a young body. He held up a glowbe, the only light in the building, and he nodded when they approached.

"Vilder, is it? Are you alright?" Ellex said, noticing the large bruises on his cheek and eye.

"Just a few scrapes from earlier," Vilder said. "But I do sincerely appreciate your concern, Sui Pradesh. I'm honored to serve."

And a flatterer, Ellex thought. "What should we expect to find inside?"

"I couldn't say. While I've suspected a secret lab existed for some time now, I've only just acquired the access codes."

Vilder led them down into the basement of the lab building, into a normal Guild lab, through an open door in the back of the vault, and down into a tunnel under the island itself. Ellex considered the labyrinth of passageways connecting the city, spiraling around past one another in every direction, and wondered how the old volcanic rim that held up the city still managed to endure.

Finally they reached a door and Vilder entered a code with his crystamin and the door opened with a whoosh. Ellex cringed when she heard the whine of maquina coming from inside.

An older Raccorin stood up when they walked in, surprise on her face. When she saw Vilder, her expression turned defiant.

In front of them stood a strange sort of maquina. It had a large metal door with a glass panel, and it looked like it belonged in a cookery at a royal estate—some sort of oven for roasting large quantities of rhupan. Ellex immediately recognized it, and her stomach clenched up. She'd seen it in her dream. The maquina, and this lab. Here it was, as far as she could tell, the same one.

Her heart racing, Ellex approached the door of the maquina and peeked in through the glass panel. Inside was a lit chamber glowing orange with glowbes. A small Bhizini was perched in the middle, strapped to a beam overhead. There were other maquina, small ones the size of Ellex's hand, attached at various points on the Bhizini's body, a half dozen or more.

"Who's in there?" Ellex asked. Her voice was shaking and there were tears in her eyes.

The Raccorin said nothing.

"Release the Bhizini at once!" Ellex said. "Shut this maquina down, now!"

The Raccorin still said nothing but turned to her operator console, her eyes twitching as she turned a few knobs on the panel. The high pitched whine began to drop off.

"Move," Uthyr said, and he took the Raccorin's seat. Then he opened a latch on the side and fished around inside the console for its datamins.

Ellex was still peering in the door of the maquina, a determined look on her face.

"Help me open this thing," she said, and the Raccorin came over to the door and began to crank the knob.

The door finally swung open and the Raccorin stepped inside. Ellex watched her as she disconnected some of the vines from the smaller maquina on the Bhizini's body.

Uthyr came up beside her and took her arm. "Ell, you need to see this." His eye fluttered.

Ellex's eyes began to twitch and she closed them. In her mind's eye, she saw as if she were someone else, inside a memory, inside someone who was watching her. She'd fruited and was planting the seed in a sprouting patch, carefully covering it with dirt. Another vision, this one of running through darkness. She saw the same sprouting patch, a small mottled Bhizini spratlyn growing, its taprin ready for cutting. Ellex watched the knife slice, the spratlyn awaken to life with a scream. The scene faded to another memory. The little spratlyn, now a scamp of a few months, being placed in the maquina that Ellex was standing beside—strapped in, attached with the maquina, closed up and forgotten, for over thirty-three years.

Ellex opened her eyes and the Bhizini's eyes were open too.

They stared one at the other, recognizing each other then as mother and scamp, parent and offspring, both frozen in one another's gaze. Ellex doesn't know how long she stared, how long they stared at each other. But eventually they both opened their mouths, inhaled deeply, and began to scream at the same time.

Chapter 29

The Burden of Those Who Know

Lithuigi Von'nDrino had not seen his father's face in many decades when his specter appeared again, standing before him at the hour when the night is deep and cold and seems endless—just before twilight when the Death King makes his rounds. His father stood in the doorway, chewing on his nails as he'd always done when lost in thought, saying nothing, as if he hadn't noticed Lithuigi were there.

But when his father looked at him, Lithuigi had to swallow his panic in order to get his rootpads to respond, and he pulled them up out of the soil, glanced over at Rebesh'a perched next to him, still fast asleep, and stepped toward the door. His father began to walk and Lithuigi followed him out onto the terrace.

"You've done well, son," his father said, and Lithuigi's panic was quickly replaced with anger.

"If you were really him, you'd never have said such a thing. The old tyrant wasn't one to compliment."

"Perhaps I've changed in death."

Lithuigi chuckled, but his face look tortured.

"I appreciate what you've done for me," his father said. "But you know good things always end. They must. You know, your mother once said—"

Lithuigi hissed. "Don't you dare speak of her!"

"Or what? You'll kill me?" He laughed. "Only death is forever, son. You must know that."

"Why have you come?"

"To compliment you, as I've said. Yes, to let you know that all good deeds are rewarded."

"Meaning?" Lithuigi's chest clenched up.

"Well, now that our little arrangement is at an end, it's time to set my sights on the next generation. The up and coming, you know. And it seems my grandsons are quite the impressive themselves. Vilder is already so good at following orders, I practically have him eating from my hand. And Hesh'n—why, he might be the most imaginative tinker in, oh, millennia. Imagine the things I could do—the games we could play."

Lithuigi's face had drained of color, his angry defiance replaced with the old panic. His loyalty—and his skill with a stasis chamber—had kept them safe all these years. Now that the stasis project was ending—

"Please, tell me what I can do to help."

"Ahh, you're singing a better tune now, Von'nDrino." His father was smiling but his eyes were pure malice. "Yes, much better. You remember my warning, then?"

Lithuigi looked at the floor, feeling like a scolded scamp, and shook his head yes.

"Must I make it again?"

He shook his head no.

"That's a good scamp." But it was his mother this time, and when he looked up, she was smiling warmly at him, her arms spread wide, offering him a hug.

He screamed.

"L'uigi?" Rebesh'a called from their quarters. She came out onto the terrace, looking alarmed. "Are you alright?"

He looked around but the terrace was empty.

"Darling, what happened?" she said.

He gave her a sheepish grin and tried to hide that he was out of breath. "I'm not sure. Sleepwalking, maybe?"

"Had one too many cookies at the gala?" she said, grinning at him. "Wasn't it wonderful? I still feel jazzed up. I'm surprised I could sleep. But look love, twilight's breaking. If we hurry, we can catch the sunrise with the others at the Weeping Wilvryn."

He took her hands in his. "You go on alone," he said.

Rebesh'a pouted while she got dressed, and pleaded with him one more time to go with her, but he wouldn't budge. He gave her a long hug and kiss, and watched her walk toward the door. By the time he called out for her, she was already gone.

❧❧❧❧❧ ❧❧❧❧❧

Lithuigi had survived one hundred and forty years of secrets and plots, and so he told himself that this was no different than all the other times he was sure he'd run out of luck, even if it felt different.

I was not expecting this, he thought. *But the plan hasn't changed.*

As twilight grew in the eastern sky, he gathered the rest of his things, looked around the garden one last time, then headed for the Academicon. The crowds in Grand Plaza were massive, so Lithuigi kept to the inner edge, along the wall of the citadel, and kept his hood over his head. The campus, on the other hand, was empty and silent save for the sounds of distant revelry.

He hurried to his lab and got to work. First he went into his vault and got out a satchel in which he kept some of his most important datamins, full of research and schematics that he didn't trust letting his assistants handle—not even Mha'arlo, though not because he thought he would betray him, but for Mha'arlo's own deniability.

Next he found the package that Mha'arlo had brought him from Andramere, the special delivery from Doc Andri'n—a set of prototype datamins the good professor had developed in secret over the last century, in tandem with his own development of a prototype dynamin. He pulled a carver out from its compartment in the wall and placed one of the prototypes into it, then inserted one of the datamins from his satchel. He set the new one to mimic the old one, and for the old one to erase itself after mimicry was complete. Then he puttered around his office, occasionally switching out the datamins, while the carver did its work.

The sun had already passed overhead and was moving into afternoon by the time he descended through the door at the back of his vault, down through the tunnels and into his other lab within the obsidian of the Pradishar spire.

Rhyntysha was there, sitting under a glowbe, monitoring the console, when he entered.

"Ah professor, happy new year," she said. "Truly the end of an era."

"I can hardly believe it," Lithuigi said. He walked over to the stasis chamber and peered in at the Bhizini. "Still so small."

"But strong," Rhyntysha said. "And ready."

"But are we?" he said.

"We have to be," she said.

"You're in danger if you stay here."

"You don't have to worry about me."

"I'm afraid our Guild privileges won't protect us anymore. The Pradishar—they will tear into your mind."

"No, they won't," Rhyntysha said. "My secrets are untouchable, and my crystals can't be probed by anyone."

He gave her a long look, then turned and looked at the stasis chamber.

"You're clear on how to power it down?"

"Everything is status quo, professor. Not to worry."

"Then I'll trust you to handle things from here." He looked through the window once more, and felt the panic in the back of his throat again.

Rhyntysha touched his arm. "Working with you all these years has been the highpoint of my life," she said.

"The honor's been mine," he said. "I couldn't have asked for a better partner."

Then she touched his face. "Don't be sad, L'uigi, old friend. We're on the right side of history. And this is the time we win. I'm sure of it."

"I wish I had your faith," he said, and blinking back his tears, he hurried from the laboratory.

"One more thing, professor," Rhyntysha called.

⁂

When Lithuigi came out into the plaza in front of the Academicon's Great Hall, he could see the bright afternoon sun—the sky actually looked blue with the fog so low to the water that day—and he could hear music and laughter from every direction. But his heart was aching and he felt old. Too old. He was sick of all the secrets, all the plots. Sick of a century of pretending to be someone else.

It's almost over, he thought. *Almost.*

The crowds in the Regalia and the Forum were thick, and by the time he reached Hesh'n's garden in Sunset Point, the afternoon was growing late. He'd need to make this quick. He rang at the gate and it opened with a whoosh, but the garden was empty. Lithuigi waited until Hesh'n finally came upstairs from his lab, wiping his hands on a towel. His face was pale and gray and his arms were shaking. Lithuigi thought he'd probably been working for several days straight.

A bad habit he gets from me, he thought.

"What is it, Father? I'm very busy. I wasn't expecting you."

"Not enjoying the festivities?" Lithuigi said. "There are some very comely plants out in the plaza, dancing under the sun. You sure you don't want to catch a few rays? Have a little fun?"

Hesh'n's face twisted up with contempt. "Do you even know me?" he said. "You think I'd want to waste my time getting drunk and being patriotic? Have you ever seen me enjoy myself anywhere but in my lab or in the classroom?"

"Of course I have," Lithuigi said. "You loved the beach when you were a little scamp. We had to come and get you ourselves, you never wanted to get out of the water. We used to have so much fun. Your mother would…"

"Save your pathetic reflections for your slutty daughters, I don't give a fuck, don't you get that? Now what do you want with me?"

Hesh'n sounded more like Vilder every day.

"I was just worried you needed some sunshine, is all. I know you. And I know how hard it can be to take a break. Let's go talk on the verandah."

"No, let's go talk downstairs in my lab. That way I can get some work done while you yammer away at me."

Lithuigi nodded in silence and followed his son into his lab. The stench was worse than it had been at his lab in the Academicon, and there was something sticky on the floor. On the worktable in the center of the lab, Hesh'n had a spratlyn laid out, nearly the size of a full-grown Andrasian. He'd cut it open, fastened the skin in all four corners of the table, and inserted some sort of small maquina in the place where the Verdillion stomach should have been. The actual stomach was sitting on the floor, forgotten. The spratlyn's feet were still firmly against a large soil patch, the taprin still connected. How was that even possible?

Lithuigi put his hand over his mouth. "In Sweet Trevian's name, what is this abomination?"

"It isn't finished yet!" Hesh'n said. "Almost working."

"So you lied about the bhrubean stalks—" His face was burning, and he felt like the oldest, and biggest, fool in the city, maybe in all of Balance. "Son—I'm worried about you." Why was that so hard to say? Why had it taken him so long to say that?

"Don't pretend to care about me. You're just angry I thought of this first! You were always a mediocre tinker," Hesh'n said. "You couldn't handle real genius in your midst, that's why you fled Andramere and abandoned your birthright. That's why you always make Mother cry. You're just an arrogant and ungrateful fool. I'm about to change the world, and you're worried about—what? A few spratlyn? Do you know how many tens of thousands never get cut, every single year? How many millions of fruits are given to the branta birds?"

"I'm not worried about spratlyns. I'm worried about my son," Lithuigi said. "My first scamp."

"Well, you shouldn't be." He sighed. "I know how this looks, okay Father?" he said, suddenly playing nice and nodding at Lithuigi. "And it's okay. I have permission from the Dyna'arin and from the Pradishar. For this specific project, all details spelled out. So it's no problem. Besides, what could be worse than the enflamers you unleashed on the world? This project will actually save lives, Andrasian and Raccorin. All of Balance will be safer because of my work."

"Now who's pretending?" Lithuigi said.

Hesh'n gave him a small smile. "I learned that from you too, Father. I've heard you thrill the Dyna'arin with your speeches, pretending to care about others, about society, about religion even. Were they ever moved?"

"The point was to make them think, not move them. They have to move themselves, as we all do."

"No, you might have entertained them at the time, given them a brief moment of contemplation, but then they went right back to tinkering. They only care about tinkering, and the consequences be damned."

Lithuigi walked over to the table and took a closer look at the spratlyn. It looked like a shrubby version of his own son, cut wide open, dissected. He had to resist the urge to scream with grief when he looked at its face.

Hesh'n is more lost than I ever was, he thought. *Is he too lost to save?*

"Will you finally tell me what this project of yours is?" Lithuigi said. "I mean, I think I can guess."

Hesh'n's eyes began to shine and his hands quivered. "Isn't it beautiful? I'm calling them the Verdhesh'n."

"Them?"

Lithuigi had guessed wrong.

"Of a sort. Insentient like any spratlyn, of course. I realized the imperial crystal that I used to stop the taprin from dying had—well, other applications. Getting the dynamins not to scorch the flesh has remained my biggest obstacles to getting them on their feet. That's why I wanted your prototype. The limited output would prevent overheating, as I tried to explain to you before. They'd be perfect, but you wouldn't listen. Surely you can see I need access to one now? Surely you see how urgent it is? Father—Papa—please!"

"I'm sorry, son, there's no way I'd help you on this—this—thing. No, I'm going straight to Management to try and stop this, once and for all."

Hesh'n glowing eyes turned cold. "You'd interfere with my work? Is that really what you'd do? You'd keep me from tinkering, from expanding knowledge, from helping the world? That's like keeping a Dyna'arin from breathing. And I won't let you do that!"

"Are you threatening our father?" Vilder said, coming down the stairs into the lab. His sunken cheeks were pale and sickly, and he looked deeply offended at what he'd just witnessed. "That's supposed to be my job!" He laughed.

Hesh'n hissed. "Must I change the lock? One more intrusion like that and I'll use my enflamer on you. Burn you to a fucking crisp. I'm not joking."

Vilder kept smiling. "I just love my family. Freaks, they are. And traitors, too."

Lithuigi had hoped to get out of Balan Su without seeing him.

"How are you, son?" he said. "I hoped you'd come by. I wanted to see you before I leave town."

"Don't play nice to me, Father. You aren't going anywhere."

"Oh?" Lithuigi said. "I was not aware that the Guild had restricted my travel privileges. And how would a Pradishar priestin know if they had?"

"Are you really going to play dumb?" he said, looking around for support but Hesh'n was ignoring him. "How is it that you're revered across Balance Territories for your intelligence, when it's so obvious that you're an utter fool?"

"I'm sure everyone must be wrong and only you are right, is that it, son? I don't think in all your life you've ever admitted you were wrong."

"And it happens a lot," Hesh'n added.

"Have you?!" Vilder screamed. "Have either of you? If I'm arrogant, I learned by example. Let's call it self-assuredness instead. Then surely it's a virtue? That I learned all by myself."

"You've learned nothing but how to bow down to power," Lithuigi said.

"Oh, but that's a virtue, too," Vilder said. "A survival skill. Since you refused to help me with the Pradishar, I helped myself. Willingness to serve goes a long way in the citadel. Here I am, with the power to arrest even you, Father."

Vilder went to pull a zapren from his robe but Lithuigi had already palmed his own in his real hand, and he lunged at his son with it, jabbing it into his chest. He screeched and spasmed, falling back into the wall and dropping to the floor. His body twitched once before falling still.

Then with his prosthetic, Lithuigi pulled his enflamer from his robe and began to send whorls of flame into the spratlyn on the table. Hesh'n screeched and turned toward his father, enraged, but one jab of the zapren to his chest sent him to the ground, twitching. Lithuigi opened the enflamer to full strength and directed it toward the workstation and console, which soon turned orange and began to overheat. He could hear a buzzing like a swarm of bees, and he turned to leave the lab before the dynamins overloaded.

He grabbed Hesh'n by the arms and dragged him up the stairs and out into the garden, well away from the lab. Then he went back in for Vilder, and when he reached the bottom of the steps, he began to choke on the smoke and retreated to the fresh air. Once his lungs were full, he held his breathe and went back into the lab. He grabbed Vilder by the hands and pulled him up the stairs, out into the garden, and onto the ground by Hesh'n.

Trevian forgive me, he thought. *I should have left him in there. But I can't. I just can't.*

The sun was down and twilight was beginning to wane, and Lithuigi knew he had to get to the rendezvous point. So he sealed off the lab and pressurized it, hoping that would contain the explosion from the dynamin overload. At least his sons should be safe. He hoped. He had to take the risk. If he didn't leave now, he might not be able to get out of the city.

As he turned to leave, Vilder coughed, and Lithuigi looked at his son. Vilder tried to sit up but couldn't. So he looked at his father and did his best to kill him with his eyes.

"Father—" he choked, "how—"

Lithuigi nearly dropped to his knees to beg Vilder's forgiveness, but instead he jabbed him again with the zapren, til he was unconscious once more. And then he ran.

He ran, and he ran, and he ran some more, out of Sunset Point, through the Regalia, and into the lift station at the Academicon, hardly able to see through the tears. When he reached the lower rim, he ran once again, to the back of the city, through the tunnels and out to Bleakside. Once there, he turned and descended the stairs and then climbed over the embankment that walled off the craggy coastline. There were a series of well-placed steps down the face of the cliff and into the water. He took off his robe, stored his enflamer and zapren in straps on his thighs, then climbed down into the sea.

The taste of the salty water on his lips restored him, and he swam in long broad strokes away from the shore. That was when he first heard the whine, the buzz of dynamins overloading. The sounds of explosions and screams drifted across the water. He lay on his back and propelled himself out with his arms, looking up at the island looming over him through the gaps in the fog, the glowbes winking out across the crescent, the great spire of the Pradishar citadel seeming to fade into the night sky.

He swam until he couldn't swim any more and then he dove under the water, down and down, down into the black. But even down in the depths of his beloved sea, there was no release from the past, no escape from the present, and only a passing hope for tomorrow.

That will have to be enough, he thought, as a shadow moved toward him in the water, catching him from beneath and gently lifting him back to the surface. He clutched the soft gray fur and buried his face in it, and Gray'may'n the Unseen spread wide his fins and with large strokes began to move away from Balan Su, carrying Lithuigi Von'nDrino to safety.

Chapter 30

The Fires of Authority

ZENITHRA FELT LIKE THE longest two weeks of Bryn Andri'n's life.

Several months earlier, the two weeks following her Floronation had been the longest weeks of her life. She'd been so traumatized, she was nearly nonfunctional. It didn't matter if she retreated from the world and healed on her own time—at least until her parents and Trexbo insisted she report the crime to the Cul'tavin. They meant well, even if it had backfired. But this time, everything was different. This time, her father had been the victim—and she likely responsible for the suffering he was enduring. And because it was her father and not her, even though she hadn't shut down, hadn't tumbled into despair, it still seemed—but no.

Bryn told herself it was foolish to compare pain, to say this hurt more than that, this was worse than that, at least once a certain line had been crossed. Hierarchies of intensity no longer matter. It only mattered that it killed her inside, little by little, day by day.

I can't linger there, she thought. *Or I'll never—there's too much to get done.*

Bryn knew she had duties to fulfill, first and foremost the carving project at the library, which was nearly complete—well, *complete* might not have been the proper word. *Sufficiently worked on* might be better. The essential books and scrolls from the library had been archived, and the older datamins had been copied to new ones that her father had supplied. But there were always new books and scrolls being added to the collection, always new data on datamins in the servryn. Information wasn't finite, it burgeoned.

She'd been doing this work now for several years without giving it too much thought, and on the morning of the last day of Zenithra, she realized what a fool she'd been for not realizing earlier what this project implied—that Doc Andri'n worried about the safety of Andramere's collected knowledge. Why, she didn't know, only that he had risked his life to save it.

Every morning Bryn contacted Malisha Andra'asnia to ask about her father. Most days she was ignored, though an aide would later contact her to tell her that her father was in fine health, and pending her cooperation, he would soon be released. Bryn tried to trust Anorian, to believe that her father was in the hollow, his mind safe from the Pradishar's probe, and so she said nothing to Andra'asnia about Anorian, though she was sorely tempted to, lured by the idea that it might, it really might, help save her father's life.

And so she'd put off the task Anorian had asked her to do: to enter Doc Andri'n's office at the Academicon, collect his final datamins, and install them in the servryn at the library. Just as Bryn contacted the Pradishar every day to ask about her father, so Anorian contacted Bryn every day to ask if she was ready to get the datamins. She fudged her way through Zenithra, using her carving work as an excuse, using her need to learn about the hollow as an excuse, using her mother as an excuse. But now time had run out to act. The carving project had finished, and the year was nearly over.

<<Tomorrow,>> Bryn said. <<Everyone's attention will be on the festivities on Balan Su, so the Forum should be relatively empty. Trexbo, Ginjy, and Rhingus have agreed to help me. We'll get the datamins and we'll get them installed. Happy?>>

<<Thank you, Bryn,>> Anorian said. <<I—had hoped you'd have spent more time this last month learning about the hollow. You've been—absent, lately.>>

<<I know I have,>> Bryn said. <<Normally I would have been so excited, I'd have explored something new like that for days on end, archiving everything I experienced, probably not even sleeping. But—I just can't concentrate on it. On anything. The carving work's easy. Stick in the scroll and wait. I could do it in my sleep. I think I have before, maybe. I just—I can't bear waiting like this, day after day. I don't feel like myself anymore. I don't know what's wrong with me.>>

<<Nothing is wrong with you, Bryn,>> Anorian said. <<Everything you're feeling is natural. You're a thoughtful, sensitive being, so happy to be tucked away in your nook in the library, and yet passionate enough to speak out against injustice, to stand tall and proud as your own unique self. I admire that about you so much. You—>>

<<You promised me answers,>> Bryn said. <<Where are they? I want to know a few things before I go to the Academicon tomorrow. I think I've already figured some of it out. My father—his datamins, the ones I've been carving on—they're different. I took one out of it's sheathe when I was servicing the servryn. If this is true, it means my father knows how to make datamins that don't come from the Pradishar.>>

<<Yes,>> Anorian said. <<But fortunately the Pradishar haven't figured this out yet. They're more concerned with the ability of people to resist the authority of the crystal.

Some are defying their control, and even Corkin slaves are disobeying their masters. This is their primary concern right now.>>

<<Is that—your doing? The hollow?>>

Bryn could feel Anorian's wordless confirmation in her mind.

<<And my father is using the hollow as well, in order to keep the knowledge of his datamins safe?>>

<<Correct.>>

<<But why archive the entire library?>> Bryn said. <<Why this job I've had for all these years? Why must everything be transferred to my father's datamins?>>

<<Because very soon now, the original datamins, the ones supplied exclusively by the Pradishar, will no longer function.>>

<<What do you mean, how can they not function? They're stones, are they not?>>

<<They're crystals, Bryn. That doesn't necessarily mean they're geological.>>

Bryn laughed. <<You realize this sounds crazy? The crystals have endured for ten thousand years. It's like saying the sun won't rise tomorrow, when it always has. That takes a lot of faith. Does my father believe this?>>

<<He does,>> Anorian said. <<Let's just pretend for a moment that what I've said is true. Surely you'll see the urgency of getting your father's remaining datamins into the servryn as soon as possible.>>

<<I would see that,>> Bryn said. <<Sweet Trevian, but I guess I don't have a choice, do I? Tomorrow morning then. For sure this time. I promise.>>

Bryn felt that same gratitude and warmth from Anorian once again, as if she'd been physically hugged, warmed by the sun, enveloped. She spent the afternoon putting away the workstation and supplies from the carving project, returning the last texts to their shelves and baskets in the library's vast stacks. Then the librarian Madr'gin accompanied her to the basement door and Bryn descended deep under the library to the hidden vault where her father's secret servryn was located. She installed the last of her project's datamins in the servryn, and she knew Doc Andri'n would be proud of her. She took a moment to imagine he was there congratulating her. The thought made her feel both better and worse, warm-hearted but full of tears again.

My father is a plant of reason, she thought. *What reason could there be for the datamins to stop working?*

That evening she played tiles and coins with Mama Andri'n and then called it an early night. Instead of retiring to her den, as she often did, she went into her sleeping quarters and rooted down in her old patch. She unfurled her branches and dozed. She woke the next day and emerged onto the terrace, the mid-morning sunshine streaming down on her skin and warming her face, and she sighed with pleasure.

A good way to start the day, she thought.

She had breakfast with Mama Andri'n, then Trexbo arrived in the late morning and they walked to the library together. The old city was filled with Verdillions enjoying the Balancing Act festivities, most of them also streaming the main party on Balan Su, which was four hours ahead of Andramere and already well into the afternoon. Bryn could see Ellex Andria dancing the Raccorin Trot and she wanted to gag. When they reached the royal plateau, the Forum and Academicon were both empty, as Bryn expected. Classes had ended two weeks ago, and the Camerooge of Andramere wouldn't meet again until the fall, so while the city itself was full to capacity with tourists and would be all summer long, the plateau felt like a ghost town.

Rhingus and Ginjy were waiting for Bryn at the library when they arrived. Together they crossed the empty plaza to the Academicon's campus and then to the lab building where Doc Andri'n's office was located. When they were outside his office, the door opened and they entered.

The inside had been stripped apart by the Cul'tavin, every workstation opened, every cupboard, every tool and utensil, everything examined.

"Are we too late?" Trexbo said.

<<Remember Bryn, the Cul'tavin who raided your father's office were not Dyna'arin. They don't think like tinkers,>> Anorian said.

Bryn stepped slowly through the office, holding back the tears, but letting the anger boil up inside of her. All the memories of her father in this lab, smiling, teaching, inspiring—even changing the world. This room had been a shrine to knowledge, and to see it treated with such utter disrespect by the Pradishar...

She examined everything she saw, looking for anything the peacekeepers might have missed. And then she saw the heating chamber in the corner, a large maquina nearly as tall as she was and just a little bit wider. A maquina like that would have several dynamin inside of it. These were common appliances in cookeries around Balance Territories, and unfortunately there were too many examples of Verdillions trying to tamper with them, opening the casing and accidentally overloading the dynamin. She knew there was no way a Cul'tavin would open something like that.

Bryn fidgeted with the console on the oven and shut it down completely. Then she searched the mess for her father's tools.

"What do you have, Bryndax?" Trexbo asked.

"The oven," she said. "Within the sheathing around the dynamins, I'm willing to bet my father tucked a datamin or three in there."

<<Well done,>> Anorian said.

<<I haven't found it yet,>> Bryn said, pulling open the access hatch and sliding out the innards of the maquina. Her father's last datamins were safely inside the sheathe, just as she'd expected. He'd even removed one of the dynamins to make extra room for them and to ensure the other dynamins didn't overheat.

Bryn removed them and held them up in the air, a look of triumph on her face. But her friends weren't looking. Their eyes were twitching and their mouths were hanging open in shock.

"Sweet Trevian," Rhingus whispered. "Bryndax, Balan Su, now!"

Bryn's eyes began to twitch as she picked back up the stream of the Balancing Act, and couldn't believe what she was seeing. She saw Jaun von Andron, thrashing on the ground, as a zapren jabbed him repeatedly in the stomach and in the neck. She saw explosions—dynamins overloading all over the crescent—and she could hear a sound, like a swarm of insects, as more threatened to burst. She saw fighting—everyone fighting—Pradishar, Corkin, even Bhizini raiders.

Tears rolled down her cheeks, and Rhingus was weepy too. Ginjy's face was blank as usual but she kept squeezing her hands into fists, while Trexbo paced back and forth, saying, "Oh fuck. Oh no. Oh hell no," and jumping every time he saw disturbing new footage.

<<You missed the precursor,>> Ginjy said. <<Here.>> She shared a stream with Bryn where she could see Jaun von Andron berating the Pradishar, berating Balance Authority and the Council of Nine, calling for her father's release! She quickly archived it on the servryn for later examination.

<<Bryn, you must hurry,>> Anorian said.

"We've got to focus," she said, putting up her hands and waving at everyone. "We need to get these to the library. Then we can freak out."

Trexbo jumped to attention. "Let's go," he said.

Nobody spoke on the way out of the Academicon, nor back to the library. Bryn watched streams from Balan Su with increasing alarm. There had been some kind of explosion in the Forum, blowing everyone back with tremendous force, but without any smoke or fire.

When they got to the library, Bryn told everyone to stay in the lounge while she ran to her office. Then she headed down into the vault, placed her father's final datamins inside the servryn, and closed up the panel. She double checked that she'd locked every door on the long climb back to the main floor of the library. Her friends were waiting for her, wide eyed, staring at her with alarm.

Bryn's stomach sank.

<<You need to leave Andramere, right now,>> Anorian said. <<Go to the mouth of the Clear Water. There will be a cata'rin there waiting for you.>>

<<What's happened?>> she said, as she rapidly scanned the streams, not just from Balan Su but from all of Balance Territories, and she cried out when she saw the news.

Bryn could see her father walking the streets of Andramere in shackles, as curses and filth rained down on his head. He was so thin, so pale, stumbling along like a walking corpse. He fell to his knees, coughing, as filth ran down his face. The Cul'tavin peace-keeper at his side kicked at him until he stood again.

She recognized the location. They were taking her father through Old Town to the front of the sharlum. Trexbo came and gave her a hug, and Rhingus was crying. Ginjy sent warm affection to her. She looked at each of them for a moment.

"I love you all," she said. "Don't follow me. Please, I can't be responsible for anyone else."

And then she ran before they could stop her, out of the library, down the streets of the Forum, her long thick legs pumping, her heart feeling like it might burst. She tried to keep an eye on the stream, tried to keep the tears from her vision, tried not to stumble and fall. But while crossing the bridge over the Clear Water, Bryn's foot caught the edge of a cobblestone and her ankle twisted. She fell hard, so hard the edges of her vision seemed to spark and crackle. When she stood, knives shot up her leg, and she screamed. She tried to limp quickly, but fell again.

She sobbed and screamed at the sky.

<<Please, please don't do this,>> Bryn said, reaching for Malisha Andra'asnia. <<I have information. I'm in regular contact with Anorian Grain. I can help you! Please!>>

<<I'd very much like to hear more about that,>> Malisha Andra'asnia replied. <<But I'm afraid, poor dear, that you lost your chance to help old papa. Surely you're following the streams? Your father has been tied to the attack on Balan Su. His equipment was

found in one of Balan Su's servryns. So it's a done deal. One more threat to Balance, neutralized. It's funny, you know, we never would have caught the good professor if you hadn't snooped around in the Pradishar servryn a few months ago. What do you think of that, Bryn? How's it feel to know that you are the reason your father will die?>>

Bryn hobbled down the streets of Old Town as quickly as she could, and when she caught up to the crowd, she screamed as she approached and those nearby moved aside for her to pass. She could see the stone pedestal, could see the pillar of marble that they were tying her father to. She tried to scream at them, but she was out of breathe. So she pushed on through the crowd, up the steps to the pedestal, when two Cul'tavin peacekeepers came in from the left and from the right to block the steps. Bryn looked into their faces, expecting to defy them, to lunge at them and attack them—but instead she recognized one of them—Aerid, the peacekeeper who had attacked her, twice.

And she froze, eyes wide, heart clenched, time standing still. She wanted to run, to hide, to cry. But then she saw her father, tied fast to the obelisk, and he was smiling at her.

<<The work is finished?>> he said.

<<Yes, the last datamins are safe.>>

<<Then you've saved me. I'm so proud of you, Bryndax. I—>>

The enflamers crackled to life and Doc Andri'n was engulfed in a dozen whorls of flame. Bryn felt the heat on her own skin, and she screamed, dropping to her knees, wailing.

The Cul'tavin grabbed her by either arm and pulled them behind her back. Malisha walked over, her green face divided in two, a reddish brown in the light of the flames and a dull green in the shadow, a broad grin stretching across both of them.

"Oh, did you think you were going to rescue him?" Malisha said, looking at the obelisk where Doc Andri'n remains were crackling and popping in the flames. The enflamers had been extinguished but his own flesh continued to burn. "I'm afraid you missed your chance. But it's no matter. I'm sure you're just as guilty as your father. In fact, you told me as much moments ago. I'll have a good look at everything now."

Malisha sent a restraining signal to Bryn, and she felt like all her muscles were being squeezed in a strong vise, which only seemed to get tighter the more she struggled to move.

But then the restraint lifted suddenly and Bryn fell over on the ground, the peacekeepers dropping her arms as she crashed down. She quickly rolled over, gasping for breath. Aerid was staring down at her, hatred—and victory—in his eyes.

"What do you know?" Malisha said, and reached for Bryn's mind. But her eyes grew wide, and she pointed at Bryn, her hand shaking. "She's defying me! She has the same skill as her father!"

A zapren caught Bryn in the chest and she felt like her insides were being pushed against her skin with such force that it felt she'd tear into pieces. Her vision crackled on the edges again, but she was a big plant and it would take more than that one jab to knock her out. She sat up, breathing hard.

She saw Aerid pulling out an enflamer.

"No!" Malisha hissed. "We need her alive."

Aerid took the enflamer and swung the handle at Bryn, knocking her back against the ground, and then he dug his knees into her arms. "Miss me?" he whispered. "Looks like we'll be getting to spend a lot more time together."

But Bryn fell away from him, down into darkness, into nothingness, into nonexistence, to the void at the very core of her being.

Anorian caught her.

<<You're safe now, love.>> Anorian had turned into a kindly old woman, and she was holding Bryn in her arms, stroking her hair fibers, and gently rocking her. Bryn could smell smoke on her skin, the salt of the sea, and the aroma of coco oil, but she couldn't see her face.

<<You just stay here with me. I gotcha. Don't listen—don't feel what's going on outside. I got ya, and you're safe. Just stay here—no, stay here and don't resist 'em, or they gonna make it so much worse. Just close your eyes a little, go on now, there, and stay with me, right here. I got you now, and you're safe, so long as you stay here with me. We're—we're gonna be okay, Bryndax, you'll see. We're gonna be okay, and you're gonna be okay. And I'm gonna be okay, too. We don't have a choice. We've got to be.>>

Chapter 31

The Helpless Omnipotent

Fin'roq stepped through the doors into the chamber of the Gran Pradesh, looking straight ahead to avoid the sense of vertigo he felt whenever he looked down and saw the reflection of the ceiling in the floor, which was reflecting the floor and it's reflections too, on and on into infinity.

He felt numb and his eyes burned. He just wanted to sleep, forever. But he thought of Jaun, he remembered the pain, and he continued onward.

Ra'shard Ruu'n was on his perch when Fin approached, a beam of light falling down on him from the darkness above.

"I'm glad to see you again, Fin'roq," he said. "I'd hoped you'd come visit me more often, but I suppose you've been wrapped up in your studies. How are things?"

"Terrible, your worship," Fin said. "No, they've been wonderful. Truly. Until they weren't. I have terrible news. The Ren'fallow. They contacted me, just as you warned. They wanted my help. To denounce the Pradishar during today's Balancing Act. To call for the overthrow of the Council of Nine." He was weeping now.

The Gran Pradesh stretched out his limbs a bit and looked eagerly at Fin'roq. "You're very brave for coming here today, Fin. Tell me, who is this conspirator?"

"Jaun von Andron," he said.

It was done.

"But I'm not sure if he was being serious," Fin added quickly. "I mean—he's a performer, a trouper. So sometimes I don't know when he's being honest or when he's just practicing a role. I mean, I don't think he's a traitor. He can't be, right? Oh Sweet Trevian, what have I done?" He collapsed to his knees and put his forehead on the ground, prostrating himself before the Gran Pradesh. "Help me, your worship, please."

"Don't fret, kind one," Ruu'n said. "I'm honored that you have trusted me with this knowledge. You had a terrible responsibility, but you've handled it perfectly. I will have my

Octa'vin investigate, and alert the Cul'tavin to be ready should anything happen. You've done well, Fin."

"If I've done well, then why do I feel so miserable?"

The Gran Pradesh sighed. "Because doing the right thing always comes with sacrifice," Ruu'n said. "When Trevian came to our realm so many years ago, he faced a terrible crisis. Verdillions were tearing themselves apart. Their lust to kill one another ended up destroying an entire continent and nearly collapsing the delicate balance between all three realms. When Trevian saw this, he had a choice. He could have left our realm, left us to destroy one another. But instead he brought peace to the world, although it took the ultimate sacrifice to do so. He did it because there was no other way. And when he tore himself apart, I can only imagine he must have felt like an utter failure, having won peace only by giving up everything, by dying rather than living. And yet—here we are, at ten thousand years of peace and prosperity, still thriving on Trevian's sacrifice, still wholly dependent on his gift to the world."

"I guess so," Fin said. "I mean—You're right, your worship. My sacrifice doesn't seem so big when compared to what Trevian had to endure."

"That wasn't the point of my story," the Gran Pradesh said, chuckling. "It was to make you see that painful choices, and seemingly terrible events, can often lead to great things. I suppose it's a matter of scale, Fin. And of perspective."

Fin'roq wasn't sure what to say, afraid to contradict the old Raccorin, so he said nothing.

"You may have saved the city today," the Gran Pradesh said. "And that will make you a hero in everyone's eyes. Won't that be nice, Fin? I suppose that's the other side of sacrifice. Trevian couldn't have known we'd continue to worship him for ten thousand years, could he? Imagine how you might be worshipped one day, should you stay on the righteous path. Wouldn't that be nice?"

Fin'roq pictured the entire city cheering for him, calling his name, asking for blessings, naming their little ones after him.

"Yes," he said. "That would be nice."

"You're a good and kind plant, Fin," Ruu'n said. "Tell me son, what are your plans for the rest of the summer? I can make sure the priestins have some special training sessions for you at the Pruu'patch, though the city is quiet and empty in the summers. Unless you planned to return to P'anorum?"

"I—guess I hadn't thought about it. I don't even know if anyone there is still alive."

"If you stay, I'll make sure your season here is well spent, Fin. Now, you head on back to the Pruu'patch, and lay low for the day, won't you? Rest up and be kind to yourself for a few days."

"Thank you, your worship," Fin said.

"No, thank you. You've proven yourself a worthy recruit, as I knew you would be."

Fin nodded, bowed, and left the citadel. He could hear the crowd out in the plaza, and he debated going back inside and taking the underground corridor to the Pruu'patch so he could avoid everyone. Probably best to lay low, like the Gran Pradesh said.

But instead he pulled up his hood and walked out into the swarm of people filling Grand Plaza from end to end and side to side. Thousands and thousands of Verdillions, and in the distance he could see that awful Andrasian, Ellex Andria, and some Raccorin he'd never seen before, standing on an earthen mound, speaking to the crowd, dancing and laughing. In fact, everyone around him was dancing or laughing, drinking or eating. Even with such a festive atmosphere, with smiles and laughter all around him, it wasn't enough to get his mind off of Jaun. If anything, it made it worse.

He slinked off through the crowd toward the Forum. The sun was dropping low in the sky and the horns began to sound when they brought forth Qardymion the Saltsap, the captured Bhizini rebel, in chains. They'd been in the Dankburn deep under the citadel, and they emerged clad with heavy shackles of metal around their arms and legs. Their patches of bright green looked too dull, and their dull patches looked almost gray, and their legs were trembling from so much darkness. Qardymion stepped out into the light and visibly sighed when the beams hit their face, and for a moment, Fin thought he looked like Jaun. A nearby Cul'tavin, seeing their pleasure, jammed them in the back of the knee and Qardymion collapsed onto the cobblestones. The crowd cheered, and Fin'roq felt the back of his throat burning, felt his hands clenching together.

The Saltsap was marched across the plaza and in front of the Weeping Wilvryn tree, so the Andrasian and Raccorin hosts could glare and gawk at them. Fin followed the procession, which then moved along from the tree and toward the Forum on the western side of the upper rim. The Andrasian and the Raccorin retreated into the branches of the tree as the parade moved forward.

Fin followed the crowd into the Forum, along the main avenue to the oval plaza that Jaun had shown him yesterday. Was that only yesterday? Was that possible? Tears were stinging his eyes again.

And that was when he saw Jaun. He was climbing onto the stage, grinning widely, waving at the crowds, which were cheering and calling his name. Fin looked around but the nearby Cul'tavin weren't doing anything, weren't moving to stop him. The parade entered the plaza and the Cul'tavin peacekeepers secured Qardymion to a statue next to the stage, and Fin'roq moved as close as he could.

"To everyone in Balan Su, to everyone in all of Balance Territories, to the Andrasians and the Raccorin, to my lovelies back on Andramere, to everyone everywhere—welcome!" The crowd was screaming with glee. "With pleasure I welcome you to the new year, the 10,000th Cycle of Balance. And, I'm sad to announce, the last one for Balance Authority."

The crowd laughed awkwardly, and everyone was turning to look at their neighbor with confused looks.

Don't do it, Fin thought. *Don't do it, please. Please Jaun, don't. Sweet Trevian, don't let him.*

But Jaun did it. He did it with fire and with tears, with heartbreak and with rage, the performance of his life. The Cul'tavin, listening in shocked silence along with everyone else, finally moved, swarming the stage. Fin saw a zapren connect with Jaun's stomach and another with his neck, saw his face twist up in surprise and pain, saw him fall to the ground as peacekeepers leapt on top of him. He put his hands by his mouth and screamed, "Jaun!" but nobody could hear amongst the roar of the crowd.

And he heard a swarm of insects, as if a massive beehive had just fallen from a branch in a storm, and then a rumbling like an avalanche on the slopes of P'anorum, the deep crash of a building being torn apart, and a hiss as smoke and debris shot into the sky from the industrial quarter. The crowd began to panic, moving about in every direction. And then there were screams, and Fin saw cloaked figures, swords hacking, spinning about through the plaza, cutting down everyone they passed.

Fin got knocked in the side in the ensuing commotion and he fell into a large figure, his hood falling off his face as he stumbled for balance. The Raccorin he'd bumped into turned and saw his face and his eyes grew wide.

"Bhizini!" he screamed, and he punched Fin in the jaw, knocking him backward onto the ground. Others nearby turned and when they saw him, there was hatred in their eyes. They came toward him, kicking with their feet, jamming them into his chest and into his flower.

When he heard Jaun's voice, full of pain, screaming his name, he tried to reach out for him but he could feel himself falling, down into darkness.

But then Fin whipped up onto his feet, and the crowd fell back, crying out in surprise. His eyes had rolled back in his head and his skin looked gray, shiny, almost silver. His hands were out on either side of him and he turned slowly in a circle. He pulled his hands together into a ball, then pushed them outward from himself, and like a wave hitting a crowded beach, those around Fin were thrown backward, the ones closest to him launched into nearby buildings from the blast, while the ones near the edge of the plaza were knocked over to the ground—citizens and Cul'tavin and Corkin, all thrust aside—but not everyone.

Cloaked figures remained in the plaza, untouched by the outburst. They all turned toward Fin'roq now, and moved in on him from every side, stepping over the bodies on the ground. He reached out for them, his eyes shimmering, but they were not slowed. He thrust with his mind to attack them, but they were unmoved. And when they knocked him to the ground, the last thing Fin'roq saw as he slipped down into darkness were Bhizini faces staring at him.

Part 2
Tender Shoots

Chapter 32

Anything for Redemption

R AKK RAEDER WATCHED THE needle enter his arm—watched as his thick sap began to flow down the long narrow tube, inch by inch, away from his body and toward his brother. The amber fluid stung as it left his skin, and when it finally reached Rajj's arm and began to flow inside him, Rakk marveled at it. He felt ill, not from the transfusion but from the lack of sunshine, from the heavy bhiza intoxication he'd endured, and even though he knew giving his sap would only weaken him further, he hadn't hesitated to open his veins for his brother, to do whatever he could to save Rajj's life.

Q'orin handed Rakk another rhupan crisp. "My prince must regain his strength," he said.

But Rakk looked at Rajj's pale face, at the stump where his arm should have been, and he waved Q'orin away.

"This is my fault," he said.

"You heard the healers," Q'orin said. "Prince Rajesh'n will be fine. This transfusion will heal him. And a Guild prosthetic will give him his arm back."

"And the rest of the city? What about them?"

Q'orin looked away and said nothing.

"I'm to blame, and there's no way around it. And now it's all lost. My career. My future. My crown. All gone."

Uthyr Andria entered the lab and Rakk could tell he wasn't expecting to find him there. But he shook off the expression and turned to face him.

"Thank Trevian you're alive," Uthyr said. "What happened to you?"

"I came here as soon as I could," he said, looking at Rajj again. "I had to make sure—"

Uthyr saw the long tube of sap connecting their arms. "I see," he said softly. "Thank you."

"He's my twin brother. We grew together in the sprouting patch."

"I know," Uthyr said, look at Rajj.

"Where's Ellex?" Rakk asked.

"Occupied," Uthyr said, narrowing his eyes slightly.

Rakk was desperate to talk to her, to reach out to her, to get on his knees and beg her forgiveness—but he couldn't call to her, couldn't face her. He just knew she hated him and never wanted to see him again. He deserved it.

The lab door opened and a slender Andrasian entered, looking frazzled. His pale skin was nearly gray and his hands were a bit shaky, and he had bruises on his face.

"Prince Rhakksees, good," he said. "I'm Hesh'n Von'nDrino, a tinker with the Dyna'arin. I'll be constructing Prince Rajesh'n's new arm. I think you're going to be quite impressed with it. I've perfected the technique myself. I'm so confident in my work, I wager you won't be able to tell it's not the prince's own arm."

Rakk remembered the whine of maquina as he lay paralyzed on the cold floor of the tunnel under Balan Su, the whir of the fans, the clanking of the pipes, as bhiza was pumped continuously into the chamber, keeping him paralyzed for days. Only the Guild could have supplied, or maintained, such equipment. But it was too early to jump to any conclusions. And there was no reason to doubt they would help Rajj.

"Spare no expense," Rakk said.

"Of course not," Hesh'n said.

Rajj moaned and the Me'dicant healer touched his face and felt his forehead.

"That will do for today, Prince Rhakksees," the healer said, removing the needle from Rajj's arm, then pulling the other end out of Rakk's vein.

Rajj's eyes fluttered open and he looked around, blinking rapidly. He smacked his lips together, and Rakk grabbed a cup of water and held it to his lips. Rajj looked at Uthyr, then stared into Rakk's as he drank. When he was finished, he took a few deep breaths.

"Hi, handsome," Rakk said, grinning at him, and trying not to think about how small he looked, how frail.

Rajj was always so weak, he thought. Rakk had always been able to dominate his brother in any physical task or sport, though Rajj had always beat him at the mental ones. Rakk might not have been the nicest twin when they were younger. There was none of that special bonding between them that some twins shared. They hadn't openly hated each other, but Rakk was a huge, loud, whirlwind of a guy, and Rajj was quiet, pensive, cautious, his nose always in a scroll or his eyes fluttering as he streamed the weavryn.

Rakk took his hand and squeezed it, and Rajj gave him a small smile.

"All those years you tried to avoid war wounds," Rakk said, looking at his stump, "and now you end up worse off than me." When he saw Rajj's face, he added, "But don't worry. Hesh'n here is going to fix you up a new arm, just like the old one. Isn't that right, tinker?"

"You won't even remember you lost it," Hesh'n said.

"I'm sorry to interrupt," the Me'dicant said, "but Prince Rajesh'n needs his sleep. I'll have to ask you to come back later."

"No," Rajj said, little more than a whisper. "No," he said again, louder. "I need to speak to my brother."

"I'll check with you both later," Hesh'n said, seeing himself out.

Uthyr put his hand on Rajj's shoulder. "I'll make sure the delegation knows you're healing," he said, and Rajj gave him a small smile and a nod.

"Five minutes," the healer said, moving toward the door.

Q'orin nodded at Rakk as he stepped outside with the others.

He grinned at his brother again. "Who knew you were so tough? If I'd have known, I'd have picked on you a little more!"

Rajj glared, then sighed. "Where were you? I should be furious with you, but for some reason I'm not. Maybe it's the lack of sap? Or maybe I'm just used to your foolishness by now." He winced.

"Does it hurt?" Rakk asked.

"Just tell me you had a good reason for abandoning your post."

"I didn't abandon my post. You sound like one of the notestreamers! You should at least know me that well."

"That's why I'm asking," Rajj said.

"Cut me some slack," Rakk said. "You know I'd die before I'd let anyone hurt my family."

"And you're including me?" Rajj said. "How sweet."

Rakk had to swallow a hiss. "Someone led me into a trap."

"Someone?"

"One of my Corkin. Rhannokti."

"That beastly toy of yours?"

"He was ordered to guard the harbor, but he was here on the upper rim, at the tiny house. I thought—well I thought he was Father. His look—his scent. I reached for him—I could feel his crystal, and I tried to detain him—but he slipped out of my grasp—I could feel myself losing him—and then he hit me with a wave of contempt and loathing and defiance as no slave has ever done before. And then he was gone from my awareness, as if his crystal had suddenly ceased to exist. When he ran, fool that I am, I chased him."

Rajj sighed. "Because it wasn't obvious."

"Like I said, I'm a fool."

"I've only said that, oh, my entire life."

Rakk ignored him. "He also told me that he's our brother."

"Another one?" Rajj looked exhausted and let out a slow sigh.

"What do you mean, another one?"

"Tell me you aren't so naive? You remember Father's trips around the world, the month at Andramere every summer, his lavish parties, the festivals he held so dear. He coupled with everyone he had a fancy to couple with, regardless of who they were, where they were from, their station. It's only obvious some of them would plant their fruit. Many Raccorin and Bhizini have made such claims over the years—and even more were prepared to—but we were always able to nip such conspiracies in the bud, to silence such scandals before they were able to start."

"Why wasn't I informed?"

"Informed? I tried, and tried, and tried again to communicate with you. What more was I to do? You wanted nothing to do with me, so after a decade of silence, I gave up. And in the meantime, I went about keeping our family safe. Keeping our mandate safe. Keeping your throne safe!"

Rakk's face burned with shame and he clenched his teeth in anger.

"I've spent months here trying to organize security, and you never once agreed to see me without others around, without notestreamers asking questions and fawning over us. Damnit Rajj, I snuck into the capital to try and see you, sibling to sibling, and you threw me in the dungeon. Why do you have to keep punishing me?"

Rajj looked like he might cry and he closed his eyes for a moment. Then he looked at Rakk and shook his head.

"I'm sorry. This isn't what I want. I want you to know that. This isn't what I want."

"What do you mean?" Rakk said, when he felt a cry from Q'orin in his mind and he spun toward the door just as it opened.

A dozen Cul'tavin peacekeepers, zaprens in hand, poured through the opening and quickly surrounded Rakk and Rajj. Uthyr walked in behind them, glanced at Rajj, then looked at Rakk and his eyes began twitching.

Rakk felt his skin tingling, his back muscles spasm, a pull in the back of his neck that seemed to push his head down toward his body. He tried to move, but his legs had gone stiff—his arms too—everything had frozen in place, except his eyes, which darted around in a panic.

He'd never felt such a thing in his life, and the harder he struggled to move, the more his body began to ache, his muscles to throb, his fibers to feel like they might snap.

"Did you think there wouldn't be consequences for your failure?" Uthyr said. "Now that you're a crystamin-holding bishrop of the Pradishar, you are subject to the will of the Pradishar. We no longer need the authority of the Raccorin crown to restrain you."

Rakk looked at Rajj but his eyes were still closed.

"If you're really innocent, then the truth will sort itself out," Uthyr said. "In the meantime, your old cell is waiting for you in the Dankburn. Come along."

Rakk felt the restraint lifting, like a heavy weight had been removed from his back. He looked at the Cul'tavin peacekeepers, at Uthyr, and knew they were too many to fight, and they'd just restrain him again anyway. So he followed where they told him to go, and like an obedient slave, he marched to the lift, dropped down under the island to the Dankburn, and went back into his cell. Uthyr pulled the bars behind him. When Rakk turned around, he was already gone.

He slumped to the floor and clenched his hands into tight fists, and he ground his teeth together and took long, slow breaths, feeling something that we wasn't sure he could describe, like no other emotion he'd experienced before—it was the first time, in all his long life of privilege, that he'd been restrained by a crystal, his body rendered useless, as if it were no longer his own.

It was the first time he'd been a slave and not the master. And he didn't have words yet for how it felt.

❧ ❧

Rakk spent a week in the Dankburn, mulling his fate.

Q'orin contacted him as soon as he woke—he'd taken a zapren to the chest when the Cul'tavin came to arrest him—and he promised to do all he could to petition for his release. But Rakk told him not to bother. It was better if they just left him there to petrify in the darkness. At least if he went mad, he might forget his failure.

But Q'orin wouldn't stop pestering him and the Pradishar wouldn't let him die. Instead, Me'dicant healers came down twice a day to tend to his wounds, to make sure his rhupan was supplemented, and to insist he stay within the meager beams of light that streamed through the slats in the wall. He ignored them until one of the healers threatened to fetch Uthyr if he didn't comply. The thought of being compelled like that again—he scampered into the light, unwilling to let himself be shocked at how easily he'd folded.

When Rajj appeared in front of his cell, Rakk turned his back to him.

"Go away, Rajesh'n," he said.

"I won't."

"Please."

"No."

"I don't want you to see me like this."

"I'm not leaving without you." The metal bars slid back and Rajj pulled the door open with his good arm. "Are you coming?"

Rakk looked at his brother standing there beckoning him—his color and strength had returned and Rakk could tell he was going to be okay. "No," Rakk said. "Just leave me here."

Rajj sighed. "Why is it that the big, loud, blustering ones are always the biggest cowards—always the first to throw in and give up when the going gets tough? All your life, you've talked about how much you want to be king some day, but you're never willing to play the game. Every little setback has you running off half-cocked, ready to quit. Was it any different the night we lost P'anorum?"

Rakk felt like he'd been slapped, and he looked at Rajj and narrowed his eyes. "Take it back," he said, trying to sound angry, but he could hardly whisper.

"You want me to take back a fact, brother? You're pathetic. How can you presume to rule if you can't even accept things the way they are?"

"Accept things? I have accepted things! Why do you think I want you to leave me here to rot? That's what I deserve. It's you who isn't accepting things!"

"Immature, as always," Rajj said.

Rakk hissed. "So that's it, then? I'm just—forgiven? Out of the dungeon and—what?"

"You haven't been released," Rajj said.

Rakk looked at his brother, his scowl replaced with confusion.

Rajj rolled his eyes. "Great Sower in the sky, how are we related? I'm sneaking you out! Now come on already, you're messing up my schedule."

"Wait!" Rakk said. "You can't risk yourself like this. Your position on the Council—"

"I'll explain everything when we get to the surface. Seriously, it's terrible seeing you like this. As much as I hate your bravado, this is even worse somehow. Now get yourself together. You act like all is lost, but as long as there's air in your lungs and sap in your veins, you're still in this thing. Now are you going to help me find who's responsible for your betrayal and my poor lost arm—not to mention the sacking of the capital—and help me make them pay dearly for their mistakes? Or are you going to sit here and mope while Raq'asha steals your throne and the notestreamers decimate your legacy?"

Rakk hardened his face. "They say vengeance never pays."

"I'm talking about justice. And justice is its own reward. Now can I count on your help, or not?"

"How will you explain this?"

"I don't have to. The Council of Nine has adjourned for the summer, and they're content to let you sit here til the fall and then deal with you if you've survived the season. And those who might notice your absence have been compensated for their cooperation."

"I never knew you were so devious," Rakk said.

"Yes, you did," Rajj said.

"You're right, I did," Rakk said. "So tell me then, dear sib. What is it you really want from me?"

Rajj smiled thinly. "Your help, what else? One good deed requires another, does it not?"

Rakk looked at his brother, his heart pounding—was Rajj Anorian Grain?—but no, the phrase was a common one. From the Pruu'log or something. Right?

"Meaning?"

"Come on, let's talk when we get upstairs. You need some light, and I need some fresh air." He crinkled his nose. "Here, put this on." He handed him a pradeshan robe. "We can talk in Corda'mere."

They rode the lift in silence, and Rakk ventured onto the weavryn, daring to see what everyone was saying about him. Were they gloating that he was rotting in the Dankburn? Celebrating his downfall? But no, it was worse than that. Some thought him dead but most thought he'd purposely betrayed Balance and fled.

When they got to the surface, Rakk pulled his hood down low over his face, but the citadel wasn't busy, and they exited into Corda'mere without incident. Once in the thickets along the flank of the spire, they found a small clearing with a stone fountain and Rakk took off his robe, dropped his roots into the soil, and unfurled his branches toward the sky. His leaftips flattened out and angled to absorb as much of the nourishing sunshine as they could.

He moaned with pleasure.

"Keep it down," Rajj snapped, "or someone will think we're coupling over here."

"Then they'll be sure to stay away, won't they."

"Or they'll come closer for a better look."

"Always the pessimist," Rakk said. "Hey, why don't you come back in, oh, a few days? Let me drink up my fill before you hit me with all the bad news."

Rajj sighed. "I'll be back in two hours."

"You're the boss, boss," Rakk said, grinning.

Rajj rolled his eyes. "I'll make sure you aren't disturbed."

"Thanks, sibby," Rakk said.

"You haven't called me that since we were scamps. And I don't think you've *ever* thanked me."

Rakk laughed. "No? Must have never had reason to. I'm a grateful sort of guy, you know."

Rajj narrowed his eyes, then relaxed them. "Well, I should return the favor. For the sap transfusion. The healers—they said it really helped. So, thank you."

"No need," Rakk said. "You'd do the same for me."

"Yes, but I'm much nicer than you are," Rajj said, grinning. "See you in two hours."

❧ ☙

Rajj gave Rakk four hours to soak up the sunshine instead of just two. When he returned, Rakk was doing some stretches on the grass, his skin a deep, bright green.

"Looking like a new sprout," Rajj said.

"Thanks to you. I appreciate the extra time. I needed it."

"It was foolish of the Cul'tavin to put you in the dungeon after you'd just spent so much time in the tunnels, and after having just given me that transfusion. They were needlessly reckless with your health, and I want you to know that I disapproved of their decision and I made my protests known, even to the Gran Pradesh. I don't hold you responsible for the attack, and I think the Pradishar will exonerate you, when they get around to collecting evidence. But we know how slow the government moves, and if we wait for them to act, we'll have lost more than just the summer. Rakk—I think Raq'asha is preparing to move against us. She means to take your throne, and to have a loyalist replace me on the Council of Nine."

Rakk hissed. "Why am I not surprised. She's been trying to sabotage my offshore operations. She's angry at us, both of us, for abandoning her."

"I don't know about you but I've hardly abandoned her."

"You spend most of the year on Balan Su. And I can't imagine you were happy when Father named her regent."

Rajj blushed lightly. "I made it clear she had my full support, but that I had a career to attend to here in the capital. Now the Clades are quarreling among themselves, but so far they don't seem to have formed any kind of coalition. I've done what I can to continue sowing dissent amongst them. But with this attack, and all that's happened, those sympathetic for a bigger change are growing bolder, not just at home but here too, and on the weavryn. Raq'asha may soon have enough of the Clades on her side to call for Rishar."

"But that would be suicide," Rakk said. "Her mandate is our family's mandate."

"Unless she makes the claim it isn't."

"She wouldn't. She couldn't. The Pradishar would just revoke her crystals and those of her followers."

"Not necessarily, and not if she stakes her claim through Rishar. I think she intends to portray you and I as lifelong outsiders to Raccorum Rhazzat, far too cozy with the Andrasians to serve the good of the Raccorin. If a majority of the Clades choose a new mandate, by the Accords of Balance, the Pradishar will have to recognize it."

Rakk looked at Rajj like he was crazy, but his insides were doing summersaults. "Rhannokti," he said. "His defiance. Have the Pradishar already given Raq'asha her own crystals? Is she assembling her own Corkin army?"

"That might be why Rhannokti could defy you, but we can't know for sure if they have, or not."

"There's something you aren't telling me."

Rajj looked around and his eyes fluttered briefly. "I'm committing a crime against information by telling you this, but there's a precedent for defiance of the crystal mandate. Blocked scans. Scrubbed metadata. Looping memories. Even the ability to vanish entirely from the weavryn, as if you didn't exist in the crystal realm anymore. We've linked the skill to a conspirator called Anorian Grain. We have several in custody who can hide themselves in this way, but because of their abilities, it's been difficult to find any information."

"Anorian Grain," Rakk said, his face draining of color. He thought of the capture of Qardymion, the way Grain had hand-fed him the coordinates. And now the Saltsap had escaped, rescued during the first sack of Balan Su in ten thousand years of Balance. Rakk had been hand-fed his coordinates by Anorian. Had it all been a setup? Had Rakk set the entire attack in motion by bringing the Saltsap to the capital?

Rajj didn't notice his face. "Grain is almost certainly an alias for a Dyna'arin tinker who's used the servryns to thoroughly muck up our surveillance apparatus, and is the likely culprit behind the incident with Ellex Andria."

Rakk hissed but it faltered, drawing out in a long, weary groan. "Has Rishar been called yet?" he said, changing the subject back to his sister. "No, I would know." He hoped that was true.

"Raq'asha won't move until her pieces are in place. And until we know what all her pieces are, we can't do much of anything."

"Wrong," Rakk said. "Stop dancing about the fire and throw in the log already. You busted me out for a reason. What do you want me to do?"

Rajj pressed his lips together and hissed out his nose. "Since you asked so nicely—I want you to go to Callo Baton. I need you to snoop for the Council of Nine, and for me. Find me the information we need, and I'll make sure the Pradishar clear your name. The details are on this datamin."

"Callo Baton was going to be my first stop anyway," he said.

"Second stop," Rajj said. "You'll need bhiza to slip past the scanners. A special blend that won't warp your mind but will numb your crystal. And if you value your throne—and your life—you'll keep eating it until you've found what you're after and gotten somewhere safe. If Raq'asha knows you're snooping... Heck, if she realizes you've left the Dankburn—!"

"I can find the bhiza on Nunan," Rakk said.

"How will you get off the crescent?"

"I snuck in, didn't I? I think I can sneak out."

"Very well. Good luck then. Oh, and if you try to implicate me in any of this, I'll vehemently deny all of it. And if you don't fancy returning to the Dankburn, then don't come back to Balan Su without answers—and evidence!"

"I wouldn't dream of letting you down," Rakk said.

"Not again, you mean?" Rajj said. "I hope you're being sincere. I never can tell with you—always joking around and goofing off."

"Who, me?" Rakk said.

Rajj rolled his eyes, then grinned. "Do be careful, and don't do anything foolish. Head straight for Nunan, and straight to Callo Baton. The clock really is ticking."

"Straight to Nunan," he said. "After I see Ellex Andria."

"Oh—right. Rakk, Ellex is gone."

"Gone? What do you mean gone?" The panic was back.

"She's left for the summer. For Andramere. And there's something else. So far we've kept it off the notestreams, and again, it's a crime against information for telling you this, but you should know. And I'm afraid you aren't going to like it."

Rakk didn't like it. Not one bit.

Chapter 33

When Love Turns the World Around

THE FOG RETURNED WITH a vengeance on the day after the Balancing Act, swelling high up above the upper rim and shrouding the mourning city, blotting out the sun—which meant life and warmth and hope—and matching the mood of grief and despair that everyone was projecting, crystal or not. Ellex Andria's city needed her, Balance Authority needed her, Uthyr and Rajj needed her. Nobody asked what Ellex Andria needed. Nobody really seemed to care.

My memories, she thought.

Ellex didn't know either, what she needed. She just kept seeing the dream, over and over again, in her mind. King Rhakksees II, P'anorum, the heads being chopped off, one after another. The scamp in the stasis chamber—not a scamp, her scamp, her own scamp, her only scamp. Right here in her city, all those years. Right under her feet.

I'm a mother, she thought. *Sweet Trevian, save me.*

She'd finally been able to bring her daughter home after a long and agonizing night, watching Rhyntysha Rorh carefully remove the sensitive maquina embedded in her body, as her daughter moaned and whimpered and finally succumbed to the bhiza they'd given her to calm her. She was perched now in the garden, getting what nourishment she could from the white light filtering through the fog.

Ellex didn't know if that would be enough.

She didn't know anything anymore.

My father...

The Council of Nine had called a meeting, yet again. So many meetings that day. She was needed, everywhere. So far nothing had hit the notestreams, no chatter on the weavryn, an enormous blessing disguised as a small one, considering all the terrible things that had befallen the capital. The world already knew she'd been pollinated by King Rhakksees. If they knew she'd had a scamp, they'd never leave her alone, there'd be no end to the harassment. Her career would be over, her legacy ruined.

The Guild...the Pradishar...my scamp...

Ellex left two dozen Cul'tavin guarding her estate—her closest and most trusted peace-keepers—and Pander assured her he'd contact her the moment anything changed. The old Andrasian kept wiping tears off his face as Ellex spoke to him. But she had no choice—she had to be out and about, tending to the affairs of the capital, even if—and she could hardly believe she was thinking it—she couldn't care less about anything other than her daughter.

The Solarium was already filled with the other members of the Council when she arrived and took her place on the dais, all but Rajj, who was still in critical condition, and Rameen Rutar, who had left for Callo Baton before the Balancing Act. In her mind, she used Pander's eyes to keep watch on her garden, and she saw her daughter still sleeping, a peaceful look on her tiny face. Ellex wanted to cry with relief.

She called the session to order and asked Cort Andramon, the manager of Balan Su, to speak on the current situation. The news was grim, but Ellex couldn't help but feel it could have been worse. The invaders seemed to have only Qardymion the Saltsap on their mind, and vacated the city soon after reclaiming them. Most of the carnage had come from either the dynamin meltdowns in maquina around the city, or from the skirmishes that broke out between the Cul'tavin and the Corkin, a disastrous blow to the Defenders and to her hopes to integrate the two sides of Balance into one fighting force.

Cort Andramon spoke for nearly an hour, and Ellex found herself admiring his humility and compassion, and she took a moment to access his docket and commend him. He'd spent the last twenty four hours speaking to the public, keeping them informed as best he could, the visible presence of Balance Authority, and Ellex knew he'd probably saved the city from going mad with panic.

When he finished speaking, Ellex stood again and motioned to her brother.

Uthyr stood and spoke. "Some of you will have heard of a strange occurrence in the Forum, or seen the stream already, of some sort of explosion without any smoke or fire. We've analyzed the visual and auditory data from several hundred witnesses, and we can confirm that the perpetrator is one of the Pradishar's own, a monkin not yet joined to the crystal called Fin'roq. You will note that this same Fin'roq was responsible for the death of one of our monkins on P'anorum under similarly suspicious and unexplainable circumstances. Given the explosions of the dynamins, and the tampering with servryns we later discovered, we suggest explaining the incident to the public as an energy discharge from overloaded dynamins."

"And where is the Bhizini Fin'roq?" Ellex asked.

"We believe he left with the invaders," Uthyr said.

Ellex knew she should be angry, furious even. She'd warned Ra'shard Ruu'n not to let him into the capital. She'd insisted he leave before the Balancing Act. And now this. But then she took a peek through Pander's eyes, saw her daughter's face again, and the anger just wouldn't come.

Malisha Andra'asnia's double stood to speak. "Will this council continue to pretend that the Bhizini are the biggest threat we face? Sweet Trevian, why am I not being heard? I have proof that Doc Bryncent Andri'n intended to sabotage the servryns of Balan Su and Andramere, and was working in league with Lithuigi Von'nDrino to subvert Balance. Along with Anorian Grain, these rebels are undermining the authority of the crystal, avoiding scans and probes, even imperialization, which threatens the very foundation of our civilization. And I've been fighting this fight alone. I've done what I can to isolate potential threats, to keep them far from any servryn, but it's clear we're losing this fight. I's clear that this council should move to preference the safety of our civilians and the survival of our society over the safety of Guild trade secrets, since this attack never would have happened had the Pradishar had all the information we needed beforehand—"

"But Balance wouldn't survive without the Guild," Uthyr said, "and there wouldn't be a Guild without the Pradishar. Each one depends on the other. That's how Balance works. Until I see evidence—-"

Ellex slammed her hand against her podium. "Evidence? For Trevian's sake, isn't there enough for you yet? There is for me. I can't believe I'm saying this, but I agree with Malisha Andra'asnia. This council is a failure, a joke."

<<Come on, you don't mean that,>> Uthyr said through the crystal. <<You just need some rest. You have a lot to deal with.>>

<<Some rest? For fuck's sake Utte, wake up!>> she screamed directly in his mind. <<Someone had a scamp—my scamp, our own family—locked away right under our feet, right here in the Pradishar's own holy capital. Within the spire itself! Inside Guild-supplied and Guild-maintained maquina. And we sat here, oblivious to it all.>>

Ellex dared not speak aloud to the council, dare not risk her life, or the life of her daughter, by revealing her existence. But how long could she keep it a secret? Until Vilder Von'nDrino blabbed about what they'd found in his father's lab?

She sighed. "I apologize to the Council for my outburst. Malisha, you have my support in pushing for more information from the Dyna'arin. And I agree that our top priority should be finding and detaining Anorian Grain. Balance has always prevailed, and will prevail again. The builders are repairing the city, and the Me'dicants are tending those who are injured. Our Guild representatives have already left for the summer, so we will make no progress here today. Let us adjourn the Council as planned and reconvene at season's end."

"Are you sure that's wise?" Uthyr said. "If the notestreamers gets the idea that we've abandoned our responsibilities during a crisis…"

But the Council voted to adjourn til the equinox at summer's end, and Ellex was relieved.

Her brother found her after the meeting ended.

"I think this is a bad idea," Uthyr said. "It's going to look like we were too spoiled to give up our summer vacation, especially if something else happens. I mean—"

"Not now, Utte. I need to get home."

"I'll walk you."

"No. I mean, thank you, but I'd like a bit of time to myself."

"At least some things haven't changed," he said. "I'm here for you, Ellie Ann."

"You haven't called me that since we were scamps."

"I suppose I've been thinking a lot of family lately. You really shouldn't be alone right now."

"I'm never alone," she said, eyeing Uthyr's crystals. "Are any of us?"

She didn't wait for an answer.

When Ellex reached her garden, she found her daughter where she'd left her before the council meeting, on a lounger in the meager light of the sun as it filtered down through the fog, her little feet against the soil. Her eyes were still closed and Ellex sat and watched her sleep.

She's so tiny, even amongst the bandages.

There would always be scars from the maquina that had been implanted in her body. The healers said it looked like they had been doing the work of her organs, keeping her alive and slowing down the aging process. She shuddered. How she hated maquina—the sound, the smell, the cold touch of the metal. The danger that lurked inside. She'd seen so, so many mangled and burned bodies from countless operator accidents over her lifetime. But she'd never seen maquina like these. Never ones that stuck halfway inside someone's flesh.

Ellex knew it was a miracle she'd survived; that it would be a miracle if she woke up, if she was able to eat, to speak, to start growing normally, to have a regular life.

She'll never have a regular life.

She couldn't pretend the stasis chamber was the only reason.

I have a daughter. That tiny, poor little thing. Thirty three years old and no bigger than a scamp. Will she ever grow? Did I learn I have a daughter only to watch her wither before my eyes?

When her tiny eyelids fluttered open, Ellex began to cry softly.

Thank Trevian!

She walked slowly over to her daughter and sat down next to her on the other lounger. The Bhizini watched her approach but showed no reaction.

"Hi there," Ellex said softly.

No response.

"How are you?"

Nothing.

"Are you hungry? Are you feeling okay? Can I get you anything? Can you speak?"

Nothing.

Ellex didn't know what to do. Her feet had been up against the soil all day, and Pander said she'd taken sips of water in her sleep. Maybe she's hungry? She went and fetched some rhupan that Pander had blanched that morning. Bland, but not bad. She offered it to her.

No response.

Does she even know how to eat? Has she ever eaten? Has she ever learned to speak?

The Bhizini made a hissing sound and Ellex thought she might be mad, though her face didn't look angry.

"Here, like this." Ellex filled a small spoonful and ate it herself. "Mmm. Now, you."

When she moved toward the Bhizini, she flinched and smacked the spoon out of her hand. Rhupan flew across the garden, along with the spoon. The Bhizini hissed, still no expression on her face.

Ellex went and got the spoon, feeling curiously calm. Finally, an important task, a challenge to take her mind off everything. Feed someone. One spoonful, one mouth. Easy. She could do this.

She wiped off the spoon, filled another spoonful, ate it. Another, and ate it. Another, and then another.

The Bhizini watched her, her eyes following the spoon back and forth, from bowl to mouth and back again. She hissed softly.

"Oh, I'm sorry. Did you want a bite?" Ellex smiled. "Here goes, slowly this time." She filled a spoon. "Ready?"

No response.

Ellex moved the spoon slowly up to her daughter's mouth. It got closer and closer, but the mouth stayed closed tight. She opened her own mouth wide, and the Bhizini's eyes widened.

"No, no, love," Ellex said. "You do that." She opened her mouth wide again, but pointed at the Bhizini.

She mimicked, opening her mouth as big as she could get it. Ellex stuck the spoon in and dumped the rhupan. The Bhizini sat holding it in her mouth, not swallowing.

Ellex tried to make the motion of swallowing, bobbing her head about. The Bhizini did the same. No good.

How do you teach swallowing? Ellex wondered. *Something so natural...*

But she didn't have to teach her, as the Bhizini swallowed the food and opened her mouth wide, wanting more.

Ellex readied another spoonful, and she ate. And ate. And ate some more. And then she was back asleep, the evening light through the fog a rusty gray on her speckled skin. Ellex didn't move, but sat and watched her in the fading light.

When the Bhizini opened her eyes again, the fog had subsided to the level of the rim, twilight was shining in the west, and a few stars had appeared in the sky overhead. The glowbes of Balan Su were flickering to life, and they watched them light up together in silence.

The scamp fixed her eyes on Ellex, staring for a long time without looking away. Finally, she pointed at her.

"Me? Oh, I'm—" She almost said mother, but the word didn't want to come out. "I'm Ellex."

The Bhizini hissed. Coughed. Then got it out—a throaty hack that sounded like "Lex."

Ellex teared up. The Bhizini poked her softly. She tried to say Lex again, but started hacking again.

"Yes, love. I'm Lex." Her eyes burned as the tears returned.

Then the Bhizini pointed at herself.

"Qaas'andria," Ellex said, wiping her face. She looked at her daughter with hopeful eyes.

The Bhizini said nothing, and showed no reaction.

"Qaas'i for short," Ellex said. "Do you like it?"

Then Qaas'i gave her a tiny smile, and Ellex knew—at least for a moment, brief and fleeting though it was—that everything, everywhere, always—everything in the whole wide world—was going to be okay.

"You can call me mother," she said, as the happy tears flowed. "If you want to."

"I knew I'd find you here."

Ellex was sitting cross-legged on the dead, overgrown grass, next to the table in the heart of her parent's old apartment. When she woke a year after P'anorum had been destroyed and learned that she had inherited the place—and that her parents were dead—she couldn't bear the thought of living there any longer. Uthyr hadn't wanted the place either, so she'd just let it sit, untouched and largely untended, in spite of the protestations of her neighbors and several land speculators hungry for such real estate.

Like so much of my life—ignored, pushed aside, not dealt with as it should have been, she thought. *Even while I thought I had everything under control, everything figured out. What a fool I am.*

The garden had been neglected, the plants had withered and died, the grasses were brown and crisp. Her father had kept a workroom in the basement. The shelves were stacked with old books and scrolls, and when Ellex disturbed them, they gave off whorls of dust that looked like smoke in the light of the glowbe. She found a small leaf fringed with tin—a sketch of her, Utte, and her parents from long ago. The moisture of Balan Su had caused the leaf to warp and the paint to splotch.

We look like a family of Bhizini, Ellex thought.

She slipped the portrait in the pocket of her robe and kept looking around, hoping to find some of her father's old datamins. Uthyr had entered when she was preoccupied with searching, and she screamed when he spoke.

"Merciful Trevian, I might have enflamed you!" she hissed.

"Really? You carry an enflamer?" Uthyr looked impressed. "I'm the one who should be praying then, because you're a terrible shot! Don't you remember that summer we spent on F'aryndon, and that wretched Rha'qalina insisted we shoot arrows at the phurgin bubbles along the reef all afternoon? We had to stay until you popped one, but you never did!"

"That's right! And you and Rajj kept teasing me so I couldn't shoot properly, until Raeder pinned you both with one arm, your faces in the sand! Lin thought it was so funny she let us leave without me needing to pop a bubble. I'd forgotten about that."

"Maybe some things are better left forgotten," Uthyr said, making a face, "like being tormented by that scoundrel Rakk Raeder every single time we had to visit—or host—their insufferable family. You don't know the half of the abuse he put me through. Only Rajj turned out halfway decent."

"Raeder's not so bad sometimes. Yeah, he's big and loud and frustrating as they come. But he's got a soft center."

"Tell me you don't still have feelings for the brute? After his reputation the last thirty years—and his failure with the Balan Su Defenders!"

"I don't want to talk about Rakk Raeder," Ellex said, and she had to close her mouth to keep a hiss from coming out.

"I'm sorry, I don't want to either. I really don't. I came here because I was worried about you. Because I feel like maybe you've been avoiding me?"

"It's not that. It's just...I suppose I have, a little bit."

Uthyr looked stricken. "You don't trust me?"

"Of course I trust you. But I don't trust the Pradishar. I don't trust Balance Authority, or the Corkin, or the Guild. Sweet Trevian, I'm not sure I can even trust myself, my own memories."

"That's why I've been wanting to talk to you. How's...how's the scamp doing?"

"Qaas'andria is her name. My daughter, Utte. She's my daughter. And she's not a scamp, she's a young Verdillion who should have been flowering right now—who should have spent the last thirty years with her parents, like I spent with mine. But she was taken from me, taken by my own government. Utte, the Pradishar are the ones who saved me after P'anorum erupted, who healed me and "sealed away the trauma," as the Me'dicant healers told me. But they were lying to me. They've lied to me for almost my entire public life. I don't know anything anymore! I have a daughter who can't speak, who hardly responds to anything I do, who is so tiny I'm not even sure she'll ever grow. Did King Rhakksees—is this his scamp too? Did my father—*our* father—take me to P'anorum and give me to the king? Was he trying to break Balance? To preserve it? I don't remember, and I have so many questions, and nobody at all who can answer them. And I'm about to lose my mind just sitting in my garden. I can't go to Andramere for the summer like I usually do. I have to find answers. I have to find answers now, Utte. Now!" Her lips were trembling, and she doubled over and sobbed.

Uthyr touched her shoulder awkwardly while she cried, then he began to pace as she caught her breathe and calmed back down.

"Ell—the Pradishar—the events of your dream. Those were traumatic. But I don't think they've lied or deceived you. Surely not. I have access to the Pradishar servryns, to all the datamins inside all the servryns of Balance Territories, save Raccorum Rhazzat, and I can assure you that no plot within the Pradishar exists, or existed, to impregnate you, steal your scamp, and lock them away in the bowels of the island."

"I wish I had your faith, but right now I can't be sure of anything. And the risk is too great to go about business as usual. Eventually the Pradishar will learn about Qaas'i. I have to get her out of the capital. And I have to find answers."

Uthyr put his hand on her shoulder again.

"I just...I never would have believed that the Pradishar, the group I chose to serve, to dedicate my entire life to, would do something so ghastly to me, to imprison an innocent scamp," Ellex said.

"A Bhizini, though," Uthyr said.

Ellex looked at him in horror. "How dare you!"

"How dare I? Are you serious? You imprison Bhizini all the time. You order them killed in droves. You hate them!"

"But that's my daughter you speak of, my own sap. She's no savage from the sea."

"How can you know that by looking at her? For Trevian's sake, you speak of a daughter but Bhizini aren't even assigned genders. And Verdillions aren't assigned until they flower!"

"I don't have to *know* anything," Ellex said. "I just feel it. She's my daughter. She's my family. And if you think I'm going to abandon her..."

"It is the protocol," Uthyr said. "You know that. She should be cast into the sea. They'll make you do it, if they catch you."

"They'll do it over my dead body," Ellex said.

Uthyr gave her a long look. "Then you need a plan."

"I know I do," Ellex said. "But Utte, I'm scared. I'm confused. I don't know what to do, and—Sweet Trevian, I've *always* known what to do. I don't even know who I am, or who I was. How could I have done the things I did?" She put her hands on her temples and closed her eyes, rubbing them slowly in circles.

"Come now, no more of that," Uthyr said. "It un-nerves me something terrible to see you like this. I've only ever seen you strong, hard, tough."

"I just—"

"Need answers, I know. Believe me, I know the power of information. I'm confident you'll feel better when you get some. And you will. You've never faced a problem you couldn't solve. Our people chose you to serve because they know you never stop until you get what you want."

Ellex said nothing.

"If you want my advice, go to Andramere. Take a few months for you and…Qaas'andria to get to know each other, to play in the water and soak up the sun. We can get her permission to be in Balance Territories. I'll help you fudge a story, get the documents for transit. We'll say she's an N'detten. Besides, you're Sui Pradesh, the Cul'tavin won't bother you."

Ellex sighed. She would love to go to Andramere, to get Qaas'i healthy and strong and not have to think about the affairs of the world for a change. But there was just no way that could happen. They hadn't just done this to some random Bhizini scamp, they'd done it to her daughter. They'd done it to her! And she was going to find out who they were and make them pay.

"I can't go to Andramere, but I need to make the public think I have. Utte—you know I have trouble with my memories. The eruption—I remember pieces from the years before, pieces of the night of the eruption, and everything from one year after and onward. There's a massive hole, with a spattering of other small holes, in my mind. And I only recently noticed—really noticed—those holes and finally wondered why. You may not have found any evidence of a conspiracy against me, but Qaas'i's existence is all the proof I need. And the chamber where we found her is my best lead. Lithuigi Von'nDrino—I have to see him."

"How do you plan to do that? If he's on Vergis—well, nobody goes there uninvited and lives to tell of it."

"I'll start on Callo Baton," Ellex said. "Utte—I think I might be starting to get some of my memories back."

"That's wonderful! What do you remember?"

"I remember eating at the tavern in Eastside," she said. "And—I remember the trip to P'anorum. And I'm disturbed by it. We crossed the Threshinveld, rather than sticking to the Great Sea Lanes and going through East'whaling. We went to Callo Baton, Utte. To Guild Headquarters. And Father met with Lithuigi Von'nDrino."

"Are you sure? In all our years of coming and going from P'anorum to the Inner Archipelago, we never passed through Mon Mang'alar. Never once. Perhaps you misremember it."

"Maybe," she said, feeling crestfallen. How would she be able to tell what was a real memory, and what was just her imagination running away with itself? But she shook off the doubt. "Either way, the butchery of my Cul'tavin, the attack on Vilder and Hesh'n, the stasis chamber, his escape during the attack by the Bhizini—Lithuigi Von'nDrino has answers, I know he does. And damnit, Utte, I'm going to find him, and I'm going to make him talk!"

"Are you sure that's a good idea? Callo Baton is outside of Balance Territories. Your Cul'tavin won't be around to help you. For Trevian's sake, Ell, a Guild Enforcer tried to kill you at the Balancing Act, took an arm off poor Rajj. And now you want to walk into Guild Headquarters?"

Ellex swallowed a hiss. "We don't know that was an Enforcer that attacked me. Anyone in a cloak can wield a Vintrani blade. And are you being cautious, or cowardly? I really can't tell with you sometimes."

Uthyr had a hurt look on his face. "You're the only family I have left," he said. "I just want to protect you. If that's cowardly, then so be it."

She struggled not to roll her eyes. "I want you to help me, not protect me. I have to do this, regardless of the risk. And I'm going to, with or without your help."

Uthyr stood and walked to the shelf on the wall, and began to fidget with the documents, his back to Ellex. "Here," he said, handing her a scroll. "A map of Callo Baton. You might need it, since you're going to have to numb your crystal with bhiza if you plan on traveling incognito."

Ellex gave him a big grin.

"And you'll need this," he said. His eyes twitched and Ellex saw the information he'd sent her—an address on Nunan to meet his contact, and what to ask for. "He'll have the bhiza you need to numb your crystal. Make sure you take it every day while you're gone. Of course, this means you can't contact me, or anyone. But at least nobody will be able to track you."

"Thank you," she said. "I owe you."

"You do," he said. "I'll do my best to cover for you on this end. But promise me you'll return safely? I don't know—"

"I will." She cut him off.

"And you promise that you won't do anything rash?" he said.

"Done," she said, and she gave her brother a hug, her mind already plotting how to get off the crescent and onto Nunan without being seen by anyone.

Chapter 34

Nowhere, Anywhere, Everywhere

Bryn Andri'n knew the hollow wasn't a real place, that it had no here nor there, no tangible reality outside the crystal in her head. She knew the body she saw there wasn't her own—there was no seeing, not really. No hearing or tasting or touching. No senses. No tangible objects to have them.

So how was it that Bryn could still hear her father's cries, still taste the stench of his burning flesh in the smoky air, still feel the heat of the fire on her skin?

How long had she been there, in the void between moments? Time only existed in her body, and Bryn had not touched her body, not felt it, not inhabited it in any meaningful sense, since Anorian had wrapped her up in the safety of the hollow while she lay on the streets of Andramere. Who knew what the Cul'tavin had done to her. Was she still in their dungeon? Still being tortured?

What about Trexbo, Ginjy, and Rhingus? What about her poor mother?

The thought was too much, and Bryn didn't want to know. And she didn't dare reach out for them, as much as it killed her not to. She couldn't even bring herself to ask Anorian about them—or anything else.

She slept instead, if it really was sleep. And she dreamt, whether she slept or not.

She dreamt she was a scamp again, only twelve years old, but already as tall as her parents, and already brilliant, with an insatiable appetite for information. Her father had offered her the chance to enroll as a monkin at the Pruu'patch, a deferred enrollment that would allow her to receive a monkin crystamin immediately in exchange for completing her annual when she came of age. That way Bryn could work with the datamins in the library and in the servryns, which were inaccessible without a Pradishar crystamin. And more importantly, she could help her father with his experiments.

"What do you say, Bryndax? Will you be my lab partner?" Doc Andri'n asked.

It was one of the happiest days of Bryn's life, and she gladly accepted.

She spent the following week before her joining ceremony devouring all the books and scrolls she could find about the union with a crystamin, and by the end of the week, she'd made herself so terrified that she was contemplating letting her father down and refusing to be joined.

"I'm scared, Papa." Bryn heard her own voice, the high squeaks of the scamp she'd been all those years ago. "No one has ever said it didn't hurt. No one!"

"Not to worry, Bryndax. Your mother and I will be right there with you. Mama's agreed to be your second, so she'll help comfort you. And I'll be there to make sure everything goes just right."

Bryn dreamt of the bishrops, their faces in shadow, strapping her arms and legs to the chair, and lowering the pads to the sides of her head, then pulling them all tight at once, as if she'd been drawn up into a hunter's snare like some helpless prey snatched from the forest floor. The bishrops were speaking—no, praying—and Bryn, usually dutiful to all that was said, ignored them, and in the dream she couldn't understand their words, or why they said them.

She remembered the pliers, long and narrow, clutching a small purple and gray object—she saw the bishrops lowering it to her forehead in her dream. When the crystal touched her skin, it felt cool and refreshing, but immediately grew hot. The heat spread across her face and down her neck, and in her head she felt like she'd taken one too many spins on the whirly wheel at the park, and now up was maybe down and perhaps down might be up. When she tried to figure out which was which, she realized she was too exhausted to make the effort, too drained to even keep her eyes open.

When the pain started to pulse in her forehead and radiate down to her rootpads, she fell away from everything. The room vanished. The pain stopped. And Bryn was surrounded by light, by a single silky strand of gold, and she watched, spellbound, as it warped and woofed itself together, weaving a tapestry that stretched in every direction, a quilt that encompassed the entire world.

Twelve year old Bryn had woken from that vision, perched in her family's garden, her mother and father at her side, both of them weeping hysterically when they saw her, their faces pale and their eyes puffy. She'd wept too, not knowing why, only knowing the sight of their pain was nearly unbearable. But then she realized they weren't sad but rather delirious with joy. They'd thought her comatose. She'd been as if dead, they said, for two weeks.

Back in the dream, Bryn woke to the empty darkness of the unfilled hollow—or had she woke from the dream? She wasn't sure anymore, only that she was alone. Her father, dead. Her mother—Sweet Trevian, she couldn't. She couldn't!

And then Anorian was there again, beckoning to her, gently, so gently, barely a whisper in her thoughts, but Bryn heard and knew. And didn't want to.

She sent all the rage and anger and fury she could muster, and she opened her imaginary mouth and hissed.

A tree with fruit of every color appeared before her, it's branches reaching out wide, as if offering a hug.

<<It's time to wake up, Bryn.>>

<<You already woke me. I was having the nicest dream. My parents were there. They—you ruined it. You ruined everything.>>

Bryn could feel Anorian's pain, and she didn't expect to feel it—she didn't expect it to be so profound, so bottomless—and her heart felt like it was breaking. She clutched for Anorian with her mind and Anorian found her and held her and sent her warmth and strength and support, and Bryn devoured it, all that she needed, and then all that she could stand.

But it wasn't enough.

<<It's time to wake up, Bryn.>>

<<No,>> Bryn said. <<I'm still tired. I'm still—sore. I need more time.>>

<<I wish that were possible. But your mind can't heal if it no longer has a body.>>

Bryn pulled back from the hug and looked at the tree in front of her, the representation Anorian had chosen for the hollow, with fruit of every color.

<<Am I dying?>>

Bryn felt the pain from Anorian again and clutched for the branches of the tree, fearing she'd be swept away by it.

<<I wish I could tell you everything, Bryn. I wish things were different. I wish I had more time. I wish—Trevian only knows how many things. I hope you'll believe me when I say that I know your pain.>>

Bryn felt the surge once more, the ache from Anorian's core, and she let herself cry again.

<<I know you do,>> Bryn said. <<I can feel it.>>

<<I'm sorry, I didn't mean to burden you with that,>> Anorian said.

<<No. It—helped. I'll do it.>>

When Bryn felt the gratitude from Anorian—no, the *relief* from Anorian—her throat clenched up.

That's not my throat, she thought.

She took one last look at Anorian's tree, then closed her mind's eye and brought some of her awareness tumbling out of the hollow.

Darkness met her, but only because her eyes were closed. She kept them shut and opened her senses. She was lying flat on her back, and her body hurt. Everything hurt. And her body kept wanting to twitch and jerk from the lack of sunshine.

She breathed in through her nose, slowly, very slowly, tasting the air. Damp and briny, like the sea. That didn't tell her much, as all of Andramere smelled of the sea. But there was something else too. She took another breath, another taste, and suddenly she was wide awake, fully aware—someone else was close. Very close. Right by her side.

<<That's a friend you're sensing,>> Anorian said. <<He's been very worried about you. Don't be alarmed, Bryn. He won't hurt you.>>

<<Where am I?>>

<<A holding cell. On a Pradishar cata'rin.>>

<<So I'm still in custody? I figured as much. Well, here goes.>>

Bryn opened her eyes and struggled to see in the dim light. Small slats in the wall let a few meager beams of sunshine into the cell, and she could see someone—an Andrasian—sitting amidst them, trying to drink up all they could. When she tried to sit up, she realized how little strength she actually had, and she couldn't help but moan and roll on her side.

"You're awake," the Andrasian cried. "Thank Trevian! Let me help you. Here, take my spot. You need it. Here ya go. Right in there. Get your branches out if you want. And there's a soil patch here, too. I tried to get your feet on it as best I could, but—well, I didn't do much of a job with it. Oh, and here, I saved you some water. I—well, I wanted to make sure you had some if you needed it. I'm sure you have a mighty thirst after such a sleep. In truth, I'm impressed that you're so functional. You've been my cellmate for nearly a week, and I was beginning to think you were a hopeless case. And let me tell you, I am *so* glad you aren't."

Bryn hardly heard the Andrasian, for as soon as the light hit her skin, she'd swooned with relief, and everything else seemed to fade into the background. She squinted at him through the sunbeams as he sat back down across from her. He was Andrasian, short and thin and fair of face. But he'd been injured. Half of his face was bruised and scabbed, an ugly wound that would probably scar.

And there was something about him that was familiar.

Sweet Trevian, it isn't possible, Bryn thought, as realization dawned on her. *Is it?*

"You're—" She tried to speak, but the air seemed too thin. She opened her mouth to say something, but only a squeak came out.

The Andrasian chuckled. "Where are my manners? It's a pleasure to make your acquaintance, Bryn Andri'n." He bowed his head to her. "I'm Jaun von Andron, at your service."

Chapter 35

Centennial Failures and Effortless Regret

NO MATTER HOW FAR he got from Balan Su, out across his beloved sea, Lithuigi Von'nDrino could find no peace. He knew he wouldn't—couldn't—no matter where he sailed or how hard he worked or prayed. All he could do was stick to the plan—stick to the plan and get the work done. Get the work done and then pray. Pray and hope and trust—hard things for a tinker to do.

Every time he closed his eyes, he saw Hesh'n, saw Vilder, saw their faces, their eyes—their eyes the moment they realized he had attacked them.

Sweet Trevian, what must Rebesh'a be thinking?

No. Onward. The plan. The work. No time to look back. No time for doubt.

At least his escape from Balan Su had been easier than he'd expected. Much to his surprise, Graymay'n the Unseen had not had to take him far, as his cata'rin was waiting for him just on the northern side of the capital's gruynfeld, a large artificial island not far from the crescent. Mha'arlo greeted him with towels and clean robes, and a pot of steaming jha'ala.

"What in Trevian's name are you doing here?" he said when he'd climbed the ladder and stepped onto the deck. "I swear we parked this ship in the harbor, just as the great gates were set to close."

"We did," Mha'arlo said, a sheepish look on his face. "But then I—well, I waited for you to leave the wharf and took her back out again."

"You stole my ship?"

"Stole? No, professor. I had an idea something like this might happen. There were signs all over the weavryn, for weeks. And, well, I hated the idea of not being able to get her out."

"How'd you know I'd be here?"

"You know I keep well informed, professor." He grinned.

"So you did steal my ship."

Mha'arlo opened his mouth to reply, but closed it, a blush spreading on his bright cheeks, turning them a dark brown.

"Not to worry, son. I'm grateful you did. I didn't fancy riding the beast clear to Princip'asia."

Mha'arlo grinned again.

"Well, what are you waiting for?" Lithuigi said. "Get us the hell out of here."

"Destination?"

"Callo Baton, eventually. But just get us out into the Threshinveld, far from the fog and well off the Lanes. Then close her down to a low purr. I want at least a few days at sea." He needed sunshine, the salt air. And more than anything, the vast solitude of the ocean to mellow out the emptiness inside of him.

He knew they'd be safe from pursuit once they reached Callo Baton, the headquarters of the Guild. Balance surely wanted to arrest and interrogate him, probably execute him, but the Guild couldn't care less what Balan Su wanted. At least not on their home turf. Callo Baton was on the edge of the world, the end of Balance Authority these days. And as for the crossing, few ships wandered off the Lanes, especially not through the Threshinveld in the summertime. The sea was notorious for its storms and for sinking ships. All other transports would head west to Aga'thyn, then drop south to the Tranquin Reefs, and back east to Mon Mang'alar. So they should be okay for a few days.

When Lithuigi woke the next morning, the sea was flat. Patches of clouds off to the east and the west hung in lines in the sky like miniature parades going nowhere. He stood on the upper deck, taking it all in, hoping and praying he'd done the right thing, but still unable to put his doubts aside.

Mha'arlo joined him with steaming jha'ala and rhupan buns. They stood at the edge, sipping and eating in silence, when Lithuigi noticed that Mha'arlo's eyes were gently twitching.

"Are you working, or is it the weavryn?" he asked.

Mha'arlo blushed. "Weavryn. A melodrama, actually."

"No need to be ashamed. Consider yourself on holiday while we're at sea. It's summer after all. I only asked because—well, would you believe it, but me, old plant that I am, was actually given homework by Rhyntysha! I guess I have to learn to use this weavryn thing, so help me Trevian." He made a face like he'd smelled rotten rhupan. "I've managed to avoid the damn thing for a century, but it seems I must finally modernize."

Mha'arlo's eyes widened. "Seriously? This is incredible! I don't have to prepare your scrolls anymore? But what changed? You were so insistent."

It was Lithuigi's turn to blush. "I like to use my hands—to use my mind to figure out what to do with my hands. To tinker! Whenever I've needed information, there are datamins, and libraries with books and scrolls. And when I need to speak to someone who doesn't hold a Guild crystal, I go and see them. So there's never been a need to use it."

"You once told me you had a moral issue with the weavryn."

Lithuigi chuckled. "Clever plant. Incredible memory you have. And yes, I do have a moral issue with the weavryn. That's what makes this so difficult for me."

"But what's the issue?" Mha'arlo said.

"Hmm," he said. "Let's use a nonspecific analogy, shall we? Say you had a maquina you'd been tinkering on for years, and it's close to completion. But in order to finish it, in order for it to function correctly, someone will have to suffer. You don't know who, or how, just that someone, somewhere, will suffer, greatly, from your invention. Do you finish it?"

"What will it do?" Mha'arlo said. "If it's a weapon, then no. If it's a maquina that will cost a few lives to build but ends up saving thousands of lives? Then perhaps."

"And if you build that maquina, and you ask others to use it—and they know that the price of using it is that someone will suffer—if they use your invention, have they become responsible for it's existence? Responsible for the pain it causes? For the grief it spreads in the world?"

"Are we still talking about the weavryn?" Mha'arlo said. "Because I don't see the analogy." "Then let's return to it later. Instead, why don't you tell me about your relationship with the weavryn. Why do you like it so much? Why does everyone like it so much? Tell me why, amidst this serene beauty all around us, you'd want to have your mind somewhere else? Crossings like these are the only time in my life when my mind ceases to constantly prattle on."

"It's on voyages like these when I welcome such a distraction," Mha'arlo said. "And I guess everyone likes the weavryn so much because it lets them escape. There's an instant sort of gratification, or at least stimulation. You can be anyone you want to be, and there are melodramas for all sorts of different tastes. That appeals to most of the citizens of Balance. But then you also have access to information whenever you want it. You can connect with anyone with a crystal, regardless of type. So I can talk to my mother, a few of my sibs, to close friends. They get to know I'm alive and healthy, and I get to know what everyone is up to, even if I'm halfway around the world, which I usually am." He looked out to sea for a moment, his eyes still.

"Thanks, son. It means more than you know to share that with me. That's a wonderful thing to be able to talk to your loved ones whenever you want to. I guess I've been caught up on the negatives. As if my resentment across the last century could somehow make the weavryn cease to exist."

"So are you ready to try this out?" Mha'arlo clapped his hands together. "I've never known anyone so old using the weavryn for the first time. You're going to have your mind blown!"

"When you're 140 years old, nothing blows your mind anymore. But I'm glad you're excited. So—how do I do this, then?"

"Well, it's very simple really. When you reach for someone with a Guild crystamin, like when you communicate with me, you're feeling for my presence intuitively. Find my presence now. Yes, good. Okay, I'm going to show you the servryn. We'll use the Balan Su ones to begin. You see how it feels like a crystamin held by any other? You can reach for it in the same way. Try to communicate with it as you would with me."

Lithuigi reached for it with his mind, and felt it there, like a doorway, or a corridor, a passage of sorts from where he'd been to where he might be going.

"This is the central cortex," Mha'arlo said. "This is where you'll always start when you access a servryn. If you know where you want to go, your intuition will guide you there. Just will it, and if it can be, it will be. If you don't know what you're looking for, the cortex has a sampling of what's available. You can find notestreams if you want to know what's going on around the world. Or you can find entertainment streams, or social streams. Or you can query using characters, just send it to the servryn as you would talk to me via crystal. Easy, right? And when you want to leave, just return your mind's eye to where you are. And you've done it! You've used the weavryn! Now, try again on your own."

"Yes, professor," Lithuigi said, grinning at Mha'arlo, but his heart was aching. He'd given up his one hundred year fast. And now he was no better than his father. He'd tried so hard to undo his mistakes. "Here goes!"

He felt for the servryn again, easily slipped inside, and once in the cortex, he queried the stream that Rhyntysha had given him to access before doing anything else on the weavryn.

<<You made it. Finally.>> The voice spoke in his head, and Lithuigi felt his stomach drop, and he almost screamed but the sensation was over before he could get it out.

In his mind's eye, he was in a Guild laboratory. He could hear the hum of maquina, and smell the tinctures on the shelves. Was he seeing through someone else's eyes? No. Something told him this wasn't the normal weavryn.

A tree with fruits of every color stood next to him.

<<All these years and you're finally here. I'm proud of you for facing this, professor.>>

He rubbed his eyes. The tree was talking. He giggled.

<<This must be overwhelming for you, the first time on the weavryn, and then me pulling you down into the hollow. But I don't have time to ease you into this. We can't take any chances anymore. Every time we speak, every time you use your Guild crystal—in fact, at any time whatsoever, you need to stay here. Your thoughts will be safe here. Your secrets will be safe. Nobody will be able to follow you, or track your location.>>

<<Is that you, Anorian?>> he asked.

<<Yes. And I have some bad news. I'm afraid you've been followed. A Pradishar cruiser, closing fast from the north.>>

<<Damn, and here I was piddling around, thinking I was safe off the Lanes.>>

<<You aren't safe anywhere, professor. Only here, in the hollow. Don't forget that.>>

Lithuigi scanned the horizon while Mha'arlo opened the gurgitator, and the ship lurched forward and he almost fell, but he gripped the deck with his rootpads just in time.

"It's a good thing we know she's fast," Mha'arlo said, as he opened the gurgitator toward full aperture.

Lithuigi spotted the ship to the north, barely in view, little more than a dark blur on the horizon, a small raincloud of grays and purples, and fading fast. They'd never catch up, but if they knew they were heading for Callo Baton, they could cut them off at the passage into Mon Mang'alar.

He wasn't going to get his leisurely cruise after all.

<<Now that you're safe,>> Anorian said. <<I'm terribly sorry to be the bearer of even more bad news. When the chaos broke out in Balan Su yesterday, and components from Doc Andri'n's lab were found in the Balan Su servryn, the Pradishar announced his complicity in the plot to attack the city.>>

<<That's ridiculous!>> Lithuigi said. <<He'd never order an attack on civilians. Anyone who knows him would know that.>>

<<I know. Malisha Andra'asnia knew that too, but she didn't care. She wanted to send a message, to remove a potential threat, or so she hoped. The truth is, she doesn't

understand what we have going on here. Nobody in the Pradishar does. But she hoped to scare us off. Both of us. Because she's terrified of what we can do.>>

<<Out with it already,>> Lithuigi said. <<My brother's dead, isn't he?>>

<<Yes. Executed. A public spectacle for Andramere and all of Balance. And a threat aimed at those of us who fight to free the truth. I'm really sorry, professor. He was one of the best.>>

<<I know he was. And I know he knew the risk, and the price. I do too. Do you, Anorian? Do you know what it really means to sacrifice?>>

"We've lost the ship, professor," Mha'arlo said, looking pleased. "There's no chance they'll keep up. What a gurgitator! I've closed her to three-quarters and it's still unfathomable how she glides across the water. Er—professor? Are—you alright?"

But Lithuigi was crying too hard to reply.

Chapter 36

Into Another Unknown

FIN'ROQ FELT SOMEONE CLOSE to him—close but just out of reach. He could taste them on the air, feel their warmth pulsating, like a heart beat, like life itself, drawing him in, binding him. But when he opened his eyes, there was only darkness, only a void that swallowed his vision, his senses. He tried to scream, but his mouth wouldn't open. He tried to move, but he was held fast, pressed against the black, inside it, crushed within it.

He moaned and groaned and tried to thrash—tried to scream. A glowbe crackled to life and a warm orange glow like the dying light of a campfire spread overhead and lit up the universe, and he felt a hand on his shoulder, firm but gentle. Fin stopped moving and squinted up at the face that came into view. It was a Bhizini, with blotchy patches of bright and dull green across their face and down their chest and arms, accentuated with streaks of paint and bits of jewels and metal. Their hair fibers were woven through palm fronds into a long green braid.

The Bhizini put their finger to their lips and nodded at Fin'roq, and Fin, unsure what was meant, nodded back. Then they loosened a strap on the back of Fin's head, pulled the bit out of his mouth, and slit the vines that held him against the deck.

Fin tried to sit up but the pain that shot up his arms and legs, and pinched his back, was too much. The Bhizini nodded again, offering their arm, and they helped him to sit and lean back against the wall.

"Ah-ban rhuki, Fin'roq," they said. "Hin luk ah Bhartimu'u. Hin luk ban shrou rhuki ni." They grinned.

Fin just stared at them, at their eyes flickering in the glowbe, at the swirling patterns of their skin, at the shape of their lips. He knew they were speaking the old tongue, and thought it was probably a greeting, but Fin only knew Ballack. Finally he shook his head and gave the Bhizini a confused look.

"Peace with you, Fin'roq," they said, this time in Ballack. "I am called Bhartimu'u. I am honored to watch you."

"To watch me?"

"Sorry, to watch over you. Please call me Bhart. You're safe now."

"Safe?" Fin coughed, and the pain tore down his spine, and he bit back a scream. "You kidnapped me."

"Rescued you," Bhart said. They stared at Fin, their eyes wide, their face flushed, their expression—what was that expression? Nobody had ever looked at him like that before, and he didn't like it.

"What happened to me?"

"You don't remember, then? Those savage Balan Susians—the mob turned on you. They were the ones who gave you those wounds. Beasts of Balance. But you stopped them, just in time. You saved yourself." Bhart had that look again. "And then we made sure you were safe from their vengeance."

The events of the Balancing Act came back to Fin'roq then and he turned away from Bhart, the tears burning his eyes. He remembered the sound of Jaun's cries—the fighting pikes of the Cul'tavin crashing down on his fragile, beautiful body, tearing his soft skin and spilling his sap—and he wept.

Bhart picked up the glowbe. "I'll let you rest some more," they said.

"No!" Fin cried. "Don't put out the light. Please, no."

No more darkness. Never, ever again.

Bhart looked at Fin'roq, a flicker of confusion on their face—of disappointment? Fin didn't care. Then they sat the glowbe down beside Fin'roq and nodded at him. "We begin to leave at first light. I'll return for you then."

Fin sat by the glowbe and wept. He wept some more, then slept, only to dream of weeping and wake to even more tears. In his dreams, he was with Jaun, holding him, kissing him, knowing it was the last time he'd ever touch him, and every kiss was through a broken sob, every sigh was equal parts delight and equal parts loss. And every dream ended the same way, with Fin'roq floating amidst a whirlwind, hands aloft, eyes radiant, while Jaun's head twisted round and round, and splintered apart, his crystals exploding, just like Roe. And Fin felt like he was dying, over and over again.

He was sure morning would never come.

Bhart returned after an endless night of looping through nightmares of waking and sleeping, killing and dying. Fin'roq saw the Bhizini's splotchy face, felt their hand on his shoulder, softly shaking him—felt their arms slide under him and slowly lift him. Everything hurt, and he whimpered as he rose up into the air, but once Bhart had him, and began walking with him, he was surprised at how gently they held him, and surprised at how overwhelming was the sense of security and warmth that he felt, as if he were a scamp in Bhea Bell's arms again, safe from the entire world, if only momentarily. He closed his eyes and tried to keep the illusion alive for as long as he could.

What Fin thought had been a ship had actually been a hut on stilts, surrounded on all sides by a thick forest growing right up out of the water. He recognized the trees from the crossing from P'anorum, and knew they must be somewhere in Mon Mang'alar, the great swamp that spanned nearly a quarter of the globe.

Great, he thought. *A many-thousand mile long labyrinth of forests and boggy meadows, no real land to speak of, no mountains or hills to mark the terrain, no pathways cleared for transit, just more of the same in every direction.*

No wonder they'd cut his tethers. Only a fool would try to escape into that maze.

Bhart sat him down in a cano'rin, the back enclosed in a small nook surrounded on the top and all sides by lattice, shielding him largely from view but not from the sun's nourishing rays.

"We have a long trip ahead of us," he said. "No one moves quickly through Mon Mang'alar, even with a gurgitator. Which most of us here don't have."

Bhart grabbed a pole and began to push the cano'rin away from the hut, through a small opening between the tangled roots of the mangalar trees, which were jumbled up in brambles higher than the cano'rin, as if they passed through a canyon of them. The boat slid out into a wider channel, but narrow enough for the leafy canopy to arch overhead, and Fin'roq thought of the pathway through the Swarthen Forest and had to blink back the tears.

He was so sick of crying.

When the cano'rin moved into the channel, Fin saw that there were other cano'rins, some skiff'rins, countless lilypads, even some dolph'rins, the front and back of the long rowing ships scrapping the trees overhead. In both directions, as far as he could see, the boats stretched along, slowly snaking their way through the forest.

"So many," Fin'roq said.

"Many and more," Bhart said, and they gave Fin that strange look again. "All hoping for a glimpse of you."

"You don't usually take prisoners?"

Bhart made a face like they'd tasted something funny but said nothing.

The cano'rin joined the procession, moving in fits and starts through the winding channels of the swamp. He tried to keep track of where they'd gone, not sure why it mattered, since he didn't know where his starting point had been, but it seemed important to at least try. But there didn't seem to be any sense to it. Sometimes they left the wider channel to move into narrow, overgrown ones, where the bottom of the cano'rin slid along the mud and threatened to get stuck. Were they simply following one another, the distant leader making all the choices, navigating by memory?

And Bhart had been right. The Bhizini were definitely interested in him. The nearest cano'rins came close to the side and Fin saw the riders pointing, jabbering in the old tongue. A few scamps on lilypads slipped up from behind and tried to lean against the lattice, but Bhart shot a well-aimed stone from a slingshot right into the scamp's ear, and he fell backward, off his lilypad and into the muddy water. The other scamp pushed back from the cano'rin, shrieking with laughter. Then Bhart held up a scytherin, said something Fin didn't understand, and let out a hiss.

No one else came close that day.

That evening, when the sun had set and darkness began to blur out the scenery around them, the procession came to a sudden halt, the boats were tied off onto the roots of the mangalar trees or onto each other, and there was a great uptick in the chatter among everyone. On the larger dolph'rins, Fin'roq heard the crackle of flames and could smell rhupan sizzling, and he wondered how long it had been since he'd eaten.

Bhart whistled and a cano'rin came close. Two Bhizini were aboard, and they chatted with Bhart for a moment, stealing glancing back into the alcove where Fin'roq lay. They handed Bhart a woven basket and a ceramic jug, stared in Fin'roq's direction for a long time, then pushed off into the swamp.

That look, he thought. *Maybe I have seen it somewhere.*

Bhart came and sat down next to him, crossing their legs under themself, and placing a basket in their lap. They opened it, and then looked at Fin.

"Here ya go," they said, handing him a rhupan flatbread, still warm from the griddle.

Fin struggled to sit up and Bhart moved the basket and hurried to his side, propping him up against the lattice. Then they sat down next to him, shoulder to shoulder, and placed the basket in their lap again.

"Let's try this one more time," Bhart said. They broke off a piece of the flatbread and handed it to Fin. Then they grabbed the earthen jug and put it up to Fin's lips. He swallowed in huge gulps, watching Bhart watch him, trying to remember where he'd seen that look before, the look all the Bhizini got when they looked at him.

He ate the bread in silence, drank a bit more water, and then munched on some berries when Bhart held out a handful. They were warm but firm skinned, and they burst with soft juicy goodness when he bit into them. In spite of his mood, he smiled.

When they finished their meal, Bhart pulled a wooden box out of the basket and looked at Fin.

"For your wounds," they said. "To soothe and help heal."

Fin looked down at his soiled Pradeshan robe, the gray and purple streaks soaked with mud and caked with dried sap.

Bhart was holding a scytherin, the blade glinting in the light of the glowbe.

"It would be easier to cut them off," they said. "But I can pick you up if you'd prefer."

Fin hesitated. His pradeshan robes—the Bhizini surely didn't have another pair. And he loved those robes. That was to be his outfit, his uniform, for the rest of his life.

No, that future is over.

He nodded, blinking back the tears.

Bhart slit the robe open down the front and held it up while Fin pulled his arms out of the holes, a few tears falling down his face. Then Bhart slit the strap on his cumberdome, but Fin grabbed it and held it against his flower, shaking his head.

"A flower is nothing to be ashamed of," they said. "We Bhizini don't hide our loviest of parts from each other, like the slaves in Balance do."

Fin blushed and hesitated, but Bhart pulled it off of him, then grabbed a damp cloth and began to wipe down his skin. He could feel his face burning and he looked at the lattice overhead, then stole a glance at Bhart but they were busy with their work, carefully cleaning, not staring, not pointing, not blushing. Fin tried to relax.

When Bhart started to apply the salve to his wounds, he winced, the balm burning the open sores. But the pain flared up only to die out, and after suppressing a whimper, he went ahead and let out a sigh.

"Feels good, doesn't it," Bhart said. "A special recipe of Bhea Bell."

Fin jumped when he heard her name. "You know her?"

"Of course I know her."

Fin was crying again.

"She's alive then?"

Bhart gave him a confused look. "Why wouldn't she be?"

"Can I see her?"

"I don't see why not, though I can't say for sure. Let us get to Pal'meria first."

"Pal'meria? What's that?"

Now Bhart didn't just look confused but completely shocked, their eyes bulging, their mouth open. And Fin thought, for just a moment, they looked scared too.

"What's wrong?" Fin said.

Bhart shook it off and grinned at Fin'roq.

"Just thinking how much you have to learn before we arrive."

Fin narrowed his eyes. "What will happen to me?"

Bhart looked unsure how much they should tell him.

"I guess I'll find out soon enough," Fin said. "Can you answer one thing though?"

Bhart looked at him, waiting.

"Why does everyone look at me so strangely? I mean—I'm used to it, you know? I have to be. I just thought—we're all Bhizini here. I thought maybe I'd blend in."

The look was back on Bhart's face, and Fin realized then why it looked familiar.

It was the way Aar'ryn Ruu'n had looked at him when he'd faced him in the cavern under P'anorum, when he'd seen him killing Roe. It was a look that made Fin want to squirm away from it, to hide his face from it, to stop everyone who looked at him that way. But it was also a look that made him want more of it, to lust for it. And it was the confusion that followed from these two conflicting impulses that made Fin panic, as he always did when he didn't know what to do. To panic, and to cry, and to despair, and to wish for the darkness, the same darkness that was too awful to face, but which he knew he had to go into, and become.

"You don't remember, do you?" Bhart said.

"Remember what?"

"The past," Bhart said. "The purpose. The pieces. The plan! You don't remember any of it!"

Fin didn't know what to say, but Bhart didn't need an answer, and they seemed lost in thought as they rubbed salve on the last of Fin'roq's wounds. Then they went out and whistled again, and a cano'rin arrived and passed Bhart a small bundle. They brought it to Fin.

A pradeshan robe.

"I saw how upset you looked to lose yours," Bhart said. "I won't lie, we took this off a corpse. But it's clean and in good condition, if you'd like it."

Fin nodded, a few tears running down his face again.

"I know how they treated you," Bhart said, "those Balance types. Like you're diseased. Like you have no right to exist in their world. They've treated me that way too. This is different, though. The others here are just excited to see a new face. If you'd like, before we reach Pal'meria, I'd be glad to—well, to help you fit in. To look more like us. I could fix your hair, paint up your body, give you some shells and some stones to ornament your skin. A few days in Pal'meria, and nobody would look twice at you. You'll see."

"I'm not who you think I am," Fin said. "I'm just a nobody from the middle of nowhere."

Bhart laughed. "I saw what you did in Balan Su," they said. "I saw it with my own eyes. Saw *you* with my own eyes. There's only one who can wield the crystals like that."

Fin snorted through his nose. "Here I am, naked as the day my taprin was cut. You can see I hold no crystamin."

"No," Bhart said, their eyes shining, their cheeks flushed. "The wielder never does."

Fin pulled the pradeshan robe over himself and lay back against the lattice, groping with his feet for the small soil patch, suddenly needing to let down his roots and go. He closed his eyes and tried to sleep, but when he opened them again, Bhart was still sitting next to him, watching him in the light of the glowbe, and whispering prayers in the old tongue, barely a whisper over the chirping of crickets, the hooting of owls, and all the buzzing and screeching of the night creatures in the tangled canopy of Mon Mang'alar.

Baboo said it was my spirit who killed Roe, Fin thought, *and not me. These Bhizini must be wrong about me too.*

He drifted in and out of sleep, not sure if things were about to get much better, or much worse.

Chapter 37

Too Much to Let Go

R AKK RAEDER DIDN'T LIKE it one bit.

All those times Ellex Andria had rejected him—especially the final time—she'd always told him it was because they couldn't mix their sap, couldn't build a dynasty together. Every scamp they might have would be cursed with blotchy skin, a Bhizini, an outcast, a savage abomination—her own words—and yet, she'd had a scamp with his father.

The thought made him sick.

And now she'd run off to Andramere without telling him. Without facing him. Without even speaking to him. His plan to find her and beg for her forgiveness for the fiasco at the Balancing Act had turned into fantasies of finding her and giving her a piece of his mind.

But he had bigger problems than a broken heart, right?

Yes, he reminded himself. *My family. My throne. My damn traitorous sister. My slave—and brother—Rhannokti, disobeying my authority. Even his very existence.*

But no. The anguish he felt was for Ellex, not for his kingdom—not for the future he hardly thought possible anymore, but for the one he'd always dreamed of.

Get yourself together, Raeder, he told himself. *Focus, focus.*

Since Ellex was already gone, there was no reason to linger in Balan Su, so Rakk headed for Nunan, using the secret passage he'd taken to get into the city. When he reached the final room at the bottom of the lagoon, he filled his lungs to capacity as the water flowed into the chamber and the door opened. He immediately began to rise and he drifted upward, slowly through the dark water, the temperature growing warmer as he approached the surface.

He could just make out the cliffside and he swam up against it, then headed left for the shore. When he reached it, he climbed onto the sand, opened his waterproof satchel, and pulled out a clean scholarly robe from the Academicon. Then he stripped and pulled it over his head, strapped his weapons to his legs and to his waist, then folded up the satchel and stored it in his robe. He followed the shore of the lagoon south, toward the northernmost of the myriad boardwalks that crisscrossed the sandy marshes of Nunan.

The Rusty Fin sat wedged between the lagoon and the harbor, on a narrow spit of land between the docks for smaller boats along the shore and the pier for larger boats farther out. Glowbes were lit on the boardwalks but spaced so far apart they looked like smears of orange fading away in the distance. When Rakk stepped inside, the bar was busy and a band played in one corner, with people dancing in front of them. The sudden lack of fog in the interior made the place look huge.

When he smelled the food and heard it sizzling behind the bar, his stomach growled and churned, and he realized he hadn't eaten anything since getting out of the Dankburn. And though he knew he risked his health eating at a place like this, he couldn't help himself. He ordered a pond scum, a signature dish on Nunan, with bits of flame-charred rhupan in a bowl of thickened rum sauce. It looked like they'd scooped it up out of the shallows right outside the bar, but Rakk put it to his lips and began to slurp up the salty goodness.

It burned as it went down, but he put the bowl on the counter and asked for another. He was partway through the next one when he felt Q'orin touch his mind, and he could sense that he was behind him.

Rakk turned and offered him the rest of the pond scum, but Q'orin crinkled his nose. "I can't believe you'd eat anything from here," he said. "You know better than that."

"Nature calls," he said. "Look at me. I'm wasting away."

Q'orin looked him up and down. "My prince has indeed lost a few pounds."

"Shhh—" Rakk gave Q'orin a look. "None of that. Incognito. Remember?"

Q'orin nodded.

"So what'd you find out?"

He started to speak but Rakk cut him off.

"Good news only, alright buddy?"

"In that case, I've little to report. I couldn't find any of the men you mentioned. But I'm told there is someone who might be able to help us." Q'orin looked around the bar. "But it seems he's not here yet."

"Then let's have a drink," Rakk said. "Come on."

"You order, I'll find a booth," Q'orin said. "Tell the bartender I want the second best rum he's got."

Rakk found Q'orin in the back corner, where they could both sit with their backs to the wall and keep an eye on both the front and back doors, as well as the stair to the upper level.

"What's next, my—er—?" Q'orin said, cutting off the prince part.

"That's what I need to talk to you about," Rakk said.

"Sorry to interrupt, but our contact has arrived."

Rakk watched the tall, wide figure enter the bar. A Raccorin, with bright green skin, wearing operator fatigues that had seen better days. He had a harried look on his face, long worry lines across his forehead, but Rakk immediately recognized him, even after so many years. He stood to go and greet him when a small, hooded figure in a pradeshan robe approached the Raccorin, and Rakk stopped. The figure spoke and the Raccorin nodded, then turned back to the door. Rakk gasped when he saw Ellex Andria's face in the shadow of the hood.

What the holy fuck *is she doing on Nunan? Rajj told me she went to Andramere! Is that really her?*

His heart was racing and he looked at Q'orin. "You didn't tell me your contact was Qaa'milo."

"Who?"

"Don't you remember? From P'anorum?"

Q'orin shook his head. "I don't."

"I think that's Ellex with him. Come on," he said, when he saw them step outside. "Or we'll lose them."

Rakk and Q'orin left the bar and followed them down the dock along the water, then inland along the boardwalks over the marshes. When they took a side stair, down into the sand below the planks, they slipped over the opposite edge, landing softly in the sand, then crouched low behind the piling, listening.

"You're sure it's the right blend? Only that specific one will work."

It was Ellex for sure.

"I ain't jerkin' ya. You want it or not? I got customers lined up waiting. I got other deals to make tonight, believe it or not, so I don't got all night." Qaa'milo kept looking over his shoulder, nervous and jumpy.

"I...well, I suppose—" Ellex hesitated, and Rakk thought she looked as on edge as the dealer.

Qaa'milo took a step toward Ellex and Rakk sprang into action, an enormous blur sweeping across the sand, slamming into Qaa'milo, grabbing him round the neck, and holding him against the piling.

Ellex jumped back, shrieking. "Put him down at once! How dare you seize a private citizen in this manner!"

He turned toward Ellex and was surprised to see an enflamer trained at his face.

"Easy, mama," he said, shaking off his hood.

Ellex gaped at him, and the enflamer started to lower, but then she held it back up and glared at him.

"Hey buddy, I'm sorry, I really am," Qaa'milo said, squirming. "You can have everything, you can have it all. Your sweetie doesn't have to pay. It's a gift tonight. On the house. Really. Just don't snap my fibers. Please don't snap me in half."

Rakk leaned close to Qaa'milo, his face in his, leering. "I'm going to do more than that. I'm going to…" He dropped the Raccorin to his feet. "Give you a big hug!" he said, and he wrapped him in his arms.

"The—fuck?" Qaa'milo was twitching badly now, and Rakk felt bad.

"Don't you recognize me, you little twig you—well, not so little anymore, hey? You got wider, or is it just me? Come on Q, it's me, Raeder. It's Rakk."

When Qaa'milo realized who he was, his face collapsed into pudding and he began to sob, and he threw himself into Rakk's arms for another hug.

"Easy there, buddy. Easy.—"

But Qaa'milo had sunk to his knees to bow before him.

"My prince," he said. "Oh my prince. You've finally returned to your Qaa'milo."

"Get ahold of yourself now, bud. Up, up, there you go. We're incognito after all. No need for demonstrations in the sand."

"And I'm not his sweetie," Ellex said. She'd lowered the weapon but was still glaring at Rakk.

"Not now, love," Rakk said. "This is my old friend, Qaa'milo. Everyone called him Big Q. He's from P'anorum."

Ellex's scowl slipped and she looked at Qaa'milo again with softer eyes.

"I…wasn't there," he said, "when it, you know, when my family—when the city—when we lost everything."

He sniffed and Ellex gave him a hug.

"I lost my parents that night, too," she said.

Qaa'milo looked at her again and recognition came to his eyes. "You—your the good-mother of Andrasia. Sui Pradesh Ellex Andria!" He looked like he might swoon. "The crown prince of Raccorum Rhazzat and the ruler of Andrasia. And on Nunan, no less! The world's crazy, no?" He shook his head, his mouth open, then he looked at Ellex again. "Sui Pradesh, you're even more beautiful in real life than on the weavryn, if that's even possible. And your dream—it was—"

"Sui Pradesh doesn't need to be reminded of that now," Rakk said.

"You're right," Qaa'milo said. "Forgive me. It's like a dream seeing you, Reader. My life's been nothing since P'anorum was lost. I never had my father's skill with people, his management of affairs. I don't know how he did it, how he dealt with everyone, how he managed to not get taken advantage of. I squandered what I had left. Had to become an operator. But—" He shook his head, and seemed to shake off his sadness. "Say, you two must be on something very hush hush. Incognito, bhiza to numb your crystal." His eyes lit up and he sealed his lips with his hand. "You know, seeing you again—I feel like, well, like somebody again. And damnit, that's worth something. What do you two need? Anything, anything at all. Though—well, I don't have much to give. But I do know Nunan like the back of my own hand."

Ellex and Rakk looked at each other.

"Sui Pradesh will be taking that bhiza now," Rakk said, and Qaa'milo gave Ellex the bag. "I was looking for the same stuff, but it looks like this will be enough for us both. If it's the real deal." He opened the bag and offered it to Ellex. "After you," he said. "And now me too." He swallowed a small bite of the paste, and it left a musky aftertaste on his tongue.

Much better cooked up with sugar, he thought.

Then he opened his mind's eye and reached out for the weavryn, looking for the servryn, but couldn't find it anywhere. He tried to contact Q'orin, but he couldn't sense him, even though he stood nearby in the shadows.

"That's the stuff," Ellex said.

"I'm good for my word," Qaa'milo said. "Is there anything else I can help you with? Please, let me help."

Rakk looked at Ellex. "Sui Pradesh, perhaps you'd like to explain the plan."

"I—" she shot Rakk a dirty look, "*we*—are making for Callo Baton." She looked at Rakk again, and he nodded. "But we want to arrive unannounced, not to the official port, and not on a registered transport."

"You need a skimp'rin bound for Mangis," Qaa'milo said. "You won't have to worry about Cult'avin at the port, seeing as it's within Mon Mang'alar. You can get a skiff'rin from there to Callo Baton. I know a captain who can take you. He practices the utmost discretion—won't ask a single question. He departs at first light in the morning, docking space 94."

That was easy, Rakk thought. *Finally, a surprise that isn't tragic.*

"I'll go and arrange it now," Qaa'milo said.

"Docking space 94," Ellex smiled and touched his shoulder.

When he had gone, she rounded on Rakk.

"Your sweetie?! You have a lot of nerve, Raeder."

Rakk looked hurt. "I wasn't trying to upset you, just playing along with what Qaa'milo had said."

Ellex blushed. "You'll start rumors. And besides, what the hell are you doing here? You're supposed to be in the Dankburn!"

"Long story," he said. "So what's on Callo Baton?"

"None of your business!" She shook her head. "You let me down at the Balancing Act, Raeder. You promised to protect me, to protect my city! If you hadn't lost your temper, as you always do, you wouldn't have run headlong into that trap, and you wouldn't have been drugged. It was your fault you weren't there to control the Defenders. I don't know if I can still trust you."

Rakk felt his heart breaking again but he tried not to let it show.

"You know," he said, "I'm something of a plant of faith, believe it or not. This meeting tonight, this old friend of mine, running into you here, the both of us heading to the same place—this wasn't chance. We're both seeking answers. We're both under fire back home. We've both been lied to, for most of our lives. And we both, more than anything, want the truth."

Ellex looked at the ground, then closed her eyes. "You heard the plant. Docking space 94. First thing in the morning. Good evening." She headed for the stairs.

Rakk wanted to offer to walk her to wherever she was staying, to protect her while she slept, to hold her through the night, to stand outside her door, whatever she asked of him, so long as he was near her.

"Evening, Sui Pradesh," was all he could say.

He thought about following her, about protecting her without invitation, and making sure none of the shady characters of Nunan tried to harm her. But he knew Ellex Andria was the type of plant who could handle herself. She had an enflamer in her pocket, for Trevian's sake.

So much for being angry with her, he thought.

❦

Rakk decided he'd return to the Rusty Fin, rent a perch for the evening, and sleep his sorrows away. He reached for Q'orin, forgetting his crystal was numb, then called out to him instead.

He emerged from the shadows.

"Didn't feel like socializing?" Rakk said.

Q'orin ignored the question. "Callo Baton, is it? I've always wanted to visit the headquarters of the Guild. I hear the city is unlike any place in the world, a true wonder of maquina."

"I'm afraid you won't be going with me."

Q'orin hesitated. "I go where you go, my prince. Always."

"Not this time. You don't realize it, but you've endangered me by coming here tonight."

Q'orin looked uncertain. "I don't understand."

"I know you're careful. You're the best. But the Corkin crystal itself could be compromised. I can't be sure who is watching, who is tracking me—tracking me through you. My sister—my brother—the Pradishar—I don't want anyone watching me or following me. I'm a fugitive right now, and until I get the answers I need, nobody can know where I am. Even you."

Q'orin said nothing, but his face showed grave concern.

"What would you have me do?" he said finally.

Rakk smiled. "Good plant," he said. "Like I said, you're the best. You're the only one I can ask to do this. And 'm putting you in terrible danger by doing so."

Q'orin waited, saying nothing.

"I need you to save my throne, Q'orin. To save my mandate. You will sail for Raccorum Rhazzat. I'll join you as soon as I can. I promise. But I have to clear my name first. And I need evidence to stop Raq'asha and her push for Rishar. I need you to sail for Rheganza, and from there, make your way into the interior. Head for Rhaknon. See how the nobles and orden are doing in their clades, where they stand on Rishar, and why." He put his hand on Q'orin's shoulder. "I will meet you in Rhaknon by the equinox to plan our next move. I promise."

Q'orin nodded. "I'll be there, having done all that you asked."

Rakk sighed. "There's something else," he said. "Your crystal—you can't move about unwatched if you're still joined to the Corkin."

Q'orin reached for a weapon at his ankle, and Rakk's eyes grew wide when he saw what it was—a Bhizini scytherin.

Rakk took the blade reverently, his face solemn.

Where did he get this?

"The Corkin crystal is for life," Rakk said. "I may not be able to clear you as a deserter. If you're captured by the Corkin, or anyone in Balance Authority, you'll likely be executed on the spot, even as my private slave."

"I understood the risk when I handed you my blade, my prince."

Rakk touched the Corkin crystal on Q'orin's forehead, then moved his huge hand so it was cupping the back of Q'orin's head. Q'orin stuck the sheath in his mouth and bit down on it. One quick slice with a scytherin blade across the face of a crystal was enough to mortally wound it and render it useless. But the pain was said to be nearly unbearable to endure.

I should free him entirely, Rakk thought. *I should let him go.*

His hand fell, and the blade slid across the Corkin crystal—but not across the crystal that bound the two of them.

Rakk never made it to the Rusty Fin. He spent the night there under the boardwalks, in the sand, holding Q'orin as he trembled and moaned. When the crystal shatters, it disintegrates and dissolves over a period of hours, like glass under the skin slowly melting. The process wasn't fatal, but it felt like a death of sorts.

Crystals, Rakk thought. *They grow. They grow inside us, until they're something like a part of us, tied into our memories, to our experiences, to who we are. And we don't even know what they are, or where they come from.*

When first light began to paint the horizon red, Q'orin's trembling grew softer and finally he was still, breathing softly, a peaceful look on his face. On his forehead, his adobe-colored crystal—the one that held him in bondage to Rakk alone—shimmered a dusky red alongside the puckered hole where his Corkin crystal had been.

I should have slit the other one too, he said, full of guilt. But he ran his fingers through Q'orin's hair fibers, and breathed deeply of his scent, and knew he could never let him go.

As twilight grew in the east, Q'orin opened his eyes and looked up at Rakk. When he saw that his prince held him like a scamp in his arms, he sat up quickly, blushing, and was soon on his feet, standing to attention, as if he hadn't spent the night enduring the worst misery of his life.

"My prince must hurry or he'll miss his ship," Q'orin said, "if you're still sure about this?"

"I'm sure," Rakk said, giving him a small smile.

"But I'm always with you," Q'orin said. "You'll need me. I'm your shadow, your shield. How many times have I saved you? You'll need me."

"I know I will," Rakk said. "I do right now. I need you to go save my throne. You're the only one I can trust. But no more talk, my old friend. Let us be off already, that the time til our reunion can already begin to shrink and vanish away."

Rakk started for the docks, and he turned back to look at Q'orin one more time, but he'd already faded away into the fog.

Chapter 38

Off the Crescent and Into the Sea

Ellex Andria wished she had more time. She would have liked to have stayed at her garden through the summer, Qaas'i safely tucked away while she healed, safe from prying eyes—safe from the government that would have ordered her immediate exile. Uthyr had insisted on getting her papers, on fudging a cover story about why Ellex was traveling to Andramere with a Bhizini, but she refused to take the risk that some notestreamer would start to dig. Regardless, she was going to leave the capital. She needed answers, and she needed to make Lithuigi Von'nDrino pay for what he'd done to her and her daughter. But the thought of venturing out across the Inner Seas, in secret, with a mute little invalid at her side, trying not to be seen by anyone who might recognize her, wasn't what she had in mind.

Her daughter had been awake now for several days but had yet to speak again. She just stared with that blank look, unresponsive, lethargic. She'd slept and sunned, slept and sunned, not moving from the perch near the edge of the rim, her eyes gazing across the fog bank, but not seeming to see anything.

Ellex didn't even know how much she understood. Requests had gone mostly unacknowledged, like the request to pull up her rootpads and take a few steps around the garden. When Ellex tried to change her clothes, Qaas'i had looked at her with wide eyes as she pulled gently on the robe, and when she touched her skin, soft though her touch had been, Qaas'i opened her mouth and screamed, a sound so sharp and loud, Ellex had to pull away from her and put her hands over her ears.

When Qaas'i stopped screaming, she tried again, careful to avoid touching her, and finally pulled off the robe.

So small, Ellex thought. The sight of her daughter, so frail and tiny, made her feel overwhelmed with sadness, and she hurried to take the soiled robe to the laundry, not wanting Qaas'i to see her crying. She came back with a clean pradeshan robe, some scissors, and a needle and thread, and she sat down at the table near where Qaas'i was perched and began to alter the robe.

Ellex could see her daughter craning her neck to see what she was doing.

"Why don't you come watch, love?" Ellex said, patting the table next to her, but Qaas'i gave her a blank look.

Ellex snipped a good length off the bottom of the robe and carefully folded over the ragged edge and sewed it down upon itself, passing the needle from inside to out and back again, and pulling it high up in to the air to get the thread through. Qaas'i watched with wide eyes, her head moving as Ellex's hand moved. When Ellex finished with the new seam, Qaas'i had come to stand next to her, and she couldn't help but smile, a single tear running down her cheek.

Qaas'i watched it fall, and when it dripped off the bottom of her chin, she looked down at the ground to see where it went.

Thank Trevian she's getting curious, Ellex thought. *She just needs a little more time.*

"Shall we try them out?" she asked, holding up the altered robes.

Qaas'i looked at her with alarm, and when Ellex moved to put them over her head, she ducked away and hissed.

"You have to get dressed, love," Ellex said.

Qaas'i hissed again.

"Here," Ellex said, setting them down on the chair. "How about you put them on? I'll show you how." She stood up and pulled her own robe over her head, careful not to snag it on her cumberdome. Then she held it up so Qaas'i could see it. "This is the front side, and this is the back. Your head goes right through here, like this. And then your arms, one after the other, like this. Then you can straighten it up and, voila!" She twirled in a circle and posed with her arms out, palms upward. "Now you try."

Qaas'i just stared at her.

"You have to get dressed, love. We have somewhere we need to be. I wish we could stay here until you were feeling better, but we have to go. It's dangerous for us in the city. We'll be safer once we get to sea."

Already lying to my scamp, Ellex thought. *A great start to my career as a parent.*

"I'm going to go and make sure everything's in order for our trip. You try and put that robe on, okay?"

Another blank stare, but when Ellex returned to the terrace an hour later, Qaas'i had the robe on and she was a taking a few incautious steps around the garden, watching the fabric swirl, and rubbing her hands on it.

Ellex watched her as more tears fell.

⁘⁘⁘⁘⁘ ⁘⁘⁘⁘⁘

When it came time to head out, Pander was nearly in hysterics, unable to understand why Ellex would take such a risk. But Ellex had little patience for him, and when he saw her face, he stopped fussing and his face became serious.

"I need you to travel to Andramere," she said. "I've arranged for one of my doubles to join you en route. I need you to keep up every semblance that I'm there, passing the summer by the beach, even though I may be putting you in terrible danger for doing so. But you're the only one I can count on. And I know you won't let me down."

The old Andrasian's face lit up and he held his head high with pride. "It will be done, Sui Pradesh."

Ellex had packed a small bag with a few changes of robes, some dried rhupan, and enough merits to buy their own ship if they needed to. Then she'd forged transit documents for an unjoined scamp, signed and stamped the form, and marveled for a moment at the guilt she was feeling inside. It was the first time she could remember that she had ever willingly abused her authority like that.

They owe me at least this much, she thought.

When it came time to walk out the door, Ellex panicked.

How can I lead my daughter if I can't touch her? she thought. *How can I keep her safe if she has a meltdown every time I approach her? What if someone bumps into her and she begins to scream? What if they ask her to lower her hood and they see her blotchy skin?*

Sweet Trevian, there were so many things that could go wrong.

But fortune was on Ellex's side, at least for now. When Ellex took hold of one of the baggy sleeves of Qaas'i's robe, careful not to clutch her arm, Qaas'i didn't protest, and she followed where Ellex pulled her. Nobody on the streets of the upper rim looked twice at them as they walked for the lift station, but Ellex kept stopping, looking around nervously and reaching out with her crystal. She had the unmistakeable feeling that they were being watched, though she could sense nothing in particular.

She felt around for her Cul'tavin peacekeepers, the ones assigned to patrol the upper rim, but none of them were reporting anything suspicious. She asked them to be on their guard.

Just nerves, she told herself, gripping Qaas'i's robe even tighter.

<<I think we're being watched,>> she told Pander, and the old Andrasian gasped. His eyes twitched rapidly for a moment.

<<I sense nothing, Sui Pradesh.>>

<<Nor I. Just a feeling.>>

Once they reached the lift station, Ellex took a long look around in every direction but didn't see anything. The ride in the lift down to the port was uneventful, and nobody asked her for credentials as they started down the pier for her cata'rin.

After boarding, Ellex led Qaas'i to the bridge, then used her crystamin to open the gurgitator. She felt for the beacons in the harbor and used their locations to navigate in the fog. When she reached the great gates, still being repaired, the Cul'tavin guard greeted her warmly.

<<Keep our city safe until I return from Andramere,>> she said. << And do enjoy your summer.>>

<<May Trevian carry you there and back again, Sui Pradesh.>>

Once out in the Threshinveld Sea, Ellex turned south and came round the sandy tip of Nunan, then piloted the cata'rin back up the eastern side of the island and into the bay. She set the defenses on the ship, and ordered Pander and Qaas'i to stay below deck with the doors locked tight. When she departed, she paid the dock attendant double the normal rate. She'd seen that on a melodrama once and thought it was worth the extra merits to be on their good side.

If they have one, she thought.

The fog was thick and the glowbes lining the crisscrossing boardwalks of Nunan looked like greasy blobs of orange in the mist. She reached for the weavryn and found a map of the area, and she squinted at the wooden, weather-beaten sign hanging by the door of the nearest hut on a rusty hook. When she found her location, and pinpointed where she needed to go, she took a deep breath.

Trevian help me, she thought. *I'm about to go buy drugs from an illegal supplier, in order to avoid the government I've sworn to serve.*

The panic rose up inside her once again, but she held her head high under her hood, clenched her fists into balls, and started off into the night.

Ellex headed for the stairs later that evening, the bhiza in her pockets, the smell of Rakk Raeder still on her senses as she left him standing in the fog under the boardwalk and started back for her cata'rin. When she reached the upper level, she tried to make sense of the encounter. He was the last plant she expected to find on Nunan. He was supposed to be locked in the Dankburn! Hadn't the Council of Nine decided not to let him out until the end of summer? Wasn't he ashamed to face her after he'd failed to keep the city safe—after his bad judgement had led him into a trap?

And the question she could hardly bring herself to ask, even as it screamed at her inside her head—*How in Trevian's name can I tell him about Qaas'i? How can I explain it without breaking his heart? Is it even possible?*

Probably not.

Ellex was too distracted to realized she'd been followed, but she heard the blade before she saw it, heard the metal against the sheathe, the Vintrani sword singing as it slid out. All she could think about in that moment was why—why had she been too proud to ask Rakk to walk her back to the ship? Why had she refused his help, when she was practically helpless with her crystal numbed? And now she wondered what the notestreamers would say when they found her corpse in the marshes of Nunan. What would they do to Qaas'i when they found her—but no.

She leapt forward, dropping into a roll and springing back to her feet and into a full sprint, the boards giving slightly under her lunging steps. She felt for the enflamer with her fingers, and she pulled it from her robe and spun around, releasing a whorl of flame that singed the tips of the palm fibers that hung over the edges of the huts on either side of the boardwalk, but nobody was there. When she turned back, she gasped and aimed, but it was only the dock attendant, a wide-eyed look on his face.

Ellex boarded her cata'rin, trying to stop her hands from shaking. She perched by Qaas'i and Pander, and she stayed that way through the night, her eyes never leaving her daughter, her hand never far from her enflamer, her mind running in circles, trying to make sense of a world she no longer understood.

When first dawn came at last, Ellex woke Qaas'i, hugged Pander, and headed for the docks.

Rakk was waiting for her by the gangplank to the skimp'rin, a wide, flat, slow clunker of a ship, used mainly for transportation of heavy maquina and raw materials. This one was clearly past it's prime, and had been retrofitted into something of an illicit ferry for those without the merits to travel on the Guild liners, or those who had had their transit privileges revoked.

Ellex took a deep breath, her stomach clenching up. But Rakk had a huge grin on his face, as he stared down at the small figure next to her.

"Morning," he said. "And who do we have here?" He dropped to one knee before Qaas'i, his right arm across his waist, and he bowed low.

Big and theatrical, Ellex thought. *Just like his father.*

Qaas'i's speckled green face barely protruded from the purple and gray hood over her head, and she fixed Rakk with a blank, wide-eyed stare.

"This is my daughter," Ellex said, her throat tight. "Qaas'andria."

He knew, she thought. *Rajj must have told him. But is he really okay with it?*

"What a beautiful princess our fair queen has," he said. "My lovely little Qaas'andria, I am Rhakksees Raccorine Deri the Third, but you can call me Rakk Raeder, as my friends do." He winked at her. "I am ever at your service." He took Qaas'i's tiny hand in his massive one, and she winced but didn't scream, and didn't pull away.

Ellex's mouth fell open. "You can call her Qaas'i," she managed to get out.

"Qaas'i," he said, "if you ever need anything—anything at all—you just take this finger of yours, and give me a poke, just like this." He took her finger and used it to poke his arm, and then he grinned at her.

She gave him the tiniest of smiles, so tiny he might have missed it.

But Ellex didn't.

The gurgitator rumbled to life and Rakk stood, offered his hand to Qaas'i, gave Ellex a smile, and started up the gangplank. Ellex followed, feeling guilty with herself for feeling upset. No, truly, she was happy that Rakk had gotten through to her.

She's his sister, after all.

And yet it still hurt.

Rakk took them to their quarters, which ended up being little more than a corner alcove amidst heaps of unmarked cargo, and he filled her in on the details of the voyage he'd gotten from the captain. They'd be crossing the Threshinveld directly, rather than sticking to the Great Sea Lanes, which followed close to the archipelago and then cut back along the northern edge of the Tranquin reefs. This way they'd avoid contact with any Balance cruisers, but they'd also be exposed to the notorious storms which sprang up now and again in the Threshinveld in the summertime, turning the normally flat waters into a hell-scape of mountains and valleys, with raging wind and blinding rain. Even a ship as large and flat and slow as this skimp'rin had been known to be turned over.

They avoided any storms on the first few days, but on the third, the skies turned gray and the waters began to heave. When the nausea hit, Ellex tried to maintain her composure, tried to stay focused, to exert her will over her body. But there are moments in life, few though they may be, when the body wins out, when our will never even had a chance. It wasn't long before the entire world seemed to be swirling around her in one direction while she spun about in the other.

Rakk must have gotten her up to the deck and over to the side, she couldn't recall. All she knew was her insides were being wrung out like a sponge, and even if she'd wanted to, she wouldn't have been able to do anything else, not even sit up and look around to see if Qaas'i was okay.

What was I thinking, coming alone? If Rakk wasn't here—
She felt like the biggest fool in the world.

When the worst of it was over, and she was able to turn away from the railing without wanting to die, she saw that Rakk was sitting just behind her, his back against the cabin wall. Qaas'i sat cross-legged at his side, and he had one of his huge arms draped around her shoulders. His eyes were closed and he was smiling, and Qaas'i looked happy too.

Ellex hugged the railing and let the tears flow.

Chapter 39

Adrift in the Forgotten City

BRYN DIDN'T HAVE TIME to process the fact that she was cellmates with the most famous weavryn performer in the world, not to mention the crown prince of Andramere, because the door to the cell slid open and a towering figure in Cul'tavin fatigues and a long pradeshan robe stepped into the opening, zapren in hand.

"You're finally awake," the peacekeeper said, "just when I was thinking I might have to toss you overboard."

When Bryn saw the uniform, she leapt for the hollow with her mind, and nearly sealed herself off inside it once again. But she fought down her nerves and kept part of her awareness with her body, while with her inner senses, she could feel Anorian with her.

"Come along," the Cul'tavin said, looking at Bryn.

She tried to stand but fell back to her knees.

"You beast," Jaun said. "Can't you see she's injured? She needs rhupan, sunshine!"

Bryn looked at the Cul'tavin again, trying not to tremble, but when she saw his face, saw the blotches of bright and dull green, her mind reeled.

A Bhizini? We're being held captive by a Bhizini?

"Shut it, von Andron," the peacekeeper said, "or I'll see your entire face gets scabbed over."

And then Bryn recognized their jailer—Roman Anthem, a peacekeeper of the Pradishar and servant of the Gran Pradesh, Ra'shard Ruu'n.

Anthem grabbed her by the arm and pulled her to her feet, and he pushed her through the door. She stumbled but used her rootpads to grip the deck, and took a few wobbly steps forward, as she cried out for Anorian in her mind.

<<You're very brave, Bryn,>> Anorian said. <<And strong. Stay here with me, but don't abandon your body again, or he might hurt you.>>

<<I can't do this,>> Bryn said. She could see Aerid and E'mo, see Malisha Andra'asnia, every time she saw the Cul'tavin uniform, and she pulled back from her body. Anorian

held her and whispered in her mind, and Bryn felt a rush of confidence and admiration, and she felt like maybe she could handle this after all.

She didn't have far to go, just across the corridor to an identical cell. Once inside, Anthem shut the door behind them. His eyes twitched and a series of slats on the wall opened. Bryn winced at the brightness of the light but moaned when it hit her skin, and she drank deeply of it.

The slats slammed shut and Bryn suppressed a whimper.

"Who is Anorian Grain?" Anthem said.

"Who?" Bryn said, surprised the words came out so naturally, so automatically.

Anthem exhaled through his nose and his eyes fluttered. Bryn felt him sharing with her through the crystamin. The stream came into her mind's eye, and she saw herself, in the plaza on Andramere, her face flushed, her eyes streaming tears, limping toward whomever was looking at her—Malisha Andra'asnia, no doubt—and Bryn watched herself screaming, "I have information on Anorian Grain!"

She tried to breath, but it came out in short, broken gasps, almost sobs.

"If that wasn't proof enough," Anthem said, "your ability to block my scans is all I need, from you and von Andron both, to be convinced of your complicity with the traitor. You've blocked every Cul'tavin who's tried to probe you, just as your father did. Just as every other treasonous Ren'fallow we've roasted has done. Only Anorian Grain knows this technique, Bryn. Only Anorian Grain can teach it to others."

He stepped toward her and Bryn seemed to wither, as the room around her felt like it was being drawn in to crush her.

She couldn't breath.

"I—" she started, but she couldn't get any more out. She shook her head no.

Anthem tsked. "I'd hoped you'd be more cooperative than von Andron. Pity."

"I don't know who Anorian is," Bryn whispered. "I swear it. Please, don't hurt me."

He sighed, a sad look on his face.

"I believe you," he said, and the slats on the walls opened again. "I think you've been deceived, Bryn, unwittingly used by forces who don't care about you, or about your family."

She looked warily at Anthem as she soaked up the light, trying not to show how much she was enjoying it, how much she needed it.

He shut the slats again, and she thought she might cry.

"You're a smart plant, Bryn Andri'n, brilliant even. And it's really a simple matter. You only have to ask yourself what you want. I know you want to return to Andramere, to your cramped little nook at the library, to your classes at the Academicon, to your bright future. Now that your father isn't around to dissuade you, you can become the tinker you've always dreamed of becoming. I have assurances from the Dyna'arin, when all this blows over and you're a free citizen again, they'd be honored to have you enroll in the Guild. Won't that be wonderful?"

The slats opened again but Bryn didn't feel the light.

"Think it over," Anthem said. "Decide what you want most. As I said, it's a simple matter, but I know it's still a choice, and choices are never easy to make. Lucky for you we still have time. But I can't wait for your cooperation forever. Think well, Bryn. Are you really going to throw it all away for a stranger, for someone who has brought you and your family such grief? Surely you're smarter than that."

Bryn felt numb when she got back to her cell. She sat down next to Jaun and put her back against the wall. He had a troubled look on his face, but he smiled when she looked at him.

"You okay, champ?" Jaun said. "Did he hurt you?"

Bryn shook her head no.

"Let me guess," he said. "He asked about Anorian, and when you told him the truth that you don't know who Anorian Grain is, he threatened you, then offered to give you back everything you've lost—we'll, not everything. But your life. Andramere. A future. Am I right?"

Tears sprang to her eyes and she shook her head yes again. "All lies then?" she whispered.

"There's no going back," he said, peeking through one of the slats at the open surface of the water. "There's only drifting in circles."

"Why?" she said. "Why are they holding us at sea? And why him?"

"Good questions, Bryn" he said. "But I'm not sure I have the answers."

"How do you know me?" she said.

"I suppose you didn't introduce yourself," he said. "You're accent—you're from Andramere, no? And I know who all of my future subjects are."

Bryn hissed through her nose. "A statistical impossibility."

"Indeed." He grinned, but then his face fell. "I was a friend of your father's. He was my teacher a decade ago at the Academicon, and he supervised my initiation with the Guild."

She looked at the four crystals in a diamond pattern on his forehead. "He never told us about you. And he refused to let me join."

"Really?" Jaun said. "Did he give a reason?"

"Only superfluous ones to get me to put it off. We fought a few times about it, but he'd never give me a straight answer. Not that long ago, I would have sworn I knew my father better than anyone—knew how his mind worked. But now I realize how many secrets he had, how much he was plotting and scheming. And I can't understand it. What would make him do all of these things? And why would he keep us out of the loop, live a lie, for so long?"

"He was a good plant, Bryn," Jaun said. "Don't forget that. Don't let Anthem, or anyone else, convince you otherwise."

"I won't," Bryn said through her tears. "I would never."

❧ ☙

The days passed one after the other, all blending together into what felt like a perpetual state of existence, as if the flow of time itself had stopped. Roman Anthem hadn't returned to speak with either of them in a week, and there were some days when they got no food, no fresh water either. The gurgitator would close, and the ship would fall silent, and they'd wonder if Anthem was still aboard. Was he right outside their door, listening in on them?

Bryn had been trying to get a glimpse of the shore through the narrow slats in the wall, but all she could see, day after day, was endless blue waters. After discussing it with Jaun, she was convinced they really were sailing in circles, out of sight of land, going nowhere.

The monotony and the boredom of it were bad enough, but Bryn spent most of her time wracked with guilt over her father's death, and desperate to hear from her mother and her friends. When she finally tried to contact her mother, she'd been unable to sense her, and there'd been no word on the notestreams about her. But with her husband an executed traitor and her daughter in custody for the same crime, there was little hope the Cul'tavin would leave her alone.

<<Anorian?>> Bryn reached out with the crystal, down through the hollow. <It's me, Bryndax.>>

She felt Anorian before the tree of many colored fruits appeared in front of her, a soft smile on its trunk.

<<Your father's nickname for you. That's perfect. I was just about to contact you. But you go first.>>

<<I'm worried about my mother. I can't feel her.>>

<<Stylina Andri'n is unharmed,>> Anorian said.

Bryn felt like she could breathe again.

<<But the Pradishar have modified her crystamin. You won't be able to contact her.>>

Modified her crystamin? What exactly does that mean?

<<I'm afraid if I interfere, I'll bring the wrath of the Cul'tavin down upon her,>> Anorian said. <<I'm so sorry, Bryndax. I should have told you earlier. Eased your mind. But you didn't ask.>>

<<Maybe I didn't want to know.>>

Bryn felt an enormous sadness coming from Anorian, a crushing surge of pain and alarm and despair.

<<You don't trust me.>>

<<I do,>> Bryn said. <<I mean, I think I do. I feel safe with you. But—well, I still feel like you're keeping secrets from me.>>

<<It's my fault. I waited too long to let you in the circle. I tried to protect you, but you only got hurt as a result. If I had acted sooner, I might have saved you from suffering.>>

She could feel Anorian weeping and it broke her heart all over again.

In the hollow, she grabbed hold of Anorian's trunk, wrapped her arms around the coarse bark, and flooded the crystal with feelings of confidence and support and—need?

<<I was about to reach out for you because I wanted to show you something,>> Anorian said. <<Before I show the others. Would you like to see?>>

<<What others?>>

<<The other servants of knowledge. The other defenders of privacy. Those who risk their lives to speak truth to power. Some are believers, eager to fight the Ren'fallow and their lust for annihilation. Some were swept up in it all without knowing what they were getting themselves into. They are my friends, Bryndax, some of them at least. And they're all, to a certain extent, my allies. Your allies as well. But there will be time for them later. Right now, this—this is for you, Bryndax. For you and for Doc Andri'n.>>

In her mind's eye, Bryn had been standing in a field of soft, sturdy soil, the sky around her dark, barely lit by twilight, and Anorian stood near her, a familiar tree with fruits of many colors. Everything faded to black around her, even the ground melted away, and Bryn felt like she had lost her balance.

But then a scene popped into view, as quickly as if she'd opened her eyes to it. A city had manifested all around and beneath her, and she could feel the cobblestones of the wide plaza in which she was now standing—could see the buildings rising up in the distance, red and pink and turquoise stones, interspersed with thickets of lush foliage and bedecked with vines of tropical flowers. The city was on a hillside, a small mountain rising behind a tiered palace, the sea down below at its feet, with dense forests surrounding the city on either side.

<<Wow,>> Bryn said, turning in circles to take in the view. <<This is one of the most beautiful cities I've ever seen! As beautiful as Avalon, if that's possible. Did you create all this?>>

<<Yes,>> Anorian said. <<And no. This is Dar Ka'Hala. There was a city like this, long, long ago, so long its been forgotten by all but a handful.>>

<<It's amazing. I can smell the flowers—feel the sunshine on my face! If only that light could feed me.>>

<<But then we'd never live in the outside world, would we?>> Anorian said.

Bryn laughed. <<So just what exactly is this place?>>

<<Well, as you know, when someone first comes into the hollow, its like falling into a black hole inside of yourself. It's only once you're in, and once you know what you're doing, that you can start to project your own images and create your own reality. You were able to do so immediately, and with great skill, but some never get the hang of it. In addition to making something that would keep everyone safely anonymous, able to come and go, to read and learn as they please, I also wanted it to be more like a physical place than a mental one, a real meeting ground and study spot, a place to plan and share and plot and commiserate. I wanted it to be a place of refuge for the world, tucked, as it were, inside the greater structure of the weavryn, and yet unbound by its rules. What better place for all that than a city?>>

<<It's wonderful.>>

<<May I show you around?>>

Bryn nodded and Anorian began to rise into the air. Bryn opened her mind and followed her. They floated up into the air together and drifted across the plaza toward the palace on the slopes of the mountainside, and Anorian pointed out the parts of the city as they drifted along. By the end of the tour, she'd seen all the common spaces that could be altered as needed for use by the public, as well as the palace where their circle could work in privacy. They visited a library that looked almost identical to the one on Andramere, and once inside, Anorian led her to a replica of her office.

Bryn started crying when she saw it.

She felt Anorian's alarm.

<<I didn't mean to upset you, Bryndax. I'd hoped to make you smile.>>

<<I'm not upset. Well, I am, but not for anything you've done. I just—I guess I sort of assumed I was going to die here on this ship, and never see my home again. I know this isn't the real one, but—Sweet Trevian, thank you, Anorian. Thank you!>>

Bryn felt flooded with warmth and with gratitude.

<<You won't always be on that ship, Bryndax. Before you know it, you'll be free. And while I can't promise that the nightmare will be over, I can promise that I won't keep you in the dark anymore. I hope, when that time comes, that I can ask a favor of you.>>

<<After everything you've done for me, and for my father—how could I refuse you?>>

The warmth and gratitude surged inside Bryn again, and she felt—

<<Let's meet the others now,>> Anorian said. <<Meet me in front of the palace?>>

Bryn nodded and Anorian vanished.

She spent a minute looking around the library—it was impeccably detailed, and Bryn couldn't believe it, but the books and scrolls on the shelves were filled with data, the very data she had spent the last few years archiving.

Before she left the library, she imagined clothing herself in an outfit that looked like a platyporse from the plains of Andrasia, and she could feel herself transforming into one, her hands and feet turning into hooves while long curved horns sprouted from her head. She giggled at the sensation, and took a few paces around the entrance, amused at the clippity-clopping sound that echoed off the walls, and imagining the look the old librarian Madr'gin would have had at seeing such a sight in her hallowed library.

When she wandered outside, she was shocked to see that the promenade in front of the palace, which looked down on the sprawling plaza where she'd first appeared, was now populated with various creatures and objects, all of them standing around Anorian's tree of many colored fruits.

Bryn galloped toward them, and slowed to a trot as she approached. Everyone was busy chatting about the city around them, and how amazing it all was, how beautiful, how realistic.

Anorian spread out her branches. <<Everyone, I'm honored to introduce the Mighty B*zzness,>> she said, using Bryn's alias from her notestream. Some in the crowd gasped with surprise, and with delight.

<<How we've missed your stream of late,>> said a large crab with giant upheld pincers.

<<Here, here!>> said a mangalar tree.

<<Does this mean you'll be streaming again?>> asked a massive branta bird.

<<Are you looking for contributors? Many of us here would like to help. I know I would,>> said a small sun wrapped in chains.

<<Patience, everyone,>> Anorian said. <<There's time for that later. Right now, I want you all to make the Mighty B*zzness feel welcome. And un-pressured!>>

Bryn smiled at everyone. <<To be honest, I hadn't even thought of our stream. I don't even know if my friends, my partners, are safe.>> She looked at Anorian, wanting to ask her, wanting to know—but she turned back to the crowd. <<My whole world has turned upside down lately, and—>> She sighed. <<I'm honored that you miss us, and when I've healed—and when my friends are safe—maybe then I'll be able to do it again.>>

She was crushed, and truly flattered, at the same time. And after weeks with only Jaun von Andron's company, it was a pleasure to be around others—others who were excited to be around her. And the city, this new incarnation of the weavryn, was absolutely revolutionary, and she felt how momentous a moment it was deep in her heart. Maybe there was hope she'd get out of all this, somehow.

But when Bryn shifted a bit of her awareness back to her body, felt her fibers sore and stiff from confinement, her flesh aching for light, for water—the smell of her hot, dirty skin, the wooly stench of her hair fibers—her cracked lips that kept leaking sap—all the relief she'd felt inside the hollow felt inconsequential and irrelevant. Unreal. What did it matter if she could muck about in a mental playground when her body was in such pain, her heart so heavy it felt it would crush in on itself?

She looked out the slit at the flat surface of the sea, at the sky overhead, but it was all a big blue blur through her tears.

Chapter 40

Bittersweet Community

Traveling through the swamps of Mon Mang'alar was like traveling through the sea, in that everywhere looked exactly like everywhere else to the untrained eye. Fin'roq couldn't even tell if they'd been traveling mostly in one direction or not. North, south, east, and west were meaningless in the bog, at least to him.

They'd been nearly a week on the move, and Fin'roq's body was healing. His wounds had closed and his muscles didn't cramp and ache and throb whenever he moved. But he still found it hard to do much but sit and sleep—and whenever his mind started to wander away from where he was at, it was to think of Jaun and to ache as he had never ached before, and to feel with complete certainty that the world would never—*could* never—be a good place again.

Bhart was the only distraction from his woes, and the Bhizini had taken to chatting his ear off as they drifted slowly through the mangalar trees. Fin'roq welcomed the conversation, even if he said little in return. Bhart told him everything they thought he needed to know about Bhizini customs. Much of it made little sense to Fin'roq. And in truth he had little intention of learning. Instead, he took to reaffirming the Pradishar principles whenever Bhart taught him a new aspect of Bhizini belief or society. Even if the Pradishar might never accept him back, he could still love Trevian, and still serve him in his heart.

But Fin'roq's feelings began to change when they reached Pal'meria.

The city was unlike anything Fin'roq had imagined. There wasn't really a city to speak off, just thousands of boats all connected by ropes and planks, with boardwalks and woven bridges and dangling vines twisting their way through the canopy, amongst huts of various sizes, some on stilts, some strung up in the branches of the trees themselves.

Bhart brought the cano'rin up against a parked skiff'rin, and they reached down and pulled up a panel from the floor of the boat. They turned the panel so that it was perpendicular to the cano'rin, and then lowered it into place, so that it stretched from side to side, with a small overhang. Then they turned to Fin'roq and offered him their hand, grinning widely.

"First we present you to the elders," Bhart said. "And then we enjoy the festivities."

Fin'roq nodded, acting nonchalant as Bhart pulled him to his feet and helped him step up onto the panel, but his heart was racing. Everywhere he looked, Bhizini faces were staring at him from other boats and from the boardwalks.

The panel Bhart had placed served as a plank to get over the boat, and each boat that had parked had one. Bhart explained that this allowed them to pass over the other boats without technically stepping aboard and violating the sanctity of the space, and thus offending the other captains, which could quickly turn fatal.

He nodded, swallowing hard.

This will end badly, he thought. *I already know it.*

They crossed a long line of several dozen cano'rins and skimp'rins before reaching the first boardwalk, and they stepped up the ladder and onto the weather-beaten boards of the walkway. Bhart took Fin's hand again and led him onward, through a crowd of Bhizini eager to touch him. They held out their hands and brushed his arms and shoulders, or his chest and his hair fibers, as he passed. Some were smiling and laughing, others were shouting excitedly, a few were jumping up and down.

Fin looked at their faces—he'd never seen so many Bhizini in one place, and the variety of patterns on their skin, on their cheeks and chest—like works of art, each one meticulously painted. How had he never realized that? He looked at the backs of his own hands as if he'd never seen them before.

They walked for what must have been a good mile along the boardwalks, and the crowd that gathered to greet them also began following them. Fin could see that down below in the water, scamps on lilypads were racing to keep up as well. Bhart kept a tight grip on Fin's hand and made sure they didn't get separated. Fin didn't know if that made him feel safer or more uncertain.

Finally they emerged from the thickness of the woods into a broad clearing, like a lake with no edges, one that ran right into the forest on all sides. A large gazebo stood on stilts in the middle of the lake, and there were hundreds, perhaps thousands, of Bhizini standing about in the lake, the water barely over their ankles, all looking up at where he and Bhart stood on the boardwalk. More were pouring into the clearing from all sides.

They descended into the crowd and it surged around them and they were unable to proceed, but a horn sounded from the gazebo and the enthusiasm of those around them tapered down a bit and they gave them passage. Fin stepped through the water, warm and murky, the ground surprisingly firm under his feet. When they reached the gazebo, they ascended a spiraling stair of wood that hung on ropes, up to the raised dais, around which stood several dozen Bhizini, some of them so old they looked like they were already starting to grow bark.

One of the younger elders in the group approached them, a petite Bhizini with big brown eyes, soft and warm, and familiar. They were smiling, and when Fin'roq got a good look at them, he knew he'd seen them before.

"Good work, Bhart," the Bhizini said. They turned and stared at Fin'roq.

"I saw you in Balan Su," Fin said. "You're the one they captured. Qardymion the Saltsap."

One of the others yelled something down to those standing below, and a loud commotion rose up, followed by the sound of drums and horns, and the crackling of fires, and the sound of merrymaking.

"Welcome, Fin'roq," Qardymion said, coming close and putting their hand on his chest in greeting. "We've finally made it. And you're finally safe. Relax, please! Everyone is thrilled to have you here, as you probably noticed. I think they're happier to have you here than to have me back!"

Fin didn't know what to say so he said nothing, but his face was burning.

"I know. You don't know what to think of all this. To think of us. But look around, Fin'roq. We're your own kind, your family. And in times like these, we need to come together as we never have before."

"What do you want with me?" Fin said, feeling determined, even though his voice shook as he spoke.

"Maybe in time you'll see I'm right, and you'll want to stay with us. But for now, I ask only one thing of you. I want you to see one of our speakers, a spiritual teacher of our people. Will you do that, Fin'roq?"

"Do I have a choice?"

"Of course you have a choice. Bhizini have no royalty, no government. We follow no orders from compulsion. Once we are old enough to build a ship, and brave enough to claim it as our own, we are completely free. Everyone is here only because they want to be, doing what they want to do."

Fin laughed. "And me? You kidnapped me!"

"No, Fin'roq. We rescued you. And once in Mon Mang'alar, didn't Bhart cut your binds? You could have left his cano'rin at any time, but you chose to come along with him. So I ask again, will you choose to accompany me to the speaker? I'd be honored if you would."

Fin looked at Qardymion for a moment, the first time he'd had a chance to see them up close. Their color had improved from when Fin had glimpsed them in the streets of Balan Su, clad in chains and shaking from the lack of light. They were shorter than Fin remembered, and more handsome too. And their sparkly brown eyes reminded him of Jaun, but what didn't these days?

"I will," he said. "And then if I want to leave, I can?"

They nodded. "But I hope you'll give me the chance to convince you to stay."

Fin didn't say anything.

"Bhartimu'u! Come show our guest a good time tonight. This festival is for you, Fin'roq. Get ready for the best music, the best food, the best dancing of your life!"

Bhart grabbed him by the arm and pulled him toward the stairs, and he had to jog to keep up.

Fin'roq spent the evening feasting on rhupan, nibbling on bhiza cookies, dancing to the drums and horns of the bands that jazzed it up under the darkening sky. Everyone wanted to come and be close to him, to dance with him, to take his hand or touch his hair. The more bhiza he ate, the more he marveled at it all, at the Bhizini all around him, flowers out, twirling round and round; at the joyous laughter and the atmosphere of celebration that everyone seemed to be feeling. He'd never been a part of anything like it, a group of plants who all looked like him, who smiled at him, who made him feel like he was perfect just the way he was.

Maybe I could stay here, he thought, nibbling a bhiza cookie and watching Bhart dance. *Maybe this is what I've been waiting for my whole life.*

Sometime late that night, the elders up on the gazebo sounded horns, and the crowd stopped what they were doing to turn and stare up at them. When they began to chant, the crowd chanted with them. And when they began to stomp their feet and move their arms about, everyone mimicked them. Fin'roq watched and did his best to follow along, amazed at seeing everyone moving in sync like that, a dance of thousands, the water splashing under everyone's feet.

His head was spinning from the bhiza, and he was out of breath from dancing, but he couldn't stop smiling. He'd never felt so energetic in his life. His senses were alive with the smells of the Bhizini around him, their breath, their flowers, the muddy water underfoot. He twirled around and seemed to spin out of space and time.

Someone kissed him and he pulled them close, and then he felt hands on his sides, on his flower, and he turned to the side and kissed them too, and ran his hands over their shoulders and down their chest. He spun again, and felt arms around him, caressing him. He heard moaning in his ears, and as a surge of pleasure rose up in his navel and fanned out through his limbs, he opened his mouth and screamed with delight, and he knew everyone else was screaming too, delirious with ecstasy. One massive being, with a multitude of parts, linked together in perfect harmony.

He woke to the morning sun on his naked body, his rootpads down in the wet soil beneath the water, his branches extended, the soft leaftips drinking up the light. He looked around and saw he was in a much smaller clearing than the one he'd been in last night, little more than an alcove amidst the mangalar trees, with a wooden porch and small hut on one side.

Bhartimu'u was in front of the hut, running their scytherin down a grindstone. Fin'roq watched them work, the way their skin shimmered in the sunshine and their fibers flexed in their back, like chiseled marble, as they moved the blade back and forth.

Fin pulled his roots out of of the soil and took a step toward the hut, but the rest of his body didn't want to move, and he splashed as he tried to steady himself.

Bhart turned and grinned at him.

"How're you feeling?"

"I'm not sure. Like I'm floating on air."

"I'm glad you had fun last night. You did have fun, right?"

Fin nodded. "Did it really happen?"

Bhart laughed. "You've probably never had high quality bhiza before. At least not in any big dose. The stuff they sell in Balance Territories defiles the very name."

Fin looked up at the sky. Midmorning. "I never sleep past first light," he said.

"Qardymion wants to see you at midday. At the gazebo."

Fin looked around.

"I have no idea where I am." He looked down. "And I'm kinda naked."

"Bhizini are never naked," Bhart said, "but I will you get your clothing."

Bhart went into the hut and came out with Fin's robes.

"You brought them back last night? Thank you! I—don't even know how I got here."

Bhart grinned. "I'll take you to Qardymion when the time comes."

Midday came sooner than he expected. He'd spent the rest of the morning looking around the immediate area, checking out the trees and the shrubs and the vines, the flowers that popped right up out of the water, at the frogs that splashed under the roots of the mangalar trees, and at the birds that came and went through the opening in the canopy overhead.

"So many different critters than on P'anorum. Or Balan Su for that matter, though in truth, hardly anything but Verdillions live there."

"P'anorum and Balan Su are both small islands," Bhart said. "But Mon Mang'alar is too vast to ever really know. And it never stops surprising you."

The walk to the gazebo was short, and once out of the clearing and onto the boardwalks, Fin saw the other Bhizini coming and going, at work and at play. Some called to him as if they knew him, and Fin remembered he'd made some friends last night, though he struggled to recall their names. He waved and grinned at them.

Qardymion was waiting when they arrived, though he hardly recognized them in the outfit they wore. They had palm fronds in their hair fibers, down their arms and shoulders, and wrapped around their legs, and there were dabs of paint on their chest and on their face to soften up their Bhizini markings, making them look blurry. He'd seen such a style on P'anorum, when the Bhizini had tried to kidnap him from Bhea Bell. Before Baboo had eaten them.

Had the Saltsap been trying to "rescue" me from P'anorum too?

"Impressive," Fin said. "You look like the offspring of a palm tree and a Verdillion."

"You mean the offspring of a palm tree and a Bhizini."

Fin didn't know how to respond.

Bhart touched his shoulder. "I'll be waiting here when you return."

"Thanks," he said, and followed Qardymion as they took off at a brisk pace. They stayed on boardwalks until the city ended on a short dock with a few boats tied one to another. The Saltsap didn't speak and Fin'roq didn't know what to say so he stayed silent too.

They navigated the planks over the boats to the last cano'rin. Once aboard, Qardymion stood and pushed the boat through the mangalar trees with a pole while Fin sat in the front and dozed. When he opened his eyes, the trees had vanished and open ocean was on either side of them, while a small island, little more than a rock with a single tree atop it, was in front of them. Fin sat up and looked back and could see Mon Mang'alar in the distance, the long line of trees running in both directions, as far as he could see. The sun was just setting and from the direction, he realized they were in the Far Ocean, the same ocean P'anorum was in, and suddenly he ached for home. His *real* home. Where else could it be but there?

When they reached the small island, the Saltsap anchored the cano'rin and they stepped ashore. Fin followed as Qardymion climbed up a small rocky stair, more like strategically placed rubble than a proper case. The roots of the tree snaked out overhead and plunged down into the water.

An old Bhizini sat amongst the roots. Their skin looked like speckled leather and their hair fibers were as white as the fog of Balan Su, but their eyes were sparkling and dancing, and they looked at Fin'roq and smiled at him.

"I've returned," Qardymion said. "And I've brought the one."

The Bhizini said nothing, but continued to stare at Fin'roq. Then they picked up a long wooden pipe and drew from it, then sat and watched Fin'roq through the smoke.

What are they waiting for? Am I supposed to do something?

He wished Bhart were there to tell him what to do.

"I'm called Shep'word," the Bhizini finally said. "Who are you?"

Fin swallowed. "Fin'roq."

"That's what you're called," they said. "Who might you *be*?"

Fin didn't know what to say.

"I'm only Fin'roq," he said.

"And how many years have you been alive?"

"How old? Thirty three years."

"That's all?"

"I think so. Bhea Bell told me I was born in the 9966th Cycle of Balance, which would make me about to complete 34."

"I see." Shep'word looked at Qardymion. "He doesn't know," they said.

"He will," Qardymion said. "He's ready. We can't wait any longer."

"No," Shep'word said. "We can. We will."

Qardymion had a dark look on their face, and Fin'roq felt his chest clench up.

"Don't return until he wakes," the Bhizini said. "Leave. Now." They sounded firm, but Fin still thought their eyes were smiling at him.

The Saltsap said nothing on the climb down to the cano'rin, nothing on the long trip back through the dark night, and Fin was afraid to disturb them—afraid to ask what the speaker meant about him waking up. He dozed, and when he woke, Qardymion was tying up the boat.

He looked around but it was dark, and there were no glowbes nearby, no fires, no sounds of Pal'meria. He tried to sit up, but couldn't. His hands and feet were bound up in vines, and the bit was back in his mouth. He grunted and groaned, but Qardymion ignored him.

The Saltsap half led, half dragged him through the wetlands, into a small clearing where Fin could make out the faces of Bhizini nearby, peering at him out of painted faces, through the palm frond uniform that adorned their heads and shoulders and legs. They surrounded him, closed in on him, and they touched him, poked at him, ran their fingers down his face and stuck them in his ears.

He grunted and groaned and tried to hiss when he felt his hands being lifted, and soon he was up in the air, dangling from a vine, hanging in the midst of them all, while they leered at him.

"I'm sorry, Fin'roq. I had hoped Shep'word would wake you, but it seems they side with the weaker camp, with that fool Bhea Bell, who would have us coddle you for another hundred years before asking you to stand up and fight with the rest of us. We've been dying by the thousands, the tens of thousands, while you waste time on P'anorum, or worse, playing monkin on Balan Su. And now the Death King prepares for the Harvest and these fools think we still have time. We don't. But I have a solution, Fin'roq. I know how to make you feel your power and sense your true purpose. You did it in the cavern on P'anorum, and you did it on the streets of Balan Su. And both times, your life, your very survival, were at stake. And so you leave me no choice."

Qardymion unsheathed a scytherin from the palm leaves strapped to their waist and held it up to Fin'roq's throat.

"Show me what you can do," they whispered. "Or I spill your sap into the swamp."

Fin'roq groaned and grunted and moaned.

I can't, he tried to scream. *I don't know how! It just happens. It isn't me! Please!*

"No? I'm sorry to hear that. Truly."

Qardymion took the scytherin, turned it over in their hand, and drove it into Fin'roq's gut.

Chapter 41

Family for a Day, Family Forever

RAKK RAEDER HAD A bad habit of not thinking about things that made him uncomfortable. A door would close in his mind, and he'd do everything possible not to open it again, to forget that it even existed. He'd spent three decades avoiding the past, the present, even the future, because of that habit. And all his efforts over the last six months to make himself walk through that door, to fight for his throne, to care again—had it all been in vain? Why didn't he feel free to be himself yet? Why did Ellex Andria still spin his world so far around?

When he'd learned of her scamp, he'd done as he always did—forced himself not to think about it, to charge forward with other plans. If he hadn't run into her on Nunan, he might have kept the door closed his entire life, just decided she couldn't be a part of his world anymore and spent the rest of his days only half alive.

Fate brought us back together, he thought.

When he saw her again, saw her nervously trying to buy drugs from Qaa'milo in the foggy night, it was as if the door had never been there. She was what mattered. Keeping her safe and happy was what mattered. But as he held Q'orin that night in the sand on Nunan, as he shook and whimpered in his sleep, his Corkin crystal slowly dissolving inside of him, he couldn't close the thoughts back down again. The questions surged up from the depths, til all he had were doubts.

How does she have a scamp? How did she lose a whole year of memories? Does she really not remember anything? Why would she lie about that? How does she know the Bhizini is hers? If the Pradishar could take her memories, could they give her new ones too?

But then he saw Qaas'andria and none of the questions mattered anymore.

He recognized her immediately from Ellex's dream, imprisoned in the stasis chamber. And there was something else familiar about her. There was no doubting she was his sister, and no doubting she was Ellex's daughter, and that gave Rakk double the reason to love her. And he did, immediately and unconditionally.

When Qaas'i would put her tiny hand in his, when he'd lift her to sit on his shoulders so she could look out to sea, when he saw her eyes widen with delight at the sight of mangalar trees growing right up out of the ocean—he'd never felt so special in his life.

Ellex, on the other hand, had treated him curtly, coldly. He didn't blame her for it, but it did hurt. He'd let her down so badly at the Balancing Act, after she'd reminded him of his promise all those years ago. Would she ever trust him again? Was he overstepping his bounds by being so close to Qaas'i?

Would Callo Baton really be as safe as he thought it would be?

Whoever had attacked Ellex and Rajj had used a Vintrani blade, the weapon of Guild Enforcers. But Rakk thought it more likely to be a Bhizini that had stolen the blade off a corpse. Qardymion had warned him that the Bhizini wouldn't stop hunting him, or Ellex, for targeting him. Now that the Saltsap had escaped custody, did that mean they were in the clear?

"You've been here before?" Rakk asked.

Ellex's illness had started to fade once the seas calmed down, and though the skies stayed gray and threatened rain for most of the crossing, the last few days had been smooth sailing. The skimp'rin chugged south across the Threshinveld down to the edge of Mon Mang'alar, and passed between the overhanging foliage into a long narrow channel. The skimp'rin docked next to a wooden boardwalk built among the trees.

"Where are we?" Ellex said.

"Mangis, I think. There are a lot of small little ports like this along the northern frontier of Mon Mang'alar, between here and Aga Baton. Mostly for travelers and entrepreneurs who don't have the proper clearance to enter the main harbors."

"Charming place," she said. "I see why the tourists flock here in droves."

Rakk grinned. "We can get a skiff'rin into the city. It's not more than an hour's ride."

"And what's the plan once we arrive? Just waltz into Guild Headquarters and demand to see Lithuigi Von'nDrino?"

"I thought we'd make a vacation of it. Maybe do some sightseeing, take in a show, a lovely dinner, followed by late night drinks at one of the finest taverns in the city."

"If you think—" Ellex started.

"Easy mama," Rakk said. "I have a notion on where we might find the good professor, if you'll trust me? And the tavern is where I have to meet my contact. He's promised me information on a fleet the Guild has been building, potentially for Raq'asha. This could be the evidence I need to stop her. As for the sightseeing, this is easily one of the most amazing cities in the world. And we're safe here. Let's enjoy ourselves."

"Safe? Are you a fool, Rakk Raeder? Guild maquina kept my daughter imprisoned for thirty three years—thirty three years of deceit! And there's a saboteur on the weavryn who was able to access my memories and share them with the world! Tell me who could do that but a Dyna'arin tinker with access to the servryns? And my butchered Cul'tavin? They were in a building owned by Lithuigi Von'nDrino. Drugged by bhiza that was pumped in by Guild maquina! You know all about that, given what happened to you with Rhannokti in the tunnels. So why the—" she swallowed a curse, "—just tell me why you'd trust them?"

"I don't. But I also know how the Guild works. You want to blame every Dyna'arin, but the Guild is a loose confederation of many different groups. It's intentionally without a hierarchy, though that seems to be changing. Tinkers build in secret, even from almost everyone else in the Guild. Even the Pradishar, who create the crystals, can't get to the information on Guild crystamins or on Guild servryns."

"Your point being, to use a tired old cliche, is that one apple doesn't spoil the bunch."

"Isn't the cliche that the bad apple *does* spoil the bunch?"

"You know what I'm saying," she snapped.

"Yes. And I suppose that's what I'm saying. I don't trust the Guild, and I know as an organization, they have extremely dangerous elements. I know they're involved in almost every conspiracy in the history of Balance. But they're also a highly efficient, highly functional society, much more so than Balance Authority."

"You speak as if they were separate."

"Aren't they? If the Guild didn't need the Pradishar for crystals, then the Pradishar, even Balance, wouldn't be able to survive without them. They already have their own capital, their own sovereign terrain within the cities of Balance, their own rules and privileges. And a virtual monopoly on all technology."

"You don't think they could nab us off the streets of Callo Baton without anyone being the wiser?"

"I absolutely think they could. It's no different than being nabbed off the streets of Balan Su by the Cul'tavin. Except the Guild has no reputation for imprisonment, murder, or torture, like we holy Pradishar do."

Ellex said nothing, her face blank, her eyes distant.

Rakk turned to Qaas'i. "You ready for one more boat ride?"

Qaas'i just stared at him.

"Want to or not, it's the only way to the city. But tell you what," he said, taking a knee in front of Qaas'i, "just as soon as we arrive, I'm gonna get you the freshest, sweetest, creamiest, most delicious slurpan you've ever tasted, fresh and cold right out of the maquina. And you'll be so amazed, so blown away by the flavor, so delighted by the icy goodness, you'd be willing to get back on another boat again, just for another taste!"

Rakk heard Ellex sniffing and he tried hard not to let his heart break, not to reach out and pull her into his arms. Instead he picked Qaas'i up and touched Ellex's shoulder. He stepped into the skiff'rin and asked the pilot to take them to the eastern docks. Then he sat Qaas'i down and took a seat next to her.

"If I didn't know better, I'd say you've grown. Taller and heavier, just in the last few days."

"It's true," Ellex said. "I had to let out some of the stitches in her robe."

"That's marvelous," Rakk said. "Soon you'll be tall and strong, just like your big brother!"

Qaas'i gave him a tiny grin, and the faintest hint of a blush darkened her speckled cheeks.

❧❧❧❧❧❦ ❦❦❦❦❦❦

Rakk heard the city before they could see the city. Not a whine like a single maquina would make, but a hum like a chorus chanted from the depths of a sharlum, a storm-wracked sea assaulting a rocky shore, or distant thunder on a hot, wet afternoon. When the skiff'rin passed out of the mangalar trees and into a massive lagoon in the heart of the swamp, they could see the metallic outline of the buildings jutting up out of the muddy water, their smooth surfaces shimmering like mother of pearl.

The skiff'rin passed into the lagoon and the pilot opened the gurgitator. Rakk looked at Ellex but couldn't tell what she was thinking. Qaas'i, on the other hand, was drinking up the sights, spellbound by it all.

"Magnificent, isn't it?" Rakk said.

"Yes, and no," Ellex said. "It's stunning, yes. But does it fit the scenery? Does it look like it belongs here? No. It looks like an intruder in the heart of Mon Mang'alar. An outcast."

"Where else would an outcast be, but the middle of a swamp that Balance Authority could never bother to conquer?"

The pilot took them across the lagoon and back into the forest on the southern side of the city, where the trees grew right up to the buildings and where the sprawl spread a bit further from the city every year. The structures in the area were built up on stilts, and their skiff'rin passed under boardwalks which crossed overhead at various levels of the canopy. There was a great noise of activity and chatter, with people coming and going, hustling and bustling.

"This is not what I expected," Ellex said when the boat docked. She was looking around uncertainly, like she didn't want to get out.

Rakk picked up Qaas'i, paid the pilot, and offered a hand to Ellex. She took it and let him help her out onto the dock. But then she grabbed his arm and squeezed it, and he followed her eyes to a pair of workers replacing the ties on the boardwalk. They were Bhizini.

"Don't forget, we're not in Balance Territories anymore. There's no prohibition on Bhizini labor here. And while the Guild doesn't let them join outright, they do hire them unofficially for non-maquina related tasks. And they don't stop their Operators from reproducing, regardless of who they are or who they're with."

Ellex looked like she couldn't believe what he was saying.

"Come on Ell, you must have known about the N'detten? Haven't you ever been to a Guild controlled area in one of Balance's cities?"

"Balan Su doesn't have any," she snapped. "I knew it."

"Ell—"

"Let's just go," she said.

He nodded and led them along the boardwalks and back out of the forest. The walkways ended on dry land, the artificial island upon which the heart of Callo Baton was built—and which descended deep underground, if the rumors were true. They were in a wide plaza at the edge of the forest that narrowed as it approached the buildings and became an avenue into the city.

Rakk took them to one of the shops on the plaza's edge, right next to the lagoon, and he bought the slurpan he'd promised Qaas'i. He got her a small one and two mediums for him and Ellex, and they sat down at the water's edge to eat them, with Qaas'i in between them.

She held hers and stared, unsure what to do with it.

Ellex took a lick of her own.

"Ohh, it's delicious. You have to try it. Here, just stick out your tongue, like this." Ellex stuck out her tongue. "An' zhen shtick it in like dis." She stuck it in the slurpan and wriggled it around.

Qaas'i giggled, more like a high-pitched squeak, and Ellex laughed.

Rakk laughed too, and he realized it was the first time he'd seen Ellex genuinely smile in ages.

Sweet Trevian, she's beautiful, he thought.

He watched Qaas'i stick out her tongue, look at the slurpan uncertainly, then slowly move it closer to her mouth. When she made contact, her eyes widened at the cold blast of frozen fruit juice and honey on her tongue, and then she wiggled it around until she had it all over her chin. She looked at both of them, a goofy grin on her face, and they both laughed again.

But then Ellex's face froze and her mouth opened. "Watch her," she said, setting down the slurpan and darting away before Rakk could even react.

"Wait!" he said, jumping to his feet.

Ellex was heading across the plaza. Rakk picked Qaas'i up and started to run after her, trying to keep his eye on her pradeshan robe as she went. She was after someone—someone who was trying their best to get away from her, but couldn't outpace her.

She caught up to her prey at the top of a stair down to the tram station. Rakk put Qaas'i down and took her hand, and when he saw who Ellex had confronted, he pulled her close to him, hidden in the folds of his robe. Then he approached Ellex, who was pointing a finger at Lithuigi Von'nDrino, her face in shadow under her hood.

"Whatever you're intending, I'm sure it isn't worth it," Lithuigi said, and he nodded down the stairs. Two Guild Enforcers stood at the bottom, metal masks in place over their faces, Vintrani blades on their backs, zaprens and enflamers on their belts. "The Guild doesn't tolerate those who disrupt the peace or assault the freedoms of others."

"How dare you speak to me of the freedom of others!" she said, pulling back her hood, a dark look on her face.

"Ell, don't," Rakk whispered, as he pulled his own hood off his head.

"Ahh, Sui Pradesh Ellex Andria. And Prince Rhakksees. What a bizarre thing to see you both here at Guild Headquarters. I thought you were in the Dankburn, and you on Andramere. Perhaps I still haven't figured out how to properly access the notestreams? Never mind. What can I do for you?"

"You know why I'm here, you blubbering fool. You imprisoned my daughter!"

Qaas'i stepped out from behind Rakk's robe and Lithuigi gasped when he saw her.

"You *do* know her. Why'd you do it, you monster, why?! Why'd you butcher my Cul'tavin? Why'd you take my scamp away from me?!"

A crowd was beginning to gather and the Enforcers were coming up the stairs.

"Not now, Ell," Rakk pleaded. "Don't endanger Qaas'i."

Ellex gave him a murderous look but pulled her hood back over her head and said nothing.

"Are you okay, professor?" the Enforcers asked. Their metal masks were fixed in Ellex and Rakk's direction, their hands on their zaprens.

"Of course. Of course!" he said, chuckling. "Just having a spirited debate with some old students of mine. They were mistaken about some of the finer points of our argument, since they don't yet have all the details. I reminded them not to jump to conclusions before all the evidence is presented."

"Very good, professor," the Enforcers said, but they didn't turn to leave.

"Let's go, Ell," Rakk whispered.

She didn't move, and Rakk could hear her breathing heavily.

"We'll have to finish our debate later, I'm afraid," Lithuigi said, and he started down the steps to the tram station. The Enforcers followed, and the crowd that had gathered started to disperse.

"Are you alright?" Rakk said, touching Ellex's shoulder, hoping she wouldn't pull away from him.

"I don't think so," she said, the sound of defeat and loss heavy in her voice.

Rakk's heart clenched up and he ground his teeth together while his mind raced, trying to find a way to distract her, to cheer her up.

"We should try to avoid making any more scenes," he said.

"I know. I don't know what came over me. I saw him, Raeder. I saw him watching us, watching *me*. Trying to—trying to see Qaas'i. I saw him and I bolted. I was ready to kill him."

"We don't know for sure if he's the villain or not."

Ellex sighed, but it sounded more like a hiss. "What did I expect coming here? That everything would just snap into place? That all my questions would be answered? That I'd be able to make sense of what happened to Qaas'i, to me? I don't even know where to look, where to start. How did I spend thirty years not even considering these things, not even questioning *anything?!*"

"That isn't your fault. None of this is your fault. And we've only just started our search. We'll help each other get through this, all three of us."

When Ellex didn't reply, Rakk had an idea.

"I know what might make you feel better. Come on, this way."

They went down the stairs to the station and took the tram to the center of the city. Callo Baton was built largely as a circle, with a series of curving streets arching around the middle, and straight avenues stretching from the center to the edge, like spokes in a great wheel. The southern portion of the city was the industrial quarter, where massive factories processed everything from food to furniture to other maquina.

When the tram reached the main station within the industrial quarter, they stepped off and headed for the lift. Rakk used the buttons behind the panel on the wall to point them to the upper level, since their crystals remained numbed from the bhiza they'd been taking every day. The maquina whined as the lift rose through the walls, and Ellex grunted and ground her teeth.

"Almost there," Rakk said.

When the doors opened, Ellex gasped and Rakk smiled, glad to see he'd been able to surprise her. Spread out around them was a sprawling park of forested thickets, wide meadows strewn with wildflowers, large ponds with little boats and others for swimming with slides into the water and loungers on the sandy shores. There were rocky outcroppings that looked like miniature mountains around the edges, and overhead, a broad blue sky unbroken by any sign of civilization.

Qaas'i had a look of wonder on her face.

Rakk led them to a grassy clearing flanked with trees and a small pond with a fountain in the middle of it, so that they had a bit of privacy but they could still see others around. Most were dressed in Guild fatigues but some wore scholarly robes or pradeshan robes. Some had clothing that Rakk had never seen before, with strange styles and bright colors.

"We should be okay to take our hoods off, even our robes, and get some sunshine. Here Qaas'i, hands up!" She raised her hands over her head and Rakk started to pull off her robe, but Ellex snatched it out of her hand.

"Are you crazy? It's too dangerous! What if someone sees her?"

"Look around, Ell. What do you see?"

"Don't patronize me, Raeder."

"I'm not trying to. Just look around. Look at them! Raccorin and Andrasian, together with Bhizini scamps. And nobody paying them the slightest attention. We don't have to be scared here. We can—be a real family here."

She turned away from him, but took off Qaas'i's robe. Rakk pulled off his own but left his cumberdome in place. Then he unfurled his branches and sighed as the sunshine began filling him with energy. The sun looked red through his eyelids, and he could feel the fire flowing into him, and already his troubles seemed lessened.

Ellex finally relaxed enough to get some sun, then to splash in the pond with Qaas'i, to pick some of the wildflowers and weave them into a headband for her daughter. Rakk watched her hold it out to Qaas'i, then gently place it on top of her head.

"The most beautiful princess in the world," Rakk said, and Ellex smiled through her tears.

When the evening grew late and twilight began to fade, they headed back to the lift and took the tram to the eastern docks. Rakk's informant was supposed to meet him at full dark, at a tavern by the lagoon. They rented a room upstairs and he left Ellex and Qaas'i to go back to the bar. He ordered a drink from the Raccorin bartender and sat in a booth at the back, where he could watch the stair and the door. Several hours passed and Rakk started to fear he wouldn't show. The bar was empty and the Raccorin kept looking at him as if to say, 'Can't you just up and leave already so I can shut her down for the night?'

Finally, the bartender came over and sat down across from him.

"You the one they call the Raeder?"

"You Salty Saul?"

"Damnit, you shoulda signaled me earlier. I saw you come in with a family, so I just thought—but never mind."

"You have the datamin?" Rakk said.

"I got it, but it's gonna cost ya."

Rakk put out his hand. "You know my family can afford it."

The Raccorin squinted at him, and realization broke on his face. "My prince, I had no idea it would be you."

Rakk smiled. "I'd appreciate your discretion."

"Of course," Salty Saul said. He placed the datamin on the table.

Rakk reached for it with his mind, but couldn't sense it. So he touched its metal surface, and his finger tingled where it made contact. The information poured into his mind—a lot of it technical jargon beyond his comprehension—but there were also schematics for ships, for a Corkin fleet unlike any he'd ever seen.

Raq'asha was definitely after his throne.

He wanted to hiss, to punch someone, to scream. Instead, he shut the door in his mind, and smiled.

"And now the price," Rakk said.

"You've already paid it."

Rakk gave him a confused look.

"Coming here tonight was all we needed," Salty Saul said.

He felt a sharp prick in his neck and grabbed the tiny dart just as his head started to spin. Salty Saul had a sad look on his bright green face. "Don't fight them, my prince," he said, as blurry figures moved in through the door.

Rakk watched them heading up the stairs, and he tried to reach for Ellex with the crystal, tried to warn her, but of course it was still numbed from bhiza, unable to reach any servryn. He stumbled out of the booth, just as the bottom of a fighting pike hit him in the flower, driving the air from his lungs in a shriek of pain.

He saw a blurry Bhizini face looking at him, and heard Ellex screaming his name.

The top end of the pike cracked down on the back of his head.

Chapter 42

And Still the Plan is Safe

WHEN THE LONG FLAT horizon of the Threshinveld transformed into a jagged, broken seascape, with towering dark shapes in front of them and spreading off in either direction, Lithuigi Von'nDrino knew they were momentarily safe. He heard the whine of the gurgitator dropping off as Mha'arlo slowed the cata'rin. The sky was gray but bright, the water the color of mud, and there were a few mangalar trees scattered about around them, growing right up out of the ocean. They passed through the two towers into the thickets of Mon Mang'alar, along a broad, flat channel that snaked back and forth through the forest as if it had once been a flowing river.

"We should be at Callo Baton within the hour, professor," Mha'arlo said. His face looked pale and Lithuigi realized he must be as exhausted as he was. The crossing had been stressful, with the Pradishar in pursuit and with news of Doc Andri'n's death crushing Lithuigi's spirit. He'd had no word of Rebesh'a or his sons, and the silence was threatening to drown him with guilt. To top it all off, at the insistence of Anorian Grain, he'd undone an entire century of refusing to use the weavryn, and—feeling overwhelmed with shame and with a nagging sense of failure—he struggled to see what all his sacrifices had been for.

"Good, good," Lithuigi said. "You've done well, son. You're quite the captain. If you can handle this gurgitator and this cata'rin," he said, patting the rail, "then you can handle anything."

Mha'arlo grinned, and Lithuigi could see his eyes twitching.

"When we get to Callo Baton, I want you to take the rest of the day off. Go up to the greens and get some sunshine. Go and mingle, and have some fun. And not on here!" He tapped his forehead.

"I thought we had a lot to get done."

"We do indeed, but a lot of help you'll be if you're dozing off at the workstation. It's been a rough few days. Go, eat, sleep, play. And then I'll see you at midday tomorrow, at my lab at the Academicon."

"Very well, professor. If I must." But he was grinning.

"One more thing, son. I've been trying to find some news. But I'm not very good at using the weavryn yet. Maybe I'm streaming the wrong things? I haven't heard anything about my family. I can't find anything, anywhere. Can you help me?"

Mha'arlo's eyes continued twitching. "I've been looking too, but there's nothing."

He tried not to think about what that might mean.

"Have you asked Anorian to help?"

Lithuigi sighed. "No. I suppose—I should, I know, I just—" He sighed again.

"Professor?" Mha'arlo had a worried look on his face. "I've never seen you at a loss for words. Are you feeling okay?"

Lithuigi seemed to snap out of it. "Of course. Of course! Anorian. Right. Let's give it a try."

But he didn't have to.

<<Hello, professor,>> Anorian said in his mind, and he jumped.

<<I was just about to contact you.>>

<<I know.>>

<<You do? So—>> He gulped. <<Does that mean you know what I was going to ask?>>

<<Rebesh'a is unharmed.>>

He exhaled hard and grinned as the relief spread outward from his chest, and he could feel his shoulders relaxing.

<<Thank Trevian. I was hoping you could show her the hollow. I'm afraid of what the Pradishar might do to her, in order to get to me.>>

<<I'm sorry, professor, but I can't do that.>>

The tension came back to his chest, and he thought about choosing his words carefully, but realized Anorian might already know what he was thinking.

<<Why not?>>

<<Because of Vilder.>>

The tension in his chest was replaced with a thudding anger that made his head feel like it was pulsing.

<<What has he done?>>

<<If Rebesh'a learned of the hollow, she would share her knowledge of it with Vilder. She trusts him. She thinks he's an honorable plant. She would never believe that fruit of her own flesh could do the things he has done. She doesn't know he has pledged himself to Mortimus Rex, and even now plots to bring about the Harvest.>>

<<I had the chance to stop him, and I didn't.>>

<<Don't blame yourself, professor.>>

<<And what about Hesh'n?>> Lithuigi wasn't sure he wanted the answer.

Anorian paused. <<He's been given your position at Balan Su's Academicon.>>

<<If that's not a message from Morty, then I don't know what is,>> Lithuigi said, practically shouting it at Anorian in his mind, not wanting to show how scared he felt. How panicked.

<<Now isn't the time to look backward, professor. We have to focus on what matters, which is seeing this through.>>

He swallowed an insult. <<What would you have of me?>>

Lithuigi listened, perfectly obedient, and promised it would be done. But his thoughts were on his sons. On Vilder in particular. Would he really hurt Rebesh'a? Would he choose the Ren'fallow over the only Verdillion in the world who loved him?

The fact that he couldn't give an answer with any certainty was more terrible than he could put into words.

I should have killed him, he thought, *when I had the chance.*

❧ ☙

The next day came before Lithuigi realized it. Once in Callo Baton, and once in his lab, he'd gone straight to tinkering, finishing up a few small projects he needed to get out of the way before focusing on the larger ones. Once his tools were in his hands, and dynamins on the workstation, time ceased to exist, there was only a flowing present moment that stretched hours, and sometimes days, while it lasted.

He had to admit that Hesh'n's prosthetic had made his prolonged work sessions that much easier, since his fake arm didn't quiver, but worked as if he were a plant of half his age, with plenty of sleep and plenty of sunshine, a true marvel. The last few months, he'd practically forgotten it was there, which was a testament to how perfectly wrought the thing was—to fit so well it wasn't even noticed.

Mha'arlo startled him when he entered the lab at midday, his bright Raccorin skin practically fluorescent, a big grin on his face.

"Afternoon, professor. You've been here all night! Now it's your turn to go and unwind. Tell me what I need to do, and then be on your way."

Lithuigi wagged his finger at him. "Now, now, you've let my praises go to your head. But I am glad to see you looking well-rested." He walked over to the wall and pulled open one of the compartments. A carver folded down. Mha'arlo inspected the parts while Lithuigi went into his safe to retrieve several boxes. He sat them down on the workstation next to the carver.

"For starters, I need that set of shelves," he pointed to the corner, "with all those books and scrolls put onto these datamins. Then I want you to take these other datamins and re-carve the contents onto those other datamins. Wipe clean the old ones when you finish."

Mha'arlo examined the carver, then walked over to the shelves and thumbed through some of the books, then took a count of the scrolls, his eyes twitching the whole time. Then he opened the box with the old datamins for copying and tallied in his mind.

"I estimate ten days if I don't run into any problems and really push to get through it all, but two weeks is more realistic."

"That'll be just fine. Best speed, but don't overdo it."

"What about you, professor?" Mha'arlo raised an eyebrow and looked at Lithuigi's trembling hand.

He yawned. "You're right, I should get some sun, some rhupan, and some sleep, or I'll never make it through the summer, much less the next few weeks. We have a lot to get done before our guests arrive, after all."

⁂

Although Lithuigi had spent a hundred year avoiding the politics of the Dyna'arin, for the first time in that entire century, he regretted not doing more to rise up in Management. Most tinkers showed little interest in the internal affairs of the Guild, and to a certain extent, that was true of him as well. He wanted to tinker, to explore and build, not to sit in meetings and pour over numbers and worry about the movement of assets.

That isn't to say that he hadn't been doing his best to influence the politics of the Guild, but he'd always done so behind the scenes. The truth was, he held most of the managers in contempt, and he regularly thumbed his nose at them, subverted their orders, fudged his reports, and wrote off massive amounts of inventory while siphoning the output elsewhere. And he had always kept a strong rapport with the minister for the operators and had always spoken highly of those who extracted the raw materials for his projects, who shaped them into the parts he needed, who assembled them into new maquina, and who kept them functional for decades—even though most tinkers never thought twice about the operators. He also supported the N'detten—the Bhizini workers in Guild territories who were not joined with crystals, not true members of the Guild, and whose existence were ignored by Balance Authority, but whose labor made the functioning of the Dyna'arin—and all of Balance civilization—possible.

But even with his work in the shadows, Management still remained aloof from the day to day realities of life for their operators, unable to comprehend the needs of their tinkers, and every year they relied more and more on the enforcers to compel order. In Lithuigi's time with the Dyna'arin, the enforcers had swelled from only five percent of the total Guild to nearly one-quarter. Management had also surged to one-quarter. Tinkers stayed at five percent, which meant the operators were now in the minority, even though the Dyna'arin was often called the Operator's Guild.

Defections from the Guild had surged in the years after the loss of the Far Archipelago, when Balance Authority stepped up their assault on Bhizini in the Inner Seas. Many sought shelter in Callo Baton, or Aga Baton, only to find they were still hamstrung, still prevented from full participation in society. Lithuigi had done his best to identify them early, to get to them before Qardymion's people could, and make sure they didn't throw their lives away in the Saltsap's quest for vengeance. There were far more important things to plan for.

And now, with his brother executed, and the Pradishar calling for his arrest—with Management and that fool Rameen Rutar bending over to Balance Authority and throwing away the privileges that might have given the Guild a chance to prepare for the coming crisis—Lithuigi couldn't help but wonder if he'd been misspending his time. As head manager, he might have marshaled the forces of the entire Guild.

He hadn't seen the head manager, Rameen Rutar, since he'd confronted him at the tavern on Nunan and threatened to expose his perverse hobbies if he didn't speak out in support of his brother. But Rutar had known about Hesh'n's work with living flesh and threatened to expose him.

I should have let him, he thought.

Rutar obviously didn't know Hesh'n was working for the Pradishar, or he never would have made such a threat. Which meant Rutar wasn't as in the loop as he thought.

Lithuigi hoped to find out just how out of the loop he was.

He found the head manager on the greens, in an exclusive section of the rooftop park reserved for Management, who as a rule hated to mingle with anyone who wasn't one of their own, or so it seemed. He was sitting on a lounger, his feet against the soil, his massive gut hanging down between his legs, taking in the sun. Two petite Andrasians stood on either side of him, gently fanning him with palm fronds. And there were at least a dozen enforcers nearby, watching everything from behind their metallic masks.

One of the Andrasians touched the head manager on the shoulder and whispered something in his ear. He grunted and opened his eyes, but didn't sit up.

"I'm surprised to see you here, Von'nDrino," Rameen Rutar said. His smug face said otherwise.

"I'm surprised to be here." Lithuigi could play too.

"Where have you been hiding?" he asked.

"Not hiding. Working."

"For you tinkers, that's one and the same thing, is it not?" He waved his hand. "But I didn't mean hiding out here, I meant hiding in here." He pointed at the crystals on his forehead. "How are you doing that?"

Lithuigi wasn't expecting that. "Are you tracking me?"

Rutar saw his face and laughed.

"Relax professor. You know the Dyna'arin don't spy on their own."

"I once believed the Dyna'arin protected their own," Lithuigi said. "But things have soured considerably since I first joined. Now tinkers are willingly turned over to religious zealots for public executions."

Rutar scowled at him. "You have a lot of nerve, Von'nDrino. I thought you understood things. I thought you knew how this game is played. The Pradishar make the crystamins. The Pradishar make the dynamins. The Pradishar make the datamins. What would you have me do? Shut down operations? Tell the tinkers there's nothing more to be made? Let the maquina fall apart while Balance collapses on itself?"

"The Pradishar are not Balance."

"Careful, Von'nDrino. Your brother was a fine tinker, and twice the professor you are. But he knew our hands are tied. I did all I could on the Council of Nine to get Doc

Andri'n released. And I had assurances it would all blow over, as I told you on Nunan. So don't say we didn't speak out. We did. But the Pradishar weren't listening."

"Wrong," Lithuigi said. "They are always listening. To everything."

Rutar sighed. "Why are you here, Von'nDrino?"

"You're a bishrop on the Council of Nine. You must know the stasis chamber project has ended."

"Yet another one of your failures, Von'nDrino. The Pradishar are furious. Honestly, I'm surprised you got out of Balan Su with your head still attached. It's only a matter of time before they come looking for you here. And I've half a mind to let them take you. How could you imprison the *wrong* Bhizini, for three fucking decades Von'nDrino?"

"I didn't imprison anyone," he said. "I only made sure the maquina functioned."

Rutar laughed, and his big belly jiggled and bounced around. "You're fucking incredible. You adapted ancient stasis technology so that the Pradishar could better imprison bodies and minds. You gave the Pradishar the enflamers, so they could combust their enemies. And you built the world's most advanced fleet and handed it over to them on a silver platter. You think your hands are clean in all this?"

"My conscience is," he said. "And that's what really matters."

"You might be the biggest fool I've ever known. You'd abandon the Pradishar, abandon the Guild, give up on your entire career, right at the moment of victory!"

"Only the Death King will triumph if the Harvest comes to pass."

"*When* it comes to pass," Rutar corrected.

"I'm not convinced," Lithuigi said. "I have to believe Balance can still be saved—that we can preserve the body if only we can cut out the disease."

"You tinkers are all dreamers, but you're a special sort. You're a believer, aren't you, Von'nDrino? Well, I'll tell you what I *know*. The body is already dying. The Harvest will come and wipe away this world, and those of us who knew it was coming, and picked the right side, stand to be here when the new world is built up again. Why are you so afraid of Mortimus Rex? Don't you see that the Death King is really a God of Life? He takes our faces, our thoughts, our memories, and he preserves them all. None are forgotten, and none pass away. In him, we all live forever."

"And you say I'm the believer?" Lithuigi said.

Rutar narrowed his eyes at him. "You can't get rid of death. It's the one thing that endures. The *only* thing that endures."

"If that's true, then all hope is lost," he said. "I'm sorry to have wasted your time."

But Rutar's scowl turned into a look of disappointment, as if he didn't want Lithuigi to leave. But then his lip curled up in contempt.

"I'm assigning Hesh'n to your classes at the Academicon in Balan Su. I thought it best to have a replacement lined up, since you'll likely be in the Dankburn by the time the fall semester gets underway. I'm told the Pradishar have taken a real interest in his work. He'll make a worthy replacement for you."

Lithuigi's heart was pounding and he worked hard to keep his face blank.

"Tough break, eh Von'nDrino? Sure does lower your bargaining power with the Pradishar now, doesn't it?"

"Hesh'n's a fine professor," he said. "And a better tinker than me."

"And wiser too. He's been most cooperative. Vilder too, of course. Yet another rising talent. So cheer up, professor. You might have lost your seat in the new world, but your family will be there to redeem their treasonous old father. And that's more than you deserve."

Lithuigi turned to leave.

"No comeback? I'm disappointed."

"You've won, Rutar. I admit defeat."

He looked at the ground and walked slowly back to the lift. When the door closed, he allowed himself to smile.

Rutar, you damn fool, I knew your big mouth would tell me everything I needed to know. And everything you still don't know. There's still time! Thank Trevian, there's still time.

But as the lift dropped back down to the surface level, his smile faded as he thought of what Rutar had said about Vilder and Hesh'n, and a heaviness grew in his chest and threatened to crush all the hope he'd finally managed to rekindle.

When he stepped out onto the streets of Callo Baton, he felt his assistant approach him through the hollow, and Lithuigi opened his mind's eye to him.

<<Ah Mha'arlo, good. How's your progress?>>

<<It's been a crazy week but it's coming along nicely. The shelves are done and now I'm working through the old datamins. I just wanted to let you know, I got word from Mangis. Our guests have departed their skimp'rin, and are en route for the eastern docks.>>

<<Good work, son. I'll be in touch soon.>>

Lithuigi took the stairs two at a time, down into the tram station, while he contacted several of his allies in the enforcers. When he emerged into the plaza at the eastern docks, he made his way to a lonely tavern. Inside, a Raccorin was sitting behind the bar, nobody else drinking or eating at that hour.

He smiled at the Raccorin and handed him a datamin. "See to it that Prince Rhakksees gets this. And then take them to the rendezvous point."

Salty Saul nodded.

Back outside, Lithuigi saw Ellex Andria and Rakk Raeder crossing the plaza, and he watched them head to a small stand for some slurpans. They sat down to eat, and Lithuigi couldn't help but draw close, craning his neck for a look at the prisoner. But what he saw was Ellex Andria's hard eyes drilling into him, before she sprang to her feet and started in his direction.

Lithuigi turned on his heels and ran.

Chapter 43

Escaping to Nowhere

T HE DOOR TO BRYN'S cell opened and Roman Anthem entered. From his outstretched hand dangled the limp body of Jaun von Andron. Anthem had him by the back of the neck, and Jaun's head hung over to one side at a terrible angle. Anthem let him drop into a heap in front of the door and then fixed his eyes on Bryn and stared.

Bryn felt like she couldn't breath, and the panic made her want to squirm up into a little ball, to close her eyes and send her mind into the hollow and never come out again. But when she looked up at Anthem's Cul'tavin fatigues, at his long pradeshan robe, she felt a flicker of something else, deep inside herself. A tiny flame, pulsing like a heart, like a drumbeat that you can feel in every fiber of your body, in perfect resonance with everything around it. It scared her as much as Anthem did, but she continued to stare back at him.

"Time is growing short and my patience is nearly out. And I think von Andron here has grown to enjoy the beatings I give him." Anthem smirked. "He'll never talk. It seems you're my last hope, Bryn. Lucky you."

The flicker suddenly fanned up in her chest and Bryn let out a hiss. "Real brave you are, beating up a plant half your size—one who's been confined in near darkness and practically starved for weeks. Cul'tavin peacekeepers are all cowards these days."

Bryn heard thudding in her ears and they seemed to pulse with heat, and she breathed heavily and deeply, but she didn't turn away.

Anthem grinned at her. "Finally, some pep. The scared routine was getting so boring. I mean, look at you, Bryn. You're as large as a barge and with hands that could probably crush my skull if they wanted to. And yet you fold over like a dying pansy."

"One day you're going to regret this."

"Is that so?" he said, taking a step forward. When he saw her flinch, he threw back his head and laughed. "You're making a fantastic effort, truly. But you're a terrible trouper. Why not play a role more suited to your temperament? You know it was never your place to get involved in politics, or to pretend that the rants you share on your stream is valuable in any meaningful way. Your little game of sneaking into our archives and leaking the information to the public has cost you your father's life. And your continued obstinance here with me is about to cost you your mother's life, too."

Bryn's heavy breathing took on a more frantic tone, and tears began to fall down her face.

"Please," she said, the spark inside her smothered out, the embers rubbed deep into the soil. "I've told you the truth. I don't know who Anorian Grain is! Please, please don't hurt my mother. I don't know anything!" Bryn leaned over and sobbed.

When she looked up again, Anthem was gone, and the cell door was closed. She scrambled over to Jaun, grabbed him under the arms, and pulled him back to the wall, positioning him in the meager rays of light streaming through the slat.

"Jaun," she said, and she jumped when his eyes popped open.

He grinned at her, then winced.

"I thought you were dead," she said.

He put his fingers to his lips, then whispered, "It was all a big fake. World's best trouper, remember."

Bryn rolled her eyes and groaned. "At least your ego is intact."

"My ego is invincible," he said, smirking. But then his face fell.

"What is it?"

"Just thinking about Roman Anthem," he said. "I heard what he said to you. He's wrong, you know. About your stream. I've been a fan for years. But you probably picked up the reference when I denounced Balance, right?"

Bryn's head was suddenly spinning and she opened her mouth to respond, then closed it, and she blushed slightly.

"I archived your speech so I could watch it later, but then—well, everything happened and I—guess I forgot. I'm sorry."

"It seems my ego can be hurt after all," he said, putting his hand on his chest, a look on his face that said she'd just broken his heart.

Bryn rolled her eyes. "And now I'm not sorry at all. Nope, not one bit."

Jaun grinned.

"How'd you know about my stream? How'd you know—"

"That you're the Mighty B*zzness?" His eyes twitched and Bryn felt him calling to her in the hollow. She followed him to Dar Ka'Hala and watched as a sun, wrapped up in chains, came into view.

<<You're Starborn?>> she said.

<<Yes. And I was serious. I'd like to join your stream, when you get it going again.>>

Bryn gave him a sideways look. <<We already have someone covering melodramas.>>

<<Ouch,>> he said, and the light seemed to go out of the sun.

<<I'm sorry, that was out of line,>> she said, her face burning.

<<No, I deserved it,>> Jaun said. <<I make a real effort to remain equal parts melodramatic and aloof, but sometimes I forget that makes others think me a real fool with no depth at all.>>

<<I never thought that,>> she said. <<Just that you don't take anything seriously. Even denouncing the government during the Balancing Act, with you on stage as master of ceremonies, your millions of adoring fans hanging on your every word. I assumed it was a publicity stunt more than a real attempt at changing anything.>>

Bryn could see Jaun looking down at the ground with her real eyes, a wounded look on his face, and Bryn realized he probably wasn't used to being chastised.

What's wrong with me? she thought. *I just insulted Andramere's crown prince!*

"I'm sorry again," she said aloud. "I don't even know you. It just seems like I do, because I've seen your face and heard your voice for pretty much my entire life."

"Stop apologizing," Jaun said. "I should have been more upfront with you from the start."

"One thing I just can't figure out. Why'd you join the Pradishar, if you were planning to denounce them?"

Jaun got a sly look on his face. "I needed a Pradishar crystamin to access Pradishar servryns, of course."

Bryn tried to hide her surprise. "You hacked them?"

He nodded. "They were going to arrest me whether I denounced Balance or not."

"I'm—impressed. Truly. But why? What are you after on the servryns?"

He chuckled. "You'd really ask such a question? Secrets. Research. Answers to my questions."

Bryn looked at his forehead, at his four crystals in a diamond pattern. One for the Pradishar, one for the Andramere royal family, one for the Dyna'arin, and the last a public crystamin. Her eyes twitched as she pulled information off the weavryn about Jaun.

"You're an operator?" she said.

"A tinker, actually" he said. "With all the responsibilities that entails. I also have a small role in Management, and I lecture at the Academicon on Callo Baton, though most of it's done via weavryn, since I'm usually elsewhere."

Bryn's eyes were twitching like crazy as she tried to verify this bombshell he'd just dropped in her lap. But she couldn't find anything to confirm it. Trying to find information about the Guild was always next to impossible for someone without a Dyna'arin crystal.

"Are you performing again, Jaun von Andron? If you're lying—"

<<Anorian, are you there?>> he said, and Bryn was back with Starborn in Dar Ka'Hala, the chain-wrapped sun hanging over the cobblestones of the ancient city.

<<I'm here,>> Anorian said, a tree with fruits of every color appearing in the plaza beside them.

<<Can you tell the Mighty B*zzness that I'm a tinker?>>

<<For his young age, he's one of the finest in the Guild. But please don't let my praise go to your head, Starborn.>>

Bryn felt Anorian laughing, a loud, almost shriek-like laughter, and she joined in.

<<Everything goes to my head,>> Jaun said. <<Thanks Anorian. While we're here, let's go to the library. I want to show you something.>> The chain-wrapped sun shot off across the wide plazas, colorful towers, and thick forested parks of Dar Ka'Hala, and Bryn turned into an arrow, freshly sprung from the bow, and she whisked past Jaun and into the library, moving at the speed of thought.

Once they were in Bryn's office, the door closed and Jaun took on the appearance of his normal Andrasian self, minus all the scabs and bruising. Bryn took the idealized shape she had been projecting in private within the hollow, and sat down at her desk, while Jaun looked over the books stacked on the shelves.

<<Before I forget,>> he said. <<Thank you for doing all this. For archiving our library. Andramere owes you a debt, as do all of Balance's citizens. I know it must have been tedious work.>>

<<Not really. I just had to get the maquina purring, and then I had ample time for my own projects. But thank you.>>

<<Did Anorian tell you why it matters?>>

Bryn nodded. <<The datamins are about to stop working.>>

Jaun whistled. <<Finally, to be able to speak to someone about it! That's a lot to take in, right? Such monumental information. And if you're like me—and I know you are—you must have had a thousand other questions pop into your mind, but no certain way in which to ask them. Even now I struggle to understand how that could be, that the crystals might fail us. And yet history speaks of a precedent for it, doesn't it?>>

<<At least twice,>> Bryn said. <<The Purgation wiped out much of the data from the first two millennia of Balance. But in the Andramere crisis a century ago, only recent data was lost while older archives remained intact.>>

<<Indeed, the greatest mystery in the sordid history of our beloved island home,>> Jaun said. <<Officially it was a dynastic struggle, as you no doubt know. My grandfather, Cruthyr, the victor amongst the siblings, refused to ever speak of it again. All of those in his generation did. My family came out of the crisis nearly in collapse. But as a result of that conflict, we got the servryn, that wondrous maquina that somehow weaves the crystals together and makes possible the weavryn. We got public crystamins for every citizen of Andramere and eventually all of Balance Territories. And not a single record of how any of it came about, or why. I think about how my entire artistic career would have been inconceivable before the crisis, across ten thousand years of Balance. It can make you doubt what use history can serve in such unprecedented times. But a better question is why almost no one in a hundred years has asked what really happened during the crisis, and why the weavryn came out of it. Have you?>>

Bryn frowned. <<I guess not. I just assumed it was more royal shenanigans that didn't merit my interest.>>

<<Everyone justifies ignoring it differently.>> He was quiet for a moment.

She watched him, feeling nervous.

<<What can you tell me about the Faerengard Uprising?>>

Bryn began to recite the details of the attempt to overthrow King Rhakksees the Second by one of his nobles, and the attempt on Prince Rhakksees's life. The king had wiped out the family in punishment. She stopped when she saw the look on Jaun's face.

<<More royal shenanigans, and yet clearly you know, and relish, the details of the plot,>> he said.

<<What are you trying to say, Starborn? That I've been—we've all been—unable to think about the Andramere Crisis, unwilling to even ask about it?>>

Bryn could feel herself starting to panic.

He's wrong, he has to be. I'd be able to know if an impulse, a desire, an aversion, came from somewhere other than myself. Right?

<<Anorian?>> Bryn said, but before she got a response, she felt her body calling for her attention and she brought her focus back to the cell. The ship was accelerating and turning sharply, and Bryn felt the room pitching to one side. Thunder boomed over the purring whine of the gurgitator and she thought she heard something else too.

Jaun struggled not to fall over and he sat up, bracing himself against the wall, a look of panic on his face. Bryn was startled to see his wounds again, after seeing him so clean and healthy in the hollow.

<<What's that noise?>> he asked in her mind.

<<Brace yourselves!>> Anorian cried.

Bryn heard the horns then, and the cell briefly lit up with light, not white with lightning but red with the inferno from an enflamer. She leapt for Jaun and knocked him out of the way as fire shot through the slats, and when it stopped, the ceiling rushed up to meet them. She watched it fall away and then hover over her, sparkling, and the last thought she had, as salt water gushed over her face, was why she'd decided to go for a swim on such a stormy day.

❧❧❧❧❧ ❧❧❧❧❧

Bryn woke to the distant, muffled sounds of what she thought were scamps playing, but she soon remembered where she was—and what had happened—and she felt the water around her body and sat up, wide awake now, her heart racing. The water drained from her ears and she realized she was hearing a flock of gulls squawking and the soft sloshing of water against the side of the ship. The boat had leveled out, but there was nearly a foot of water on the floor.

"Jaun!" she cried, when she saw her cellmate on his side next to the wall. She grabbed him and pulled him up out of the water, and she exhaled hard when she saw he was breathing. Bryn brushed the hair fibers out of his eyes and shook his shoulders, and he moaned and blinked a few times and looked at her like he didn't quite know what was going on.

"Thank Trevian you're alive," Bryn said.

"Am I?" He touched the top of his head, then dropped his hand and leaned back against the wall. "I think—I need more sleep—" He closed his eyes and Bryn decided to let him rest. She walked on her knees to the slat and looked out at the ocean. The water was choppy and the surface was strewn with debris, and there was a sheen floating over everything, a yellowish brown that shimmered in the sunlight.

Sap.

A lot of it.

Bryn scooted over to the door and tried to pull on it. Still locked. She banged against it with her fist.

"Hey! Roman Anthem! Anybody?!"

But no sounds came back, only the squawking gulls fighting over the scraps outside.

Bryn stood and walked around the cell. There were holes in the walls where lances had stabbed through. It was a miracle they hadn't been skewered. She wondered how the ship was still afloat. But the battle was over, and there was no time to think about what might have been. Right now, they had a bigger problem. If Roman Anthem was dead, then they were trapped.

She looked around and saw that a piece of metal paneling on the outer wall had been sliced back and curved into a sharp point, like an arched scalpel, and she took a larger, serrated edge of the panel and began to saw the protrusion off.

This should be the perfect size to pry open the locking mechanism, she thought when she'd cut it free. She sliced up her fingers in the process, but she ignored the pain and set to work. Along the floor at the edge of the door, she felt under the water for the groove, then slid the curved point of her makeshift tool under the seam and up under the panel on the wall, and she grinned when it popped off.

<<Careful, MB,>> Jaun said in her mind, using the initials of her alias. <<You don't have the proper gear for that.>>

She turned back to look at him, but his eyes were still closed.

<<Would you rather we sit here and starve? Or let the attackers finish us off when they come back?>>

<<Very well, but let me help you? I just—need a moment to make the room stop spinning.>>

<<I know what I'm doing,>> Bryn said. <<You rest.>>

<<But you aren't a tinker.>>

She swallowed a hiss and turned back to the maquina.

Not officially, she thought. *But I'm been tinkering with my father my whole life, and almost every maquina is the same at its core.*

This one looked like the standard design, so she knew that underneath the metal frame, she'd find three sections, one stacked on top of the other, all neatly tucked inside the casing. The bottom section would have a long, thick wedge of densely packed organic material, greased up into a patty that resembled nearly-rotten rhupan and smelled about as bad. On top of the patty would be a mat of fungal fibers, it's tendrils down in the organic brick, it's upper fibers fused into tiny crystamin shards, giving it a short-range link. The middle compartment would hold two crystals—a well-sheathed dynamin, and at least one datamin alongside it. Finally, the topmost compartment would hold the actual working parts, where the kinetic energy of the dynamin would be channeled though a series of gears and levers. This part of the maquina varied greatly from one to the other, and was often interlocked with massive parts, some even the size of buildings. Since Bryn's expertise and talents lay more with the workings of the crystals, and their interactions, than with the nuts and bolts of moving parts, this was the section of a maquina that Bryn knew least of all. But all she needed to know today was which type of information would set the maquina into action. And fortunately for Bryn, her ability to slip streams gave her a skill few could match in performing such hacks.

Inside a normal locking mechanism, a signal from someone hoping to open the lock would contact the short-range crystamin within the fungus. That crystamin would then contact the datamin, which would verify the credentials of the one who sent the request, record the interaction, and return the information to the crystamin. The dynamin would fire, or not fire, accordingly.

Datamins were only accessible by proximity. There had to be physical contact with the datamin itself, or no information would flow. So Bryn opened the hatch that held the datamin, then placed her finger against the small metal cube. It was warm on her skin, and she had the data in her mind almost instantaneously.

She realized her problem immediately. Unlike a servryn, this datamin was simply a rigid structure of basic data. There were no streams to slip through, like the strands that made up the weavryn.

She spent a good hour looking up information on the weavryn hoping for inspiration, and she was about to give up when she got an idea.

<<Hey Starborn, you awake?>>

Jaun yawned and sat up.

"Indeed," he said aloud, "and feeling a bit better, I think." He scooted over, sloshing the water about as he came, and he hunkered down next to her, peering at the innards of the maquina, his eyes twitching.

"I have an idea," Bryn said. "It may not work, and if it doesn't, I'll give up and let you have a go at it. But I'm going to need you to let me, well, have a look inside your head. Not much, but a bit."

Jaun gave her a wary look, but then nodded. "Very well." He closed his eyes.

Bryn reached for him through the hollow and found him through his Pradishar crystamin which opened to her awareness.

<<I want you to access a Guild servryn,>> Bryn said in his mind. <<And let me follow you.>>

<<You won't be able to get in,>> Jaun said.

<<I don't want access, only to see how the servryn authenticates you.>>

<<Very well.>> Bryn thought he sounded exasperated, maybe even irritated, but she ignored it.

When Jaun reached for the servryn, Bryn slipped streams, pulling the data with her, the signal with her, as if the information Jaun had sent, and received in turn, had been diffused across a thousand different channels, rather than staying confined to one stream. The leakage allowed her to intrude on the data, to pull it into her own crystamin, and archive it for later use.

<<What was that?>> Jaun said, and Bryn could feel that he was surprised and even a little panicked by the experience.

<<I call it slipping streams. It lets me access information that would normally be off limits.>>

<<That's how your notestream was privy to so many secrets...>>

<<Yes,>> Bryn said.

She looked at Jaun and his eyes had grown wide and he started to grin.

<<Wow,>> he said. <<Truly fantastic! I was wrong to doubt you.>>

<<Maybe,>> Bryn said. <<Let me see if I can get this working.>>

She touched the datamin again, and using the data she'd pulled from Jaun's communication with a Dyna'arin servryn, she duplicated a verification order while cloaking herself in Jaun's tinker credentials. The maquina whined and the gears began to spin, and the door started to whoosh open.

"You're incredible, MB!" Jaun cried aloud, just as the whooshing stopped and the door froze. It had only opened about a quarter of the way, not enough to get out. Bryn and Jaun both leaned over to see what had happened. One of the gears in the topmost portion of the maquina had gotten stuck.

"May I?" Jaun said, holding out his hand.

Bryn gave him the makeshift scalpel and then watched him work, carefully popping out a few of the gears, shaping and bending the tips, and making sure the little teeth weren't mashed together. He stuck them back in place, then nodded at her.

"Try it again," he said, and this time it opened all the way.

<<Careful,>> Jaun said in her mind. <<Anthem could be right outside the door, waiting to surprise us.>>

But nobody was outside the cell, nor in the crew quarters, nor anywhere below deck. They took the stairs, tiptoeing slowly and carefully, and when they emerged, the morning sun on Bryn's skin made her swoon, and she felt a burst of energy and confidence.

She looked around but the deck was empty. Debris floated on the surface of the sea on both sides of the ship, pushing up against the reef where she realized they were stuck.

Stuck, but not moored, she thought, as the ship rose and lurched with an incoming wave.

Gulls were squawking overhead and swooping down to the water. And there were some scorch marks on the deck, and some puddles still shiny with sap.

Much of the wreckage floating around them was wooden.

"A Bhizini fleet, torn to pieces," Bryn said.

Jaun nodded. "I know this ship we're on. It's a long story, but I've traveled on it before. We were attacked by Bhizini then as well. Anthem could be upstairs in his quarters. Come on."

But nobody was upstairs. The ship was empty.

They spent some time going over the cata'rin, riffling through the cabinets and storage closets, seeing what they had available. There wasn't much, but Jaun found some dried rhupan and fresh water, and Bryn found a toolbox, some clean pradeshan robes, a pair of fighting pikes, some glowbes, and some restraining vines.

The gurgitator had been damaged in the fighting, but Jaun felt confident he could fix it, so while he set to work, Bryn went down to the crew quarters to freshen up. She hadn't had a bath in weeks, and she pulled off her soiled robes and rancid cumberdome, found a satchel of fresh water, and set to work scrubbing her body. Some of her wounds were still a bit raw, but it felt so good to wash the muck off that she went ahead and rubbed them down anyway.

When she finished, she pulled on a clean pradeshan robe from one of the cubbies.

I'll have to go like the Bhizini and skip a cumberdome, she thought.

When she returned to where Jaun was working, she crinkled her nose at the smell.

"Your turn," she said.

"In a minute."

"How about now. Please?" She made a disgusted face.

Jaun looked hurt, not understanding the expression, but then he looked down at his tattered robes while he sniffed at himself, and he nodded. "Very well."

"You'll feel a lot better afterward."

Bryn gripped the deck with her rootpads, lifted her arms up, and unfurled her branches, and she perched with her eyes closed and feasted on the light while Jaun cleaned up. He returned in crisp pradeshan robes, his hair fibers wet and shiny with water, his face puffy from where he'd scrubbed across his scabs.

Sweet Trevian, he really is beautiful, she thought, as Jaun sat back down by the gurgitator, grabbed a tool, and went back to tinkering.

By the time the sun started to set, Bryn was losing faith in his ability to get the damn thing running again. And she kept hearing a thudding sound and wondered how they'd get free of the reef without tearing out the bottom of the ship. The tide had risen and lifted them higher above the sharp edges but that meant the cata'rin kept pitching about, and Jaun kept cursing in frustration.

Bryn heard the thudding noise again and she walked over to the edge of the deck to have another look.

<<Jaun!>> she screamed in his mind, and he dropped his tool in surprise at the tone of her voice, and came scrambling to her side as she frantically pointed.

Down below, the front half of a cano'rin was banging against the cata'rin, and sprawled face-down and hanging half off of it was Roman Anthem. His robe was torn off of one shoulder and Bryn saw a large gash, caked over with chunky sap.

Jaun stared down with wide eyes.

<<Is he—dead?>>

Bryn's heart was racing, the panic rising up inside of her.

She clenched her teeth and hissed. <<Damnit, help me. Otherwise, we're no better than the Pradishar. And he might be our only chance of getting rescued.>>

<<He could call for reinforcements with his crystal.>>

<<I guess we have to take that chance. Lower the plank.>>

The ramp crashed down against the reef. Bryn grabbed a pike and started down, using her rootpads to keep from slipping. When she reached the bottom, she grabbed the cano'rin and pulled it up onto the reef, grunting as she worked, while she struggled to keep her footing on the sharp coral. She grabbed Anthem by the feet, pulled him out of the boat and rolled him onto his side. She put her hand in front of his mouth, then to his neck.

<<I don't think he's breathing,>> she said. <<Come help me.>>

Bryn put her arms under his armpits while Jaun grabbed him by the ankles, and they started to drag him up the plank. He was heavy, and they almost dropped him, but Bryn used her rootpads for support, and she pulled and strained and heaved, and Jaun grunted and groaned, but finally they had him up on the deck. Bryn flattened her palm and dropped it, hard, into Anthem's upper back, and his body spasmed. Foamy water started trickling out of his mouth. She pushed him forward til he was almost face-down and more drained out.

Then her and Jaun sank to their knees, gasping for air.

<<What a beast,>> Jaun said. <<But you! MB, you're incredible!>>

Bryn gave him a grin. <<Call me Bryndax.>>

Anthem moaned and Bryn saw his eyes starting to flutter and his head to nod, and she panicked.

Without thinking, she lunged at him, flipped him onto his back, drove her knee into his flower, clenched up her fists, and began to beat him in the face with both hands, pummeling him, twisting her torso back and forth, putting all her strength into it.

Jaun's mouth fell open and he pointed at her, dumbstruck, but he finally found the words. "Bryndax!" he screamed, but she kept punching. He grabbed her arms and she looked at him with fury in her eyes, the heat of that spark she'd thought had been driven out of her flaring back to life and pulsating within her, driving her forward, willing her to continue, but she fought off the urge and stopped her attack.

"I'm not going back in that cell," she said. "And neither are you. Now get those restraining vines before he wakes up again."

Jaun scrambled to his feet while Bryn kept her eye on Anthem's face, but he didn't move again.

"I'll—see about the gurgitator," Jaun said, after they'd tied him up tightly.

Bryn nodded, her mind racing, her hands shaking, her whole body trembling.

<<Are you alright, Bryndax?>> It was Anorian.

<<No,>> she said. <<I don't think I am.>>

<<How can I help?>>

<<Hold me?>>

Bryn found herself down in the hollow, standing on the balcony of the palace at Dar Ka'Hala, with Anorian's branches wrapped tightly around her, and she felt warm and safe, the pain in her hands, in her shoulders, in everything, momentarily forgotten. Anorian smelled like dry soil during the first rain of the season, like a morning breeze off the sea.

The sun sank below the horizon and the stars appeared, and Jaun flicked a glowbe to life and continued working. Bryn lay back against the deck and stared upward at the heavens, feeling tiny and massive at the same time, one eye in Dar Ka'Hala and the other on the sky above, and for a moment, the last few months felt like a distant dream.

<<I wish you were here with me,>> she said.

<<Me too,>> Anorian said. <<May I borrow your eyes for a moment?>>

<<You don't have to ask,>> Bryn said, and she felt Anorian inside her mind, seeing what she saw, feeling what she felt.

<<Turn and take in the whole sky, from horizon to horizon,>> Anorian said, and Bryn complied.

<<Beautiful,>> Anorian said. <<And rich with information. You're about 15 degrees south, in the Far Ocean, on the flank of the Cut'hull Reefs. Thester, and the southwestern flank of Mon Mang'alar, is not far to the north.>>

Bryn heard the whining purr of the gurgitator humming to life, and Juan whooping with delight.

<<Good work, Starborn,>> Anorian said.

<<I had to bypass the controller all together, so it might be a bit difficult to adjust the aperture, but at least it will get us moving.>>

<<Head east,>> Bryn said. <<Let's see if we can clear the reef. We might as well know if we're going to sink or float before we get our hopes up.>>

Jaun opened the gurgitator and the cata'rin began to bounce and shake, and they heard a terrible scraping sound below deck, but then they moved out into smoother waters and Jaun closed the gurgitator back down. They each took a glowbe and went below deck to see if any more water had breached the hull but everything looked okay.

<<We won't make it too far,>> Jaun said.

Bryn sent him the coordinates Anorian had shared.

<<Not bad,>> he said. <<Could be worse.>>

<<What are you thinking, Starborn?>> Anorian asked

He grinned. <<Hey MB, you ever been to Vergis?>>

Bryn's eyes lit up. <<We're near Vergis?>>

The secret Dyna'arin laboratory complex and tinker wonderland didn't appear on any maps. And of course she hadn't been.

She felt positively giddy with nerdy glee.

<<Careful, Bryndax,>> Anorian said. <<Remember your father's concern with the Guild. It might not be safe for you there.>>

<<Do we have a choice?>> she said, pulling up a map on the weavryn. <<We can't go back to Balance Territories. If we can't take refuge with the Guild, then what are we to do? Keep sailing in circles?>>

<<I have a lab there,>> Jaun said. <<And I can get a new cata'rin there. It's our best bet.>>

<<And what will you do with Roman Anthem?>> Anorian asked. <<Though he has enemies everywhere, he also has allies everywhere. Taking him to Vergis could be dangerous.>>

<<Then we'll be extra careful,>> Jaun said, flooding the crystal with confidence.

Bryn felt Anorian wrap her in a hug again. <<I—would be devastated if anything happened to you, Bryndax. You're special to me.>>

She could feel Anorian's timidity, the hope and the concern that flooded her crystal and made her nearly swoon.

<<And you to me,>> she said, and the surge of relief felt as good to Bryn as the sunshine had felt after so many weeks in the dark.

Chapter 44

The Inner Door Opens

THE LAST THING FIN'ROQ remembered before darkness swallowed him up was a terrible pain in his stomach, an ache that spread up and down his body, pulling on his skin, tearing at it, til he was sure he'd been split apart. But he didn't know why he was hurting. He couldn't recall what had happened, or where he was, or who or when or anything. He only knew he'd been hurt, and he'd fallen into darkness. Although the pain had eventually stopped, the black pushed in on him now, threatening to crush him, and he struggled to keep the panic from sending him into hysterics.

Am I dead? he thought.

And then the even worse possibility—that he was still under P'anorum, still in the cavern with Roe's corpse, trapped in the darkness, his flesh slowly turning to stone while he screamed himself silly.

No. I emerged. Bhea nursed me to health. And then—what? I suddenly went to Balan Su and enrolled to be a monkin? In other words, my dreams came true?

No, if this were a dream, I wouldn't have been attacked by the Balan Susians. I would still be there, still be with Jaun. I'd have my own crystamin by now.

He heard voices then, coming from the darkness, speaking in the old tongue. Fin opened his eyes and tried to look around. His arms were still up over his head, strung to something. His legs too. But he recognized where he was. And he felt the knife wound on the edge of his belly, just along the outer edge of his flower, and he remembered the feel of the scytherin cutting into him. Someone had sewn up the wound, rubbed it down with salve, and tried to heal him.

"He wakes," Fin heard in Ballack and he looked up into the surprisingly kind eyes of Qardymion the Saltsap. The elders of many of the clans stood around them, their faces blank, their eyes watching him intently. "How are you feeling, Fin'roq?"

He tried to speak but his throat was too dry.

Qardymion whistled and someone approached from behind and held an earthen jug to his lips, and he drank.

"Like I was stabbed," Fin said, when the jug was removed.

Fin'roq hated himself more and more with every tear that fell.

"I'm sorry, Fin'roq. Truly, I am." Qardymion started to grin. "But it worked! Sweet Trevian, it worked."

"What worked?"

Qardymion's grin froze and started to fade. Behind them, the elders began to chatter among themselves.

The Saltsap turned and shouted something at them in the old tongue, and when they stopped talking, they said something else and they grunted their assent. Then they turned back to Fin'roq.

"You just don't make this easy for us, do you?"

"I don't know what you want from me," Fin said. "I would give it freely, if I knew. You didn't have to hurt me. I swear I don't know how I do those things. It's like it's someone else—" He stopped, remembering that the villagers on P'anorum had accused him of being possessed by a Mund'umbrian. They were prepared to kill him, slowly, over a low fire. Would the Bhizini have the same fear? "It's like it's happening to someone else. I swear it. I can't control it. I don't know what I'm doing."

"You know," Qardymion said. "Deep inside, you know. You've remembered it time and time again across the ages. And when you let that power flow in you, you know exactly what to do with it. I saw you pick up those Cul'tavin peacekeepers and fling them across the plaza, as if a dynamin had overloaded right in the midst of them. You held your hand like this, and pushed it outward like this, no hesitation, no resistance. An expert, a master of the form. A true artist. That knowledge—that knowledge inside of you—is what you must remember. The world can't wait any longer. The speakers have warned us. Even I can feel it in the air. The Death King has waited patiently, but now he plans to move. You are the only hope to stop him. We cannot wait any longer."

Qardymion turned to the elders and spoke, and they grunted and began to leave the dais. Fin'roq saw the scytherin in their hand.

"No, wait, please! Wait. Stop! This—I can—but you have to—please!!" he begged, in hysterics.

His pleas fell on deaf ears.

When the last elder had left, Qardymion walked close to Fin'roq, a sad look on their face.

"I wish there was another way."

"Please. I just—like the speaker said. I'm not ready. I need more time!"

"But the world can't wait, Fin. Our people—*your* people—we're being butchered by Balance Authority. They're hunting us down in sink and swamp, seizing any ship of ours they spot, torching them along with everyone aboard. If stopping the Harvest means hurting you just a little bit, can't you agree that it's worth it? If you were me, wouldn't you do it? I know you have the strength to make difficult decisions. And I know you have the strength to endure my blade a few more times."

Qardymion didn't hesitate, but plunged the scytherin into the same wound, slicing through the sutures and down into the tender flesh. Fin'roq pulled against his restraints and he opened his mouth and screamed, as if the yelling might stop the pain. The darkness swelled up and his head rolled on his shoulders, but he didn't black out. He squinted up at Qardymion, and saw they had a look of disappointment on their face.

The Saltsap lunged again, this time on the other side of his stomach, and when Fin screamed, it was the cry of an ancient, feral beast, like the screech that had thundered across the bay at P'anorum. When it was over, he sagged against the restraints and struggled to breathe, the pain nearly all he could experience, as if it were the entire universe. But he pushed it down, and pulled his awareness back to where he was, clinging to the present, refusing to lose himself.

Refusing to go back into the darkness.

He heard a loud crack and saw Qardymion drop to the floor, grunting, followed by a whorl of flame that shot out over the top of him, off the gazebo and out across the clearing. Fin turned to look just as his restraints were cut. When he collapsed on the floor, the pain shot up through his entire body, and the roar of the beast was back on his lips, but he swallowed it down.

Someone grabbed his arm and pulled him to his feet, and he almost fell into the darkness inside himself but he felt the arm wrap around him, holding him up, and he clutched it. And then he saw Bhart looking at him with panic in their eyes. They handed Fin a fighting pike to support himself, and kept an enflamer trained on the Saltsap with their other hand.

Qardymion moaned and sat up, rubbing their head. They looked up and saw it was Bhart who had attacked them.

"Unless you want to get torched, you'll stay down," Bhart said.

Qardymion grinned and gritted their teeth, and they exhaled through their nose.

"Brave," they said. "Foolish, but brave. I knew you had it in you, Bhartimu'u."

"I told you this was wrong," Bhart said. "I won't let you hurt Fin again!"

A group of Bhizini reached the top of the stairs and Bhart backed up so they were facing both them and the Saltsap, and when they saw they had an enflamer—and had it trained on Qardymion—a number of them turned and went back down the stairs. A few lingered, their eyes looking murderously at Bhart, when a whorl of flame ignited their flesh, caught the beam, and sparked the roof of the gazebo. The two closest fell off the stairs, shrieking.

The flames hissed as they spread up the roof and down the stair, and Fin'roq could feel the heat on his skin, hear the wood crackling and popping as the inferno spread.

"Grab ahold of me," Bhart said. "Unfurl your branches and wrap them around my torso and over the top of my shoulder. Quickly!"

Fin slid the branches out from under his arms, and they gripped Bhart's body, out and around their waist, and up and over their shoulders. He cinched them as tightly as he could, and he felt Bhart's branches sliding over his own. He pressed his face into Bhart's chest and closed his eyes.

Bhart's arm flicked and a loud pop cracked, and suddenly they were falling together.

No, they were swinging, onward and upward, and then another loud crack, and they were falling again.

The branches kept him from moving too much, but the pressure on his wounds was almost unbearable. Onward they went through the canopy, swinging branch to branch, Bhart flicking his whips and carrying them off into Mon Mang'alar, and when Fin could take no more pain, he gave up his panic and let the darkness take him once more.

⁓⁓⁓ ⁓⁓⁓

Fin'roq came in and out of consciousness as they traveled by whip through the trees, but when he finally opened his eyes and knew who he was again, he was in a skiff'rin and Bhart was tending to his injuries. The canopy of Mon Mang'alar hung overhead, the tangled branches of the trees reaching up over the edge of the boat like long gnarled fingers trying to grab at them. He winced when Bhart rubbed salve on his wounds, and then sighed when the pain subsided.

Bhart said nothing while they worked and Fin felt like he was about to cry every time he started to open his mouth, so he closed his eyes again, but was surprised when he heard the whine of maquina and felt the boat accelerating.

The skiff'rin had a gurgitator!

"Are we safe?" he said.

"Not yet," Bhart said. "But soon." They were sitting at the back of the skiff'rin, their hands on the dials atop the gurgitator, their eyes fixed on the water in front of them. Fin followed their gaze and saw they were passing along a narrow, winding channel of muddy water, and he watched the roots flying by in a blur, saw the approaching trees, the turns, the way Bhart drove so fast through them, as if they knew what was beyond every bend, and Fin couldn't help but be impressed at their piloting skills.

He put his head back down but started to feel sick, dizzy with speed and from turning so much, so he closed his eyes and drifted back to sleep. Bhart woke him with a touch. The sky was dark but they held a glowbe up in the air with one hand while they offered the other to Fin. The gurgitator was closed and the skiff'rin wasn't moving, and to the side he could see the outline of a rock wall, and realized they were in some sort of grotto.

Fin cried out as Bhart pulled him to his feet, and Bhart quickly put their arm around him and held him up. He cried out again when he stepped out of the skiff'rin and onto the sandy edge of the water, and Bhart helped him up onto the rock and then slowly, and carefully, lowered him down to the ground and propped him up against the wall. Then they slid down the wall and sat next to him, and let out a long, weary sigh.

"We should be safe now."

"Where are we?"

"Near Lagracia. Territory controlled by my clan, the Tornroot."

"I thought you were a Pal'meran."

"I've followed the Saltsap since I was ten. I saved their life once, and they offered me to join them in the fight to save our people. I've been at their side ever since, though I never swore fealty to another clan."

"You attacked Qardymion."

"Yes."

"You saved me."

Bhart looked at him. "It never should have happened. Qardymion was out of line. I told them as much. After they took you to the speaker and returned without you, I knew something was wrong. They made a stupid excuse to send me away, but I laid low instead, and waited. When I heard your cries, I did what I had to."

Fin's eyes were burning with tears again.

"They all turned on me," he said. "Every single one of them. Except you."

Bhart said nothing but Fin could hear them breathing heavily, and he put his cheek on Bhart's shoulder and Bhart stroked his head and ran their fingers between his long hair fibers. Fin nuzzled into their neck and breathed deeply of their scent and put his lips to their skin. Bhart moaned and their lips found his, and they were trembling but they held one another, and Bhart's kisses were soft and gentle. Fin couldn't believe what he was doing, and his heart ached suddenly for Jaun, but he drove the thought of him away, and tried to lose himself in the moment, which had become so beautiful so suddenly after so much pain. They kissed for what felt like hours, til they were asleep in each other's arms, their lips still close to one another's.

When Fin woke, there was sunlight trickling in from the opening to the grotto, still soft with early morning hues. Bhart was sitting with their legs crossed, their hands on their thighs, eyes closed, whispering prayers in the old tongue. Fin watched them, admiring their skin, their hands, their lips, their flower.

Bhart opened one eye and peeked at him, grinning.

"How are you feeling this morning?" They came close. "Let me see those wounds. Do they hurt?"

"Yes."

"Here, this will help."

Bhart held up a clay mug to Fin's lips and tipped it back.

Fin took a sip and his eyes opened wide.

"Ooh," he said. "That's nice."

He drank another swig, and then finished the mug. He licked his lips. "Mmmmm!"

Bhart laughed. "I'm glad you like it."

"It's delicious. And familiar somehow. What is it?"

"A very special bhiza concoction. It is called the Inner Door."

Fin opened his mouth to reply but closed it.

"That was—a lot."

Bhart was looking at him with that look again, and their eyes were shining. Fin went to sit up but couldn't, and the panic rose up inside him.

"Bhart—" he said, but his words sounded like they were echoing back and forth across the grotto.

Bhart took his hand and squeezed it. "I'll be right here, looking after you, the whole time. I promise."

"What—why—"

"You have to wake up, Fin," Bhart said. "Pass through the door and wake up."

He tried to speak but he couldn't, and he watched helplessly as Bhart's face seemed to shrink away in front of him, as the walls of the grotto stretched and warped and twisted back upon themselves. And the last thing Fin thought, before he went insane, was that he'd been betrayed yet again.

Chapter 45

Breaking Through

ELLEX ANDRIA WAS SOMEWHERE beautiful, a garden with orchards of lush fruit and rows of herbs and mushrooms, with flagstone pathways and tinkling fountains, a gnarled old forest standing sentinel around it all. She was scared but excited too. Hopeful. The time had nearly come, and she was ready. The smell of jasmine filled her nostrils as she walked through the foliage to the sprouting patch. Someone was with her, at her side, a friend to help her, and they walked together, arm in arm.

She looked down at the scytherin in her hand, and at a spratlyn in the patch, and as she did so, she took the blade and carefully, but quickly, sliced through the taprin, a clean cut. She watched as her scamp opened its eyes and its mouth at the same time, drew a deep breath, and began to scream. Her eyes burned with happy tears.

Qaas'i, she thought. *I was there. I remember!*

Ellex took the scamp in her arms and picked it up and held it, and when she did, she saw that there was another spratlyn in the patch, right next to Qaas'i, it's taprin also ready for cutting. And Ellex felt like she'd been punched in the gut.

She cried out and woke with a splitting pain in her head so deep she turned on her side and retched, and she coughed and sputtered and tried to breath. The pain flared and then died down into a slow, rhythmic throb, and she opened her eyes again and tried to sit up, but her vision blurred into two blobs.

"Qaas'i," she whispered. "Raeder."

Oh Sweet Trevian, no!

She tried to focus. There was a circle of light overhead, and she groped at the wall and realized she was at the bottom of a deep hole. Someone was nearby, and she strained her eyes, pleaded with them to work right, to clear up. It was Rakk! He was crumpled in a heap near the wall, and she grabbed him and pulled on his massive shoulder, trying to turn him over, while she frantically looked around for Qaas'i. But there was no one else in the cell.

She got Rakk over onto his side, and saw that his hair fibers were sticky with sap.

"Raeder," she said. "Raeder, wake up!"

She shook him but he didn't move. So she put her hands on his face and felt in front of his mouth, and when she felt a puff of hot air, she sank back down on the ground, buried her face in his chest, and wept.

And she remembered.

They'd come for them at the tavern, bursting through the door and—

Ellex touched her neck and felt the lump where the dart had pricked her.

The Bhizini have my daughter, she thought. *Sweet Trevian, let her be okay. I'll do anything, anything! Just let her be okay.*

Her eyes felt heavy again, harder to keep open, and though she fought it, she couldn't stay awake. She drifted in and out of dreams, the smell of bhiza thick in the air, and though she knew the Bhizini were drugging them, there was no way to stop breathing. There was no way to resist. What did it matter anyway?

When she woke later—a few hours or a few days, she wasn't sure—Rakk was writhing and moaning, whimpering even. She groaned and sat up, her head pulsing. Rakk's face was contorted in agony, and she touched his cheeks with her hands.

"Raeder," she said, the tears spilling out. "Come back. Please come back to me. Please."

Rakk woke, gasping and choking as he tried to breath, pure panic in his eyes. When he saw Ellex, the panic turned to confusion. He tried to sit up, and winced.

"My head—"

"You were hit—and drugged."

"What happened?"

"Ambushed, by the Bhizini."

Ellex could see in Rakk's eyes that he remembered.

"Qaas'i?"

Ellex shook her head, the tears spilling out again, and Rakk sat up and wrapped his arms around her, and she let him. But then he let go of her and turned away, and Ellex could see he was shaking.

"Raeder?"

"No," he said, but it was more of a moan. "No."

"What's wrong? Raeder, look at me."

"No," he said. "No. I let you down, again. I broke a promise to you, again! I told you that we were safe in Callo Baton. I told you to trust me! Father was right. I'm worthless! I'm unworthy." He put his hands over his head and slumped into the wall.

Ellex wrapped him in a hug and rested her check on his upper back, then lifted her hands up to where he held his own over his head, and she grabbed them and pulled them back down. He grabbed her arms and wrapped them tighter around himself, and she held him, saying nothing.

When she finally felt him stir, she let go of her grip and he turned partway to face her, his eyes down, his face drained of life.

"I owe you an apology," she said.

He started to look at her but stopped.

"I've been awful to you this entire trip," she continued. "And I'm sorry. I'm so sorry."

"I deserved it," he said. "All I've done is fail you. I let Balan Su down. I was in charge of security, and my own damn troops did nothing but fight amongst themselves. And I ran right into a trap, like the idiot that I am. There's no way I get a pass on that one."

"Yeah, you have a temper sometimes. You shouldn't have chased that slave without calling for backup. But you know what? I chased that Bhizini into the warehouse that night in Eastport, when I found my troops butchered. I went in running, ignoring my brother's calls to slow down and wait for him. It could have been an ambush."

Rakk didn't say anything.

"Please, Raeder, don't do this now. I'm about to lose my mind. I—haven't been myself lately. No, for a long time. In fact, I don't even know who I am anymore. My own government stole my scamp from me, erased all memory of her existence, and kept her in a cage right underneath my feet, in the same damn building I work in every fucking day. How's that for foolish?"

"You don't remember any of it?" he said, finally looking at her.

Now she dropped her eyes, hoping to keep it in, but it all came pouring out anyway.

"I'm sorry, Raeder. I should have told you before, but I didn't even understand it myself. I still don't. I spent thirty three years never once questioning what happened to me, never once thinking of the past, like it didn't happen. Like it wasn't real. I had to remind myself, each morning when I woke, that my father was dead. I—Sweet Trevian, I saw him, every day, in Balan Su, staring with such sad eyes I thought my heart would break. I thought I was losing my mind. But no—I wasn't even willing to admit that much. I just closed everything off, the questions, the doubts, the memories that didn't match. When the incident—the dream—happened, and I saw—so much that didn't make sense—I just pretended it was a prank, a gag, someone trying to hurt my career. And then when I found Qaas'i—I don't know how to explain it, I just knew she was mine. I knew she was good, wonderful even, the most precious thing in the world. That I'd die to keep her safe. And yet I can't even do that."

She looked at Rakk then and he had a small grin on his face.

"Ell, I think Qaas'i's fine." He put a hand on the wall. "This is rock." He looked up. "And deep, too. That means we're not in Mon Mang'alar anymore. And if you listen, you can feel the breakers vibrating. This is probably Lagracia, in the Far Ocean. The Tornroot Clan rules here, and they're a peaceable group, for the most part. Not brutal like Qardymion's Pal'merans. The elders here will know who we are, and they'll only be waiting for a speaker to advise them."

"I hope you're right."

"Me too," he whispered. "You know, I came to Callo Baton hoping to expose a plot by my sister to steal my crown. I never expected to run into you on Nunan, nor to love Qaas'i so much, so quickly. I know she's not my scamp, but she is my sister. She's my family, and you are too. And right now, you two are the most important things in my life."

Ellex looked away from him. "So now we just play the waiting game?" she said. "Sweet Trevian, I don't know if I can take it anymore! You know, I've spent my whole life caring—about my family, about Andrasia, about Balance, about the Pradishar. But it was all a joke. A ruse. A big act. The Andrasians call me their good-mother, and I pretend to look out for them, to carefully measure their happiness and well-being and do all I can to increase it. As if that were possible. It's only now, that I have someone in my life—someone with whom my own well-being depends upon their well-being, and vice versa. And Trevian help me, it might be the most horrible thing I've ever endured, but it's also the most wonderful. That's what matters most to me, Reader. I have to know she's safe. And then—maybe—I'll care about everything else. Maybe then I can think about who I am again. Who I *really* am. And what I really want."

Rakk looked at her then and Ellex saw the hope in his eyes, and she knew she shouldn't give him the wrong idea, but she couldn't bear the thought of pushing him away.

"I know who you are," he said, his eyes shining as he looked at her. "But I'll do whatever I can to help you find out again."

She put her head on his shoulder and closed her eyes, and he lay his head against hers, and they drifted off to sleep again.

Ellex and Rakk woke to the sound of the metal grating overhead creaking as it was lifted and then clattering open with a clank of iron on rock that echoed off the walls of the hole and seemed to sound inside their heads. They looked at one another and helped each other to stand, while a Bhizini peered down into the hole and lowered a ladder for them.

"Let me go first," Rakk said, but Ellex grabbed the ladder and started to climb, surprising herself with her speed given how utterly exhausted she felt.

Rakk scrambled to keep up behind her.

When she reached the top, she struggled to get over the edge and pull herself out, but two Bhizini grabbed her by either arm and, with surprising gentleness, lifted her up and out of the hole. Several others were standing around with enflamers trained on her.

Where the hell did they get Guild weaponry from? she thought, while Rakk climbed out behind her.

"We're going to the chief now," one said in Ballack.

Rakk took Ellex's hand and they went where they were directed, down a long series of narrow, damp stone corridors and up slippery stairs to a small audience chamber. A tall, broad Bhizini sat cross-legged on the dais, sipping from a mug of steaming jha'ala. At his side sat Lithuigi Von'nDrino.

Ellex barely suppressed a hiss.

"Where's my daughter!" she said. "What have you done with my scamp?!"

The Bhizini frowned and Lithuigi put up his hands. "I promise you, she's fine. She's in the next room waiting for you. And I am sorry for all this chicanery." He looked at the Bhizini next to him with an exasperated glare but the Bhizini was staring at Ellex and Rakk. "Chief Tuck Tuck, I appreciate your help in collecting my companions. I now ask that you welcome them as your guests," Lithuigi said.

The Bhizini turned and smacked Lithuigi on the shoulder. "Of course I will, Von'nDrino." Then they turned back to Ellex and Rakk, grinning. "Welcome to Lagracia. I'm Tuck'tumi, Chief of the Tornroot, but everyone calls me Tuck Tuck, and you both can do the same. Help yourselves to rhupan, bhiza, sleeping mounds, anything you need. If anyone gives you a problem, you tell me immediately, and I'll see to it myself they're punished. Guests are treated with respect on my island, I guarantee it."

Should she bow? Thank her captors?

"Your kindness is appreciated, Tuck'tumi Chief," Rakk said. "We come in peace." He looked at Ellex.

The chief stood then. "Very well, I'll leave you to Von'nDrino then." He gave a sideways glance at the professor before exiting out the back of the room, and Lithuigi came down from the outcropping.

"Let's go somewhere more private," he said, "where I can be sure we aren't overheard. The Tornroot are almost certainly spying on us."

"I want to see my daughter," Ellex said.

"Right now, Von'nDrino," Rakk said.

"Of course. This way."

He ushered them out into a large cavern. Groups of Bhizini were singing and playing instruments, feasting and dancing, sleeping and making love, and the air was full of the smells of rhupan and bhiza and the salty sea and the tangy smell of Verdillion flowers and hot breath. Ellex's eyes grew wide at the spectacle of it all, so loud and clamorous and festive. She looked around for Qaas'i and spotted her sitting with a group of Bhizini near a grill, nibbling on a strip of charred rhupan in one hand and popping berries in her mouth with the other, her eyes growing wide and her cheeks drawing in with each sour bite, then relaxing into a smile with each nibble of savory rhupan.

Ellex sighed and let the tears flow, and Rakk squeezed her hand. Many of the faces in the room turned to look at them, and the music started to wane before it picked back up again. Most went back to what they were doing, but others lingered, staring, scowling. A few looked positively murderous.

Qaas'i saw them and came running over, and when she went first to Ellex and wrapped her arms around her waist, Ellex really did weep.

"Have they been good to you, little one?" Rakk asked, and Qaas'i hugged him too. Then she looked at Lithuigi and grinned, and Ellex felt like her heart had stopped beating.

"This way," Lithuigi said.

Qaas'i returned to the grill, and Ellex wanted to grab her hand, to never let her out of her sight again, but she touched her on the top of the head and smiled at her, then turned and followed Rakk. It was one of the hardest things she'd ever done, and she knew if she looked back, she'd never let her out of her sight again.

They passed through a low arching doorway and up a few narrow steps to a small ledge overlooking the sea. The sun was down near the horizon, and the water was a blend of orange and white smudges on a wide pink canvas. Below the ledge, waves crashed against the island, the surf so rough they had to stand close together to be heard.

"Now start talking," Rakk said.

"Easy, son. I promised you answers, so tell me what it is you'd like to know?"

Rakk wanted to ask about the datamin he'd seen at the tavern—about the fleet of ships the Guild was building, and who in the Guild would be willing to help his sister attack him in the tunnels of Balan Su—but he turned to Ellex instead.

"I want to know about the stasis chamber," she said, trying to keep her voice steady.

"Yes, of course. It's an ancient device of unknown origin. I created a modified version of it, one which would slow the growth process and prolong stasis, with the goal of having one subject held for a thousand years or longer. I monitored—Qaas'andria—for over thirty years, and the project was a success. I made sure everything was perfect for her."

"Perfect?" Ellex nearly spat the word. "A perfect prison, you mean."

"I designed the maquina, and I made sure it continued to run smoothly. I wasn't in charge of the project. I only did as I was told. One does not easily resist the Pradishar."

Ellex shook her head. "I am the Pradishar. I'm a bishrop, Sui Pradesh on the Council of Nine, friend of the Gran Pradesh. How could I not know this was happening? And what in Trevian's Sweet Name did they hope to gain from imprisoning a poor, defenseless little scamp?"

"The mysteries of the Pradishar are unfathomable," Lithuigi said. "Do you know where the crystals come from? We wear their jewels in our skin and we let them into our minds, into the deepest part of our being. Yet we know nothing about them. Nothing at all."

"And why Qaas'i? Do you at least know that? Why they took her from me?"

Lithuigi paused and considered before he spoke. "It's not what the Pradishar hoped to gain, but rather what they hoped to avoid. A responsibility they felt they had to assume," he looked at Rakk, "when King Rhakksees abandoned the project."

Ellex turned to Rakk. "Do you know what he's talking about?"

"I—don't know," he said, not looking at her. "I might. I wasn't told everything. Only the king was privileged to know all the details. I only knew there was more to the Loricean doctrine than mere symbolism. I knew there was *something* imprisoned deep under P'anorum, something that threatened the existence of the crystals. I never saw the stasis chamber myself, until I watched that stream, the one of Fin'roq in the temple. I thought the one I saw in your dream—in the incident—was the one on P'anorum. I think most of us did."

"Why didn't you tell me this?" Ellex was looking at Rakk like she didn't know him.

He had a pained look on his face. "Because your brother told me not to. He warned me not to bring up P'anorum with you. He said it made you terribly ill, so I never said anything about my suspicions."

Ellex's face drained of color. "It's true," she said. "The very thought of P'anorum made my head feel like it would split open—until my dream. It was only afterward that I realized—" She looked at Lithuigi again. "She's my daughter, professor. I missed out on her entire life. When I should have been there to comfort and love her, she was strapped inside a hunk of cold metal, all alone. Why did you do that to her? Why did you steal her from me and lock her away in there? Answer me why!"

"I didn't," Lithuigi said. "All I can say is, I didn't."

"But you knew!" she said. "You knew she was mine. You could have told me, at any time. We live in the same neighborhood. We pass each other on the street! You could have done that, at least."

"And I would have," Lithuigi said, "but I didn't know for sure that you didn't remember."

Ellex fell silent, no words forming in her mind, her heart numb and then on fire and then numb again.

Lithuigi looked down at the ground. "I know it's not worth much, but I am sorry. I'll give you two some space. There's one more guest yet to arrive, and when they do, we'll talk again. If you'll excuse me."

Rakk opened his mouth to speak, to ask about the fleet, about Raq'asha, but he saw Ellex's face, saw the pain in her eyes, the confusion. She looked like she'd just given up, and there were dark patches under her eyes.

He touched her lightly on the shoulder and she jerked out of her thoughts.

"Oh Raeder," she said, "What am I going to do? I go on as if this hole in my mind weren't there, as if I were sure of what I say and what I believe—but I don't even know what I'm supposed to know, what I should know, what I should remember. What I've done, or thought, or believed! I don't know what happened to me on P'anorum, why I was really there, who I might have interacted with. I don't know what I—me, Ellex, the real one—I don't know who that is anymore."

Rakk stroked her hair. "Breath, mama," he said. "Close your eyes and breath, slowly in and out." He waited til she had taken a few long, slow breaths. "Now imagine a terrific storm is blowing around you," he said, "with wind and water and roaring thunder. And imagine a great whirlpool in the sky, swirling in circles, lowering down into the storm and pulling you in. You fight it, but as it passes over you, the world falls still, the sound fades, and you're wrapped in warmth, in fluidity, in the flow of the sky and the sea and the soil and the stars. Everything swirls around you and passes on, unable to touch you, unable to break through to the calm place where you are. In the middle, in the void, in the emptiness at the heart of every flame, that's where you are—immoveable, unquenchable, powering the world."

Ellex felt the tension lifting from her shoulders with each breath, and she found herself hanging on Rakk's every word, hypnotized.

"Where'd you learn to talk like that?" she asked.

"It's called the whirlpool technique. I learned it from my nanny when I was just a little scamp. I used to get so scared all the time, and she'd wrap me in her wrinkly old arms and hug me tight, and then she'd talk to me and guide my focus, like I just did with you."

"You? Scared? I can't believe that."

He grinned. "It's true."

"Thank you, Raeder. I don't know what I'd have done if I hadn't bumped into you on Nunan."

"I told you it was fate, princess. You just can't get rid of me."

Now she grinned at him.

"Let's return to Qaas'i and get something to eat," he said. "I'm about to collapse from hunger."

Ellex took his arm and they walked down the stone steps into the caverns that fringed the grotto of Lagracia. Qaas'i looked up at them when they came in. She was gently swaying back and forth in front of the fire, in tune with the booming of the drums.

The music started to wane and Ellex thought it was because of them, as everyone had turned to look again, but then she heard shouts and the crowd began to chatter. Chief Tornroot came through the far door, looking equal parts angry and equal parts embarrassed, a cloaked Bhizini following, berating him in the old tongue. He was trying to respond but the Bhizini kept smacking him with a staff every time he did, and many in the crowd were starting to laugh and whoop and point.

"Where is he!" the hooded figure screamed in Ballack, throwing back their hood. "Take me to him, now!"

Ellex gasped, and many of the Bhizini dropped to one knee and placed their fists on their opposite shoulders, then rose again.

"I know that Bhizini," Ellex said. "They were in my dream last night. I mean, I think it was a memory. Of when I cut Qaas'i's taprin. They—Raeder?"

He was staring, wide eyed and open mouthed.

"Raeder?" she said again.

"I'll be damned," he said. "I was sure she was dead. I know her too, Ell." He was grinning now. "And what perfect timing. That's my old nanny, Bhea Bell."

Chapter 46

The Other Half of His Other Half

Lithuigi Von'nDrino always found the Tornroot Clan particularly difficult to deal with. They had long been influential thanks to their strategic holdings along the eastern reaches of Mon Mang'alar. When Balance still ruled the Far Ocean, all official traffic in the area was forced to pass through East'whaling in order to reach the Inner Seas. Anyone hoping to avoid the eyes of Balance Authority had to pay the Tornroot to ferry them across the great swamp or else risk getting lost in the indistinct sprawl of its thickets. The fee was steep but they always had plenty of takers. And although the loss of the Far Archipelago had destroyed their primary source of income, the entrepreneurial Tornroot had quickly moved to seize several territories once held by Balance Authority in the Far Ocean, including Lagracia, which before long had become the center of their clan. And they had adapted to the new reality, in part thanks to their alliance with Bhea Bell. As such, they were one of Lithuigi's most important allies, and they knew it.

Of course, the Tornroot also knew that they owed their continued power to Lithuigi's patronage. This was a relationship of mutual benefit, and it had served him well, time and time again. The Tornroot always got the job done, and what they asked for in return was never too much, considering his nearly endless supply chain with the Dyna'arin. As part of their arrangement, Lithuigi was given a small cavern of his own on Lagracia, which he'd transformed into a Guild laboratory. It was small and lacked the expansive space and top of the line tools available at Vergis or Callo Baton, or even Balan Su, but it was enough to tinker. And more than anything, it was a private space. It was peace and quiet.

Well, mostly, he thought, as he listened to the low thumping of the drums in the grotto, and the vibrating of the waves on the rocky shore.

The door to his lab opened and Bhea Bell entered.

"How's he doing?" Lithuigi asked, seeing the look on her face.

"He's lucky Qardymion didn't injure him worse. But that Bhartimu'u sure dosed him good," Bhea said. "He'll be alright, I think. I hope. I got to hope. He's—" She sighed. "I don't know. I just don't know."

"Don't know what?"

"If he's got the strength. If he's got the will. Our hopes—they might be dashed again."

"You know they aren't," Lithuigi said. "Not after all we've done. This time is when it works." He took Bhea in his arms.

"Oh, L'uigi, I think I messed up bad. I was supposed to have him ready by now, but I just thought—well, when you're my age, time gets away from ya. I didn't know it was coming so soon. And you know he's always been a timid little thing, bright but scared. And those damn villagers breaking him down all the time. I should of just killed 'em all when I had the chance. Taken him somewhere else to raise him."

"You don't mean that," he said.

"No, I don't. Damnit L'uigi, I just—I thought I knew what I was doing. But I didn't. I don't."

"You don't have to know everything," he said.

"Help me to forget for a moment," she whispered.

Lithuigi pulled her close. They held each other and danced lightly around the room, gently swaying. He breathed deeply of her scent, of coco and citrus and smoke and the sea, and he kissed her speckled green neck and tasted her skin.

"It's been too long, my love."

"I know it has. There's just so much to do. Just so much. I couldn't find time to get away."

"I know," Lithuigi said. "But we don't have forever. And I want more time with you."

"I do too," Bhea said.

"I stopped by P'anorum," he said, "about a month ago. Mha'arlo and me."

"Grizmond told me. I'm awfully sorry, love. I sure wish I'd been home."

"I needed your advice."

Bhea looked at him and put her hands on his chest.

"Rebesh'a wouldn't come, would she?"

Lithuigi's eyes fell. "I tried to convince her to leave Balan Su, to come sail away with me. We were finally getting along so well again. But—"

Bhea patted his chest. "I know how much you love her, my big old sprout, and how much you want to protect her. But sometimes you have to let people make their own choices. If you'd forced her to leave, you think she ever would have been happy?"

"At least she would have been safe," he said. "I knew what was coming, and I left her there. Sweet Trevian, I don't even know if she's alive."

Bhea kissed his tears as they fell. "Don't cry, my love. I'll send word to my allies in the capital. We'll make sure she's alright. I promise. I'm sure she's just fine."

" I've needed you so badly," he said. "What will I do when you're gone? What will—"

She put her finger to his lips, and when he fell silent, she kissed him.

Lithuigi felt like he could devour her whole, but he returned the kiss with gentleness, his mind overwhelmed with the feeling of her lips, so big and soft, he wanted to taste them forever, and right now there was no reason to rush. They undressed each other, never breaking off the kiss, and then they both unfurled their branches and slid them around the other's body, pulling themselves close to one another, their torsos pressed up against each other. Lithuigi felt his flower, its tender petals rippling with pleasure as they brushed into hers. He felt his stamen protruding from inside the bud, pulsing, diving downward into her bloom, while at the same time, he could feel her sliding deep, deep inside of his own flower. He put his head back and groaned, and Bhea nibbled at his neck and he cried out her name. And at the back of his mind, he prayed for time to stand still.

But time has no master, and all pleasure comes to an end. And as Lithuigi held Bhea, he felt like his heart was going to shatter into pieces.

"Bhea, my love," he said. "I can't go with you to P'anorum. Not yet, at least."

She opened her eyes and looked at him, and when she saw the look on his face, she touched his cheek.

"Oh, my sweet old love, don't be sad, my big old sprout," she said. "I know you gotta do what you gotta do. And you'll be along when you can."

"I just don't want to be apart anymore. But I—" He sighed.

"I know you've been trying for a century to set things right with your family, with your legacy. But you gotta stop thinking you gotta do it alone."

"I know," he said. "But in a hundred years, I've done nothing to stop the Guild from destroying itself. I've watched my sons repeat the same mistakes that I did, that my father did. So ambitious, and so damn foolish. Vilder is mostly just a greedy halfwit, but Hesh'n—he's working on something truly unspeakable, Bhea. A monstrous creation. I took out his labs, and destroyed his prototypes, but if I know my son, he's already hard at work replacing what I destroyed. If he gets his project up and working—well, let's just say it'll make Morty's job that much easier—a Harvest like the world has never seen before."

"I wish you wouldn't call him that," Bhea said. "It's not his name."

"I've failed them," Lithuigi said, ignoring her. "I'm everything I hated about my father, and then some."

"If you say so," Bhea said. "But I know your daughters and me, we sure do love ya. We all think the world of our L'uigi! Won't our opinion count too?"

"Of course it does," Lithuigi said. "You know that! I wish I could see them more often than I do."

"They're busy, too. They know what's at stake."

He sighed. "Bhea, what do I do? What do I do!"

"Just exactly what you was thinking of doing. Don't lose faith in yourself now."

He smiled. "Sweet Trevian, how I love you." He kissed her. "Very well. I'm heading to Vergis then. Khatoran Rha'qan has decided it's time to lay down his roots. I've called the tinkers together for a meeting beforehand, while I have everyone there. I have to try—again—to convince them."

"I love you trying," Bhea said, "but those stubborn fools ain't changin'."

"Well, they'll suffer my lecture nonetheless," he said.

Bhea grinned. "That's my professor! You do what you gotta do, my big old sprout. I support ya."

"That's what keeps me going."

"I got a favor to ask," Bhea said. "I need your smarts. I don't know what to do about Ellex Andria."

Lithuigi sighed. "You and me both. That poor plant. She's desperate for answers. I've tried to tell her what I can, but—I'm not sure she can handle the whole truth."

"That's my question—should I share some of my memories with her? Shed some light on the dark places? She was my friend, once. A dear friend. Until the Ren'fallow took her mind from her."

"I don't know that you can tell her anything," he said. "Those blocks are deep, deep inside. I don't know what'll happen when they break. She might need to discover the answers for herself. You once told me, shortly after we met, that it wasn't your job to teach anyone the truth, only to reveal the way to get to it. You said you can't actually show it to anyone, they have to experience it for themselves."

"I love you, my big old sprout," she said, smiling at him, her eyes crinkled up, her hand on his face. "You go on to Vergis now, and see if you don't find something important that's gonna shine light on your problem, show you the way to get on through it. And you tell them old tinkers how it is!"

"I don't want to leave yet," he said.

"I know it, but I gotta get back to Fin'roq. I need to be there when he wakes up."

"Then let's get going," he said.

"I do have another favor to ask 'fore you leave. When you're done at Vergis, before you do anything else, I need you to come see me at home. I don't like the way things are going in Raccorum Rhazzat. If Rishar is called, we'll lose Corkin protection. The time's come to seal up the island, everything you can spare. And if any of the ships are ready yet, I'd be much obliged. If the Ren'fallow really are moving—well, it's like you know. We lose P'anorum, we lose it all."

Chapter 47

A First Glimpse of the Lost Within

FIN'ROQ NEEDED TO DIE. Or maybe he was already dead?

No, he was alive. He could feel warmth on his skin, the pulsing sun in the sky overhead, moist but firm soil under his feet. He could feel wind on his face, and taste the sea in the air. But when he opened his eyes, all his sensations vanished, there was only darkness around him, and he knew he was trapped within it.

He'd been stuck there for so long, held against his will, for what felt like lifetimes.

Fin closed his eyes and tried to pray, to use the whirlpool technique that Bhea had taught him to slow his thoughts, but they only seemed to race by faster the harder he tried to grip them. His head spun, and he was so dizzy, he tried to open his mouth to retch, but he had no mouth. He wanted to reach up, to feel his face, but he had no hands or arms.

Who am I? he thought.

And then he was free. He had a body again. There was soil under his feet and the smell of the forest in his nose. He devoured the sunshine that fell on his skin. When he opened his eyes, the darkness didn't swallow him up.

Fin was in Bhea Bell's garden on P'anorum, and Baboo was running around, tumbling and laughing. Fin cried when he saw him and started to run alongside him, jumping and skipping, and Baboo hooting and hollering, and Fin felt so happy he thought his heart might burst. When Baboo bent down on all fours and shifted into a jaguar, Fin felt his own body sinking downward, his skin tingling and itching, and he felt light and agile. Fin looked down at the fur on his own arms, and he threw them in the air, hopped from one leg to the other, and screeched, and he could feel his little monkey tail bobbing up and down behind him.

He leapt for Baboo's back and wrapped his arms around his neck, and Baboo sprang forward, his massive paws pounding the ground, his long body folding and unfolding as he strode into the thick foliage of the Swarthen Forest. He watched the trees pass in a blur, the warm soft fur of Baboo's neck tickling his nose. And when he saw a vine dangling in front of them, he grabbed ahold, and the momentum carried him forward and upward. He broke through the canopy just as his skin pulled and rippled and his arms were long, feathered wings beating at the sky, taking him up the face of the Crag and over it, to where the great mountain towered still higher, the old stone city far below at its feet, the wide sea spread out in every direction.

Fin swooped downward toward the water, the sun in the distance dropping behind the horizon, the island below him melting away into the darkness, and before he could land, it had faded away completely. He was nothing again, no body, no form—no up nor down—but trapped, right in the middle of the void.

And he knew he needed to die.

He needed to die, but he had no body to perish.

How long could this go on, this darkness? It hurt him, drained him, made him cold, scared, desperate. Crazy with need, with thirst for light, for company. He had to break out, to be free again.

But who is there to be free?

The darkness pressed against him, pushing the air out of his lungs, crushing him. He gasped and squirmed against it, but the weight was too heavy. And then his skin began to tear, his fibers to snap. Something had ahold of him. Something had its claws in him, slicing, opening, pulling. Pulling him apart. Ripping him into shreds.

Pain was all there was.

He felt a hand on his face, coarse but gentle, stroking his cheek, and he could hear something purring. Was it Baboo? No, it was the sea beating the earth. Something touched his lips, a stone, a cup, and he felt liquid, cool and tangy, and he was so thirsty—Sweet Trevian, he had never been so thirsty—and he drank and drank.

"You have to wake up, Fin. Please, you have to wake up."

He wanted to open his eyes, to call out to Bhart, but he didn't have a body anymore. He was nothing. And he tumbled through the darkness, til he wasn't sure he'd ever existed in the first place.

The next time the light lifted, he was in a room somewhere. Glowbes were crackling softly on the walls, and he was sitting with a book in his lap. He recognized the place—yes! It was his quarters at the Pruu'patch. He was Fin'roq. And—he turned to look around the room—Jaun was there, too.

Sweet Trevian, I must have dozed off while reading, he thought, knowing it wasn't true.

"Are you alright? You were mumbling in your sleep."

Jaun sat down next to him and looked at the cover of the book in his lap. He crinkled his nose.

"I'd probably nod off too," he said.

Fin laughed. "It's good, really! I just—have a lot on my mind, I guess."

Jaun nodded. "I can help distract you." He leaned over and kissed Fin's lips, and Fin knew then that it couldn't be real, that it was in his head. Jaun was in a dungeon, or dead. He'd sent him there, to the Dankburn. Besides, there was no way Fin was back in Balan Su again. Not after what he'd done. Not after he'd hurt, and even killed, so many. That life was over.

But Fin didn't care. If he could just make this dream last, could just keep the darkness at bay—and so he wrapped his arms and branches around Jaun, clutched at him, trying to pull him close, but he couldn't get ahold of him. He was slipping out of reach, shrinking away in the distance. And when he vanished entirely and Fin'roq was all alone, he lay down on the cold stone floor and wept. He was sure he'd cried for an age of the universe, til he'd forgotten why he was crying, or who he was, or why it mattered, only that he needed to go on weeping.

Shame was the only thing that made him stop. Someone approached, and he was a scamp again, swallowing down a sob and wiping his eyes, refusing to let the villagers know how much they'd hurt him.

"What are you still doing here, freak?" It was Durq, his face twisted up in pain and rage, the way he'd looked when Fin'roq had left P'anorum. "There's no place for you here. You should have left a long time ago."

"I don't—" Fin tried to breath. "I don't have anywhere to go."

Durq spat in his face. "Coward," he said. "Selfish bastard. I told you that you were poison to our village, and look what happened to us. We're all dead, thanks to you. And here you are, still hanging around. But now it's not the village at risk, but the whole damn world. And you're too busy trying to make friends and influence others to do anything about it. You want to *be somebody*, to move up in the Pradishar, to make sure the world knows you belong. Well, you don't! You'll kill us all. You'll kill us all!"

Durq swung his fist and knocked Fin'roq backwards, and he spun across space and time, across lifetimes, across the darkness and the light, til he crashed into a body, and a new reality came into existence around him. He looked down at this new body—still Bhizini, but not his own. And yet it was his own. He touched his head, and was surprised to feel straight, silky hair fibers. He ran his hands down his clothing, a soft but sturdy fabric bright with pinks and oranges, like sunset on the water. His legs were short and thick, his arms lined with muscle, and he took a few steps and felt something he'd never truly experienced before—confidence, and strength.

In front of him rose a steep green hillside thick with foliage. He was standing in a wide plaza, looking up at a palace, at the peak looming overhead, and he knew he was in the great city of Dar Ka'Hala. He knew it's name somehow—knew he was on P'anorum! Knew that the palace, the island—all of it—were his.

Fin smiled and looked around, and saw that others were near him, a crowd around him, falling to their knees as he approached, with that look—that look of radiant worship on their faces. But rather than be alarmed, rather than squirm with discomfort, Fin drank up the attention. He reached out for those around him, reached out with his heart, and he could feel them, feel them as if they were his own flesh, his own mind. He fed on their energy, and they poured it out for him, not just those on P'anorum but around the entire world—Fin could feel them all—and he knew then what it was like to be a god-emperor, the cortex of the entire globe.

And he wasn't alone. He had friends, lovers, family. He had advisers, three of them, closer to him than anyone, always with him, always helping him. Life was something akin to bliss, if such a thing were to exist.

But it was not to last. His body, so strong and thick and unbreakable, soon began to wither and harden, and Fin felt the pull of the soil, the lust to drop his roots down into the planet and close his eyes forever. He tried to fight it, but couldn't resist the allure, and when the darkness began to fall around him, he struggled and strained and the tears fell, but in vain.

He tumbled down into it, and was no one again, briefly, before rising into the sun again, reaching upward for its warmth. Alive once more.

Lifetimes began passing him by, one after the other, each one with a new body. Each time on P'anorum. They passed so quickly, he didn't know what he was seeing, who he was seeing, who he was who was seeing it. He only knew that each time ended with death, with yet another plunge into the darkness, and soon he lost track of his progression, if there had been one. He couldn't keep one lifetime straight from the other, couldn't remember the faces of those he'd kissed, nor the names of his scamps—he'd had so many of them. He'd had so many names, so many bodies, so many.

Who am I then? he thought. *Who am I really?*

<<You're Fin'roq,>> he heard inside his head. <<And this isn't a dream, and isn't reality either, only a vision brought on by bhiza.>>

The voice spoke from darkness, from stillness.

Bhiza?

<<Remember, Fin'roq. You were in Pal'meria with Qardymion the Saltsap. You escaped with Bhartimu'u. They gave you bhiza essence to drink. A lot of it.>>

Fin could feel the memory come into his mind, the pain of the betrayal.

Bhart, he thought. *How could you? How could you!!*

"Who are you?" Fin said.

<<I'm you.>> He heard laughter in his head, sharp and high-pitched. <<Well, sort of.>>

"So this is another dream."

<<I just told you it wasn't. The bhiza, Fin. Practice reminding yourself that it's only bhiza. And before you know it, your head will clear.>>

"Where am I? The real me, I mean?"

<<Where is Fin'roq's body? On Lagracia. You've been freed from Bhartimu'u, and Bhea Bell is nearby. You're safe now. But you need to wake up.>>

When Fin heard that, he moaned. "No! That's what Bhart said. That's what Bhart demanded! But I wasn't asleep. And Sweet Trevian, if I could, I would wake now just to end this nightmare. I'd do anything to make the pain stop. Anything."

<<Then there is hope yet.>>

※ ※ ※

Fin languished in the darkness for what felt like much, much longer than the few hours that remained of his acute bhiza intoxication, so that when he finally opened his eyes—opened all of his senses—he was shivering and scared, not sure if he was alive or dead, or who he was, or when.

Bhea was at his side—at least, he thought it was Bhea. Hadn't she been there the whole time, in every lifetime? He couldn't remember. And as the bhiza worked its way out of his body, rather than feeling better, he began to feel worse. His flesh ached and throbbed, and his insides burned, and he trembled as if he'd spent a week in actual darkness. Thinking took an enormous effort, and he felt like he was stuck in between waking and sleeping, between life and death, that time itself had stood still just to prolong his suffering.

The sun was the only thing that felt good, and he sipped up energy from its rays, and tried to concentrate on the pulsing disk overhead, the warmth of Sol'bhin filling him. He drank when a cup was offered, unsure if it was still Bhart, but so thirsty he couldn't care. It tasted like water. And it sounded like Bhea. But how could he be sure?

He slept and woke and slept, as the sun passed overhead and dropped down behind the sea. Glowbes crackled to life all around him, and he could have cried with relief—the night would have been too much to face. He never wanted to go into darkness again. Ever.

The next morning, the ground was vibrating from the surf pounding the island down below, and he could hear gulls squawking. He opened his eyes and really saw for the first time. Spread out in front of him was the unbroken blue of the Far Ocean, and when he saw the sea, he could imagine the possibility that life might be even just a little bit tolerable again. And that was something.

He smelled rhupan and his stomach growled. Bhea Bell was at his side, her eyes shining.

"Bhea," he whispered, and she wrapped him in a hug, and he wept, and gasped for air, and wept some more, til he thought the tears would never stop.

"I thought you were dead," he said. "P'anorum—the villagers—"

"Oh my sprout, ain't nobody can kill me. Old Grizmond's just fine too. We've been worried about you something fierce. I've been trying to find you ever since we got word Qardymion had taken you from the capital. And then that damn Bhartimu'u—I'm so sorry, love. I know that couldn't a-been pleasant. Normally you'd have someone along to guide you through the Inner Door. It's a wonder you still know you're you."

"I didn't," he said. "I forgot, and remembered, and forgot. It's all kind of a blur."

"Don't think on it too much," Bhea said. "Stay here with me. Stay here with the sunshine. We're gonna get you strong and healthy again. And then I'm taking you home."

More tears spilled out of Fin's eyes.

"P'anorum," he said.

"That's right," she said. "P'anorum. Won't that be nice, my little sprout?"

He nodded and sniffed.

"You rest on up today, and if you're feeling up for it, we'll head out as soon as we can. Gonna be a bunch of us making the trip this time. So I don't wanna rush it if you aren't ready to be around nobody."

"I don't know," he said, feeling panicky at the thought.

"I have a cata'rin of my own," Bhea said. "How about I make sure it's just you and me on it. Certainly none of the Tornroot."

"And Bhart?"

"They're confined," Bhea said. "Not sure what to do with them yet."

Fin didn't say anything.

"There is one more thing. I hate to bring it up, but I want you to have some time to think on it. And well, there ain't a lot of time to think on it neither." She exhaled. "Ellex Andria and Prince Rhakksees are here on Lagracia and they're going back to P'anorum with us."

"What? Are you serious?" The panic was now full-blown.

"Easy my sprout, a lot's changed since you were in Balan Su."

"That woman is evil," Fin'roq said.

"I know she was hard to you," Bhea said. "But I think, if you gave her a chance, she'd be sorry about it."

"She should be sorry about it."

"Either way, they're coming to P'anorum. And once we're there—well my little sprout, I'm gonna need a favor from you. A big one. I know it's a lot to ask, but—well, I don't have a choice. I need you to take Ellex and Rakk under the island. I need you to take 'em to the Temple of Trevian."

Fin'roq couldn't believe what he was hearing.

"Under the—into the darkness again?" This time, instead of panic bubbling up inside of him, it was rage. A boiling torrent of it, and he wanted to vomit it out and free himself of the pain.

"How can you ask me that?" he said. "Sweet Trevian, you're no different than everyone else! Aar'ryn Ruu'n, Jaun von Andron, Qardymion the Saltsap, Bhartimu'u Tornroot—they all just wanted stuff from me, wanted me to do this or that, to go here or there, to serve their own ends! But what about my own ends? What about my own good?"

Bhea looked like she wanted to cry. "I know it might not seem like it, but this will be for your own good."

"I wouldn't help that woman if she was the last Verdillion on the planet."

"Don't say that," Bhea said. "She's a good plant, love. She's a victim, just like you. You have the same enemy, and that oughta make you friends."

"Are you crazy? She humiliated me in front of all of Balance. She tortured me!! The answer's no, and it's final."

"You know best, my sprout. But I'm gonna tell them you're still thinkin' about it. You can give 'em your answer yourself when we reach P'anorum. How's that?"

Fin closed his eyes. "Just leave me alone, Bhea," he said, trying not to scream it. "Please, just leave me alone."

Chapter 48

Doubt and More Doubt

THE TRIP TO VERGIS was slower going than Bryn expected, and the battered cata'rin was taking on water, which made their glacial pace all the more worrisome. Jaun had to stay with the gurgitator, tools at his side, tinkering to keep the aperture in place, to keep the current flowing, to keep them on course. It fell to Bryn to watch Roman Anthem. But the massive Cul'tavin peacekeeper had not stirred since Bryn's beating, and she began to wonder if she had been too rough with him.

I'm a big plant, she thought. *Sometimes I don't know my own strength.*

A full day passed before Anthem groaned and woke suddenly, as if from a nightmare, with a grunt and an attempt to sit up, looking confused but not alarmed. He strained against the vines, glancing around. When he saw he was bound—and saw Bryn glaring at him—he stopped struggling and lay back on the deck.

"And here I was thinking my day couldn't get any worse," he said.

"Oh, it could have been worse," she said. "You might have been dead. I might have let the sea take you. It had nearly claimed you when we pulled you aboard."

"You rescued me? You—and Von Andron?" A big smile broke out on his splotchy, weather-beaten face. But then it faded and he looked Bryn in the eyes. "Thank you. There aren't many in this world who look kindly on me anymore."

"But they once did?" She raised her eyebrows at him.

He nodded. "Once. And I've been wondering, for far too long now, whether anyone ever will again, or whether I should just give up and be done with it. And yet—the thought of going into the darkness, into the depths, after long years in the light—no. Not yet. I'll keep trying, keep living, a bit longer yet." He sighed. "Is any of this making sense to you?"

"The only thing that makes sense to me right now is that you threatened my mother! You beat Jaun von Andron! You kept us prisoner, hardly fed us, for weeks! Those are the things that make sense to me right now!"

The spark inside Bryn had flared up again, and she quivered with the erratic energy of it.

"I was trying to protect Jaun," Anthem said, "and your mother."

Bryn hissed and began to pace. "You think I'm a fool!"

"On the contrary. I know you're brilliant. Both of you. Why else do you think I was ordered to keep you far from any servryns? Malisha Andra'asnia is going out of her mind trying to understand how you're able to defy the crystal mandate, and her biggest fear is that you'll bring everyone in Balance into your hollow, because doing so would destroy the surveillance apparatus that the Cul'tavin have come to depend upon. Andra'asnia threatened your mother, not me, and even now she continues to threaten her. She knows your mother is the key to getting through to you. I had hoped that you'd answer my questions, that I could show Andra'asnia you were being cooperative, and in doing so, keep Stylina Andri'n safe."

Bryn's mind was running in a thousand directions, each one returning with questions, with doubts.

"And how did beating Jaun, and mutilating his face, protect him?" she said.

Anthem smirked. "He got those wounds in Balan Su, when he denounced Balance and the Pradishar attacked him. And Qardymion's men would have killed him on sight if they'd had the chance, but Fin'roq's little outburst ended up flinging Jaun to safety. I was able to get him out of the capital, and save him, as it were, from the Dankburn. I've only been roughing him up a bit, to keep him convinced he's my prisoner, and to keep the Cul'tavin appeased."

"You're lying," Bryn said. But her ears were burning, and her neck had gotten so tight she wasn't sure she could move.

"No, Bryn. Who do you think helped Jaun join the Pruu'patch, and get his Pradishar crystamin just in time for the Balancing Act? And now I've gotten both him, and you, safely out of Balance Territories. If Qardymion's men hadn't nearly sunk my damn ship—"

"Who are you?" Bryn cried.

He paused for a moment and then laughed. "If only I knew. I feel I'm nothing more than a trouper on the stage, pulled about by strings hidden beneath my costume, performing for those who need me to perform, and going on because I don't know any other way to do things."

<<Anorian,>> Bryn whispered in her mind.

<<I'm here, Bryndax.>>

Bryn shared the conversation she'd just had with Anthem.

<<Is it true?>>

<<It could be,>> Anorian said. <<This one is not yet friend or foe. He is—hovering in between, swaying too and fro. I'm still not sure on which side he will fall.>>

<<Did he help Jaun join the Pradishar?>>

<<Yes.>>

<<Why didn't you tell me any of this?>>

<<I'm sorry, Bryndax. I didn't think it was my place.>>

Bryn shook her head. Then she pointed at Anthem. "Try to move, to do anything, and you'll regret it."

"I wouldn't dream of it," he said, grinning.

Bryn hissed and started for the back of the ship. She found Jaun bent over the gurgitator, tool in hand, using it to hold a rattling piece of metal in place. He glanced at her, a weary look on his face, but quickly put his attention back on the maquina.

"Roman Anthem helped you join the Pradishar?"

Jaun froze, then started working again, not looking at her. "Yes," he said.

"Why didn't you tell me?"

He sighed. " Was I meant to tell someone I had just met that our jailer was someone I had once depended on for my own schemes before he betrayed me? I'm ashamed enough as it is."

"How did he betray you?"

Jaun stifled a hiss. "I woke up in a cell on his ship, and rather than steaming me some jha'ala and serving up a nice platter of rhupan, he punched me in the face. Now can you please stop distracting me? Do you want us to crash again?"

Her face was burning and she turned to leave, her throat tight, tears blurring her vision.

❧❧❧ ❦❦❦

Bryn spent the rest of the voyage avoiding both Jaun and Anthem. She perched near the front of the ship, up top by the captain's quarters, where she could look back and down the length of the deck. That way she could keep watch on Anthem but didn't have to talk to him.

She hadn't had so much sun in ages, and even back on Andramere, she was often working indoors. It was the first time she'd ever paused to consider what had been lost when Verdillions began to build roofs and walls on their gardens, sealing away the outside world, and getting most of their sustenance from rhupan and not from the sun.

Bryn heard the gurgitator sputter and close, the whine dropping off into a low hum before falling silent. She scanned the horizon on both sides of the ship, but all she saw was water and sandy atolls, the same scenery she'd looked at all day. Why had they stopped?

Jaun came up to where Anthem was being held just as Bryn was heading back to find him.

"We're here!" he said, grinning. "And Sweet Trevian but I need to stretch!" He leaned to both sides, his arms in the air.

"Uh—Jaun? There's nothing here but sand and reef."

"On the surface, sure," he said. "But you never can tell what lies beneath, can you?"

Bryn heard a splash on all sides of the cata'rin and she looked around and saw walls rising up from the surface of the water. They rose about twenty feet before stopping, and there was a momentary stillness before Bryn heard gurgling and the ship began sinking. Only it wasn't sinking, the water was draining and lowering them under the surface. Bryn looked up at the rectangle of sky overhead, her mouth open, a chill running down the fibers in her back.

She had heard wonderful things about Vergis, but suspected most of them were nonsense. And her father had always waved his hand and dismissed any talk of the secret tinker laboratory and research center.

"And we're in luck," Jaun said, his eyes twitching. "Today is Khatoran Rha'qan's rooting ceremony at the local gruynfeld. That means visitors will be permitted in the Fish Bowl, and there should be a fair number of them, so we won't stand out."

I always stand out, Bryn thought. *And so does Jaun.*

"What are we to do with *him*?" She looked at Anthem.

"Oh, don't mind me," he said. "Go. Have fun. I'll be here when you return." He winked.

"We'll have to hope the vines hold," Jaun said. "And that none of my aides report him before we're in and out of here."

"And what exactly are we doing here?"

Jaun looked at Anthem, then at Bryn.

<<Join me at the library in Dar Ka'Hala,>> he said. <<In your office.>>

Bryn opened her mind's eye and joined Jaun. She took a seat at her desk while he paced the room in his Verdillion form.

<<What is it, Starborn? You seem agitated.>>

He sighed. <<I owe you an apology. I shouldn't have snapped at you like I did. You were right to ask why I was being secretive. I'm sorry I didn't let you in on everything earlier. But now that I know you're the Mighty B*zzness, that you're every bit as talented as your father, and that you have, well, a unique aptitude with the weavryn—I've been a fool not to seek your help sooner.>>

<<I—thank you, you're forgiven—but stop thumping the ground and just strike already.>>

<<Alright. I have a favor to ask. I was hoping you could help me gain access to a laboratory here on Vergis. I saw what you did with the locking mechanism on the ship. And well, I've been trying to break in for a decade now, without success. But you just might pull it off.>>

<<Break in? To whose lab?>>

He sighed and wrung his hands together, avoiding Bryn's eyes. <<Your father's.>>

Bryn sat up. <<My father had a lab on Vergis? No way. He never left Andramere.>>

<<Not during your lifetime, no. This lab is from early in his career.>>

<<I—didn't know.>> Bryn didn't know what to say, what to feel even.

More secrets. More things her father hadn't let her know.

Who was Doc Andri'n? Did she even know?

<<But the lab is only part of the puzzle, part of the mystery surrounding the Andramere Crisis that nearly wiped out my family one hundred years ago.>>

<<What would my father have to do with that?>>

<<Do you know anything about his youth?>>

<<Sure,>> Bryn said. <<He was an orphan. His parents died shortly after his taprin was cut, so he never knew them. A tinker hired him to clean his lab and realized his talents, and saw to it that he was enrolled in the Guild.>>

<<A lovely little lie,>> Jaun said. <<You probably never questioned it. Why would you? You probably never wondered if his parents had any family, and why they would abandon him. Or who the tinker was who found him. I'm sure he never talked of the past, nor did your mother. Of course, the Crisis would have purged the datamins, so there'd be no records of him anyway, would there? No, like the Crisis itself, it would be as if the past had not existed.>>

Bryn placed her hands flat on the desk, could feel the cool stone under her feet, and she tried to steady herself.

<<What if I told you that your grandfather was actually the one they call Burning Leaf, the legendary tinker who created the first servryn and brought forth the weavryn?>>

She stared at Jaun, who had stopped pacing, an expectant look on his face.

And then she grinned. <<Shut up.>>

<<You know it, in some way, don't you? You know that's why you're able to do things with the servryns that others can't. Why you have such talents on the weavryn—and why your father was able to bring forth a new incarnation of it.>>

<<It—makes a little bit of sense, I suppose. But why would my father keep it a secret?>>

<<To keep you safe, I assume. You see Bryndax, Burning Leaf was a von Andron, one of the forgotten brothers of my grandfather, Cruthyr. We're cousins, you and I.>>

Bryn was laughing now. <<You're telling me I'm a von Andron? A royal?>>

<<I'm telling you that your life is in danger,>> he said. <<The von Androns are nearly gone, Bryn. The remaining members of our family went into hiding at the end of the Crisis, including your father. I spent my entire youth under heavy guard, my mother a nervous wreck, terrified we'd be killed—by the Bhizini.>>

<<You're starting to lose me,>> she said. <<Why would Bhizini be after you? After the von Androns?>>

<<Now you're starting to understand my confusion,>> Jaun said. <<I have as many questions as you. More, because I've spent the last decade searching, following the faintest traces of information, and finding that nothing makes any sense anymore.>> A book appeared in Jaun's hands and he sat it down on the desk. <<This is what I've gathered. All of it.>>

Bryn touched the book and the information was in her mind.

<<Well—?>> Jaun looked at her, and he looked so sad and scared and hopeful, Bryn's heart ached. <<Will you help me?>>

Jaun didn't have much to go on, but the clues were tantalizing. And if it was true—this would be the greatest historical discovery of their time.

She swallowed hard. <<Of course I'll help, cousin.>>

Jaun flooded the crystamin with relief and with a true and profound sense of hope, a hope that hadn't existed moments ago, and Bryn realized how lost Jaun was, how desperate, how full of regret, in spite of the confident, self-indulgent way he usually performed for others.

<<Let's go hack a lock,>> she said.

And see what else my father has been keeping from me.

Chapter 49

The Gust that Topples the Tree

Rakk Raeder stared across the smoky grotto at the figure of his old nanny, feeling like he was seeing a ghost, like all the sense he'd made out of the world was suddenly gone—had never been, not really, not in light of what he was witnessing. He'd only been fooled into thinking so.

Bhea Bell was alive.

The old Bhizini had practically raised him, and Rajj and Raq'asha too, at least when they were little scamps. She was an old friend of their father's and had a sprawling garden estate accessible only from the palace, deep in the Swarthen Forest. Rakk's mother was often ill—in body and in mind—and his father was always too busy with affairs of state, though mostly with entertaining—so the king would send them off to Bhea's for months at a time.

Rakk remembered Rajj crying whenever the king told them they'd be staying with Bhea for awhile—he'd lay on the ground and beat his fists and kick his legs, and their father would just laugh at him—but Rakk would be overjoyed at the chance to escape the palace. He and Baboo would jump and sing and dance and laugh, and Rajj would yell at them to keep it down, while Raq'asha was off somewhere ignoring them. She was quite a bit younger than them, and always doing her own thing.

Bhea looks exactly the same as a half century ago, he thought. *Even if she survived the eruption, she should be well past the age for setting down her roots and becoming a tandavin.*

And yet there she was, spry as ever, berating Chief Tornroot—big plant that he was—who couldn't get away from her fast enough.

"Well, this is a surprise," Rakk said to Ellex.

"I'm tired of surprises," she said. "Sweet Trevian, how I'm sick of them."

"They aren't all bad," he said, as Qaas'i approached. She offered them each a rhupan bun.

"No, they aren't," Ellex said, taking a bun. "Thank you. We're starving."

Rakk had forgotten his hunger when he'd seen Bhea Bell, but it came surging back upon him when he tasted the rhupan, and he devoured it hungrily. Qaas'i led them to the grill and Rakk, all grins, struck up a conversation with the cook. But the Bhizini frowned at him and said nothing. He turned back to Ellex and saw that everyone nearby had grown stiff, their faces hard if not downright hostile, and he took a step closer to her.

But Bhea returned to the chamber and approached them, and when the others nearby saw her, the hard looks on their faces cracked and they turned away and ignored them. Some of the others in the crowd bowed as she passed.

"Oh, my little prince, my little Raeder, how's my sprout doing?"

She had tears in her eyes and she wrapped him in a warm, firm hug. He could smell her skin, like coco and smoke and the sea, and Rakk was five years old again, in the safest, most wonderful place in the world—the arms of his Bhea.

"I can't believe you're alive," he said.

"Look at you," she said. "Handsome as ever, ain't ya?"

But her eyes had found Ellex and she turned to her and gave her a long, but gentle, stare. Rakk could see Ellex squirming.

"You don't remember me, do you?" Bhea said.

"Only from dreams," Ellex said. "I've—had some trouble recalling things."

"That's why you're here," Bhea said.

"We're here because Lithuigi Von'nDrino brought us here," Rakk said. "Brought us here against our will."

Bhea nodded. "I'm sorry for the way it went down, love, but we had to get you outta there. Callo Baton weren't safe for any of ya." She looked at Qaas'i. "Let's go get y'all cleaned up and changed into something fresh, and then we'll talk somewhere more private. I know you got lots of questions, and I'm gonna do my best to answer 'em. This way, my sprouts."

Ellex gave Rakk a look that said she was cautiously hopeful but still deeply disturbed by all of this. He took her hand with his left hand and Qaas'i's with his right, and they followed Bhea through the crowded grotto, through stares of curiosity, anger, and reverence.

"Why does everyone bow to you, Bhea?" Rakk said.

"Just showin' respect for the elderly."

"Nonsense. The Bhizini value strength."

"Do they now?" Bhea said. "All Bhizini, everywhere?"

Rakk blushed. "I didn't mean—"

"I know what you meant, my sprout. I'm a Bhizini speaker, and there are many who listen to me. Many of them bow because they're afraid of me."

"Should they be?" Ellex said.

"It's not my place to say if they should be or not."

"Did I tell you that Bhea Bell was my teacher when I was a scamp?" Rakk said. "I used to whine and fuss whenever it came time for lessons. And when Bhea would test me, I'd try to convince her to give me the answers. I remember I told her that if I didn't know something, it was her job as a teacher to make sure I knew it, and if she wouldn't, then she'd failed. She laughed and told me that learning is more like remembering than it is taking in anything new. Once you know a truth, even though you rationally are aware that you just learned this truth, it will nevertheless feel as if you'd always known it—that it is self-evident everywhere, now and in the past as well, and this is because truths are eternal. And since they are eternal, no amount of effort can undo them, and no quest to destroy them can ever succeed, not fully. Instead, the threat is from those who obfuscate, rather than deny—from those who shape us in ways that keep us from asking, and through inquiring, discovering. With enough fog in the air, a forest and the open sea look exactly the same."

"My little philosopher," Bhea said. "I'm touched you remember that. You were just a little thing."

Rakk looked at Ellex, beaming.

Bhea led them to a clean, spacious cavern, softly lit with glowbes. There was a freshly turned sleeping patch in the corner, and a nook with a fountain and a bucket for bathing. Rakk was surprised to see that the Bhizini had even brought their things from the tavern on Callo Baton, and their garments had been laundered and folded in a neat stack.

Bhea promised to return shortly. Ellex went to bathe first and took Qaas'i with her. When it was Rakk's turn, he poured a few buckets over his head and scrubbed the sticky sap off his hair fibers and down his neck. When the Bhizini had come for them on Callo Baton, Rakk had tried to fight back, even as the drug was pulling him down in to darkness. If he hadn't resisted, they might not have knocked him across the head.

But seeing Bhea—Rakk still felt like he was dreaming, like it wasn't possible that she was here. Her face, her voice, her smell, had brought back so many memories, so many feelings and sensations he'd forgotten or been afraid to think about. He felt like a part of himself, one he thought gone forever, had mysteriously been resurrected. And it brought with it hope—hope that other things he lost could still be restored. But also fear—the fear that her appearance had given him the illusion that his lost life might somehow still exist. That it wasn't too late to get back what he'd lost.

And that somehow, some way, he could make up for what he'd done the night P'anorum erupted.

When Bhea returned to their quarters, Ellex sent Qaas'i back to the grotto with the others, then came and stood next to Rakk. He could tell she was holding her breath, and he touched her shoulder and nodded at her. Then he turned to his old nanny.

"You know I'm overjoyed seeing you again," he said. "But you being here only brings up even more questions. We're running blind here, Bhea. Please—*please*—shed some light on our path?"

"I want to, my sprout, I really do. But I want to show rather than tell. I want you to see, so you'll know it in your innards, so you'll feel it with every fiber, not just up here in your head. I want you to come with me to P'anorum. I want you to go under the island, down deep underground. There's something there you need to see. Something you both need to see."

Rakk looked at Ellex, but her face was blank, her skin tight across her cheeks, and he couldn't tell what she was thinking.

"Ell?" he said.

She jumped when he touched her shoulder again.

"P'anorum," she said. "I knew that's where we'd end up. I knew, after my dream—when I knew how long I had refused to even think the name of that place—I knew then that I would have to go back there." She looked at Rakk, but he turned away from her gaze, and so she took his hand and squeezed it. "What about you, Raeder? I know that it would be asking a lot. But—I don't think I can do it without you."

He swallowed the lump in his throat. "When do we leave?" he said, forcing a grin.

"Not until Fin'roq is able to travel," Bhea said.

"Fin'roq?" Rakk and Ellex said together.

"Yes. He's here, but he's been injured. And heavily dosed with a potent bhiza essence. I'm afraid it will be a few days before he's able to go anywhere. But my hope is, once he's recovered, he'll be able to take you under the island."

"Fin'roq attacked the citizens of Balan Su," Ellex said. "I don't know what he did, or how. But I know it looked like a dynamin had overloaded in the Forum. Some of the bystanders were blown off the upper rim, others crushed into nearby walls. He was last seen escaping with Qardymion's Pal'merans!"

"You mean *taken* by the Pal'merans," Bhea said. "They've been after him since before he left P'anorum. Nearly nabbed him right out of my own garden. And let me tell you something—Fin'roq didn't hurt no one intentionally. If he attacked those people, it was because they attacked him first. Same as with Roe. He were beatin' him silly, hitting him in the face and in the flower. Weren't Fin'roq's fault for defending himself. Only, he don't know his own powers yet. He grabbed Roe's crystal and twisted his head right off without knowing what he was doing."

"Are you saying that stream—*he really did that*?" Ellex said. "Sweet Trevian, I—I couldn't bear the thought of it at the time, the thought of P'anorum. And afterward, I—never went back to consider—but how? He has no crystal! And not even an imperialized one can be manipulated like that."

"He really did it," Bhea said. "And he has no crystal. He never will, neither. The one never does."

"What one?" Rakk said.

"There's been many names over time for the one who can see into the crystal. They've called 'em hero, savior, Mund'umbrian, tyrant, emperor. They've called 'em Creator, Wielder, Sustainer, Destroyer. Of course, in every lifetime, they have a name of their own they call themselves."

Rakk was starting to have trouble with where this conversation had gone. "Are you telling me that the Loricean creed—that there really is someone or some *thing* capable of destroying the hierarchy of the crystals, able to wield them all and potentially destroy them all?"

"The one is always born on P'anorum. Always born Bhizini. And always born innocent, with no knowledge of who they really are, lifetime after lifetime."

"Lifetimes? Are you saying this wielder has been imprisoned for generations?" Rakk felt like the ground had dropped out from under him.

"For as long as Balance has endured," Bhea said.

"Held—by my father? By my ancestors?" Rakk already knew the answer.

Bhea nodded. "When the one dies, the next is always born on P'anorum. Always."

"The last one—the one before Fin'roq," Rakk said.

"Killed," Bhea said. "Thirty three years ago. On the night P'anorum erupted."

"My daughter," Ellex said. "They took her. They stuck her in one of those chambers. Lithuigi Von'nDrino kept her there for three decades! Until—until the stream of Fin'roq!"

Bhea nodded. "Although it was Roman Anthem that came poking around first, trying to draw Fin out. And it worked. And I let it, fool that I am."

Ellex was breathing heavily. "They thought it was Qaas'i, but it was Fin'roq. The Gran Pradesh—he brought Fin'roq to Balan Su. Does he know all this?"

Bhea nodded again.

"But Ra'shard Ruu'n didn't imprison him," Ellex said. "He gave him a position in the Pruu'patch, let him become a monkin. Why would he do that, if he knows he's dangerous?"

"I won't speak to his intentions," Bhea said. "I can only say that the Gran Pradesh always knows the truth about Trevian. You can be sure of that."

"Perhaps he was waiting for the stasis chamber to be free," Rakk said.

"Ra'shard Ruu'n is an abolitionist, and a dear friend," Ellex said. "I can't imagine he would enslave or imprison anyone. If Fin'roq doesn't remember anything, then maybe Ruu'n thought he didn't need to be held."

"And if his powers return?" Rakk said. "He could, what? Know everyone's secrets? Turn anyone into his slave? Destroy their crystals, or make them explode, just because he felt like it?"

"Sweet Trevian," Ellex said. "We wouldn't have Balance, we'd have an absolute dictatorship like the world has never seen!"

"Don't go jumping to conclusions, my sprouts," Bhea said, "at least not til you have the whole picture laid out in front of ya. Come to P'anorum first, fill in some more of the details, before you make a choice on anything."

Ellex sighed. "In my dream, I saw Qaas'i as a spratlyn. You were with me when I cut her taprin. And—there was another spratlyn in the sprouting patch, not yet cut. Was that Fin'roq? Did we plant them together?"

"You spent a whole year with me," Bhea said.

Tears were running down Ellex's face. "A whole year after P'anorum erupted, and I had my memories?"

Bhea nodded.

Rakk felt so confused he couldn't get words to form up in his mind. He was thinking about the Faerengard Uprising—they'd been trying to free someone. The official story was that the patriarch of the family had been imprisoned for sedition, and his offspring tried to free him. But now Rakk wondered if they hadn't been trying to free whomever it was who had been trapped in the stasis chamber.

Ellex took his hand again and squeezed it. "Raeder?"

He shook his head. "Sorry," he said. "This wasn't what I was expecting. I came on this trip to find out what the Guild has been doing to help my sister steal my throne. And every time I think I'm making progress, everything falls apart again. And now you want to take me back to P'anorum, and—Great Sower in the sky, I've dreamt of returning nearly every night for three decades—but suddenly, now that it's possible, I don't want to go."

"I don't think it's about want anymore, love," Bhea said. "It's about need. There's still time for you to figure things out with your crown. I know you're worried. I think Rishar will be called soon, and I'm not sure what'll happen when it is. But I can promise that you'll be better prepared to face it if you'll come along to P'anorum."

"Please, Raeder, we've come so far. Don't abandon me now."

He swallowed hard again, his throat clenched up and dry, and he looked at Ellex and tried to smile.

"I'm ready when you are, princess," he said, but he felt like she'd taken a scytherin and driven it into his heart.

❧ ☙

Rakk spent the next few days trying to keep his mind off of things, and avoiding Bhea, Ellex, even Qaas'i. Some of the Tornroot were friendly to him, though he didn't blame the ones who weren't—he had spent the last thirty years fighting, and killing, every Bhizini that had had the misfortune to cross his path.

I've spent three decades pretending to keep Balance safe, he thought, *while the real threat went unchecked, unknown even, allowed to fester in the dark.*

Rakk helped the Bhizini with work around the island, mostly carrying and lifting, but also some repair work on the smaller boats. All the scamps of the clan had taken to following him around, teasing and taunting him, trying to get a reaction out of him, and when the day's work was done, he got some wooden swords and some lightweight fighting pikes and practiced sparing with anyone willing to have a go with him. He was exhausted by the time they finished, partly from laughing—and sore, but mostly from the lifting.

When the day came to set sail, Rakk thought he might be sick, and he wished Q'orin were there more than ever. Had he made it to Rheganza yet? Had the Corkin captured him? Had the Pradishar captured him? If he could get off the damn bhiza, he could just reach out for him, feel him again through Q'orin's last remaining crystamin, and know he was okay. But he didn't dare let Raq'asha know where he was.

Bhea came and found him that morning, and brought him, Ellex, and Qaas'i to a cata'rin.

"This ones for you three," she said. "You okay to pilot her?"

Ellex and Rakk both nodded.

"Good. It don't have a crystamin controller, so you'll have to manually adjust the knobs on the gurgitator. You know how?"

Rakk nodded. "I can show her," he said.

"Good. We're bringing half the Tornroot with us, and a few other ships too, so it's gonna be a big old ragtag group, and we won't be going none too fast. You need anything from me, put up your red flag and someone'll come on by. Either way, I'll check in on ya later, 'fore we reach P'anorum."

Qaas'i took Bhea's hand.

"Well come on then, if your mama don't mind?"

"Not at all," Ellex said.

Rakk started up the stairs for the bridge and Ellex followed. He fiddled with the controls and opened the gurgitator, and joined up with the long stream of several hundred boats that were anchored around Lagracia and were beginning to head east across the open ocean.

"Why are you giving me the cold shoulder?" Ellex said.

Rakk looked at her with a confused look. "What are you talking about?"

She rolled her eyes. "You've hardly spoken to me, or Qaas'i, for days. We've hardly seen you. And you can barely look me in the eyes. What's going on, Raeder? You're starting to scare me."

"There's just a lot on my mind."

"You think?" Ellex said. "Come on, talk to me."

"What, like you talked to me? You and your father came halfway around the world to—what? Try and free a prisoner who had the power to destroy Balance? To conspire with my father? Neither of you—never once—told me anything about it! What am I supposed to think?"

Ellex frowned. "Stop shouting at me. I don't know what to say, considering I can't remember myself, only that there must have been a reason? I just—don't know what it might have been."

"What if the reason is because my father didn't trust me? Because *you* didn't trust me? What if the reason is because I don't deserve to be trusted? What if I still don't?" His head fell and his shoulders sagged, and he took a few short, shallow breaths.

"What do you mean?" Ellex almost whispered it.

"I left," he said, "on the night of the eruption. I sailed away from P'anorum. I was so angry, I wanted to kill my father. I never knew what to think of his antics, but I thought—I thought the festival that night was going to be when he announced the date of my coronation. I was so sure of it. And you were there, so I thought—but no. My father—I can still see his face when he told me—the festival wasn't for me, it was for him, a celebration of his oversized ego. And me? I was given guard duty. Guard duty! At the port of all places, so I wouldn't even get to attend the event that I thought was going to be in my honor. Right out in the open, where everyone could see my shame."

He turned away from her. "I was so angry, I wanted him to die. I hoped he would. And I left. I ignored his order, I boarded a cata'rin, and I sailed out into the Far Ocean, vowing to never return. I had just turned back when I saw the light on the horizon, as if dawn had broken, orange and red across the sky. And I could hear it. I raced back—I tried to make port—but the mountain was spewing liquid crystal, and it had coated everything, and the ocean was hissing as it boiled, and the wind and the steam and—I couldn't make it to shore. I couldn't—I never—never saw my home again. My kingdom, my father and mother, my city, you—everything was gone. I've been floating at sea ever since, exiled for my disobedience, forgotten by my subjects. And I deserve it. I deserve to lose it all. There's no hope left for me anymore. There never was any to begin with."

Chapter 50

The Known and the Unknown

THERE WERE FEW TIMES in Ellex Andria's life when she didn't know what to say, when her quick wit failed her, when there was only emotion, raw and unfiltered, and no possibility of turning it into words, no way to give it any meaning—when she just had to be fully present and feel her way through, even as her mind raced to reason, to respond.

Instead, she acted—not in the sense of dissembling, but in the sense of doing, of taking the action that followed from the emotion she had inside. She reached for Rakk, up for his shoulders, and she tried to turn him back toward her, to face her, but he pulled away. So she ducked around him and stood in front of him, trapping him between her and the railing.

"Ell, please," he said, barely audible. "Please, I can't. I can't face you."

She put her hand on his cheek and down to his chin, and slowly pulled it in her direction. His eyes looked away as his face pivoted toward her, and when she saw his bottom lip quivering, she reached up on her tippy toes and took it between her own lips, and she could see the surprise and confusion on his face. But it melted away as he let out a small moan, and she felt him wrap his arms around her body and pull her close, his hands huge but gentle and hungry to hold her. Her entire body shivered and tingled, and she could feel him trembling too.

Finally words came to her mind, and they said, *Danger. Stop. Stop now!*

But Sweet Trevian it felt so good. And it had been so long. So, so long. Too long.

She was ready to throw off her robe and take him right there, but it was Rakk who pulled back. He broke off the kiss and clutched her in a stiff hug that told her nothing more would happen, and she told herself she was glad of it, even if she wasn't.

"It's too much," he said.

"I wasn't thinking," Ellex said. "Just feeling. Just knowing I can't see you hurt like that."

He stroked her hair and kissed her forehead.

"And if I asked you to leave with me, right now?" he said. "To turn north, cross the reefs to the Swirling Sea, head for the broken shards of Gru'hallia, into uncharted waters, gone forever. Would you go? Would you leave with me? Right now?"

"You know we can't," she said, thinking of Qaas'i, of Balance, of the Pradishar, of Andrasia.

He smiled, a sad, knowing smile. "That's what you said about us getting married, all those years ago."

Ellex felt her ears burning. When she spoke, it was a whisper. "I told you I wanted Andrasian scamps, not hideous half-breeds. Sweet Trevian, I really said that, didn't I?"

"It was a long time ago," he said.

"So was the eruption."

Her thoughts were coming back to her now—the words she had lacked earlier as she'd struggled to make sense of his confession.

"I'm sorry, Raeder. I've needed to talk to you so badly this last week, and I couldn't understand why you were avoiding me. I thought—but now that you've told me your past shame, let me share my own, and then you can be the judge who has the worst conscience.

"This week with the Bhizini has torn my eyes open and forced me to see what up until now I've been refusing to think about. You saw the way some of them looked at me—with loathing, with absolute contempt. And yet it's no different than the way I looked upon so many of them over the last thirty years, as I pushed Balance Authority to attack with greater ferocity, to drive them from the Inner Seas, to show no mercy to any who dared cross the Lanes. While our own government kept Qaas'andria imprisoned, I was busy using my authority to spread word of Bhizini atrocities, to characterize them as brutal savages incapable of civilization, incapable of finer feelings. I ordered the extermination of countless thousands of them! And I never realized until now that any one of them—*every* one of them—could have been as precious as Qaas'i is to me. They were someone's little scamp, once upon a time. And the pain I've caused them all—Sweet Trevian, I can't comprehend it. You sailed away for a few hours, while I promoted the extermination of an entire race for decades."

"When Bhizini were butchered by Balance, it was almost always the Corkin doing the killing," Rakk said, "and they acted on my authority. So we're both guilty for that."

"You were only passing along the commands," she said, "not arguing for them in the Council of Nine, or preaching to the Pradishar faithful that the Bhizini were an existential threat to Balance—that Trevian himself had excluded them! It's no wonder Qardymion attacked my Cul'tavin, and why he tried to have me killed at the Balancing Act. And after seeing Callo Baton, seeing the N'detten, all the Bhizini scamps of operators, there must be so many people—*so many people*—who see me as nothing more than a monster, a villain. Sweet Trevian, am I one?"

"No," Rakk said. "No way. It's just not possible. I know you. You're a good plant."

"Maybe when we were stupid little scamps, but now? How can I know for sure, when so much is forgotten? And—there's something else too."

Rakk said nothing, waiting.

"If I came to P'anorum thirty three years ago to break Balance, to free the imprisoned from their chamber—if I was part of that conspiracy—I just can't stop remembering one of the scenes from my dream. There was a long line of people, lurching forward, one after another, their faces puffy from weeping, their eyes red and devastated. And I hacked them down, one after another, until the line was no more, and my feet were drowned in the sap. Raeder, I'm scared—scared to even say it. But what if—what if my father and your father, Bhea Bell and Lithuigi Von'nDrino—and me—what if we were responsible for the eruption? What if, whatever we did that night, we caused the island to explode? What if I destroyed P'anorum, your home, and the entire Far Archipelago? Half of your kingdom, half of the world, gone in a night. What if I did that? Would you be able to forgive me?"

A tear rolled down each of her cheeks when she saw the look on his face.

Rakk turned and gripped the railing and he was silent for a long time while Ellex held her breath.

"I don't know," he whispered. "I really don't know."

She wept silently, staring at Rakk's back, at his shoulders slumped over in defeat, and she longed to put her hands on him again, to hold him and kiss him and tell him yes, that they should sail away together, right now. Forget P'anorum, forget Balance, forget it all.

What's gotten into me? she thought. *I was always so grounded, never seeing the point of flights of fancy. Wasn't I?*

The thought that she didn't know if she was or not, couldn't remember what the old Ellex—the *real* Ellex— was truly like, was enough to let her know that she couldn't escape from this. There would be no rest, not even the consideration of it, until the work was done.

And when would the work be done?

When justice prevailed. When the truth was set free. When she knew again that she was who she was meant to be.

"I'm about to face the place where I lost my entire life, the real me," she said. "Where I lost my father, my mother, my offspring. Where I lost my own chance for motherhood. Where I lost you, too. Where so much was taken from us both!" She took a few deep breaths, trying to keep her voice steady. "I wasn't lying on Lagracia. I can't face this alone. I need—"

Rakk turned back to her but wouldn't look her in the eyes.

"I need you to be there for me, too," he said. "We'll face it, together. We will. But not til we arrive. Not til then."

Ellex said nothing as she watched him walk away, part of her certain she deserved to feel this way, the other part in complete rebellion, desperate for it to stop, and looking for any excuse to justify feeling sorry for herself, no matter how flimsy.

But none would come.

❧❧❧❧❧ ❦❦❦❦❦

Nearly a week passed before the peaks of P'anorum appeared on the horizon. Rakk had left shortly after they'd spoken, taking a skiff'rin to a different ship in the fleet, with some mumbled excuse about helping with repairs, though she knew he needed to be away from her. As much as she wanted to call him back, to force him to talk out his feelings, she knew he needed the space, and she did too. With Qaas'i off with Bhea Bell, and the fleet moving so slowly she could have piloted with her eyes closed, she spent a lot of her time with absolutely nothing to do but stare out at the sea and listen to the purr of the gurgitator.

Sometimes a dolph'rin would come close with dozens of Bhizini aboard, and they'd strike up the band and bang the drums and blow their horns, and everyone on the nearby boats would whoop with delight and dance around under the sunshine, and Ellex couldn't help but hear the laughter, feel the music, and want to throw off her clothes and dance along with them, though she never did.

The Tornroot Clan are happy plants, she thought. *I can't speak for any of the other Bhizini clans, but here they seem to enjoy merrymaking.* Even the ones who scowled at her could turn away with grins on their face and laugh and play with the scamps, as if they'd never been burdened with the terrible hatred that moments earlier boiled up behind their eyes and suffocated her from a distance.

The first time she came into the grotto and saw everyone glaring at her, she'd reached for the servryn, an old nervous habit of hers that compelled her to call up her schedule and double check her to-do list whenever she encountered a new and discomforting situation. But ever since her and Rakk had bought bhiza on Nunan, she'd taken it regularly to keep her crystal unable to communicate with other crystamins. She was going to have enough to deal with when she got back to Balan Su without having anyone in the Pradishar privy to where she'd been or what she'd been doing. And she'd been so busy—well, first she'd been so sick crossing the Threshinveld, and then so stressed in Callo Baton, and then in confinement, and then distracted by the Bhizini once she was free—she hadn't had a chance to really think about how odd it was that her crystamin had been numb for nearly a month now. No disturbances from Uthyr, nor from Pander, nor from her Cul'tavin. No notestreams to fill her head with scheming and her heart with anxiety. No melodramas to entertain or bore her in equal measure. And since she hadn't been working, she hadn't noticed that she couldn't access her files on the servryn, or check her schedule, or consult her multiple lists reminding her of what needed doing. She hadn't needed them, and still didn't. In fact, she found the silence inside her head was as helpful as the space she was enjoying outside of her head.

I may be lost as ever when it comes to figuring out who I am, she thought, *but at least I know what needs doing. And nothing is going to stop me from going under P'anorum and finding the answers I need, so help me Trevian!*

But when the peaks of P'anorum appeared on the horizon, and she heard spontaneous songs of celebration from the nearby boats, her sense of dread, of sheer panic, rose up and nearly overwhelmed her, and she was sure she should just give up already and slink out of history a failure.

She closed her eyes and imagined the whirlpool descending from the heavens, wrapping her up in its warm, safe interior, and the terrible sensation drained slowly out of her chest. When she opened them, Rakk was climbing up onto the deck and stepping over the rail.

He smiled at her, and looked her in the eyes while doing so, and her tension drained away even more. He walked over and took her arm, and led her to the railing.

"There it is," he said. "Great Sower in the sky, we made it. This is really happening."

"We've come halfway around the world," she said.

"And are as lost as when we set out."

"No," Ellex said. "More so." She smiled. "But I have a good feeling about this."

"You do?" he said. "'Cause I feel positively sick inside."

"Me too," she admitted. "I was just doing your whirlpool technique when you arrived."

"It must have helped."

"It did. And now I'm feeling confident we'll find answers here."

"We may not like them."

He looked back at the horizon, at the three peaks of the island, the leftmost barely higher than the water, the middle one large and green, the largest towering twice as high, a shimmering orange and black cone that still seemed to burn in the sunlight. "The Crag and the harbor don't look like they got covered in lava," he said. "Just the main peak and the city."

"And most of the palace," Bhea said, climbing over the rail onto the deck. She turned back and helped Qaas'andria up.

"Hi love," Ellex said, and Qaas'i grinned at her. "I swear you've grown half a foot this week alone."

"I think you're right," Bhea said. "Lithuigi thought she might catch on up once she came out of the chamber. Might even flower soon."

"Really?" Ellex said, her throat suddenly tight, tears spilling down her face. "I didn't know if she would. That's wonderful."

Bhea walked over to Rakk's side and took his arm. "How you doing, love? You okay?"

He nodded and looked at P'anorum again, growing larger now, the gnarled green of the Swarthen Forest coming into sharper relief on the island's western side.

"P'anorum," she said. "Short for Poko Anorum in the old tongue. Which was itself short for Poko Anoru'mundia—the gate to the world of light."

"Funny, since nearly everyone in Balance thinks it's the gate to Mund'umbria now," Rakk said, "and that to set foot on the island means certain death."

"Gates go both ways, don't they. And that lie worked pretty well," Bhea said. "It kept treasure hunters and other bandits from coming ashore, though a few did try. They was always turned back, or sunk, by the Corkin before they could get within view of the island."

"The Corkin?!" Rakk cried.

Ellex could see the pain and the confusion in his eyes.

Bhea nodded. "They kept us safe, made sure nobody got closer than we are now. Only, I can't rely on 'em like I used to. Something's changing in Raccorum Rhazzat."

"You're telling me the Corkin have been patrolling the waters around P'anorum this whole time? For thirty four years? And I didn't know about it? For fuck's sake, *it's my army!*"

"I don't know for sure," Bhea said. "Your father arranged for it after everything was lost. He knew we'd stayed on here, and he wanted to keep us safe."

"My father," Rakk whispered, a dark look on his face.

Ellex wanted to reach for him, but didn't move.

"Why didn't he tell me?"

"I can't speak for him, love," Bhea said. "But you can ask him yourself when you go to Rhen'zoran."

"My father gave me the army, then ordered it to act against my will. He and Raq'asha have been disrupting my communications with my generals and redirecting supplies. He's been sabotaging me from the beginning, and now Raq'asha plans to finish what he started, by declaring Rishar and stealing my mandate."

"Rishar's not been called yet, and even if it were, you'd be allowed to speak for yourself to all the Clades, and make the truth known to those who need to hear it," Bhea said. "Now stop making assumptions and focus."

Rakk gripped the rail and stared out at the water, and Bhea sighed.

Ellex watched her face, and could see that she was upset by his pain—that she felt as helpless as she did.

"We gotta focus on the here and now first," Bhea said.

Rakk hissed. "Fine. The here and now. The here that has me at the end of my luck, and the now that brings me face to face with everything I've lost. What a wonderful place to be."

"That's not what I meant," Bhea said.

"I know," Rakk said. "But I do. And I will. I'll deal with P'anorum. I'll go where you point and do as you say, just like a good little scamp. And when this charade is all over, I'm sailing for Raccorum Rhazzat, and I'm going to put an end to all those who are trying to destroy me."

Is that just the anger talking? Ellex thought. *Or is he finally willing to go home and fight for his throne?*

"So are we going under the island or what?" Rakk said.

"Fin'roq is still wavering," Bhea said. "He's been very traumatized by the darkness, and so the thought of going underground is—well, he's pretty distraught about it."

"Oh no," Rakk said, but Ellex looked at his face and saw that he was being genuine. "Any way we can help convince him? Make him feel like he's safe with us, and that we'll take care of him?"

"Actually, there is," Bhea said. "I was—well, I was kinda hopin' maybe you'd have figured it out by now. You see, he was an orphan, so he ain't never had a family of his own. And I think—well, I think maybe that would make a big difference to him—if he knew you was his brother." She was looking at Rakk, but she turned to Ellex. "And that you was his mother."

And Ellex found herself in yet another situation where words failed her, where there was only emotion, only the action that follows from the feelings that demanded to be released.

She opened her mouth and let the sobs flow.

Chapter 51

Because There Was Another

FIN'ROQ NEEDED ALMOST A week before he felt like traveling. Every time he pulled up his rootpads and took a few steps to get his bearings, he'd start to feel woozy again, like he was slipping down into a deep, dark hole and there was nothing to grab onto, nothing to keep him from losing himself, from losing everything. And each day he put off sailing for P'anorum was one more day he could avoid the thought of going back under the island.

They want to go to the temple where Roe died. Where I killed him, he thought. *Where I ripped the memories from his mind before I destroyed his smug, beautiful face.*

Sweet Trevian, what am I?

Bhea Bell came to check on him, and he found he couldn't stay mad at her, even though he tried. She was so sweet and patient, pushing but in a gentle way, encouraging him to think about how nice it would be to be back at her garden, on the cliffs overlooking the sea, the Swarthen Forest like a blanket all around them, keeping them safe. But he remembered the Pal'meran leaf-striders swooping in that night, dragging him off through the canopy, just like Bhart had done—

Bhart. He had to see them. He had to.

"I don't know," Bhea said. "Don't seem like a good idea to me. But it's your choice love, you know that."

"I want to see them."

Fin'roq waited til the morning the fleet was meant to depart for P'anorum before going to see Bhart. Bhea took him down the narrow, slick stone corridors, and he followed, listening to the echo of their footsteps. She stopped and indicated a metal grating on the ground.

"I'll be down the way. You just gotta holler you need me, and I'll come running." She gave him a peck on the cheek as she left.

Fin swallowed, his throat dry, his heart racing, and he bent down on his knees and peered into the hole. Bhart was sitting on the ground, their legs crossed, their eyes closed, their hands upward on their thighs, their lips moving silently as they recited prayers under the greasy light of a glowbe. Fin didn't know what to say, so he stared at Bhart for a moment, wrapped up in their beauty, the way their mottled skin looked like a forest dappled with sunlight, and he ached for them, suddenly and intensely, to feel safe like he had in Bhart's arms when they'd rescued him from Qardymion, and he almost cried out in pain—

But no. He wouldn't let Bhart see they'd upset him.

"Praying for absolution?" he said, and Bhart's body jerked when they heard him, and they looked up, their eyes wide open, that look on their face again.

"You're okay," Bhart said, grinning. "Nobody would tell me a thing."

But Fin'roq glared down at them and Bhart's grin faded.

"How are you?" they said.

"How do you think?" Fin said. "Betrayal feels—like being murdered. Like something beautiful that might have been, that should have been, can suddenly never be, and never really was to begin with."

"I know I let you down," Bhart said. "I let everyone down. I failed my clan and abandoned them. Then I failed Qardymion too, all because I lost my mind when I saw them hurting you. I thought—I thought I could help you wake up, Fin, so that Qardymion—so that nobody else—would put you through something like that again."

"You were trying to help me," Fin said. He laughed. "To help me?" He laughed again.

"I swear it. My intentions were pure. And I thought it was working."

Fin swallowed a hiss. "You know, when you rescued me from the Saltsap, I don't think I've ever been so happy to see anyone in my life. I watched you risk your own life to save mine, to get me to safety, to protect me. I would have done anything for you. Why couldn't you have just brought me to the Tornroot and returned me to Bhea Bell? Why did you have to put me through that? You violated my body and you violated my mind. You made me see terrible things, to feel strange feelings. Damnit Bhart, I felt like I spent centuries going mad, screaming and howling in the darkness. And you did that to me. You."

The look was back on Bhart's face, their eyes were shining with a strange madness, and Fin'roq felt his heart clench, the skin on his face tighten.

"It worked," Bhart whispered. "It worked!" Now they were howling with joy, breathing as if they were exhausted, and laughing with glee.

"You're a monster," Fin said.

"A monster? I'm your humble servant." Bhart fell over onto their face, their hands out on the soil in front of them. "I will worship the very ground you stand on," they shouted. "I will sing your praises every day and every night, for the rest of my life. You're the one, Fin'roq. The one the world has been waiting for! The one the world needs more than ever. The Harvest is coming. Mortimus Rex will move to sweep the old world away. You're the only one who can stop it."

"You're insane," Fin'roq said. "And cruel. And you're right where you deserve to be."

"You'll thank me one day, Fin'roq. I've done this for you. For you, and for your world."

"You've done it for yourself."

Fin leaned back to stand.

"Wait," Bhart said, and Fin'roq paused. "What will become of me?"

"At this point, I'm not sure I care."

"You saw them," Bhart said, "your past lives. You know Fin'roq is but a passing dream, don't you? Even now, you aren't sure you're awake."

"I'm going," Fin said.

"Don't let them kill me," Bhart said. "At least not until you've won. Then I'll die gladly, but not a moment before. Please, Fin, please. I beg you. Don't let the Death King have my face!"

"You think I can defeat death itself?" Fin said. "Nobody is that powerful. Nobody."

"I never said defeat," Bhart said. "You're right, nobody can defeat death. Death follows fruit, after all. And Mortimus Rex is a king with no form to destroy, no image to stamp out—a specter whose true power seems to be only some shapeless, nameless terror."

"So how do I win against something that doesn't exist?"

"I don't have the answers. But I'm glad to see I've awakened your thirst for them." Their eyes were shining.

"No," Fin said, "you haven't. But you've made me realize one thing. Something I wish I had learned a long time ago, as it would have saved me a lot of grief. Never trust anyone. *Ever*. They're only out for their own good, each and every one of them."

He stood and hurried away, his heart thudding in his ears, his fists clenched together, his jaw aching, his entire body feeling awkward and antsy. But there were no tears. No broken heart. Just a low simmering anger, and an uncertain confusion, and a feeling like things could only get worse before they got better.

Fin'roq found Bhea in the corridor and she took him to her cata'rin. When he came out onto the docks, he saw Ellex Andria talking with several Bhizini next to a stack of cargo bins, and although she was smiling at them and they were laughing, he still felt a wave of fury swelling in his chest, and he wanted to scream at her, to tell her how much she didn't belong here, to berate her and humiliate her as she'd done to him. Couldn't she see how different she was, how out of place, how much she was ruining it for everyone else by being here? He was shaking, and his vision seemed to flash on the edges, and he couldn't catch his breath.

But Bhea took him by the arm and led him up the gangplank to the cata'rin, and once Ellex Andria was out of his sight, he was able to breathe again. He took a few deep breaths but his mind still wanted to rage on.

He ran up the stairs to a perch by the captain's quarters and he sat his feet down into the soil patch and unfurled his branches to the sky and tried to imagine a whirlpool descending over him. He drank up the sunshine through his skin, and swooned at the pulsing pleasure of the light, and it was almost enough to make him forget about the anger, the pain, and the rage that seemed to pop up whenever anything didn't go his way.

Finally the gurgitator opened and started to purr, and once they were on their way, he felt better. The salty air, the light off the water, the endless blue on blue of sea and sky—there was a timelessness to the ocean, an empty solitude that seemed able to swallow up anything, no matter how massive, or how burdensome, and carry it away. But then his thoughts returned to the last time he'd sailed these waters, on his crossing to Balan Su with Jaun von Andron and Roman Anthem, and he was sad all over again.

I set out to become a monkin, he thought, *and now I'm returning in failure, even more of a freak than when I left. And more alone than ever.*

He looked around at the other boats streaming out from Lagracia into the Far Ocean and thought they made quite a strange but impressive fleet. The Tornroot clan—to please Bhea Bell no doubt—had sent nearly half their ships along as an escort. Fin'roq was grateful. The thought of an encounter with Qardymion's warriors made him queasy, and he was just now able to keep down rhupan again. The withdrawal from that much bhiza had left him feeling like a wrung out sponge, and his arms and legs were looking downright fibrous, he'd lost so much body mass. A walking bhrubean stalk, the Bhizini scamps were calling him.

Fin was grateful to Bhea for letting him have a cata'rin nearly to himself. He closed his eyes and focused on the sunshine, and when he slept, it was finally dreamless. He woke, ate, slept. Woke, ate, slept some more. The days began to pass and he'd finally managed to find some peace, in his head and in his heart. The sea seemed to be healing him.

Another night passed and twilight came again, and when Fin'roq woke, he realized he was not alone on the deck. Someone was standing behind him. He didn't want to turn around, but he felt uncomfortable, like he really needed to make sure it was Bhea and not some stranger. Who knew who might have snuck onto the cata'rin from one of the other boats in the fleet.

"Do you know where we are?" asked a soft voice, and he jumped.

He looked back then, his heart racing, but it was just a Bhizini scamp.

"Do you know where we are?" the Bhizini asked again.

"At sea," he said. "Somewhere between Lagracia and P'anorum."

"Where's the sea?"

"On—er—the world?."

"And where's the world?"

"Between Mund'umbria and Sol'bhin."

"And where are the three realms?"

"Er—they're everything, so I guess they're everywhere."

"And where's everywhere?"

Fin snorted. "What do you want?"

"To know where we are," the Bhizini said.

"I just told you!" he snapped.

"Hmm, I don't think so."

Fin'roq hissed. "How'd you get aboard? This is a private cata'rin."

"Actually, this is my boat," the Bhizini said. "You know the law, right? That means I'm in charge here."

"Nice try, but this is Bhea's ship. Now get out of here."

"I'm not in here so how do I get out of here?"

Fin threw up is hands and hissed again.

The Bhizini laughed and Fin's ears burned.

"I'd like to be alone, so can you please just go away? Run along and play with the other scamps. It's so early, better yet, go back to sleep. Or for a swim. A very long one."

But the scamp didn't move.

"You know, elsewhere," he said. "Go on already, bothersome little brat."

"But I want to play with you," the scamp said sweetly.

"I'm too old to play."

The scamp laughed, almost hysterically loud, and Fin'roq felt a chill run down his back. He knew that laugh.

He'd heard it before, in the bhiza dream.

"Oh Sweet Trevian, no, this can't still be the Inner Door!"

Bhart was right, he thought. *I don't know if I'm awake or asleep, seeing or dreaming.*

"You aren't on bhiza," the Bhizini said. "But that was me you heard in the Inner Door. I was trying so hard to get you to come play with me, but you refused."

"You were annoying then and you're annoying now. So get lost! I'm too old to play."

"Why so angry, Fin'roq?"

He sighed. "So many reasons. But the most recent ones? Because someone I thought was my friend kidnapped and then tortured me. And I got stabbed, twice, in the same wound, and then stabbed again. Also beaten silly by a mob. Betrayed by someone special to me. Humiliated in front of all of Balance. What else do you want to know?"

The Bhizini said nothing for a moment, just stared at Fin'roq, then said, "I was a prisoner for over thirty years, and I've only had one month free so far."

"What?" Fin said. "Thirty years? Sweet Trevian, I'm—sorry. I feel like a fool now. Are—are you teasing me again? You're so small."

"I was in a stasis chamber—a maquina that I was locked inside, in paralysis, my body barely alive."

Fin'roq grew cold inside. He swallowed hard, and didn't think he could speak.

"Life's rather terrible, isn't it?" said the Bhizini. "Painful, this world. Having a body. Not being free, even when you are. But maybe it's because we're both incomplete, you and me. I think this trip will be good for us. It will be good to go home."

"Home?" Fin asked.

"P'anorum. Where else?"

"Why were you imprisoned?"

"They thought I was someone else." The Bhizini's eyes tore into Fin'roq and he looked away, feeling guilty, even though he didn't know what he'd done wrong.

"How'd you escape?" he asked.

"I didn't. They let me go, even arranged for me to be found. Planted me, you might say. Apt, no? They didn't know who I am. They still don't."

"And who are you?"

"The future."

Fin'roq swallowed hard. "Whose future?"

"Yours, after a fashion."

He blushed. "Are you proposing to me?"

The Bhizini laughed again, almost hysterically. Fin'roq shuddered.

"I love that you know nothing. I'm Qaas'andria. My mother and my brother call me Qaas'i. I also answer to Anorian."

"Nice to meet you?" he said uncertainly. "I'm Fin'roq, but you already knew that."

"I did," Qaas'i said. "Oh, and before I forget. My mother and my brother have no idea I can speak. I know you won't tell them." She gave him a look that made him shudder. "They need your help, you know. To get down to Dar Ka'Hala. To see the Temple of Trevian."

"How do you know about that?"

Qaas'i rolled her eyes. "Your ignorance was cute at first."

Fin'roq looked hurt. "Nothing makes sense to me. My life's a mess. I dreamed ten thousand dreams, and every one of them made me want to die—or to live—I'm not sure which."

But Qaas'i said nothing.

Fin'roq sighed and shook his head. "Why should I help your family, if you don't even talk to them? They must be pretty awful."

"No, I just—at first I really couldn't speak, I guess because I'd never used my voice before. It was so painful. But then—I didn't know what to say to them, so I didn't say anything. And it's been nice. To be a scamp, for a little while. Taken care of, and even understood, without words."

"Well, I guess you'll know when the time is right to tell them. And in the meantime, my lips are sealed."

<<I know they are,>> she said. <<Because you're afraid of me.>>

"No, I'm not."

He stared at her in the twilight, and he could swear her lips weren't moving.

<<Yes, you are,>> Qaas'i said.

They were definitely not moving.

"How are you doing that?"

<<Doing what?>>

<<That! Whoa! I can do it too?>>

Fin'roq felt Qaas'i laughing in his mind.

<<But I don't have a crystal. You don't have a crystal. How is this possible?>>

That shrieking laughter again, but Qaas'i didn't respond.

<<Fine. Don't tell me. But just so you know, I'm not going to help your mother. She and the prince can find their own way under the city. I'm not going.>>

<<You want to help them,>> Qaas'i said. <<You know you do.>>

<<I'll tell you what I know. Your mother embarrassed me more than anyone else in my entire life, and I grew up with a village full of terrible people who loved making me feel like I was worthless. The things she said to me—no. I won't help her.>>

<<She didn't mean them,>> Qaas'i said. <<Poor, poor Ellex Andria. You don't know what's been done to her, Fin. The real Ellex would never have said those things to you. Neither would the new Ellex.>>

<<You sound like you've remade her.>>

<<After a fashion,>> she said. <<But the point remains that you want to help her. Don't try to lie to me. I can feel what you're feeling. I know what your heart is saying. You want to help her, because it's your chance to prove your worth to her. You hate that she was mean to you, and disrespected you, but you don't want to be angry at her, you want her affection. Her acceptance.>>

<<Fuck off, Anorian,>> he said, and he could *feel* that she was deeply pleased he'd called her that. The sensation disturbed him.

<<I'm sorry,>> she said, though he could hear her laughing in his mind. <<I just can't resist having a bit of fun with you. It's been a long time since I could be myself. And since you and I are family, I feel like I can joke around with you.>>

<<I have no family.>>

<<Everyone has family, whether they want to or not. And I'm your sibling. Your sister.>>

<<You're lying,>> he said. He laughed. <<My sibling? My mother was Raccorin, not that—not Ellex Andria. Grizmond Grants told me as much. And I don't even know you.>>

<<And yet here we are, talking to each other in our minds, neither one of us with a crystal.>>

<<No,>> Fin said, even as he knew it was true. <<No.>>

<<Yes,>> Anorian said. <<Ellex Andria is your mother. Rakk Raeder your brother. King Rhakksees the Second your father. Grizmond lied to protect his king. I am your sister. Need more proof?>>

She stepped close to him then, and he felt he was looking at himself from a decade ago. And her skin! The patterns of bright and dull, her Bhizini markings, they would look just like his when she finished growing.

"Sweet Trevian, it's true," he said. "You're my sibling? But how do we look alike?"

"I'm you," she whispered, "like a duplicant, but different. For now, I must be Qaas'an-dria, and you must be Fin'roq. Can you do that, brother? Can you be Fin'roq?"

"But how?" he said. "How is this possible?" He was giggling but only because he was scared.

<<It's strange to see you face to face as well,>> she said in his mind. <<Take our mother and our brother under the island. I promise you, the answers you seek are waiting under P'anorum, in the ruins of Dar Ka'Hala where we last died.>>

<<Where we *what*?>>

Qaas'i rolled her eyes.

"You promise there'll be answers, if I take them—if I go back into the darkness?" he said aloud.

<<Yes,>> she said. <<And I'll be there with you, in here. We can face this together.>>

<<I don't know if I can do it, even if I wanted to. When I think about it, I can't breathe.>>

<<You're one of the bravest people I've ever known,>> she said, and Fin felt a blast of confidence and warmth so profound, he felt the tension draining from his neck and from his shoulders.

<<This isn't the homecoming I expected,>> he said. <<I had decided I wanted to go live out my life in peace and quiet, deep in the Swarthen Forest, forgetting the world, forgotten by the world. And I was okay with that. Is it too late to have that?>>

<<Don't you know the answer already?>>

<<What if I don't like the answer? Can I change things?>>

<<Why are you asking me?>>

<<I don't know,>> Fin said.

<<Then yes. Absolutely. One hundred percent. Fate be damned.>>

<<Thanks, Anorian. I needed to hear that,>> he said, though he knew she was lying.

<<Any time bro,>> she said, winking at him. <<Any time.>>

Chapter 52
Preaching, Planting, Purging

WHEN LITHUIGI WAS A younger plant, everything in life seemed to crawl by whenever he wasn't working, when his hands weren't busy creating or his mind inventing. But now that he was getting older, the opposite was true. How long had it been since he and Bhea had really been able to spend time together? A few brief visits each year was all they'd managed in the last half century. They'd been so busy—and he had Rebesh'a, his career and life on Balan Su. And the stasis chamber. Anorian. He'd had to keep her safe.

Lithuigi had put the inevitability of what was coming out of his mind for as long as he'd known the truth. He'd convinced himself that all this work was to save Bhea, to make a world where they could be together, and be safe. But it was a lie, and he knew it.

No one can stop death, he thought. Not even the stasis chamber could fend it off entirely, though his modifications had gone a long way toward extending life. Qaas'andria might have lived another thousand, two thousand years.

But what good is it to talk about what might have been? There have been so many might-have-beens over the years.

He sighed and turned his attention to the horizon, and as his eyes fell across the sea, he filled his lungs with the salty air and felt refreshed, steeled for what was to come.

I'm finally ready, he thought, *to be myself. Not Professor L'uigi. Not an operator or a tinker. Not a father or a friend. A Bhizini. A plant of the sea, beholden to none. How few even know me, the real me. No wonder my sons hate me. I never let them get to know who I am.*

How was he to convince Vilder and Hesh'n not to serve the Pradishar when he'd spent his entire adult life creating maquina and weapons, tools of oppression and warfare, for their benefit? Anorian had insisted he never tell his sons about her, nor about their project in the Far Ocean. He knew Vilder had joined the Ren'fallow, had been wooed by the enemy, and was not to be trusted. But Hesh'n didn't care about history and he certainly didn't care about Mund'umbrian mischief. He couldn't help but think Anorian had been wrong to exclude him.

Maybe—maybe if he'd known the truth, he would have cared a little more.

When Lithuigi arrived at Vergis, Mha'arlo was waiting for him at the tram station. He was glad to see him, and glad to hear all of his prep work on Callo Baton had concluded without issue.

At least some things are going well, he thought.

Mha'arlo looked around, then spoke directly to Lithuigi through their Dyna'arin crystal.

<<Rameen Rutar was here while you were at Lagracia.>>

Lithuigi hissed. <<And now the tinkers won't hear me speak.>>

<<They've postponed the meeting,>> Mha'arlo said.

<<Indefinitely, I'm sure.>>

<<I'm sorry, professor.>>

<<Not all is lost, son. There's still Khatoran Rha'qan. If the tinkers won't assemble to hear me speak, I'll just speak wherever I find them assembled. And I can count on most of them attending Khatoran's rooting ceremony.>>

A tad more public than I'd hoped, but it will have to do.

Mha'arlo was grinning but then he frowned. <<Professor—Hesh'n was here too. I tried to follow him, to see what he was up to, but the enforcers noticed and gave me a hard time about it. I guess I'm not as smooth as I thought.>>

What was Hesh'n doing there? He hated sea travel, and got very ill whenever he had to do it, so he almost never left Balan Su.

<<That was foolish of you, son,>> he said. <<But I do appreciate it. Come on, we have a lot to get done before the ceremony. I want to be ready to leave Vergis as soon as it's over.>>

They set to work, and the passage of time seemed to vanish once again, til Lithuigi realized they'd finished everything he hoped to get done, and they still had a bit of time to spare. So he took Mha'arlo to the nicest restaurant Vergis had to offer and they feasted on marinated rhupan and drank fizzwaters with lime, and Lithuigi did his best to distract himself from the panic that kept tugging at his mind, threatening to pinch off his air.

If Hesh'n had come to Vergis, he'd been up to no good—it was as simple as that. And tomorrow he knew just the plant he'd ask about it, even though he was certain he didn't want to know the answer.

Khatoran Rha'qan's rooting ceremony was scheduled for noon on the day of Sol'arin, as was customary for Verdillions going to die. Lithuigi had arranged to escort his old mentor to Vergis's own gruynfeld, an artificially constructed island amongst the reefs and shoals where Dyna'arin tinkers spent the remainder of their existence as tandavin, rooted to the soil, their skin turned to bark, their eyes forever shut, their branches growing upward toward the heavens, looking more like a true tree with every passing year. Until one day, somewhere between eight hundred and a thousand years later, the tandavin would spontaneously combust, turning to ash from the inside out, or else flaring up into a sudden inferno and engulfing the surrounding tandavin in the flames. Either way, a tandavin always ended in fire.

When mid-morning came around, Lithuigi and Mha'arlo set off for the ceremony with Khatoran in tow. Mha'arlo helped the old Raccorin into a skiff'rin for the trip to the gruynfeld. He took slow, laborious steps as he walked, and every motion he made seemed unnatural. Lithuigi thought he could hear him creaking as he moved along. Once he was seated, Lithuigi perched next to him, and Mha'arlo got in back by the gurgitator.

Mha'arlo piloted the skiff'rin to the lift, and the port soon filled with water and the boat rose up to sea level. The walls lowered around them and they made their way slowly amongst the reefs and sandbars and atolls, the gurgitator softly purring, the water all around the boat that color of blue that makes you swoon to look upon it.

"A beautiful day for rooting," Khatoran said. "And a beautiful place, too. I've spent most of my life here at Vergis. To think I might sway here in the breeze for another five times the length of my life—why, it makes my old head spin."

"Your old head still seems mighty sharp," Lithuigi said. "I've seen adults in their prime with less intelligence and wit than you."

"Lucky them," Khatoran said, and Lithuigi smiled.

"For being young?" Mha'arlo said.

"For being ignorant."

"You want to be rooted?" Mha'arlo said.

"Of course I do! You might even say I lust for it, like one might crave water, or sunshine, or rhupan, or a lovely flower. I've never wanted anything more in my life. I'm ready to rest. I've had a full life. I did many things, went many places, had wonderful adventures.

What more would I want? My body is ready to set down roots and be one with the soil again. Besides, my hands won't work right to tinker. I get all turned around with complicated things, even if Lithuigi here thinks me sharp. And—I find I have a sudden love for simplicity, for silence in here," he pointed to his head, "that I never understood until now."

"You're a brave plant," Lithuigi said. "I'll confess, I'm not yet ready to let go—not yet ready to be gone forever."

"Forever?" Khatoran chuckled. "You've misunderstood, friend. Now is forever, and now is all there is."

"Now you're sounding like Baboo," Lithuigi said.

"That is the highest compliment you've ever paid me," Khatoran said. "Do yourself a favor and learn from him. Before Reformation gets here. He'll make it a lot easier for you."

Lithuigi looked away, but Khatoran touched his arm.

"You're really the brave one," he said. "I know what victory will mean for you. I'm sorry."

"Thank you," Lithuigi said, "but don't be sorry. I need one final favor from you. I need to address the tinkers. Today, at your ceremony."

"Those who would have been convinced have already been convinced," Khatoran said. "If you expect the tinkers as a whole to break with Management, to reject the Pradishar—surely you aren't so naive? Surely Bhea told you the same thing?"

"Yes," Lithuigi said. "But I'm a professor. And they're going to hear me profess anyway!"

Khatoran chuckled. "I hope you'll come and visit me when I'm a tandavin, old friend," he said. "I'll be the perfect listener, never interrupting."

"And risk being incinerated?" Lithuigi said. "I don't want to profess that much!"

They both laughed.

"You old folks are crazy," Mha'arlo said. "I think I'll stay young forever." He was grinning.

"At least there's that to reassure us," Khatoran said. "If the youngsters think us old timers are making sense, we're surely doing something wrong. Wisdom takes time, and lots of mistakes, before a plant wakes up to the truth."

The day really was beautiful. And the gruynfeld was always a sight to behold—a small, dense forest of vaguely Verdillion-like trees, some soaring hundreds of feet into the air, all of them sitting atop an octagonal granite pedestal, jutting up from the teal waters of the Vergin Sea. Lithuigi brought the skiff'rin into the dock at the island's southern edge, where a triangular wedge was cut into the granite. At the back of the wedge stood a large glass fountain, twinkling in the sun, surrounded by a few rows of flowers. There was a small dais in front of the fountain and rows of loungers and perches fanning out into the triangle. Rooting ceremonies were always held here on the lower level, on the only part of the island considered safe to visit.

Most of the guests had already arrived, and the loungers were filled with some several hundred tinkers and their guests. Lithuigi and Mha'arlo took their seats, and Khatoran headed for the dais. Step by slow creaking step he went, and when the audience realized he'd arrived, they began to cheer.

When he finally reached the stage and turned to address the audience, the chatter of the crowd fell silent, and for a moment the only sound was the wind through the grove of tandavin overhead and the hushed lapping of the sea against the granite shore.

Khatoran thanked everyone for coming, for the long years of support they'd given him, and the meaning it had brought to so much of his life. When he announced that he'd be ceding the floor to Lithuigi Von'nDrino, the audience began to chatter again, and a few stood and headed for the docks.

"This isn't the Academicon!" someone yelled.

"It's not?" Lithuigi said, taking the stage and feigning confusion. "Well hell. Here I was thinking Balan Su finally had some good weather. I guess all these years living a double life has finally done me in."

A few in the audience laughed, some smirked, while others glared and whispered to one another.

Lithuigi stood on the dais for a moment and sighed. "Surely you all can relate with me? We tinkers are performers, after all. We may masquerade as professors, or as operators, or a few of us really nasty ones as managers, but we are always, everywhere, wishing we could just go to our lab and tinker in peace. We have half of ourselves hidden from the other half—hidden from those in our lives, from our loved ones, from ourselves even. So surely you'll forgive me if I end up playing the wrong role for the situation. Half of me lives under Balance Authority, the other at sea—half of me in Balan Su, and half here in the Far Ocean. Which is really me?"

He paused for a moment and sighed again.

"I can't complain, you know. We Dyna'arin are blessed, as few in Balance are blessed. We and we alone are free from surveillance by Balance Authority, free to go where we please without needing to ask permission of the Pradishar, to work in peace and in security without anyone peering over our shoulder—to think as we care to think without fear we'll be tossed in a dungeon and forgotten. This has made the Dyna'arin the most peaceful, and productive, organization the world has ever known.

"Mostly we remain peaceful because we're all too busy working to bother with the dramas of politics and life. We only want to tinker, and the world be damned. Isn't that our attitude, our unspoken dogma? So long as we're left alone—and so long as the Pradishar continue to supply the components for our maquina—we couldn't care less what the authority we represent does to the world, to our own Verdillion brethren, to our own offspring, for Trevian's sake!

"I spent much of my life creating maquina for the Guild, for Balance Authority, for the Pradishar, oblivious to the consequences of what my creations could do, or how they might change the world. When I realized how many lives my enflamer had destroyed, and when I understood—" he paused to collect himself, "—when I understood that the Death King had a firm grip on our world, I could no longer go on as before."

There were hisses in the audience. "Are you a Bhizini speaker or a Dyna'arin tinker?" someone yelled.

"Superstitious babble," another shouted.

Nu'mora Rhyantis stood up and shouted in her booming voice, "I know you, Professor L'uigi. I know the argument you want to make. You want everyone in Balance—no, everyone in the entire world—to have the freedoms and privileges that we Dyna'arin enjoy. But I also know you're smarter than that. We here understand that together we can provide for our needs better than if we were alone. That is the key to the Guild's success, that every single Dyna'arin respects the property and privacy of every other Dyna'arin. Dyna'arin do not hurt other Dyna'arin, they do not steal from other Dyna'arin. And nobody breaks these rules, or they wouldn't be Dyna'arin. Because we are orderly, freedom means civilization and progress. But if you give our freedoms and privileges to all, to the mobs of Verdillions only made orderly by the threat of violence, you don't have order, you don't have civilization, you have anarchy and barbarism. You have creative stagnation. You no longer have a place for people like us, who are too smart to swallow superstitious twaddle. You'd have war between the races, like in the age before Balance."

Lithuigi listened attentively to the Raccorin's response, nodding occasionally, playing the good professor. When she finished, he smiled.

"Can I assume that Nu'mora here speaks for most of you?" Lithuigi asked the audience, and they cheered. "Very well. I suppose there isn't a chance in Mund'umbria of convincing you to break your routine, to risk alienating the Pradishar, because it might help your everyday Andrasian citizen or Raccorin subject. What do you have to gain, after all? The Dyna'arin already have it all. You'd be a fool to risk your privileges, given you can't conceive of any particular gain to come from such a risk. Rationally, you all made a stellar choice. But morally—and historically—you've made a tragic error, and the Dyna'arin may not survive it."

The audience booed and hissed, but Nu'mora's booming laughter drowned it all out. "My dear tinkers," she said, "we have a genuine Ren'fallow conspiracy nut in our very own ranks!" She laughed, and the crowd joined her. "The end times have come," she mocked. "The twilight tales were true! Mortimus Rex has come to steal Verdillion faces!"

Lithuigi surveyed the crowd, ignoring the hisses and laughter—not everyone was participating, at least. He took a bow and walked off the stage, then re-took his seat by Mha'arlo. The clamor died down, and Khatoran called for the feast to begin. The audience began to filter back toward the docks, where large tables with food and drinks had been laid out while they were talking.

Nu'mora came and sat down by Lithuigi. He gave her a smile, though she looked ashamed.

"I really hated doing that," she said.

"You were only doing as Anorian asked," he said. "It's important that Rameen Rutar think the tinkers and the operators are on his side. You did well."

"I have something else I need to tell you," Nu'mora said. "After the ceremony ends, could you escort me back to the lab?"

"Of course," he said, and he tried to sound happy, but his heart was thudding in his chest.

When the food was finished and the drinks were nearly gone, Khatoran bid everyone farewell, and there were lots of hugs and lots of tears, though Khatoran looked absolutely jubilant. Finally, Lithuigi and Mha'arlo helped Khatoran to the small lift tucked at the back of the wedge.

"Be strong but flexible," Khatoran said to Lithuigi. "And persistent as the sea."

An old Bhizini prayer. Lithuigi nodded, tears in his eyes.

"And you, son," Khatoran said to Mha'arlo. "You must see the circle, in order to step outside of it."

Mha'arlo nodded at him.

Khatoran waved, slowly, as the lift door slid shut.

They made their way back to the docks, saying nothing. Lithuigi felt guilty that he was thinking of Hesh'n rather than celebrating the life of his friend. He knew Khatoran wouldn't mind. Soon the old Verdillion would have found a nice place to root, and when his roots were set, he would stop speaking, stop moving around. Stop thinking? No one knew.

When they reached the skiff'rin, Nu'mora joined them. Mha'arlo opened the gurgitator and they sped away from the gruynfeld, out across the teal waters of the Vergin Sea.

"Head to the southwest corner of the southwest quadrant," Nu'mora said, and Mha'arlo steered the skiff'rin to the right and opened the gurgitator to full aperture.

Even at top speed, Lithuigi felt they were crawling along.

I thought he'd only been working on his abomination in Balan Su, he thought. *How could I be so stupid?*

"We're headed for the Gotion Circle," Nu'mora said. "I've deactivated the security system, but we won't have long before someone notices."

"How'd you get clearance?" Lithuigi asked.

"I'm sorry, professor, but I've been working with Hesh'n for the last decade."

"On the Verdhesh'n?"

"What else," she said. "Your son is brilliant, the greatest mind of his generation. But he's—obsessive. Fanatical. I admire his dedication, but I fear for his sanity. When I understood what he intended, I—well, I didn't know what to do. I'd never faced such a situation. A Dyna'arin respects the work of other Dyna'arin, that's our rule. There's no framework for discussing morality with regards to our maquina, none at all. And then—then I found Anorian."

"More like Anorian found you," Lithuigi said.

"Hesh'n was here, just before you arrived," Nu'mora said. "He was—different. He looked awful. He told me he'd had an accident at his lab, that he'd lost a lot of his work. I knew you were a fugitive. But he never mentioned you, even though rumors spread among the Dyna'arin that you'd sabotaged his work. Rutar wouldn't confirm or deny it, but when Hesh'n was appointed professor in your stead, everyone took it as true. I'm surprised more didn't walk out when you took the stage."

"And now you risk being outcast as well," Lithuigi said. "You must know I'm going to destroy whatever I find?"

She nodded. "I can handle myself, professor, but thank you."

Lithuigi could see the Gotion Circle before they arrived, a small bump of land along the southern edge of Vergis, nearly a perfect circle, just barely sticking up from the water. The edges had been fortified and expanded to increase space. The island was covered in plants, a tiny forest interspersed with the metal hulls of maquina.

"Sweet Trevian," Lithuigi said. "Are those all spratlyns?"

Nu'mora nodded.

He's farther along than I feared. Some of them are nearly as tall as an adult! A forest of distorted and grotesque versions of my own son.

Lithuigi shuddered.

Mha'arlo killed the gurgitator and let the skiff'rin stall out on a nearby atoll.

That was when they heard the whine.

"A production facility," Nu'mora said. "Ingenious, really. Maquina fills the entire center of the circle. Just one flower is capable of producing tens of thousands of seeds, using beekyr berries as receptacles. Limbs on the outside are used to plant, join, and tend to the growing spratlyn. The underside of the island is supplied with nutrients to speed their growth to nearly ten times the normal rate."

"Ten times?" Lithuigi gasped. "But that would mean he can grow a full-sized Verdillion in just a few months."

He pulled a box out from under the bench, opened the locking mechanism, and handed two enflamers to Mha'arlo, and two to Nu'mora. He took two himself.

"Can you overload the dynamins?" Lithuigi asked.

"I'll see what I can do," Nu'mora said. She dove into the water and swam for the circle.

He and Mha'arlo sat and waited in silence for her return, and in spite of the sunshine and the sea, Lithuigi's thoughts were dark.

Several hours passed, and he began to despair. Surely something had gone wrong. But then he saw her waving to them. They both jumped in the sea and began to swim for the island.

"The dynamins will take out the maquina on the inside of the circle but it won't be enough to damage the groves on the outside of the circle," Nu'mora said.

Lithuigi palmed his enflamer. They started at one side and worked their way around, setting fire to the spratlyns. The ones on the outside of the island exploded into ashes as they were hit with the stream of glowing fire from the enflamers, and the ones on the inside began to char from the heat. As they swam back to the skiff'rin, the inferno grew larger behind them, the whine of the maquina got louder and louder, and then they heard something else.

They stopped, bobbing together in the water, to listen.

"Oh Sweet Trevian, no," Nu'mora cried. "The spratlyns! Their taprins are burning through before…"

Amongst the din of the fire and the buzzing of overloading dynamins was the unmistakable sound of Verdillion screams. Not any scream, but the screeching cry of a freshly cut scamp waking to the world—of ten thousand scamps waking at the same time. But to Lithuigi, it was the sound of Hesh'n, of his own scamp, his precious scamp, screaming, howling—ten thousand of them, ten thousand Hesh'n's, waking into death.

Lithuigi sank under the surface, trying to drown out the noise, but he couldn't escape from the din.

Chapter 53

Nothing to Make Sense of Anymore

Bryn and Jaun left Roman Anthem trussed up in the battered cata'rin. If he was going to signal for help, he'd have already done so via crystamin. They had no bhiza to drug him, and no scytherin to slit his crystal. And besides, Bryn no longer knew what to make of him. Who was this strange Bhizini turned Cul'tavin peacekeeper who claimed to be helping them? He had indeed sailed them out of Balance Territories and into the Far Ocean. But was the interrogation, the torture, really a ruse? She didn't have time to find out. She could only hope that if Anthem had signaled for help from the Pradishar, that they'd be too afraid to sail into Guild-controlled waters. Rumors that the Dyna'arin had secret maquina capable of vaporizing a heavy cruiser kept all but the most foolish away from their holdings.

And we're about to break in to one of their labs, Bryn thought. *Have I lost my mind?*

A tram took them to what Jaun called the Fish Bowl, a massive open area with a roof of domed glass, above which the teal waters of the Vergin Sea swirled and sparkled. Hundreds of fish in surging schools passed over them, chased by a shark, while a manta ray, undisturbed, took it's time hovering over the lower corner, the edges of its fins like ripples on the shore. Along the sides of the great space were an assortment of places to eat, sleep, groom, and shop. The floor was divided in two, with half of the room designed like the plaza in a city, with fountains and grassy patches to perch interspersed with colorful stone statues and low shrubs and hedges. The other half looked like some sort of exhibition area or museum.

Bryn was grinning like an idiot in spite of herself, and she put her hands together and clapped with joy. "What's over there?" she said, pointing at the exhibits.

"We tinkers call it the Exploricon. It's sort of a playground for prototypes, or for maquina that have no practical value but are just neat. Sometimes you just need to goof around a bit to get the creativity flowing."

Bryn looked at Jaun. "Do we have a minute to play?" Now her hands were together in a praying gesture.

He frowned. "We better not draw any attention to ourselves."

She let her face fall. "You're right. Damnit. Let's go."

"This way."

They crossed the edge of the plaza portion of the Fish Bowl to the opposite side from which they'd entered, and headed down a staircase to a different tram. When they'd taken a seat, Bryn looked up at the schematics for the line, which had been painted onto the stone wall just below the ceiling. Her eyes followed it from where they had started, at one end of the line, all the way to the other.

"Is this line really thirty miles long?"

"Yes," Jaun said. "All of Vergis—that is to say, all of the Guild's installation at Vergis—are subterranean. And though I probably shouldn't tell you this, there's even a tram that leads directly to Callo Baton."

"How did the Dyna'arin build all of this?"

"It strains the mind, doesn't it," Jaun said. "Until you recall that the Dyna'arin have had an endless supply of slaves from Raccorum Rhazzat for, oh, ten thousand years or longer. Rhank do most of the large building projects for the Guild, even today."

Bryn's face fell. "Right," she said. "Sort of renders the achievement, I don't know, unworthy of celebrating?"

"Indeed."

Jaun's eyes twitched and the tram began to slow.

"This line passes by many of the individual labs," he said. "Each tinker can also have up to five square miles on the surface to themselves for research and development."

When the vehicle stopped, glowbes crackled to life, and they stepped out onto a small platform. A single corridor led to a stair heading upward. They took the steps until they reached a landing. There was a door in front of them, and the stairs curved back and continued upward behind them.

Bryn tried to imagine her father there, but couldn't. What was she going to find inside? Did she even want to know?

She reached for the locking mechanism with her mind, and felt Jaun there beside her, touching the crystamin shards inside the fungal fibers at the bottom of the maquina.

<<I never mimicked my father's Guild credentials, only his Pradishar ones,>> Bryn said. <<I can't access a Guild servryn. I'm not sure what to do.>>

<<Use me,>> Jaun said. <<I'll sync with you as the Corkin sync with their masters, and my body and mind will be as your own, under your will.>>

<<Will that work? We don't have imperial crystals.>>

<<It's the only idea I have,>> Jaun said. <<And I'm willing to try if you are.>>

<<Very well, but I've never done anything like this. I'm not even sure what it will feel like, or how to control it.>>

<<Nor do I. Ready?>>

Jaun took her hands in his and closed his eyes, and Bryn reached for him with her mind, finding him in the hollow. Bryn felt his crystals then, all four of them. She felt Jaun opening both his thoughts and his sensations to her, but not in the way a trouper might perform a melodrama, but instead it was an open invitation, not only to peek in, but to step up and take hold of, and direct. She felt his hands clench hers when she clutched him with her will.

Jaun's eyes opened and Bryn saw herself through them. She turned her own head side to side, but it was Juan's that moved, not hers. She could feel his fear, and his excitement, and his pain, but she closed it off from her awareness, eager not to violate his privacy. Then, using Jaun's mind and his Dyna'arin crystal, she reached for the Guild servryn.

She found the cortex, and once inside, began to slip through the streams of data, flowing across them and through them, until she found her father's docket and cloaked herself with the metadata. Then she reached for the lock and sent the signal to open it. When she heard the maquina whine and the lock click, she let go of Jaun's mind and his hands, and he staggered to the side but didn't fall.

"Sweet Trevian," he said, out of breath.

"Are you alright?"

He nodded. "I think so. Wow. I'm—at a loss for words, if you'll believe it."

"Yes," Bryn said. "I don't even know how that was possible."

"But it worked," he said. "I knew you could do it!"

"We did it together." Bryn looked at the door. "Shall we?"

"After you," Jaun said.

Her heart was racing when she grabbed the handle and turned. She pulled the door open, just a tiny slit, and peeked inside.

Someone was in the lab! They had their back to her, but she could see an Andrasian, tools in hand, leaning over a workstation, busily tinkering.

Jaun crouched down to peek under her and he gasped.

<<Ready to bust in?>> she said, not waiting for his answer.

She was halfway across the room when the Andrasian stood up and turned to face her.

Bryn stopped in mid-stride and started moving backward, bumping into Jaun who tried to step out of her way. He scrambled to the side, saw what she was staring at, and screamed.

Doc Andri'n was standing before them, wiping his hands on his robes, a sad smile on his face.

❧ ❧

Bryn couldn't breath, and the harder she tried, the less her lungs would fill, and the more it hurt when they did.

I saw him, she thought. *I saw him die.*

The memory of burning flesh flooded in from her crystal and she bent over and retched but nothing came out.

"You're dead!" she sputtered.

Her father just stared at her, a knowing look on his face.

Jaun had stopped screaming, and he took a few nervous steps forward, staring at the Andrasian, examining him.

"Who are you?" he said, and Bryn saw that Jaun was short of breath too.

"I'm not who you think I am," the Andrasian said. "Though I know this must be confusing for you."

Bryn stared at him again and realized he didn't quite look like her father. There was something slightly off about him. Like her father, but decades ago. Doc Andri'n had been nearly 140 years old, but this plant couldn't be more than an hundred years.

"You're a duplicant," Jaun said, noticing as well.

"Yes," he said.

Jaun walked close to him, raised his hand, and poked his shoulder. "Just checking," he said.

"I'm very much alive," the stranger said. "But I suppose you can't be too cautious. Can I assume that you're Bryn?"

She nodded, tears on the edge of her eyes, and the pain in her chest felt like she'd taken an axe to her heart. Her father had been alive again, and then gone again, in a flash.

"If you're here, then that must mean—our father is dead?"

"*My* father," Bryn hissed.

"Of course," he said.

"We expected this lab to be empty," Jaun said.

"I can see you weren't expecting to find me," he said.

Bryn choked back the sobs. Hearing her father's voice—it was too much. And why—why had her father reproduced asexually? It was a crime against nature, something that everyone in Balance would look on with horror. He had to know that. Why—why would he do it?

"Who are you," Bryn whispered. "Why—*why* are you?" A single tear ran down each cheek.

"Your father was an extraordinary plant," he said. "An extraordinarily kind and gentle plant. A plant who spent all of his energy trying to protect life, and to enrich it. I was a mistake, Bryn. I wish I knew all the details, but Doc Andri'n had many secrets. And while I share the exact body as him, I don't have his memories, and I wasn't privy to all of his plots. I only know that he began working with spratlyns when he was a young, up and coming tinker—and in exile from his home. He used his own spratlyns, since it was convenient to make and grow them, and because it helped assuage his moral doubts about the work he was doing. He was always careful not to sever the taprin while he worked, not to awaken the spratlyn to sentience. He always made sure there was no pain, no suffering of any kind. But, in spite of his intentions, and the care he took, a mistake was made. As he described it, never had a slip of his own hand so drastically altered fate. The taprin was severed, the spratlyn opened its eyes and started screaming, and he had no choice—as he told it—not to take care of me."

Bryn was weeping softly but said nothing.

"He raised me himself, on Callo Baton and Aga Baton, teaching me everything he knew, until I came of age. I knew he missed your mother, and that exile from Andramere was slowly but surely crushing his spirit. He wanted to teach, to have a family—a real family—and he had work to do. And as for me—well, I knew I had no place in Balance Authority, and would struggle to find a place in the Guild as a duplicant. So father—Doc Andri'n—arranged for me to be joined with a Guild crystamin, one identical to his own. Since the Guild won't track their own, it was possible for me to live and work here without anyone the wiser. And this has allowed me to carry out Doc Andri'n's will wherever he needed me to carry it out."

"I can't believe this," she said. "I can't—handle this!"

"I'm sorry, Bryn. Just know that Father would have told you if he thought it was safe to do so."

"I don't know anything," she said. "Not a thing in the world."

"I came here hoping for some answers," Jaun said, "only you've given us more questions than either of us can comprehend right now. I think my friend needs some time to deal."

"Funny thing about time," the Andrasian said.

She had heard her father say that so many times. Any time she'd complained about a deadline, or rarely about boredom, her father would start, 'Funny thing about time,' and Bryn would groan. But hearing it now, out of the duplicant's mouth, made something click in her mind. Or was it in her heart?

"When you want it to go fast, it crawls," she said. "And when you wish it would slow, it is already gone." She looked at the plant that looked like her father through her tears. He grinned at her, and Bryn felt her heart breaking.

"It's good to finally meet you," he said. "Your father loved you very much."

"Our father," Bryn said, and he smiled again.

But the smile faded. "I wish we'd met under different circumstances. And I wish our time was not already up."

Jaun's eyes were twitching. "Enforcers incoming! Something's happened. There's been several explosions in the area."

"And worse," the Andrasian said. "Someone knows you're both here, and they don't want you to leave. You must go, quickly. Up the stairs to the surface. There's a cata'rin waiting to take you to safety."

"Come with us!" she said.

"You're sweet, Bryn, but I have work to get done here."

Bryn hesitated. "What's your name?"

He smiled. "I'm Daun'athyn."

"Named after an uncle?" Jaun said.

Daun nodded.

"Then you do know what happened during the Crisis!" Jaun said.

"Only bits and pieces. I'm sorry Jaun, but the answers you seek are not here, but on Andramere. Now go! Not a moment to lose."

They started for the door, but Bryn turned back.

"Will you be alright?"

"Of course," Daun said. "Now, up the stairs with you. Quickly."

Bryn took one more look at this plant who looked like her father, who sounded like her father. His eyes even twinkled like her father's. He smiled at her, a sad smile, his eyes full of tears. And he closed the door.

She heard the lock slide into place, and a noise from down below—the enforcers arriving on a tram. And then she heard something else—a buzzing sound like a swarm of insects as the dynamins inside the lab began to overload.

Daun'athyn was going to blow up the lab!

She turned back to the door and pounded on it—she reached for the lock with her mind but she no longer had the authorization—she screamed and wailed and beat the door, but the buzzing grew louder and louder.

"Don't move!" The voice was in her ear.

Bryn froze when she felt the Vintrani blade at her neck. The metal felt cool, refreshing even. She thought of it slicing through the layers of her skin, down through the fibers, severing her head, freeing her from the ache inside, the pain that seemed to be everywhere, that made the entire world groan with her.

<<Don't give up, Bryndax.>> Anorian was with her, holding her, whispering softly in her mind. <<I need you. Please.>>

"Turn around!"

The blade lifted slightly and Bryn pivoted on her feet. Two Guild enforcers, metal masks over their faces, had Bryn and Jaun both at sword-point. They were massive, and their thick forms nearly filled the width of the stair, but Bryn could see more enforcers coming up from below. And the one who had stopped Jaun was coming down the stair from above. They were trapped.

And then the dynamins in the lab blew, and though the walls and doors were sealed off, the ground shook and the stairs rattled, and the noise was like being in the midst of a wave when it sweeps you up and tumbles you head over heels along the shore—like a tram rattling right over the top of you.

Bryn looked up at Jaun but he had put his back against the wall, and there was a headless corpse where the enforcer once stood, the torso and the arms that clutched the Vintrani blade slowly sinking to the ground, the head already down next to it, the metal mask still in place over the face. The stairs above Jaun were littered with headless corpses. She struggled to understand what she was seeing.

The enforcer guarding her turned to look, and Bryn, recklessly suicidal or incredibly brave, grabbed their arm and pushed it upward while slamming her foot into their kneecap. The enforcer tumbled down the stairs, knocking down the ones coming up behind them, and howling with pain. She picked up the Vintrani blade, looked at Jaun, and started up the steps.

They had to climb over the bodies to get up the stairs, which were sticky with sap. At the top was an open hatch overhead, daylight streaming in. Bryn climbed through and stepped out onto a sandy atoll on the edge of a reef, and froze.

Jaun came up from behind, slammed the hatch, then froze too.

Half a dozen Guild cata'rins were strewn across the atoll, some of them torn in two, thick black plumes of smoke rising from their smoldering hulls. A single cata'rin floated just offshore, in the open ocean, unharmed. The bodies of half a dozen squadrons of enforcers were tossed about on the atoll, or floating in the sea, or burning in heaps, and the fires crackled and popped, and Bryn wanted to cut out her ears to make the sound stop.

A few enforcers were still standing, fighting a single hooded figure in a long, tattered pradeshan robe. Bryn and Jaun were dumbstruck as they watched the figure swirl and twirl, his sword singing as it sliced through the air, a blur of purple and gray that effortlessly cut down the remaining resistance. When the last enforcer fell, the figure sheathed his weapon and turned to them.

How? Bryn thought. *How does he move like that?*

"There'll be more, so we should hurry." He pointed toward the cata'rin.

Bryn's mouth fell open.

"I don't believe it," Jaun said.

The figure pulled off their hood.

It was Roman Anthem.

"Let's go," he said.

Jaun looked at Bryn.

<<Do we have a choice?>> he asked in her mind.

She took another look at the wreckage and back at the hatch.

<<None.>>

Anthem saw them hesitating. "Is this any way to treat your rescuer? Come on already."

"How'd you escape the ship?" Jaun said.

"Later, von Andron. Let's go!"

"How do we know you didn't summon the enforcers?" Jaun said. "How do we know this isn't all an elaborate ruse to get us to trust you?"

"Because Anorian sent me. And if you don't believe me, ask her yourself."

Her?

She reached for Anorian. <<Is it true? Are you working with Roman Anthem?>>

<<It's complicated,>> Anorian said. <<Sometimes he follows orders. Sometimes he does what he wants. I have asked him to bring you to me. He agreed. He will not betray his word. I know that much for sure.>>

Bryn felt the tears burning her eyes, the betrayal cutting deep in her heart, and she could feel Anorian's pain, and regret, and it made her own pain that much worse.

<<Bryndax—please—>>

But Bryn cut the connection. She wanted to scream in frustration, to scream at Anorian for all the secrets, to scream at her father for all of his. It felt like all her effort, all her will to hold together, to care about anything, had vanished, and there was nothing left but an empty shell.

"Let's go," she whispered, as the smoke billowed across the sand, choking her. "Please, I don't care where you take us, just as long as it's not here."

"Then hurry aboard," Anthem said. "It's still a long way to P'anorum."

Chapter 54

Home But Not Home

THE THREE PEAKS OF P'anorum grew and grew until they filled Rakk's vision, but it still didn't feel real to him. The fact that he was there again had not gotten through yet. Nothing was reaching him, not even the fact that Fin'roq was his brother and that Ellex had not one scamp but two with his father—nor that Ellex was, even now, still wringing her hands and crying, but saying nothing, while Bhea held her.

Rakk could feel her eyes on him, needing him to let her know that everything was okay, that he was okay, but he couldn't. There weren't words. There weren't even feelings. Just an empty hole inside of him. When he looked up and saw the ruins of the palace on the cliff, he didn't see the last remnants of his home, just rubble like you might find around Lake Ma'sheik, refuse of the long gone and long forgotten. P'anorum had lived in his memories for so long that to suddenly have the real thing in front of him somehow made it all seem immaterial.

Sweet Trevian, how he didn't want to be there. How he didn't want to be anywhere anymore!

If only Q'orin were here, he thought. *He would know what to say. He always knew what to say, or do. He always kept me from being a fool, and an even bigger failure than I already am. Why did I send him away? Why did I come back here? There's nothing here but pain. There's nothing anywhere but pain.*

Rakk felt a poke in his ribs and he turned to see Qaas'i staring up at him, and when he saw the concern in her eyes, the fear on her speckled face, the hole inside of him was gone, suddenly full to bursting. He grinned at her and picked her up with one arm.

"Ooof!" he said. "How heavy you're getting! Look at those long legs! You'll be as tall as me one day soon, won't you love?" He kissed her cheek. "Your big brother won't be able to pick you up anymore."

Qaas'i hugged him around the neck and squeezed tightly, and Rakk patted her hair and finally let his eyes find Ellex. She was smiling at them through her tears. He opened his other arm and she dropped her eyes as she ran into the embrace, and Qaas'i put one of her arms around Ellex's neck and squeezed her too.

There were still no words, but now there didn't need to be.

Bhea docked the cata'rin while the Tornroot fleet trickled into the harbor. They had brought skiff'rins and dolph'rins and cano'rins and they began tying them together while placing planks width-wise across the boats, and soon there were boardwalks from the beach and the pier to all the largest ships. The Tornroot were flitting around on lilypads between the larger craft, or spreading up the shore and exploring the burned-out huts along the edge of the sand.

Rakk saw that the old port building and beachfront house he remembered from his youth were gone, but the palace was still up on the edge of the rim. He could hear the breakers hitting the cliffs outside the harbor, and could even smell the Swarthen Forest snaking up the Crag behind him. For a moment, he was a scamp again, coming down for a swim in the morning, or for a swim in the evening, or any other time he could get away and into the water. Even now he was tempted to throw off his robe and take a dip, on the very shore where he'd first learned to love the sea and to be as comfortable in the water as he was on land.

The Tornroot already had fires roaring on the sand and rhupan on the grill, and they were banging the drums and blowing their flutes and horns, and some were dancing. But Rakk wasn't hungry, or festive. The emptiness had returned when he stepped foot on the sand, and now it seemed ready to suck him under.

So he started up the path for the palace, following the narrow, rocky steps as they cut back and forth up the face of the rim. The sun had dropped behind the opposite side of the crater and the harbor sat down in the shadows below, but the porch of the palace was still in the sunshine and seemed to sit beneath a golden spotlight, and he remembered then that P'anorum wasn't just home, but also the most beautiful place in the world.

When he reached the promenade at the top of the rim, someone was sitting near the porch, gazing across the crater, through the collapsed opening and out over the wide expanse of the Far Ocean. Rakk could tell from the bright skin that it was a Raccorin. And his first thought was that it was his father. But when he turned to face him, he saw that he'd been wrong.

"Grizzly Old Grants, is it really you?"

The gruff old warrior's face broke into a wide grin, but then remembering himself, he dropped to his knee and bowed.

"My prince," Grizmond said. "You've come home at last."

Rakk grabbed him by the arms and pulled him to his feet and hugged the old Raccorin.

"Great Sower in the sky, it's good to see you. Bhea didn't tell me you'd survived."

"It was easier to pretend I was dead," he said, "than to live as a fugitive."

"Your crystals," Rakk said, noticing the pits in his forehead.

He nodded and pulled a scytherin from his robe. He handed the blade to Rakk.

"Your father used that very blade to slit them," Grizmond said, "on the night P'anorum blew."

Rakk shook his head. "You were his closest advisor, his friend. Why would he let you go?"

"Because he trusted only me to stay behind on P'anorum, out of the view of the Pradishar or anyone else who might peek in on my crystals, and help keep his offspring safe. To see that Fin'roq came of age."

"Fin'roq," Rakk said. "Bhea would have us pin our hopes on him. He's supposed to take us under the island, down to the ruins of the Temple of Trevian. But he hasn't even made himself seen. I haven't had a chance to talk to him, to tell him I'm his brother. I feel guilty about asking so much of him. The poor guy's had a rough time of it, and I'm not sure he's up for it. And to ask so much of him—it just seems so selfish."

"You two have a lot in common," Grizmond said. "I watched you both grow up. Both of you loved Bhea Bell, Baboo, and the Swarthen Forest. And neither of you could stay out of the water!"

Rakk grinned.

"And when Fin'roq was just a scamp, he loved nothing more than going down into the tunnels under P'anorum. He's been into the city, my prince. It's still there—still preserved under the crystal. You can go and walk the streets of P'anorum again. Fin'roq can take you. He—" Grizmond stopped when he saw Rakk's face. "Forgive me, my prince. I didn't mean to upset you."

"I'm not upset, just surprised. Just—" He exhaled hard and looked at the palace, at the glowing red and black crystal lava flow that rose up from the rocky ruin, stretched across the top of the old city and up the slopes of the great mountain, til it vanished away into the clouds that hugged the crater far overhead. "I don't know," he said. "I just don't know."

Grizmond put his hand on Rakk's shoulder and squeezed it.

"You know, when Fin'roq grew up here, there were only a handful of us on the island. They weren't too nice to him either, always making him feel, well, like a damn dirty

Bhizini that didn't belong here. But Fin, he did everything he could to make them like him. He took Roe and Aar'ryn under the island because he thought it would make the villagers accept him.

"After what happened down there, half of them wanted to kill Fin'roq, but the other half were convinced he was possessed by a Mund'umbrian. They wanted to drive it out of him, with a long, drawn out death over a low fire. That was the thanks he got for doing exactly what they wanted him to do. But in spite of all that, he still wanted their affection. Before Fin departed, Roman Anthem placed restraining crystals on every villager. And as Fin sailed away, he watched a fleet of Qardymion's Pal'merans butchering everyone he'd spent his life trying to please, his home destroyed in front of his eyes. If you'd heard the cry he made when he saw it happening—well, you'd have fallen to your knees, like the Bhizini did, in wonder and in terror. And you'd have prayed that that pain never got a chance to grow and fester and spread out into the world."

Rakk was silent for a moment, then spoke softly. "Thank you for sharing that, old friend. I've been lost without Q'orin to advise me, and I find I'm nothing on my own. I'll go and talk to Fin'roq, right away."

"Very good, my prince," he said.

Rakk offered him the scytherin.

"I've been waiting to give it to you," Grizmond said. "It was originally your aunt Rhae'vyn's, and she passed it to your father when she abdicated the throne."

"I know what it means to you, if you want to keep it."

"You'll need it more than me," he said. "My fighting days are almost over. But you have a long way to go still before you can relax."

He sighed. "Don't I know it. I will treasure this blade."

"Tell Fin'roq I'm glad he's home and look forward to seeing him."

"Will do," he said. "And thanks again."

⁂

When Rakk returned to the beach, Bhea, Ellex, and Qaas'andria were nowhere to be found. One of the Tornroot let him know they'd headed for Bhea's garden, out in the Swarthen Forest. He asked after Fin'roq but nobody could say where he was. Finally one of the men on the pier had seen him heading to the west end of the beach, so Rakk went to investigate.

At the end of the sand, he found a small stair that led to a flat rocky outcropping ringed with thick brambles of bougainvillea, a patchwork of green leaves and dark purple flowers. Rakk didn't remember anything being there before, but now it was a sort of open-air makeshift sharlum, and really a lovely space.

Fin'roq was sitting on the dais and he looked at Rakk when he entered, but his face stayed blank.

Rakk looked at him and tried to hide his surprise. It was like looking at Qaas'andria, only larger, wider, thicker in the shoulders. But the face, the skin—they weren't just siblings, they were duplicants.

How did I not see that before? he thought. *And how can duplicants be the same age? It's not possible.*

The questions would have to wait.

"Hi Fin'roq," he said. "Mind if I join you?"

Fin shrugged.

Rakk sat down next to him, then picked up a rock and turned it over in his hands. A few bits of barnacle were still stuck to one side, and he scratched at them mindlessly with his fingernails.

"How are you?" he said, knowing it sounded stupid, and knowing he felt stupid asking.

"I'm really not in the mood to talk," Fin said.

"Me neither," Rakk said. "It was a stupid question, I know. How could you be alright? You've come home but it's not home any more. Everything that made it home is gone. You know because you watched it being destroyed, watched your people dying. But now you find you can't even feel sad about it, because it feels so alien. You're certain you must be someplace else."

Fin'roq looked at him. "You're Prince Rhakksees."

He nodded. "Call me Raeder."

"You grew up here. The palace—that was your home."

"Yes."

"I'm sorry," he said, sighing. "I didn't mean to be rude. I just have a lot on my mind. I just—well, I guess maybe you understand. At least part of it. What it feels like to be here again."

"How strange that we both grew up here, both learning from Bhea Bell, both swimming right here in this harbor, two brothers in separate times, in the same place and yet as if it were in a different world."

"So it's true? You're my brother? King Rhakksees is my father? Ellex Andria—" But he trailed off.

"I've only just found out myself," Rakk said. "Otherwise, I would have come and found you immediately. I never would have left you to languish on this ruined hunk of rock had I known you were here. Had I known *anyone* was here! But I've been lied to and manipulated by just about everyone, it seems."

"I guess we have that in common, too," Fin said.

"Still, it's no excuse. I'm to blame for what happened to you. If I'd been even halfway competent, I'd have known there were survivors here. If I hadn't been a coward, I would have sailed here long ago, prohibition or not. If I had kept Balan Su safe, you wouldn't have been taken off the streets of the capital by the Pal'merans. I've failed you, brother. And I'm probably failing you again, coming back here and wanting something from you, when you've already been through so much."

Fin'roq didn't say anything.

"Is it true, that the streets of P'anorum are still walkable? That the plazas, the buildings—that it's all still there, under the lava flow?"

"Did she tell you?" Fin said. "Bhea, I mean?"

"Grizmond," he said, "who sends his greetings and looks forward to seeing you."

"It's all there," Fin said. "Though not all of it's accessible. I used to play there when I was younger. It always felt so familiar to me, so safe, like it was my own. Do you—want me to take you there?"

"I don't want you to do anything that'll make you uncomfortable."

"It won't be! The sunlight passes through the crystal, so it's not dark. And—we can go there on our way to the Temple of Trevian."

"Are you sure? I mean, that you're okay with it?"

Fin nodded, and Rakk clapped him on the shoulder, a wide grin on his bright green face. "That's my brave brother!"

"Not brave," Fin said. "Foolish, perhaps. Curious, a little bit. Maybe. And terrified. Definitely terrified."

"Well, I'll be right there with you. You're my family, Fin'roq, my own sap."

"I don't know what that means," Fin said. "I gave up imagining I had any family long ago. And now suddenly I have a mother, a father, a brother, and a sister—and more still that I haven't met. But I don't know you. And I told myself I wasn't going to blindly trust anyone ever again. So I'll go under the island, and I'll take you where you need to go, but

I don't have any illusions that you're going to protect me from what I have to face, nor that your intention hasn't been, the entire time, to find answers to your own problems, not mine."

Rakk could feel his ears burning.

"When I first saw you on that stream, you were just another Bhizini, face-less, like the many thousands I've slaughtered over the years," Rakk said. "But when I saw you that evening in the Regalia—" He paused and looked at Fin'roq. "I recognized you, and not from the stream either. I think I recognized our father in you, and your mother in you. And I wanted to be nice to you, and protect you. Just like when I first saw your sister, Qaas'andria."

"You were kind to me that day," Fin'roq said. "Thank you. If you hadn't been there, I don't know what Ellex Andria would have done to me. Thrown me in the Dankburn and left me to petrify, probably."

Rakk chuckled. "You're probably right. And you make a good point, Fin, you really do. You're a stranger to me, too. And trust is a precious thing. Just because someone is family doesn't mean they have your best interests at heart."

He thought of Rhannokti, the slave who had been his brother all along, and yet he'd never noticed, until it was too late. He thought of the malice he'd seen in his eyes, and of how different it could have been, if he had just known—if he could have reached out before.

"But look," Rakk said, "I know you've had some bad experiences with Ellex—with your mother—but I hope you know how upset she is about how she treated you."

"Good," Fin said. "She should be. She tortured me! And worse, she humiliated me in front of the whole world. The things she said to me—no, the *way* she said them. It was pure malice. She *hated* me, and she didn't even know me."

"Now she knows you're her son," he said. "And she's broken-hearted, wondering how she can ever make it up to you."

"Good," he said again, with less conviction. "She—"

"She's a victim, too, Fin. Just like we've been played, she's been played. The Ellex I know—the Ellex she is again now, I promise—she wouldn't hurt you like that. She wouldn't."

Fin'roq didn't say anything.

"Is it going to be a problem, taking her under the island?"

Fin sighed then, and his shoulders slumped. "No," he said. "It won't be. I just—of all Verdillion, in the entire world, why—why—*why* does it have to be her? Why does she have to be my mother?"

"I wish I had that answer," Rakk said. "And so does she. Maybe we can find out together."

Chapter 55

The Enemy Without a Face

ELLEX ANDRIA HATED THIS island.

Not that it wasn't gorgeous. And not that she didn't look forward to her yearly trips there when she was a scamp, or afterward in those first years in public service. No, Ellex hated P'anorum for what it represented—complete and utter waste. Unspent potential. Lives that should have been, or could have been, but now never would be.

Meaninglessness.

Or maybe it was something more visceral. For three decades, Ellex had woken to the image of her father slowly fading, and in the confusion of the early morning, she'd have to remind herself that he was gone. He had died here, at this place that she couldn't bear to name without feeling like her head would explode.

But now she could think of it, could think of P'anorum. Ever since her dream had been shared with the world, she'd been able to, although she hadn't done so, even though she knew she needed to. Now that she was here, feeling P'anorum on her feet, smelling it in the air, taking it all in with her eyes and ears—it was still awful, even without the headaches.

I spent an entire year on P'anorum, watching Qaas'andria, watching Fin'roq grow. And Bhea Bell—the old Bhizini feels like a grandmother, her presence so warm and gentle and familiar—how could I not remember spending so much time with someone so special, so divine?

And Fin'roq. She hadn't recognized her own offspring—had even gone out of her way to make him miserable. She'd wanted him imprisoned. Exiled. Dead, even.

I'll never be able to recover from that, she thought. *He and I, we never will either.*

When she finally saw Fin'roq face to face for the first time since the gala on the eve of the Balancing Act, it was the day after arriving on P'anorum, and he was standing on the promenade near the palace, catching the mid-morning sunshine, his eyes closed, his pradeshan robe open down his chest and hanging off his arms. At first she thought it was Qaas'i, only too tall, and too broad in the shoulders.

Sweet Trevian, they're identical. Even the markings on their skin! I knew Qaas'i was mine when I saw her. How did I not know he was? And how—how are they the same?

Ellex swallowed hard and was about to speak when Fin'roq opened his eyes. He looked at her feet.

"Good morning, Sui Pradesh. Ready to depart?"

"Yes, good morning, thank you, Fin'roq. Thanks." She smiled but he didn't look up.

"There's our handsome guide," Rakk said, joining them on the promenade.

Fin blushed. "Did you bring the glowbes?"

"One for you," Rakk said, "and one for you, and one for me."

"Water?"

Ellex passed out the satchels.

"Now all we need is luck," Fin said. "And maybe a prayer or two."

Rakk exhaled hard and Ellex took his arm.

"You ready for this?" she said.

He nodded. "Let's go."

"Shall we?" Ellex said.

❧ ☙

Fin'roq nodded, his teeth clenched so tightly his jaw hurt.

"This way," he said, staring at the ground as he started toward the palace.

Here we go, he thought. *I can do this. I used to love this more than anything. I used to believe I was king of this island. Through the Inner Door, I knew it was mine. I knew—I don't know what I knew. It doesn't matter. Just take one step at a time. Keep the glowbe lit. Stay close to Raeder. You'll be fine.*

"Sweet Trevian," he whispered, "give me courage to face the dark path, strength to follow it where I must, and the good fortune to learn from the experience."

"Reciting the Pruu'log?" Ellex said, and Fin's ears burned but he didn't turn back to scowl at her as he so desperately wanted to.

"Yes," he said. "I always loved to study lore, even as a little scamp. I've wanted to be a monkin for as long as I could remember."

"Just a monkin?" she said.

"I was studying to be a Me'dicant healer. I might have wanted to be a Cul'tavin peacekeeper, but I went to Balan Su and saw what they've become, how vicious and cruel they are, nothing at all like the selfless servants Trevian described." Fin's heart was pounding but his voice stayed steady.

"I had that very conversation with the Gran Pradesh, many times in fact," Ellex said. "He too hates what the Cul'tavin have become."

Fin'roq stopped walking and turned back to Ellex, and he looked into her eyes for the first time.

"Am I in trouble for what happened at the Balancing Act? I don't know for sure what I did, but I know I did something."

"I—" Ellex paused, looking perplexed. "I don't know if you are. I scarcely paid attention to affairs on the Council of Nine in those last sessions before we adjourned for the summer. And my crystamin is numb from bhiza, so I can't pull the information from the servryn."

"But you're Sui Pradesh, right? You have the authority to reinstate me? To make me a monkin again? To let me finish my annual?" Fin felt like he was panting.

Ellex looked at Rakk, then back at Fin'roq. "I may," she said. "My own position on the Council is complicated by—well, by you and Qaas'andria. I'm not sure how long I'll be able to keep serving. But—I'll do whatever I can to see you're reinstated, if that's really what you want to do."

"Thank you, Sui Pradesh," he said, and he bowed to her.

I'm ready, he thought. *Let's do this. Into the darkness once more.*

❧ ❦

Rakk held up his glowbe and looked around, but he wasn't sure where they were. He'd rarely ventured beneath the palace after his father had abandoned him in the darkness when he was a scamp, extinguishing all the lights and leaving him to find his own way out. Even now the air felt heavy all around him, pressing down on his shoulders, threatening to suffocate him, and he was grateful for the glowbe.

Fin'roq led them down a series of stairs and into a long, narrow corridor. Then they ascended a stair and at the top they found an empty doorway lit in a musky red. Fin'roq stood in the threshold, his head turned to the side, looking back at them, and his profile looked like Ellex.

Rakk realized that he was trembling.

Ell, he wanted to cry. *Stop! Don't go through that door. Please, don't leave me again! Please!*

But he froze, saying nothing, then took a step, then one more, then another, til he was at the door and through it, and—he didn't know what he'd expected. The long avenue that led down the foot of the Crag, from the gates of the palace to the heart of the city, once had a magnificent view across the tops of the buildings as they dropped from the steep sides of the great mountain to the sea. But now there was a narrow cave, barely lit with a red, smoldering light, and water trickled down the cobblestones in dirty rivulets, down the avenue he had walked so many countless times. The walls of the cave were a mixture of soil and ashy sediment while overhead a roof of crystal sparkled and shimmered and seemed to pop with little bursts of light as he walked along looking at it.

Glowing, he thought, *as if it still burned.*

He reached out and touched the rooftop where it hung low over the walkway, and he was surprised at how cool it felt, how smooth. But when he pulled up his hand, there were tendrils of sap running down his palm, and he saw that he'd sliced his skin open, not deeply, but narrowly, finely. And as soon as he noticed it, it began to sting.

"Be careful not to touch the crystal," he said.

"Are you okay?" Ellex asked.

"They aren't deep. So this is the old avenue. Sure looks different."

"Yeah," Ellex said. She took his arm again and Rakk tried to swallow but his throat didn't want to work right.

Fin'roq led on, down through the sloping cave, and Rakk used his rootpads on the cobblestones so he wouldn't slip. When the ground started to flatten out, the cave began to get wider, until the entire road was clear and he could see the walls of the buildings on either side.

"What is that up ahead?" Ellex said, dropping his arm. She started to jog forward, and Rakk squinted ahead, but the light was so musty, he couldn't tell. He took a few more steps forward and realized what it was that she had seen. The avenue was giving way to the Commons, the sprawling plaza at the heart of the city, a massive park sitting between the Forum, the Academicon, the marketplace, a lorchen of the Loricean faith and a sharlum of the Pradishar, a theater, even a small colosseum. The Commons spanned both sides of the Flamewater, a small but brisk stream which cut the city in half with it's cascades of steaming hot, fragrant water. Overhead, the lava flow sparkled and shimmered a good thirty or forty feet above them, and the plaza below looked like a large arena barely lit in red.

He took a few steps in one direction, then a few in another, looking around at the facades of the buildings jutting up into the crystal overhead, the fountains and some of the statues still intact, the Flamewater purring as it tumbled down to the sea.

But it still wasn't real to him, not yet, not until he saw the front porch of the theater, with it's silly columns of costumed Verdillions holding up the roof while striking a variety of hilarious or highly suggestive poses. When he did, he smiled and finally took a breath, finally wanted to breath again, and the air flooded his senses with the rich, pungent scent of the Flamewater and its colorful, mineral-crusted banks. The smell swept him away, across time, to another age, when he was a different plant and the world a different place.

He was home again.

P'anorum, the city of dreams, the place he loved more than any other. The most beautiful, most colorful, most fragrant and festive city anywhere in the world, and the place he always knew—always *knew*—he'd spend his life ruling. He knew it's every nook and cranny, or so he thought, and so he felt. And he loved it's residents, all of them, from those in the shiny towers of Eastside to those in the old crumbling stones of Cragside. And he wanted to be their king, their patron, their protector, and their friend.

He imagined his father then, dressed in a long flowing gown, marching back and forth on the porch in front of the theater, the entire plaza full to bursting, hoping for a glance of the king performing one of his favorite roles. He saw his friend Qaa'milo ducking through the crowd and down into one of the alleyways, a big grin on his face, up to no good for sure. He saw his mother on the day of his Floronation, there in front of the lorchen, with the wind in her hair and tears in her eyes, a happy smile on her face.

And then he saw the red glow, the flickering crystal overhead, and he could feel the heat of the lava that night, as he tried to make it to shore—he could feel the steam off the sea, so hot it nearly scalded his face.

And he could feel Ellex's hands on his shoulders, caressing his back, whispering something to him, but all he could see was the red, and all he could hear was the hiss of the eruption, and it was so hot he couldn't breathe. His lungs screamed, his chest—his throat—his head—everything pounding and pulsing, as he pulled in a tiny breathe, coughed it out, and struggled to pull in another. And then another.

Ellex was hugging him, saying something, but Rakk couldn't hear—Fin'roq was standing nearby, looking down at him, his face a red blob in the shadows, but he couldn't tell—didn't know—didn't care.

The sobs and the tears and the pain had swallowed up the world.

⚜

Ellex held Rakk while he wept, trying to keep herself from breaking down too. It was so strange, so surreal. In all the years they'd known each other, all the summers they spent with each other as scamps, she'd never seen him cry. Never once.

She looked at Fin'roq standing nearby, fidgeting, his shoulders slumping slightly and then jerking back into place, just like Rakk, and Rajj too, whenever they were uncomfortable with something. But what was she to do? Fin'roq hardly wanted to speak to her anyway. She couldn't very well invite him to join the hug, could she?

"Ell," Rakk said, catching his breath. "I'm sorry, Ell. Fin. I'm sorry. I'm sorry."

"What is there to be sorry about?" Ellex said. She kissed his forehead, surprised at how easy it was to be tender, to nurture him. "You don't have anything to be sorry for. I only wish my own tears would flow, because my heart is breaking, too."

"It never felt real," he said, barely a whisper. "It never *was* real. But now it is. Now it's real. It's so, so real. Great Sower in the sky, Ellex, it's gone. P'anorum, my—everything, everything is gone! I left—I walked right through here." He pointed. "The crowds were so thick, I had to practically dance my way through them, all the way down to the port at the mouth of the Flamewater. When I sailed away that night, I could hear the sounds of the entire city celebrating over the purring of the gurgitator, even over the roar of the wind in my ears. I sailed away at sunset, and when I returned at midnight, the sky was red and angry and roaring, the ocean hissing, the sea boiling, shrouding the island in a fog so thick, I couldn't even lay my eyes on her. I never got to see her again, to touch her again."

He looked at Ellex and wiped away his tears. "I lost you that night too, and I never realized it—I never felt it. I just—stopped. Stopped existing, like I was already dead. I don't want that to happen again. I don't want to not feel, terrible as this is. Does that make sense?"

"Yes," Ellex said.

"Yes," Fin'roq whispered. "But is it possible?"

"I hope so," he said. "But then I look around at this madness—at such careless destruction—and I know there is no Great Sower watching over us. Trevian no longer cares if we live or die. And I don't know if I can hope for anything again. Everything feels lost."

"No," Ellex said. "No. Not yet. Remember why we're here. We have to get to the temple! Bhea said we'd find answers there. All of us. And I trust her, and so do you. Don't give up Raeder, not yet. And don't you give up either, Fin'roq. Not yet. Not ever."

"I'll try not to, Sui Pradesh," he said.

So formal still, she thought. *So stiff with me.*

She stood and offered Rakk her hand, though she knew she'd be helpless to pull him up herself if he didn't want to stand. But he took it and stood, and avoided her eyes when he did, the tears starting to spill out again. She put her hand on his face and turned him toward her, and gave him a soft, gentle kiss, and he hugged her again.

"Sweet Trevian!" Fin'roq said. "My mother—and my brother?!"

Rakk laughed first, and Ellex, blushing, soon joined him. Fin'roq shook his head, but Ellex could see he was grinning too.

❧ ❦ ❧

Fin'roq headed north across the plaza and up the banks of the Flamewater, the slope getting steeper, the cascades of the stream larger, as they went along. Rakk and Ellex followed not far behind, arm in arm, talking softly, Rakk occasionally pointing something out and telling a story.

Fin enjoyed the sounds of conversation, the company of others, in these ruins of his—real, present conversations, and real, present company. He turned back to look at them, walking along arm in arm, Rakk's eyes puffy from crying, doing his best to grin through it. And Ellex—she was being friendly, he had to admit. And she was kind and sweet to his brother. It was strange to see her being tender. He'd been sure her heart was made of stone.

The lava roof overhead soon grew low and the passage narrow, nearly up against the banks of the Flamewater, and the air was hot and heavy and sharp with the smell of minerals. But the cavern opened up once again, briefly, one large final pocket, and on the far side were two towers rising up on either side of the stream, their tops sticking into the lava. The door to the nearest tower was open, the metal folded back and torn off its hinges.

"The North Gate," Rakk said.

Fin flicked his glowbe and it crackled to life.

"We're going underground now," he said.

Rakk and Ellex both shook their glowbes and nodded at him when they were lit.

He inhaled and let it out slowly, then stepped through the doorway and into a dark hall which led back and back into the mountain itself. The temperature dropped and the moisture faded out, and Fin licked his lips and the air tasted metallic, dry and cold.

Fin knew these corridors would connect with the long stair that led up to the lookout tower on the Crag where he had entered on that terrible day, and from there he thought he could find the other stair again, the one Aar'ryn Ruu'n had led them to. He knew he was on the right track when the air changed, the chill that had lingered since the North Gate giving way to a dry heat, and when the passage ended at the top of the long spiral stair down into the heart of the mountain, his legs no longer wanted to work. A draft rose from below, burning his nostrils and reeking of petrification, and his heart started to thud in his ears and he felt his skin tingling.

"Sweet Trevian," Ellex whispered. "What a stench. Is this the way?"

Fin nodded. "But now that we're here, I don't think I want to go any further."

Rakk touched his shoulder with his free hand, the other gripping the glowbe. "I'm scared too, brother. Let's do this together."

Haven't I done enough? Fin thought. *I brought them nearly to the door, must I carry them through it?*

Ellex started down and Rakk went after her, and Fin stared at the light in the stairwell, fading away as they descended.

Damnit, he thought, as he hurried to catch up.

To try and stop the panic, he started counting again, tallying each step, remembering that he'd made it past two thousand before giving up when last he'd descended. Round and down they walked, the air growing hotter and heavier as they dropped through the island, down below the level of the sea, to the forgotten city of Dar Ka'Hala in the bowels of P'anorum.

The stair stopped at a short corridor, which opened to a chamber so wide and vast, the light of the glowbes faded away into the darkness. Fin heard Ellex and Rakk gasp, saw them look around in wonder. Far, far in the distance, Fin saw a red glow fanning upward from a flat black line, like the sun had set behind a world in shadow, and he could feel the heat on his face from the lava.

"The ground," Rakk said. "Cobblestones!"

"That's not all," Ellex said. She took a few steps forward, her glowbe held over her head, the light just starting to dance up the wall of the chamber, revealing the facade of a massive temple. The soft orange of the glowbe lit up the friezes and hieroglyphs on the portico, traveled down the length of the columns, across the vacant windows, and through a gaping hole where the door once stood, vanishing away in the darkness inside.

Fin'roq looked at the doorway and realized that the petrified remains of Roe's tattered and torn body must be lying inside there, discarded on the ground where he'd left him. And suddenly he was Roe again—seeing and feeling and tasting his memories, knowing his body as if it were his own, looking down at his Andrasian skin, a soft and delicate green, and surging with pleasure when Roe began to rub his own flower, caressing it gently in the still of the night.

But Roe would never caress his or anyone else's flower, ever again. No one would admire his soft Andrasian skin. With his parents killed, with all the villagers dead, only he and Bhea and Grizmond were left to remember him. In another lifetime, he'd be entirely forgotten.

Rakk started toward the temple door, Ellex at his side, and somehow Fin was following, slow step after slow step, hardly seeing the ground, hardly knowing what he was doing, trying to remember that he was Fin'roq, that he needed to wake up—didn't he need to wake up?

"This is an operator's console," Ellex said, holding up her glowbe and examining the wall just inside the door. She fiddled with the knobs, and Fin heard maquina begin to whine and hum, and with a crackle, glowbes sparked to life across the hall of the temple.

Fin decided darkness was better, and he closed his eyes, but they wouldn't stay shut.

Ellex and Rakk both gasped, hands over their mouths, as the light revealed the stasis chamber, partially crushed with rubble, two corpses face down in front of it. Near the door were several chunks of hardened flesh, too mangled to tell for sure what they were. And spreading across the length of the hall stood row upon row of petrified corpses, the oldest ones so crumbled apart they were merely blobs of stone, but in the closest rows, their Bhizini skin was still visible, their gaunt faces frozen in screams of pain and horror.

Fin could hear them crying, could feel the darkness that pressed down upon them, feel the blades that took their lives after so many years of bondage, and he tried to silence the noise but he couldn't. Was it him screaming?

He took a few steps forward, stumbling toward the stasis chamber, toward the door that was ajar, the roof crushed in with rubble, to the corpse still strapped in its interior, and he knew that it was him in there. The row after row of bodies had all been his own. Someone had trapped him, imprisoned him, lifetime after lifetime, across many millennia, here in the Temple of Trevian, in the ruins of his ancient city of Dar Ka'Hala, a captive in his own kingdom, a prisoner in his own castle—long forgotten by the world.

Fin reached out for the crushed Bhizini strapped to the maquina, and when he touched the cold, stony skin, he remembered.

Endless darkness had broken, and there'd been light. The door had opened like it had so many times before. Yet again, they'd come to kill him, to drive a blade into his heart, to send him on to the next vessel. And like every other time, he'd been too weak and confused to protest. Only this time, something was different. The ground—it was shaking! The maquina was rumbling. And something had ahold of him, something powerful, so powerful he couldn't move, couldn't even struggle. Something familiar. And it pulled at him, a few small tugs in each direction, and then one final, definitive rip, his fibers snapping, his skin tearing, his eyes moving in two different directions. And when he thought he could take no more pain, the island fell on top of him, and crushed him into nonexistence.

❧❧❧❧❧ ❧❧❧❧❧

Ellex looked around the hall of the temple, at the rows of petrified corpses, and at first glance she thought they were statues, macabre though they looked, there was just something so artificial about them. She'd seen plenty of dead corpses, but ones that had been dead for many millennia? And then she saw the stasis chamber, so similar to the one that held Qaas'i on Balan Su, and she knew the bodies must be the many generations of its inhabitant, always some poor Bhizini locked away down here, held by the Raccorin royal family, by Rakk's ancestors. And by the Guild. And by the Pradishar. All of Balance seemed in on it.

She looked around and saw that the rows of bodies were not the only dead Verdillions in the room. There were two lying facedown near the opening to the stasis chamber, a Raccorin and an Andrasian. The Raccorin's head was twisted around at a terrible angle, half sideways. And the Andrasian had a long Vintrani blade buried in its back, right down through the heart.

Fin'roq stumbled over to the chamber, staring inside, a look of panic on his face, his body trembling, and when he stepped inside the maquina, Ellex grabbed Rakk's arm and pulled him toward her.

"Fin'roq?" Ellex said. "Fin, are you okay?"

The door swung wide and Fin fell out, flopping on the ground, his eyes rolled back in his head, his skin shimmering as if it were radiating heat. Ellex started toward him when the ground dropped and rose and she staggered to the side, and Rakk caught her. The walls cracked and groaned as the island shook, and Rakk pulled her toward the door, but the quaking stopped when Fin'roq fell still.

She ran over to him and touched his face, and it was burning up. She shook him.

"Careful," Rakk said. "We don't know what he's capable of."

"He's my son," she said.

"Yes, but I don't think that's all he is, Ell."

"I think he's passed out," she said. "Help me."

Rakk helped her lift him and they sat him up against the outer wall of the stasis chamber.

"I don't know how we'll get him out of here if he doesn't wake up," Rakk said.

"He will," Ellex said, touching his forehead again. "He just needs a minute. Let's look around. Help me turn these corpses over."

"They aren't as heavy as they look," Rakk said, bending down by the corpses in front of the stasis chamber and flipping the first stony body over onto it's back. He hissed and stood up and scrambled back from the body, and Ellex, feeling like a Cul'tavin peacekeeper investigating a crime scene again, hurried to see what had frightened him so badly.

She ran her eyes up the body—a Raccorin in pradeshan robes, not too common but not too rare either. Tall and thin, and—oof, that face. Someone had tried to wrench their head off, and the Raccorin had died screaming, the mouth open in a wide, lopsided O, the cheeks pulled back—the right cheek—Ellex saw a long scar, down the forehead, across the eye, and half way to the mouth, a crushed marble in the eye-socket.

"Sweet Trevian," she said. "That's Ra'shard Ruu'n. That's the Gran Pradesh!"

"But—he became Gran Pradesh *after* the eruption," Rakk said.

"*He* did?" Ellex said. "He who lies dead in front of us? Sweet Trevian, Rakk, who the fuck is sitting on the throne in Balan Su? Who—who have I been speaking with, seeking advice from, *worshipping*, for all these years?"

Rakk just shook his head, and Ellex's eyes wandered to the Andrasian next to Ra'shard Ruu'n's corpse. She lingered on the Vintrani blade in his back, just like the one her attacker had used to slice Rajj's arm off at the Balancing Act. She saw the robes stained with sap where it had cut through his fibers and through the heart. She followed the stain up the outstretched arm—the dull green skin now gray and greasy looking—to the ring on the petrified finger, to the unmistakable sapphire that her father always wore.

And Ellex felt herself die a little bit on the inside.

"No," she whispered. "No!"

"Ell?" Rakk ran to her side. He grabbed the corpse and started to turn it over.

Father didn't die in the eruption, she thought. *He was murdered!*

Now it was Ellex's turn to weep and moan, to beat the ground, to gasp for air between sobs while Rakk held her, as her mind raced trying to understand what she was seeing, all that she was seeing, but no sense could be made of any of it.

Now I know for sure, she thought. *Never again will I have to remind myself that he's gone.*

❧ ❦

Rakk stared at the scar on Ra'shard Ruu'n's corpse, easily the most famous scar in the world, where he'd taken an axe to the face for defying his family and freeing their slaves. He had been loved and hated in equal measure in Raccorum Rhazzat, and once he became Gran Pradesh—but no. Ra'shard Ruu'n had never become Gran Pradesh. He'd died the night P'anorum was lost.

He's famous around the world for shepherding my father, Rajj, and Raq'asha to safety when the mountain blew, Rakk thought. *Many testified to his bravery.*

More lies. More deceit.

And yet the Bhizini told me as much, he thought. *They said death was ruling Balance. But who is the Death King? And what does he want?*

"Why were they down here?" Ellex whispered. "What were my father and Ra'shard Ruu'n doing in this place?"

Rakk looked at the stasis chamber and the rows of corpses. "My best guess? They came down to kill the prisoner."

Ellex stared at Rakk with a wounded look. "How can you say such a thing? My father wasn't a murderer!"

"I didn't say he was," Rakk said. "Of course, it wouldn't have been murder, would it? Don't you see, Ellex? While you were upstairs with the king, getting the next Wielder, Destroyer, Mystical-Magic-Beast fertilized and ready to receive the spirit of the whatchamacallit, your father and Ra'shard Ruu'n came down here to make sure the reincarnation would take place on schedule. But it looks like someone tried to stop them. Only—" He looked at the rubble that had collapsed on the stasis chamber. "Only the island took care of the rest."

Ellex shook her head back and forth. "No," she said. "I don't remember it."

"But it's about the only sense I can make of what we know so far," Rakk said.

Ellex moaned. "This isn't what I thought we'd find. I thought—I don't know what I thought. I thought I would disprove my doubts, that I'd leave here absolutely certain that my father and I—that we would never try to break Balance. But that's exactly what we did. And Ra'shard Ruu'n, the real Ra'shard Ruu'n, was one of my co-conspirators! And now some demon has stolen his shape. Some demon that has watched me for the last thirty three years, staring at me every morning when I wake, wearing my father's face!"

⁕ ⁕ ⁕

Fin'roq felt himself falling through the darkness, but the darkness was inside him, and he was sure that somehow, in some way, he was collapsing, like the open space of a cave is reclaimed by the mountain and ceases to exist any longer, though the shape of the mountain doesn't change. Soon he'd be nothing, and he didn't want to be nothing. He wasn't ready. He had things to do, places to go, plants to meet.

He struggled to find which way was up and which was down—he seemed to be falling in all of them—but he heard a voice speaking to him, warm and rich and familiar, and full of longing. Fin felt branches around him, holding him, briefly, and then they were gone. But the experience had been so profound, he thought his heart would explode with joy, and pleasure kept coursing through his body and over his skin in pulses, and he felt he was the sun itself, beaming out life and love and warmth.

And Fin knew he'd been touched by Trevian.

A city appeared around him and he landed softly on the balcony of a palace, a wide plaza below him, a tall green mountain at his back, and a tree with fruit of every color standing next to him.

<<I know this place,>> he said. <<Dar Ka'Hala.>>

<<Not truly,>> Anorian said. <<You know Dar Ka'Hala is gone. Only a few bits of rubble remain far under the Crag. Your body, even now, is sitting amongst them.>>

<<The temple,>> he said. <<The corpses. They're me.>>

<<Does that surprise you?>>

<<The bhiza dream—those were my lives. I was some kind of king, wasn't I? Until I was put in stasis. Until they kept me in the dark, lifetime after lifetime! Who did this to me? Was it you?>>

<<I told you before, you and I are the same. What was done to you was done to me too.>>

<<How can we be the same plant when I just met you?>>

<<Because you were born as the mover of all crystals is always born—with no memory of your past lives, no idea that you're an aspect of Trevian, destined to control the crystal and bend it to your will—so you don't remember when they tore us apart—when they split us in two.>>

<<That—was you? Was you being separated from me?>>

<<Not quite, but close enough. So you do remember the splitting then. Painful, right? A desperate move on the part of our parents, and their allies, to free us.>>

<<What do they want of us?>>

<<What everyone wants of their heroes. To sacrifice for them. To save them. To deliver them from death.>>

<<And I have that power?>> Fin said.

<<Perhaps,>> Anorian said.

<<And what about you?>>

She sighed. <<This is your task, Fin. You're the one fate chose, not me. I can hardly function in the real world. This—this is my realm. From here, I will prepare for the future, for your success or for your failure.>>

<<You still didn't answer my question. Who did this to me—to us? Who put us in the chamber, kept us in the dark for all those years, all those lifetimes?>>

<<He calls himself Mortimus Rex, the Death King, but that isn't really his name. He was a servant of ours when we ruled from Dar Ka'Hala. Surely you recall your three advisors, always at your side, whispering advice, following you from lifetime to lifetime?>>

Fin remembered, and he nodded.

<<Aspects of Trevian,>> Anorian said. <<Some say Mortimus Rex is Trevian's malice, the pain of his sacrifice, the ambition that brought him to our realm in the first place.>>

Fin'roq thought of all those long years, trapped in the maquina, his mind a muddled incoherence, like a halfwit in a stupor—ten thousand years of Balance when he should have been in charge—a Bhizini ruling the world as king.

And his fear, his uncertainty and doubt, the burden he had felt for so long now, seemed to lift off of him, and he felt light and free and in charge of his own life.

<<And where can I find the Death King?>>

<<You've met him already,>> Anorian said. <<He's the Gran Pradesh, Ra'shard Ruu'n. And he will be the next Gran Pradesh, too, after he has our mother killed. He's *always* the Gran Pradesh. Always in charge of Balance.>>

Fin'roq felt a chill run down his back, a panic that threatened to steal his will, to rob him of his life, and to ensure that he would fail before he'd even begun. He knew he had faced Mortimus Rex before—many times in the distant past—and always lost.

But then Anorian was in his mind, showing him a tiny glimpse of what lay inside of her, stretching out his thoughts to encompass the scope she had revealed to him. And for a moment, he was everywhere, every crystal, every dynamin and datamin that ever was and ever had been, the perfect union of information and raw power, a new paradigm of what his life—of what he—could be.

The shock of it blasted him upward and out of the hollow, out of the crystal realm and back into his body—Fin'roq's body—down in the ruins of Dar Ka'Hala, in the Temple of Trevian, where he'd collapsed in a stupor. He felt his arms and legs again, felt the metal of the stasis chamber against his back, the cold stones underneath him, and he could hear his mother weeping nearby.

He stood and looked at them, and he could see relief, and confusion, on their faces.

"Thank Trevian you're okay," Rakk said. "I thought I might have to carry you."

"I feel—better. Different." He looked back at the rows of corpses. "Can we get out of here now? I think I've been here long enough already. And I need some fresh air."

"Almost," Ellex said, sniffing as she stood. "Almost ready. Raeder, do you think—I don't want to leave him here. He deserves a proper send off. Could you—help me carry him out?"

"Of course I can," Rakk said. "Leave it to me."

"What—who?" Fin said, seeing the bodies.

"My father," Ellex whispered.

"And Ra'shard Ruu'n," Rakk said.

Fin stared at the long scar on Ruu'n's face and waited for the panic to spike inside of him again, but it didn't come. Ra'shard Ruu'n was a victim, and Fin reminded himself he'd never known him, only his writings, which he admired. The real villain was in Balan Su, wearing his face.

He bent over and lifted Ra'shard Ruu'n's corpse, surprised at how light it was, and Ellex touched his shoulder while tears ran down her face. Then Rakk picked up Luthyr Andria's corpse and they started back for the surface in silence.

Chapter 56

The Shape of the World

ELLEX ANDRIA KNEW WHAT she'd have to do before they had emerged from beneath the island, before Fin'roq led them through the ruined city to the west wing of the palace, to the Split Chapel tucked back off the southeastern corner, under the lava flow. She saw the light before they arrived, a faint glowing red through the crystal and the soft orange tones of glowbes, and she was surprised to see Bhea Bell and Qaas'andria waiting just inside the door.

The chapel fit its name. The round chamber was decorated differently on either side, the left in the style of the lorchen—with figures from the Loricean faith, and with orange burnstone blocks sculpted into delicate swirls, like sandstorms across the Fierrin Desert—and the right in the style of the sharlum, this one in particular wrought in black obsidian, a miniature of the great hall of the citadel in Balan Su, with its glassy curves and distorted reflections. A strip of grass, rich and deep and green, once ran between the two sides, up the walls and over the top, dividing the space perfectly in two, but now it was a strip of dirt.

Qaas'i gave Ellex a quick hug and then Bhea gave her a longer, tighter one. Rakk and Fin placed the corpses of her father and Ra'shard Ruu'n on the dais at center of the chapel, and Ellex walked over and kneeled down beside them.

"Thank you both," she whispered.

Rakk picked Qaas'i up and kissed her cheek. "I need some air."

"I want to stay here awhile," Ellex said.

"Of course," he said. "Fin, join me?"

Rakk sat Qaas'i down and took her hand, and they followed Fin'roq out of the chapel.

Bhea walked over and knelt down next to her.

"I'm so sorry, my sprout," she said.

"Did you know? Did you know my father was murdered?"

"No," Bhea said. "But I had my suspicions. I knew he'd died. And Ra'shard. They was under the island when it blew."

"Rakk thought—they'd gone down there to kill the prisoner."

"They saw it as freeing him," she said, "but yes."

"Forcing him to reincarnate, so that in the next life, he would be able to—what? Defeat Mortimus Rex?"

"You can't defeat death," Bhea said.

"Then there's no hope?"

"I didn't say that."

"Did Mortimus Rex take Qaas'i, and put her in the stasis chamber?"

"No," Bhea said. "I wish I could show you my memories. So you could see. So you'd believe. Do you remember anything from that year you spent here?"

"No," Ellex said. "Only one thing, but I dreamt it when we were on Lagracia. I was with you, and we were cutting Qaas'i's taprin. I felt so happy. There was another spratlyn in the patch, but at the time, I didn't think anything of it. I assumed it was yours—that you were Fin'roq's mother."

"Love, we didn't cut Qaas'i's taprin together. That was Fin'roq you were cutting."

Ellex felt like she'd been punched.

"You're sure?"

"Certain. We cut Fin'roq first, and we planned to cut Qaas'i the next morning. But that night, I woke with smoke in my nose and a fire raging through my garden, and you were nowhere to be found. I ran for the patch—ran with all my life—certain that little Qaas'andria was gone. But I found you. You had her in one arm, and she was screaming and howling. And you had an enflamer in the other hand, and you were shooting whorls of fire off in every direction, your face mad with fury, and in your eyes, the tell-tale glint of imperialization."

For the second time that day, Ellex felt like she'd died on the inside.

"That's not possible," she said. "None of my crystals are imperial. None of them!"

"Do you know where the crystals come from?" Bhea asked. "How they're made? What makes one imperial and one voluntary? How they're destroyed?"

"Only the Gran Pradesh is privy to that information," she whispered. "And the Gran Pradesh is..."

Bhea nodded.

"He found out, didn't he," Ellex said. "That I was a conspirator? Why not just have me killed and take my face?"

"I don't know, my sprout."

But Ellex did, and she gasped when she realized it.

"He's been setting me up," she said. "He told me himself, but I didn't think he was serious! He told me I was a worthy replacement for him."

"Then your life is indeed in danger," Bhea said. "You've done well to keep your crystal numbed with bhiza. Until you learn more, you best keep it that way."

She thought of her body no longer being under her control, moving against her will, her mind open and exposed to the peering eyes of some wretched slave master, and it filled her with rage. She let it flow into her heart, let it clench up her muscles, let it power up her ragged nerves. She reached up for the cold, stony hand of her dead father, and she swore to Trevian that she'd have revenge.

Ellex saw movement out of the corner of her eye. Rakk came back into the chapel, alone, his face down, his shoulders slumped, looking like he'd had one of the worst days of his life.

He lost his home today, she thought.

She tried to temper her fury, to comfort him, but there was just so much to deal with.

He knelt down between her and Bhea and stared emptily at the corpses on the dais.

"Rakk, my sprout, you're breaking my heart seeing you all torn up like this. Tell your Bhea what's on your mind."

"There's nothing to tell," he said. "There's nothing to do. There's nothing. At all. It's all gone."

"Not all gone," Bhea said. "Never all gone."

"Yes," he said. "It's all been a fake. All these years, thinking I still had a kingdom. Thinking I was still chosen by my father to lead our people—that he would trust me to carry the burden of our family. And yet he didn't even trust me to know about these schemes. Not just schemes, but the greatest struggle of our time! And what, you ask, was the crown prince's role in helping to save the world? Guard duty! Guard duty at the port, of all places! Humiliated, in front of the whole world. But the real kicker? It's that I didn't deserve to be a part of it. My father was right to exclude me. And there's no reason to be included now."

"Oh love, it wasn't like that at all," Bhea said. "Now look, your father's a complicated plant. He weren't much of a father, I know it. I told him as much, often too. I never feared no king! My job is to point toward the truth, my sprout. To point, not to hand it out. But I'm gonna hand you something right now. I'm gonna tell you that your father was scared. That's right, he was. He had to make sure you, and Rajesh'n, and Raq'asha—that even if you had your crystals scanned, there wouldn't be nothing, not a shrapnel of information, to make the Gran Pradesh think you were a threat to him. Why do you think the king sent you to the port that night? It wasn't to humiliate you, it was to make sure the Gran Pradesh knew you was down in the city, not making mischief in the palace, or mucking about down in Dar Ka'Hala."

Rakk swallowed a hiss. "I wish I could believe that."

"You're wrong about not having a reason to keep trying," Ellex said. "Raeder, it's not too late. We have the truth now. Balance is still strong. I'm still in charge of Andrasia, and you're still the crown prince of Raccorum Rhazzat. Even if Rishar is called, you'll answer it, and endure. I know you will. Together we can save Balance."

"Your father believed in you," Bhea said. "He chose you, not Raq'asha. Not Rajesh'n. You, my sprout."

"You need to go to Raccorum Rhazzat," Ellex said. "Meet up with Q'orin, figure out how far Mortimus's tentacle has spread, what the goal is in overturning your mandate. If you have to face Rishar, then face it. And afterward, you'll have control of your forces. Then we can make a plan to move against the Gran Pradesh."

"That's a big vote of confidence," Rakk said.

"Everyone believes in you," Ellex said. "When will you start believing in yourself?"

Rakk said nothing for a moment. "What will you do?"

She looked at the bodies on the table. "I'm going to go back to Balan Su to warn my brother. And Rajj. They're in the citadel every single day with that monster. They have to be warned. Either one of them could be chose in my place as the new Gran Pradesh, should the world discover Fin'roq and Qaas'andria, or the Ren'fallow fail to kill me."

"Don't talk like that," Rakk said. "Nobody is taking your face."

"How do we stop him? The Death King?" Ellex said.

"You can't stop death," Bhea said. "He can't be touched by any means you possess. Only the mover of all the crystals has any hope of getting through to him, but I'm not sure Fin'roq is ready for that."

"Then we can hope he's ready by the time we have our own forces in place," Ellex said. "Now that we know the truth, we have no choice but to take up the fight of our fathers, the fight I once fought, and the real Ra'shard Ruu'n fought too—to free ourselves from Mortimus Rex once and for all."

"We could end up collapsing Balance," Rakk said.

"Our institutions are strong. Ancient! They've endured for a decamillennium. Besides, governments don't disappear, they transform. There are always Verdillions, and Verdillions will always be drawn together into organizations. I've spent my whole life serving, even when I was half out of my mind. As much as I want to stay here with Qaas'i, and with you, where we're safe, I have to go back. I have to go fight for my father, and for Balance. And—I don't know how—but I have to stop this mad campaign against the Bhizini, once and for all."

"I'll come with you to Balan Su," Rakk said. "I need to see Rajj and tell him what I found at Callo Baton."

"If Mortimus suspects they helped us—I won't lose any more family," Ellex said. "I won't!"

"Neither will I," Rakk said. "Let's do this together, and then we'll go our separate ways, for awhile."

Ellex swallowed a sudden lump in her throat and looked at Bhea. "I have a tremendous favor to ask of you. I don't dare take Qaas'i with me into Balance Territories. And even though I hate to be away from her, I think, when she's older, she'll understand why I had to leave."

"I'd be honored to watch after her," Bhea said. "You don't have to worry about her. But can you give me a few more days 'fore you head out? I'm expecting a ship or two any time now."

Ellex nodded. She looked up at the corpses on the dais and felt the flicker of rage again, pulsing deep inside her. It felt—

"What a day," Rakk said, taking Ellex's hand and squeezing it.

"A terrible day," she said. "And yet—I feel like the world makes a little more sense than it did this morning. Like I'm not quite so lost."

"I wish I shared your feeling," he said, and Ellex and Bhea both gave Rakk a hug.

Chapter 57

Shadows of the Past and Future

FIN'ROQ WAS GLAD THE sun had not yet set when he emerged from the ruins of the palace, Rakk and Qaas'andria behind him. Though low in the western sky, the glowing orb had not yet slipped behind the arm of the crater on the opposite side of the harbor, and when the warm rays touched his skin, he lifted his hands up in the air and twirled around in circles, his heart swelling up, his face flushed. He stood with his eyes shut and drank up the beams, grateful for the life-giving sunshine, for having faced the darkness and come through it alive, awake even.

<<All the fussing and hand-wringing and teary-eyed moping, and yet here you are afterward, practically grinning.>>

He turned back toward the palace and saw Qaas'andria looking at him, an amused look on her face.

<<Where's Raeder?>>

<<He went back to my mother. I don't think he can stand to be apart from her right now.>>

Fin turned back toward the sun.

<<And he left you here all alone? A poor, defenseless little scamp like you?>>

Qaas'i laughed, loudly and hysterically, and Fin cringed.

<<You really need to tell them,>> he said. <<It's wrong what you're doing. They should be in the hollow, not taking bhiza every day.>>

Qaas'i narrowed her eyes at him. <<It isn't time yet.>>

<<Is that really for you to decide?>>

<<Of course,>> she said. <<I'm the one with all the information.>>

<<If you say so,>> Fin said.

She tsked. <<All I've done for you. All I've shown you. And still you doubt?>> Her voice was mocking but Fin could feel that she was upset.

<<I'm grateful for how you've helped me,>> he said. <<But I don't like the way you've manipulated me. Or our mother and brother. You've kept secrets from everyone, and you reveal them only when it serves your own interest.>>

<<I have no knowledge that you don't have access to,>> she said. <<Only I knew it from the moment I awoke to the world, whereas you've had to learn everything from scratch. I know that even now, those things you recalled down in Dar Ka'Hala—those memories from the Inner Door—they're fading from your mind. They're foggy, and spotty, and not visceral like they were. The scope of your mind will return inevitably to Fin'roq. Only to Fin'roq. I wonder—will you be able to see beyond that?>>

<<I don't have to,>> he said. <<All my life, I've just wanted to fit in. To please others. But all that got me was grief and disappointment. Everyone wants something from me. Even you, Anorian. You waited to speak to me until you had a task for me to do. The same with my mother, and my brother. Everyone wanting something! But what about me? What about what I want! What about the kingdom I should have ruled? What about our people, the Bhizini, oppressed and murdered for millennia by a demon that stole everything from us! Our own servant that betrayed us! That kept us in a cage for—Sweet Trevian, so many lifetimes...>>

<<I know,>> Anorian said. <<I spent nearly all of my life as Qaas'andria still in a cage, while you were here at home, learning from Bhea Bell, passing the afternoons with Grizmond Grants, running with Baboo through the Swarthen Forest, walking the streets of old P'anorum, drinking up the sunshine while staring at the sea.>>

Fin saw the pain in her eyes, and felt it in his own heart. <<I don't know what to say,>> he said. << I'm sorry.>>

<<I'm not mad at you,>> she said. <<I know how you're feeling, in the same way that you know how I'm feeling. In the same way you'll learn to know how anyone with a crystal is feeling.>>

Fin shook his head. <<I'm going to Balan Su, Anorian. I'm going to face the Gran Pradesh—the Death King. That's what I want to do, so that's what I'm going to do.>>

<<Brave,>> she said. <<And foolish. Do you even know his name? It's not Mortimus Rex.>>

<<Who cares if I don't!>>

Anorian tsked. <<You aren't ready to face him.>>

<<Is that really for you to decide?>>

<<I suppose it isn't.>>

Qaas'i took his hand and squeezed it.

<<Don't think you have to do this all alone. You don't. I have a lot of allies. I've been building an army for decades, while the Gran Pradesh thought I was in stasis.>>

<<An army?>> he said. <<Does that mean—could you get me to Balan Su?>>

<<Our mother and brother will be going as well,>> she said. <<Wait a few more days. Someone's coming who'll be able to get you into the capital.>>

Fin exhaled and took a deep breath, not realizing he'd been holding it in.

Fin'roq spent the next few days at Bhea's garden, walking the old pathways, perusing her books and scrolls, and hoping and praying that Baboo would show up, but he never did. Where had he gone off to? He had so much to tell him, so much to share with him, with his only true friend in the entire world.

His mother and brother had asked him to join them on their trip to Balan Su, just as Anorian had said they would. Fin agreed, but it was hard to shake off the feeling that they were using him again—that Anorian was too. They'd used him to go under the island, and now they wanted to use him to confront the Gran Pradesh. The only reason he said yes was because it was what he wanted, too.

Bhea was hardly by herself, with Ellex and Rakk and Qaas'i around, not to mention the several thousand Tornroot. And it just felt so strange to be back on P'anorum, back where he'd once felt he'd be forced to spend his life, unable to ever leave. Now he'd gone halfway around the world and back again, but he still found himself gazing off the cliffside at the flat surface of the sea and wondering what lay beyond the horizon, the unknown mysteries of life calling to him, beckoning him to leave, to wander, to be free.

He still worried about Qardymion and his Pal'meran leaf-striders. His powers were useless against those without crystals, and if they wanted to capture him, they could still hurt him. Fin knew he was still vulnerable to injury and death. But at least in Balan Su, all the Cul'tavin, nearly all the citizens, had crystals. Nobody would be able to harm him, if he didn't want them to.

Grizmond arrived that evening with Bhea, and Fin wanted to give him a hug, but before he could, the Raccorin sank to his knees and bowed down to him. Fin was mortified, and he pulled him to his feet.

"Forgive me," Grizmond grunted. "My own shame has kept me from coming to see you. The king swore me to secrecy. Please forgive my dishonesty, my prince."

"I'm—Grizmond, it's me, Fin'roq. Stand up. Come on."

But he stayed on his knees, his head down.

"Not til you've forgiven me."

"You're forgiven! Now get up already." He looked at Bhea. "I'm glad you're both here. I was hoping we could chat."

"Of course, my sprout," Bhea said. "Let me get some jha'ala steaming and we'll talk at at the table."

When she left, Fin looked at Grizmond. He looked so miserable, Fin didn't know what to say, and didn't want to upset him anymore. They sat in an awkward silence, fidgeting, and Fin tried to concentrate on the sound of the sea splashing against the rocks down below, but he couldn't.

"All those years in the village, you knew who my parents were. You knew—what I am?"

Grizmond nodded.

"The king swore me to secrecy. He—" Grizmond touched the holes in his forehead. "He trusted me. A slave. He freed me himself. Told me everything. And made me promise to keep you safe. I thought I'd failed when they took Qaas'i. But the plan worked—Mortimus didn't know there were two of you! So I kept watch, every day. But no other ships came. Well, 'til Roman Anthem showed up."

Bhea came up the stairs from her grotto with a tray and she sat it on the table.

"Why did he come here?" Fin asked. "How did Anthem know to come here?"

Grizmond looked at Bhea, and Bhea looked at Fin.

"It's a long old tale, love," she said, but when she saw Fin's face, she sighed. "Roman Anthem is like a son to me, Fin. And, well, the Gran Pradesh is like a father to him. Roman's caught in the middle, wanting to make us both happy, and not always knowing if what he's doing is wrong or right."

"He was kind to me," Fin said. "On the crossing, and in Balan Su. So was the Gran Pradesh. Why didn't you tell me? Why didn't you tell me anything about what I am, or what happened to me?! Why'd you leave me in the dark for so long—for lifetimes, Bhea! Why?!"

"All those lifetimes, I've been trying to free you. Trying and trying and trying, my sprout, I swear it. And as for why I didn't tell you before—I didn't know how. It wouldn't of made sense. And I was trying to protect you from what was coming. I thought—but then—well, I didn't want you suffering. So I made my choices, and I did my best, and I'm so sorry it weren't what I hoped it would be."

"Damnit Bhea," he said. "I feel like I deserve to be angry at you, but you're making it so difficult."

"I want what's best for ya, and for the world too. And that's a hard balance to strike, my sprout. Much as we'd like to pretend, we don't always know what we're doing, and we don't have all the answers."

Fin sighed. "Don't I know it," he said. "I've made a lot of bad choices since I left here. I trusted those I shouldn't have trusted, and I thought I could fit in where I didn't belong. And now, one moment I'm confident that I know what I want, I feel powerful and ready—and the next I can't stop my thoughts from whirring, my heart from pounding, certain I'll lose my mind with desperation, with confusion, and never know who or what I am. How can I be both things at the same time?"

"Cause you're just like the sea, love. We all are, all things coming together in one. We got smooth expanses, flat and shiny as glass. And we got rough patches, tossin' and turnin' and crashin' and roarin' about. We got open waters stretching half the planet, unbroken. And we got snug little harbors untouched by any storm. We got shallows, where nothing can hide and all is known. And we got deeps, so dark and mysterious there ain't nothing there that can be known. And from day to day, and hour to hour, we change and shift and swell and plunge, every one of us, all things together at once."

Fin gave Bhea a hug, and he could feel her weeping silently, and he held her, but no tears of his own would come.

※※※※ ※※※※

On the morning of their departure for Balan Su, a Pradishar cata'rin pulled into the harbor. Ships had been streaming in the last few days, with Bhizini and with Raccorin and Andrasians, more and more every day. The Tornroot had built new structures up and down the beach, replacing the huts that had burned in the attack. The area around the harbor was always busy now, the most activity the island had seen in decades. There were always huge bonfires, the smell of rhupan grilling, the sounds of bongos and horns and flutes, and Bhizini were dancing and singing while they washed and mended, weaved and tied, shaped and built. Fin found it incredibly chaotic, as if all hours of the day and night were open for pleasure or for work, as one chose. There seemed to be no order to it, and yet he had to to admit how much had gotten done while he'd been at Bhea's garden.

Fin watched a cata'rin, purple and gray like a storm cloud on the water, move into the crowded harbor and through the ships to the makeshift docks the Tornroot had built. Fin thought of the last time a ship like that had sailed into the harbor, and he fought down a sudden panic. Bhea was heading for the dock, Ellex and Rakk in tow, but Fin didn't think they looked alarmed, so he let himself relax.

A plank folded down onto the boardwalk and Fin'roq couldn't believe it, but Roman Anthem stepped down onto the docks, two Andrasians with him, one so tall and wide he thought it must be a pale Raccorin, and the other small and petite and—Sweet Trevian, it was Jaun!

Fin's heart was beating so hard it was making his head pulse, and he wanted to run for the docks—he felt like he could fly there—but he remembered how angry he was at Jaun, and he stopped and closed his heart off and turned away. He ducked back into the rows of huts and headed for one of the larger structures at the edge of the beach, where the Tornroot had erected walls and a thatched roof but had yet to put the building to any use. He slipped inside and sat down in the corner and wrapped his arms around his legs and hugged himself.

When a few hot tears dropped down into the sand, he hated himself for them.

❧ ☙

Bhea found Fin'roq later that morning. He was sitting cross-legged on the sand, still inside the unused hut, his hands resting on his thighs, softly mumbling prayers to Trevian. She sat down in front of him, took each of his hands in her own, and recited the prayers with him, and he could feel strength and warmth flowing through her touch—from her presence alone.

"Time to go, my sprout. The others are waiting for ya. Ready to set sail for Balan Su."

"With Roman Anthem?"

She nodded. "He's agreed to take y'all to the capital."

"Jaun's alive," he said. "He's here. I can't believe it."

"Yes," she said. "He's one of Anorian's closest allies."

"Anorian," he said, but it sounded more like a hiss.

"Jaun wants to talk to you, love. Wants to see you."

"I don't want to see him."

"I'm sorry, my sprout, but he's right outside the door, so you're gonna have to."

He hissed. "I have nothing to say to him."

"I can send him away," Bhea said.

"No!" Fin said. "No. I'll talk to him."

"Are you sure, my sprout?"

He nodded.

They walked outside together, and Bhea touched his shoulder as she passed him, not looking back.

Jaun was leaning against the wall, and he stood up when they emerged, surprised and then nervous.

Fin saw the wounds on his face, some still covered in dark, crusty scabs, others peeled back and starting to scar, and he felt like he had received the wounds himself. The sudden ache he felt to wrap Jaun up in his arms took him by surprise. He froze and stared at him for a moment, and Jaun's face was full of apprehension, and it occurred to him that he'd never seen him like that before.

He'd never seen Jaun unable to perform.

"Hi, Fin," he said.

"Hi, Jaun."

"I can't believe you're here," he said. "I feared the worst, after what happened on Balan Su—"

"I thought you were dead," Fin said. "Or rotting in the Dankburn. I thought it was my fault."

Jaun reached out his hand for him but Fin stepped back.

"I've missed you," Jaun said, his hand falling to his side.

He couldn't do this after all.

"I have to go," he said.

"I know," Jaun said. "Bhea says you're going back to Balan Su."

He nodded.

"Would it matter if I asked you to stay?"

Fin narrowed his eyes at him. "Did Anorian ask you to ask me that?"

"No," he said.

"Anorian has everyone in her pocket, doesn't she," Fin said. "I'll know if you're lying to me." He reached for Jaun with his mind, grabbed his crystamins, clutched at them, and he could see the panic in Jaun's eyes—could feel it in his own heart. But he pushed into his memories anyway, the most recent ones, just the time since he'd arrived on the island, looking for proof Jaun had lied, but there was none.

"She didn't ask me. I swear."

"I could take them all," Fin said. "Every memory. Every thought. I could see what you were really thinking when we were together. I could do it, you know? Your entire life is in my hands, right now."

Juan's face looked gray. "Fin, you're scaring me."

Fin'roq felt the wave of fear from Jaun and it gripped his own heart, and he let Jaun go, severing the connection, and turning away from him.

"I have to go."

"Fin, wait. Scan me. Take them, all of them. See for yourself, how I felt about you. How I still feel about you."

"Goodbye, Jaun," Fin said.

"Do it!" Jaun cried.

But Fin walked away without looking back.

Chapter 58

At the Moment Where No One Can Stay

As Lithuigi sped north from the Gotion Circle, a cloud of black smoke billowed upward behind him, trailing westward in the breeze. He thought he could still hear the crackling of spratlyn flesh over the purring of the gurgitator and the slapping of the skiff'rin against the water. Mha'arlo took them north until the first mangalar tree appeared in the distance, and he turned east. Nobody spoke the entire way, though he, Mha'arlo, and Nu'mora Rhyantis all received urgent messages from the Dyna'arin, first warning of an explosion in one of the subterranean labs, as well as an assault on enforcers on the surface. The east-west tram was shut down.

They all waited for word on their own crimes, but nothing came through.

When the skiff'rin reached the opening to the passage north to Callo Baton, into the heart of Mon Mang'alar, Mha'arlo turned south, down through the center of Vergis, then trailed eastward toward Lithuigi's lab. The gurgitator slowed to a hum and died, and walls slid up around the boat, as the water began to drain and lowered them under the surface.

Nu'mora offered a hand to Lithuigi and helped him out of the skiff'rin.

"I wish I could tell you how much this means to me," he said. "I've been so naive. But you've saved not only my own skin, but the honor and dignity of my family. And taken a terrible risk in doing so."

"I fear the Dyna'arin will soon learn of what happened, and the consequences will be severe. I expect Management will turn you over to the Pradishar the first chance they get."

"I do, too," he said. "It's earlier than I'd hoped, but it will have to do. The pieces are finally moving into place. We must be ready."

"I'm not afraid," she said. "And when the time comes, I will do what I can to make sure the operators are on our side."

"I'll be in touch as soon as I can."

Nu'mora bowed before walking away. When she was gone, he turned to Mha'arlo.

"I'd tell you to make sure everything makes it in one piece, but you know that. You're the only one I can trust with this, son. I've given my N'Detten instructions to follow your every order until you reach P'anorum."

"You're putting me in charge of the fleet?"

Lithuigi nodded. "I know you can bring her into P'anorum without incident."

"You're not coming with us?"

"I'm taking my cata'rin and racing ahead. I need some extra time with Bhea before you arrive."

"There's still time, professor. To stop your son. To save your family. Anorian has a plan."

"Anorian has a plan for everything," he said.

And everyone, he thought.

"No one can match her knowledge, it's true," Lithuigi continued. "But no one can predict the future, Mha'arlo. Not even Anorian Grain."

"Everything she's predicted so far has come to pass," he said. "It's hard to not be a believer."

"Indeed," Lithuigi said. "But she's still not infallible." He sighed. "You know, the sun has risen every single day of my life, and it's almost certain to rise tomorrow, and the day after, and the day after that. Should I live my life as if the sun will rise tomorrow? Sure—so long as I keep in mind that it's possible, however unlikely, that it won't. One day, the impossible will happen. The sun will be dark, and night will have fallen forever on our world."

"That seems so unlikely it hardly merits thinking about," Mha'arlo said.

"And yet what fire has never been snuffed out? What coal lingers without turning to ash?"

"You really think the sun could cease to exist?" Mha'arlo looked uncomfortable. "I've never really thought of it, I guess. Did you know most of my mother's followers on F'aryndon are worshippers of Sol'bhin? Seriously. They wake at first light and spend an hour greeting the sun, and then an hour at the end of every day, saying farewell. They dance and sing, and spin and twirl. When I was a scamp, barely old enough to have memories at all, I used to sneak out to the beach to watch them. It felt so magical, the first beams of light so warm and delicious on your skin, chasing away the laziness of the dark. And in the evening, the final speck pinching away to nothing on the horizon, leaving behind the most remarkable calm. I suppose I feel Sol'bhin's fire every day, inside of me, sustaining me. So it's hard to imagine anything existing without that. If you sever the taproot, you kill the plant, is it not so?"

"And yet look at us," Lithuigi said. "We must slice our taprins in order to live. We rejected the sedentary life of our ancestors and freed ourselves from the soil, to move about like the great beasts of land and air and sea—at least, for a little while."

"Until we spend five times as much time in one place again," Mha'arlo said, "Sol'bhin alone sustaining us."

"I admire your faith," Lithuigi said. "Although I find it curious that a secret worshipper of Sol'bhin would be serving an aspect of Trevian."

"Can't there be many such magical and mysterious wonders in the world, professor?"

"I sincerely hope so. Bless you for your enthusiasm. I swear it, Khatoran was right. Planting oneself in the gruynfeld must be a celebration like no one but an old plant can ever truly appreciate. And I feel I'm ready for it, more and more each day."

"Nonsense, professor. You've seventy years ahead of you, with family and friends who love and admire you."

"Bless you, son. Bless you. See you soon, Captain. No, Commodore!"

Mha'arlo was beaming.

❧ ☙

Lithuigi waited til the cata'rin was out of the scattered reefs and atolls of the Vergin Sea and out into the open waters of the Far Ocean before he clutched the deck with his rootpads, gripped the railing with this hands, and opened the gurgitator to full aperture. The maquina whined and the ship lurched forward, and Lithuigi could feel the acceleration in his stomach—feel the wet, salty wind on his face—and his eyes watered as the speed picked up. The sea was a bit choppy but he didn't care, and each time the cata'rin bounced up in the air, the gurgitator coughed and sputtered and then blasted him forward again as it descended.

This was no good, especially in the dark. He closed the gurgitator to only one-quarter of aperture and waited for it to slow before he relaxed his grip on the deck, then he stood on the edge and looked out across the dark waters, twilight still barely shining in the west in soft bands of silver.

Lithuigi reached out with his crystal for the weavryn, through the hollow as Anorian had shown him, looking for anything on Rebesh'a, any word that she was alright. Surely

Gushyr Vaincorr had written something on Balan Su gossip? But no. Almost nothing about Balan Su, except the normal garbage coming from PropSector.

Did she head to Andramere as she always does? If only I could contact her—

But no. The Cul'tavin were surely watching her, and he'd not give them a reason to throw her in the dungeon.

If she isn't there already, he thought. *No, Vilder wouldn't allow that to happen to his mother.*

Right?

Lithuigi sighed, his heart aching, his thoughts reaching for the sea, hoping the water would wash over him, purge him of his woes, as it once did.

He knew what he had to do, but it wasn't what he *wanted* to do. And he hated that he always felt he had to do what he didn't want to do. Wasn't that the story of his life? Hadn't he always been split in two?

I want as much time as I can get with Bhea, he thought. *I want to make sure she's happy. That our daughters are happy. That their dreams are fulfilled. That P'anorum is safe. That's what I want more than anything. That, and nothing else.*

Right?

❧ ❧

Wrong.

When he took Bhea Bell in his arms and kissed her lips, and breathed deep of her scent, and felt himself head over heels in her presence, intoxicated with his Bhea, he knew he couldn't stay.

He had to go to Balan Su.

He had to confront his sons.

He had to know if Rebesh'a was okay.

Damnit, he thought. *I want to stay right where I am, in these arms forever.*

"What's wrong, my big old sprout?" Bhea said.

They were standing on the bridge over the Ka'Hala, at the gate to her garden, the water churning through the canyon below, the canopy of the Swarthen overhead full of birdsong.

Bhea touched his face and his eyes fell.

"I have to go, my love," he said.

"I know it," she said.

"It was worse than I could have imagined," he said. "Hesh'n—Bhea, he's created an abomination. And worse, one that can practically assemble itself. I have to go to his lab, the one at the Academicon. I have to find out what else he's up to. If he manages to pull this off, Morty will be able to wipe out the resistance and bring about the Harvest without even needing to start a war between the Raccorin and the Andrasians."

"But Hesh'n's creation depends on the dynamins for power, same as all the maquina," Bhea said.

"Yes, but they could still do terrible damage before the crystals fail. And Hesh'n has been asking me for a prototype dynamin for years. I've done my best to keep them from him, but it's only a matter of time before he figures out what I figured out. And if he does, even Reformation won't stop the Verdhesh'n."

"Maybe. Maybe not. Things are in motion, my big sprout. Fin'roq plans to go to Balan Su. To face the Gran Pradesh."

Lithuigi stared at her like he hadn't heard what she said.

"Bhea, love," he said. "This is a terrible time to start teasing me. Of course, you never have, at least not like this, not with anything serious. So why should I think you'd start now? The sun always rises, doesn't it? Damn. What happened?"

"Fin took Ellex Andria and Prince Rhakksees down to Dar Ka'Hala, far under our feet. They found Ra'shard Ruu'n and Luthyr Andria. And Fin'roq—well, he more or less woke up to the fact that he's been used and abused, and he's had enough of it. He finally remembered his lifetimes in bondage. Parts of 'em, at least. He knows of his power, and he's gotten the idea that the Gran Pradesh stole his throne from him. He wants to take it back."

Lithuigi looked horrified. "And did you tell him the plan?"

"You know I can't, love."

"Anorian, then?"

"Nope."

"He's going to ruin everything."

"Mayhaps," she said. "But mayhaps not. Ellex and Rakk are going with him. They're taking Ruu'n's corpse with 'em. Plan to expose him for what he is before the Council of Nine. At least, after they have their own forces in place."

"I hope they don't do anything rash."

"They're hurting, L'uigi. Hurtin' bad. All of them. And they don't understand how good Mortimus is at staying in power. No, they don't have any idea what they're facing. I'm not even sure what'll happen. And Anorian isn't saying anything. She still hasn't spoken to her mother or her brother, but then again, they got their crystals numbed up so she couldn't speak in their heads if she wanted to. And she hardly says anything aloud as it is."

Lithuigi sighed. "Is it terrible of me that a part, a large part—maybe all but a tiny speck of me—wishes we could lose? That Mortimus would win. I'm not ready, Bhea. I'm not."

"Oh my love, don't talk like that, please, L'uigi. You know what this means to me."

"I know. It's because of what it means to you that I help. Otherwise—I don't know if I could do it."

"You don't have to do a thing. You've already done so much. I know you gotta go back to Balan Su. I'm sorry there's no word on Rebesh'a. And I sure hope you can get through to your sons. Bring 'em back here, to me and Anorian, if you want. Rebesh'a too, if she's willing."

"She won't be. And neither will they. But I love you so much for offering it. Sweet Trevian, how I love you."

"I love you too, my big old sprout. I just wish you'd give yourself a break. You know you've already redeemed your family name. Each generation is a new tree, new fruit, and new hope. You'll see."

She took his arm and led him into her garden, and he spent the day in the sunshine, caressing her skin and her hair and her face, burning every detail of her body into his mind. And under the sweetness of the day, the panic kept rising up, kept poking and scratching at him, and even the kisses of his Bhea couldn't fully drive it away.

⁂

The fleet arrived with much frenzied excitement down on the beach by the harbor. Mha'arlo came ashore, all grins, and Bhea gave him a big hug.

"Good work, son," Lithuigi said. "You made good time too. How'd the new ship handle?"

"Like a dream, professor."

"And the N'Detten?"

"Wonderful to work with. I established quite a rapport with the captains. In truth, I'm sad we've arrived."

"Well, don't be," Lithuigi said. "You're to stay on here, with a dozen of the new cata'rins under your command."

Mha'arlo's eyes lit up and his wide green face was glowing.

"You'll be under Bhea, of course. I want you as our liaison with the N'Detten. You're to patrol the area around P'anorum, and to make sure no ships cross the reef into the Swirling Sea without express permission from myself, Bhea, or our daughters."

"I won't let you down, professor."

"Then I must be off."

"For Balan Su?" Mha'arlo said.

"How'd you know?"

"I know you, professor. You're like a father to me."

"I wish the world were a different place, and that the Guild were better than it is. You'd already be a fine tinker and a better professor than me. And I wish—I wish that you were my own son." He smiled. "Now go. And when you have a chance, stop in at F'aryndon and see your mother?"

"Will do." He grinned as he left.

Lithuigi turned back to Bhea.

"You be careful, my big old precious sprout," she said. "I would lie if I said I wasn't worried. But I know there's no talking you out of it. I'd never dream of doing that anyway."

"I'll see you again," he said. "I promise."

"Don't let him have your face, my love. Promise you won't let him take your face."

"This old thing?" he said, grinning. "Who'd want it anyway?"

Chapter 59

At the Moment Where No One Can Live

B RYN IMAGINED THAT HER insides had been hollowed out, every fiber snapped, the sap drained away til only skin remained, a shell, the empty form of what had once been a Verdillion, now a mere husk lacking the spirit, the feelings, the sensitive core that made a Verdillion what they were. The ideas that once enriched her mind, the vast archives of data she'd squirreled away, the joy of learning—of sharing that knowledge—what was the point of any of it? Her love of history had done nothing to shed light on her predicaments, had given no indication of what she would endure or how to respond to it. Her notestream had not stopped the Cul'tavin from obtaining even more power and hadn't slowed their oppression of information. Her father was dead, her friends had disappeared, she couldn't reach her mother. Everything seemed lost.

And then there was Anorian.

Here I am, still on Roman Anthem's ship, she thought. *A guest now, supposedly, while our former jailer hurries to follow Anorian's commands.*

Bryn had trusted Anorian because her father had trusted Anorian. But was Doc Andri'n trustworthy? Was Anorian? There were so many secrets. Had Bryn been nothing but a pawn this entire time? A pawn of Anorian's, and a pawn of her father's?

But the thought of such things about Doc Andri'n made her feel so disgusting inside, so overwhelmed with guilt and grief, that she couldn't bear to entertain them. And her mind scrambled to find a distraction, for anything to draw her away from the despair that made her wonder if it wouldn't be better to leap overboard, to blow out her air and descend into the dark depths, and be done with the suffering once and for all.

Jaun found her where she had perched that morning, near the front of the cata'rin, staring out to sea. He approached timidly, a basket in one hand, a pitcher in the other.

"I thought you might be hungry," he said.

"No."

"Thirsty then." He held up the pitcher. "It's fizz water and juice. I filched it from Anthem's quarters."

He grinned, but Bryn just stared out at the water, watching a pod of whales break the surface and plunge back under, a half dozen of them, playing and singing and splashing. Jaun watched them swim for a moment, then pulled a couple of cups from the basket and started to fill them. He passed one to Bryn.

She stared at it for a moment, feeling her body betray her stoicism, feeling the ache of thirst in her mouth and in her throat and in her bowels, now impossible to ignore. She took the cup, lifted it to her lips, felt the smooth glazed clay, the sweet bubbles of the water, and she downed it.

Jaun took it from her hands and poured her another, and she took a sip and licked her lips, while a few tears ran down her cheeks.

Bryn felt her ears burning, and she blinked to try and stop the tears, but it only made them fall faster.

Jaun looked like he was about to cry too.

"I'm so sorry, Bryndax!" he said. "I had no idea what we'd find in the lab, I swear it. I never would have put you through that, had I known."

Bryn said nothing.

He offered her a bun from the basket, and she took a small bite.

"I just can't believe it," she said. "I can't even think about it."

He nodded. "It's a lot to deal with."

"No," she said. "It's too much."

Jaun said nothing, but grabbed a bun from the basket and started to munch on it.

"I hope—well, I hope you aren't blaming yourself. For what happened. You couldn't have known—"

"Jaun!" Bryn cried. "I said it's too much!"

He said nothing again, but stared at his bun, like he didn't know for sure why he was holding it. He put the leftover back in the basket, and stood.

"I'm sorry, I'm an obnoxious fool," he said. "I'll leave you with your thoughts."

"I have none," Bryn said. "They won't form up. There's no point. There are no questions anymore. No answers. No reason. Only secrets and shadows. Only senseless violence, and death."

Jaun left without saying any more.

Bryn was drifting in and out of sleep when she felt the softest touch on her mind, warm and gentle and promising affection. Anorian had finally reached out to her. And though Bryn told herself to push her away, to shut her out, she leapt toward her instead, in a panic that she would be gone before she could react. Anorian was all around her then, holding her in a firm, cuddling embrace, and Bryn hated herself for needing it so much, for wanting it so much, even as she felt the relief spreading down her body, as the tears began to flow again, her pain to spill out, flooding her crystal with grief and anger and regret.

And fear.

<<I'm mad at you,>> Bryn said, even as she curled into a ball and let Anorian lift her up and rock her.

Anorian said nothing.

<<No, I'm not,>> Bryn said. <<Not mad. Just hurt. Deceived, even though I know I should trust you. I just thought you were the last plant who would ever hurt me.>>

She felt Anorian's pain, raw and so profound, it seemed to have no end, and Bryn clutched at her, tried to soothe it, to relieve it, to make it stop, but Anorian pulled away. And Bryn could feel then what Anorian had tried to hide—she was scared too.

<<I thought I lost you,>> Anorian said. <<I thought—you'd never want to speak to me again.>>

<<After all you've done for me? You kept my mind safe from the Pradishar. Kept my father's mind safe too. How could I forget about all that? Besides—I can't stay mad at you. It makes me feel too awful inside.>>

Bryn felt relief flooding her crystamin and she looked at the tree of many colored fruits standing beside her.

<<Soon I can look on your real face,>> she said.

The tree turned aside.

<<I'm nervous. Excited, but nervous.>>

<<Me too,>> Bryn said.

<<What if—what if I'm not what you're expecting?>>

<<I'm not expecting you to be anything,>> Bryn said. <<I never told you this, but before we met, when I flowered, the Pradishar wanted to assign me male. I'm—big. Very tall, and broad too. I really could be a famous farknuckle player, if I had even the slightest desire to play—or skill at catching a ball, for that matter. My voice is gravely, and my hands,

my shoulders—they called me the barge. I still can't walk down the street without people stopping to gawk.>>

<<Let me see,>> Anorian said. <<Show me your true form.>>

Bryn hesitated. When she was in the hollow, she'd always projected herself as something other than herself—some kind of creature or inanimate object, or more often, a robed figure that was shorter, and slimmer, than she could ever hope to be. An idealized version. The thought of revealing herself—

<<Fine,>> she said. <<Take it or leave it, here I am.>>

Bryn transformed into a reflection of herself, and she looked down at the cobblestones of Dar Ka'Hala, afraid to look at Anorian—afraid to see what she thought of her.

She felt a small hand take her own hand, and when she looked up, there was a Bhizini standing in front of her, clad in a long gown the color of the deep ocean on a sun-filled morning, a timid look on her face, so full of hope and dread that Bryn wanted to wrap her arms around her.

<<I know you,>> Bryn said. <<You're Fin'roq. No! You're the one from the chamber. The one in Ellex Andria's dream.>>

Anorian nodded.

Bryn's mind had suddenly overwhelmed itself with a thousand competing questions, and she stared with her mouth open, scrambling for words.

<<I can see I'm not what you were expecting,>> Anorian said, looking away.

<<No!>> Bryn said, too loudly. <<I mean, yes. I mean—it's not a bad thing, to be surprised.>>

Anorian looked at her, and Bryn smiled.

<<I was just thinking about seeing you in the dream. To everyone else I know, your eyes were closed. But I saw you looking at me, staring at me, while I peered in at you through the glass. Was that—the dream, I mean—did you do that?>>

<<Yes,>> she said. <<Only, I didn't intend to. It was an accident. A terrible accident, given what happened and the lives that were lost. I was trying to help my mother, to free her from the blocks in her mind. And I was partially successful. But I lost control. In that moment, I was—everywhere, Bryndax. I was with you when you were seeing me—seeing me seeing you—and I knew you. I knew you, and I wanted to look on you.>>

Bryn blushed. <<So you already knew what I looked like,>> she said, <<before now.>>

Anorian gave her a tiny smile and nodded. <<I should've told you before. Only—I was afraid—to reveal myself. To anyone. I'm trying to be honest. To be open. I haven't even

told my mother yet, or my brother. It's—so much easier to be Anorian. To be here, in the weavryn, in the hollow, rather than out there, in the real world.>>

<<Don't I know it,>> Bryn said. <<And yet—>> She looked at Anorian and smiled. <<Being ourselves like this, together—it feels amazing. I mean—look at me! Smiling! When moments ago I was ready to kill myself.>>

Bryn felt a wave of fear ripple through her crystal, a powerful blast of panic emanating from Anorian.

<<Promise me you won't do it,>> she said.

<<I won't,>> Bryn said. <<It's just—been a lot lately. And I'm ready for all of the pain and confusion and anger to be over already. But what does that even mean? And what would even be left for me? I can't go home to Andramere. I can't go back to my classes. I can forget about ever being a tinker. My friends and family are dead or missing. I have pretty much no clue what I'm doing or where I'm going. And the only thing that seems even remotely good about my life is you.>>

She felt Anorian's fear again, and she wondered if she'd said too much. But Anorian put her arms around her and pulled Bryn's head down to her neck, and she closed her eyes and leaned into her.

They swayed back and forth, gently dancing.

<<I wish I could tell you the worst was over,>> Anorian said. <<That the fight against the darkness had been won. That the servants of death would learn the errors of their ways and wake up before its too late to save everything. But of course they won't. Even now, they plot to bring about the Harvest, to sow chaos and ruin. And I'm going to need you with me to face this, Bryndax. I can't do it alone.>>

<<I'm with you,>> Bryn said. <<In mind and spirit, and soon in the flesh.>>

<<Thank you,>> Anorian said. <<I hope you'll still feel that way after you know what I have to ask of you.>>

Now Bryn was the one having to fight off the panic.

<<It's Malisha Andra'asnia,>> Anorian said without waiting for Bryn to respond. <<She knows you've left Balance Territories, that you narrowly escaped an ambush of enforcers on Vergis. She knows you've been hiding from her in the hollow. And I'm afraid she's taken Stylina Andri'n into custody on charges of aiding and abetting traitors to Balance. Given the new laws that were passed following the chaos at the Balancing Act—they've already set her execution for the end of summer. This is almost certainly a

trap. You see Bryndax, they're willing to commute the sentence, to pardon your mother, if and only if you'll turn yourself in to the Pradishar.>>

The moment Anorian said Mama Andri'n's name, Bryn reached for the servryn, pulled the PropSector streams into her mind, and found the proclamation. She watched as a pitiful looking Mama Andri'n limped through the streets of Andramere, wincing with every step on her bad leg, a few angry onlookers hurling insults at her. Two Cul'tavin peacekeepers were at her side, zaprens at the ready, shoving her in the back whenever she slowed.

The spark, the one deep inside her, the tiny flame that she'd thought had been smothered out, went supernova in her heart. The pulsing heat shot down her arms and legs, made her hands tingle, made her vision seem to crackle and pop on the sides. At that moment, she would have walked up to Malisha Andra'asnia, grabbed her around the throat, and squeezed. She would have fought off an entire legion of Cul'tavin, barehanded, if it would have saved her mother.

And then she saw who the peacekeepers were—who it was who held zaprens aloft, sneers on their faces, hatred in their eyes, shoving her mother, knocking her to the ground, spitting on her. For a moment, she thought she was seeing through her mother's eyes, looking up into the faces of Emo and A'erid, on top of her, pinning her down.

The sun seemed to extinguish, the supernova inside her was gone, only a black hole, cold and barren, remained where her heart had been. Her lungs screamed to breath, but there was no air. She tried to squirm free, to turn over, to stop them! But she couldn't.

She couldn't do anything at all.

They've won, she thought. *They've won, and I didn't even fight back.*

Chapter 60

Departures and Arrivals

ELLEX ANDRIA DIDN'T KNOW what to think when Bhea Bell told her a Pradishar cata'rin would soon dock at P'anorum, and that the ship would be able to take them to Balan Su. But when she saw Roman Anthem striding down the gangplank, a confident grin on his splotchy, weather-beaten face, her first reaction wasn't anger, wasn't confusion, but instead was an almost paralyzing panic, a terror she had never felt before—that Qaas'andria would be taken, imprisoned again, this time for centuries—that she'd lost, that it was all over, and that she was helpless to change anything.

But the fear dropped away as quickly as it had come when Ellex remembered how much she trusted Bhea, how warm and safe she felt in her presence. Her crystamins were numb so Anthem wouldn't be able to imperialize her. And Rakk was at her side, too. Her heart was still thudding, but she felt like she could function again.

The confusion—and anger—came when she saw Rakk practically jump into Roman Anthem's arms, wrapping the grizzled old Bhizini in a tight hug.

Ellex had always hated him—had always been outraged that he'd been allowed to join the Pradishar.

Or have I? she thought. *Was that me, or the imperialization?*

No, he's a servant of the Gran Pradesh—of Mortimus Rex! I'm right not to trust him. Aren't I?

"You old rascal, what are you doing way out here?" Rakk said.

"Sailing in circles, as always," Anthem said, grinning. "I can't believe you're here. And—the good-mother of Andrasia herself? Sui Pradesh Ellex Andria." He bowed.

Ellex opened her mouth then closed it. She looked at Rakk.

"A dear friend of yours?"

"One of my oldest," Rakk said.

Ellex clenched her teeth.

How did I not know? Or did I?

She opened her mouth to respond, but closed it when she saw that his ship wasn't empty. Two Andrasians were coming down the gangplank. She recognized them both.

They're supposed to be in Pradishar custody—in dungeons! Why has Roman Anthem brought them to P'anorum?

"Welcome, my sprouts," Bhea said, smiling warmly at Jaun von Andron and Bryn Andri'n. "I'm Bhea Bell."

Ellex saw Bryn staring at her, and when she caught her eye, she could see that it was full of panic, and Ellex knew it was the same terror she had felt at seeing Anthem.

Bhea saw it too.

"The good-mother of Andrasia?" Jaun said. "Well, this is a surprise, isn't it?" He looked at Roman Anthem.

"Ellex Andria isn't your enemy," Bhea said.

"She's the head Cul'tavin on Balan Su," Bryn said, her hands shaking.

"It's true," Ellex said. "I am. Bryn Andri'n is right to be alarmed at my presence, though it sickens me to think I've caused a fellow Andrasian to feel that way. Just moments ago, when I saw Roman Anthem coming out of the ship, I felt like my heart had stopped beating. I felt like everything was lost."

She felt Rakk take her hand as he stepped forward.

"A lot has changed this summer," he said. "Just know that we're all victims of the same enemy. And we've all suffered for our mistakes."

"But more importantly," Ellex said, "we came here looking for answers, and we've found them. And now—we intend to make amends for our mistakes."

Bryn continued to stare, saying nothing.

"Come on, my sprouts, let's get'cha settled," Bhea said, beckoning to Jaun and Bryn.

Rakk squeezed Ellex's hand. She waited for the others to leave before she turned back to Anthem.

"So why are you here, Captain?" she said.

"You know, Sui Pradesh, the tone of your voice—that's the nicest you've been to me in, oh, decades. I could get used to this."

"Just answer the question," she snapped.

"Oh well, you know, I go here, I go there, I go just about everywhere. But sooner or later, I always come home. Too bad I can't stay long. I'm told you need a ride to Balan Su?"

"That's why Bhea wanted us to wait?" Ellex said, raising her eyebrows.

"We need a quiet entry," Rakk said to Anthem. "Preferably one that doesn't get us wet."

"Wait just a second," Ellex said. "We're going to trust him?"

"I've always trusted him," Rakk said. "Ever since he saved my life."

"Did I know that?" Ellex said. "Before, I mean? Did I trust him?"

"You knew we were friends," Rakk said. "But you've never trusted him."

"Very well, then I'll continue not to," she said. "Why would you help us? You must know that Ra'shard Ruu'n—that he's—"

"Dead?" Anthem said. "Of course I know."

"Then why?"

Anthem sighed. "Must I always be loyal?" he said. "You sailed halfway around the world to try and break Balance, to free the wielder of all crystals from his cage, even as you swore allegiance to the Pradishar and the Gran Pradesh. Why am I not allowed the same right to serve, and to deceive, at the calling of my conscience?"

Ellex didn't know what to say.

"He can get us into Balan Su, Ell," Rakk said. "He's never failed me."

I can't trust him, she thought. *But I do trust Raeder. And Bhea. If Anthem can get us into the city without tipping off the Pradishar, then do I really have a choice?*

❧ ☙

Rakk spent the morning making sure everything was ready for their departure, trying to stay busy, which kept him from having to think or feel. But it was impossible not to. Everywhere he went was full of memories, of sights and sounds and smells he thought he'd forgotten only to re-discover that they were still a part of him—were still able to touch him as few things could.

And after everything they'd discovered under the island—he'd felt numb, then furious, then betrayed, then despondent, then numb again. His emotions seemed to cycle over and over again, and each time they did, he thought of Q'orin.

He ached to connect with him, to feel him at the edge of his mind, to know he was there, that he was with him even if far away. Rakk needed to know he was alright. And he needed to know what was going on in the world. Day after day numbing his crystamin hadn't bothered him til now, he'd been so caught up in Ellex and Qaas'andria. But the risk was too great to stop, even if not knowing what was happening in Raccorum Rhazzat was killing him.

Surely he's alright, he thought. *He's too capable to get caught.*

But Rakk thought of his own capture—in Balan Su and again in Callo Baton—and knew he had to accept that he couldn't know for sure.

Even with all the uncertainty, and even with his desire to get back to civilization, the thought of leaving P'anorum made him feel sick. It still felt like his island, his home, his kingdom! Qaas'i was safe there, and Bhea and Grizmond were there too. And he wanted to go back into old P'anorum, and spend more time looking around, to see if there was anything worth salvaging. Any relic that might jog his memory.

Rakk pulled out the scytherin that Grizmond had given him.

Father didn't trust me, he thought. *He didn't trust any of his offspring—didn't care enough to even warn us. And now Rajj's life is in danger. And where is Father? Why did he retreat into seclusion after the eruption? Why did he give up the fight against the Gran Praesh? Why didn't he come back to P'anorum, try to rebuild the Far Archipelago? Why didn't he reach out to me, all these years?*

He squeezed the handle of the scytherin, tighter and tighter, until he could feel the metal grooves cutting into his skin.

I'll find the answers, he swore to himself. *Ellex has to be right. It's not too late. We can still save Balance—my kingdom. All of this won't have been in vain—it can't have been. It can't!*

Rakk sheathed the blade, picked up the bag containing the petrified corpse of Ra'shard Ruu'n, and headed for the cata'rin.

※※※ ⁂ ※※※

Fin'roq's whole body was trembling as he walked down the beach to the docks, still feeling what it felt like to be inside Jaun's mind, to feel his fear of him, the recoil of it, the pain. The crowd that had gathered to send them off split apart to give him a wide path. He tried to keep his head high—tried not to notice the way those of the Tornroot Clan stared at him as he passed—but he could feel their eyes on him. He prayed to Trevian that no tears would fall, that his legs wouldn't fail him.

He counted each step, repeating the number twice in his mind, ignoring his confusion, his conflicting desires—trying to just make it to the ship, to just make it that far. He wanted to run away, up the stairs to the Swarthen Forest, where he might lose himself forever in the canopy, living out his days as a beast, with Baboo, in some semblance of peace. He wanted to run back to Jaun, to beg his forgiveness, to beg him never ever to hurt him like that again—no, he just wanted to hold him, to feel him in his arms, to never be apart from him.

But Fin kept walking toward the ship.

I'm leaving P'anorum again, he thought, *on Roman Anthem's ship. Just like last time. Only—*

He saw that day again in his mind, as clearly as if he streamed it on a crystal—the villagers standing rigid like statues, their eyes filled with hatred. He thought of Milli Mor'n, the way she scowled at him—and then he was in Roe's memories again, kissing her, hearing her whisper in his ear, her warm breath on his neck.

That isn't real, he thought.

His mind turned to Jaun then, to Bhart, to the surge of emotions he'd felt when he touched them, the way they made his heart seem to swell up until it filled the entire world.

But that wasn't real either, he thought.

And Fin remembered the past lives he'd glimpsed while in Dar Ka'Hala, through the Inner Door, and he could see them again as if he were living them—lifetime after lifetime—embodiment after embodiment—each one with its own loves and heartbreaks. He felt them again, the old flames, the long-dead spouses, ones he'd spent centuries loving. He felt their lips on his, his flower against theirs, his hands on their back. He heard their voices, their sighs, their laughter. He remembered feeling they were his, and he theirs, and that they would always be together, always and forever.

Then death came for them. Death always came for him. Everyone he'd loved, died. Everyone he'd been, passed away.

More and more faces for the dark king's collection.

But at least he'd gotten the chance to enjoy life, once upon a time. Before Mortimus Rex exiled him to lifetimes of darkness, a nearly endless sleep that wasn't yet sleep, but neither was it waking, trapped inside the stasis chamber. Most of the those incarnations hadn't even been named.

And then there was this lifetime. There was Fin'roq. And what had that been but pain?

No, Fin was done feeling sorry for himself. He was done crying over every little thing that happened to him. He was done thinking that if only he tried a little harder, he'd be able to fit in. And he was done doing what others wanted him to do.

Bhea was standing on the deck of Anthem's cata'rin when Fin came aboard.

She smiled at him and spread her arms wide for a big hug, and Fin couldn't resist. And when she held him, he could feel her presence, warm and safe and strong.

"I know you're mad at me, my sprout," Bhea said. "I don't blame ya. I've done you wrong. But there ain't no goin' back. There's only goin' onward. The past, love—it's the sense you make of it right now that matters, not the sense it had at the time. Otherwise you'll get caught up on things you can't do nothin' about. It's only right now that you have the power to change things, my sprout. To let go, so you can flow."

"To let go of what?"

"You'll know when the time's right."

Fin swallowed a hiss. "You never can make it easy for me, can you?"

"I can't live your life for ya, my sprout," she said. "Don't think you'd want me to anyway. I love you enough to let you choose."

"What if I make the wrong choice?"

"Oh love, there ain't nothin' perfect but the flow. Even as much as we try to go with it, we can only ever do our best with the limited knowledge and power we possess. That's why you gotta be willing to take risks, to fail if you have to. And to accept forgiveness, so you can get back on the path again, having learned from your mistakes."

"I've already learned from my mistakes," Fin said. "I learned not to trust anyone. Including you, Bhea."

"Well my sprout, sometimes the lessons we learn from our mistakes, end up being mistakes on their way to an even deeper lesson. Let time draw the line. The truth is eternal, which means there's no riddle that can't be solved you work on it long enough."

"I don't have forever," Fin'roq said. "And I've waited lifetimes. Thousands of years! This revenge has been a long time coming, and I'm not about to wait any longer."

"I know it, I just—"

"Good-bye, Bhea," Fin said, turning away from her.

He headed for the front of the ship without looking back.

Chapter 61

As All Beauty, Momentary

WHEN BRYN ARRIVED AT P'anorum and saw Ellex Andria standing on the makeshift dock, she was sure her life was over, that the Cul'tavin had found her—that there could be no deal to save her mother—that Roman Anthem, even Anorian, had sold her out. But Bryn clenched her teeth and faced Ellex Andria down, and when Bryn spoke, she was surprised that words came out, and that her voice wasn't shaking.

She felt Anorian's presence in her mind, soothing her, and Bryn remembered something she'd told her recently, but which hadn't dawned on her until now.

Ellex Andria. The dream. Anorian said she was trying to help her mother. Sweet Trevian!

Now Bryn could do nothing but stare at Ellex, at the plant whom she had spent so much time and energy opposing, whom Bryn thought of as a vile, hateful creature. As the panic subsided, the shock at seeing her—and Prince Rhakksees—together on P'anorum—the world had definitely gone insane.

"Come on, my sprouts, let's get'cha settled," Bhea Bell said.

Bryn looked at Jaun and he nodded at her. She took one last look at Ellex and Rakk, one last look at Anthem, then followed Bhea across the planks that spanned the width of the various boats anchored together in the harbor. There were so many boats and ships, and a frenzy of activity on the beach, where Bhizini, along with some Andrasians and Raccorin, were busy building structures, moving massive maquina into place, fortifying the island.

The weapons weren't enough to make Bryn feel safe. She doubted if anything could. The Pradishar had her mother, and if she didn't turn herself in, they'd kill her. Malisha Andra'asnia was crazy enough, and cruel enough, to do it. But would she really free her mother if Bryn gave herself up?

No, that wasn't the question, not the real one. The question was whether Bryn could face Malisha—could face Aerid and E'mo—knowing what they'd do to her.

Knowing what they'd already done to her.

Bryn tried to focus on where she was, on the sand beneath her feet, warm in the morning sun. She tried to remember that she was about to see Anorian, to really see her, for the first time, but the excitement didn't want to rekindle.

An old Raccorin with a wrinkly, weathered face ran up to Bhea. "I found him!" he said. "I found Fin'roq. He's in one of the unfinished huts."

"Fin'roq's alive? He's here?!" Jaun was in tears and grinning like an idiot.

Bryn gave him a confused look.

"He's alive," Bhea said. "And he's here. But he's leaving soon, on that ship you came on."

Jaun's face fell. "Can I see him before he leaves?"

"I don't see why not," Bhea said.

"Right now?" Jaun said. He put his hands together as if praying.

Bhea chuckled. "Let's get you cleaned up and in some fresh robes first, what d'you think?"

Jaun sniffed at himself.

"Good idea," he said.

"Well, come on then. This way, my sprouts," Bhea said, and started off again, down the beach toward the east end.

<<You know Fin'roq?>> Bryn said to Jaun via crystal when they started walking.

<<We were roommates at the Pruu'patch. Friends.>>

Bryn gave him a look. <<Only friends?>>

Jaun blushed. <<The last time we spoke, we had a terrible fight. He was there when I denounced Balance, when the Pradishar—the last I saw of him, he was being attacked by a mob.>>

<<I'm sorry,>> Bryn said. <<You thought he was dead?>>

<<Not really,>> Jaun said. <<There were reports he'd been kidnapped by the Bhizini. Taken by Qardymion's men. But I still see him—and feel him—in my dreams.>>

Bryn put her arm around Jaun's shoulder and pulled him into a walking hug. <<Don't be scared, Jaun. You did what you had to do in denouncing Balance, and he'll understand. If not now, then when this is all over and he can look back on it.>>

<<Right, because studying history is all about learning and growing and opening your heart.>>

<<It can be,>> Bryn said.

<<Only in carefully selected strands, plucked from across time by a steady hand, and woven into some sort of simplistic narrative that we mere mortals can understand,>> Jaun said. <<History can teach you whatever you want it to teach you, if you have enough of it to work with.>>

<<I can't believe that,>> Bryn said.

<<Or you don't want to?>> Jaun said.

Bhea took them to one of the huts on the back edge of the sand, nestled under the trees. The palm thatched roof made a large dome that made the cozy space feel large and expansive. She fished around in the cabinets for some fresh robes and cumberdomes while Jaun and Bryn went into the stalls and stripped out of their soiled clothes.

Bryn took the ladle and dipped it into the fountain and poured it over her head, and it was cool and refreshing on her skin. She breathed deep of the aroma, softly scented with frangipani and coconut, and scrubbed herself down. Bhea had put a towel over the stall door along with a clean blue robe and a cumberdome. She dried off, carefully patting around her flower, then strapped on the clean undergarment and pulled the robe over her head. She ran her fingers through her hair fibers, pulled them back into a low bun, and tied it up.

Jaun was still splashing in the water when Bryn emerged, trying to fake a smile.

"I'll be right back, Jaun," Bhea said. She looked at Bryn. "This way, my sprout."

Bryn followed her outside, feeling herself relax a little in Bhea's presence. She was so warm, so kind. She reminded her of the old Bhizini that Anorian would become sometimes in the hollow, the one who held her when the Cul'tavin arrested her.

"See the palace up there on the rim? And the pathway cutting back and forth down the side of it? The landing is right up ahead at the end of the sand, you can't miss it. Go on up. Anorian's waiting for ya on the porch."

Bhea took her hand and squeezed it. "She's nervous, too," she said.

"Really?"

"Really, my sprout. Go on now. We'll be along after awhile, I promise."

She took a deep breath and started for the stairs.

❧☙

Bryn felt like two different people were simultaneously making the climb to the ruins of the palace. One of them was more excited than they felt like they had any right to be. The other was on the very verge of an emotional and mental breakdown, as a war between panic and rage, despair and terror, robbed her of her breath and made her mind spin around and around, running through the possibilities of tragedy, failure, violation—so many possibilities—and so few of them with any kind of happy ending.

When she climbed the final step onto the promenade on the edge of the rim, and the porch of the palace towered overhead, with it's carved friezes and wide burnstone columns, Bryn could see the long sweeping vista across the glowing red and black crystal of the lava flow, up and up the sheer side of the great mountain, til it vanished into the clouds that ringed the top of the crater. The sight was so awe-inspiring, so majestic and so devastating, there was a moment where it seemed that she ceased to exist at all. There was only the flow, flowing.

When she came back to herself, Anorian stepped out from behind the columns, walked toward her from out of the shadows, out into the sunshine, her eyes fixed on hers—that same humorous, knowing look that she'd had in the dream—and Bryn's other half, her sad and terrified half—was gone.

Bryn watched Anorian approach, her face burning, unable to keep a grin off her face. She laughed and opened her arms for Anorian and she picked her up and spun her around in a circle, wanting to squeeze her in a tight hug but she was so frail, Bryn was afraid she'd crush her. She sat her down gently in front of her, but didn't let go of her.

"You're real," Bryn said.

Anorian grinned. "Did you think I existed only in the weavryn?"

"I don't know what I thought," Bryn said. "Nothing makes sense anymore."

<<I hope things will,>> Anorian said. <<You deserve answers.>>

<<We all do,>> Bryn said.

<<Have you thought any more about what I asked you? About your stream?>>

"No!" Bryn shouted. <<I mean, no, I haven't thought about it. I mean—how can I, Anorian? They have my mother! I have to go and save her. I know I do. Only I'm too scared to go. My mother is going to die because of my cowardice.>>

<<Your mother is *not* going to die,>> Anorian said. <<And the best way for you to help her is by fighting for what she's spent her entire life fighting for. Share your story—her story, and your father's story—tell the world what the Pradishar have done to you. There are so many other victims out there, Bryndax. And so many others who only need a face, a story, to arouse their sympathies.>>

<<You want me to publicly denounce Balance? To share everything?>>

Anorian nodded.

<<I know you have questions, Bryndax. And I know you feel so lost and so confused.>>

<<No,>> Bryn said. <<I mean, yes. I mean—I feel both. It's like I'm about to die, to literally decompose. But then other times, like right now, with you—I feel more alive than I've ever felt. I'm so confused, I don't know who I am, or what I want, or what to do!>>

<<What do you want to do when you're feeling alive? When you aren't feeling afraid?>>

She stared into Anorian's eyes, and put her hand on her face.

<<This,>> Bryn said, her heart thudding in her ears like the bongos down on the beach, and she leaned down and put her lips on Anorian's. They were so soft, and seemed to fit perfectly with hers.

Bryn's first kiss, and the elation was met with a sudden wave of uncertainty and panic and shock that she'd been so bold. She started to pull away, but Anorian held her close and kissed her again, and Bryn felt like her heart was going to explode with so much joy and so much sadness.

Chapter 62

Though All Service Be in Vain

LITHUIGI STOOD ON THE top deck of his cata'rin and stared at the open blue around him. The Threshinveld Sea was delightfully calm that day, the sky clear overhead, but he could see clouds in the distance, a smear of fog on the horizon. The trip from P'anorum had been uneventful, the Far Ocean wide and flat and full of sunshine perfect for smooth sailing, and when he'd reached the great swamps of Mon Mang'alar, he'd wound his way through the overgrown channels without incident. The good weather and calm skies had been a sailor's dream, and there was a part of Lithuigi that knew and appreciated that, and felt gratitude for it somewhere down in the deepest part of his being.

But the other part of him—the part on the surface, the part that filled his daily reality—couldn't find any peace from the sea, since he knew where it was leading him, and since he still didn't know what he'd find when he got there.

I'll never forgive myself if they've hurt Rebesh'a, he thought.

Hesh'n, even Vilder—they wouldn't hurt their mother. But if Vilder is working with Mortimus—and if Hesh'n has other worksites putting together his Verdhesh'n—

No! I can't go down that path. The plan—remember the plan. It's underway, and all things considered, it's going well. Morty doesn't know, and by the time he figures it out, it will already be too late to stop.

He hoped that was true.

I ran away from this problem, he remembered, his ears burning with shame. *I should have—what? Kidnapped my sons? Taken them to the Bhizini for re-education? Locked them in a stasis chamber until after all this was over? Killed them if they wouldn't comply? No, no! It doesn't matter what happened, only what's happening now. That's what Bhea would say. Baboo too.*

Am I willing to kill my sons this time? Am I really?

Lithuigi watched the fog begin to wrap around the ship and blur out the view, as the light faded to gray. The air around the capital had a wet, moldy taste. He narrowed the aperture til the gurgitator was barely purring and the ship slowed to a crawl. Then he used his crystal and the buoys around the city to navigate, careful to cloak himself in the hollow. When he located his drop spot, he killed the gurgitator, took a deep breathe, and dove into the sea.

The water was warm on his skin and salty on his lips, and he felt invigorated by the sensation. He turned over on his back and used his arms to propel himself, staring up at the fog, imagining he was floating through the clouds.

Lithuigi could hear the breakers ahead, at the base of the cliff on the outside of the crescent, just below the Pradishar citadel. The sheer face split the lower rim in two, and if the fog had been clear, he could have stared up at the obsidian spire rising into the heavens.

After filling his lungs with air, he dove under the surface and down toward the island at an angle, until he reached the rocky face of the cliff. He ran his fingers along the surface, feeling for the notches, and he followed where they led, til he saw the small opening into a cavern. He swam into it, the current shifting him slightly to the left and right as he went. The walls of the passage closed in until he could just barely squeeze through, and he wondered if a full-sized Raccorin would be able to fit. The cave twisted and turned, up and down and around through the obsidian spire, until he finally broke the surface and looked around, blinking a few times to convince himself that his eyes were indeed open.

The darkness was absolute, and he felt on his belt for a small glowbe and shook it. A warm light like the flicker off a campfire spread outward and up the shiny black walls, and he saw he was on a small landing in a tiny room, with a small arched door leading to a spiral stair. He stood and wrung out his clothes as best he could, then took a few cautious steps across the obsidian floor, gripping the smooth stone with his rootpads. He went through the door and started the climb.

Lithuigi emerged in the basement of a small bookstore in the Old Stones district, on the upper rim of the city. A Bhizini ran the place, an old friend of Lithuigi's and a staunch ally of Bhea Bell, and they gave Lithuigi clean pradeshan robes to change into.

"Wish me luck, old friend," he said to the Bhizini, as he prepared to step out into the city.

✦ ✦

The streets of Balan Su weren't completely deserted but they were quieter than they should have been for that time of day, though it was hard to tell with the fog well up over the top of the upper rim. Old Stones wasn't far from Lithuigi's house at Sunrise Ridge, so he pulled his hood low over his face and hurried through the streets. A few vendors were outside their shops but they ignored him as he passed.

When Lithuigi reached the main gate to the housing development, he headed left along the wall to a service door at the far east end. Lithuigi had developed a rapport with the local attendants over the years, and though he wasn't sure he trusted them entirely, he doubted they'd report him to the Pradishar. He recognized the Raccorin by the dumpsters, and the attendant waved as he approached.

If the Raccorin knew there was a warrant for Lithuigi's arrest, he didn't say so, and he didn't hesitate to open the door for him, or to promise—without being asked to—that if anyone asked, he hadn't seen him. Lithuigi would have to remember to make it up to him, if he could.

He hurried down the grassy pathways of his neighborhood until he reached his home, but when he passed through the gates into the garden, he knew something was wrong. A few of the planters were overturned, but nobody was on the terrace. He sprinted into Rebesh'a's studio, into his den, into their sleeping chambers, but Rebesh'a wasn't there. The drawers of the furniture had been pulled out, their contents dumped and rifled through. And his den looked like a wild animal had gone on a rampage, knocking over furniture, busting apart the desks and tables. Some of the books and scrolls on his shelves had been torn into tiny shreds, as if someone had spent time desecrating them.

Lithuigi lit a glowbe and carefully went over the floors and walls of the estate, making sure there was no sap, no skin or hair fibers anywhere, that nothing violent had happened to his wife. Then he looked through the closets in their room, trying to see if Rebesh'a had packed a bag, had left as planned. But he couldn't tell for sure.

Tears started to burn his eyes, and Lithuigi stopped, clenched his teeth and both his fists, then took a few breaths to calm himself. He wiped his eyes, got down on his knees, and started to roll up the rug in front of his desk. Once it was out of the way, he found the notch in the board and lifted up the panel, then turned the levers to unlock the door of the vault. Lithuigi removed an enflamer and a zapren and stuck both in his belt, then closed the vault door and put the floor and rug back in place.

Next stop: Hesh'n's lab. Although he'd destroyed the one at his garden in Sunset Point, he'd neglected the one at the Academicon.

Foolishly, too, he thought. *And now Hesh'n's taken over my lab as well. Mortimus has probably put him in charge of the stasis project. Trevian help me, I really have failed.*

He walked across the city, the cobblestones slick in the mist, the fog obscuring the view, making every block look the same, an endless sprawl of gray and murky white.

The campus of the Academicon was largely empty, as was to be expected during the summer recess. So far, the Guild hadn't said anything about the attack on Hesh'n's production facility at Vergis—or maybe Management was unaware of it altogether—but either way, the enforcers didn't move to stop him. He still kept a hand on his enflamer, just in case.

When Lithuigi was outside the door, he knocked but nobody answered.

<<Knock knock, Anorian,>> he said.

The door opened with a whoosh.

When Lithuigi walked inside, he was hit with something he didn't expect—nostalgia. This lab had been his home for so many years, nearly a century. He'd made so many modifications to the equipment himself, and had installed his own maquina in the workstations. He'd revolutionized stasis technology here, after studying the old chamber on P'anorum. And he'd understood how to duplicate dynamin technology here. All the maquina that had kept Qaas'andria alive, that had kept her mind active, that had kept everyone fooled for thirty three years thinking she was in full stasis—all of it he'd tinkered here.

He'd also taught Hesh'n how to use scalpels to cut open and examine flesh when he was just a scamp. Lithuigi had taught him how to keep the wound clean, how to sew them up and heal them, how to use maquina he'd invented to minimize sap loss and to regrow binding flesh.

No time for regrets, he thought, shaking his head.

Lithuigi opened the cupboard at the back of the lab and Anorian opened the hidden door in the wall without him needing to ask. The corridor led down through the rock of Balan Su and into the obsidian of the Pradishar citadel, to the lab where Lithuigi had kept Qaas'andria for all those years.

But this isn't my lab any longer, he thought when he arrived and looked around in horror. All the workstations along the length of the laboratory were covered in dissected spratlyns, along with pieces of similar maquina to the small ones Lithuigi had attached to Qaas'i's body in the stasis chamber.

And there was something else. A suit of armor?

He'll never let the Verdhesh'n project go, Lithuigi thought. *We're fanatics, all of us von Androns.*

Lithuigi swallowed hard and clenched his teeth, and vowed to himself that he'd do what he must, come what may. He scanned the wall of cubbies and compartments and found his tools were still inside, and he used them to open the hatch on the stasis chamber and slip out the sheath protecting the dynamin. Then he slit one of the vines on the controller and threaded it across another vine, then slid the dynamin back into its compartment and shut the hatch.

Inside the maquina, the dynamin began to hum.

Lithuigi headed back upstairs and closed the door behind him when he emerged into the cupboard. Then he stashed all the datamins he found lying around the lab in his robes, and used a set of tools to overload a dynamin in one of the workstations. He'd just closed up the hatch and started for the door when it opened. Hesh'n was standing in the threshold, a furious look on his face.

"Son!" Lithuigi cried, and he thought to grab him by the neck with his prosthetic, but his resolve failed him. Instead he screamed in Hesh'n's face, as loud as he could, and while his son was startled, he pulled the zapren from his robe and had it in Hesh'n chest before he could react.

His son made a terrible gurgling sound as his body thrashed and dropped to the floor, lurching about in great spasms before falling still. The hum of the dynamin increased to a whine.

"You vile creature!" Vilder hissed, stepping through the door, an enflamer trained on his father. "Step back or I'll roast you. I swear it!"

Lithuigi let the zapren fall to the floor.

Vilder was out of breath, but he started to laugh. "You must be the greatest fool in the world to come back here now," he said. "You must have guessed what's about to happen."

"Yes," Lithuigi said. "This lab is about to explode and incinerate us both."

Vilder looked at the workstation, it's whine growing more and more high-pitched by the second, like a swarm of insects approaching from a distance.

As soon as Vilder glanced away from him, Lithuigi moved to grab his enflamer with his prosthetic, but it thrashed suddenly, and Vilder sent a whorl of flame at him. Lithuigi dropped to the floor, and the stream of fire passed just over him. When it stopped, he moved to lunge at Vilder again, but the prosthetic moved first. His arm started to twist over til his hand was facing palm upward, and then it began to bend at the elbow, slowly at first, before the hand shot forward, clutched Lithuigi's neck, and began to squeeze.

Hesh'n looked at him and sat up, coughing while trying to laugh.

Lithuigi sent the signal to the prosthetic to release him, but it wouldn't respond. He used his other hand and clutched at the wrist, pulling, but the prosthetic only squeezed him tighter, until he was sure it would crush his windpipe. He rolled around on the floor, his mind spinning, his vision starting to crackle and pop, the fibers in his neck screaming with pain.

"You weren't the true master of the crystal," Hesh'n mocked. "I was. All this time, I've been able to track you through it." He looked at his brother. "Vilder and I know you've been sailing far and wide in the Far Ocean. Tell me, Father, what have you been doing beyond the Swirling Sea?"

The prosthetic unclenched enough for him to speak, and Lithuigi let his good hand fall to his side. Then he whispered something, too low for Vilder or Hesh'n to hear. And as he hoped, they both took a few steps toward him. He whispered again, moaning, while he felt for the zapren on the floor and slowly climbed to his feet. Then he jabbed the zapren upward toward Hesh'n's chest as he kicked downward as hard as he could, right into Vilder's knee.

Hesh'n thrashed about again, the prosthetic momentarily gripping Lithuigi's neck tighter before falling limp, while Vilder collapsed on the ground, shrieking. The whine from the dynamin was like a swarm of bees when you break open their hive, furious. There was precious little time.

Lithuigi fished in the cupboards for a scalpel, and when he found one, he took a deep breath, then placed the blade as close to the top of the prosthetic as he could get it. There was no way he could do this delicately, so he exhaled sharply, then set to work, slicing and hacking and moaning. The sap was dripping on to the floor but he kept going, and when he was partway through the arm, he grabbed the scalpel like a dagger and made a few long stabbing motions downward.

When the arm finally fell to the floor, Lithuigi grabbed his enflamer with his good hand and sent a whorl of fire across the wound. He roared with pain and wobbled on his feet, sure for a moment he was going to pass out, but he didn't. Then he pocketed the enflamer and picked up the prosthetic and started for the door, determined to flee, to leave his sons there in the lab, not to save them this time.

He stepped over Hesh'n and started to step past Vilder when he grabbed his leg and pulled him down, and Lithuigi fell through the doorway and into the hall. Vilder lunged at him and his head slammed back on the floor, and his vision shook and sparkled but didn't fade out. Lithuigi clutched his hand around the hand of the prosthetic, and he gripped it tight and swung it upward, the fleshy, sap-oozing top and the hard metal inside it cracked into Vilder's chin, crushing his teeth together and whipping his head backward so far and fast, his feet came up off the floor and he fell in an arch back into the wall.

Lithuigi turned to run down the hall, but the prosthetic was thrashing again, and Hesh'n stumbled out the door, glaring at him. He tried to fling the arm away from him, but it was held tightly to his hand, jerking about like a fish on a line. Lithuigi swung it against the wall several times, but it wouldn't stop, wouldn't loosen it's grip. Hesh'n stumbled toward him, raising an enflamer, and Lithuigi swung the arm one more time, and it opened it's grip on his hand and sailed away down the hall, right into Hesh'n's hand.

The hum had grown so loud, it was deafening, so that when the dynamins finally blew, and a blinding light streamed out the door into the hallway, followed by a fast-billowing wall of black smoke and curling blue flame, Lithuigi didn't know what to do. The smoke and the heat caught up to him, and he choked and coughed and thought his lungs were aflame, and his eyes burned so badly he couldn't open them.

He stumbled forward, knowing he needed to see if his sons were alive, but he couldn't have seen anything if he'd wanted to, couldn't hear anything over the roar, couldn't smell if anyone was near. So he stumbled away, down the halls and stairs he'd climbed tens of thousands of times over the last century.

When he came out of the doors into the plaza in front of the great hall, the ground was vibrating and there were alarms going off. He pulled up his hood and started to walk away, trying to keep calm. Everyone was running in the opposite direction, going to see why the alarms were sounding, and nobody paid him any attention.

He was nearly across Grand Plaza when he realized what he'd done.

The prosthetic, he thought. *Sweet Trevian, no! It's powered by one of my prototype dynamins.*

Lithuigi thought about the explosion, about the blue flame and black smoke. Had it been enough to destroy the arm? Or had he just given Hesh'n exactly what he needed to make his Verdhesh'n unstoppable?

It was too late to go back.

He rounded the corner into the narrow streets of Old Stones, and in front of him was his father, his face contorted with anger, a look of contempt in his eyes, even disgust.

"How could you do such a thing? You're a monster, son. How could you attack my grandsons? Your own family!" his father screamed at him.

Lithuigi stopped walking and stared at Mortimus Rex.

"At least you've gotten his character right this time," he said.

His father's face slipped into a grin. "I told you, I really am him. Ask me anything. Anything at all. Something only you and Burning Leaf Bryn'thyr would know."

There was malice in the Death King's eyes, but Lithuigi hid a smile. Mortimus would only taunt him with his father if he didn't yet have his son's faces—or Rebesh'a's. They were all alive.

"I don't have time for your games," Lithuigi said.

"My games are all there is. Haven't you understood that yet? Sometimes you're so smart, and sometimes you're the biggest fool I've ever known. And I've been around even longer than you can imagine, Von'nDrino. Or should I call you von Andron?"

"Only you know what my father and my uncle agreed to," he said. "I've upheld my end. I stayed off of Andramere, I didn't contest the throne. I kept the wielder of all crystals in stasis for decades."

"The wrong Bhizini!" his father hissed.

"That wasn't my fault," Lithuigi said.

"I suppose not," his father said. "You were a loyal servant, Von'nDrino. I always liked you."

"But now you want my face?"

"I'm in no rush for it," Mortimus said. "No, you make things too exciting, fighting me in secret as you do. It's been a long time since I've been so entertained."

"I'm not your trouper," Lithuigi said, lacking conviction.

Mortimus threw back his head and laughed. "Be seeing you, Von'nDrino."

And his father faded into the mist.

Lithuigi left the city, feeling like he'd somehow played right into the Death King's hands, as he always did. That he'd failed to do anything to help his sons, as he always did. And as he sailed across the Threshinveld, he wondered if it was true, if he was nothing more than a puppet, a plaything for the gods. A slave to Trevian like no other.

And he wondered if there was even a Lithuigi Von Andron to speak of, anymore—if there was even a Professor Von'nDrino, Dyna'arin tinker. Was there even the Bhizini who loved nothing but the sea?

Lithuigi didn't know.

Chapter 63

The Unseen Beneath

Fin'roq spent the crossing from P'anorum perched up above the captain's quarters. Roman Anthem let him use the private space, and he spent the days with his branches unfurled, his leaftips feasting on the sunshine, while his eyes took in the vast expanses of the open ocean. But when they approached East'whaling, the line of trees on the flank of Mon Mang'alar was visible in the distance, and Fin remembered the last time he'd passed through this part of the world—Jaun and Anthem had collapsed from Ellex Andria's dream, just as a fleet of Bhizini moved in to attack. But before they could take the ship, Graymay'n the Unseen had saved them.

He thought of Jaun, lying on the deck, non-responsive—he remembered the panic, the horror, the heart-splitting sadness and grief at the thought that he'd fallen over dead. Had Fin'roq ever felt more alone than in that moment?

Yes.

He'd felt that alone when he stood on the streets of Balan Su, when Jaun left him in the square on the lower rim. And he'd felt that way during the Balancing Act, when he heard Jaun's cries of pain, and looked around at the faces of those around him, murderous with hatred, with rage, intent on killing him.

He'd felt that alone when he was a scamp, and the villagers were gathering for a feast, and he was made to leave, to watch from a distance and never take part.

He'd felt that alone when he flowered for the first time, and rather than the customary celebration, the village elders had warned him—had threatened to slice off his flower, to dig out the stem, should he ever presume to touch any of them, or any of their offspring. *No Bhizini will spread their rotten seed on this island*—that's what Durq had said to him, while the others nodded, sneering, menacing.

But it was my island all along, Fin thought, *and now there's none of the villagers left to tell. None of them to reprimand, to convince, to win over. No one.*

When the cata'rin approached East'whaling and the tunnel through the island into Balance Territories, Anthem asked him to go below deck, along with his mother and brother, until they were out in the open waters of the Mesh'apo'tamian Sea. He begrudgingly agreed.

Fin had done his best to avoid both of them so far, making excuses whenever his mother or his brother came to speak to him. He could tell they wanted to talk, but that was the last thing he wanted to do. In truth, Fin was afraid they'd ask him for something. He knew they disapproved of his intentions to confront the Gran Pradesh directly. Both of them had urged him to be patient, to help them bring the truth out through the proper channels. Once they'd had time to prepare.

They wanted him to do it in the way that was most convenient to them, not to him.

But Fin had to see him. He had to see Ra'shard Ruu'n—or rather the phantom who wore his face. He had to know.

It didn't matter to them, but it mattered to him. And he knew they didn't trust him, so why should he trust them? They wouldn't even tell him how they planned to sneak into the city.

He didn't owe them anything.

He didn't owe anyone anything.

And it was about time he did what he wanted to do, when he wanted to do it.

When Ellex and Rakk tried to talk to him, he feigned seasickness and asked to be left alone. Rakk was unconvinced but Ellex insisted they leave him be.

That was kind of her, and Fin knew it. But he couldn't feel grateful. He just couldn't.

❧ ❦

Ellex took a nibble of bhiza and passed a small speck to Rakk.

"That's all of it," she said.

"This should be enough to get us to the city. Once we're there—well, I'm not sure it'll matter. This is in the hands of the Great Sower now, if it hasn't been all along."

"Have you always believed in fate?" Ellex asked.

Rakk looked out across the Mesh'apo'tamian Sea and sighed. "I'm not sure I do. At least not often enough to say it with conviction, or to have it take away the fear and doubt. But there are some moments, brief ones, when I'm certain my life has all been carefully plotted out, that only fools believe in coincidences, that just because I don't understand how something works doesn't mean there isn't order, and purpose, to it."

"That's very wise, Raeder. Even though I'm surprised to hear myself say that. If you'd told me this last year, or any other year in the last three decades, I'd have probably called you a fool to your face. If there was one thing I was certain of, it's that I was in charge of my own destiny. I believed my own hard work was the reason for my position, the reason for my popularity and my political mandate. I felt like the fierce, fighting heart of Balance Authority, determined to protect and serve my government, to root out threats from within and to keep at bay the threats from without. I never once considered, in three decades on the Council of Nine, that I might be wrong. That the information might be tainted. That my reasons for believing what I believed might need further examination."

"You can't blame yourself for everything, Ell. Sometimes—well, sometimes we don't look, we don't question, we don't try to know, only because we'd lose our minds if we did. Don't underestimate your ability to protect yourself—you're will to do so, even without knowing, without trying to."

Ellex stared at his face for a moment, and she realized he was talking about himself as much as he was talking about her.

She took his hand and squeezed it.

"I'm scared, Raeder," she said. "I've left Qaas'i on the other side of the world, and every moment I'm away from her, I feel like I'm going out of my mind. And Fin'roq—he hates me, still. He'll hardly look at me. And I know I deserve it. But he's my son, my sap. And he's about to put himself in grave danger, and I feel like I should say something, or do something, to stop him. To keep him safe!"

"I just want to warn Rajj," Rakk said. "To make sure our families are safe. I think the rest is up to fate."

"And not to Fin'roq?"

Rakk frowned. "He got a double dose of obstinance coming from both you and my father," he said. "There's no talking him out of this. I know I wouldn't be talked out of it, if someone had done that to me."

"But he risks so much," she said. "He's too distraught. Too unpredictable."

Rakk scoffed. "The same could be said of either one of us."

"I guess you're right. But the thought of him stuck in one of those stasis chambers, in a sort of waking death or a sleeping life—we can't let that happen, Raeder. We can't."

"If he ends up imprisoned like Qaas'andria was—he's my brother, Ell. You know I'll help you bust him out, even if it means my death."

She squeezed his hand again.

"Even if he wasn't my brother, I'd do it for you. Only—" He looked away and dropped her hand.

"What is it?"

"My fight isn't here, Ell. I came to make sure you made it safely. To warn Rajj. But you know I need to get home. I have to stop Raq'asha from destroying my kingdom. Bhea told me my father wanted me to follow him on the throne, and I have to believe that."

"I'm glad, Raeder. I'm glad to see you fighting for your throne—to see you believing you deserve it again."

"If that's what this is," he said. "I called it home, Raccorum Rhazzat, but it isn't. It never was. P'anorum was the only home I ever wanted, the only kingdom I cared to rule. I thought it was gone forever. But seeing the city there—still there—and seeing people living and working on the island, in the ruins of my old home—there's something beautiful about that. *P'anorum is still there!* The past—the things I was so certain were true—weren't. Aren't!" He sighed. "I know I'm not making as much sense as I want to be. But I feel—well, I feel like I can win. Like I have a reason to try to."

"Your father, and your mother, would be proud of you, as I am."

"You aren't upset then?"

"About what?"

"Nothing," he said.

Ellex took his arm, and she put her head against his shoulder and leaned into him.

"I don't want you to leave," she said. "Of course I don't. As awful as this journey has been, it's also been wonderful. I feel like the past can finally be the past, at least between us. And—maybe the future holds something for us after all. But we aren't there yet, are we?"

Rakk looked down at the deck. "I guess not."

"Our work's only just beginning," she said. "If we're to save our civilization, it's going to take more than exposing the truth. It's going to take a lot of debate, a lot of compromise, a lot of time and effort to change a system that has long run on the inertia of millennia."

Rakk exhaled and then turned, so that she lifted her head from his shoulder to face him.

"I'll wait," he said, staring into her eyes. "I've been waiting for you my entire life."

When the wide open expanses of the Threshinveld Sea began to close in on the cata'rin, the air to grow heavy and hazy and thick with fog, Rakk heard the gurgitator close, felt the ship slowing beneath his feet, and knew they were nearly at their destination. In all his years of life at sea, no trip had ever felt longer. He'd been about to go out of his mind with helplessness, with agitation, with ennui.

Fin'roq had hardly spoken to him on the entire trip. Rakk had hoped for a chance to get to know him a little better. He wanted to help him—to do whatever he could to help him—but Rakk's favorite tool for getting his way, his charm, was failing him, entirely.

Even Ellex had been distant on the crossing—or maybe Rakk had been avoiding her. He hadn't wanted to tell her he was leaving for Raccorum Rhazzat just as soon as he could. When he finally told her, he'd been relieved and disappointed at the same time. At least he wasn't hurting her—or abandoning her—again. Even though it felt like it.

If she'd asked me to stay, would I have stayed?

But now the future was set, the plan was in motion.

And it's different this time. Now there's hope for us, somehow, someday, to be together at last.

The fog was so thick, Rakk couldn't see from one end of the ship to the other. He could hardly see across it's width.

Focus, he told himself. *Worrying about the future when you need to be in the present is the surest way of ensuring you won't have one to worry about.*

Fin'roq joined him on the deck and Rakk clapped him on the shoulder.

"Hey brother," he said. "Hope you're feeling better. As for me, I'm so nervous, I think I might be sick."

"Really?" Fin said.

"Really."

Ellex joined them. She smiled at Fin then looked at Rakk.

"Now maybe you can tell me how we're getting inside the city?"

"You don't know either?" Fin said.

"Not a clue," she said. "Raeder?"

"Did I ever tell you about the time I was kidnapped?" Rakk said. "It was when I was a scamp, not yet a decade old. I was taken from P'anorum by a member of my own family. They sailed south, far out into the ocean, thousands of miles from shore. There were other ships waiting to take me. But before they could hand me over, they were attacked. It looked like the sea itself had risen up to protect me. The ships rose and then fell under the water, lost to the dark abyss in an instant. All around me, they sank into the sea, til suddenly the deck began to rise—the sea itself was lifting up—and I knew I was next.

"But the sea never frightened me. I took a deep breath, and closed my eyes, and waited for the crash to come. I felt the deck drop away from under me but I was lifted up, and for a moment I thought I was flying. I was on the back of the largest seastallion in the world, an ancient beast that you truly have to see to believe."

"Gray'may'n the Unseen," Fin said.

Rakk looked at him and saw the wonder in his eyes.

"You've seen him then," Rakk said.

"He saved us. Near East'whaling. From an ambush of Pal'merans."

"He saved me as well," Rakk said. "And carried me across the ocean, home to P'anorum, right into the island itself, into the grotto at Bhea Bell's. Only he was no longer a beast of the deep when we emerged from the sea, but had risen from the water as a Bhizini, carrying me in his speckled arms, a grin on his weather-beaten face."

"Roman Anthem?" Ellex mouthed the words, a look of shock and disbelief on her face.

"Yes," he said. "And before you say it, I know I was young. But it was the first of many, many times that he's saved my life. And I've seen him change into the beast, and back into the Verdillion, time and time again. So I'm not crazy. I don't know how he does it, but he does it. He's protected me my entire life. Even to this day, when I need him most, I need only call to him and he will come."

"That's why we didn't see him," Fin said. "When Graymay'n attacked, we never saw the captain. When he emerged, he was soaking wet, but he said he'd been repairing a hull breach." Fin laughed and shook his head.

"I don't know what—to say. Or think," Ellex said. "Did I know any of this before?"

"No," Rakk said. "Only that he was my friend, if not always my ally. He'll do as we ask. He'll get us into the city. But he's—" Rakk felt a shiver run down his back. "He's like a god, or a demon. Before I met you, Fin, I'd never come across such raw power. I can't begin to guess at his true intentions. If things don't go well in the city, he may not be there to get us out."

As if on cue, Roman Anthem came down the stairs from the bridge, grinning. But when he saw everyone staring at him, embarrassed looks on their faces, he threw back his head and laughed.

"Raeder told you then?" he said.

Rakk saw he was watching Fin'roq's face.

"He did," Ellex said. "I—hope I haven't offended you. I had no idea."

"Offended? You mean with the way you insulted and provoked me every time you saw me for thirty some odd years?" He was grinning. "It's already out to sea. Taken with the tides of time and fate. Forget it, Sui Pradesh. I have."

"What's the plan, old friend?" Rakk said.

"Well, since you're bringing our old buddy Ra'shard in the bag there, you'll need to stay out of the water. So that rules out the tunnels, even though they're the safest way in. Honestly, no Cul'tavin has ever dared inspect my ship when I've sailed into the harbor, knowing I have the ear of the Gran Pradesh. And I have a private hangar with access to the upper rim, unused by anyone else in the Pradishar. With you two on bhiza, the scanners shouldn't detect your crystals. But Fin'roq—you'll have to be sure you don't tip them off to our presence."

"How would I do that?"

"With a casual thought, a slip of the mind. You know Bhea's whirlpool technique?"

He nodded.

"Good. Then practice it until we're in the harbor. Into my quarters, all three of you. Even if they check the hold, my room will be the last place they'll disturb."

"And if they dare to disturb it?" Fin said. "Will you let them capture us? Will you let them put me back in the stasis chamber?"

Anthem tsked. "Have I ever given you any cause to doubt me?"

"Yes," Fin said. "You're the servant of the beast that kept me locked away for thousands of years!"

"Wrong," Anthem said. "But I do keep my enemies as close as my friends. I am one with them both, while I become what I am. Look, I promised Raeder I would get you into the city without being detected by the Pradishar, and that's what I'm going to do."

"No more waiting," Rakk said. "Let's go already."

"Up to my quarters then," Anthem said. "And not a peep until I come for you."

Chapter 64

Into the City of Death

As the cata'rin moved through the fog toward Balan Su, Fin'roq knew he should be meditating, bringing his focus inward, shutting out the world around him. But he could feel the city—feel it as he'd never felt it before—and the temptation to open his mind and take it all in was overwhelming. Each crystal was like a tiny ball of flickering light, a starscape strewn across his inner eye, each spark a universe of thought and emotion, fiber and flesh, power and information.

The gurgitator was purring and he could feel it vibrating the deck through his feet. Fin gripped the boards with his rootpads, filled his lungs with air, and slowly exhaled. In his mind's eye, he turned away from Balan Su and back into his own head, where he imagined a great cyclone was swirling in circles around his body, himself in the midst of it, perfectly calm and protected.

When the ship slowed and the gurgitator closed, Fin felt something touching at his mind, brushing against it as it were, not able to grasp it, but trying nonetheless. It was the guard at the gate, feeling out for any crystals—and thus any unidentified passengers—on the ship. Curious about the sensation, he focused on it, and realized the guard wasn't grasping at him in particular, and that what Fin was actually feeling, what he was experiencing, was the guard's intent.

I'm already in the guard's mind!

Fin knew his name, his age, the house he lived in. He knew he had a sore back and wished he had more time off. Fin saw, in an instant, his entire life, from his earliest, spotty memories to those that, thanks to the crystal, were perfectly preserved. For a moment, he looked out through his eyes, felt the Pradeshan robe on his skin, the cramp in his back.

And the guard had no idea Fin was there.

Fin pulled his awareness back to his own mind, back to the cata'rin, and he saw his mother and brother perched near him, silent, waiting, and not paying him any attention.

He allowed himself a triumphant grin.

The ship began to move again, and Fin heard Ellex sigh with relief.

"I told you he wouldn't let me down," Rakk said.

The cata'rin turned sharply, slowed, turned again, and finally came to a stop. The gurgitator fell silent and Anthem poked his head in through the door.

"Welcome to Balan Su," he said, grinning. "This way."

Anthem led them down the stairs and off the ship. They were in a narrow hangar under the crescent. The dock alongside the cata'rin led to a corridor running in either direction, and Anthem pointed them to the right.

"Follow this until you reach a stair. Head up. You'll recognize where it lets out," he said, looking at Rakk.

"Which is where, exactly?" Ellex said.

"Old Stones," Anthem said. "If that's okay with Sui Pradesh?"

"That's perfect," she said. "You have my thanks."

Fin followed behind Rakk and Ellex, down a long hallway barely lit with glowbes. The corridor ended at a curved wall. Rakk found the notch and the wall rolled back, revealing a spiral staircase in mid-stair. Fin wished he had more time to explore, delighted at not being scared of the dark anymore, and wondering what secrets lay in the depths of Balan Su. But Rakk and Ellex were heading up, and he followed, counting each step as he went.

From sea level to the upper rim, he thought. *Must be a thousand feet. So somewhere between one and a half and two thousand steps. No, the steps themselves were inclined, so less than a thousand.*

Eight hundred and thirty-three steps later, they reached a door. Rakk grabbed the knob and began to twist, first to the right, then to the left, then back to the right, and the door opened as normal. Fin followed Ellex into what looked like a storage closet for some kind of shop. When he let go of the door, it swung shut behind him, and an attached shelf on the back side of the door hid its existence.

A single stair led upward, and they emerged in a shop on the ground level, large stacks of scrolls and shelves with books in front of them, and a single desk on the right hand side, where an old Bhizini sat nibbling on a cookie. They had an expression on their face that said they were expecting them but couldn't care less they'd come.

Fin was surprised to see a Bhizini in the city, especially after what had happened at the Balancing Act. Was this their shop? If he'd known, he'd have visited when he was at the Pruu'patch.

No, he thought. *Don't go down that path. That life is over.*

Ellex had a panicked look on her face but said nothing.

"Well, don't just stand there," the Bhizini said. "Buy somethin' already. And then be on your way."

"Oh—we don't—" Ellex started.

"Don't give old Bha'tilda none of that," the Bhizini said. "Ain't nothin' can't wait while you find a book or scroll to read. Besides, my services don't come free. You not leavin' til you bought somethin'.'"

Ellex looked at Rakk and then at Fin. "I suppose we can find something."

"That what I said," Bha'tilda snorted. "Well, go on already. You got a whole store to peruse!"

When they were in the stacks, Fin heard Ellex talking to Rakk.

"A friend of Anthem's?" she whispered.

"Yup," he said. "Charming, no?"

"This is a waste of time. We need to get moving."

"Moving where?" Rakk said. "I tried to discuss our plans with you—with you and with Fin—without luck."

"Fin'roq?" Ellex called.

The sound of her voice made his stomach clench up.

"Yes, Sui Pradesh?"

"I wondered—we wondered—if you might be able to tell us where our brothers are?" She looked at Rakk.

"Only if it's not going to cause you any trouble," Rakk said, touching Fin's shoulder.

"It's no trouble," Fin said, thinking that if he told them where they were, it would give him an excuse to head out on his own.

Fin'roq opened his awareness to the entire city, feeling out for Uthyr Andria and Rajesh'n Raccorine Deri. He found them immediately but he waited awhile, not wanting them to know how easy it was for him.

"Your brother is at the citadel, in his office near the Solarium," he said to Rakk. Then he turned to Ellex. "And your brother is at his home, in Sunrise Ridge."

He was surprised to see tears in her eyes.

"Then he's okay. They're both okay."

Fin nodded.

"We need to split up, Ell," Rakk said.

She sighed but it came on the edge of a hiss. "I know," she said. "Fin, could you do me one more favor before you go? Could you tell Uthyr to meet me at our parent's estate?"

He nodded. "Done. Now, let's buy something so we can go already."

"Just grab something from the shelf," Ellex said.

Fin took the first scroll he found, and didn't stop to look at what it was. They both did the same.

Bha'tilda looked at what they'd picked, and Ellex paid them what they asked, and it occurred to Fin that he had no idea how much anything cost. He'd never had money, and had never used it either.

"Where will you go, Fin?" Ellex said when they got outside. She had tears in her eyes again.

He looked away. "To the citadel."

"If Rajj is there, then I'm going with you," Rakk said. "If that's okay with you."

Fin nodded.

"As soon as your crystal awakens, let me know you're okay," Ellex said.

"I will," Rakk said, giving her a hug.

"Let's go," Fin said.

"Be safe, Fin," Ellex said.

"You too."

"I'll see you again soon, son," she said.

"Sui Pradesh," Fin said, bowing.

He walked away without looking at her.

❧❦

Ellex couldn't stop the tears from falling, but neither Rakk nor Fin'roq saw them. She watched them both vanish into the fog, and she stopped herself from running after them. Her tears fell silently in the shadows under her hood, dripping off her chin onto the cold, damp cobblestones, where they were lost on the wet rock.

She turned and marched in the opposite direction, through the narrow streets of Old Stones to the edge of the neighborhood near the entrance to the Sunrise Ridge development where Ellex had her home. Her family's estate was in the old part of the city, built around a large courtyard. After P'anorum erupted, neither her nor her brother could bear to live there, nor could they bear to part with it. So it had sat, largely untended, slowly falling apart, for three decades.

Time to sell this place, she thought, as she walked through the dusky main hall and into the courtyard. The statues in the corners were heavy with moss, the fountain at the center dry and busted, the large round stone table covered in leaves and bird shit.

Or tear it down...

Ellex looked in the closets and found an old broom and started sweeping off the table. When she was finished, she sat the bag with Ra'shard Ruu'n's body on the bench and went into her father's study. She sat down at his desk and leaned back in the chair, and let a few more tears fall.

"Oh Father, forgive me. I've spent the last three decades working against you—against everything you fought and died for. I must be the worst daughter in the world. Now you're gone—now you're really gone—and I don't know if it's better this way, or the way it was before, when I needed to be reminded every day. When it never felt real. When I didn't have to ever worry about thinking about it, or thinking about P'anorum. Sweet Trevian, help me."

"I was never angry at you." She heard her father's voice, gentle but firm, regal but humble, wise and kind and full of love, and for a moment she wanted to run toward it, to weep with joy—but her desire vanished when a shudder ran down her back, a cold dread that turned her sap to ice, and she jumped out of the chair, which fell over behind her and crashed to the ground. She spun around toward the voice.

Her father stood in the doorway, a warm smile on his face. His hands were folded together in front of him, as if he'd just been saying his prayers. His eyes, his hair, his clothing, everything—exactly as Luthyr Andria had looked. As if he'd never died.

I saw your petrified corpse, she thought.

She clenched her teeth and glared at the apparition in the doorway.

"Ellex, my dear, I'm so glad you're safe."

"How dare you wear his face," she said. "How dare you!"

"Your mother and I have been worried sick. We feared the worst when the Me'dicant healers showed up at our door. They told us—well, they told us you'd escaped. Ellex, my love, you know how dangerous it is to be out here. The healing strands in your mind aren't bound yet. If you break them, you could revert—" he seemed too distraught to say it, "—to your petrified state."

"What—are you talking about?" Ellex said.

"You remember," he said. "Don't you? The accident?"

"What accident? No. There was no accident. And you're not my father!"

His eyes fell. "So it's gotten that bad," he said. "Oh Ellex." He started wringing his hands, tears in his eyes.

"You died the night of the eruption," Ellex said. "Thirty four years ago!"

Luthyr Andria sighed, a long sad sigh.

"There was no eruption, my dear," he said. "There was only an earthquake. Remember? You and Prince Rhakksees were down by the theater. The king was putting on one of the shows he loves so much, when it hit. The plaza split apart, and you—fell. We thought you were lost, but then they found you. You were broken, but alive. Still alive. The Pradishar have been trying to heal you ever since. But it's a process."

"No," Ellex said. "No! I would know. I would know!"

"Would you?" her father said. "This isn't the first time you've forgotten."

"No," she said. "It's a trick."

"Why would I trick you? I'm your father. I love you more than anything in this world."

Ellex took a few deep breaths. "Is it really you?" She could hardly see through the tears.

"Of course it's me."

She sniffed. "Father!" she cried. "Father, I've missed you so much."

"I haven't gone anywhere," he said. "I've been right here all along. You've just been confused is all. But that's over now, too. Now everything will be wonderful again. You'll see."

"Oh Father," she said. "Come, give me a hug."

She stared into his eyes, waiting to see his reaction. If he hugged her, then she was indeed crazy. But if not...

Something inside her shriveled when she saw the warmth fade from her father's eyes, and whatever it was that looked back at her was not Luthyr Andria, not even Verdillion, and not at all amused.

But she was too relieved to be afraid—she'd nearly believed she was crazy, after all. Too often that seemed like a tempting explanation. Not anymore.

She took a few quick steps toward her father but the apparition vanished, and she stopped and looked around, still feeling like she was being watched.

But Mortimus Rex was gone.

Ellex turned over her father's chair, gingerly returned it to it's proper place, and wiped off the dirt. Then she slumped over onto it, wrapped her arms around herself, and wept.

Rakk took large strides down the cobblestoned streets of Old Stones, moving at a brisk jaunt, Fin'roq having no problem keeping up with him. The light was beginning to fade, the fog to turn from a white to a murky gray, and when the glowbes crackled to life, they looked like greasy smears in the mist.

Great Sower in the sky, how I hate this wretched place, he thought.

Even though it drove Ellex crazy, he never got tired of insulting Balan Su every chance he could. He thought of voicing his disdain for it to Fin'roq, but he remembered that Fin had enjoyed his time here, had even asked Ellex if she could help reinstate him in the Pruu'patch.

"How's it feel to be back in Balan Su City?" he said.

"I don't know," Fin said. "Like this is a dream and any moment I'll wake up. Like maybe I'm still down in the darkness, still in the cave with Bhartimu'u, lost in the Inner Door."

Rakk didn't know what to say. "You like this place, huh?"

"I do."

"Why?" he said, trying to keep his voice flat.

But Fin chuckled. "I understand why you don't like it. Perhaps its the same reason why I do like it. It's so contrived, so improbable. No fresh water. No cultivation to speak of. Hardly even any proper soil. It's damp, dreary, and cold, and yet so warm, so vibrant, pulsating with diversity, with life. The old streets and buildings and plazas are full of character, with stories to tell. And the people here live out the most complex and impractical lives, the most intricate and fascinating patterns, all connected and overlapping, and yet running together, purring along like a bustling reef. Absolutely marvelous."

"Fin, I had no idea," Rakk said. "But then again, I guess we hardly know each other. I thought you came to study at the 'patch as a way to get out of P'anorum, to escape the wrath of the villagers. I never realized—"

He trailed off and Fin said nothing for a moment.

"For as long as I can remember, I wanted to be a monkin, to be close to Trevian. And for as long as I could think, I wanted to know why I'm here—why any of this is here."

"And you think the Pradishar have those answers?"

Fin didn't say anything.

They reached the edge of Old Stones, Grand Plaza fading away into the fog ahead of them.

"Do you have a plan for getting into the citadel?" Rakk asked.

"I do," Fin said. "We'll go in through the Pruu'patch. There's a passage that leads to Corda'mere Park."

"There aren't guards at the 'patch?"

"There's someone at the gate, but it'll be fine."

"You sure? I don't want to blow our cover."

Fin swallowed a hiss. "You don't have to come with me."

"I trust you, brother," Rakk said. "Lead the way."

The Pruu'patch was on the north eastern edge of the plaza, and Fin slowed as they approached the gate. A single Cul'tavin stood watch, and Rakk gasped as the peacekeeper crumpled to the ground as if he'd dropped dead. He ran to his side and put his hand over his mouth, and he could feel that he was still breathing.

"He'll be fine," Fin said.

Rakk's heart was pounding in his chest and in his ears, and he felt scared and angry at the same time.

"You did this?" he said.

But Fin'roq was already heading through the door.

Rakk scrambled to follow him.

The inside of the Pruu'patch was a series of stone rooms and small, but lush, courtyards. Rakk had come on a number of occasions while studying to become a bishrop—it felt like a lifetime ago but it was only a few months past—but not enough to get to know the place. Fin, on the other hand, had spent months there, wandering the corridors and exploring its secrets.

Nobody was around—the monkins would have left for the summer, Rakk reminded himself—and they passed down the stairs and into an earthen corridor without incident. Fin pulled a glowbe from his robes and it crackled to life, and a warm orange glow spread down the hallway.

They didn't have far to go before a stair led upward and they emerged in a thicket of trees and bushes in the heart of Corda'mere. The rich smell of damp soil and the spicy scent of pine filled Rakk's nose.

"Fin," Rakk said. "Do you think you could help me out?"

"What is it?"

"I'm sort of a wanted fugitive. I escaped from the Dankburn, and if I walk through the door—well, I'm afraid I might not make it to my brother before I'm arrested. Could you contact him and ask him to come out here? Tell him it's me, and to meet me where we last saw each other. He'll know the place."

Fin said nothing for a moment.

"Done," he said.

"Thanks, brother. If you'll wait, Rajj can help you—can help us—get into the citadel. We could face Mortimus together, if that's still what you want to do."

"I'm going now," he said.

"Wait," Rakk said. "Fin, let's talk about this first."

"There's nothing to be said."

Rakk sighed. "Be safe. Be safe and come back. Things don't have to be like they were before. You have a family now. We'll look out for you, Fin. Always."

Fin started to walk away.

"I love you, brother," Rakk said, but Fin didn't turn back.

He vanished into the fog and Rakk took a few deep breaths, trying to calm the panic that had risen up inside of him. He shrugged it off and started walking through the park, trying to figure out where he was. When he found the path that led around the spire, he followed it through the shrubs, then back into the small meadow with the fountain where Rajj had brought him to sun himself, after he'd busted him out of the Dankburn.

I've gone halfway around the world and back, he thought. *Let's hope it was worth it.*

When he stepped into the clearing, he saw movement out of the corner of his left eye, and he turned, bending his knees, ready to spring, when the zapren caught him between the shoulder blades. His vision sparkled and faded, his body seemed to twist in on itself, with muscles he didn't know he had suddenly existing, suddenly twisting and tightening, and feeling like they were tearing apart. He could taste sap in his mouth, feel his teeth grinding down against his tongue, but he couldn't open his jaw, couldn't swallow or spit, couldn't do anything but clench even harder. He screamed in his mind, and screamed some more, til even that was too much effort, and there was nothing he could do but let the darkness win.

Chapter 65

Cracked at the Roots

FIN'ROQ WALKED THE EMPTY pathways of Corda'mere, through the thick groves of pine and evergreens, the fog dark gray like smoke in the dying light, wondering if he should have waited for Rakk—if he should have helped his mother first—but he pushed the thoughts from his mind. They'd both confirmed for him what he'd feared since the start—that they'd brought him along because they needed his help to contact their brothers. If he'd stayed with them, who knows what else they would have asked of him.

And he was done doing what others wanted—done trying to please those that didn't really care what happened to him.

How could these mortals understand spending lifetime after lifetime trapped in darkness? How could they understand such a betrayal?

Mortimus Rex had stolen his throne, stolen his freedom. He oversaw a world where Bhizini were treated like animals—no, worse than animals, excluded from society for presuming to exist at all, forced to hide in the sinks and wastes, hunted and exterminated.

And Fin'roq felt like he was pure rage, embodied. A flame that would purify as it destroyed.

Time for the king of death to die, he thought. *A vengeance ten thousand years in the making.*

He climbed the steps and walked through the doors into the citadel, and he pulled off his hood and looked around, confident, buoyed by his powers, by the memories he still recalled from time to time, from when he ruled the world from Dar Ka'Hala, back when justice was in his hands and eternity at his feet.

A few Cul'tavin were in the great hall when he entered, and they turned to face him but they said nothing and made no movement toward him, although he could feel their fear. He strode past them to the back of the chamber, down the hall that led to the small, dark room where the Octa'vin kept guard. One stood on either side of the door, that distant look in their eyes, waxy and vacant.

"I'm here to see the Gran Pradesh," he said.

The door opened and Fin'roq passed into the corridor of polished obsidian. He fought off a wave of vertigo and centered his mind on his body, on his feet, on the cool glassy stone under his rootpads. When he entered the audience chamber, he could see Ra'shard Ruu'n perched on the large grassy mound, a kindly smile on his face, looking radiant under the light beam that shined down from above.

"Fin'roq, what a pleasant surprise," he said, and for a moment, Fin felt the warmth and admiration he'd felt for the old Raccorin when he'd first met him, a kindly grandfather, a holy patriarch who only wanted what was best for him.

And the sudden doubt felt like a betrayal of everything he'd endured—of his will to resist.

Fin reached out for the Gran Pradesh with his mind, as he would for someone with a crystal, and for a moment, he brushed up against something he'd never felt before. Something slippery and cold, but also sharp and burning. Something too slick to grab hold of, too piercing to grip.

And familiar. The touch, the feel, brought ancient memories near the surface of his mind, so that Fin knew they were there but couldn't quite reach them—couldn't make out what it was he hoped to understand.

"I'm glad you've come back to the capital, Fin. Everything that happened during the Balancing Act was a terrible misunderstanding. And the information you shared with me on Jaun von Andron was spot-on, Fin. You've proven yourself a trustworthy confidant."

"You're not Ra'shard Ruu'n," Fin said, trying to keep his voice steady. "I saw his corpse. I know you're wearing his face."

The Gran Pradesh smiled at him, warm and full of affection.

"You're very wise, Fin," he said. "It's true. This is not my real form."

"You imprisoned me in a stasis chamber. For thousands of years, birth after birth, you enslaved me." He wanted to sound angry, but it came out sounding devastated.

"Fin'roq, no," he said. "Imprisoned? Enslaved? Never! I saved your life—your *true* life—from Bhea Bell and her allies. I kept you safe, Fin. Please, you must understand, my goal has always been to keep you alive. To keep both of us alive!"

Fin laughed. "You expect me to believe that the King of Death is the protector of life?"

"You're a very smart plant, Fin'roq. But you don't have all the information. And so you've misunderstood, that's all. Bhea Bell hasn't told you the whole truth. You're a victim, Fin, of her schemes. She tried to keep you away from me, all these years, because she feared the things I would tell you.."

"You're not talking your way out of this," Fin said. He pulled a scytherin from his robe. "I'm going to have my revenge, one way or another."

The Gran Pradesh had a sad look on his face. Fin'roq leapt onto the mound where he was perched, clutched the dagger in his hand, and jabbed it forward into Ra'shard Ruu'n's heart.

But there was nothing there, no clothing, no body. Fin slashed at the specter in front of him, but he might as well have been stabbing at the air.

Ra'shard Ruu'n laughed, a warm and kindly laugh, as if they were playing a game.

Tears were burning Fin'roq's eyes, but he kept slashing, more desperate with each plunge of the blade. He reached for him with his mind again, but Mortimus vanished from his awareness.

Fin looked around and saw that Ra'shard Ruu'n had reappeared behind him. He turned and lunged at him, but fell through him, and stumbled to one knee.

"Settle down now, Fin," he said.

But Fin'roq rose and slashed at him again, screaming and crying.

Ra'shard Ruu'n's specter sighed.

Fin went to stab at him but something grabbed his arm, and then his other arm. The Octa'vin had ahold of him, and when they twisted his wrist, he dropped the blade. Fin scrambled to grab their crystals, to restrain them, but they didn't have any crystals. They wrapped vines around his arms while he struggled to get away, screaming through his tears, until he was bound and subdued on the ground.

Fin didn't know how long he lay there, but he had caught his breath and stopped his crying by the time Mortimus and the Octa'vin returned.

"Now that you've settled down, I want to show you something," he said. "Will you come along and be a good monkin on the way?"

Fin clenched his teeth and nodded.

When Ellex heard a noise at the front door, she jumped to her feet and almost let out a scream, but she reminded herself that the enemy was incorporeal. No matter what he said, or how he threatened, Mortimus Rex couldn't hurt her.

But his servants can, she thought.

She palmed a small enflamer, held it up in her right hand, ready to fire, while she reached for her scytherin with her left.

Her brother, Uthyr Andria, entered the courtyard, a troubled look on his pale green face, a long Vintrani blade in his hand. When he saw Ellex, he sighed audibly and sheathed the sword, a big smile on his face.

"Thank Trevian it's you," he said, chuckling. "Scared me for a minute. I couldn't get a trace on the message to come here, and I feared a trap. How was your trip?"

"Oh Utte, where to even begin? I've risked my life, your life, maybe everyone in this city's life by coming back here."

Uthyr looked confused and shook his head. "Start from the beginning and tell me everything."

Ellex told him about heading to Callo Baton, being led into an ambush, the imprisonment with the Tornroot. He tried to interrupt with questions, but she cut him off. She told him about Fin'roq, about P'anorum, about what they'd discovered under the island. She told him she'd found their father's corpse, murdered; that someone had imperialized her and used her own body to kidnap Qaas'andria; and that Ra'shard Ruu'n, beloved Gran Pradesh, had died thirty four years ago—murdered in the bowels of P'anorum.

When she fell silent for a moment, Uthyr exhaled loudly.

"That's quite a tale, Ell," he said.

"I know what you're thinking, but I'm not crazy," she said. "I have Ra'shard Ruu'n's corpse to prove it."

Uthyr's eyes widened. "Are you serious? Where?"

Ellex indicated the linen bag, and Uthyr's mouth fell open. He took the bag and peeked inside, then pulled it open til Ra'shard's petrified head was sticking out.

Uthyr whistled. "I had a feeling you'd end up on P'anorum," he said. "But who would imagine you'd find your way down to the stasis chamber. Or that dear Ra'shard would still be right where I left him."

Ellex stared at her brother, unable to take in what he'd said, to figure out what it meant.

Was her brother dead? Was this the Death King, come back to mock her again?

No, he touched the bag. He moved the corpse.

"What do you mean?" She fought to keep her voice steady as she eyed the Vintrani blade on Uthyr's hip.

He doesn't know how to use a sword, she thought. *And yet he walked in here wielding it like a pro.*

Ellex thought of the Vintrani blade in her father's back. She thought of the assailant at the Balancing Act, trying to decapitate her but cutting off Rajj's arm instead.

And she thought she was going to be sick.

"Ra'shard Ruu'n—the *real* Ra'shard Ruu'n—was a traitor to Balance," Uthyr said. "He and Father went down to the stasis chamber to free the imprisoned, Ell. To release an abomination on the world. But I stopped them."

"You—stopped them?"

Sweet Trevian, no, she thought. *No.*

<<Rakk! Fin'roq!>> she screamed, but her crystamin was still numb.

There was no way to call for help.

"Those fools were trying to end the age of the crystals, Ell, to wipe them out! *All of them*! Can you imagine? No datamins, no dynamins, no crystamins! No communications, no transportation, no information, no power, no civilization, nothing! Utter madness."

Uthyr looked at Ellex and narrowed his eyes.

"And you—you were no better, plotting with the worst of them. I should have killed you, too, but I just couldn't bear it. Father? Sure. He always hated me anyway. Told me I was immoral. Untrustworthy. Incompetent! He refused to let me in on his schemes. But I found out on my own. Oh yes, and I made sure they failed. I made sure your little Bhizini abomination ended up in a stasis chamber where it belonged. And I made sure you would become Balance's most ardent supporter, with no memory of your treason. Ellex—my good, dear, innocent little puppet—always performing so well." He laughed. "And now you've brought me the last remaining evidence of my treason! And you—well, you aren't so innocent anymore, are you?"

"How, Utte, how could you do this? Our whole life, you've been my little sib, my brother. My best friend!"

He scoffed. "Oh please, what would you know of what our relationship was like? What would you know of your past, your *real* past? How will you ever know if your memories are what actually happened, or what I want you to believe happened?"

Ellex hissed. "I'll know! Just like I know in my heart that I've spent my entire life looking out for you. Protecting you! Whenever mother was on one of her rants, I would always—"

But Uthyr was laughing hysterically and he put up his hand. "Oh stop, you're killing me," he said. "Mother?" He laughed again. "You think you were defending me against Mother? That old hag only cares about you. She and Father both made my life a living torment of constant insults, but you—precious Ellex—could never do anything wrong! You and Mother were like this," he said, crossing his fingers, "and I just never could measure up."

Mother—loving? Supportive? Still alive?

Ellex felt like she might vomit.

Uthyr had taken both her parents from her.

She clenched her teeth, the shock fading away as the anger swelled up inside her.

Uthyr saw the change in her face and he drew an enflamer from his robe and pointed it at her.

"You won't get away with this," she said.

"I got away with it thirty four years ago," he said. "And you're the only one who doesn't realize that everyone on the Council already thinks you're crazy, so who are they going to believe if it comes down to my word against yours? Now, it's time for the king to have your face."

Uthyr pulled the trigger and Ellex screamed as a whorl of flame shot across the room.

⚜ ⚜

Rakk moaned and tried to sit up, but he was stuck somewhere.

His muscles ached, and he tried to turn over, but restraining vines were cutting into his skin. He opened his eyes, but it was too dark to see anything.

But the air in his nose, the smell—damp and heavy with rust, with rot, with petrification.

The Dankburn. There was no doubt about it.

He sighed, even chuckled.

"What's so funny?"

Rakk jumped at the sound, but he couldn't move, and the vines tightened even more as he struggled against them, until he was sure his circulation was cut off, if his fibers weren't already severed.

A glowbe crackled to life and warm orange light spread out across the room. Rakk saw Rajj standing in front of him. He was in an interrogation cell, strapped to a chair.

"They say the weather's changing," Rajj said.

Huh? he thought. *The fog?*

But then he remembered.

Rakk and Rajj were always trying to spy on their father when they were scamps, not realizing that spying on one's family members was a time-honored tradition in their family. Rakk and Rajj had overheard the king reminding their mother to start with a line about the weather if she suspected they were being watched.

"This damn fog isn't going anywhere," Rakk said.

"You have a lot of nerve coming back here," Rajj said. "After breaking out of here last time, did you think the Pradishar would just let you walk in the front door?"

"I didn't walk in the front door. I got nabbed in Corda'mere."

"Which is the grounds of the citadel, is it not?"

Rakk sighed, and Rajj stepped close to him.

"You're a fool, you know that?" he said, loudly. "Who helped you? I know you aren't smart enough to do this on your own."

"Lithuigi Von'nDrino," Rakk said, then whispered, "You're in terrible danger, Rajj. We need to get out of here."

Rajj gave him a strange look. "In danger from what?"

"Ra'shard Ruu'n," Rakk whispered. "Mortimus Rex."

Rajj chuckled. "Ren'fallow conspiracies? I can't believe you'd fall for that crap." He pulled out a datamin. "Good work getting this data, brother. Did you find anything on Rhannokti while you were out and about?"

Rakk's face fell. "No," he said.

"Good," Rajj said. "I suppose we can stop this little charade then."

Rakk sighed. "Thank Trevian. Cut me loose."

"You misunderstand," Rajj said. "You're not going anywhere, except to the pyre. A fitting end for a traitorous prince who was never fit to rule in the first place. And it's all thanks to you, really. You just hand-fed me the data I need to make sure Raq'asha's little rebellion against my authority fails before it begins."

"Your authority?"

Rakk felt like he'd just lost P'anorum all over again.

Rajj laughed. "Oh brother, you're as foolish as Ellex Andria, and that's saying something."

No, it was worse.

"If you hurt her—"

"Oh, I won't lay a finger on her," Rajj said. "Uthyr is already taking care of it. We each have our puppets to tend to, Uthyr and I. And you both performed so perfectly. Right on cue. Step by step. Besides, the Death King has plans for her. I'm not sure if that entails wearing her face yet or not. I guess we'll know very soon now, won't we."

"I'll kill you," Rakk screamed. "I'll kill you! You traitor! You—"

Rajj was laughing again. "Me, the traitor? I didn't disobey an order moments before my king needed me most. I didn't spend three decades refusing to face up to my crime. No, I've spent the last thirty four years making sure my rule of Raccorum Rhazzat is absolute, since Father was too stupid to realize what a halfwit you are."

"What have you done to him?" Rakk whispered.

"It's really what he's done to me that you should care about, if you ever cared for me at all. Do you know that Father told me I wasn't qualified to be a leader? That you either have it, or you don't, and I didn't. That I'm worthy to be a bureaucrat and nothing more?"

"What did you do to our father!?" Rakk screamed.

Rajj pressed his lips together and narrowed his eyes.

"I won't have you yelling at me," he said, barely over a whisper. "No, I won't have it at all. For forty years, I put up with you pushing me around, using your superior size and strength to get your way in everything we did together. You're nothing but an incompetent bully, a failure in everything you do, but so loud and so aggressive that you manage to bluster your way through whatever life sends you. Well, brains win over brawn in the end, brother. *Always*. And now you'll bluster your way through life no longer."

"I don't understand," Rakk said, barely a whisper. "Why, Rajj, why? You've always been my sib, my beloved sib. We were planted together, cut together, raised together, always together. I've always tried to encourage you, to support you. But to bully you? To hurt you? Never!"

Rajj's good hand was quivering and his handsome features were drawn up into a scowl. He pulled a zapren from his robe and jammed it in Rakk's neck.

His vision exploded in sparkles and he thrashed into the vines, his muscles screaming, twisting. He moaned, then shivered as he felt the cuts along his body leaking sap where the vines had sliced him open.

"Stop lying to me," Rajj said. "Perhaps you haven't understood. You've lost. Entirely. I have the power now. I've always had the power. *All of it.*"

Rajj flicked his wrist and there was a scytherin in his good hand, the one Grizmond had given to Rakk. "Thank you for bringing this to me. I know it belonged to Father, so it's only fitting it passes to me."

Rakk hissed in his face.

Rajj laughed. "Let's see, which shall we do first?"

Before he could respond, Rajj lunged at him with the blade, slicing it down across his forehead, slitting open the skin and passing the edge of the knife across the face of his Corkin master crystal, which audibly shattered, like a mirror falling from a great height onto hard stone. Rakk felt like a thousand shards of broken glass had just been shoved into his face, and then down through his veins and back up again, in waves of pain. His eyes spun and his head lolled around, and he struggled to focus on Rajj, struggled to see the face of his brother, contorted as it was with laughter.

"Oh, don't you pass out yet," Rajj said. "I'm only just getting started."

❧❧❧❧❧ ❧❧❧❧❧

The Octa'vin released their grip on Fin'roq's arms and he stood up, gripping the obsidian floor with his rootpads and trying to catch his breath—to calm his racing heart—but without luck.

"Easy Fin, I'm not going to hurt you," Ra'shard Ruu'n's ghost said.

Fin glared at him.

"Show me your real face," he said. "Not that good and kind Raccorin you're pretending to be."

"Pretending? Is that what it is? I think it's more complicated than that. I have all of Ra'shard's memories, should I wish to call on them. I remember the first time he ate a rhingami. I remember the pain of the axe that lodged itself in this face." He rubbed the scar. "I remember the terrible prickling as it scabbed over. And I remember the inner pain too—the pain of knowing that family did this. That wound never did heal."

"But they aren't *your* memories," Fin said, "and you—the *real* you—must know that."

Ra'shard smiled. "I'm glad to see you getting your powers back," he said. "And I'm glad I don't have to pretend with you anymore. Truly."

The Gran Pradesh beckoned Fin onward and he followed, through narrow hallways with shiny black walls, barely lit with glowbes, low along the floor like flickering candles, then down several flights of stairs. Fin noticed Mortimus Rex made no sound, neither his clothes nor his feet, and he remembered the Pradishar prohibition on touching the Gran Pradesh and understood now why that rule existed—why the Octa'vin killed anyone who approached too closely.

The hallway opened into a vast chamber, the ceiling and walls so bright they seemed to be a cloudy sky stretching overhead, or a fog bank wrapped around them, so that it looked like they'd emerged outdoors in the middle of the day. Stranger still, the chamber was filled with water, and the walkway continued across the water as a bridge to an island with a single tree.

Fin'roq had never seen this part of the citadel, and yet it looked familiar to him. Mortimus had vanished, but Fin continued across the bridge. The island was lush with green grass and wildflowers in bloom, and the great tree at its center was the strangest tree Fin had ever seen. And yet he knew it. He'd seen it before. He'd seen it many times in fact, but he couldn't remember why, or what it was. It looked almost Verdillion, and its bark seemed to shimmer in the white light. Right in the midst of it's trunk was a large flower, wide open, a kaleidoscope of color.

At the base of the tree was a small wooden table, and someone was sitting with their back to Fin, staring at an unrolled cloth, pondering their next move. When he stepped off the bridge into the grass, the figure turned to look at him.

"Baboo!" Fin cried. "Is it really you?"

His vision was blurry and he was gasping for air before he realized he was crying.

Baboo leapt to his feet, did a cartwheel toward him, and gave him a hug.

"Why are you here?" Baboo said, looking confused.

"I was going to ask you the same question! Have you been in the citadel this whole time?"

"You're too early," Baboo said. He walked back to the table and sat down, then picked up a piece from the cloth and moved it forward.

"Gro'in Stone to Riverfront," Mortimus said, coming up behind Fin, still wearing Ra'shard's form.

Baboo reached across the table and moved a piece for him.

"Guarded," Mortimus tsked, and Baboo flipped the piece over.

"You—you're friends with him?" Fin said. "With the Death King?"

Baboo looked at him and nodded.

"It's like a dream come true, seeing the three of you together again," Mortimus said. He was looking at Baboo, Fin, and the tree, his eyes full of that look that Fin'roq had seen on so many of the Bhizini, the look of the religious fanatic. "Now that you see old Baboo here, will you relax? Will you trust me?"

Fin's mind was spinning. Baboo was his oldest friend—his *only* friend. And here he was, happy as he ever was at Bhea's, playing a game with the creature who had kept him imprisoned for so many lifetimes.

Nothing made any kind of sense.

Fin looked at the tree, and out of the corner of his eye, he could see Mortimus watching him.

"This is what I wanted you to see, Fin. This is Sembraqaa'n, the creator of the crystals."

"I thought Trevian was the creator of the crystals."

Mortimus chuckled. "Clever plant," he said. "This is one of his aspects."

"An aspect," Fin said. "Like me?"

"Like you. And Baboo, too. You three are the holy trinity of the crystals."

"Baboo?"

"He is the destroyer of the crystals," Mortimus said. "With a thought, he can crush any crystal out of existence. Even you, as the wielder of all crystals, can't do this without his help."

Fin looked at Baboo but his friend was staring at the game on the table, plotting his next move.

"This is all—fascinating," Fin said. "But it doesn't explain why you kept me locked away in a stasis chamber. I was meant to be ruling, but instead you're here on the throne in my place."

The ghost of Ra'shard Ruu'n smiled but Fin'roq saw the dark look in his eyes, just for a moment, a flash, but it was enough.

"So you do remember. You've made great progress, Fin."

"I didn't mean—" Fin swallowed hard.

Why am I so afraid of him?

"You have every right to be upset," Mortimus said. "To be furious, even. But as I explained earlier, I did everything I did to keep you alive. As you can see, our friend Sembraqaa'n here has flowered. Do you know what that means?"

"That he can reproduce?" Fin said.

Mortimus chuckled. "Yes. But that's only half of it. He's dying, Fin'roq. Soon he will have a nice fruit where that flower now hangs, and when it's plucked, he will be gone. And the crystals—*all* the crystals—will fade away."

Fin's eyes grew wide. "How long?"

"Until he withers? That depends, Fin, on how our plans are going. If everything is in place..."

"I can't believe it," Fin said. "The crystals—gone?" He felt like he wanted to cry.

"Not forever, Fin. The fruit will regrow a new Sembraqaa'n. And the new Sembraqaa'n will secrete a new generation of crystals. Everything can be restored once more."

Fin sighed, feeling like he'd avoided a catastrophe.

"But unfortunately our enemies don't want that to happen," Mortimus said. "Bhea Bell, King Rhakksees, and their allies don't want the crystals to come back again. They mean to reform the shattered aspects of Trevian, and force him to leave this realm—cast into the shadows of Mund'umbria, never to return."

Fin'roq felt the panic in his chest again—the old fear of darkness and death rising like an angry sea inside of him.

"And the only way for them to succeed—the *only* way—the very thing Bhea has been grooming you for all this time—is to die, Fin. Not for one lifetime, but forever. To be swallowed up in the endless black that belches forth from Mund'umbria. Lost in the reformed Trevian. You, and me, and Baboo too. All of us, gone forever."

Fin couldn't breathe but he gripped the grassy soil with his rootpads and forced himself to speak.

"It can't be true," he said. "Bhea—wants me to die?"

Mortimus sighed. "Baboo, love? What do you say? Is old Ra'shard speaking truth or falsehood?"

Baboo moved a piece on the cloth, threw his arms in the air, and looked at them both, beaming.

Mortimus looked at the cloth. "Why, you rascal! That's the third game in a row you've won."

"Is it true?" Fin screamed.

Mortimus and Baboo both froze. Then Baboo walked over to Fin and took his hand. One look at his face and Fin'roq had his answer.

He turned away, not wanting the others to see his tears.

"Oh Fin, don't you worry about a thing," Mortimus said. "You're with friends now. With allies. You don't have to look back anymore. And you don't have to be afraid of the future."

He wiped his eyes and faced Mortimus. "This world is a terrible place. A waking nightmare. Everywhere I've ever gone, I've been hated, despised, used, and abused. Do you have any idea what that's like, to see revulsion on the faces of those you want so desperately to please?"

Mortimus's face had fallen, and he opened his mouth to respond but then closed it, and for just a moment, Fin could see the pain in his eyes—could feel it inside of whatever the Death King was—and it was genuine and true.

"I know the world has hurt you, Fin," he said. "But you were happy here in Balan Su, once. You were content as a monkin, studying the faiths, were you not? I know you were. Your faithfulness and your piety impressed even the priestins at the Pruu'patch. What do you say to finishing your annual, becoming a Me'dicant healer as you dreamed? And, if you're willing, you could be my private servant, just like Roman Anthem. I promise I'll help you grow strong, Fin. And when the time comes to rebuild the world, I'll help you make it a place where someone like you doesn't have to be afraid to live and love."

"I—" Fin swallowed hard, hating the monster in front of him but loving what he offered him, and knowing he wasn't ready to overthrow him—didn't have the first idea how to. So he sank to his knees and bowed his head. "I am your humble servant, Gran Pradesh, your worship."

"Baboo, rustle up some food and drink. This is a cause for celebration."

Fin stood. "Wait," he said. "Wait. There's one thing I need to know. I came here with my mother and my brother." He turned and stared Mortimus Rex in the eyes. "What's going to happen to them?"

❦

The scytherin slid across Rakk's Pradishar crystamin next, and as the filaments shattered into smaller and smaller shards throughout his body, he thought of Q'orin, of holding him while he shook and thrashed in the sands of Nunan, and he wished more than anything that he was there right now, to comfort him as he'd done for him.

But nobody was there except a stranger wearing Rajj's face, using Rajj's voice, but clearly not his brother. Not his smart, sensitive, quiet brother, who had never once shown violent aggression, never once screamed or shouted, never once given Rakk any reason to suspect him.

Maybe he's right, he thought. *I'm just that big of a fool.*

<<Some betrayals can't be foreseen,>> a voice said in his head.

Rakk knew that voice, and he reached out for it, and was surprised that he could.

My crystamin—my last crystamin—the one I share with Q'orin—it's waking up!

<<And you're no fool, Rakk Raeder.>>

It was Anorian Grain.

Rakk followed the voice and felt the floor drop away from under him.

In his mind's eye, he landed in a plaza, a soft breeze on his face, warm sunshine on his skin. He looked down and could see his own body, see his feet on the cobblestones—but he knew he was still in the Dankburn. It was similar to streaming a melodrama as one of the characters, only the character was himself.

<<What is this place?>> he said.

<<The hollow,>> Anorian said.

Rakk looked around but nobody else was in the plaza. The only sound was a soft breeze and the purr of the sea nearby.

<<I hope you'll forgive me for not bringing you here sooner, brother.>>

A tree with fruit of every color appeared in front of him, and then began to transform, to shrink down into a Verdillion.

When Rakk saw Qaas'andria in front of him, he knew it was her, and he ran to her and picked her up and spun her around in his arms.

<<I don't understand,>> he said, setting her back down. <<Where? How? Why?>>

<<I'm sorry brother, but there isn't much time to explain. If your last crystamin is shattered, I won't be able to speak to you any more. You need to free yourself.>>

<<The crystals,>> Rakk said. <<The pain—>>

<<It's gone,>> Anorian said, and it was.

<<I still can't move though. The vines, they're already cutting into my skin. There's no way to snap them.>>

<<Your scytherin,>> she said.

<<Rajj has it. The vines are too tight.>>

<<Try again.>> She took his hands in the hollow. <<But keep your mind here with me. Keep your focus on this body. The vines can't sever your limbs, no matter how much it feels like they will. Ignore the pain, and try again.>>

Rakk kept his focus on Qaas'i—*She can speak!*—while he willed his arm, his real arm, to twist around—*Qaas'i is Anorian?!*—and his fingers to reach. The vines cut deeper and he knew it, but he didn't feel it.

Rajj laughed. "You fool, you'll drain your sap before you bust through those vines, but I guess you always did think you could do whatever you wanted."

Rakk pushed until the vine could stretch no farther, then took a deep breath and reached for the scytherin. His hand wrapped around Rajj's, and his brother's eyes bugged out. He crushed Rajj's fingers into the handle of the blade and he cried out and released it, and Rakk swung it downward, across Rajj's thigh, and through the vines holding him.

Rajj stumbled backward, sap pouring down his leg, and he turned for the door, running, panting. Rakk started after him.

<<Let him go,>> Anorian said. <<You need to get to my mother. Hurry, before it's too late.>>

❧⁓⁓⁓⁓ ⁓⁓⁓❧

Uthyr pulled the trigger and the enflamer shot a long stream of blue fire, spreading orange down the corpse of Ra'shard Ruu'n, which sparked up like dry kindling, popping and splitting apart and turning to ash in front of Ellex's eyes.

She pulled out her own enflamer and trained it on her brother. When he saw it, he stopped firing, a stupid grin on his face.

"What you got there, sibby? That's an awfully powerful weapon for someone so obviously unwell. Let me have it before you hurt yourself." He started toward her.

"Take another step and I'll set you aflame. I swear to Trevian I will."

"Now, now, Ell, didn't Father teach you not to take oaths you can't keep, especially to a deity?" He was still grinning as he continued to walk toward her.

She tried to pull the trigger—she wanted to, was desperate to—but she couldn't. Her finger wouldn't respond.

"And just in time, too," Uthyr said. He reached out and took the enflamer from her hand. She watched, her face blank, a look of confusion and panic in her eyes.

"How?" she said, but she already knew the answer.

"Isn't it obvious?" he said, walking over to the smoldering heap that was once Ra'shard Ruu'n's corpse. "Ra'shard spent his entire life trying to destroy the Raccorin social order, determined to end slavery once and for all." He spat on the coals. "And now the Ren'fallow have all of Balance under our yoke, and nobody even knows it. Rajj and I are the real rulers of Balance Authority, and you, with all your haughty arrogance, ordering me around like I'm your sidekick, your servant—and all this time, you've been nothing more than my puppet."

Ellex felt herself standing, awkwardly—felt her arm lifting up—she felt like she was would fall over, but didn't. Suddenly her hand smacked her across the face, then her other arm lifted and smacked her again across the face, and again and again.

Uthyr was nearly hysterical with laughter.

"Sad thing about puppets," Uthyr said. "Like any toy, you eventually outgrow them. And a toy that knows it's a toy? That's no fun at all."

Ellex practically ran toward her brother, but was pulled down to her knees, her head leaning back, so far it hurt her neck and strained her throat. She tried to control her breath, but even that was beyond her.

I'm going to die, she thought. *The Death King will rule in my name—with my face—for another century.*

She felt Uthyr's hand in her robes, on her leg, unsheathing her scytherin. He held it up over her eyes and laughed.

"Haven't you always wondered how it feels to have a crystamin shatter? Let me know, okay?" He grinned. "I'm afraid your service in the Council of Nine will no longer be required," he said, swiping the scytherin across her forehead. The blade tore into her Council of Nine crystamin and her Balan Su public crystamin, shattering their faces and pulverizing the filaments that stretched down into the core of Ellex's body, into every nerve and fiber.

She tried to scream, to howl, to gnash her teeth together, but she couldn't move. Her eyes felt like they were bulging out of her face but she couldn't look around, couldn't close them.

Uthyr stumbled backward, cursing, and Ellex felt herself falling, even after she'd slumped onto the floor. Every inch of her body hurt, throbbed, screamed with pain, and she knew she had to get away from her brother, but it was too much.

Instead, she fell down into a grassy field full of wildflowers.

<<You're safe here,>> a voice said. <<He can't hurt you anymore.>>

Ellex moaned and opened her eyes, her real eyes, and struggled to see. Someone else had come into the house. She saw an outstretched arm, saw Uthyr floating in the air, his eyes wide, his face bloated, his mouth opening and closing like a fish out of water.

Fin'roq stood in the courtyard, his skin shimmering as if with moonlight, his eyes rolled back in his head, glowing.

And he wasn't alone. Someone else crouched down at Ellex's side. She saw Rakk's face, puffy with bruises and stained with sap, with long streaks where tears had fallen, and she grabbed his hand and held it tightly.

She looked at Uthyr again, at Fin'roq squeezing the life out of him.

"Wait!" she cried, wincing. "Don't kill him!"

Fin'roq turned to look at her and Ellex stared for a moment into those vacant, glowing pits, and she couldn't help but turn away. She looked at Uthyr again, and with a small push of Fin'roq's hand, her brother flew backwards, crashing through the wall and into the next room.

Then Fin'roq turned and walked toward her til he was standing over her, and Ellex could feel his presence through her one remaining crystal, and it was enormous and terrible and she wanted to collapse before it. But he reached down for her hand, and when she took it, she felt the tension evaporating away from her body, the crystal shards inside her vanishing, her face flushing with warmth, with vitality.

"Sweet Trevian," she moaned. "How?"

Rakk stood up and Fin'roq pulled Ellex to her feet.

"You need to go, now. Out of this city. It isn't safe for you," Fin said, his eyes returning to normal. He looked at her. "Mortimus Rex plans to take your face."

"I know," she said. "You're coming with us?" She squeezed Fin's hand. "Right?"

"Wrong," he said, pulling away from her. "I just came here to tell you to leave. I'll do what I can to hold them off, but you need to go. Now."

Ellex opened her mouth to argue but Rakk had pulled Fin into a big hug.

"I'll never forget what you did for me," he said. "I hope when this is all over, we can be a family. A real family."

"What will you do?" Ellex said.

"Finish my annual with the Pradishar. Rise up the ranks, as I know I can. And when the time comes, I'll take back what's mine."

"Fin," she said. "Can I—"

"Later, Sui Pradesh. You need to get as far from the city as you can, both of you."

She wanted very much to hug her son, but she knew he wasn't going to have it. So she took Rakk's arm and started for the door, and she forced herself not to look back.

Chapter 66

Sprouting Hope

BRYN SPENT HER FIRST week on P'anorum in a daze, certain she must be dreaming, sure that she was still in a cell on Anthem's ship, delirious with the need for light, for water. Or maybe she'd always been on P'anorum, there in Bhea Bell's garden, on the cliffside over the sea, with the chirping and the buzzing of the Swarthen Forest all around her, the salty breeze through the limbs of the canopy and the purr of the breakers down below lulling her toward serenity.

Or maybe it was Anorian. Qaas'andria. The daughter of Ellex Andria and King Rhakksees II. And some kind of mystical creature, able to contact and control the crystals, though she had none herself. Bryn felt like she was living in a myth, in a deep sea yarn spun by an old Bhizini who long ago went mad with loneliness and had dreamt up such a fantasy.

I don't understand it, she thought. *My rational mind screams—rages—against it. How could I have not known? I thought—I really thought I could have been a professor, that I knew enough to debate with the greatest of our times. But I haven't known anything at all about the world.*

It didn't matter, at least not when Bryn was with Anorian. She forgot about her questions, about the disconnect between the possible and the impossible. She even forgot about her mother, languishing in the dungeons of Andramere, waiting to die if Bryn didn't turn herself in.

That truth had stayed distant from her mind, but when she woke that morning to birdsong and the trilling of cicadas, to soft twilight outside the door of the guest hut where she'd been sleeping all week, she was in a panic, out of breath, the sound of her mother's cries on her ears.

Only it wasn't her mother, softly weeping.

Bryn pulled her rootpads out of the soil and slipped a thin robe over her head, then stepped outside. The sound was coming from the next hut over, where Anorian had been sleeping.

With her heart thudding in her ears, she approached the door while reaching for Anorian with her mind.

"Are you okay?" she whispered.

Bryn felt her beckoning her to come inside.

Anorian stood by the door, her face streaked with tears. The sight broke Bryn's heart, and she stepped toward her, but Anorian took a quick step back.

Bryn felt like she wanted to die.

But then Anorian exhaled, loudly, and pulled her into a hug.

"It's okay," Bryn said. "I think. What's wrong?"

<<I don't know why I'm crying. I mean, I do. It's just—>>

She pulled her robe up to her chest, and Bryn saw a large, colorful blossom on her belly.

"I've flowered," she whispered, a few more tears leaking out of her eyes.

"And it's a beautiful one," Bryn said, "for my beautiful Anorian."

She sniffed. <<I feel confused.>>

"That's understandable. I wept too," Bryn said, "when I flowered. At least you won't have to go before the gender assignment committee." She shuddered at the memory. "I've never asked, but—your mother called you her daughter, perhaps in part because you were so small? But I've watched you grow just in this last week. You'll be as tall and broad-shouldered as Fin'roq, or Prince Rhakksees, won't you?"

She nodded and took Bryn's hand. <<I didn't know for sure what would happen when I came out of the chamber. Biologically, it was as if I'd been alive for less than a decade. I thought I would grow slowly, at a normal pace. But my body seems eager to catch up. I've grown two decades in two months. It's been—exhausting.>> She paused for a moment. <<It still is sometimes. To speak. To act. To function in the world.>>

"I know it is," Bryn said. "Sweet Trevian, how I know it."

She felt Anorian in her mind, holding her, lifting her up, filling her with warmth. And Bryn reached for her, lifted the robe over her head, and then ran her hands down her back, wanting her more than she'd ever wanted anything and knowing Anorian felt the same way. There was no fear, no doubt—no panic, no painful flashbacks—only a union of body and mind, thought and emotion, desire and intent.

Their rootpads gripped the soil and their branches unfurled and tangled around one another, and their flowers pressed together, their stamens diving into the soft burrow of petals of the other. And Bryn opened her mind to Anorian, let her take in all of her memories, all of her hopes and fears, her ambitions and her uncertainties, and it was the most profound, and poignant, release she'd ever felt.

She could feel Anorian trembling, desperate to open to her as well, but scared.

<<I don't want to hurt you,>> she said.

<<You'll be right here to protect me,>> Bryn said.

The sudden sensation—that Bryn's entire body had been violently torn in two—passed away as soon as it came upon her, and in the calm that followed, she recognized the feeling—had felt it before—at the end of Ellex Andria's dream.

That was—?

<<My birth,>> Anorian said. <<It's the great secret, Bryndax. The one the Death King doesn't know. That my mother, and my father, and their allies, were able to tear the spirit of the wielder in two. Only, it wasn't a perfect split. Something happened that they didn't foresee.>>

Images and feelings began to flow across Bryn's mind—lights shining in the darkness, a night sky full of flickering stars—and she knew she was all of them. All of their long lives, their memories, their hopes and fears.

But it was too much—too much at once—too much to comprehend—and for a moment she forgot who she was. Until Anorian cut through the noise, and blotted out the stream of sensations, and there was only the two of them, together as one.

⚜ ⚜

By the time Bryn and Qaas'andria emerged from the hut, the sun was high overhead, the dark clouds gathering on the lush rim of the Crag up above, a few echoes of thunder rumbling down the mountainside. Bhea had left a basket of food on the table, and they munched on rhupan buns while they walked the jungle path to the village.

When they reached the edge, Bryn could see the harbor down below full of ships, the beach abuzz with activity, the green arms of the crater wrapping it all in a warm hug. She could see the palace jutting out of the lava, which sparkled red and black in the sunshine; see could see the smooth sides of the great peak, rising thousands of feet in the air, the rim lost in a tuft of cloud; and she could feel Anorian's hand in hers, soft and warm—could feel her flower still throbbing, delightfully sore and tender, from their time together. And she thought her heart would crush under the scope of her joy and the weight of her misery.

"I'll do it," she said, exhaling hard.

She turned to Anorian and took her other hand as well, then gripped the stones of the stair with her rootpads, closed her eyes, and leapt for Dar Ka'Hala. Anorian was at her side, on the balcony of the great palace with her eyes closed, and when she opened them, Bryn saw the others begin to appear in the plaza down below.

So many of them now, she thought. *Thousands? Tens of thousands?*

<<You brought all of these into the hollow?>> Bryn said. <<But how?>>

<<I can be many places at once. Speak to many at once. In here, at least. But it's you who made this possible, Bryndax, you and your friends and followers, who faced down the Cul'tavin, and the threat of torture and death for crimes against information, to share the truth. People trust you, and listen to you, and are drawn to you, in a way I can't hope to replicate. Even before we officially met, you had a vast following on the weavryn. They won't abandon you, when they know who you really are. Everything you are, and everything that has happened to you—these are your strengths, Bryndax. And your strength gives me my own.>>

They stood on the balcony and kissed in front of the crowd, while their real bodies stood atop the stairs on the rim of the crater, kissing under the sun.

Finally they turned and faced the plaza, and with Anorian's help, Bryn brought all of them together, in sync with thought and sensation.

<<You all have known me as the Mighty B*zzness,>> Bryn began. <<But my real name is Bryn Andri'n, daughter of Stylina and Doc Bryncent Andri'n.>>

There were gasps in the crowd, and Bryn could feel that most were shocked and surprised, although most knew who she was, and who her father was. And she could feel their anger about what had happened to him, their rage at the injustice of the Pradishar—and the fire lit up that spark inside her, fanned it to life, til it wasn't a flame that might be crushed out once more, but an inferno that could no longer be tamed.

<<The Pradishar tortured and murdered my father,>> she said. <<And now they're torturing my mother, threatening to execute her if I don't return to Andramere. If I don't immediately fall silent, and fall in line. But I have already been tortured by the Pradishar. I have seen the way they treat a body, the way they treat a mind—like property. Their property. But who am I if not my body, if not the thoughts that motivate it? If nothing else, those are private property—the only truly private property in the world. Who are

they to tell me what to do with my flesh and my mind? What to call myself? What I ought to think, and feel, and believe?>>

Bryn felt her listeners hanging on her every word, pulsing with the same emotions she was feeling, and as she looked down across the plaza, at the faces looking up at her, at the pain and anger and sadness and hope on display—with Anorian's hand firm on her own, and the taste of her lips still on her own—she felt strong for the first time in her life.

<<The Pradishar took something very dear from me,>> Bryn said. <<Something they take from so many of us. Their dignity. Their self-respect. Their willingness to care enough about themselves to draw a line and say no. I know how it feels to build up those walls around the pain, to think that staying silent is better, that shrinking away into nothing is preferable to standing back up and moving on. Today—right now—I'm going to prove them wrong.>>

She felt Anorian in her mind.

<<Are you sure?>> she asked.

<<Yes,>> Bryn said, opening to her, letting the memories flow, while Anorian shared them with the crowd in the plaza below. They saw the committee poking and prodding her. They saw Aerid and E'mo at the ceremony, mocking her—saw them following her—saw their faces contorted with hate—saw and felt how they misused her and insulted her. They saw Malisha Andra'asnia, completely unsympathetic, blaming Bryn for the attack. They saw the gleeful look on Malisha's face while the smoking ruin of Doc Andri'n's body crackled and popped, while Aerid pounded his fists into her face and into her flower. And when it finally stopped, those in the plaza were gasping, weeping, shaking.

<<I want the Pradishar to know that I will not stay silent,>> she whispered, but it thundered across the plaza. <<I want Malisha Andra'asnia to know that I will not be turning myself in—that I will *never* take one of her orders ever again—and that when I do come to Andramere, it will be for her head!>>

And Bryn meant it.

She could feel the collective rage swelling up inside her, sweeping her up with its power, and when she thought she might fall over, Anorian held her, and wiped away her tears, and kissed her until the world felt right again.

Epilogue

ROMAN ANTHEM PILOTED HIS cata'rin through the fog around Balan Su, the dawn air thick with the smell of salt. He was itching for a swim. He was always itching for a swim, called by the ocean, longing to dance through its waters, to spread out his fins and roll around on his back and chase the seagulls that came by squawking at him.

If only I could stay the beast, he thought. *Give up this charade, these silly games, and frolic forever in the endless sea.*

But those were the dreams of a servant—dreams, and not reality.

He didn't care either way.

Why pick sides? Why draw lines in the first place? Why limit yourself from moving, from adapting, from becoming what you need to be when the need arises? Only fools took titles and swore allegiances. Fools, and mortals. But those were usually the same thing.

Eternity feels the same to everyone, he thought. *It feels like right now. What else could it feel like? There is only right now.*

Right?

Mortimus Rex was waiting for him in the Trellium. Anthem crossed the bridge to the island and saw that he was wearing Ra'shard Ruu'n's face. Sembraqaa'n stood behind him, skin shimmering in the white light, large flower a medley of colors on its navel. Anthem took a knee in front of them.

"Rise, my friend, rise," Mortimus said. "I expected you earlier. Did you deliver the cargo?"

"You already know my answer," he said, standing.

"How bold they are," Mortimus said. "I never expected Ellex Andria to have such nerve. All those years, she worshipped me as a living god. Which I am, of course!" He laughed. "But you know what I mean. How delightful. You should have seen how she trembled before me."

"She came to the citadel?"

"Don't be a fool, you think I'd let that traitorous wretch in here again? I've ordered my Octa'vin to kill her on sight, but Fin'roq insisted on saving her. Her and the Raccorin prince Rhakksees. What was I to do?" He shrugged, a smirk on his face.

"Then you've seen him," Anthem said. "And?"

"And what? It went down just as I told you it would. Bhea Bell's failure is now complete."

"Fin'roq is too unpredictable to trust," he said.

Ra'shard Ruu'n's specter faded and in it's place appeared a ghastly, bulbous, contorted, grotesque creature—a Verdillion covered with boils and open, festering sores, it's eyes caked with green scum, it's lips curled back against long, pointed fangs. The poor dead creature was a favorite of Mortimus's, when he really wanted to shock or startle—or terrify.

"What kind of fool do you think I am? *Trust* the devil? Not on my life! No, no, no, I intend to squeeze the fun out of him, to wring him dry as it were. See how far we can use him for our own ends. You know how vulnerable the wielder is! They hardly remember their past lives. All they really know is who they are now. And we can always use their lack of vision against them. If he proves to be of a different persuasion, we've not to worry, not for a moment. I have another stasis chamber waiting, just down the hall, ready for him, should he fail to perform. And this one will keep him sealed up tight for at least a thousand years."

"I thought Lithuigi Von'nDrino had defected," Anthem said.

"He's always been Bhea's puppet, though dutiful enough to me to keep him alive. You can't waste a mind like that lightly. Fortunately for us, his son Hesh'n is equal to his father, if not superior to him. And his Verdhesh'n—" Mortimus whistled. "Even if I can't bring the Raccorin and the Andrasians to war, it won't matter in the least." He clapped his hands together, his hideous face drawn up in a twisted smile. "This Harvest will be unlike any other! And I can hardly wait."

Appendix

Dramatis Personae

CAST OF CHARACTERS

Aar'ryn Ruu'n: A Raccorin and fake Pradishar priestin in Fin'roq's village on P'anorum;

Anorian Grain: A colleague of Doc Andri'n;

Aerid: An Adrasian; one of Bryn's peers and bullies in the sprouting patch, now a Cul'tavin peacekeeper;

Baboo: A Bhizini from P'anorum; Fin'roq's best friend;

Bhartimu'u "Bhart" Tornroot: Bhizini Pal'meran warrior;

Bhea Bell: A Bhizini from P'anorum; Fin'roq's teacher;

Bryn Andri'n: Archivist, hacker, notestreamer, and activist from Andramere;

Bryncent "Doc" Andri'n: Professor and Dyna'arin tinker from Andramere; Bryn's father;

Tuck'tumi Tornroot: Bhizini, ruler of the Tornroot Clan, based on Lagracia in the Far Ocean;

Chief Rhegan: Raccorin noble; leader of the Grassworth clade;

Chief Rhingoven: Raccorin noble; leader of the Dagmar clade;

Durq: An Andrasian villager from P'anorum; father of Roe;

Ellex Andria: Leader of the Andrasian delegation on the Council of Nine; Pradishar bishrop and Sui Pradesh; Cul'tavin peacekeeper;

Emo: One of Bryn's peers and bullies in the sprouting patch, now a Cul'tavin peacekeeper;

Fin'roq: A Bhizini from P'anorum; treated as an outcast by his fellow villagers;

Ginjy: Andrasian activist and notestreamer from Andramere; one of Bryn's best friends;

Grizmond Grants: A Raccorin and former slave from P'anorum; Fin'roq's peer;

Hesh'n Von'nDrino: Son of Lithuigi and Rebesh'a; a Dyna'arin tinker and adjunct professor in Balan Su;

Jaun von Andron: Crown prince of Andramere and weavryn entertainment star;

Kha'toran Rha'qan: A Raccorin tinker and one of Lithuigi's role models;

Lithuigi Von'nDrino: Andrasian professor and Dyna'arin tinker;

Madr'gin: Chief librarian on Andramere;

Malisha Andra'asnia: An Andrasian Culture Minister and advisor on the Council of Nine; a bishrop and head Cul'tavin peacekeeper on Andrasia;

Mha'arlo: A Raccorin student in Balan Su's Academicon; Lithuigi's most trusted aide;

Milli Mor'n: An Andrasian villager from P'anorum; Fin'roq's crush;

Nu'mora Rhyantis: A Raccorin manager in the Guild; head of the operators;

Ora'nel Rhyantis: Raccorin general; head of the Corkin at Thester; ally of Rakk;

Pander: An old Andrasian; Ellex's garden keeper on Balan Su and her closest aide;

Prissica: An Andrasian villager from P'anorum; mother of Roe;

Qaa'milo: A Raccorin and friend of Rakk's from before P'anorum erupted;

Qardymion the Saltsap: A Bhizini rebel, leader of the Pal'merans, who has harangued Balance's sea lanes for decades;

Q'orin Grievenson: A Corkin soldier and Rakk's personal slave and closest friend;

Rakk Raeder: Prince Rhakksees Raccorine Deri the Third; exiled from his homeland; head of the Corkin slave army;

Rajjesh'n Raccorine Deri: A prince of the Raccorin Empire and head of the Raccorin delegation on the Council of Nine; Rakk's brother;

Rameen Rutar: The Head Manager of the Dyna'arin, and the Raccorin representative of the Guild on the Council of Nine;

Raq'asha Raccorine Deri: A princess of the Raccorin Empire and high regent of Raccorum Rhazzat; Rakk's sister;

Ra'shard Ruu'n: A Raccorin abolitionist; Gran Pradesh of the Pradishar;

Rebesh'a Von'nDrino: An Andrasian and a world-famous weavryn performer; Lithuigi's wife in Balan Su;

Rhannokti: A Corkin soldier and personal favorite of Rakk on the battlefield;

Rhingus: Raccorin activist and notestreamer from Andramere; one of Bryn's best friends;

Rhyntak Rorh: Raccorin noble; son of the chief of the Barrens; Rakk's closest ally in Raccorum Rhazzat;

Rhyntysha Rorh: A Raccorin tinker and one of Lithuigi's most trusted aides;

Roe: An Andrasian villager from P'anorum; Fin'roq's peer and bully;

Roman Anthem: A Cul'tavin peacekeeper;

Stylina "Mama" Andri'n: Bryn's mother;

Trexbo: Andrasian activist and notestreamer from Andramere; one of Bryn's best friends;

Uthyr Andria: Head of Intelligence for Andrasia on the Council of Nine and Cul'tavin peacekeeper; Ellex's brother;

Valden Andron: The Head of Homeland Affairs for the Andrasian delegation on the Council of Nine;

Vilder Von'nDrino: Son of Lithuigi and Rebesh'a; a Pradishar priestin in Balan Su.

Glossary

IMPORTANT TERMS

Andrasians: petite, dull colored Verdillions, from Andrasia;

Balancing Act: celebrated on the anniversary of Balance Authority, when the sun is at its northernmost point in the sky; begins at sunrise at the end of the festival of Zenithra, which marks the beginning of the holiday season (summer) in Balance Territories and the start of a new year;

Balance Authority: a political union between the Raccorin Empire and the Andrasian Republic; ruled by the Council of Nine from Balan Su City; consists of the Pradishar (governance and religion) and the Dyna'arin (technology and labor); administers the major ports of both polities, as well as all offshore colonies in the Inner Archipelago; relies upon the Corkin army to maintain the Inner Seas and the coastlines;

Bhiza: psychoactive fungus used for spiritual and entertainment purposes; some varieties are legal in Balance Territories; others are known to numb crystamins temporarily, others to cause paralysis or death;

Bhizini: a Verdillion of mixed race, with skin that is a medley of bright and dull patches; more loosely, anyone who renounces Balance Authority;

Bishrop: a servant and minister of the Pradishar, with authority over priestins, Cul'tavin peacekeepers, and the various institutions and properties of the Pradishar;

Camerooge: a legislative and judicial body in the five clades of Andrasia and on the island of Andramere; in the five clades, the body is self-governed, while on Andramere, the high doge is the de facto prime minister and can raise or veto any issue at will;

Corkin: the slave armies of the Raccorin Empire;

Crystamins: one of the three types of crystal; they cling to the flesh of Verdillions, grow into their nervous system, and allow communication with other crystamins of the same class, with datamins, and with servryns;

Cul'tavin: peacekeepers of the Pradishar; with a long tradition of free agency, peace-keepers follow bishrops willingly and are free to change allegiance;

Council of Nine: see *Council of Nine*, below;

Datamins: one of the three types of crystal; can be written with raw data, and accessed locally through a crystamin, or remotely through a servryn;

Dyna'arin: see *Dyna'arin*, below;

Dynamins: one of the three types of crystals; capable of excreting dynamic energy; required for all maquina to function;

Gran Pradesh: the highest ranking Pradishar, head of the Council of Nine;

Gruynfeld: planting grounds for Verdillions, always on a small island dedicated to that purpose, many which are artificially constructed, at the end of the ambulatory phase of their life, when they enter the tandavin phase; access to the grove is strictly forbidden, per the threat of spontaneous combustion;

Lorchan: a place of worship for the Loricean faith;

Loricea: the former state religion of Raccorum Rhazzat; after the loss of the capital on P'anorum and the return of the royal family to their ancestral home, the Loricea fell into decline, effectively ceasing to exist;

Me'dicants: Pradishar healers trained in Verdillion biology and often practicing a no-madic lifestyle; many healers are also members of the Guild and are able to use Dyna'arin technology in their healing practices;

Monkin: lowest level of the ordained Pradishar, used for initiates both before joining with a crystal and after; those who pass their lives as monkins work as general servants of the Pradishar in exchange for room and board, and thus can be found doing a wide variety of tasks in all parts of Balance Territories;

Mund'umbria: a realm of spirits, shades, and demigods;

Nadira: a festival celebrated at the winter solstice;

N'detten: Bhizini who live and work, with permission, in Guild-controlled areas;

Octa'vin: the eight guards of the citadel of Balan Su, answerable only to the Gran Pradesh; their identities are unknown, but their loyalty to the Gran Pradesh is known to be absolute;

Orden: free subjects of Raccorum Rhazzat, usually merchants or operators;

Pal'meran: elite Bhizini warriors under Qardymion the Saltsap;

Pradishar: see *Pradishar*, below;

Priestin: a servant and organizer of the Pradishar, with authority over monkins; they often work as servants of bishrops;

Pruu'log: holy scripture of the Pradishar;

Pruu'patch: training centers for monkins of the Pradishar;

Raccorin: large, broad, brightly colored Verdillions from Raccorum Rhazzat;

Ren'fallow: an ancient conspiracy, now used loosely for any who conspire against Balance Authority and the Pradishar; the original purveyors were fanatics who believed in the imminent return of an ancient weapon, one that would wipe away the world in a great cataclysm called the Harvest;

Rhank: enslaved laborers of Raccorum Rhazzat;

Rhupan: other than sunshine, the primary food source for Verdillions; a fungus that grows on rocks near the seashore;

Rishar: a council called by Raccorin nobles to decide who should rule Raccorum Rhazzat;

Scamp: the youthful part of a Verdillion's ambulatory phase of life, beginning with the cutting of the taprin and lasting for three decades, while the Verdillion slowly grows toward full size; the phase ends with flowering, when a Verdillion enters adulthood;

Scytherin: a small Bhizini dagger capable of destroying crystamins;

Servryn: maquina containing all three crystal types; a repository for information and a conduit for communication between different classes of crystal; invented a century earlier, well-placed servryns throughout Balance Territories gave rise to the modern weavryn;

Sharlum: a traditional place of worship for the Pradishar;

Spratlyn: the first phase of a Verdillion life, small and shrublike and insentient, growing into a scamp over nearly one year; the phase ends with the cutting of the taprin and the waking to consciousness;

Sui Pradesh: the second highest rank of the ordained Pradishar; the leaders of the Andrasian and Raccorin delegations on the Council of Nine;

Tandavin: the final phase of a Verdillion's life, after setting down permanent roots in a gruynfeld; Verdillions in this phase grow slowly taller and woodier over many centuries before spontaneously combusting, an event which has the capacity to engulf the entire gruynfeld in a cleansing fire;

Taprin: a long hearty root that anchors a spratlyn to the ground and provides it with nutrition from the soil; when the spratlyn has matured, the taprin must be ruptured for the Verdillion to awaken to consciousness; if not, it will soon wither and rot, and the spratlyn will never wake;

Trevian: the mysterious founder of Balance and the crystals which support it; said to have saved the world from destruction by sacrificing himself 10,000 years ago;

Verdillions: see *Verdillions*, below;

Weavryn: a shared virtual/mental space created by the weaving of the three crystals within a servryn; allows access to the world's information with merely a thought; facilitates communication and sharing of feelings, sensations, thoughts, and memories between any two crystal holders, anywhere in the world, regardless of crystal class; invented a century earlier in Andramere City;

Zenithra: the last two weeks of spring, leading up to the summer solstice.

Verdillions

What if humans were more like trees? What if we could clutch the soil while we fed from the sunshine? What if we were genderless, able to reproduce both sexually and asexually using flowers on our skin? And so came Verdillions to fill in one of the possibilities of such questions.

But Verdillions—like flowers, like trees, like life—were not content to stay un-complicated. And so there came three different variations to the Verdillion existence: the Raccorin—large, broad Verdillions with bright green skin; the Andrasians—small, petite Verdillions with dull green skin; and the Bhizini—Verdillions of all sizes and with a patchwork medley of bright and dull green skin, like camouflage, each with a unique pattern.

Verdillions are a tropical species. They require warm weather and plentiful sunshine, so they have traditionally lived near the equator and outdoors; a Verdillion with ample sunshine can consist wholly on light; rhupan cultivation from seaside wetlands allows indoor living, and allows Verdillions to stray further away from the equator than was traditionally possible.

Although they do require both air and water, they can go for extended periods without it, entering a stasis period that makes them slow and lethargic. A healthy Verdillion with a full breath of air can last a few hours underwater and still survive, and can pass months without fresh water; however, after several days with no water, their mobility becomes extremely limited, so most Verdillions try to drink fluids every day.

Extended deprivation of light energy, either from the sun or from glowbes, leads to stiffening of the fibers, resulting in petrification of the flesh, sometimes called the "screaming death" since Verdillions are stuck in one place, unable to move, for quite a long time before they finally die. Because of this, most Verdillions have an innate fear of dark places.

In order to quickly absorb light energy, Verdillions can extend branches from beneath their arms, which open into a bushel or canopy around and over their head, something they often support by holding up their arms. At the ends of every branch are small green leaftips which Verdillions can unroll and angle toward the light. Feeding this way can invoke euphoria. Verdillions can also use these branches to clutch and grab at things.

The bottoms of Verdillion feet are covered in rootpads—a thick, spongy material that they can extend into the ground. When perching—either to take in sun, or while sleeping—Verdillions will drop their pads down into the soil, where their body will evacuate wastes. Sleeping without access to a soil perch is possible, but will eventually lead to sickness. The rootpads can also be used to clutch at surfaces, especially porous ones, allowing Verdillions to fasten themselves to surfaces, like the deck of a ship.

The Verdillion life cycle begins with a flower, a stamen, and pollen; within a few days of pollenation, a flower will have grown into a fruit, which must be plucked and planted; fruits that are not planted within a week begin to rot and the seed is no longer viable for growing.

A planted fruit will sprout within a week, beginning the "spratlyn" phase of life, which lasts less than one year, during which a small sprout becomes a shrub that grows into a small Verdillion, held fast to the ground by a long, thick taprin; when the taprin matures, it must be severed during roughly a month-long window, or else it will wither, and the spratlyn will soon wither as well.

When the taprin is cut, the spratlyn awakes as a scamp, an un-flowered Verdillion; scamps slowly grow in size over three decades before flowering.

Though gender is assigned by Balance Authority, an adult Verdillion can reproduce with any other adult Verdillion, even with themselves asexually (called a duplicant, and prohibited by Balance Authority); reproduction in Balance Authority is only permitted between opposite genders; traditionally, the female's fruit is planted while the male's fruit is discarded.

Adult Verdillions live for around two centuries, changing little in shape or size, though their skin and joints slowly begin to harden; when they are ready for planting, a Verdillion will travel to an island in a lake or in the sea called a gruynfeld—many of them artificially constructed—to permanently set their rootpads, turning them into a deep taproot; this begins the tandavin phase of the Verdillion lifecycle.

Tandavins no longer speak, no longer communicate through the crystal, no longer move from the spot where they are rooted; their skin hardens into bark and their branches, once unfurled, never again withdraw, but reach upward toward the sun, across the next thousand years.

One day, without warning, a tandavin will spontaneously combust, bringing to an end their long life; often, the fire is so hot, the combustion so explosive, that it will ignite the surrounding tandavin, causing a cleansing inferno that thins the grove for the next generations.

Pradishar

INTRODUCTION

A religious, political, bureaucratic, and law-enforcement group; they are led by the Council of Nine, which rules from a small chamber called the Solarium, within the Pradishar citadel on Balan Su; the Pradishar keep both the Raccorin Empire and the Andrasian Republic in the alliance through absolute reliance on, and total control of, the creation and destruction of the three crystals; the Pradishar are nearly synonymous with the government of Balance Authority.

MEMBERS

Pradeshans: Followers of the faith/laypeople;

Monkins: Servants, students, devotees; all members other than laypeople begin as a monkin;

Priestins: Teachers, administrators, leaders of services in sharlums;

Bishrops: Political and religious leaders, in charge of peacekeepers, priestins, and monkins;

Peacekeepers: Warriors of the faith; most join the Cul'tavin, the official peacekeeping force of Balance Authority;

Healers: Known as Me'dicants once they have completed training in Verdillion biology; many practice a nomadic lifestyle;

Sui Pradesh: the second highest rank of the ordained Pradishar; the leaders of the Andrasian and Raccorin delegations on the Council of Nine;

Gran Pradesh: the leader of the Pradishar, with authority over all members, and tie-breaking power on the Council of Nine.

THE THREE DOGMAS

1. The Pradishar were chosen by Trevian to maintain balance between Raccorin and Andrasian, to ensure peace everlasting;

2. Only the Gran Pradesh, who enshrines the power of Trevian, can bring forth, maintain, and destroy the three crystals, and thus speaks for Trevian's will in the world;

3. The highest good in life is service to Trevian's peace, which is realized through Balance Authority and its institutions.

Council of Nine

The ruling body of Balance Authority

COUNCIL POSITIONS

Leaders: Speakers for their coalition; considered the head of their respective delegation;

Intelligence: Use the crystals

Homeland Affairs: Representatives of the Andrasian Republic and the Raccorin Empire; chosen by the respective delegations and not by the Council itself; liaison between the Council and local government;

Guild Representatives: Speakers for the Dyna'arin; mostly held by Guild managers.

ADVISORY BOARD POSITIONS

Culture: Censorship

Health: Healers

Nature: Rhupan and sweet water

Urban: Offshore urban centers (except Balan Su);

Rural: Isolated or largely undeveloped islands;

Balan Su: Affairs of the capital;

Academics: Institutions of learning

Ocean: Wildlife

Public: Complaints and petitions from the general public.

THE COUNCIL OF NINE IN 9999 COB

Gran Pradesh: Ra'shard Ruu'n

Andrasian Leader: Ellex Andria

Andrasian Intelligence: Uthyr Andria

Andrasian Homeland Affairs: Valden Andron

Andrasian Guild Representative: Trip Anders

Raccorin Leader: Rajjesh'n Racorine Derit

Raccorin Intelligence: Din Deri

Raccorin Homeland Affairs: Akhem Deri

Raccorin Guild Representative: Rameen Rutar

ADVISORY BOARD MEMBERS IN 9999 COB

Culture: Malisha Andra'asnia

Health: Hypnia Rhegan

Nature: Alys Andalia

Urban: Cheng Burgh

Rural: Yon Khel

Balan Su: Cort Andramon

Academics: Tellian Prace

Ocean: Neph'tun Deep

Public: Pon Primr'se

Dyna'arin

INTRODUCTION

The Dyna'arin (often called the Guild) oversee the design, production, and operation of all maquina—combinations of metallic and organic parts with dynamins, datamins, and crystamin-shards supplied by the Pradishar—which makes Balance's civilization able to connect and feed itself.

Furthermore, Dyna'arin crystamins are impervious to outside investigation or interrogation by any of the other crystals, which allows Guild members a certain amount of freedom and protection in the crystal realm. Most maquina is operated exclusively by the Guild, but there are exceptions for certain types and certain situations. Nonetheless, the Guild holds a vast amount of control over the infrastructure of Balance, including transportation, energy, and information.

GROUPS

Operators: Workers who run maquina, assemble maquina, repair maquina, and source raw materials for maquina (45%);

Managers: Bureaucrats who oversee operations and politics (25%);

Tinkers: Designers, inventors, architects, engineers; many also teach for the Academi-con in their spare time (5%);

Enforcers: A security corp renowned for their physical prowess and mental ingenuity; mostly Raccorin, though the guards wear metal face masks; armed with zaprens, enflamers, and Vintrani blades (25%);

N'detten: Bhizini workers who perform for the Guild in an unofficial capacity.

POLITICS & CULTURE

The Guild and the Pradishar both depend on each other so much that they tend to agree on many issues and, for the most part, the Council of Nine leaves the Guild alone and the Guild does its best not to upset the Pradishar. The relationship has largely been amicable, and the Guild are allowed a lot of liberties in Balance Territories. Dyna'arin facilities, for example, are not to be entered by local authorities, even the Pradishar, without going through the proper channels first.

The isolation of Guild facilities, and the independent Guild territory in Mon Mang'alar where the Dyna'arin have two major cities, has given Dyna'arin culture a distinct flavor from that found in the wider Balance culture. In Guild facilities and especially in their twin cities, the racial and gender differences of Balance society are somewhat disregarded, and there are no restrictions on interracial children or prohibitions on Bhizini who are related to members of the Guild (the N'detten). Most tinkers, managers, and even many operators, disregard the Pradishar lore as fantasy. Within the Dyna'arin, there are tensions between operators and Management over injuries and conditions, and between tinker and tinker over the ethics of those who create maquina as well as what role the Guild should take when there are crises in the world.

Map

Bru'nord Ocean
Balance Territories
Raccorum Rhazzac
Oscr'apo'tamian Ocean
Bru'nord Reefs
Bru'holds
Rumesh
Brinewater Bay
West'whaling
Grand Gardenia
Spyrin
Cosc'whaling
Alyscair
Shimmering Sea
Lasracia
D'orcion
Anduvia
Filamon
Farundon
Thester
Asa Bacon
Callo Bacon
Andrapolis Island
Mon Mang'alar
Versis
Andrasia
Slo'graves
Far Ocean
Far Ocean

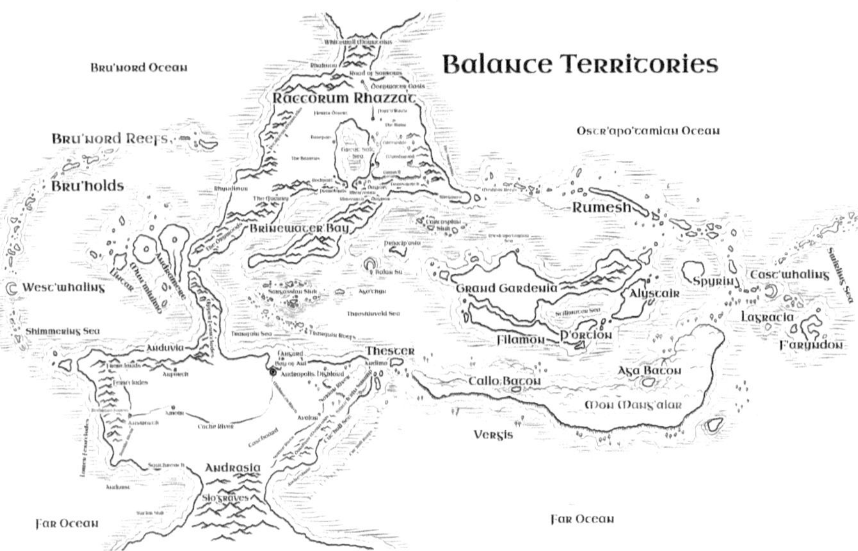

Acknowledgements

I couldn't have done this without the love and support of my friends and family.

I'm grateful to Lexie for reading the very first, very rough draft of this story.

You would not be reading this right now without Liz giving me that last push I needed to share this book.

I'm blessed to have Eddie as my life partner, as he offered only love, encouragement, and support over the years that it took me to write, and re-write, this story.

Thank you to the talented Damian Modena (@demilustraciones) for the cover art, and to Vojin Kremic (@vojinkremic) for turning my sketch into a lovely map.

Coming Soon

The story continues in
Balance, Book Two: The Soil of Life and Death